W9-BFH-647

STARK AND HIS PEOPLE . . .

Willie the "Boss"—a ham-fisted, hard-drinking, pile-driving powerhouse of a dictator.

Sadie Burke—his long-standing mistress and a motivating force behind his rise to power.

Jack Burden—the Boss's press agent. He was expected to carry out orders—no matter what.

And an endless parade of swindlers, fixers, power brokers, and henchmen in the corrupt cavalcade of American politics.

"Characters, thought, and action . . . form a narrative whole that has power to excite the imagination, the emotions and the mind . . . There are not too many good political novels. This is one."

—Saturday Review of Literature

"The finest American novel in more years than one would like to remember."

—New Republic

D.M.G.

ALL THE KING'S MEN

Robert Penn Warren

Mentre che la speranza ha fior del verde.
LA DIVINA COMMEDIA, PURGATORIO, III

*This low-priced Bantam Book
has been completely reset in a type face
designed for easy reading, and was printed
from new plates. It contains the complete
text of the original hard-cover edition.*
NOT ONE WORD HAS BEEN OMITTED.

ALL THE KING'S MEN

*A Bantam Book / published by arrangement with
Harcourt Brace Jovanovich, Inc.*

PRINTING HISTORY

*Harcourt, Brace edition published August 1946
Fourteen printings through October 1965*

*Bantam edition / November 1951
2nd printing .. November 1951
New Bantam edition / April 1955
2nd printing .. November 1955
3rd printing ...... March 1957
4th printing ...... April 1958
Bantam Classic edition / June 1959
20 printings through July 1967
Bantam Modern Classic edition / January 1968
29 printings through November 1970
Bantam edition / November 1971*

31st printing ...... July 1972	*36th printing ... October 1974*
32nd printing ... August 1972	*37th printing ...... May 1975*
33rd printing ... January 1972	*38th printing ...... May 1976*
34th printing ... October 1973	*39th printing ... October 1976*
35th printing ...... June 1974	*40th printing ..... April 1977*
	41st printing .. November 1977

*All rights reserved.
Copyright 1946, © 1974 by Robert Penn Warren.
This book may not be reproduced in whole or in part, by
mimeograph or any other means, without permission.
For information address: Harcourt Brace Jovanovich, Inc.,
757 Third Avenue, New York, N.Y. 10017.*

ISBN 0-553-11705-X

Published simultaneously in the United States and Canada

*Bantam Books are published by Bantam Books, Inc. Its trade-
mark, consisting of the words "Bantam Books" and the por-
trayal of a bantam, is registered in the United States Patent
Office and in other countries. Marca Registrada. Bantam
Books, Inc., 666 Fifth Avenue, New York, New York 10019.*

PRINTED IN THE UNITED STATES OF AMERICA

To
JUSTINE and DAVID MITCHELL CLAY

Chapter One

MASON CITY.

To GET there you follow Highway 58, going northeast out of the city, and it is a good highway and new. Or was new, that day we went up it. You look up the highway and it is straight for miles, coming at you, with the black line down the center coming at and at you, black and slick and tarry-shining against the white of the slab, and the heat dazzles up from the white slab so that only the black line is clear, coming at you with the whine of the tires, and if you don't quit staring at that line and don't take a few deep breaths and slap yourself hard on the back of the neck you'll hypnotize yourself and you'll come to just at the moment when the right front wheel hooks over into the black dirt shoulder off the slab, and you'll try to jerk her back on but you can't because the slab is high like a curb, and maybe you'll try to reach to turn off the ignition just as she starts the dive. But you won't make it, of course. Then a nigger chopping cotton a mile away, he'll look up and see the little column of black smoke standing up above the vitriolic, arsenical green of the cotton rows, and up against the violent, metallic, throbbing blue of the sky, and he'll say, "Lawd God, hit's a-nudder one done done hit!" And the next nigger down the next row, he'll say, "Lawd God," and the first nigger will giggle, and the hoe will lift again and the blade will flash in the sun like a heliograph. Then a few days later the boys from the Highway Department will mark the spot with a little metal square on a metal rod stuck in the black dirt off the shoulder, the metal square painted white and on it in black a skull and crossbones. Later on love vine will climb up it, out of the weeds.

But if you wake up in time and don't hook your wheel off the slab, you'll go whipping on into the dazzle and now and then a car will come at you steady out of the dazzle and will pass you with a snatching sound as though God-Almighty had ripped a tin roof loose with his bare hands. Way off ahead of you, at the horizon where the cotton fields are blurred into the light, the slab will glitter and gleam like water, as though the road were flooded. You'll go whipping toward it, but it will always be ahead of you, that bright, flooded place, like a mirage. You'll go past the little white metal squares set on metal rods, with the skull and crossbones on them to mark the spot. For this is the country where the age of the internal combustion engine has come into its own. Where every boy is Barney Oldfield, and the girls wear organdy and batiste and eyelet embroidery and no panties on account of the climate and have smooth little faces to break your heart and when the wind of the car's speed lifts up their hair at the temples you see the sweet little beads of perspiration nestling there, and they sit low in the seat with their little spines crooked and their bent knees high toward the dashboard and not too close together for the cool, if you could call it that, from the hood ventilator. Where the smell of gasoline and burning brake bands and red-eye is sweeter than myrrh. Where the eight-cylinder jobs come roaring around the curves in the red hills and scatter the gravel like spray, and when they ever get down in the flat country and hit the new slab, God have mercy on the mariner.

On up Number 58, and the country breaks. The flat country and the big cotton fields are gone now, and the grove of live oaks way off yonder where the big house is, and the white-washed shacks, all just alike, set in a row by the cotton fields with the cotton growing up to the doorstep, where the pickaninny sits like a black Billiken and sucks its thumb and watches you go by. That's all left behind now. It is red hills now, not high, with blackberry bushes along the fence rows, and black-jack clumps in the bottoms and now and then a place where the second-growth pines stand close together if they haven't burned over for sheep grass, and if they have burned over, there are the black stubs. The cotton patches cling to the hillsides, and the gullies cut across the cotton patches. The corn blades hang stiff and are streaked with yellow.

There were pine forests here a long time ago but they are gone. The bastards got in here and set up the mills and laid the narrow-gauge tracks and knocked together the company commissaries and paid a dollar a day and folks swarmed out of the brush for the dollar and folks came from God knows where, riding in wagons with a chest of drawers and a bedstead canted together in the wagon bed, and five kids huddled down together and the old woman hunched on the wagon seat with a poke bonnet on her head and snuff on her gums and a young one hanging on her tit. The saws sang soprano and the clerk in the commissary passed out the blackstrap molasses and the sow-belly and wrote in his big book, and the Yankee dollar and Confederate dumbness collaborated to heal the wounds of four years of fratricidal strife, and all was merry as a marriage bell. Till, all of a sudden, there weren't any more pine trees. They stripped the mills. The narrow-gauge tracks got covered with grass. Folks tore down the commissaries for kindling wood. There wasn't any more dollar a day. The big boys were gone, with diamond rings on their fingers and broadcloth on their backs. But a good many of the folks stayed right on, and watched the gullies eat deeper into the red clay. And a good handful of those folks and their heirs and assigns stayed in Mason City, four thousand of them, more or less.

You come in on Number 58, and pass the cotton gin and the power station and the fringe of nigger shacks and bump across the railroad track and down a street where there are a lot of little houses painted white one time, with the sad valentine lace of gingerbread work around the eaves of the veranda, and tin roofs, and where the leaves on the trees in the yards hang straight down in the heat, and above the mannerly whisper of your eighty-horsepower valve-in-head (or whatever it is) drifting at forty, you hear the July flies grinding away in the verdure.

That was the way it was the last time I saw Mason City, nearly three years ago, back in the summer of 1936. I was in the first car, the Cadillac, with the Boss and Mr. Duffy and the Boss's wife and son and Sugar-Boy. In the second car, which lacked our quiet elegance reminiscent of a cross between a hearse and an ocean liner but which still wouldn't make your cheeks burn with shame in the country-club parking lot, there were some reporters and a photographer and Sadie Burke, the Boss's secretary, to see they got there sober enough to do what they were supposed to do.

Sugar-Boy was driving the Cadillac, and it was a pleasure to watch him. Or it would have been if you could detach your imagination from the picture of what near a couple of tons of expensive mechanism looks like after it's turned turtle three times at eighty and could give your undivided attention to the exhibition of muscular co-ordination, satanic humor, and split-second timing which was Sugar-Boy's when he whipped around a hay wagon in the face of an oncoming gasoline truck and went through the rapidly diminishing aperture close enough to give the truck driver heart failure with one rear fender and wipe the snot off a mule's nose with the other. But the Boss loved it. He always sat up front with Sugar-Boy and looked at the speedometer and down the road and grinned to Sugar-Boy after they got through between the mule's nose and the gasoline truck. And Sugar-Boy's head would twitch, the way it always did when the words were piling up inside of him and couldn't get out, and then he'd start. "The b-b-b-b-b—" he would manage to get out and the saliva would spray from his lips like Flit from a Flit gun. "The b-b-b-b-bas-tud—he seen me c-c-c—" and here he'd spray the inside of the windshield—"c-c-com-ing." Sugar-Boy couldn't talk, but he could express himself when he got his foot on the accelerator. He wouldn't win any debating contests in high school, but then nobody would ever want to debate with Sugar-Boy. Not anybody who knew him and had seen him do tricks with the .38 Special which rode under his left armpit like a tumor.

3

No doubt you thought Sugar-Boy was a Negro, from his name. But he wasn't. He was Irish, from the wrong side of the tracks. He was about five-feet-two, and he was getting bald, though he wasn't more than twenty-seven or -eight years old, and he wore red ties and under the red tie and his shirt he wore a little Papist medal on a chain, and I always hoped to God it was St. Christopher and that St. Christopher was on the job. His name was O'Sheean, but they called him Sugar-Boy because he ate sugar. Every time he went to a restaurant he took all the cube sugar there was in the bowl. He went around with his pockets stuffed with sugar cubes, and when he took one out to pop into his mouth you saw little pieces of gray lint sticking to it, the kind of lint there always is loose in your pocket, and shreds of tobacco from cigarettes. He'd pop the cube in over the barricade of his twisted black little teeth, and then you'd see the thin little mystic Irish cheeks cave in as he sucked the sugar, so that he looked like an undernourished leprechaun.

The Boss was sitting in the front seat with Sugar-Boy and watching the speedometer, with his kid Tom up there with him. Tom was then about eighteen or nineteen—I forgot which—but you would have thought he was older. He wasn't so big, but he was built like a man and his head sat on his shoulders like a man's head without that gangly, craning look a kid's head has. He had been a high-school football hero and the fall before he had been the flashiest thing on the freshman team at State. He got his name in the papers because he was really good. He knew he was good. He knew he was the nuts, as you could tell from one look at his slick-skinned handsome brown face, with the jawbone working insolently and slow over a little piece of chewing gum and his blue eyes under half-lowered lids working insolently and slow over you, or the whole damned world. But that day when he was up in the front seat with Willie Stark, who was the Boss, I couldn't see his face. I remembered thinking his head, the shape and the way it was set on his shoulders, was just like his old man's head.

Mrs. Stark—Lucy Stark, the wife of the Boss—Tiny Duffy, and I were in the back seat—Lucy Stark between Tiny and me. It wasn't exactly a gay little gathering. The temperature didn't make for chitchat in the first place. In the second place, I was watching out for the hay wagons and gasoline trucks. In the third place, Duffy and Lucy Stark never were exactly chummy. So she sat between Duffy and me and gave herself to her thoughts. I reckon she had plenty to think about. For one thing, she could think about all that had happened since she was a girl teaching her first year in the school at Mason City and had married a red-faced and red-necked farm boy with big slow hands and a shock of dark brown hair coming down over his brow (you can look at the wedding picture which has been in the papers along with a thousand other pictures of Willie) and a look of dog-like devotion and wonder in his eyes when they fixed on her. She would have had a lot to think about as she sat in the hurtling Cadillac, for there had been a lot of changes.

We tooled down the street where the little one-time-white houses were, and hit the square. It was Saturday afternoon and the square was full of folks. The wagons and the crates were parked solid around the patch of grass roots in the middle of which stood the courthouse, a red-brick box, well weathered and needing paint, for it had been there since before the Civil War, with a little tower with a clock face on each side. On the second look you discovered that the clock faces weren't real. They were just painted on, and they all said five o'clock and not eight-seventeen the way those big painted watches in front of third-string jewelry stores used to. We eased into the ruck of folks come in to do their trading, and Sugar-Boy leaned on his horn, and his head twitched, and he said, "B-b-b-b-as-tuds," and the spit flew.

We pulled up in front of the drugstore, and the kid Tom got out and then the Boss, before Sugar-Boy could get around to the door. I got out and helped out Lucy Stark, who came up from the depths of heat and meditation long enough to say, "Thank you." She stood there on the pavement a second, touching her skirt into place around her hips, which had a little more beam on them than no doubt had been the case when she won the heart of Willie Stark, the farm boy.

Mr. Duffy debouched massively from the Cadillac, and we all entered the drugstore, the Boss holding the door open so Lucy Stark could go in and then following her, and the rest of us trailing in. There were a good many folks in the store, men in overalls lined up along the soda fountain, and women hanging around the counters where the junk and glory was, and kids hanging on skirts with one hand and clutching ice-cream cones with the other and staring out over their own wet noses at the world of men from eyes which resembled painted china marbles. The Boss just stood modestly back of the gang of customers at the soda fountain, with his hat in his hand and the damp hair hanging down over his forehead. He stood that way a minute maybe, and then one of the girls ladling up ice cream happened to see him, and got a look on her face as though her garter belt had busted in church, and dropped her ice-cream scoop, and headed for the back of the store with her hips pumping hell-for-leather under the lettuce-green smock.

Then a second later a little bald-headed fellow wearing a white coat which ought to have been in the week's wash came plunging through the crowd from the back of the store, waving his hand and bumping the customers and yelling, "It's Willie!"

5

The fellow ran up to the Boss, and the Boss took a couple of steps to meet him, and the fellow with the white coat grabbed Willie's hand as though he were drowning. He didn't shake Willie's hand, not by ordinary standards. He just hung on to it and twitched all over and gargled the sacred syllables of *Willie*. Then, when the attack had passed, he turned to the crowd, which was ringing around at a polite distance and staring, and announced, "My God, folks, it's Willie!"

The remark was superfluous. One look at the faces rallied around and you knew that if any citizen over the age of three didn't know that the strong-set man standing there in the Palm Beach suit was Willie Stark, that citizen was a half-wit. In the first place, all he would have to do would be to lift his eyes to the big picture high up there above the soda fountain, a picture about six times life size, which showed the same face, the big eyes, which in the picture had the suggestion of a sleepy and inward look (the eyes of the man in the Palm Beach suit didn't have that look now, but I've seen it), the pouches under the eyes and the jowls beginning to sag off, and the meaty lips, which didn't sag but if you looked close were laid one on top of the other like a couple of bricks, and the tousle of hair hanging down on the not very high squarish forehead. Under the picture was the legend: *My study is the heart of the people.* In quotation marks, and signed, *Willie Stark.* I had seen that picture in a thousand places, pool halls to palaces.

Somebody back in the crowd yelled, "Hi, Willie!" The Boss lifted his right hand and waved in acknowledgment to the unknown admirer. Then the Boss spied a fellow at the far end of the soda fountain, a tall, gaunt-shanked, malarial, leather-faced side of jerked venison, wearing jean pants and a brace of mustaches hanging off the kind of face you see in photographs of General Forrest's calvarymen, and the Boss started toward him and put out his hand. Old Leather-Face didn't show. Maybe he shuffled one of his broken brogans on the tiles, and his Adam's apple jerked once or twice, and the eyes were watchful out of that face which resembled the seat of an old saddle left out in the weather, but when the Boss got close, his hand came up from the elbow, as though it didn't belong to Old Leather-Face but was operating on its own, and the Boss took it.

"How you making it, Malaciah?" the Boss asked.

The Adam's apple worked a couple of times, and the Boss shook the hand which was hanging out there in the air as if it didn't belong to anybody, and Old Leather-Face said, "We's grabblen."

"How's your boy?" the Boss asked.

"Ain't doen so good," Old Leather-Face allowed.

"Sick?"

6

"Naw," Old Leather-Face allowed, "jail."

"My God," the Boss said, "what they doing round here, putting good boys in jail?"

"He's a good boy," Old Leather-Face allowed. "Hit wuz a fahr fight, but he had a lettle bad luck."

"Huh?"

"Hit wuz fahr and squahr, but he had a lettle bad luck. He stobbed the feller and he died."

"Tough tiddy," the Boss said. Then: "Tried yet?"

"Not yit."

"Tough tiddy," the Boss said.

"I ain't complainen," Old Leather-Face said. "Hit wuz fit fahr and squahr."

"Glad to seen you," the Boss said. "Tell your boy to keep his tail over the dashboard."

"He ain't complainen," Old Leather-Face said.

The Boss started to turn away to the rest of us who after a hundred miles in the dazzle were looking at that soda fountain as though it were a mirage, but Old Leather-Face said, "Willie."

"Huh?" the Boss answered.

"Yore pitcher," Old Leather-Face allowed, and jerked his head creakily toward the six-times-life-size photograph over the soda fountain. "Yore pitcher," he said, "hit don't do you no credit, Willie."

"Hell, no," the Boss said, studying the picture, cocking his head to one side and squinting at it, "but I was porely when they took it. I was like I'd had the cholera morbus. Get in there busting some sense into that Legislature, and it leaves a man worse'n the summer complaint."

"Git in thar and bust 'em, Willie!" somebody yelled from back in the crowd, which was thickening out now, for folks were trying to get in from the street.

"I'll bust 'em," Willie said, and turned around to the little man with the white coat. "Give us some cokes, Doc," he said, "for God's sake."

It looked as if Doc would have heart failure getting around to the other side of the soda fountain. The tail of that white coat was flat on the air behind him when he switched the corner and started clawing past the couple of girls in the lettuce-green smocks so he could do the drawing. He got the first one set up, and passed it to the Boss, who handed it to his wife. Then he started drawing the next one, and kept on saying, "It's on the house, Willie, it's on the house." The Boss took that one himself, and Doc kept on drawing them and saying, "It's on the house, Willie, it's on the house." He kept on drawing them till he got about five too many.

By that time folks were packed outside the door solid to the middle of the street. Faces were pressed up against the screen door, the way you do when you try to see through a screen into a dim room. Outside, they kept yelling, "Speech, Willie, speech!"

"My God," the Boss said, in the direction of Doc, who was hanging on to one of the nickel-plated spouts of the fountain and watching every drop of the coke go down the Boss's gullet. "My God," the Boss said, "I didn't come here to make a speech. I came here to go out and see my pappy."

"Speech, Willie, speech!" they were yelling out there.

The Boss set his little glass on the marble.

"It's on the house," Doc uttered croakingly with what strength was left in him after the rapture.

"Thanks, Doc," the Boss said. He turned away to head toward the door, then looked back. "You better get back in here and sell a lot of aspirin, Doc," he said, "to make up for the charity."

Then he plowed out the door, and the crowd fell back, and we tailed after him.

Mr. Duffy stepped up beside the Boss and asked him was he going to make a speech, but the Boss didn't even look at him. He kept walking slow and steady right across the street into the crowd, as though the crowd hadn't been there. The red, long faces with the eyes in them watching like something wary and wild and watchful in a thicket fell back, and there wasn't a sound. The crowd creamed back from his passage, and we followed in his wake, all of us who had been in the Cadillac, and the others who had been in the second car. Then the crowd closed behind.

The Boss kept walking straight ahead, his head bowed a little, the way a man bows his head when he is out walking by himself and has something on his mind. His hair fell down over his forehead, for he was carrying his hat in his hand. I knew his hair was down over his forehead, for I saw him give his head a quick jerk once or twice, the way he always did when he was walking alone and it fell down toward his eyes, the kind of motion a horse gives just after the bit is in and he's full of beans.

He walked straight across the street and across the patch of grass roots and up the steps of the courthouse. Nobody else followed him up the steps. At the top he turned around, slow, to face the crowd. He simply looked at them, blinking his big eyes a little, just as though he had just stepped out of the open doors and the dark hall of the courthouse behind him and was blinking to get his eyes adjusted to the light. He stood up there blinking, the hair down on his forehead, and the dark sweat patch showing under each arm of his Palm Beach coat. Then he gave his head a twitch, and his eyes bulged wide suddenly, even

8

if the light was hitting him full in the face, and you could see the glitter in them.

It's coming, I thought.

You saw the eyes bulge suddenly like that, as though something had happened inside him, and there was that glitter. You knew something had happened inside him, and thought: *It's coming.* It was always that way. There was the bulge and the glitter, and there was the cold grip way down in the stomach as though somebody had laid hold of something in there, in the dark which is you, with a cold hand in a cold rubber glove. It was like the second when you come home late at night and see the yellow envelope of the telegram sticking out from under your door and you lean and pick it up, but don't open it yet, not for a second. While you stand there in the hall, with the envelope in your hand, you feel there's an eye on you, a great big eye looking straight at you from miles and dark and through walls and houses and through your coat and vest and hide and sees you huddled up way inside, in the dark which is you, inside yourself, like a clammy, sad little foetus you carry around inside yourself. The eye knows what's in the envelope, and it is watching you to see you when you open it and know, too. But the clammy, sad little foetus which is you way down in the dark which is you too lifts up its sad little face and its eyes are blind, and it shivers cold inside you for it doesn't want to know what is in that envelope. It wants to lie in the dark and not know, and be warm in its not-knowing. The end of man is knowledge, but there is one thing he can't know. He can't know whether knowledge will save him or kill him. He will be killed, all right, but he can't know whether he is killed because of the knowledge which he has got or because of the knowledge which he hasn't got and which if he had it, would save him. There's the cold in your stomach, but you open the envelope, you have to open the envelope, for the end of man is to know.

The Boss stood up there quiet, with the bulge and glitter in the eyes, and there wasn't a sound in the crowd. You could hear one insane and irrelevant July fly sawing away up in one of the catalpa trees in the square. Then that sound stopped, and there wasn't anything but the waiting. Then the Boss lounged a step forward, easy and soft-footed.

"I'm not going to make any speech," the Boss said, and grinned. But the eyes were still big and the glitter was in them. "I didn't come here to make any speech. I came up here to go out and see my pappy, and see if he's got anything left in the smokehouse fit to eat. I'm gonna say: Pappy, now what about all that smoked sausage you wuz bragging about, what about all that ham you wuz bragging about all last winter, what about—" That's what he was saying, but the voice was different, going up

9

in his nose and coming out flat with that little break they've got in the red hills, saying, "Pappy, now what about—"

But the glitter was still there, and I thought: *Maybe it's coming.* Maybe it was not too late. You never could tell. Suddenly, it might be there, he might say it.

But he was saying, "—and so I'm not going to make any speech—" In his old voice, his own voice. Or was that his voice? Which was his true voice, which one of all the voices, you would wonder.

He was saying, "And I didn't come here to ask you to give me anything, not even a vote. The Good Book says, 'There are three things that are never satisfied, yea, four things say not, it is enough—'-" and the voice was different now—" 'the grave, and the barren womb, the earth that is not filled with water, and the fire that saith not, it is enough.' But Solomon might have added just one little item. He might have just made his little list complete, and added, the politician who never stops saying, Gimme."

He was lounging back on himself now, and his head was cocked a little to one side, and his eyes blinked. Then he grinned, and said, "If they had politicians back in those days, they said, Gimme, just like all of us politicians do. Gimme, gimme, my name's Jimmie. But I'm not a politician today. I'm taking the day off. I'm not even going to ask you to vote for me. To tell the God's unvarnished and unbuckled truth, I don't have to ask you. Not today. I still got quite a little hitch up there in the big house with the white columns two stories high on the front porch and peach ice cream for breakfast. Not that a passel of those statesmen wouldn't like to throw me out. You know—" and he leaned forward a little now, as if to tell them a secret—"it's funny how I just can't make friends with some folks. No matter how hard I try. I been just as polite. I said, Please. But *please* didn't do any good. But it looks like they got to put up with me a spell longer. And you have. Before you get shet of me. So you better just grin and bear it. It's not any worse'n boils. Now, is it?"

He stopped, and looked all around, right down at them, moving his head slow, so that he seemed to look right in a face here and stop for just a split second, and then to move on to another one a little farther. Then he grinned, and his eyes blinked, and he said, "Huh? What's the matter? Cat got yore tongue?"

"Boils on the tail!" somebody yelled back in the crowd.

"Dammit," Willie yelled right back, "lie on yore stummick and go to sleep!"

Somebody laughed.

"And," yelled Willie, "thank the good Lord who in his everlasting mercy saw fit to make something with a back side and a front side to it out of the skimpy little piece of material provided in your case!"

"You tell 'em, Willie!" somebody yelled back in the crowd. Then they started to laugh.

The Boss lifted up his right hand about as high as his head, out in front of him, palm down, and waited till they stopped laughing and whistling. Then he said: "No, I'm not here to ask you for anything. A vote or anything else. I reckon I'll be back later for that. If I keep on relishing that peach ice cream for breakfast in the big house. But I don't expect all of you to vote for me. My God, if all of you went and voted for Willie, what the hell would you find to argue about? There wouldn't be anything left but the weather, and you can't vote on that.

"No," he said, and it was another voice, quiet and easy and coming slow and from a distance, "I'm not here to ask for anything today. I'm taking the day off, and I've come home. A man goes away from his home and it is in him to do it. He lies in strange beds in the dark, and the wind is different in the trees. He walks in the street and there are the faces in front of his eyes, but there are no names for the faces. The voices he hears are not the voices he carried away in his ears a long time back when he went away. The voices he hears are loud. They are so loud he does not hear for a long time at a stretch those voices he carried away in his ears. But there comes a minute when it is quiet and he can hear those voices he carried away in his ears a long time back. He can make out what they say, and they say: Come back. They say: Come back, boy. So he comes back."

His voice just stopped. It didn't trail off like a voice coming to a stop. One second it was there, going on, word by word, in the stillness which filled the square and the crowd in front of the courthouse and was stiller for the grinding of the July flies in the two catalpas rising above the heads of the people who had crowded up on the patch of grass roots. The voice was going there, word by word, then suddenly it was not there. There was only the sound of the July flies, which seems to be inside your head as though it were the grind and whir of the springs and cogs which are you and which will not stop no matter what you say until they are good and ready.

He stood there a half minute, not saying a word, and not moving. He didn't even seem to be noticing the crowd down there. Then he seemed, all at once, to discover them, and grinned. "So he comes back," he said, grinning now. "When he gets half a day off. And he says, Hello, folks, how are you making it? And that's what I'm saying."

That's what he said. He looked down, grinning, and his head turned as his eyes went down in the crowd, and seemed to stop on a face there, and then go on to stop on another face.

11

Then he started walking down the steps, as if he had just come out of that dusky-dark hallway beyond the big open doors behind him and was walking down the steps by himself, with nobody there in front of him and no eyes on him. He came straight down the steps toward where his gang was standing, Lucy Stark and the rest of us, and nodded at us as though he were simply passing us on the street and didn't know us any too well anyway, and kept right on walking, straight into the crowd as though the crowd weren't there. The people fell back a little to make a passage for him, with their eyes looking right at him, and the rest of us in his gang followed behind him, and the crowd closed up behind us.

People were clapping now, and yelling. Somebody kept yelling, "Hi, Willie!"

The Boss walked straight across the street, through the crowd, and got into the Cadillac and sat down. We got in with him and the photographer and the others went back to their car. Sugar-Boy started up and nosed out into the street. People didn't get out of the way very fast. They couldn't, they were so jammed in. When we nosed out into the crowd, the faces were right there outside the car, not more than a foot or so away. The faces looked right in at us. But they were out there and we were inside now. The eyes in the red, slick-skinned long faces, or the brown, crinkled faces, looked in at us.

Sugar-Boy kept pecking at his horn. The words were piling up inside him. His lips started to work. I could see his face in the driver's mirror, and the lips were working. "The b-b-b-b-as-tuds," he said, and the spit flew.

The Boss had sunk in on himself now.

"The b-b-b-b-as-tuds," Sugar-Boy said, and pecked at his horn, but we were easing out of the square now to a side street where there weren't any people. We were doing forty by the time we passed the brick schoolhouse on the outskirts of town. Seeing the schoolhouse made me remember how I had first met Willie, about fourteen years before, back in 1922, when he wasn't anything but the County Treasurer of Mason County and had come down to the city to see about the bond issue to build that schoolhouse. Then I remembered how I had met him, in the back room of Slade's pool hall, where Slade sold the needle beer, and we were sitting at one of those little marble-topped tables with wirework legs, the kind they used to have in drugstores when you were a boy and took your high-school sweetie down on Saturday night to get that chocolate banana split and rub knees under the table and the wirework would always get in the way.

There were four of us. There was Tiny Duffy, who was almost as big back then as he was to get to be. He didn't need any sign to let you know what he was. If the wind was right, you knew he was a city-hall slob long before you could see the whites of his eyes. He had the belly and he sweated through his shirt just above the belt buckle, and he had the face, which was creamed and curded like a cow patty in a spring pasture, only it was the color of biscuit dough, and in the middle was his grin with the gold teeth. He was Tax Assessor, and he wore a flat hard straw hat on the back of his head. There was a striped band on the hat.

Then there was Alex Michel, who was a country boy from up in Mason County but who was learning fast. He had learned fast enough to get to be a deputy sheriff. But he wasn't that long. He wasn't anything, for he got cut in the gut by a coke-frisky piano player in a cribhouse where he had gone to take out a little in trade on his protection account. Alex was, as I have said, from up in Mason County.

Duffy and I had been in the back room of Slade's place waiting for Alex, with whom I had the hope of transacting a little business. I was a newspaperman and Alex knew something I wanted to know. Duffy had called him in, for Duffy was a friend of mine. At least, he knew that I worked for the *Chronicle,* which at that time was supporting the Joe Harrison outfit. Joe Harrison was Governor then. And Duffy was one of Joe Harrison's boys.

So I was sitting in the back room of Slade's place, one hot morning in June or July, back in 1922, waiting for Alex Michel to turn up and listening to the silence in the back room of Slade's place. A funeral parlor at midnight is ear-splitting compared to the effect you get in the middle of the morning in the back room of a place like Slade's if you are the first man there. You sit there and think how cozy it was last night, with the effluvium of brotherly bodies and the haw-haw of camaraderie, and you look at the floor where now there are little parallel trails of damp sawdust the old broom left this morning when the unenthusiastic old Negro man cleaned up, and the general impression is that you are alone with the Alone and it is His move. So I sat there in the silence (Duffy was never talkative in the morning before he had worried down two or three drinks), and listened to my tissues break down and the beads of perspiration explode delicately out of the ducts embedded in the ample flesh of my companion.

Alex came in with a fellow with him, and I knew my little conversation was not promising. My mission was of some delicacy, not fit for the ear of a stranger. I figured that might be the reason Alex had his friend in tow. Maybe it was, for Alex was cagey in an amateurish sort of way. In any case, he had the Boss with him.

Only it was not the Boss. Not to the crude eye of the *homme sensuel.* Metaphysically it was the Boss, but how was I to know?

13

Fate comes walking through the door, and it is five feet eleven inches tall and heavyish in the chest and shortish in the leg and is wearing a seven-fifty seersucker suit which is too long in the pants so the cuffs crumple down over the high black shoes, which could do with a polishing, and a stiff high collar like a Sunday-school superintendent and a blue-striped tie which you know his wife gave him last Christmas and which he has kept in tissue paper with the holly card ("Merry Xmas to my Darling Willie from your Loving Wife") until he got ready to go up to the city, and a gray felt hat with the sweat stains showing through the band. It comes in just like that, and how are you to know? It comes in, trailing behind Alex Michel, who is, or was before the piano player got him, six-feet-two of beautifully articulated bone and gristle with a hard, bony, baked-looking face and two little quick brown eyes which don't belong above that classic torso and in that face and which keep fidgeting around like a brace of Mexican jumping beans. So Fate trails modestly along behind Alex Michel, who approaches the table with an air of command which would deceive no one.

Alex shook my hand and said, "Hi, pal," and slapped me on the shoulder with a palm that was tough enough to crack a black walnut, and paid proper obeisance to Mr. Duffy, who extended a hand without rising; and then, as a sort of afterthought, Alex jerked a thumb toward his trailing companion and said, "This is Willie Stark, gents. From up home at Mason City. Me and Willie was in school together. Yeah, and Willie, he was a bookworm, he was teacher's pet. Wuzn't you, Willie?" And Alex whickered like a stallion in full appreciation of his own delicious humor and nudged the teacher's pet in the ribs. Then, controlling himself, he added, "And he's still teacher's pet, ain't you, Willie, ain't you?"

And he turned to Duffy and me, and explained, before mirth again took him and Slade's back room again resounded with the cheerful note of the breeding paddock, "Willie—Willie—he married a school-teacher!"

That idea seemed monstrously funny to Alex. Meanwhile, Willie, unable to complete the amenities of the situation, bowed to the blast and stood there with the old gray felt hat in his hand, with the sweat showing around the band outside where it had soaked through. Willie's large face, above the stiff country collar, didn't show a thing.

"Yeah—yeah—he married a school-teacher!" Alex reaffirmed with undiminished relish.

"Well," said Mr. Duffy, whose experience and tact were equal to any situation, "they tells me school-teachers are made with it in the same place." Mr. Duffy lifted his lip to expose the gold, but made no sound, for, Mr. Duffy being a man of the world and serene in confidence, his style was to put forth his

14

sally and let it make its way on its intrinsic worth and to leave the applause to the public.

Alex provided the applause in good measure. I contributed only a grin which felt sickly on my face, and Willie was a blank.

"Gawd!" Alex managed, when breath had returned to him, "Gawd, Mr. Duffy, you are a card! You shore-Gawd are." And again he vigorously nudged the teacher's pet in the ribs to spur his laggard humor. When he got no result, he nudged again, and demanded flatly of his ward: "Now ain't Mr. Duffy a card?"

"Yes," Willie replied, looking at Mr. Duffy innocently, judicially, dispassionately. "Yes," he said, "Mr. Duffy is a card." And as the admission was made, albeit belatedly and with some ambiguity of inflection, the slight cloud which had gathered upon Mr. Duffy's brow was dissipated with no trace of rancor left behind.

Willie took advantage of the momentary lull to wind up the ritual of introduction which Alex's high spirits had interrupted. He transferred his old gray hat to his left hand and took the two steps necessary to bring him to the table, and gravely extended his hand to me. So much water had flowed beneath the bridges since Alex had jerked his thumb toward the stranger from the country and said, "This is Willie Stark," that I had almost forgotten I hadn't known Willie all my life. So I didn't catch on right away that he was out to shake hands. I must have looked at his outstretched hand inquiringly and then given him a blank look, and he just showed me his dead pan—it was just another pan, at first glance anyway—and kept on holding his hand out. Then I came to, and not to be outdone in courtesy of the old school, I hitched my chair back from the table and almost stood all the way up, and groped for his hand. It was a pretty good-sized hand. When you first took it you figured it was on the soft side, and the palm a little too moist—which is something, however, you don't hold against a man in certain latitudes—then you discovered it had a solid substructure. It was like the hand of a farm boy who has not too recently given up the plow for a job in the crossroads store. Willie's hand gave mine three decorous pump-handle motions, and he said, "Glad to meetcha, Mr. Burden," like something he had memorized, and then, I could have sworn, he gave me a wink. Then looking into that dead pan, I wasn't sure. About twelve years later, at a time when the problem of Willie's personality more imperiously occupied my rare hours of speculation, I asked him, "Boss, do you remember the time we first got acquainted in the back room of Slade's joint?"

He said he did, which wasn't remarkable, for he was like the

15

circus elephant, he never forgot anything, the fellow who gave him the peanut or the fellow who put snuff in his trunk.

"You remember when we shook hands?" I asked him.

"Yeah," he said.

"Well, Boss," I demanded, "did you or didn't you wink at me?"

"Boy—" he said and toyed with his glass of Scotch and soda and dug the heel of one of his unpolished, thirty-dollar, chastely designed bench-made shoes into the best bed-spread the St. Regis Hotel could afford. "Boy," he said, and smiled at me paternally over his glass, "that is a mystery."

"Don't you remember?" I asked.

"Sure," he said, "I remember."

"Well," I demanded.

"Suppose I just had something in my eye?" he said.

"Well, damn it, you just had something in your eye then."

"Suppose I didn't have anything in my eye?"

"Then maybe you winked because you figured you and me had some views in common about the tone of the gathering."

"Maybe," he said. "It ain't any secret that my old schoolmate Alex was a heel. And it ain't any secret that Tiny Duffy is as sebaceous a fat-ass as ever made the spring groan in a swivel chair."

"He is an s.o.b.," I affirmed.

"He is," the Boss agreed cheerfully, "but he is a useful citizen. If you know what to do with him."

"Yeah," I said, "and I suppose you think you know what to do with him. You made him Lieutenant Governor." (For that was in the Boss's last term when Tiny was his understudy.)

"Sure," the Boss nodded, "somebody's got to be Lieutenant Governor."

"Yeah," I said, "Tiny Duffy."

"Sure," he said, "Tiny Duffy. The beauty about Tiny is that nobody can trust him and you know it. You get somebody somebody can trust maybe, and you got to sit up nights worrying whether you are the somebody. You get Tiny, and you can get a night's sleep. All you got to do is keep the albumen scared out of his urine."

"Boss, did you wink at me that time back at Slade's?"

"Boy," he said, "if I was to tell you, then you wouldn't have anything to think about."

So I never did know.

But I did see Willie shake hands that morning with Tiny Duffy and fail to wink at him. He just stood there in front of Mr. Duffy, and when the great man, not rising, finally extended his hand with the reserved air of the Pope offering his toe to the kiss of a Campbellite, Willie took it and gave it the three pumps which seemed to be regulation up in Mason City.

16

Alex sat down at the table, and Willie just stood there, as though waiting to be invited, till Alex kicked the fourth chair over a few inches with his foot and said, "Git off yore dogs, Willie."

Willie sat down and laid his gray felt hat on the marble top in front of him. The edges of the brim crinkled and waved up all around off the marble like a piecrust before grandma trims it. Willie just sat there behind his hat and his blue-striped Christmas tie and waited, with his hands laid in his lap.

Slade came in from the front, and said, "Beer?"

"All around," Mr. Duffy ordered.

"Not for me, thank you kindly," Willie said.

"All around," Mr. Duffy ordered again, with a wave of the hand that had the diamond ring.

"Not for me, thank you kindly," Willie said.

Mr. Duffy, with some surprise and no trace of pleasure, turned his gaze upon Willie, who seemed unaware of the significance of the event, sitting upright in his little chair behind the hat and the tie. Then Mr. Duffy looked up at Slade, and jerking his head toward Willie, said, "Aw, give him some beer."

"No, thanks," Willie said, with no more emotion than you would put into the multiplication table.

"Too strong for you?" Mr. Duffy demanded.

"No," Willie replied, "but no thank you."

"Maybe the school-teacher don't let him drink nuthen," Alex offered.

"Lucy don't favor drinking," Willie said quietly. "For a fact."

"What she don't know don't hurt her," Mr. Duffy said.

"Git him some beer," Alex said to Slade.

"All around," Mr. Duffy repeated, with the air of closing an issue.

Slade looked at Alex and he looked at Mr. Duffy and he looked at Willie. He flicked his towel halfheartedly in the direction of a cruising fly, and said: "I sells beer to them as wants it. I ain't making nobody drink it."

Perhaps that was the moment when Slade made his fortune. How life is strange and changeful, and the crystal is in the steel at the point of fracture, and the toad bears a jewel in its forehead, and the meaning of moments passes like the breeze that scarcely ruffles the leaf of the willow.

Well, anyway, when Repeal came and mailmen had to use Mack trucks to haul the applications for licenses over to the City Hall, Slade got a license. He got a license immediately, and he got a swell location, and he got the jack to put in leather chairs kind to the femurs, and a circular bar; and Slade, who never had a dime in his life after he paid rent and protection, now stands in the shadows under the murals of undressed

17

dames in the midst of the glitter of chromium and tinted mirrors, wearing a double-breasted blue suit, with what's left of his hair plastered over his skull, and keeps one eye on the black boys in white jackets who tote the poison and the other on the blonde at the cash register who knows that her duties are not concluded when the lights are turned off at 2:00 A.M., and the strains of a three-piece string ensemble soothe the nerves of the customers.

How did Slade get the license so quickly? How did he get the lease when half the big boys in the business were after that corner? How did he get the jack for the leather chairs and the string ensemble? Slade never confided in me, but I figure Slade got his reward for being an honest man.

Anyway, Slade's statement of principle about the beer question closed the subject that morning. Tiny Duffy lifted a face to Slade with the expression worn by the steer when you give it the hammer; then, as sensation returned, he took refuge in his dignity. Alex permitted himself the last luxury of irony. Says Alex: "Well, maybe you got some orange pop for him." And when the whicker of his mirth had died away, Slade said: "I reckin I have. If he wants it."

"Yes," Willie said, "I think I'll take some orange pop."

The beer came, and the bottle of pop. The bottle of pop had two straws in it. Willie lifted his two hands out of his lap where they had decorously lain during the previous conversation, and took the bottle between them. He tilted the bottle slightly toward him, not lifting it from the table, and affixed his lips to the straws. His lips were a little bit meaty, but they weren't loose. Not exactly. Maybe at first glance you might think so. You might think he had a mouth like a boy, not quite shaped up, and that was the way he looked that minute, all right, leaning over the bottle and the straws stuck in his lips, which were just puckered up. But if you stuck around long enough, you'd see something a little different. You would see that they were hung together, all right, even if they were meaty. His face was a little bit meaty, too, but thin-skinned, and had freckles. His eyes were big, big and brown, and he'd look right at you, out of the middle of that thin-skinned and freckled and almost pudgy face (at first you would think it was pudgy, then you would change your mind), and the dark brown, thick hair was tousled and crinkled down over his forehead, which wasn't very high in the first place, and the hair was a little moist. There was little Willie. There was Cousin Willie from the country, from up at Mason City, with his Christmas tie, and maybe you would take him out to the park and show him the swans.

Alex leaned toward Duffy, and said confidingly, "Willie—he's in poly-ticks."

Duffy's features exhibited the slightest twitch of interest, but the twitch was dissipated into the vast oleaginous blankness which was the face of Duffy in repose. He did not even look at Willie.

"Yeah," Alex continued, leaning closer and nodding sideways at Willie, "yeah, in poly-ticks. Up in Mason City."

Mr. Duffy's head did a massive quarter-revolution in the direction of Willie and the pale-blue eyes focused upon him from the great distance. Not that the mention of Mason City was calculated to impress Mr. Duffy, but the fact that Willie could be in politics anywhere, even in Mason City, where, no doubt, the hogs scratched themselves against the underpinnings of the post office, raised certain problems which merited passing attention. So Mr. Duffy gave his attention to Willie, and solved the problem. He solved it by deciding that there wasn't any problem. Willie was not in politics. Not in Mason City or anywhere else. Alex Michel was a liar and the truth was not in him. You could look at Willie and see that he never had been and never would be in politics. Duffy could look at Willie and deduce the fact that Willie was not in politics. So he said, "Yeah," with heavy irony, and incredulity was obvious upon his face.

Not that I much blame Duffy. Duffy was face to face with the margin of mystery where all our calculations collapse, where the stream of time dwindles into the sands of eternity, where the formula fails in the test tube, where chaos and old night hold sway and we hear the laughter in the ether dream. But he didn't know he was, and so he said, "Yeah."

"Yeah," Alex echoed, without irony, and added, "Up in Mason City. Willie is County Treasurer. Ain't you, Willie?"

"Yes," Willie said, "County Treasurer."

"My God," Duffy breathed, with the air of a man who discovers that he has built upon sands and dwelt among mock shows.

"Yeah," Alex iterated, "and Willie is down here on business for Mason County, ain't you, Willie?"

Willie nodded.

"About a bond issue they got up there," Alex continued. "They gonna build a schoolhouse and it's a bond issue."

Duffy's lips worked, and you could catch the discreet glimmer of the gold in the bridgework, but no word came forth. The moment was too full for sound or foam.

But it was true. Willie was the County Treasurer and he was, that day long ago, in the city on business about the bond issue for the schoolhouse. And the bonds were issued and the schoolhouse built, and more than a dozen years later the big black Cadillac with the Boss whipped past the schoolhouse, and then Sugar-Boy really put his foot down on the gas and we headed out, still on the almost new slab of Number 58.

We had done about a mile, and not a word spoken, when the Boss turned around from the front seat and looked at me and said, "Jack, make a note to find out something about Malaciah's boy and the killing."

"What's his name?" I asked.

"Hell, I don't know, but he's a good boy."

"Malaciah's name, I mean," I said.

"Malaciah Wynn," the Boss said.

I had my notebook out now and wrote it down, and wrote down, *stabbing*.

"Find out when the trial is set and get a lawyer down. A good one, and I mean a good one that'll know how to handle it and let him know he God-damn well better handle it, but don't get a guy that wants his name in lights."

"Albert Evans," I said, "he ought to do."

"Uses hair oil," the Boss said. "Uses hair oil and slicks it back till the top of his head looks like the black ball on a pool table. Get somebody looks like he didn't sing with a dance band. You losing your mind?"

"All right," I said, and wrote in my notebook, *Abe Lincoln type*. I didn't have to remind myself about that. I just wrote because I had got in the habit. You can build up an awful lot of habits in six years, and you can fill an awful lot of little black books in that time and put them in a safety-deposit box when they get full because they aren't something to leave around and because they would be worth their weight in gold to some parties to get their hands on. Not that they ever got their hands on them, I never needed money that bad. But I had the habit of saving them. A man's got to carry something besides a corroded liver with him out of that dark backwood and abysm of time, and it might as well be the little black books. The little black books lie up there in the safety-deposit box, and there are your works of days and hands all cozy in the dark in the little box and the world's great axis grinds.

"You pick him," the Boss said, "but keep out of sight. Put one of your pals on him, and pick your pal."

"I get you," I replied, for I got him.

The Boss was just about to turn around and divide his attention between the highway and Sugar-Boy's speedometer, when Duffy cleared his throat and said, "Boss."

"Yeah?" the Boss said.

"You know who it was got cut?"

"No," the Boss said, getting ready again to turn around, "and I don't care if it was the sainted uncut maiden aunt of the Apostle Paul."

Mr. Duffy cleared his throat, the way he always did in late years when he was congested with phlegm and an idea. "I happened to notice in the paper," he began. "I happened to notice

20

back when it happened, and the feller got cut was the son of a doctor up in this neighborhood. I don't recall what his name was but he was a doctor. The paper said so. Now—" Mr. Duffy was going right on talking to the back of the Boss's head. The Boss hadn't paid any mind, it seemed. "Now, it would appear to me," Mr. Duffy said, and cleared his pipes again, "it would appear to me maybe that doctor might be pretty big around here. You know how a doctor is in the country. They think he is somebody. And maybe it got out how you was mixed up with trying to get the feller Wynn's boy off, and it wouldn't do you any good. You know, politics," he explained, "you know how politics is. Now it—"

The Boss whipped his head around to look at Mr. Duffy so fast all of a sudden there wasn't anything but a blur. It was as though his big brown pop eyes were looking out the back of his head through the hair, everything blurred up together. That is slightly hyperbolic, but you get what I mean. The Boss was like that. He gave you the impression of being a slow and deliberate man to look at him, and he had a way of sitting loose as though he had sunk inside himself and was going down for the third time and his eyes would blink like an owl's in a cage. Then all of a sudden he would make a move. It might just be to reach out and grab a fly out of the air that was bothering him, that trick I saw an old broken-down pug do once who hung around a saloon. He would make bets he could catch a fly out of the air with his fingers, and he could. The Boss could do that. Or he would whip his head at you when you said something he hadn't seemed to be listening to. He whipped his head round now to Duffy and fixed his gaze on him for an instant before he said quite simply and expressively, "Jesus." Then he said, "Tiny, you don't know a God-damned thing. In the first place, I've known Malaciah Wynn all my life, and his boy is a good boy and I don't care who he cut. In the second place, it was a fair fight and he had bad luck and when it's like that by the time the trial comes up folks are always feeling for the feller who's being tried for murder when he just had bad luck because the fellow died. In the third place, if you had picked the wax out of your ears you'd heard me tell Jack to prime the lawyer through a pal and to get one didn't want his name in lights. As far as that lawyer knows or anybody else knows, he's been sent by the Pope. And all he wants to know anyway is whether the foliage he gets out of it has those little silk threads in it. Is all that clear or do you want me to draw a picture?"

"I get you," Mr. Duffy said, and wet his lips.

But the Boss wasn't listening now. He had turned back to the highway and the speedometer and had said to Sugar-Boy, "God's sake, you think we want to admire the landscape? We're late now."

Then you felt Sugar-Boy take up that last extra stitch.

But not for long. In about half a mile, we hit the turn-off. Sugar-Boy turned off on the gravel and we sprayed along with the rocks crunching and popping up against the underside of the fender like grease in a skillet. We left a trail of dust for the other car to ride into.

Then we saw the house.

It was set on a little rise, a biggish box of a house, two-story, rectangular, gray, and unpainted, with a tin roof, unpainted too and giving off blazes under the sun for it was new and the rust hadn't bitten down into it yet, and a big chimney at each end. We pulled up to the gate. The house was set up close to the road, with a good hog-wire fence around the not very big yard, and with some crepe myrtles in bloom the color of raspberry ice cream and looking cool in the heat in the corner of the yard and one live oak, nothing to brag on and dying on one side, in front of the house, and a couple of magnolias off to one side with rusty-looking tinny leaves. There wasn't much grass in the yard, and a half dozen hens wallowed and fluffed and cuck-cucked in the dust under the magnolia trees. A big white hairy dog like a collie or a shepherd was lying on the front porch, a little one-story front porch that looked stuck on the box of the house, like an afterthought.

It looked like those farmhouses you ride by in the country in the middle of the afternoon, with the chickens under the trees and the dog asleep, and you know the only person in the house is the woman who has finished washing up the dishes and has swept the kitchen and has gone upstairs to lie down for half an hour and has pulled off her dress and kicked off her shoes and is lying there on her back on the bed in the shadowy room with her eyes closed and a strand of her hair still matted down on her forehead with the perspiration. She listens to the flies cruising around the room, then she listens to your motor getting big out on the road, then it shrinks off into the distance and she listens to the flies. That was the kind of house it was.

One time I had wondered why the Boss never had the house painted after he got his front feet in the trough and a dollar wasn't the reason you got up in the morning any more. Then I figured the Boss knew best. Suppose he had painted it up, then the next fellow down the road would be saying to the next one, "Seen Old Man Stark got his house painted? Yeah, putten on airs. Hit looks lak hit wuz good enuff fer him to live in all his life lak hit wuz, and his boy gits up thar in the cappy-tell, and hit ain't good enuff no more. Fust thing you know and Old Man Stark'll be going to the privy in the house and maken 'em cook cabbige out behind the barn." (As a matter of fact, Old Man Stark was going to the privy in the house, for the Boss had put in running water and a bathroom. Water pumped by a little automatic electric pump. But you can't see a commode from the road when you pass by. It doesn't hit you in the eye or run out and bite you in the leg. And what the voter doesn't know doesn't prey on his mind.)

Anyway, if he had painted the house it wouldn't have made half as good a picture as it was going to make that day with Willie and his Old Man on the front steps, with Lucy Stark and the boy and the old white dog.

The old man was on the front steps now. By the time we got through the front gate, which had a couple of old plow points hung on a wire to pull it shut and clank to announce the visitor, and had started up the path, the old man had come out the door. He stopped on the steps and waited, a not very tall old man, and thin, wearing blue jean pants and a blue shirt washed so much that it had a powdery pastel shade to it and a black bow tie, the kind that comes ready-tied on an elastic band. We got up close and could see his face, brown and tooled-looking, with the skin and flesh thin on the bone and hanging down from the bone to give that patient look old men's faces have, and his gray hair plastered down on his narrow, egg-thin old skull—the hair still wet as though he had given it a dab with the wet brush when he heard the car, just to be looking right at the last minute—and slow blue eyes in the middle of the brown folded skin. The blue of the eyes was pale and washed out like the blue of the shirt. He didn't have any whiskers or mustache, and you could see that he had shaved pretty recently, for there were two or three little nicks, with the little crusts of blood on them, where the razor had got tangled in the folds of the brown, dry skin.

He stood on the steps, and for any sign he gave we might as well have been back in the city.

Then the Boss went up to him, and put out his hand, and said, "Hello, Pappy. How you making it?"

"Gitten along," the old man said, and shook hands, or rather putting out his hand with that same motion from the elbow which Old Leather-Face had had in the drugstore back in Mason City, he let the Boss shake it.

Lucy Stark went up to him, not saying anything, and kissed him on his left cheek. He didn't say anything either when she did it. He just reached his right arm a little more around her shoulder, not quite a hug, just putting his arm there, and you could see his knobby, crooked, brown old hand, which looked too big for the wristbone, and the hand gave her shoulder two or three little tired, apologetic pats. Then the hand dropped away and hung at his side beside the blue jean pants leg, and Lucy Stark stepped back. Then he said, not very loud, "Howdy, Lucy."

"Howdy, Papa," she said, and the hand hanging beside the

jean pants jerked as though it were getting ready to reach out and pat her again, but it didn't.

I suppose it didn't have to, anyway. Not to tell Lucy Stark what Lucy Stark already knew, and had known without words ever since the days when she had married Willie Stark and had come out here and had sat by the fire at night with the old man, whose wife had been dead a long time then and who hadn't had a woman in the house for a long time. That they had something in common, Old Man Stark and Lucy Stark, who had loved and married Willie Stark, the Willie Stark who at that moment when she and the old man sat wordlessly before the fire was upstairs in his room with his face bent down over a law book, his face puzzled and earnest and the tousle of hair hanging, and who was not with them by the fire, but was up there in that room, but not even in that room, either, but in a room, a world, inside himself where something was swelling and growing painfully and dully and imperceptibly like a great potato in a dark, damp cellar. What they had in common was a world of wordless silence by the fire, a world which could absorb effortlessly and perfectly the movements of their day and their occupations, and of all the days they had lived, and of the days that were to come for them to move about in and do the things which were the life for which they were made. So they sat there in their common knowledge, while the chunk on the hearth stewed and hissed and crumbled, and were together in the down beat and pause of the rhythm of their lives. That was what they had in common now, and nothing could take that away. But they had something else in common: they had in common the knowledge that they did not have what they had. They did not have Willie Stark, who was what they had.

The Boss was introducing Mr. Duffy, who was delighted to meet Mr. Stark, yes, sir, and introducing the gang who had just come up in the second car. Then the Boss jerked a thumb at me, and said to his father, "You recollect Jack Burden, don't you?"

"I recollect," the old man said, and we shook hands.

We all went into the parlor, and sat around on a few pieces of stuffed horsehair furniture, which had an acid, mummy smell in your parched-out nostrils, or on straight split-bottom chairs, which Old Man Stark and the Boss had fetched in from the kitchen, and the motes of dust swam in the rays of light striking in under the shades on the western windows of the room through the one-time white but now yellowish lace curtains, which looped uncertainly from their rods like fish nets hung up to wait for mending. The gang of us sat around, and moved our thighs on the horsehair or on the split-bottom and stared down at the unpainted boards of the floor or at the design on the linoleum mat in the middle of the floor as though we were attending a funeral and owed the dead man some money. The

24

linoleum mat was newish, and the colors were still bright—reds and tans and blues slick and varnished-looking—a kind of glib, impertinent, geometrical island floating there in the midst of the cornerless shadows and the acid mummy smell and the slow swell of Time which had fed into this room, day by day since long back, as into a landlocked sea where the fish were dead and the taste was brackish on your tongue. You had the feeling that if the Boss and Mr. Duffy and Sadie Burke and the photographer and the reporters and you and the rest got cuddled up together on that linoleum mat it would lift off the floor by magic and scoop you all up together and make a lazy preliminary circuit of the room and whisk right out the door or out the roof like the floating island of Gulliver or the carpet in the Arabian Nights and carry you off where you and it belonged and leave Old Man Stark sitting there as though nothing had happened, very clean and razor-nicked, with his gray hair plastered down damp, sitting there by the table where the big Bible and the lamp and the plush-bound album were under the blank, devouring gaze of the whiskered face in the big crayon portrait above the mantel shelf.

Then the nigger woman brought in a pitcher of water on a tray, with three glasses, slipping her feet in old tennis shoes dryly along the boards. Lucy Stark took one glass and Sadie Burke another, and the rest of us just passed around the third glass.

Then the photographer took a secret look at his watch, and cleared his throat, and said, "Governor—"

"Yeah?" the Boss answered.

"I just reckoned—if you and Mrs. Stark is rested and all—" he made a sitting-down bow in the direction of Lucy Stark, a bow from the waist that was quite a feat and gave the impression he had had a couple too many for the heat and was passing out in the chair—"if you all—"

The Boss stood up. "All right," he said, grinning. "I just reckon I get you." Then he looked at his wife questioningly.

Lucy Stark stood up, too.

"All set, Pappy," the Boss said to the old man, and the old man stood up, too.

The Boss led the way out to the front porch. We all tailed him out like a procession. The photographer went to the second car and unpacked a tripod and the rest of his plunder and got it rigged up facing the steps. The Boss was standing on the steps, blinking and grinning, as though he were half asleep and knew what kind of a dream he was going to have.

"We'll just take you first, Governor," the photographer said, and the rest of us eased off the porch and out of range.

The photographer hid his head under the black cloth, then he popped out again all agog with an idea. "The dog," he said, "get

25

the dog in there with you, Governor. You be petting the dog or something. Right there on the steps. It'll be swell. It will be the nuts. You be petting that dog, he's pawing up on you like he was glad to see you when you come home. See? It will be the nuts."

"Sure, the nuts," the Boss said.

Then he turned toward the old white dog, which hadn't moved a muscle since the Cadillac pulled up at the gate and was lying over to one side of the porch like a worn-out fur rug. "Here, Buck," the Boss said, and snapped his fingers.

But the dog didn't show a thing.

"Here, Buck," the Boss called.

Tom Stark prodded the dog with his toe for a little encouragement, but he might just as well have been prodding a bolster.

"Buck is gitten on," Old Man Stark said. "He ain't right spry any more." Then the old man went to the steps and stooped down with a motion which made you expect to hear the sound of old rusty hinges on a barn door. "Hi, Buck, hi, Buck," the old man wheedled without optimism. He gave up, and lifted his gaze to the Boss. "If he was hongry now," he said, and shook his head. "If he was hongry we could guile him. But he ain't hongry. His teeth gone bad."

The Boss looked at me, and I knew what I was paid to do.

"Jack," the Boss said, "get the hairy bastard up here and make him look like he was glad to see me."

I was supposed to do a lot of different things, and one of them was to lift up fifteen-year-old, hundred-and-thirty-five-pound hairy white dogs on summer afternoons and paint an expression of unutterable bliss upon their faithful features as they gaze deep, deep into the Boss's eyes. I got hold of Buck's forelegs, as though I were girding myself to shove a wheelbarrow, and heaved. It didn't work. I got his front end up for a second, but just as I got him up, he breathed out and I breathed in. One gust of Buck was enough. It was like a gust from a buzzard's nest. I was paralyzed. Buck hit the porch boards and lay there like the old polar-bear rug he resembled.

Then Tom Stark and one of the reporters shoved on the tail end and I heaved on the front end and held my breath and we got Buck the seven feet to the Boss. The Boss braced himself, and we heaved up the front end, and the Boss got a gust of Buck.

That gust was enough.

"God's sake, Pappy," the Boss demanded as soon as he had mastered his spasm, "what you been feeding this dog?"

"He ain't got any appetite," Old Man Stark said.

"He ain't got any appetite for violets," the Boss said, and spat on the ground.

"The reason he fell," the photographer observed, "was because his hind legs gave down. Once we get him propped we got to work fast."

"We?" the Boss said. "We! What the hell you mean *we*. You come kiss him. One whiff would curdle milk and strip a pine tree. *We*, hell!"

The Boss took a deep breath, and we heaved again. It didn't work. Buck didn't have any starch in him. We tried six or seven times, but it was no sale. Finally the Boss had to sit down on the steps, and we dragged Buck up and laid the faithful head on the Boss's knee. The Boss put his hand on Buck's head and looked at the photographer's birdie. The photographer shot it, and said, "It is the nuts," and the Boss said, "Yeah, the nuts."

The Boss sat there a few seconds with his hand on Buck's head. "A dog," the Boss said, "is man's best friend. Old Buck, he's the best friend I ever had." He scratched the brute's head. "Yeah, good old Buck," the Boss said, "the best friend I ever had. But God damn it," he said, and stood up so quick that Buck's head slid off his knee, "he don't smell a bit better'n the rest of 'em."

"Is that for the record, Boss?" one of the reporters asked.

"Sure," the Boss said. "He smells just like the rest of 'em."

Then we cleared Buck's carcass off the steps, and the photographer settled into the grind. He took the Boss and the family in every possible combination. Then he got his rig together, and said: "Governor, you know we want a picture of you upstairs. In the room you used to have when you were a kid. It will be the nuts."

"Yeah," the Boss said, "the nuts."

That was my idea. It would be the nuts all right. The Boss sitting there with an old schoolbook in his hands. A good example for the tots. So we went upstairs.

It was a little room, with bare board floor and tongue-and-groove beaded walls, which had been painted yellow one time, but had the paint crazing off the wood now in the sections where any paint was left. There was a big wooden bed with a high head and foot standing somewhat off the perpendicular, and a white counterpane on the bed. There was a table—a pine table—and a couple of straight chairs, and a stove—the kind of tin stove they call a trash-burner, pretty rusty now—and against the wall beyond the stove a couple of home-made bookcases, crammed with books. Third readers and geographies and algebras and such in one of them, and a lot of crummy old law books in the other.

The Boss stood in the middle of the floor and took a good look, all around, while the rest of us hung around the door bunched up like sheep and waited. "Jesus," the Boss said, "put the old white thunder-mug under the bed and it'll look just like home."

I looked over at the bed, and the crockery wasn't there. It was the only prop missing. That and a kid with a pudgy face and freckles on his face and sandy hair falling down on his forehead, bending down at the table by a coal-oil lamp—it must have been a coal-oil lamp then—and a pencil in his hand, tooth marks on the pencil where he'd been gnawing at it, and the fire in the trash-burner getting low, and the wind pounding on the north side of the house, pounding down off the Dakotas a thousand miles away and across the plains which were icy and pearl-blind with the snow polished hard under the wind and glimmering in the dark, and across the river bottoms, and across the hills where the pine trees had stood once and moaned in the wind but where there wasn't anything to break the wind now. The sash in the window on the north wall of the room would rattle under the wind, and the flame in the coal-oil lamp would bend and shiver in what current of air sneaked in, but the kid wouldn't look up. He would gnaw his pencil, and hunch down. Then after a while he would blow out the lamp and pull off his clothes and get into bed, wearing his underwear. The sheets would be cold to the skin and stiff-feeling. He would lie there and shiver in the dark. The wind would come down a thousand miles and pound on the house and the sash would rattle and inside him something would be big and coiling slow and clotting till he would hold his breath and the blood would beat in his head with a hollow sound as though his head were a cave as big as the dark outside. He wouldn't have any name for what was big inside him. Maybe there isn't any name.

That was all there was missing from the room, the kid and the thunder-mug. Otherwise it was perfect.

"Yeah," the Boss was saying, "it's sure gone. But it's O.K. by me. Maybe sitting over running water puts phlegm in your gut like the old folks say, but it would sure have made learning law a hell of a lot more comfortable. And you wouldn't have to waste so much time."

The Boss was a slow mover. Many's the time we've settled affairs of state through a bathroom door, the Boss on the inside and me on the outside sitting on a chair with my little black notebook on my knee and the telephone ringing to beat hell.

But now the photographer started arranging things. He got the Boss to sit at the table and pore over a dog-eared reader, and he fired off his flash bulb and got that. And he got a half dozen more, the Boss sitting in a chair by the trash-burner, holding an old law book on his knees, and God knows what else.

I wandered off downstairs and left them preparing the documents for posterity.

When I got to the bottom of the stairs I could hear voices in the parlor, and figured it was the old man and Lucy Stark and

Sadie Burke and the kid. I went out the back way, to the back porch. I could hear the nigger woman puttering around in the kitchen, humming to herself about her and Jesus. I walked across the back yard, where there wasn't any grass. When the fall rains came there wouldn't be anything here but a loblolly with the crazy marks made in it by hens' feet. But it was dust now. There was a chinaberry tree beside the gate letting you into the back lot, and as I went through the gate the berries scattered on the ground crunched under my feet like bugs.

I went on down the lot, past a row of gable-shaped chicken coops, made of wood which had been split out like shingles, and set on cypress chunks to keep them out of the wet. I went on down to the barn and stable lot, where a couple of able-bodied but moth-eaten mules hung their heads in the unflagging shame of their species beside a big iron pot, the kind they use for cooking up molasses. The pot was a water trough now. There was a pipe sticking up beside it with a faucet on it. One of the Boss's modern improvements you couldn't see from the road.

I went on past the stables, which were built of log, but with a good tin roof, and leaned on the fence, looking off down the rise. Back of the barn the ground was washed and gullied somewhat, with piles of brush chucked into the washes here and there to stop the process. As though it ever would. A hundred yards off, at the foot of the rise, there was a patch of woods, scrub oak and such. The ground must have been swampy down there, for the grass and weeds at the edge of the trees were lush and tropical green. Against the bare ground beyond it looked too green to be natural. I could see a couple of hogs lounging down there on their sides, like big gray blisters popped up out of the ground.

It was getting toward sunset now. I leaned on the fence and looked off west across the country where the light was stretching out, and breathed in that dry, clean, ammoniac smell you get around stables at sunset on a summer day. I figured they would find me when they wanted me. I didn't have the slightest notion when that would be. The Boss and his family, I reckoned, would spend the night at his pappy's place. The reporters and the photographer and Sadie would get on back to the city. Mr. Duffy—maybe he was supposed to put up in Mason City at the hotel. Or maybe he and I were supposed to stay at Pappy's place too. If they put us in the same bed though, I was just going to start walking in to Mason City. Then there was Sugar-Boy. But I quit thinking about it. I didn't give a damn what they did.

I leaned on the fence, and the posture bowed my tail out so that the cloth of my pants pulled tight and pressed the pint against my left hip. I thought about that for a minute and admired the sunset colorations and breathed the dry, clean, ammoniac smell, and then pulled out the bottle. I took a drink and put it back. I leaned on the fence and waited for the sunset colorations to explode in my stomach, which they did.

I heard somebody open and shut the gate to the barn lot, but I didn't look around. If I didn't look around it would not be true that somebody had opened the gate with the creaky hinges, and that is a wonderful principle for a man to get hold of. I had got hold of the principle out of a book when I was in college, and I had hung on to it for grim death. I owed my success in life to that principle. It had put me where I was. What you don't know don't hurt you, for it ain't real. They called that Idealism in my book I had when I was in college, and after I got hold of that principle I became an Idealist. I was a brass-bound Idealist in those days. If you are an Idealist it does not matter what you do or what goes on around you because it isn't real anyway.

The steps came closer and closer, padded in the soft dust. I didn't look up. Then I felt the wire of the fence creak and give because somebody else was leaning against it and admiring the sunset. Mr. X and I admired the sunset together for a couple of minutes, and nothing said. Except for the sound of his breathing I wouldn't have known he was there.

Then there was a movement and the wire shifted when Mr. X took his weight off it. Then the hand patted my left hip, and the voice said, "Gimme a slug." It was the Boss's voice.

"Take it," I said. "You know where it lives."

He lifted up my coattail and pulled out the bottle. I could hear the gurgle as he did the damage. Then the wire shifted again as he leaned against it.

"I figured you'd come down here," he said.

"And you wanted a drink," I replied without bitterness.

"Yeah," he said, "and Pappy doesn't favor drinking. Never did."

I looked up at him. He was leaning on the fence, bearing down on the wire in a way not to do it any good, with the bottle held in both hands, corked, and his forearms propped over the wire.

"It used to be Lucy didn't favor it either," I said.

"Things change," he said. He uncorked the bottle and took another pull, and corked it again. "But Lucy," he said, "I don't know whether she's changed or not. I don't know whether she favors it or not now. She never touches it herself. Maybe she sees it eases a man's nerves."

I laughed. "You haven't got any nerves," I told him.

"I'm a bundle of nerves," he said, and grinned.

We kept on leaning against the fence, watching the light lying across the country and hitting the clump of trees down the rise. The Boss leaned his head a little forward and let a big globule of spit form at his lips and let it fall through the space between his forearms down to the board hog trough just over the fence from us. The trough was dry, with a few odd red grains of corn and a few shreds of shucks lying in it and on the ground by it.

"Things don't change much around here, though," the Boss said.

That didn't seem to demand any response, and so I didn't give it any.

"I bet I dumped ten thousand gallons of swill into that trough," he said, "one time and another." He let another glob of spit fall into the trough. "I bet I slopped five hundred head of hogs out of this trough," he said. "And," he said, "by God, I'm still doing it. Pouring swill."

"Well," I said, "swill is what they live on, isn't it?"

He didn't say anything to that.

The hinges of the gate up the lot creaked again, and I looked around. There wasn't any reason not to now. It was Sadie Burke. She was plowing her white oxfords through the dust as though she meant business, and every time she took a stride it looked as though she were going to pop the skirt of her blue-striped seersucker suit, she was in such a rush. The Boss turned around, looked at the bottle in his hand, then passed it to me. "What's up?" he asked her when she got within ten feet.

She didn't answer right away, but came up close. She was breathing hard from the rush. The light hit her on her slightly pock-marked face, which was damp now with perspiration, and her chopped-off black hair was wild and electric on her head, and her big, deep, powerful black eyes burned right out of her face into the sunlight.

"What's up?" the Boss demanded again.

"Judge Irwin," she managed to get out with what breath she had after the rush.

"Yeah?" the Boss said. He was still lounging against the wire, but he was looking at Sadie as though she might draw a gun and he was planning on beating her to the draw.

"Matlock called up—long-distance from town—and he said the afternoon paper—"

"Spill it," the Boss said, "spill it."

"Damn it," Sadie said, "I'll spill it when I get good and ready. I'll spill it when I get my breath. If I'm good and ready, and if you—"

"You're using up a lot of breath right now," the Boss said with a tone of voice which made you think of rubbing your hand down a cat's back, just as soft.

"It's my breath," Sadie snapped at him, "and nobody's bought it. I damned near break myself down running out here to tell you something and then you say spill it, spill it. Before I can get my breath. And I'll just tell you when I get good and ready. When I get my breath and—"

"You don't sound exactly wind-broke," the Boss observed, leaning back on the hog wire and grinning.

"You think it's so damned funny," Sadie said, "oh, yeah, so damned funny."

The Boss didn't answer that. He just kept leaning on the wire as though he had all day before him, and kept on grinning. When he grinned like that it didn't do much to soothe Sadie's feelings, I had observed in the past. And the symptoms seemed to be running true to form.

So I decorously withdrew my gaze from the pair, and resumed my admiration of the dying day on the other side of the hog lot and the elegiac landscape. Not that they would have bothered about me if they had anything on their minds—neither one of them. Powers, Thrones, and Dominations might be gathered round, and if Sadie felt like it she would cut loose, and the Boss wasn't precisely of a shrinking disposition. They'd get started like that over nothing at all sometimes, the Boss just lying back and grinning and working Sadie up till those big black glittering eyes of hers would almost pop out of her head and a hank of her black hair would separate from the tangle and hang down by her face so she'd have to swipe it back with the back of a hand. She would say plenty while she got worked up, but the Boss wouldn't say much. He'd just grin at her. He seemed to take a relish in getting her worked up that way and lying back and watching it. Even when she slapped him once, a good hard one, he kept on looking at her that way, as though she were a hula girl doing a dance for him. He relished her getting worked up, all right, unless she finally landed on a sore spot. She was the only one who knew the trick. Or had the nerve. Then the show would really start. They wouldn't care who was there. Certainly not if I was there, and there wasn't any reason for me to avert my face out of delicacy. I had been a piece of furniture a long time, but some taint of the manners my grandma taught me still hung on and now and then got the better of my curiosity. Sure I was a piece of furniture—with two legs and a pay check coming—but I looked off at the sunset, anyway.

"Oh, it's so damned funny," Sadie was saying, "but you won't think it's so damned funny when I tell you." She stopped, then said, "Judge Irwin has come out for Callahan."

There wasn't any sound for what must have been three seconds but seemed like a week while a mourning dove down in the clump of trees in the bottom where the hogs were gave a couple of tries at breaking his heart and mine.

Then I heard the Boss say, "The bastard."

"It was in the afternoon paper—the endorsement," Sadie elaborated. "Matlock telephoned from town. To let you know."

"The two-timing bastard," the Boss said.

Then he heaved up off the wire, and I turned around. I figured the conclave was about to break up. It was. "Come on," the Boss said, and started moving up the hill toward the house, Sadie by his side popping her seersucker skirt to keep up with him, and I trailing.

About the time we got to the gate where the chinaberry tree was and the berries on the ground popped under your feet, the Boss said to Sadie, "Get 'em cleared out."

"Tiny was figuring on having supper out here," Sadie said, "and Sugar-Boy was gonna drive him to Mason City in time for the eight-o'clock train to town. You asked him."

"I'm un-asking him," the Boss replied. "Clear 'em all out."

"It'll be a privilege," Sadie said, and I reckoned she spoke from the heart.

She cleared them out, and fast. Their car went off down the gravel road with the springs flat on the rear axle and human flesh oozing out the windows, then the evening quiet descended upon us. I went to the other side of the house where a hammock made out of wire and barrel staves, the kind they rig up in that part of the world, was swung between a post and the live oak. I took off my coat and hung it on the post, and dropped my bottle into the side pocket so it wouldn't break my hip bone when I lay down, and climbed into the hammock.

The Boss was down at the other end of the yard where the crepe myrtles were, prowling up and down on the dusty grass stems. Well, it was all his baby, and he could give it suck. I just lay there in the hammock. I lay there and watched the undersides of the oak leaves, dry and grayish and dusty-green, and some of them I saw had rusty-corroded-looking spots on them. Those were the ones which would turn loose their grip on the branch before long—not in any breeze, the fibers would just relax, in the middle of the day maybe with the sunshine bright and the air so still it aches like the place where the tooth was on the morning after you've been to the dentist or aches like your heart in the bosom when you stand on the street corner waiting for the light to change and happen to recollect how things once were and how they might have been yet if what happened had not happened.

Then, while I was watching the leaves I heard a dry, cracking sound down toward the barnyard. Then it came again. Then I figured out what it was. It was Sugar-Boy off down in the lot playing with his .38 Special again. He would set up a tin can or a bottle on a post, and turn his back to the post and start walking away, carrying his baby in his left hand, by the barrel, the safety on, just walking steadily away on his stumpy little legs with his always blue serge pants bagging around his underslung behind and with the last rays of the evening sun faintly glittering on his bald spot among the scrubby patches of hair like bleached lichen. Then, all of a sudden, he would stop walking, and grab the butt of the play-pretty with his right hand, and wheel—all in one quick, awkward motion, as though a spring had exploded inside him—and the play-pretty would go bang, and the tin can would jump off the post or the bottle would spray off in all directions. Or most likely. Then Sugar-Boy would say, "The b-b-b-bas-tud," and shake his head, and the spit would fly.

There would be a single cracking sound and a long wait. That meant he had hit it the first try, and was trudging back to the post to set up another. Then, after a spell, there would be another crack, and a wait. Then, one time, there came two cracks, close together. That meant Sugar-Boy had missed the first try and had got it on the second.

Then I must have dozed off, for I came to with the Boss standing there, saying, "Time to eat."

So we went in and ate.

We sat down at the table, Old Man Stark at one end and Lucy at the other. Lucy wiped the perspiration-soaked wisp of hair back from her face, and gave that last-minute look around the table to see if anything was missing, like a general inspecting troops. She was in her element, all right. She had been out of it for a long time, but when you dropped her back in it she hit running, like a cat out of a sack.

The jaws got to work around the table, and she watched them work. She sat there, not eating much and keeping a sharp eye out for a vacant place on any plate and watching the jaws work, and as she sat there, her face seemed to smooth itself out and relax with an inner faith in happiness the way the face of the chief engineer does when he goes down to the engine room at night and the big wheel is blurred out with its speed and the pistons plunge and return and the big steel throws are leaping in their perfect orbits like a ballet, and the whole place, under the electric glare, hums and glitters and sings like the eternal insides of God's head, and the ship is knocking off twenty-two knots on a glassy, starlit sea.

So the jaw muscles pumped all around the table, and Lucy Stark sat there in the bliss of self-fulfillment.

I had just managed to get down the last spoonful of chocolate ice cream, which I had had to tamp down into my gullet like wet concrete in a posthole, when the Boss, who was a powerful and systematic eater, took his last bite, lifted up his head, wiped off the lower half of his face with a napkin, and said, "Well, it looks like Jack and Sugar-Boy and me are going to take the night air down the highway."

Lucy Stark looked up at the Boss right quick, then looked away, and straightened a salt shaker. At first guess it might have been the look any wife gives her husband when he shoves back after supper and announces he thinks he'll step down town for a minute. Then you knew it wasn't that. It didn't have any question, or protest, or rebuke, or command, or self-pity, or whine, or oh-so-you-don't-love-me-any-more in it. It just didn't have anything in it, and that was what made it remarkable. It was a feat. Any act of pure perception is a feat, and if you don't believe it, try it sometime.

But Old Man Stark looked at the Boss, and said, "I sorta reckined—I reckined you was gonna stay out here tonight." There wasn't any trouble figuring out what he said, though. The child comes home and the parent puts the hooks in him. The old man, or the woman, as the case may be, hasn't got anything to say to the child. All he wants is to have that child sit in a chair for a couple of hours and then go off to bed under the same roof. It's not love. I am not saying that there is not such a thing as love. I am merely pointing to something which is different from love but which sometimes goes by the name of love. It may well be that without this thing which I am talking about there would not be any love. But this thing in itself is not love. It is just something in the blood. It is a kind of blood greed, and it is the fate of a man. It is the thing which man has which distinguishes him from the happy brute creation. When you get born your father and mother lost something out of themselves, and they are going to bust a hame trying to get it back, and you are it. They know they can't get it all back but they will get as big a chunk out of you as they can. And the good old family reunion, with picnic dinner under the maples, is very much like diving into the octopus tank at the aquarium. Anyway, that is what I would have said back then, that evening.

So Old Man Stark swallowed his Adam's apple a couple of times and lifted his misty, sad old blue eyes to the Boss, who happened to be flesh of his flesh though you'd never guess it, and threw in the hook. But it didn't snag a thing. Not on Willie.

"Nope," the Boss said, "I gotta shove."

"I sorta reckined—" the old man began, then surrendered, and tailed off, "but if'n it's business—"

"It is not business," the Boss said. "It is pure pleasure. At least I'm aiming for it to be before I'm through." Then he laughed and got up from the table, and gave his wife a smack of a kiss on the left cheek, slapped his son on the shoulder in that awkward way fathers have of slapping their sons on the shoulder (there is always a kind of apology in it, and anybody, even the Boss, who slapped Tom Stark on the shoulder had better apologize, for he was an arrogant bastard and when his father that night slapped him on the shoulder he didn't even bother to look up). Then the Boss said, "Don't wait up," and started out the door. Sugar-Boy and I followed. That was the first news I had had that I was going to take the night air. But it was all the warning you usually got from the Boss. I knew enough to know that.

The Boss was already sitting in the front by the driver's seat when I got to the Cadillac. So I got in the back, and prepared my soul for the experience of being hurled from one side to the other when we hit the curves. Sugar-Boy crawled under the wheel, and touched the starter, and began to make a sound like "Wh-wh-wh-wh—" A sound like an owl tuning up off in the swamp at night. If he had enough time and the spit held out, he would ask, "Where to?" But the Boss didn't wait. He said, "Burden's Landing."

So that was it. Burden's Landing. Well I ought to have guessed that.

Burden's Landing is one hundred and thirty miles from Mason City, off to the southwest. If you multiply one hundred and thirty by two it makes two hundred and sixty miles. It was near nine o'clock and the stars were out and the ground mist was beginning to show in the low places. God knew what time it would be when we got back to bed, and up the next morning to face a hearty breakfast and the ride back to the capital.

I lay back in the seat and closed my eyes. The gravel sprayed on the undersides of the fenders, and then it stopped spraying and the tail of the car lurched to one side, and me with it, and I knew we were back on the slab and leveling out for the job.

We would go gusting along the slab, which would be pale in the starlight between the patches of woods and the dark fields where the mist was rising. Way off from the road a barn would stick up out of the mist like a house sticking out of the rising water when the river breaks the levee. Close to the road a cow would stand knee-deep in the mist, with horns damp enough to have a pearly shine in the starlight, and would look at the black blur we were as we went whirling into the blazing corridor of light which we could never quite get into for it would be always splitting the dark just in front of us. The cow would stand there knee-deep in the mist and look at the black blur and the blaze and then, not turning its head, at the place where the black blur and blaze had been, with the remote, massive, unvindictive indifference of God-All-Mighty or Fate or me, if I were standing there knee-deep in the mist, and the blur and the blaze whizzed past and withered on off between the fields and the patches of woods.

But I wasn't standing there in the field, in the dark, with the mist turning slow around my knees and the ticking no-noise of the night inside my head. I was in a car, headed back to Burden's Landing, which was named for the people from whom I got my name, and which was the place where I had been born and raised.

36

We would go on between the fields until we hit a town. The houses would be lined up along the street, under the trees, with their lights going out now, until we hit the main street, where the lights would be bright around the doorway of the movie house and the bugs would be zooming against the bulbs and would ricochet off to hit the concrete pavement and make a dry crunch when somebody stepped on them. The men standing in front of the pool hall would look up and see the big black crate ghost down the street and one of them would spit on the concrete and say, "The bastard, he reckins he's somebody," and wish that he was in a big black car, as big as a hearse and the springs soft as mamma's breast and the engine breathing without a rustle at seventy-five, going off into the dark somewhere. Well, I was going somewhere. I was going back to Burden's Landing.

We would come into Burden's Landing by the new boulevard by the bay. The air would smell salty, with maybe a taint of the fishy, sad, sweet smell of the tidelands to it, but fresh nevertheless. It would be nearly midnight then, and the lights would be off in the three blocks of down-town then. Beyond the downtown and the little houses, there would be the other houses along the bay, set back in the magnolias and oaks, with the white walls showing glimmeringly beyond the darkness of the trees, and the jalousies, which in the daytime would be green, looking dark against the white walls. Folks would be lying back in the rooms behind the jalousies, with nothing but a sheet over them. Well, I'd put in a good many nights behind those jalousies, from the time I was little enough to wet the bed. I'd been born in one of those rooms behind the jalousies. And behind one set of them my mother would be lying up there tonight, with a little fluting of lace on the straps of her nightgown, and her face smooth like a girl's except for the little lines, which you wouldn't be able to make out in the shadow anyway, at the corners of her mouth and eyes, and one bare arm laid out on the sheet with the sharp, brittle-looking, age-betraying hand showing the painted nails. Theodore Murrell would be lying there, too, breathing with a slightly adenoidal sibilance under his beautiful blonde mustache. Well, it was all legal, for she was married to Theodore Murrell, who was a lot younger than my mother and who had beautiful yellow hair scrolled on top of his round skull like taffy, and who was my stepfather. Well, he wasn't the first stepfather I had had.

Then, on down the row, behind its own live oaks and magnolias, there would be the Stanton house, locked up and nobody behind the jalousies, for Anne and Adam were in town now, and grown up and never went fishing with me any more, and the old man was dead. Then on down the row, where the open country began, would be the house of Judge Irwin. We

37

wouldn't stop before we got there. But we'd make a little call on the Judge.

"Boss," I said.

The Boss turned around, and I saw the chunky black shape of his head against the brightness of our headlights.

"What you gonna say to him?" I asked.

"Boy, you never know till the time comes," he said. "Hell," he amended, "maybe I won't say anything to him a-tall. I don't know as I've got anything to say to him. I just want to look at him good."

"The Judge won't scare easy," I said. No, I didn't reckon the Judge would scare easy, thinking of the straight back of the man who used to swing off the saddle and drop the bridle over a paling on the Stanton fence and walk up the shell walk to the veranda with his Panama in his hand and the coarse dark-red hair bristling off his high skull like a mane and the hooked red nose jutting off his face and the yellow irises of his eyes bright and hard-looking as topaz. That was nearly twenty years before, all right, and maybe the back wasn't as straight now as it had been then (a thing like that happens so slowly you don't notice it) and maybe the yellow eyes were a little bleary lately, but I still didn't reckon the Judge would scare easy. That was one thing on which I figured I could bet: he wouldn't scare. If he did, it was going to be a disappointment to me.

"No, I don't count on him scaring easy," the Boss said. "I just want to look at him."

"Well, God damn it," I popped out, and came up off my shoulder blades before I knew it, "you're crazy to think you can scare him!"

"Take it easy," the Boss said, and laughed. I couldn't see his face. It was just a black blob against the glare of the headlights, with the laugh coming out of it.

"I just want to look at him," the Boss said, "like I told you."

"Well, you sure picked a hell of a time and a hell of a long way to go look at him," I said, not feeling anything but peevish now, and falling back on my shoulder blades where I belonged. "Why don't you get him to see you in town sometime?"

"*Sometime* ain't ever *now*," the Boss said.

"It's a hell of a thing," I said, "for you to be doing."

"So you think it's beneath my dignity, huh?" the Boss asked.

"Well, you're Governor. They tell me."

"Yeah, I'm Governor, Jack, and the trouble with Governors is they think they got to keep their dignity. But listen here, there ain't anything worth doing a man can do and keep his dignity. Can you figure out a single thing you really please-God like to do you can do and keep your dignity? The human frame just ain't built that way."

"All right," I said.

38

"And when I get to be President, if I want to see somebody I'm gonna go right out and see 'em."

"Sure," I said, "in the middle of the night, but when you do I hope you leave me at home to get a night's sleep maybe."

"The hell I will," he said. "When I'm President I'm gonna take you with me. I'm gonna keep you and Sugar-Boy right in the White House so I can have you all handy. Sugar-Boy can have him a pistol range in the back hall and a brace of Republican Congressmen to be caddy for him and set up the tin cans, and you can bring your girls right in the big front door, and there's gonna be a member of the Cabinet to hold their coats and pick up hair pins after 'em. There's gonna be a special member of the Cabinet to do it. He's gonna be the Secretary of the Bedchamber of Jack Burden, and he will keep the telephone numbers straight and send back any little pink silk articles to the right address when they happen to get left behind. Tiny's got the build, so I'm gonna get him a little operation and put flowing silk pants on him and a turban and give him a tin scimitar like he was a High Grand Shriner or something, and he can sit on a tuffet outside your door and be the Secretary of the Bedchamber. And how you like that, boy, huh?" And he reached back over the back of the front seat and slapped me on the knee. He had to reach a long way back, for it was a long way from the front seat of the Cadillac to my knee even if I was lying on my shoulder blades.

"You will go down in history," I said.

"Boy, wouldn't I!" And he started to laugh. He turned round to watch the lit-up road, and kept on laughing.

Then we hit a little town and beyond it a filling station and lunch stand. Sugar-Boy got some gas and brought the Boss and me a couple of cokes. Then we went on.

The Boss didn't say another word till we hit Burden's Landing. All he said then was, "Jack, you tell Sugar-Boy how to find the house. It's your pals live down here."

Yes, my pals lived down there. Or had lived down there. Adam and Anne Stanton had lived down there, in the white house where their widowed father, the Governor, lived. They had been my friends, Anne and Adam. Adam and I had fished and sailed all over that end of the Gulf of Mexico, and Anne, who was big-eyed and quiet-faced and thin, had been with us, close and never saying a word. Adam and I had hunted and camped all over the country, and Anne had been there, a thin-legged little girl about four years younger than we were. And we had sat by the fire in the Stanton house—or in my house—and had played with toys or read books while Anne sat there. Then after a long time Anne wasn't a little girl any more. She was a big girl and I was so much in love with her that I lived in a dream. In that dream my heart seemed to be ready to burst,

39

for it seemed that the whole world was inside it swelling to get out and be the world. But that summer came to an end. Time passed and nothing happened that we had felt so certain at one time would happen. So now Anne was an old maid living in the city, and even if she did look pretty good yet and wore clothes that didn't hurt her any, her laugh was getting brittle and there was a drawn look on her face as though she were trying to remember something. What was Anne trying to remember? Well, I didn't have to try to remember. I could remember but I didn't want to remember. If the human race didn't remember anything it would be perfectly happy. I was a student of history once in a university and if I learned anything from studying history that was what I learned. Or to be more exact, that was what I thought I had learned.

We would go down the Row—the line of houses facing the bay—and that was the place where all my pals had been. Anne, who was an old maid, or damned near it. Adam, who was a famous surgeon and who was nice to me but didn't go fishing with me any more. And Judge Irwin, who lived in the last house, and who had been a friend of my family and who used to take me hunting with him and taught me to shoot and taught me to ride and read history to me from leather-bound books in the big study in his house. After Ellis Burden went away he was more of a father to me than those men who had married my mother and come to live in Ellis Burden's house. And the Judge was a man.

So I told Sugar-Boy how to get through town and to the Row where all my pals lived or had lived. We pulled through the town, where the lights were out except for the bulbs hanging from the telephone poles, and on out the Bay Road where the houses were bone-white back among the magnolias and live oaks.

At night you pass through a little town where you once lived, and you expect to see yourself wearing knee pants, standing all alone on the street corner under the hanging bulbs, where the bugs bang on the tin reflectors and splatter to the pavment to lie stunned. You expect to see that boy standing there under the street lamp, out too late, and you feel like telling him he ought to go on home to bed or there will be hell to pay. But maybe you are home in bed and sound asleep and not dreaming and nothing has ever happened that seems to have happened. But, then, who the hell is this in the back seat of the big black Cadillac that comes ghosting through the town? Why, this is Jack Burden. Don't you remember little Jack Burden? He used to go out in his boat in the afternoon on the bay to fish, and come home and eat his supper and kiss his beautiful mother good night and say his prayers and go to bed at nine-thirty. Oh, you mean old Ellis Burden's boy? Yeah, and that woman he married out of Texas—or was it Arkansas?—that big-eyed thin-faced woman who lives up there in that old Burden place now with that man she got herself. What ever happened to Ellis Burden? Hell, I don't know, nobody around here had any word going on years. He was a queer 'un. Damn if he wasn't queer, going off and leaving a real looker like that woman out of Arkansas. Maybe he couldn't give her what she craved. Well, he give her that boy, that Jack Burden. Yeah.

You come into the town at night and there are the voices.

We had got to the end of the Row, and I saw the house bone-white back among the dark oak boughs.

"Here it is," I said.

"Park out here," the Boss said. And then to me, "There's a light. The bugger ain't in bed. You go on and knock on the door and tell him I want to see him."

"Suppose he won't open up?"

"He will," the Boss said. "But if he won't you make him. What the hell do I pay you for?"

I got out of the car and went in the gate and started up the shell walk under the black trees. Then I heard the Boss coming after me. We went up the walk, with him just behind me, and up the gallery steps.

The Boss stood to one side, and I pulled open the screen and knocked on the door. I knocked again; then looking in through the glass by the door I saw a door open off the hall—where the library was, I remembered—then a side light come on in the hall. He was coming to the door. I could see him through the glass while he fumbled with the lock.

"Yes?" he asked.

"Good evening, Judge," I said.

He stood there blinking into the dark outside, trying to make out my face.

"It's Jack Burden," I said.

"Well, well, Jack—well I'll be jiggered!" And he put out his hand. "Come in." He even looked glad to see me.

I shook hands and stepped inside, where the mirrors in the peeling gold frames glimmered on the walls in the rays of the not bright side light, and the glass of the big hurricane lamps glimmered on the marble-top stands.

"What can I do for you, Jack?" he asked me, and gave me a look out of his yellow eyes. They hadn't changed much, even if the rest of him had.

"Well," I began, and didn't know how I was going to end, "I just wanted to see if you were up and could talk to—"

"Sure, Jack, come on in. You aren't in any trouble, son? Let me shut the door first, and—"

He turned to shut the door, and if his ticker hadn't been in good shape for all his near three score and ten he'd have

41

dropped dead. For the Boss was standing there in the door. He hadn't made a sound.

As it was, the Judge didn't drop dead. And his face didn't show a thing. But I felt him stiffen. You turn to shut a door some night and find somebody standing there out of the dark, and you'll take a jump, too.

"No," the Boss said, easy and grinning, taking his hat off his head and stepping inside just as though he'd been invited, which he hadn't been, "no, Jack isn't in any trouble. Not that I know of. Nor me either."

The Judge was looking at me now. "I beg your pardon," he said to me, in a voice he knew how to make cold and rasping like an old phonograph needle scraping on an old record, "I had forgotten for the moment how well your needs are provided for."

"Oh, Jack's making out," the Boss said.

"And you, sir—" the Judge turned on the Boss, and slanted his yellow eyes down on him—for he was a half a head taller —and I could see the jaw muscles twitch and knot under the folds of red-rusty and seamed skin on his long jaw, "do you wish to say something to me?"

"Well, I don't know as I do," the Boss remarked, offhand. "Not at the moment."

"Well," the Judge said, "in that case—"

"Oh, something might develop," the Boss broke in. "You never can tell. If we get the weight off our arches."

"In that case," the Judge resumed, and it was an old needle and an old record and it was scraping like a file on cold tin and nothing human, "I may say that I was about to retire."

"Oh, it's early yet," the Boss said, and took his time giving Judge Irwin the once-over from head to toe. The Judge was wearing an old-fashioned velvet smoking jacket and tuxedo pants and a boiled shirt, but he had taken off his collar and tie and the gold collar button was shining just under the big old red Adam's apple. "Yeah," the Boss went on, after he'd finished the once-over, "and you'll sleep better if you wait before going to bed and give that fine dinner you had a chance to digest."

And he just began walking down the hall toward the door where the light was, the door to the library.

Judge Irwin looked at the Boss's back as the Boss just walked away, the Palm Beach coat all crumpled up where it had crawled on the Boss's shoulders and the old sweat-stains of the afternoon showing dark at the armpits. The Judge's yellow eyes were near to popping out of his face and the blood was up in his face till it was the color of calf's liver in a butcher shop. Then he began to walk down the hall after the Boss.

I followed the pair of them.

The Boss was already sitting in a big old scuffed leather easy chair when I went in. I stood there against the wall, under the bookshelves that went up to the ceiling, full of old leather books, a lot of them law books, that got lost in the shadows up above and made the room smell musty like old cheese. Well, the room hadn't changed any. I could remember that smell from the long afternoons I had spent in that room, reading by myself or hearing the Judge's voice reading to me, while a log crackled on the hearth and the clock in the corner, a big grandfather's clock, offered us the slow, small, individual pellets of time. It was the same room. There were the big steel engravings on the wall—by Piranesi, in the heavy, scrollwork frames, the Tiber, the Colosseum, some ruined temple. And the riding crops on the mantel and on the desk, and the silver cups the Judge's dogs had won in the field trials and the Judge had won shooting. The gun rack, over in the shadow by the door, was out of the light from the big brass reading lamp on the desk, but I knew every gun in it, and knew the gun's feel.

The Judge didn't sit down. He stood in the middle of the floor and looked down at the Boss, who had his legs stuck out on the red carpet. And the Judge didn't say anything. Something was going on inside his head. You knew that if he had a little glass window in the side of that tall skull, where the one-time thick, dark-red, mane-like hair was thinned out now and faded, you could see inside and see the wheels and springs and cogs and ratchets working away and shining like a beautiful lot of well-kept mechanism. But maybe somebody had pushed the wrong button. Maybe it was just going to run on and on till something cracked or the spring ran down, and nothing was going to happen.

But the Boss said something. He jerked his head sideways to indicate the silver tray with the bottle and the pitcher of water and a silver bowl and two used glasses and three or four clean ones which sat on the desk, and said, "Judge, I trust you don't mind Jack pouring me a slug? You know, Southern hospitality."

Judge Irwin didn't answer him. He turned to me, and said, "I didn't realize, Jack, that your duties included those of a body servant, but, of course, if I am mistaken——"

I could have slapped his face. I could have slapped that God-damned handsome, eagle-beaked, strong-boned, rubiginous-hided high old face, in which the eyes weren't old but were hard and bright without any depth to them and were an insult to look into. And the Boss laughed, and I could have slapped his God-damned face. I could have walked right out and left the two of them there, alone in that cheese-smelling room together till hell froze over, and just kept on walking. But I didn't, and perhaps it was just as well, for maybe you cannot ever really walk away from the things you want most to walk away from.

"Oh, nuts," the Boss said, and stopped laughing, and heaved himself up out of the leather chair, and made a pass at the bottle and sloshed out some whisky into a glass and poured in some water. Then he turned round, and grinning up to the Judge, stepped toward me and held out the glass. "Here, Jack," he said, "have a drink."

I can't say that I took the drink. It got shoved into my hand, and I stood there holding it, not drinking it, and watched the Boss look up at Judge Irwin and say, "Sometimes Jack pours me a drink, and sometimes I pour him a drink and—" he stepped toward the desk again—"sometimes I pour myself a drink."

He poured the drink, added water, and looked again at the Judge, leering with a kind of comic cunning. "Whether I'm asked or not," he said. And added, "There's lots of things you never get, Judge, if you wait till you are asked. And I am an impatient man. I am a very impatient man, Judge. That is why I am not a gentleman, Judge."

"Really?" replied the Judge. He stood in the middle of the floor and studied the scene beneath him.

From my spot by the wall, I looked at both of them. *To hell with them*, I thought, *to hell with both of them*. When they talked like that, it was to hell with both of them.

"Yeah," the Boss was saying, "you're a gent, and so you don't ever get impatient. Not even for your likker. You aren't even impatient for your drink right now and it's likker your money paid for. But you'll get a drink, Judge. I'm asking you to have one. Have a drink with me, Judge."

Judge Irwin didn't answer a word. He stood very erect in the middle of the floor.

"Aw, have a drink," the Boss said, and laughed, and sat again in the big chair and stuck out his legs on the red carpet.

The Judge didn't pour himself a drink. And he didn't sit down.

The Boss looked up at him from the chair and said, "Judge, you happen to have an evening paper round here?"

The paper was lying over on another chair by the fireplace, with the Judge's collar and tie on top of it, and his white jacket hung on the back of the chair. I saw the Judge's eyes snap over there to it, and then back at the Boss.

"Yes," the Judge said, "as a matter of fact, I have."

"I haven't had a chance to see one, rushing round the country today. Mind if I take a look?"

"Not in the slightest," Judge Irwin said, and the sound was the file scraping on that cold tin again, "but perhaps I can relieve your curiosity on one point. The paper publishes my endorsement of Callahan for the Senate nomination. If that is of interest to you."

"Just wanted to hear you say it, Judge. Somebody told me, but you know how rumor hath a thousand tongues, and how the newspaper boys tend to exaggeration, and the truth ain't in 'em."

"There was no exaggeration in this case," the Judge said.

"Just wanted to hear you say it. With your own silver tongue."

"Well, you've heard it," the Judge said, standing straight in the middle of the floor, "and in that case, at your leisure—" the Judge's face was the color of calf's liver again, even if the words did come out cold and spaced—"if you have finished your drink—"

"Why, thanks, Judge," the Boss said, sweet as chess pie, "I reckon I will take another spot." And he heaved himself in the direction of the bottle.

He did his work, and said, "Thanks."

When he was back in the leather chair with the fresh load in the glass, he said, "Yeah, Judge, I've heard you say it, but I just wanted to hear you say something else. Are you sure you took it to the Lord in prayer? Huh?"

"I have settled the matter in my own mind," the Judge said.

"Well, if I recollect right—" the Boss ruminatively turned the glass in his hands—"back in town, when we had our little talk, you sort of felt my boy Masters was all right."

"I made no commitment," the Judge said sharply. "I didn't make any commitment except to my conscience."

"You been messing in politics a long time, Judge," the Boss said, easy, "and—" he took a drag from the glass—"so has your conscience."

"I beg your pardon," the Judge snapped.

"Nuts," the Boss said, and grinned. "But what got you off Masters?"

"Certain features of his career came to my attention."

"Somebody dug up some dirt for you, huh?"

"If you choose to call it that," the Judge said.

"Dirt's a funny thing," the Boss said. "Come to think of it, there ain't a thing but dirt on this green God's globe except what's under water, and that's dirt too. It's dirt makes the grass grow. A diamond ain't a thing in the world but a piece of dirt that got awful hot. And God-a-Mighty picked up a handful of dirt and blew on it and made you and me and George Washington and mankind blessed in faculty and apprehension. It all depends on what you do with the dirt. That right?"

"That doesn't alter the fact," the Judge said from way up

there where his head was, above the rays of the desk lamp, "that Masters doesn't strike me as a responsible man."

"He better be responsible," the Boss said, "or I'll break his God-damned neck!"

"That's the trouble. Masters would be responsible to you."

"It's a fact," the Boss admitted ruefully, lifting his face under the light, and shaking his head in fatalistic sadness. "Masters'd be responsible to me. I can't help it. But Callahan—now take Callahan—it sort of seems to me he's gonna be responsible to you and Alta Power and God knows who else before he's through. And what's the difference? Huh?"

"Well—"

"Well, hell!" The Boss popped straight up in the chair with that inner explosiveness he had when, all of a sudden, he would snatch a fly out of the air or whip his head at you and his eyes would snap open. He popped up and his heels dug into the red carpet. Some of the liquor sloshed out of his glass onto his Palm Beach pants. "Well, I'll tell you the difference, Judge! I can deliver Masters and you can't deliver Callahan. And that's a big difference."

"I'll have to take my chance," the Judge said from way up there.

"Chance?" And the Boss laughed. "Judge," he said, and quit laughing, "you haven't got but one chance. You been guessing right in this state going on forty years. You been sittting back here in this room and nigger boys been single-footing in here bringing you toddies and you been guessing right. You been sitting back here and grinning to yourself while the rest of 'em were out sweating on the stump and snapping their suspenders, and when you wanted anything you just reached out and took it. Oh, if you had a little time off from duck hunting and corporation law you might do a hitch as Attorney General. So you did. Or play at being a judge. You been a judge a long time. How would it feel not to be a judge any more?"

"No man," Judge Irwin said, and stood up there straight in the middle of the floor, "has ever been able to intimidate me."

"Well, I never tried," the Boss said, "yet. And I'm not trying now. I'm going to give you a chance. You say somebody gave you some dirt on Masters? Well, just suppose I gave you some dirt on Callahan?—Oh, don't interrupt! Keep your shirt on!"— and he held up his hand. "I haven't been doing any digging, but I might, and if I went out in the barn lot and stuck my shovel in and brought you in some of the sweet-smelling and put it under the nose of your conscience, then do you know what your conscience would tell you to do? It would tell you to withdraw your endorsement of Callahan. And the newspaper boys would be over here thicker'n blue-bottle flies on a dead dog, and you

46

could tell 'em all about you and your conscience. You wouldn't even have to back Masters. You and your conscience could just go off arm in arm and have a fine time telling each other how much you think of each other."

"I have endorsed Callahan," the Judge said. He didn't flicker.

"I maybe could give you the dirt," the Boss said speculatively. "Callahan's been playing round for a long time, and he who touches pitch shall be defiled, and little boys just will walk barefoot in the cow pasture." He looked up at Judge Irwin's face, squinting, studying it, cocking his own head to one side.

The grandfather's clock in the corner of the room, I suddenly realized, wasn't getting any younger. It would drop out a *tick,* and the *tick* would land inside my head like a rock dropped in a well, and the ripples would circle out and stop, and the *tick* would sink down the dark. For a piece of time which was not long or short, and might not even be time, there wouldn't be anything. Then the *tock* would drop down the well, and the ripples would circle out and finish.

The Boss quit studying Judge Irwin's face, which didn't show anything. He let himself sink back in the chair, shrugged his shoulders, and lifted the glass up for a drink. Then he said, "Suit yourself, Judge. But you know, there's another way to play it. Maybe somebody might give Callahan a little shovelful on somebody else and Callahan might grow a conscience all of a sudden and repudiate his endorser. You know, when this conscience business starts, ain't no telling where it'll stop, and when you start the digging—"

"I'll thank you, sir—" Judge Irwin took a step toward the big chair, and his face wasn't the color of calf's liver now—it was long past that and streaked white back from the base of the jutting nose—"I'll thank you, sir, to get out of that chair and get out of this house!"

The Boss didn't lift his head off the leather. He looked up at the Judge, sweet and trusting, and then cocked his eyes over to me. "Jack," he said, "you were sure right. The Judge don't scare easy."

"Get out," the Judge said, not loud this time.

"These old bones don't move fast," the Boss murmured sadly, "but now I have tried to do my bounden duty, let me go." Then he drained his glass, set it on the floor beside the chair, and rose. He stood in front of the Judge, looking up at him, squinting again, cocking his head to one side again, like a farmer getting ready to buy a horse.

I set my glass on the shelf of the bookcase behind me. I discovered that I hadn't touched it, not since the first sip. *Well, to hell with it,* I thought, and let it stand. Some nigger boy would get it in the morning.

Then, as though he had decided against buying the horse, the Boss shook his head and passed around the Judge, as though the Judge weren't a man at all, or even a horse, as though he were the corner of a house or a tree, and headed for the hall door, putting his feet down slow and easy on the red carpet. No hurry.

For a second or two the Judge didn't even move his head; then he swung round and watched the Boss going toward the door, and his eyes glittered up there in the shadow above the lamp.

The Boss laid his hand on the doorknob, opened the door, and then, with his hand still on the knob, he looked back. "Well, Judge," he said, "more in pain than wrath I go. And if your conscience decides it could gag at Callahan, just let me know. In, of course——" and he grinned——"a reasonable time."

Then he looked over at me and said, "Let's haul ass, Jack," and started on down toward the front door, out of sight.

Before I could get into low gear, the Judge swung his face in my direction, and focused his eyes on me, and his upper lip lifted under that nose to form a smile of somewhat massive irony, and he said, "Your employer is calling you, Mr. Burden."

"I don't use any ear trumpet yet," I said, and pulled off toward the door, and thought to myself: *Christ, Jack, you talk like a snot, Christ, you are a smart guy.*

I had just about made the door, when he said, "I'm dining with your mother this week. Shall I tell her you still like your work?"

Why don't he lay off? I thought, but he wouldn't, and that lip lifted up again.

So I said, "Suit yourself, Judge. But if I were you I wouldn't go around advertising this visit to anybody. In case you changed your mind, somebody might figure you had stooped to a low political deal with the Boss. In the dark of night."

And I went out the door and down the hall and out the hall door and left it open but let the screen door slam.

God damn him, why hadn't he laid off me?

But he hadn't scared.

We left the bay, and lost the salt, sad, sweet, fishy smell of the tidelands out of our nostrils. We headed north again. It was darker now. The ground mist lay heavier on the fields, and in the dips of the road the mist frayed out over the slab and blunted the headlights. Now and then a pair of eyes would burn at us out of the dark ahead. I knew that they were the eyes of a cow—a poor dear stoic old cow with a cud, standing on the highway shoulder, for there wasn't any stock law— but her eyes burned at us out of the dark as though her skull were full of blazing molten metal like blood and we could see

48

inside the skull into that bloody hot brightness in that moment when the reflection was right before we picked up her shape, which is so perfectly formed to be pelted with clods, and knew what she was and knew that inside that unlovely knotty head there wasn't anything but a handful of coldly coagulated gray mess in which something slow happened as we went by. We were something slow happening inside the cold brain of a cow. That's what the cow would say if she were a brass-bound Idealist like little Jackie Burden.

The Boss said, "Well, Jackie, it looks like you got a job cut out for you."

And I said, "Callahan?"

And he said, "Nope, Irwin."

And I said, "I don't reckon you will find anything on Irwin."

And he said, "You find it."

We bored on into the dark for another twenty miles and eighteen minutes. The ectoplasmic fingers of the mist reached out of the swamp, threading out from the blackness of the cypresses, to snag us, but didn't have any luck. A possum came out of the swamp and started across the road and might have made it, too, if Sugar-Boy hadn't been too quick for him. Sugar-Boy just shaded the steering wheel delicately to the left, just a fraction. There wasn't even a jounce or twitch, but something thumped against the underside of the left front fender, and Sugar-Boy said, "The b-b-b-b-bas-tud." Sugar-Boy could thread a needle with that Cadillac.

At about the end of that eighteen minutes and twenty miles, I said: "But suppose I don't find anything before election day?"

The Boss said, "To hell with election day. I can deliver Masters prepaid, special handling. But if it takes ten years, you find it."

We clocked off five miles more, and I said, "But suppose there isn't anything to find?"

And the Boss said, "There is always something."

And I said, "Maybe not on the Judge."

And he said, "Man is conceived in sin and born in corruption and he passeth from the stink of the didie to the stench of the shroud. There is always something."

Two miles more, and he said, "And make it stick."

And that was all a good while ago. And Masters is dead now, as dead as a mackerel, but the Boss was right and he went to the Senate. And Callahan is not dead but he has wished he were, no doubt, for he used up his luck a long time back and being dead was not part of it. And Adam Stanton is dead now, too, who used to go fishing with me and who lay on the sand in the hot sunshine with me and with Anne Stanton. And Judge Irwin is dead, who leaned toward me among the stems of the tall gray marsh grass, in the gray damp wintry dawn, and said, "You ought to have led that duck more, Jack. You got to lead a duck, son." And the Boss is dead, who said to me, "And make it stick."

Little Jackie made it stick, all right.

Chapter Two

THE LAST time I saw Mason City I went up there in that big black Cadillac with the Boss and the gang, and we burned up that new concrete slab, and it was a long time ago—nearly three years, for it is now into 1939, but it seems like forever. But the first time I went up there it was a lot longer time ago, back in 1922, and I went up there in my Model-T, hanging on to the steering post to stay in the saddle when I sideslipped in the gray dust, which plumed out behind for a mile and settled on the cotton leaves to make them gray too, or when I hit a section of gravel, holding my jaws clamped tight to keep the vibration from the washboard from chipping the enamel off my teeth. You'll have to say this for the Boss: when he got through you could drive out for a breath of air and still keep your bridgework in place. But you couldn't that first time I went to Mason City.

The managing editor of the *Chronicle* called me in and said, "Jack, get in your car and go up to Mason City and see who the hell that fellow Stark is who thinks he is Jesus Christ scourging the money-changers out of that shinplaster courthouse up there."

"He married a school-teacher," I said.

"Well, it must have gone to his head," Jim Madison, who was managing editor of the *Chronicle,* said. "Does he think he is the first one ever popped a school-teacher?"

"The bond issue was for building a schoolhouse," I said, "and it looks like Lucy figures they might keep some of it for that purpose."

"Who the hell is Lucy?"

"Lucy is the school-teacher," I said.

"She won't be a school-teacher long," he said, "Not on the Mason County payroll if she keeps that up. Not if I know Mason County."

"Lucy don't favor drinking either," I said.

"Was it you or the other guy popped Lucy?" he demanded. "You know so much about Lucy."

"I just know what Willie told me."

"Who the hell is Willie?"

"Willie is the fellow with the Christmas tie," I said. "He is Cousin Willie from the country. He is Willie Stark, the teacher's pet, and I met him in the back room of Slade's place a couple

51

of months ago and he told me Lucy didn't favor drinking. I'm just guessing about her not favoring stealing."

"She don't favor Willie being County Treasurer either," Jim Madison allowed, "if she is the one putting him up to what he is doing. Doesn't she know how they run things up in Mason County?"

"They run 'em up there just like they run 'em down here," I said.

"Yeah," Jim Madison said, and took the foul, chewed, and spit-bright butt of what had been a two-bit cigar out of the corner of his mouth and inspected it and reached out at arm's length and let it fall into the big brass spittoon which stood on the clover-deep, Kelly-green carpet which bloomed like an oasis of elegance in the four floors of squalor of the Chronicle Building. He watched it fall, and said again, "Yeah, but you leave down here and go on up there."

So I went up to Mason City in the Model-T, and kept my jaws clamped tight when I went over the washboard and hung to the steering post when I went over the sideslipping dust, and that was a very long time ago.

I got to Mason City early in the afternoon and went to the Mason City Cafe, Home-Cooked Meals for Ladies and Gents, facing the square, and sampled the mashed potatoes and fried ham and greens with pot-likker with one hand while with the other I competed with seven or eight flies for the possession of a piece of custard pie.

I went out into the street, where the dogs lay on the shady side under the corrugated iron awnings, and walked down the block till I came to the harness shop. There was one vacant seat out front, so I said howdy-do, and joined the club. I was the junior member by forty years, but I thought I was going to have liver spots on my swollen old hands crooked on the head of the hickory stick like the rest of them before anybody was going to say anything. In a town like Mason City the bench in front of the harness shop is—or was twenty years ago before the concrete slab got laid down—the place where Time gets tangled in its own feet and lies down like an old hound and gives up the struggle. It is a place where you sit down and wait for night to come and arteriosclerosis. It is the place the local undertaker looks at with confidence and thinks he is not going to starve as long as that much work is cut out for him. But if you are sitting on the bench in the middle of the afternoon in late August with the old ones, it does not seem that anything will ever come, not even your own funeral, and the sun beats down and the shadows don't move across the bright dust, which, if you stare at it long enough, seems to be full of glittering specks like quartz. The old ones sit there with their liver-spotted hands crooked on the hickory sticks, and they

52

emit a kind of metaphysical effluvium by virtue of which your categories are altered. Time and motion cease to be. It is like sniffing ether, and everything is sweet and sad and far away. You sit there among the elder gods, disturbed by no sound except the slight *râle* of the one who has asthma, and wait for them to lean from the Olympian and sunlit detachment and comment, with their unenvious and foreknowing irony, on the goings-on of the folks who are still snared in the toils of mortal compulsions. *I seen Sim Saunders done built him a new barn.* Then, *Yeah, some folks thinks they is made of money.* And, *Yeah.*

So I sat there and waited. And one of them said it, and another one leaned and shifted the quid and answered, and the last one said, "Yeah." Then I waited again for a spell, for I knew my place in the picture, and then I said, "They tell me there's gonna be a new schoolhouse." Then I waited another spell while the words died away and it was as though I hadn't said anything. Then one of them let the ambeer drop to the dry ground, and touched the spot with the end of the hickory stick, and said, "Yeah, and steam heat, hear tell."

And Number Two: "Give them young 'uns pneumonia, steam heat."

And Number Three: "Yeah."

And Number Four: "If'n they git hit built."

I looked across the square at the painted clock face on the courthouse tower, which was the clock the old ones kept time by, and waited. Then I said, "What's stopping 'em?"

And Number One: "Stark. Thet Stark."

And Number Two: "Yeah, thet Willie Stark."

And Number Three: "Too big fer his britches. Gits in the courthouse and gits his front feet in the trough, and gits too big fer his britches."

And Number Four: "Yeah."

I waited, then I said, "Wants 'em to take the low bid, they tell me."

And Number One: "Yeah, wants 'em to take the low bid and git a passel of niggers in here."

And Number Two: "To put white folks out of work. Builden hit."

And Number Three: "You want to work longside a nigger? And specially him a strange nigger? Builden schoolhouse or backhouse, how so be hit?"

And Number Four: "And white folks needen work."

And Number One: "Yeah."

Yeah, I said to myself, *so that is the tale,* for Mason County is red-neck country and they don't like niggers, not strange niggers anyway, and they haven't got many of their own. "How much could they save," I asked, "taking the low bid?"

53

And Number One: "Couldn't save enuff to pay fer bringen no passel of niggers in here."

"Putten white folks out of work," Number Two said.

I waited till it was decent, then I got up and said, "Got to be moving. Good afternoon, gentlemen."

One of the old ones looked up at me as though I had just come and said, "What you work at, boy?"

"I don't," I said.

"Porely?" he asked.

"Not porely," I said. "It is just I lack ambition."

Which was God's truth, I reckoned, as I walked on down the street.

I reckoned, too, that I had killed enough time and I might as well go on to the courthouse and get my story in the way I was supposed to get it. All this sitting around in front of harness shops was not the way any newspaperman would go about getting his story. There isn't ever anything you get that way which you can put into a newspaper. So I went on over to the courthouse.

Inside the courthouse, where the big hall was empty and shadowy and the black oily floor was worn down to humps and ridges under your feet and the air was dry and dusty so that you felt in the stillness that you were breathing into yourself the last shrunk-up whispers still hanging in the air from all the talk, loud and little, there had been in there for seventy-five years— well, inside there, just off the hall I saw some men sitting in a room. Above the doorway there was a tin sign with the letters about faded off. But they still said *Sheriff*.

I went into the room where the three men were cocked back in split-bottom chairs and an electric fan set on top of the roll-top desk was burring away with little effect, and said howdy-do to the faces. The biggest face, which was round and red and had its feet cocked on the desk and its hands laid on its stomach, said howdy-do.

I took a card out of my pocket and gave it to him. He looked at the card for a minute, holding it off near arm's length as though he were afraid it would spit in his eye, then he turned it over and looked at the back side a minute till he was dead sure it was blank. Then he laid the hand with the card in it back down on his stomach, where it belonged, and looked at me. "You done come a piece," he said.

"That's right," I said.

"What you come fer?"

"To see what's going on about the schoolhouse," I said.

"You come a piece," he said, "to stick yore nose in somebody else's bizness."

"That's right," I agreed cheerfully, "but my boss on the paper can't see it that way."

"It ain't any of his bizness either."

"No," I said, "but what's the ruckus about, now I've come all that piece?"

"It ain't any of my bizness. I'm the Sheriff."

"Well, Sheriff," I said, "whose business is it?"

"Them as is tending to it. If folks would quit messen and let 'em."

"Who is *them?*"

"Commissioners," the Sheriff said. "The County Commissioners, the voters of Mason County done elected to tend to their bizness and not take no butten-in from nobody."

"Yeah, sure—the Commissioners. But who are they?"

The Sheriff's little wise eyes blinked at me a couple of times, then he said, "The constable ought to lock you up fer vagruncy."

"Suits me," I said. "And the *Chronicle* would send up another boy to cover my case, and when the constable pinched him the *Chronicle* would send up another one to cover that case, and after a while you'd get us all locked up. But it might get in the papers."

The Sheriff just lay there, and out of his big round face his little eyes blinked. Maybe I hadn't said anything. Maybe I wasn't there.

"Who are the Commissioners?" I said. "Or maybe they are hiding out?"

"One of 'em is setten right there," the Sheriff said, and rolled his big round head on his shoulders to indicate one of the other fellows. When the head had fallen back into place, and his fingers had let go my card, which wafted down to the floor in the gentle breeze from the fan, the little eyes blinked again and he seemed to sink below the surface of the roiled waters. He had done his best, and now he had passed the ball.

"Are you a Commissioner?" I asked the fellow just indicated. He was just another fellow, made in God's image and wearing a white shirt with a ready-tied black bow tie and jean pants held up with web galluses. Town from the waist up, country from the waist down. Get both votes.

"Yeah," he said.

"He's the head man," another fellow said, reverently, a little old squirt of a fellow with a bald knotty old head and a face he himself couldn't recollect from one time he looked in the mirror to the next, the sort of a fellow who hangs around and sits in a chair when the big boys leave one vacant and tries to buy his way into the game with a remark like the one he had just made.

"You the Chairman?" I asked the other fellow.

"Yeah," he said.

"You mind telling me your name?"

"It ain't no secret," he said. "It is Dolph Pillsbury."

"Glad to know you, Mr. Pillsbury," I said and held out my hand. Not getting up, he took it as though I had offered him the business end of a cottonmouth moccasin in shedding time.

"Mr. Pillsbury," I said, "you are in a position to know the situation in regard to the schoolhouse contract. No doubt you are interested in having the truth of that situation made public."

"There ain't any situation," Mr. Pillsbury said.

"Maybe there isn't any situation," I said, "but there's been a right smart racket."

"Ain't any situation. Board meets and takes a bid what's been offered. J. H. Moore's bid, the fellow's name."

"Was that fellow Moore's bid low?"

"Not egg-zackly."

"You mean it wasn't low?"

"Well—" Mr. Pillsbury said, and his face was shadowed by an expression which might have been caused by a gas pain, "well if'n you want to put it that a-way."

"All right," I said, "let's put it that way."

"Now look a-here—" and the shadow passed from Mr. Pillsbury's face and he sat up in his chair as suddenly as though he had been stuck by a pin—"you talk like that, and ain't nuthen done but legal. Ain't nobody can tell the Board what bid to take. Anybody can come along and put in a little piss-ant bid, but the Board doan have to take it. Naw-sir-ee. The Board takes somebody kin do the work right."

"Who was it put the little piss-ant bid in?"

"Name of Jeffers," Mr. Pillsbury said peevishly, as at an unpleasant recollection.

"Jeffers Construction?" I asked.

"Yeah."

"What's wrong with Jeffers Construction?"

"The Board picks the fellow kin do the work right, and it ain't nobody's bizness."

I took out my pencil and a pad of paper, and wrote on it. Then I said to Mr. Pillsbury, "How's this?" And I began to read to him: "Mr. Dolph Pillsbury, Chairman of the Board of County Commissioners of Mason County, stated that the bid of J. H. Moore for the construction of the Mason County School was accepted, even though it was not the low bid, because the Board wanted somebody 'who could do the work right.' The low bid, which was submitted by the Jeffers Construction Company, was rejected, Mr. Pillsbury stated. Mr. Pillsbury stated further—"

"Now look a-here—" Mr. Pillsbury was sitting very straight up as though it were not a pin this time but a hot tenpenny and in the brown—"now look a-here, I didn't state nuthen.

56

You write it down and claim I stated it. Now you look a-here—"

The Sheriff heaved massively in the chair and fixed his gaze upon Mr. Pillsbury. "Dolph," he said, "tell the bugger to git out of here."

"I didn't state nuthen," Dolph said, "and you git out!"

"Sure," I said, and put the pad in my pocket, "but maybe you can kindly tell me where Mr. Stark is?"

"I knowed it," the Sheriff exploded and dropped his feet off the desk with a noise like a brick chimney falling, and heaved up in the chair and glared apoplectically at me. "That Stark, I knowed it was that Stark!"

"What's wrong with Stark?" I asked.

"Jesus Gawd!" roared the Sheriff, and his face went purple with the congestion of language which couldn't get out.

"He's biggety, that's what he is," Mr. Dolph Pillsbury offered. "Gits in the courthouse and gits biggety, he—"

"He's a nigger-lover," the little old bald, knotty-headed fellow submitted.

"And him, him—" Mr. Pillsbury pointed at me with an air of revelation—"I bet he's a nigger-lover, comen up here and sashayen round, I bet he—"

"No sale," I said. "I like mine vanilla. But now you've raised the subject, what's nigger-loving got to do with it?"

"That's it!" Mr. Pillsbury exclaimed, like the man overboard seizing the plank. "The Jeffers Construction now, they—"

"You, Dolph," the Sheriff bellowed at him, "why don't you shut up and tell him to git out!"

"Git out," Mr. Pillsbury said to me, obediently but without great vigor.

"Sure," I replied, and went out and walked down the hall.

They ain't real, I thought as I walked down the hall, *nary one.* But I knew they were. You come into a strange place, into a town like Mason City, and they don't seem real, but you know they are. You know they went wading in the creek when they were kids, and when they were bigger they used to go out about sunset and lean on the back fence and look across the country at the sky and not know what was happening inside them or whether they were happy or sad, and when they got grown they slept with their wives and tickled their babies to make them laugh and went to work in the morning and didn't know what they wanted but had their reasons for doing things and wanted to do good things, because they always gave good reasons for the things they did, and then when they got old they lost their reasons for doing anything and sat on the bench in front of the harness shop and had words for the reasons other people had but had forgotten what the reasons were. And then they will lie in bed some morning just

57

before day and look up at the ceiling they can scarcely see because the lamp is shaded with a pinned-on newspaper and they don't recognize the faces around the bed any more because the room is full of smoke, or fog, and it makes their eyes burn and gets in the throat. Oh, they are real, all right, and it may be the reason they don't seem real to you is that you aren't very real yourself.

But by that time I was standing in front of a door at one end of the cross hall and was looking up at another tin sign, and knew from it that I had arrived at the one-man leper colony of Mason City.

The leper was sitting in the room, not doing anything, all by himself. There wasn't anybody to sit and spit and jaw with him under his electric fan.

"Hello," I said, and he looked up at me as though I were a spook and the word I had used were in a foreign language. He didn't answer me right off, and I figured he was like one of those fellows who gets marooned on a desert island for twenty years and when the longboat is beached and the jolly tars leap out on the sand and ask him who the hell he is, he can't say a word because his tongue is so rusty.

Well, Willie wasn't that bad off, for he finally managed to say hello, and that he remembered me from our meeting in Slade's place a few months back, and to ask me what I wanted. I told him, and he grinned a grin more wistful than happy and asked me why I wanted to know.

"The editor told me to find out," I said, "and why he wants me to find out only God knows. Maybe it is because it is news."

That seemed to be enough to satisfy him. So I didn't tell him that beyond my boss the managing editor there was a great high world of reasons but to a fellow like me down in the ditch it was a world of flickering diaphanous spirit wings and faint angel voices I didn't always savvy and stellar influences.

"I reckon it is news," Willie allowed.

"What's been going on around here?"

"I don't mind telling you," he said. He began telling me and he finished telling me about eleven o'clock that night with Lucy Stark, after she had put the kid to bed, and me sitting with him in the parlor out at his pappy's place, where he had asked me to spend the night, and where he and Lucy ordinarily lived in the summer and where they were going to live that winter too instead of in a room in town because Lucy had just been fired from her teaching job for the coming year and there wasn't any reason to be in town and be spending good money for rent. And there was very likely to be another reason for there not being any reason to stay in town, for Willie was coming up for re-election and his chances looked about as good as the chances of a flea making a living off a carved marble

58

lion on a monument. He had only got the job in the first place, he told me, because Dolph Pillsbury, the Chairman of the Board of County Commissioners, was a sort of secondhand relative of old Mr. Stark, by marriage or something, and Pillsbury had had a falling-out with the other fellow who wanted to be Treasurer. Pillsbury about ran the county, he and the Sheriff, and he was sick of Willie. So Willie was on his way out, and Lucy was already out.

"And I don't care if I am," Lucy Stark said, sitting there in the parlor, sewing by the lamp on the table where the big Bible and the plush-bound album were. "I don't care a bit if they won't let me teach any more. I taught six years, counting that term I was out and having little Tommie, and nobody ever said I wasn't all right, but now they write me a letter and say there're complaints about my work and I don't show a spirit of co-operation."

She lifted her sewing and bit off the thread in the way women do to make your flesh crawl. When she leaned over, the light hit her hair to show up the auburn luster lurking in the brown which the operator of the recently established Mason City Beauty Shoppe hadn't been entirely able to burn out with the curling tongs when she gave the marcel treatment. It was too bad about Lucy's hair, even if the luster was still there. She was still girlish then, about twenty-five but not looking it, with a nice little waist coming straight up out of the satisfactory and unmeager hips and a nice little pair of ankles crossed in front of the chair, and her face was girlish, with soft, soothing contours and large deep-brown eyes, the kind that makes you think of telling secrets in the gloaming over a garden gate when the lilacs are in bloom along the picket fence of the old homestead. But her hair was cut off at about neck level and marcelled the way they did it back then, which was a shame because the face she had was the kind that demanded to be framed by a wealth of long and lustrous-dusky tresses tangled on the snow-white pillow. She must have had plenty of hair, too, before the massacre.

"But I don't care," she said, and lifted her head out of the light. "I don't want to teach in a schoolhouse they build just so somebody can steal some money. And Willie doesn't want to be Treasurer either, if he has to associate with those dishonest people."

"I'm going to run," Willie said glumly. "They can't keep me from running."

"You can give a lot more time to studying your law books," she said to him, "when you aren't in town all the time."

"I'm going to run," he repeated, and jerked his head with that sharp motion he had to get the lock of hair out of his eyes. "I'm going to run," he repeated again, as though he

59

weren't talking to Lucy, or to me, but to the wide sweet air or God-Almighty, "if I don't get a single God-damned vote."

Well, he did run when the time came, and he got more than one vote, but not many more, and Mr. Dolph Pillsbury and his pals won that round. The fellow who was elected against Willie that fall didn't hang his hat up in the office before he had signed the check for the advance payment to J. H. Moore, and J. H. Moore built the schoolhouse. But that is getting ahead of the story.

The story, as Willie told it, was this: The Jeffers Construction Company had low bid at one hundred and forty-two thousand. But there were two more bids in between the Jeffers bid and the Moore bid, which was one hundred and sixty-five thousand and a lot of nickels and dimes. But when Willie kicked about the Moore business, Pillsbury started the nigger business. Jeffers was a big-time contractor, from the south of the state, and he used a lot of Negro bricklayers and plasterers and carpenters in some of his crews. Pillsbury started howling that Jeffers would bring in a lot of Negroes—and Mason County, as I said, is red-neck country—and worse, some of the Negroes would be getting better pay, being skilled laborers, than the men he would pick up around Mason City for some of the work. Pillsbury kept the pot boiling.

He kept it boiling so well that the public overlooked the fact that there were two bids in between Jeffers and Moore and the fact that Pillsbury had a brother-in-law who had a brick-kiln in which Moore had an interest and that in the not distant past a lot of the bricks had been declared rotten by the building inspector on a state job and had been refused and there had been a lawsuit and that as sure as God made little green apples with worms in them, bricks from the same kiln would be used in the schoolhouse. The kiln owned by Moore and Pillsbury's brother-in-law used convict labor from the state pen and got it cheap, for the brother-in-law had some tie well up in the system. In fact, as I picked up later, the tie was so good that that building inspector who squawked about the bricks on the state job got thrown out, but I never knew whether he was honest or just ill-informed.

Willie didn't have any luck bucking Pillsbury and the Sheriff. There was an anti-Pillsbury faction, but it didn't amount to much, and Willie didn't add to its numbers. Willie went out and buttonholed folks on the street and tried to explain things to them. You could see Willie standing on a street corner, sweating through his seersucker suit, with his hair down in his eyes, holding an old envelope in one hand and a pencil in the other, working out figures to explain what he was squawking about, but folks don't listen to you when your voice is low and patient and you stop them in the hot sun and make them do arithmetic. Willie tried to get the *Mason County Messenger* to print something, but they wouldn't. Then he wrote up a long statement of the case as he saw it about the bids, and tried to get the *Messenger* to print it on handbills in their job-printing shop, paid for, but they wouldn't do it. So Willie had to go to the city to get the work done. He came back with his handbills and hired a couple of kids to tote them from house to house in town. But the folks of one of the kids made him stop as soon as they found out, and when the other kid didn't stop, some big boys beat him up.

So Willie toted them around himself, over town, from house to house, carrying them in an old satchel, the kind school kids use, and knocked on the door and then tipped his hat when the lady of the house came. But most of the time she didn't come. There'd be a rustle of a window shade inside, but nobody would come. So Willie would stick a handbill under the door and go to the next place. When he had worked out Mason City, he went over to Tyree, the other town in the county, and passed out his bills the same way, and then he called on the crossroads settlements.

He didn't dent the constituency. The other fellow was elected. J. H. Moore built the schoolhouse, which began to need repairs before the paint was dry. Willie was out of a job. Pillsbury and his friends, no doubt, picked up some nice change as kickback from J. H. Moore, and forgot about the whole business. At least they forgot about it for about three years, when their bad luck started.

Meanwhile Willie was back on Pappy's farm, helping with the chores, and peddling a patent Fix-It Household Kit around the country to pick up a little change, working from door to door again, going from settlement to settlement in his old car, and stopping at the farmhouses in between, knocking on the door and tipping his hat and then showing the woman how to fix a pot. And at night he was plugging away at his books, getting ready for the bar examination. But before that came to pass Willie and Lucy and I sat there that night in the parlor, and Willie said: "They tried to run it over me. They just figured I'd do anything they told me, and they tried to run it over me like I was dirt."

And laying her sewing down in her lap, Lucy said, "Now, honey, you didn't want to be mixed up with them anyway. Not after you found out they were dishonest and crooked."

"They tried to run it over me," he repeated, sullenly, twisting his heavy body in the chair. "Like I was dirt."

"Willie," she said, leaning toward him a little, "they would have been crooks even if they didn't try to run it over you."

He wasn't paying her much mind.

"They'd be crooks, wouldn't they?" she asked in a tone

which was a little bit like the patient, leading-them-on tone she must have used in the schoolroom. She kept watching his face, which seemed to be pulling back from her and from me and the room, as though he weren't really hearing her voice but were listening to another voice, a signal maybe, outside the house, in the dark beyond the screen of the open window.

"Wouldn't they?" she asked him, pulling him back into the room, into the circle of soft light from the lamp on the table, where the big Bible and the plush-bound album lay. The bowl of the lamp was china and had a spray of violets painted on it.

"Wouldn't they?" she asked him, and before he answered I caught myself listening to the dry, compulsive, half-witted sound the crickets were making out in the grass in the dark.

Then he said, "Yeah, yeah, they'd be crooks, all right," and heaved himself in the chair with the motion of one who is irritated at having a train of thought interrupted.

Then he sank back into whatever he was brooding over.

Lucy looked at me with a confident birdlike lift of her head, as though she had proved something to me. The secondary glow of the light above the circle of light was on her face, and if I had wanted to I could have guessed that some of that glow was given off softly by her face as though the flesh had a delicate and unflagging and serene phosphorescence from its own inwardness.

Well, Lucy was a woman, and therefore she must have been wonderful in the way women are wonderful. She turned her face to me with that expression which seemed to say, "See, I told you, that's the way it is," and meanwhile Willie sat there. But his own face seemed to be pulling off again into the distance which was not distance but which was, shall I say, simply himself.

Lucy was sewing now, and talking to me while looking down at the cloth, and after a little Willie got up and started to walk up and down the room, with his forelock coming down over his eyes. He kept on pacing back and forth while Lucy and I talked.

It wasn't very soothing to have that going on across one end of the room.

Finally, Lucy looked up from her sewing, and said, "Honey—"

Willie stopped pacing and swung his head at her with the forelock down over his eyes to give him the look of a mean horse when he's cornered in the angle of the pasture fence with his head down a little and the mane shagged forward between the ears, and the eyes both wild and shrewd, watching you step up with the bridle, and getting ready to bolt.

"Sit down, honey," Lucy said, "you make me nervous. You're just like Tommie, you can't ever sit still." Then she laughed, and with a sort of shamefaced grin on his face he came over and sat down.

She was a fine woman, and he was lucky to have her.

But he was also lucky to have the Sheriff and Dolph Pillsbury, for they were doing him a favor and not knowing it. He didn't seem to know it either at the time, that they were his luck. But perhaps the essential part of him was knowing it all the time, only word hadn't quite got around to the other and accidental parts of him. Or it is possible that fellows like Willie Stark are born outside of luck, good or bad, and luck, which is what about makes you and me what we are, doesn't have anything to do with them, for they are what they are from the time they first kick in the womb until the end. And if that is the case, then their life history is a process of discovering what they really are, and not, as for you and me, sons of luck, a process of becoming what luck makes us. And if that is the case, then Lucy wasn't Willie's luck. Or his unluck either. She was part of the climate in which the process of discovering the real Willie was taking place.

But, speaking vulgarly, the Sheriff and Pillsbury were part of Willie's luck. I didn't know it that night in Pappy's parlor, and I didn't know it when I got back to town and gave Jim Madison my tale. Well, Willie began to appear in the *Chronicle* in the role of the boy upon the burning deck and the boy who put his finger in the dike and the boy who replies "I can" when Duty whispers low "Thou must." The *Chronicle* was turning up more and more tales about finagling in county courthouses around the state. It pointed the finger of fine scorn and reprobation all over the map. Then I began to grasp the significance of what was going on in that world of reasons high above the desk of Jim Madison, and caught the glint of those diaphanous spirit wings and the fluting whispers of the faint angel voices up there. In brief, this: The happy harmony in the state machine was a thing of the past, and the *Chronicle* was lined up with the soreheads, and was hacking away at the county substructure of the machine. It was starting there, feeling its way, setting the stage and preparing the back-drop for the real show. It wasn't as hard as it might have been. Ordinarily the country boys in the county courthouses have plenty of savvy and know all the tricks and are plenty hard to pin anything on, but the machine had been operating so long now without serious opposition that ease had corrupted them. They just didn't bother to be careful. So the *Chronicle* was making a good show.

But Mason County was Exhibit Number One. On account of Willie. He gave the touch of drama to the sordid tale. He became symbolically the spokesman for the tongue-tied population of honest men. And when Willie was licked at the polls of Mason County, the *Chronicle* ran his picture, and under it the line KEEPS HIS FAITH. And under that they printed the statement which Willie had given to me when I went back up to Mason City after the election and after Willie was out. The statement went like this:

"Sure, they did it and it was a clean job which I admire. I am going back to Pappy's farm and milk the cows and study some more law for it looks like I am going to need it. But I have kept my faith in the people of Mason County. Time will bring all things to light."

I had gone up there to see what he had to say, but didn't have to go out to the farm. I ran into Willie on the street. He had been building some fence and had busted his wire stretcher and had come in to town to get a new one. He was wearing an old black felt hat and overalls which hung down around his can as though he were little Droopy-Drawers smiling up from the play pen.

We went to the drugstore and had a coke. We stood in front of the soda fountain and I put my pad in front of Willie by his old hat and gave him a pencil. He licked the point and his eyes glazed as though he were getting ready to do sums on his slate, and then leaning up against the marble, with his overalls drooping, he wrote out the statement in his big round, scrawly hand.

"How's Lucy making out?" I asked him.

"Fine," he said. "She likes it out there and she's company for Pappy. It suits her all right."

"That's fine," I said.

"It suits me, too," he said, not looking at me but across the fountain at his own face in the big mirror. "The way it is it all suits me just fine," he said, and looked at the face in the mirror, which was freckled and thin-skinned over the full flesh but under the shaggy forelock was untroubled and pure like the face of a man who tops the last rise and looks down at the road running long and straight to the place where he is going.

As I said, if a man like Willie can be said to live in the world of luck, Dolph Pillsbury and the Sheriff were his luck. They ran it over Willie and got the new schoolhouse built by J. H. Moore. J. H. Moore used the brick out of the kiln owned by the distant relative of Pillsbury. It was just another big box of a schoolhouse with a fire escape at each end. The fire escapes weren't the kind which looks like a silo and which has a corkscrew-shaped chute inside for the kiddies to slide down. They were iron stairs attached to the outside of the building.

There wasn't any fire at the schoolhouse. There was just a fire drill.

About two years after the place was built, it happened. There was a fire drill, and all the kids on the top floors started to use the fire escapes. The first kids to start down on the fire escape at the west end were little kids and they couldn't get down the steps very fast. Right after them came a batch of big kids, seventh and eighth graders. Because the little kids held up the traffic, the fire escape and the iron platform at the top got packed with kids. Well, some of the brickwork gave and the bolts and bars holding the contraption to the wall pulled loose and the whole thing fell away, spraying kids in all directions.

Three kids were killed outright. They were the ones that hit the concrete walk. About a dozen were crippled up pretty seriously and several of those never were much good afterward.

It was a piece of luck for Willie.

Willie didn't try to cash in on the luck. He didn't have to try. People got the point. Willie went to the triple funeral the town had for the kids who got killed, and stood modestly in the background. But old Mr. Sandeen, who was father of one of the dead kids, saw him back in the crowd and while the clods were still bouncing off the coffin lids Mr. Sandeen pushed back to him and grabbed him by the hand and lifted up one arm above his head and said, loud, "Oh, God, I am punished for accepting iniquity and voting against an honest man!"

It brought down the house. Some women began to cry. Then other people began to come up and grab Willie by the hand. Pretty soon there was scarcely a dry eye in the crowd. Willie's weren't dry, either.

It was Willie's luck. But the best luck always happens to people who don't need it.

He had Mason County in the palm of his hand. And in the city his picture was in all the papers. But he didn't run for anything. He kept on working on his father's farm and studying his law books at night. The only thing he did about politics was to get out and make some speeches for a fellow who was running in the primary against the Congressman who had always been a pal of Pillsbury. Willie's speeches weren't any good, at least the one I heard wasn't any good. But they didn't have to be good. People didn't bother to listen to them. They just came to look at Willie and clap and then go vote against the Pillsbury man.

Then one day Willie woke up and found himself running for Governor. Or rather, he was running in the Democratic primary, which in our state is the same as running for Governor.

Now it wasn't any particular achievement to be running in the primary. Anybody who can scrape together a few dollars for the qualifying fee can offer for election and have the pleasure of seeing his name printed on the ballot. But Willie's case was a little different.

There were then two major factions in the Democratic party in the state, the Joe Harrison outfit and the MacMurfee outfit.

Harrison had been Governor some time back, and MacMurfee was in then and was going to try to hold the job. Harrison was a city man and practically all of his backing was city backing. MacMurfee wasn't exactly a hick, having been born and bred in Duboisville, which is a pretty fair-sized place, maybe ninety thousand, but he had a lot of country backing and small-town backing. He had played pretty smart with the cocklebur vote and mostly had it. It was due to be a close race. That situation was what got Willie into the show.

Somebody in the Harrison outfit got the idea, which God knows he didn't invent, of putting in a dummy who might split the MacMurfee vote. This had to be somebody who had a strong appeal in the country. So that was Willie, who could throw some weight up in the north end of the state. There wasn't any deal with Willie, it developed. Some gentlemen from the city called on him up in Mason City, driving up there in a fine car and striped pants. One of them was Mr. Duffy, Tiny Duffy, who was a lot grander now than he had been back that day when he and Willie had first met in the back room of Slade's beer parlor. The gentlemen from the city persuaded Willie that he was the savior of the state. I suppose that Willie had his natural quota of ordinary suspicion and cageyness, but those things tend to evaporate when what people tell you is what you want to hear. Also there was the small matter of God. People said that God had taken a hand in the schoolhouse business. That God had stepped in on Willie's side. The Lord had justified him. Willie was not religious by any ordinary standards, but the schoolhouse business very probably gave him the notion—which was shared by a lot of the local citizenry —that he stood in a special relation to God, Destiny, or plain Luck. And it doesn't matter what you call it or if you go to church. And since the Lord moves in a mysterious way, it should not have surprised Willie that He was using some fat men in striped pants and a big car to work His will. The Lord was calling Willie, and Tiny Duffy was just an expensively dressed Western Union boy in a Cadillac instead of on a bicycle. So Willie signed the receipt.

Willie was ready to ride. He was a lawyer now. He had been for some little time, for after he had lost out as County Treasurer, he had buckled down to his books pretty seriously, in what time he could spare from farming and peddling his Fix-It Household Kit. He had sat up there in his room late at night in summer, dog sleepy but grinding his eyes into the page, while the moths tapped and blurred at the window screen and tried to get onto the flame of the oil lamp which sizzled softly on his table. Or he had sat up there on winter nights while the fire died out in the rusty trash-burner stove and the wind beat on the north side of the house, coming down a thousand miles through the night to shake the room where Willie sat hunched over the book. Long back, he had spent a year at the Baptist College over at Marston, in the next county, long back before he had met Lucy. The college wasn't much more than a glorified grade school, but there he had heard the big names written on the big books. He had left the college with the big names in his head, because he didn't have any money. Then the war had come and he had been in it, stuck off somewhere in Oklahoma in a camp, feeling cheated, somehow, and feeling that he had missed his chance. Then after the war there had been the working on his father's place and reading books at night, not law books, just what books he could get hold of. He wanted to know the history of the country. He had a college textbook, a big thick one. Years later, showing it to me, he prodded it with his finger, and said, "I durn near memorized every durn word in it. I could name you every name. I could name you every date." Then he prodded it again, this time contemptuously, and said, "And the fellow that wrote it didn't know a God-damned thing. About how things were. He didn't know a thing. I bet things were just like they are now. A lot of folks wrassling round." But there had been the great names, too. There had been a notebook, a big cloth-bound ledger, in which he wrote the fine sayings and the fine ideas he got out of the books. A long time later he showed me that, too, and as I thumbed idly through it, noticing the quotations from Emerson and Macaulay and Benjamin Franklin and Shakespeare copied out in a ragged, boyish hand, he said with that same tone of amiable contempt, "Gee, back in those days I figured those fellows who wrote the books knew all there was. And I figured I was going to get me a chunk of it. Yeah, I figured I would sweat for me a chunk of it." He laughed. And added, "Yeah, I thought I was the nuts."

He had been going to get a chunk of all there was. But in the end it was a chunk of law. Lucy came into the picture, and then the kid Tom, and there was working, and later the court-house, but in the end he got a chunk of law. An old lawyer over at Tyree helped him, lending him books and answering questions. There had been about three years of that. If he had just been trying to squeeze by the bar with as little as possible he could have done it a lot sooner, for back in those days, or now for that matter, it didn't take any master mind to pass the bar examination. "I sure was a fool," Willie said to me once, talking about those times, "I thought you had really to learn all that stuff. I thought they meant for you to learn law. Hell, I got down to that bar examination and I looked at the questions and I nearly busted out laughing. Me sitting up there bearing down on those books, and then they gave me those little crappy questions. A corn-field nigger could have answered them if he'd been able to spell. I ought to have looked twice at some of the lawyers I'd seen and I'd have known a half-wit could pass it. But, oh, no, I was hell-bent on learning me some law." Then he laughed, stopped laughing, and said with a touch of the grimness which must have belonged to the long nights up there in his room when he bent over the trash-burner or heard the moths batting soft at the screen in the August dark: "Well, I learned me some law. I could wait." He could wait. He had read the books the old lawyer over at Tyree had, and then he bought new books, sending away for them with the money he grubbed out of the ground or got with his patented Fix-It Household Kit. The time came in the end, and he put on his good suit, blue serge and slick in the seat, and caught the train down to the city to take the examination. He had waited, and now he really knew what was in the books.

He was a lawyer now. He could hang the overalls on a nail and let them stiffen with the last sweat he had sweated into them. He could rent himself a room over the dry-goods store in Mason City and call it his office, and wait for somebody to come up the stairs where it was so dark you had to feel your way and where it smelled like the inside of an old trunk that's been in the attic twenty years. He was a lawyer now and it had taken him a long time. It had taken him a long time because he had had to be a lawyer on his terms and in his own way. But that was over. But maybe it had taken him too long. If something takes too long, something happens to you. You become all and only the thing you want and nothing else, for you have paid too much for it, too much in wanting and too much in waiting and too much in getting. In the end they just ask you those crappy little questions.

But the wanting and the waiting were over now, and Willie had a haircut and a new hat and a new brief case with the copy of his speech in it (which he had written out in longhand and had said to Lucy with gestures, as though he were getting ready for the high-school oratorical contest) and a lot of new friends, with drooping blue jowls and sharp pale noses, who slapped him on the back, and a campaign manager, Tiny Duffy, who would introduce him to you and say with a tin-glittering heartiness, "Meet Willie Stark, the next Governor of this state!" And Willie would put out his hand to you with the gravity of a bishop. For he never tumbled to a thing.

I used to wonder how he got that way. If he had been running for something back in Mason County he never in God's world would have been that way. He would have taken a perfectly realistic view of things and counted up his chances. Or if he had got into the gubernatorial primary on his own hook, he would have taken a realistic view. But this was different. He had been called. He had been touched. He had been summoned.

And he was a little bit awe-struck by the fact. It seems incredible that he hadn't taken one look at Tiny Duffy and his friends and realized that things might not be absolutely on the level. But actually, as I figured it, it wasn't incredible. For the voice of Tiny Duffy summoning him was nothing but the echo of a certainty and a blind compulsion within him, the thing that had made him sit up in his room, night after night, rubbing the sleep out of his eyes, to write the fine phrases and the fine ideas in the big ledger or to bend with a violent, almost physical intensity over the yellow page of an old law book. For him to deny the voice of Tiny Duffy would have been as difficult as for a saint to deny the voice that calls in the night.

He wasn't really in touch with the world. He was not only bemused by the voice he had heard. He was bemused by the very grandeur of the position to which he aspired. The blaze of light hitting him in the eyes blinded him. After all, he had just come out of the dark, the period when he grubbed on the farm all day and didn't see anybody but the family (and day after day he must have moved by them as though they weren't half-real) and sat at night in his room with the books and hurt inside with the effort and the groping and the wanting. So it isn't much wonder that the blaze of light blinded him.

He knew something about human nature, all right. He'd sat around the county courthouse long enough to find out something. (True, he had got himself thrown out of the courthouse. But that wasn't ignorance of human nature. It was, perhaps, a knowledge not of human nature in general but of his own nature in particular, something deeper than the mere question of right and wrong. He became a martyr, not through ignorance, not only for the right but also for some knowledge of himself deeper than right or wrong.) He knew something about human nature, but something now came between him and that knowledge. In a way, he flattered human nature. He assumed that other people were as bemused by the grandeur and as blinded by the light of the post to which he aspired, and that they would only listen to argument and language that was grand and bright. So his speeches were cut to that measure. It was a weird mixture of facts and figures on one hand (his tax program, his road program) and of fine sentiments on the other hand (a faint echo, somewhat dulled by time, of the quotations copied out in the ragged, boyish hand in the big ledger).

Willie went around the country in a good secondhand automobile, which had been bought on the eighteen-payment plan, and saw his face on the posters nailed to telephone poles and corncribs and board fences. He'd get to town, and after he'd been to the post office to see if there was a letter from Lucy and after he had had a session with the local politicos and done some handshaking (he wasn't too hot at that, too much talk about principles and not enough about promises), he would hole up in a hotel room ($2.00 without bath) and work some more on his speech. He kept on polishing and revising the damned thing. He was hell-bent on making each one a second Gettysburg Address. And maybe after he had tinkered with it awhile, he would get up and start pacing in his room. He would pace and pace, and pretty soon he would start to say his speech. If you were in the next room, you could hear him pacing and speeching, and when he stopped pacing you knew he had stopped in front of the mirror to polish up a gesture.

And sometimes I'd be in the next room, for I was supposed to cover his campaign for the *Chronicle*. I'd be lying there in the hole in the middle of my bed where the springs had given down with the weight of wayfaring humanity, lying there on my back with my clothes on and looking up at the ceiling and watching the cigarette smoke flow up slow and splash against the ceiling like the upside-down slow-motion moving picture of the ghost of a waterfall or like the pale uncertain spirit rising up out of your mouth on the last exhalation, the way the Egyptians figured it, to leave the horizontal tenement of clay in its ill-fitting pants and vest. I'd be lying there letting the smoke drift up out of my mouth and not feeling anything, just watching the smoke as though I didn't have any past or future, and suddenly Willie would start in the next room. Tramping and mumbling.

It would be a reproach, an affront, a cause for laughter and a thing for tears. Knowing what you knew, you would lie there listening to him getting ready to be Governor, and want to stuff the pillow slip in your mouth to stop the giggles. The poor half-witted bastard and his speech. But the voice would keep on going over there beyond the wall, and the feet would keep on tramping, back and forth like the feet of a heavy animal prowling and swinging back and forth with a heavy swaying head in a locked-up room, or a cage, hunting for the place to get out, not giving up and irreconcilably and savagely sure that there was going to be a loose board or bar or latch sometime, not now but sometime. And listening to it, you wouldn't be so sure for a minute the bar or board would hold. Or the feet would not stop and they were like a machine, which was not human or animal either, and were tramping on you like pestles or plungers in a big vat and you were the thing in the vat, the thing that just happened to be there. The plungers didn't care about its being you, or not being you, in the vat. But they would continue until there wasn't any you, and afterward for a long time until the machine wore out or somebody switched off the juice.

Then, because you want to lie down in the late afternoon on
70

a strange bed in a shadowy room and watch the smoke drift up and not think about anything, what you've been or what you're going to be, and because the feet, the beast, the plungers, the half-wit won't stop, you jerk yourself up and sit on the edge of the bed and feel like swearing. But you don't. For you are wondering, with the beginnings of pain and insufficiency, what it is inside that won't let the feet stop. Maybe he is a half-wit, maybe he won't be Governor, maybe nobody will listen to his speeches but Lucy, but the feet won't stop.

Nobody would listen to the speeches, including me. They were awful. They were full of facts and figures he had dug up about running the state. He would say, "Now, friends, if you will bear patiently with me for a few minutes, I will give you the figures," and he would clear his throat and fumble with a sheet of paper and backbones would sag lower in the seats and folks would start cleaning their fingernails with their pocket knives. If Willie had ever thought of talking to folks up on the platform just the way he could talk to you face to face when he got heated about something, leaning at you as if he meant every damned word he said and his eyes bugging out and shining, he might have swayed the constituency. But no, he was trying to live up to his notion of a high destiny.

It didn't matter so much as long as Willie was playing the local circuit. The carry-over of the schoolhouse episode was still strong enough to mean something. He was the fellow on the Lord's side and the Lord had given a sign. The Lord had knocked over the fire escape just to prove a point. But when Willie got down in the middle of the state he began to run into trouble. And when he hit a town of any size he found out that the folks didn't care much which side of a question was the Lord's side.

Willie knew what was happening, but he didn't know why. His face got a little thinner, and the thin skin seemed to draw back tighter over the flesh, but he didn't look worried. That was the funny part. If ever a man had a right to look worried, it was Willie. But he didn't. He just looked like a man in a kind of waking dream, and when he walked out on the platform before he began talking his face looked purified and lifted up and serene like the face of a man who has just pulled out of a hard sickness.

But he hadn't pulled out of the sickness he had. He had galloping political anemia.

He couldn't figure out what was wrong. He was like a man with a chill who simply reckons that the climate is changing all of a sudden, and wonders why everybody else isn't shivering too. Perhaps it was a desire for just a little human warmth that got him in the habit of dropping into my room late at night, after the speaking and the handshaking were over. He would sit for a spell, while I drank off my nightcap, and not talk much, but one time, at Morristown, where the occasion had sure-God been a black frost, he did, after sitting quiet, suddenly say, "How you think it's going, Jack?"

It was one of those embarrassing questions like "Do you think my wife is virtuous?" or "Did you know I am a Jew?" which are embarrassing, not because of anything you might say for an answer, the truth or a lie, but because the fellow asked the question at all. But I said to him, "Fine, I reckon it's going fine."

"You think so, for a fact?" he asked.

"Sure," I said.

He chewed that for about a minute and then swallowed it. Then he said, "They didn't seem to be paying attention much tonight. Not while I was trying to explain about my tax program."

"Maybe you try to tell 'em too much. It breaks down their brain cells."

"Looks like they'd want to hear about taxes, though," he said.

"You tell 'em too much. Just tell 'em you're gonna soak the fat boys, and forget the rest of the tax stuff."

"What we need is a balanced tax program. Right now the ratio between income tax and total income for the state gives an index that—"

"Yeah," I said, "I heard the speech. But they don't give a damn about that. Hell, make 'em cry, make 'em laugh, make 'em think you're their weak erring pal, or make 'em think you're God-Almighty. Or make 'em mad. Even mad at you. Just stir 'em up, it doesn't matter how or why, and they'll love you and come back for more. Pinch 'em in the soft place. They aren't alive, most of 'em, and haven't been alive in twenty years. Hell, their wives have lost their teeth and their shape, and likker won't set on their stomachs, and they don't believe in God, so it's up to you to give 'em something to stir 'em up and make 'em feel alive again. Just for half an hour. That's what they come for. Tell 'em anything. But for Sweet Jesus' sake don't try to improve their minds."

I fell back exhausted, and Willie pondered that for a while. He just sat there, not moving and with his face quiet and pure, but you had the feeling that if you listened close enough you would hear the feet tramping inside his head, that something was locked up in there and going back and forth. Then he said, soberly, "Yeah, I know that's what some folks say."

"You weren't born yesterday," I said, and was suddenly angry with him. "You weren't deaf and dumb all the time you had the job in the courthouse in Mason City. Even if you did get in because Pillsbury put you there."

He nodded. "Yeah," he said. "I heard that kind of talk."

72

"It gets around," I said. "It's not any secret."

Then he demanded, "Do you think it's true?"

"True?" I echoed, and almost asked myself the question before I said, "Hell, I don't know. But there's sure a lot of evidence."

He sat there a minute longer, then got up and said good night and went to his room. It wasn't long before I heard the pacing start. I got undressed and lay down. But the pacing kept on. Old Master Mind lay there and listened to the pacing in the next room and said, "The bastard is trying to think up a joke he can tell 'em at Skidmore tomorrow night and make 'em laugh."

Old Master Mind was right. The candidate did tell a joke at Skidmore. But it didn't make them laugh.

But it was at Skidmore that I was sitting in a booth in a Greek cafe after the speaking, having a cup of coffee to steady my nerves and hiding out from people and the cackle of voices and the smell of bodies and the way eyes look at you in a crowd, when in came Sadie Burke and gave the joint the once-over and caught sight of me in the booth and came back and sat down across from me in the booth.

Sadie was one of Willie's new friends, but I had known her from way back. She was an even better friend, rumor had it, of a certain Sen-Sen Puckett, who chewed Sen-Sen to keep his breath sweet and was a fat boy, both physically and politically speaking, and had been (and probably still was) a friend of Joe Harrison. Sen-Sen, according to some guesses, was the fellow who originally had had the bright idea of using Willie as the dummy. Sadie was a lot too good for Sen-Sen, who wasn't, however, a bad looking fellow. Sadie herself wouldn't have been called good looking, certainly not by the juries who pick out girls to be Miss Oregon and Miss New Jersey. She was built very satisfactorily but you tended to forget that, because of the awful clothes she wore and the awkward, violent, snatching gestures she made. She had absolutely black hair, which she cut off at a crazy length and which went out in all directions in a wild, electric way. Her features were good, if you noticed them, which you were inclined not to do, because her face was pocked. But she did have wonderful eyes, deep-set and inky-velvety-black.

Sadie wasn't, however, too good for Sen-Sen because of her looks. She was too good for him because he was a heel. She had probably taken him up because he was good looking and then, again according to rumor, she had put him into political pay dirt. For Sadie was a very smart cooky. She had been around and she had learned a lot the very hard way.

She was in Skidmore with the Stark party that time because she was attached to the Stark headquarters troop (probably as a kind of spy for Sen-Sen) in some such ambiguous role as secretary. As a matter of fact, she was around a lot, and made a good many of the arrangements and tipped off Willie about local celebrities.

Well, now she came up to my booth in the Greek restaurant with that violent stride which was characteristic of her, and looked down at me, and demanded, "Can I sit with you?"

She sat down before I could reply.

"Or anything else," I replied gallantly, "stand, sit, or lie."

She inspected me critically out of her inky-velvety-black, deep-set eyes, which glittered in the marred face, and shook her head. "No thanks," she said, "I like mine with vitamins."

"You mean you don't think I'm handsome?" I demanded.

"I don't care about anybody being handsome," she said, "but I never did go for anybody that reminded me of a box of spilled spaghetti. All elbows and dry rattle."

"All right," I said. "I withdraw my proposal. With dignity. But tell me something, now that you mention vitamins. You figure your candidate Willie has any vitamins? For the constituency?"

"Oh, God," she whispered, and rolled her eyes to heaven.

"All right," I said. "When are you going to tell the boys back home it's no go?"

"What do you mean, no go? They're planning on a big barbecue and rally at Upton. Duffy told me so."

"Sadie," I said, "you know damned well they'd have to barbecue the great woolly mastodon and use ten-dollar bills instead of lettuce on the buns. Why don't you tell the big boys it's no go?"

"What put that in your head?"

"Listen, Sadie," I said, "we've been pals for a long time and you needn't lie to uncle. I don't put everything I know in the papers, but I know that Willie isn't in this race because you admire his oratory."

'Ain't it awful?" she demanded.

"I know it's a frame-up," I said. "Everybody knows but Willie."

"All right," she admitted.

"When are you going to tell the boys back home it's no go, that they are wasting dough? That Willie couldn't steal a vote from Abe Lincoln in the Cradle of the Confederacy?"

"I ought to done it long ago," she said.

"When are you going to?" I asked.

"Listen," she said, "I told them before this thing ever started it was no go. But they wouldn't listen to Sadie. Those fat-heads—" and she suddenly spewed out a mouthful of cigarette smoke over the rounded, too red, suddenly outcurling and gleaming underlip.

74

"Why don't you tell them it's no go and get the poor bastard out of his agony?"

"Let them spend their God-damned money," she said fretfully, twitching her head as though to get the cigarette smoke out of her eyes. "I wish they were spending a lot more, the fat-heads. I wish the poor bastard had had enough sense to make them grease him good to take the beating he's in for. Now all he'll get will be the ride. Might as well let him have that. Ignorance is bliss."

The waitress brought a cup of coffee, which Sadie must have ordered when she came in before she spotted me. She took a drag of the coffee, and then a deep drag of the cigarette.

"You know," she said, jabbing out the butt savagely in the cup and looking at it and not at me, "you know, even if somebody told him. Even if he found out he was a sucker, I believe he might keep right on."

"Yeah," I said, "making those speeches."

"God," she said, "aren't they awful?"

"Yeah."

"But I believe he might keep right on," she said.

"Yeah."

"The sap," she said.

We walked back to the hotel, and I didn't see Sadie again, except once or twice to say howdy-do to, until Upton. Things hadn't improved any before Upton. I went back to town and left the candidate to his own devices for a week or so in between, but I heard the news. Then I got the train over to Upton the day before the barbecue.

Upton is way over in the western part of the state, the capital of the cocklebur vote which was supposed to come pelting out of the brush to the barbecue. And just a little way north of Upton there was a coal pocket, where a lot of folks lived in company shacks and prayed for a full week's work. It was a good location to get a sellout house for the barbecue. Those folks in the shacks were in such a shape they'd be ready to walk fifteen miles for a bait of fresh. If they still had the strength, and it was free.

The local I rode puffed and yanked and stalled and yawned across the cotton country. We'd stop on a siding for half an hour, waiting for something, and I watched the cotton rows converging into the simmering horizon, and a black stub of a burnt tree in the middle distance standing up out of the cotton rows. Then, late in the afternoon, the train headed into the cut-over pine and sagebrush. We would stop beside some yellow, boxlike station, with the unpainted houses dropped down beyond, and I could see up the alley behind the down-town and then, as the train pulled out again, across the back yards of houses surrounded by board or wire fences as though to keep out the openness of the humped and sage-furred country which seemed ready to slide in and eat up the houses. The houses didn't look as though they belonged there, improvised, flung down, ready to be abandoned. Some washing would be hanging on a line, but the people would go off and leave that too. They wouldn't have time to snatch it off the line. It would be getting dark soon, and they'd better hurry.

But as the train pulls away, a woman comes to the back door of one of the houses—just the figure of a woman, for you cannot make out the face—and she has a pan in her hands and she flings the water out of the pan to make a sudden tattered flash of silver in the light. She goes back into the house. To what is in the house. The floor of the house is thin against the bare ground and the walls and the roof are thin against all of everything which is outside, but you cannot see through the walls to the secret to which the woman has gone in.

The train pulls away, faster now, and the woman is back there in the house, where she is going to stay. She'll stay there. And all at once, you think that you are the one who is running away, and who had better run fast to wherever you are going because it will be dark soon. The train is going pretty fast now, but its effort seems to be through a stubborn cloying density of air as though an eel tried to swim in syrup, or the effort seems to be against an increasing and implacable magnetism of earth. You think that if the earth should twitch once, as the hide of a sleeping dog twitches, the train would be jerked over and piled up and the engine would spew and gasp while somewhere a canted-up wheel would revolve once with a massive and dream-like deliberation.

But nothing happens, and you remember that the woman had not even looked up at the train. You forget her, and the train goes fast, and is going fast when it crosses a little trestle. You catch the sober, metallic, pure, late-light, unriffled glint of the water between the little banks, under the sky, and see the cow standing in the water upstream near the single leaning willow. And all at once you feel like crying. But the train is going fast, and almost immediately whatever you feel is taken away from you, too.

You bloody fool, do you think that you want to milk a cow? You do not want to milk a cow.

Then you are at Upton.

In Upton I went to the hotel, toting my little bag and my typewriter through the gangs of people on the street, people who looked at me with the countryman's slow, full, curious lack of shame, and didn't make room for me to pass until I was charging them down, the way a cow won't get out of the way of your car in a lane until your radiator damned near bats her in the underslung slats. At the hotel I ate a sandwich and went up to my room, and got the fan turned on and a pitcher of ice water sent up and took off my shoes and shirt and propped myself in a chair with a book.

At ten-thirty there was a knock on the door. I yelled, and in came Willie.

"Where you been?" I asked him.

"Been here all afternoon," he said.

"Duffy been dragging you round to shake hands with all the leading citizens?"

"Yeah," he said, glumly.

The glumness in his voice made me look sharply at him. "What's the matter?" I asked. "Don't the boys around here talk nice to you?"

"Sure, they talk all right," he said. He came over and took a chair by the writing table. He poured some water into one of the glasses on the tray beside my bottle of red-eye, drank it, and repeated, "Yeah, they talk all right."

I looked at him again. The face was thinner and the skin was pulled back tighter so that it looked almost transparent under the clusters of freckles. He sat there heavily, not paying any attention to me as though he were mumbling something over and over in his mind.

"What's eating you?" I asked.

For a moment he didn't act as if he had heard me, and when he did turn his head to me there seemed to be no connection between the act and what I had said. The act seemed to come from what was going on inside his head and not because I had spoken.

"A man don't have to be Governor," he said.

"Huh?" I responded in my surprise, for that was the last thing I ever expected out of Willie by that time. The showing in the last town (where I hadn't been) must have been a real frost to wake him up.

"A man don't have to be Governor," he repeated, and as I looked at his face now I didn't see the thin-skinned, boyish face, but another face under it, as though the first face were a mask of glass and now I could see through it to the other one. I looked at the second face and saw, all of a sudden, the heavyish lips laid together to remind you of masonry and the knot of muscle on each cheek back where the jawbone hinges on.

"Well," I replied belatedly, "the votes haven't been counted yet."

He mumbled over in his mind what he had been working on. Then he said, "I'm not denying I wanted it. I won't lie to you," he said, and leaned forward a little and looked at me as though he were trying to convince me of the thing which I was already surer of than I was of hands and feet. "I wanted it. I lay awake at night, just wanting it." He worked his big hands on his knees, making the knuckles crack. "Hell, a man can lie there and want something so bad and be so full of wanting it he just plain forgets what it is he wants. Just like when you are a boy and the sap first rises and you think you will go crazy some night wanting something and you want it so bad and get so near sick wanting it you near forget what it is. It's something inside you—" he leaned at me, with his eyes on my face, and grabbed the front of his sweat-streaked blue shirt to make me think he was going to snatch the buttons loose to show me something.

But he subsided back in the chair, letting his eyes leave me to look across the wall as though the wall weren't there, and said, "But wanting don't make a thing true. You don't have to live forever to figure that out."

That was so true I didn't reckon it was worthwhile even to agree with him.

He didn't seem to notice my silence, he was so wrapped up in his own. But after a minute he pulled out of it, stared at me, and said, "I could have made a good Governor. By God—" And he struck his knees with his fist—"by God, a lot better than those fellows. Look here—" and he leaned at me—"what this state needs is a new tax program. And the rate ought to be raised on the coal lands the state's got leased out. And there's not a decent road in the state once you get in the country. And I could save this state some money by merging some departments. And schools—look at me, I never had a decent day's schooling in my life, what I got I dug out, and there's no reason why this state—"

I had heard it all before. On the platform when he stood up there high and pure in the face and nobody gave a damn.

He must have noticed that I wasn't giving a damn. He shut up all of a sudden. He got up and walked across the floor, and back, his head thrust forward and the forelock falling over his brow. He stopped in front of me. "Those things need doing, don't they?" he demanded.

"Sure," I said, and it was no lie.

"But they won't listen to it," he said. "God damn those bastards," he said, "they come out to hear a speaking and then they won't listen to you. Not a word. They don't care. God damn 'em They deserve to grabble in the dirt and get nothing for it but a dry gut-rumble. They won't listen."

"No," I agreed, "they won't."

"And I won't be Governor," he said, shortly. "And they'll deserve what they get." And added, "The bastards."

"Well, you want me to hold your hand about it?" Suddenly, I was sore at him. Why did he come to me? What did he expect me to do? What made him think I wanted to hear about what the state needed? Hell, I knew. Everybody knew. It wasn't any secret. What it needed was some decent government. But who the hell was going to give it? And who cared if nobody did or ever did? What did he come whining to me for about that? Or about how bleeding much he wanted to be Governor because he lay and thought about it in the night? All that was in me as I suddenly felt sore at him and asked him snottily if he expected me to hold his hand.

He was looking at me slowly, giving me the once-over, reading my face. But he didn't look sore. Which surprised me, for I had wanted to make him sore, sore enough to get out. But there wasn't even surprise in his look. "No, Jack," he finally said, shaking his head, "I wasn't asking you for sympathy. Whatever happens I'm not asking you or anybody else for sympathy." He shook himself heavily, like a big dog coming out of the wet, or waking up. "No, by God," he said, and he wasn't really talking to me now, "I'm not asking anybody in the world for it, not now or ever."

That seemed to settle something. So he sat down again.

"What are you going to do?" I asked.

"I got to think," he replied. "I don't know and I got to think. The bastards," he said, "if I could just make 'em listen."

It was just at that time Sadie came in. Or rather, she knocked at the door, and I yelled, and she came in.

"Hello," she said, gave a quick look at the scene, and started toward us. Her eye was on the bottle of red-eye on my table. "How about some refreshment?" she said.

"All right," I replied, but apparently I didn't get the right amount of joviality into my tone. Or maybe she could tell something had been going on from the way the air smelled, and if anybody could do that it would be Sadie.

Anyway, she stopped in the middle of the floor and said, "What's up?"

I didn't answer right away, and she came across to the writing table, moving quick and nervous, the way she always did, inside of a shapeless shoddy-blue summer suit that she must have got by walking into a secondhand store and shutting her eyes and pointing and saying, "I'll take that."

She reached down and took a cigarette out of my pack lying there and tapped it on the back of her knuckles and turned her hot lamps on me.

"Nothing," I said, "except Willie here is saying how he's not going to be Governor."

She had the match lighted by the time I got the words out, but it never got to the cigarette. It stopped in mid-air.

"So you told him," she said, looking at me.

"The hell I did," I said. "I never tell anybody anything. I just listen."

She snapped the match out with a nasty snatch of her wrist and turned on Willie. "Who told you?" she demanded.

"Told me what?" Willie asked, looking up at her steady.

She saw that she had made her mistake. And it was not the kind of mistake for Sadie Burke to make. She made her way in the world up from the shack in the mud flat by always finding out what you knew and never letting you know what she knew. Her style was not to lead with the chin but with a neat length of lead pipe after you had stepped off balance. But she had led with the chin this time. Somewhere way back inside of Sadie Burke there had been the idea that I was going to tell Willie. Or that somebody was going to tell Willie. Not that she, Sadie Burke, would tell Willie, but that Willie would be told and Sadie Burke wouldn't have to. Or nothing as specific as that. Just floating around in the deep dark the idea of Willie and the idea of the thing Willie didn't know, like two bits of drift sucked down in an eddy to the bottom of the river to revolve slowly and blindly there in the dark. But there, all the time.

So, out of an assumption she had made, without knowing it, or a wish or a fear she didn't know she had, she led with her chin. And standing there, rolling that unlighted cigarette in her strong fingers, she knew it. The nickel was in the slot, and looking at Willie you could see the wheels and the cogs and the cherries and the lemons begin to spin inside the machine.

"Told me what?" Willie said. Again.

"That you're not going to be Governor," she said, with a dash of easy levity, but she flashed me a look, the only S O S, I suppose, Sadie Burke ever sent out to anybody.

But it was her fudge and I let her cook it.

Willie kept on looking at her, waiting while she turned to one side and uncorked my bottle and poured herself out a steady-er. She took it, and without any ladylike cough.

"Told me what?" Willie said.

She didn't answer. She just looked at him.

And looking right back at her, he said, in a voice like death and taxes, "Told me what?"

"God damn you!" she blazed at him then, and the glass rattled on the tray as she set it down without looking. "You God-damned sap!"

"All right," Willie said in the same voice, boring in like a boxer when the other fellow begins to swing wild. "What was it?"

"All right," she said, "all right, you sap, you've been framed!"

He looked at her steady for thirty seconds, and there wasn't a sound but the sound of his breathing. I was listening to it.

Then he said, "Framed?"

"And how!" Sadie said, and leaned toward him with what seemed to be a vindictive and triumphant intensity glittering in her eyes and ringing in her voice. "Oh, you decoy, you wooden-headed decoy, you let 'em! Oh, yeah, you let 'em, because you

80

thought you were the little white lamb of God—" and she paused to give him a couple of pitiful derisive *baa's*, twisting her mouth—"yeah, you thought you were the lamb of God, all right, but you know what you are?"

She waited as though for an answer, but he kept staring at her without a word.

"Well, you're the goat," she said. "You are the sacrificial goat. You are the ram in the bushes. You are a sap. For you let 'em. You didn't even get anything out of it. They'd have paid you to take the rap, but they didn't have to pay a sap like you. Oh, no, you were so full of yourself and hot air and how you are Jesus Christ, that all you wanted was a chance to stand on your hind legs and make a speech. My friends—" she twisted her mouth in a nasty, simpering mimicry—"my friends, what this state needs is a good five-cent cigar. Oh, my God!" And she laughed with a kind of wild, artificial laugh, suddenly cut short.

"Why?" he demanded, still staring steadily at her, breathing hard but not showing anything. "Why did they do it? To me?"

"Oh, my God!" she exclaimed and turned to me. "Listen to the sap. He wants to know why." Then she swung to him again, leaning closer, saying, "Listen, if you can get this through your thick head. They wanted you to split the MacMurfee vote. In the sticks. Do you get that or do you want a picture? Can you get that straight, you wooden-head?"

He looked at me, slow, wet his lips, then said, "Is it true?"

"He wants to know if it's true," Sadie announced prayerfully to the ceiling. "Oh, my God!"

"Is it true?" he asked me.

"That's what they tell me," I said.

Well, it hit him. There was no denying it. His face worked as though he might try to say something or might bust out crying. But he didn't do either one. He reached over to the table and picked up the bottle and poured out enough into a glass to floor the Irish and drank it off neat.

"Hey," I said, "take it easy, you aren't used to that stuff."

"He ain't used to a lot of things," Sadie said, shoving the bottle toward him on the tray. "He ain't used to the idea he's not going to be Governor. Are you, Willie?"

"Why can't you lay off?" I said to her.

But she didn't even notice me. She leaned toward Willie, and repeated, coaxingly this time, "Are you, Willie?"

He reached for the bottle and did it again.

"Are you?" she demanded, not coaxing now.

"I was," he said, looking up at her, the blood up in his face now, the tousle of hair hanging, his breath coming heavy. "I was," he said, "before, but I'm not now."

"Not what?" she said.

"Not used to it."

"You better get used to it," she said, and laughed, and shoved the bottle in his direction.

He took it, poured, drank, set the glass down deliberately, and said: "I better not. I better not get used to it."

She laughed again, that wild artificial laugh, chopped off the laugh, and echoed, "He says he better not get used to it. Oh, my God!" Then she laughed again.

He sat there heavy in his chair, but not leaning back, the sweat beginning to pop out on his face and run down slow and shining over the flesh. He sat there, not noticing the sweat, not wiping it away, watching her laugh.

All at once he heaved up out of the chair. I thought he was going to jump her. And he must have thought so too, for her laugh stopped. Right in the middle of the aria. But he didn't jump her. He wasn't even looking at her. He flung his glance wide around the room, and lifted his hands up in front of him, as though he were ready to grab something. "I'll kill 'em!" he said, "I'll kill 'em!"

"Sit down," she said, and leaned quickly toward him to give him a shove on the chest.

His pegs weren't too steady, and he went down. Right in the chair.

"I'll kill 'em," he said, sitting there, sweating.

"You won't do a God-damned thing," she announced. "You won't be Governor and you won't get paid for not being and you won't kill them or anybody else, and you know why?"

"I'll kill 'em," he said.

"I'll tell you why," she said, leaning. "It's because you're a sap. A triple-plated, spoon-fed, one-gallus sap, and you—"

I got up. "I don't care what kind of games you play," I said, "but I don't have to stay here and watch you."

She didn't even turn her head. I went to the door, and out, and the last I heard she was defining what kind of a sap he was. I figured that that might take anybody some time.

I took in a good deal of Upton that night. I saw the folks coming out of the last show at the Picture Palace, and I admired the cemetery gate and the schoolhouse by moonlight, and I leaned over the railing of the bridge over the creek and spit in the water. It took about two hours. Then I went back to the hotel.

When I opened the door of the room, Sadie was sitting in a chair by the writing table, smoking a cigarette. The air was thick enough to cut with a knife, and in the light of the lamp on the table the blue smoke drifted and swayed and curdled around her so that I got the impression I might have been looking at her sitting submerged in a tankful of soapy dishwater at the aquarium. The bottle on the table was empty.

For a second or two I thought that Willie had left. Then I saw the finished product.

It was lying on my bed.

I came in, and shut the door.

"Things seem to have quieted down," I remarked.

"Yeah."

I walked over to the bed and inspected the item. It was lying on its back. The coat was pushed up under the armpits, the hands were crossed piously on the bosom like the hands of a *gisant* on a tomb in a cathedral, the shirt had pulled up some from its moorings under the belt and the two lowest buttons had come unbuttoned so that a triangular patch of slightly distended stomach was visible—white, with a few coarse dark hairs. The mouth was parted a little, and the lower lip vibrated with a delicate flabbiness at each measured expulsion of breath. All very pretty.

"He rared around some," Sadie said. "Telling me what he was going to do. Oh, he's gonna do big things. He's gonna be President. He's gonna kill people with his bare hands. Oh, my God!" She took a drag on her cigarette and spewed the smoke out and then fanned the backwash away from her face with a savage, slapping motion of her right hand. "But I quieted him down," she added, with an air of grim, suddenly spinsterish, satisfaction, the kind your great-aunt used to wear.

"Is he going to the barbecue?" I asked.

"How the hell do I know?" she snapped. "He wasn't screaming about any little detail like a barbecue. Oh, he's a big operator. But—" She paused, and did the drag and spew and fanning routine—"I quieted him."

"It looks like you slugged him," I observed.

"I didn't slug him," she said. "But I hit him where he lives. I finally got across to him the kind of sap he is. And that quieted him."

"He's quiet now, all right," I said, and walked over toward the table.

"He didn't get that quiet all of a sudden. But he got quiet enough to sit in a chair and hang on to the bottle for support and talk about how he'd have to break the news to some Goddamned Lucy."

"That's his wife," I said.

"He talked like it was his mammy and would blow his nose for him. Then he said he was going right to his room and write her a letter. But," she said, and looked over at the bed, "he never made it. He made the middle of the floor, and then heaved for the bed."

She rose from the chair and went over to the bed and looked down at him.

"Does Duffy know?" I asked.

"I don't give a damn what Duffy knows," she said.

I went over to the bed, too. "I guess we'll have to leave him here," I said. "I'll go over to his room and sleep." I leaned over and hunted for his room key in the pockets. I found it. Then I took a toothbrush and some pajamas out of my bag.

She was still standing by the bed. She turned to me. "It looks like you might at least take the bastard's shoes off," she said.

I laid down my truck on the side of the bed, and did it. I picked up the pajamas and toothbrush and went over to the table to switch off the lamp. Sadie was still by the bed. "You better write that letter to that Mamma Lucy," she said, "and ask where to ship the remains."

As I laid my hand on the switch, I looked back at Sadie standing there looking down at the remains, with the left arm, the arm toward me, hanging straight down and a cigarette hanging out of the tips of two fingers and unreeling its spinner of smoke slowly upward, and with her head leaning forward a little while she expelled smoke meditatively over her again outthrust and gleaming lower lip.

There was Sadie, who had come a long way from the shanty in the mud flats. She had come a long way because she played to win and she didn't mean to win matches and she knew that to win you have to lay your money on the right number and that if your number doesn't show there's a fellow standing right there with a little rake to rake in your money and then it isn't yours any more. She had been around a long time, talking to men and looking them straight in the eye like a man. Some of them liked her, and those that didn't like her listened when she talked, which wasn't too often, because there was a reason to believe that when those big black eyes, which were black in a way which made it impossible for you to tell whether it was a blackness of surface or a blackness of depth, looked at the wheel before it began to move they could see the way the wheel would be after it had ceased to move and saw the little ball on the number. Some of them liked her a lot, like Sen-Sen. That had at one time been hard for me to get. I saw a package done up in the baggy tweed or droopy seersucker suit, according to the solstice, and the pocked face with the heavy smear of lipstick and the black lamps in it and above it the mob of black hair which looked as though it had been hacked off at ear length with a meat cleaver.

Then one time, suddenly, I saw something else. You see a woman around for a long time and think that she is ugly. You think she is nothing. Then, all of a sudden, you think how she is under that baggy tweed or droopy seersucker. All of a sudden, you see the face which is there under the pock-marked mask and is humble, pure, and trusting and is asking you to lift the mask. It must be like an old man looking at his wife and just

84

for a second seeing the face he had seen thirty years before. Only in the case I am talking about it is not remembering a face which you have seen a long time back but discovering a face which you have never seen. It is future, not past. It is very unsettling. It was very unsettling, temporarily. I made my pass, and it didn't come to a thing.

She laughed in my face and said, "I've got my arrangements, and I stick to my arrangements as long as I've got my arrangements."

I didn't know what the arrangements were. That was before the day of Mr. Sen-Sen Puckett. That was before the day when she gave him the benefit of her gift for laying it on the right number.

Nothing of this passed through my mind as I put my hand on the switch of the lamp and looked back at Sadie Burke. But I tell it in order that it may be known who the Sadie Burke was who stood by the bed meditating on the carcass as I laid my hand on the switch and who had come the way she had come by not leading with her chin but who had led with her chin that night.

At least, that was the way I figured it.

I turned the switch, and she and I went out the door, and said good night in the hall.

It must have been near nine the next morning when Sadie beat on my door and I came swimming and swaying up from the bottom of a muddy sleep, like a piece of sogged driftwood stirred up from the bottom of a pond. I made the door and stuck my head out.

"Listen," she said without any build-up of civilities, "Duffy's going out to the fairgrounds, and I'll ride with him. He's got a lot of big-shotting to do out there. He wanted to get the sap out pretty early, too, to mingle with the common herd, but I told him he wasn't feeling too good. That he'd be out a little later."

"O.K.," I said, "I'm not paid for it, but I'll try to deliver him."

"I don't care whether he ever gets there," she said. "It won't be skin off my nose."

"I'll try to get him there anyway."

"Suit yourself," she said, and walked off down the hall, twitching the seersucker.

I looked out the window and saw that it was going to be another day, and shaved, and dressed, and went down to get a cup of coffee. Then I went to my room, and knocked. There was some kind of a sound inside, like an oboe blatting once deep inside a barrel of feathers. So I went in. I had left the door unlocked the night before.

It was after ten by that time.

Willie was on the bed. In the same place, the coat still wadded up under his armpits, his hands still crossed on his chest, his face pale and pure. I went over to the bed. His head didn't turn, but his eyes swung toward me with a motion that made you think you could hear them creak in the sockets.

"Good morning," I said.

He opened his mouth a little way and his tongue crept out and explored the lips carefully, wetting them. Then he grinned weakly, as though he were experimenting to see if anything would crack. Nothing happened, so he whispered, "I reckon I was drunk last night?"

"That's the name it goes by," I said.

"It's the first time," he said. "I never got drunk before. I never even tasted it but once before."

"I know. Lucy doesn't favor drinking."

"I reckon she'll understand though when I tell her," he said. "She'll see how it was I came to do it." Then he sank into meditation.

"How do you feel?"

"I feel all right," he said, and pried himself up to a sitting posture, swinging his feet to the floor. He sat there with his sock-feet on the floor, taking stock of the internal stresses and strains. "Yeah," he concluded, "I feel all right."

"Are you going to the barbecue?"

He looked up at me with a laborious motion of the head and an expression of question on his face as though I were the fellow who was supposed to answer. "What made you ask that?" he demanded.

"Well, a lot's been happening."

"Yeah," he said. "I'm going."

"Duffy and Sadie have already gone. Duffy wants you to come on out and mingle with the common herd."

"All right," he said. Then, with his eyes fixed on an imaginary spot on the floor about ten feet from his toes, he stuck his tongue out again and began to caress his lips. "I'm thirsty," he said.

"You are dehydrated," I said. "The result of alcohol taken in excess. But that is the only way to take it. It is the only way to do a man any good."

But he wasn't listening. He had pulled himself up and padded off into the bathroom.

I could hear the slosh of water and the gulping and inhaling. He must have been drinking out of the faucet. After about a minute that sound stopped. There wasn't any sound at all for a spell. Then there was a new one. Then the agony was over.

He appeared at the bathroom door, braced against the doorjamb, staring at me with a face of sad reproach bedewed with the glitter of cold sweat.

"You needn't look at me like that," I said, "the likker was all right."

"I puked," he said wistfully.

"Well, you didn't invent it. Besides, now you'll be able to eat a great big, hot, juicy, high-powered slab of barbecued hog meat."

He didn't seem to think that that was very funny. And neither did I. But he didn't seem to think it was especially unfunny, either. He just hung on the doorjamb looking at me like a deaf and dumb stranger. Then he retired again into the bathroom.

"I'll order you a pot of coffee," I yelled in to him. "It'll fix you up."

But it didn't. He took it, but it didn't even take time to make itself at home.

Then he lay down for a while. I put a cold towel on his forehead and he closed his eyes. He laid his hands on his breast, and the freckles on his face looked like rust spots on polished alabaster.

About eleven-fifteen the desk called to say that a car and two gentlemen were waiting to drive Mr. Stark to the fairgrounds. I put my hand over the receiver, and looked over at Willie. His eyes had come open and were fixed on the ceiling.

"What the hell do you want to go to that barbecue for?" I said. "I'm going to tell 'em to hist tail."

"I'm going to the barbecue," he announced from the spirit world, his eyes still fixed on the ceiling.

So I went down to the lobby to stall off two of the local semi-leading citizens who'd even agreed to ride in the gubernatorial hearse to get their names in the paper. I stalled them. I said Mr. Stark was slightly indisposed, and I would drive him out in about an hour.

At twelve o'clock I tried the coffee treatment again. It didn't work. Or rather, it worked wrong. Duffy called up from out at the fairgrounds and wanted to know what the hell. I told him he'd better go on and distribute the loaves and fishes and pray God for Willie to arrive by two o'clock.

"What's the matter?" demanded Duffy.

"Boy," I said, "the longer you don't know the happier you'll be," and hung up the phone.

Along toward one, after Willie had made another effort to recuperate with coffee and had failed, I said, "Look here, Willie, what you going out there for? Why don't you stay here? Send word you are sick and spare yourself some grief. Then, later on, if—"

"No," he said, and pushed himself up to a sitting position on the side of the bed. His face had a high and pure and trans-

87

parent look like a martyr's face just before he steps into the flame.

"Well," I said, without enthusiasm, "if you are hell-bent, you got one more chance."

"More coffee?" he asked.

"No," I said, and unstrapped my suitcase and got out the second bottle. I poured some in a tumbler and took it to him. "According to the old folks," I said, "the best way is to put two shots of absinthe on a little cracked ice and float on a shot of rye. But we can't be fancy. Not with Prohibition."

He got it down. There was a harrowing moment, then I drew a sigh of relief. In ten minutes I repeated the dose. Then I told him to get undressed while I ran a tub of cold water. While he was in the tub I called down for the desk to get us a car. Then I went to Willie's room to get some clean clothes and his other suit.

He managed to get dressed, taking time out now and then for me to give a treatment.

He got dressed and then sat on the edge of the bed wearing a big label marked, *Handle with Care—This End Up—Fragile.* But I got him down to the car.

Then I had to go back up and get a copy of his speech, which he'd left in his top bureau drawer. He might need it, he said after I got back. He might not be able to remember very well, and might have to read it.

"All about Peter Rabbit and Wallie Woodchuck," I said, but he wasn't attending.

He lay back and closed his eyes while the tumbril bumped over the gravel toward the fairgrounds.

I looked up the road and saw the flivvers and wagons and buggies ranked on the outskirts of a grove, and the fair buildings, and an American flag draped around a staff against the blue sky. Then, above the sound of our coffee-grinder, I caught the strains of music. Duffy was soothing the digestion of the multitude.

Willie put out his hand and laid it on the flask. "Gimme that thing," he said.

"Go easy," I said, "you aren't used to this stuff. You already—"

But he had it to his mouth by that time and the sound of it gargling down would have drowned the sound of my words even if I had kept on wasting them.

When he handed the thing back to me, there wasn't enough in it to make it worth my while putting it in my pocket. What collected in one corner when I tilted it wouldn't make even a drink for a high-school girl. "You sure you don't want to finish it?" I asked in mock politeness.

He shook his head in a dazed sort of way, said, "No, thanks," and then shivered like a man with a hard chill.

So I took what was left, and threw the empty pint bottle out of the window.

"Drive in as close as you can," I told the boy at the wheel.

He got in pretty close, and I got out and gave Willie a hand, and paid the kid off. Then Willie and I drifted slowly over the brown and trodden grass toward a platform, while the crowd about us was as nothing and Willie's eyes were on far horizons and the band played "Casey Jones."

I left Willie in the lee of the platform, standing all alone in a space of brown grass in a strange country with a dream on his face and the sun beating down on him.

I found Duffy, and said, "I'm ready to make delivery, but I want a receipt."

"What's the matter with him?" Duffy wanted to know. "The bastard doesn't drink. Is he drunk?"

"He never touches the stuff," I said. "It's just he's been on the road to Damascus and he saw a great light and he's got the blind staggers."

"What's the matter with him?"

"You ought to read the Good Book more," I told Duffy, and led him to the candidate. It was a touching reunion. So I melted into the throng.

There was quite a crowd, for the scent of burning meat on the air will do wonders. The folks were beginning to collect around in front of the platform, and climb up in the grandstand. The local band was standing over to one side of the platform, now working over "Hail, Hail, the Gang's All Here." On the platform were the two local boys who didn't have any political future, who had come to the hotel that morning, and another fellow who was by my guess a preacher to offer up a prayer, and Duffy. And there was Willie, sweating slow. They sat in a row of chairs across the back of the platform, in front of the bunting-draped backdrop, and behind a bunting-draped table on which was a big pitcher of water and a couple of glasses.

One of the local boys got up first and addressed his friends and neighbors and introduced the preacher who addressed God-Almighty with his gaunt rawboned face lifted up above the blue serge and his eyes squinched into the blazing light. Then the first local boy got up and worked around to introducing the second local boy. It looked for a while as though the second local boy was the boy with the button after all, for he was, apparently, built for endurance and not speed, but it turned out that he didn't really have the button any more than the first local boy or the preacher or God-Almighty. It just took him longer to admit that he didn't have it and to put the finger on Willie.

Then Willie stood all alone by the table, saying, "My friends," and turning his alabaster face precariously from one side to the other, and fumbling in the right side pocket of his coat to fish out the speech.

While he was fumbling with the sheets, and looking down at them with a slightly bemused expression as though the stuff before him were in a foreign language, somebody tugged at my sleeve. There was Sadie.

"How was it?" she asked.

"Take a look and guess," I replied.

She gave a good look up to the platform, and then asked, "How'd you do it?"

"Hair of the dog."

She looked up to the platform again. "Hair, hell," she said, "he must have swallowed the dog."

I inspected Willie, who stood up there sweating and swaying and speechless, under the hot sun.

"He's on the ropes," Sadie said.

"Hell, he's been on 'em all morning," I said, "and lucky to have 'em."

She was still looking at him. It was much the way she had looked at him the night before when he lay on the bed in my room, out cold, and she stood by the side of the bed. It wasn't pity and it wasn't contempt. It was an ambiguous, speculative look. Then she said, "Maybe he was born on 'em."

She said it in a tone which seemed to imply that she had settled that subject. But she kept on looking up there at him in the same way.

The candidate could still stand, at least with one thigh propped against the table. He had begun to talk by this time, too. He had called them his friends in two or three ways and had said he was glad to be there. Now he stood there clutching the manuscript in both hands, with his head lowered like a dehorned cow beset by a couple of fierce dogs in the barnyard, while the sun beat on him and the sweat dropped. Then he took a grip on himself, and lifted his head.

"I have a speech here," he said. "It is a speech about what this state needs. But there's no use telling you what this state needs. You are the state. You know what you need. Look at your pants. Have they got holes in the knee? Listen to your belly. Did it ever rumble for emptiness? Look at your crop. Did it ever rot in the field because the road was so bad you couldn't get it to market? Look at your kids. Are they growing up ignorant as you and dirt because there isn't any school for them?"

Willie paused, and blinked around at the crowd. "No," he said, "I'm not going to read you any speech. You know what you need better'n I could tell you. But I'm going to tell you a story."

And he paused, steadied himself by the table, and took a deep breath while the sweat dripped.

I leaned toward Sadie. "What the hell's the bugger up to?" I asked.

"Shut up," she commanded, watching him.

He began again. "It's a funny story," he said. "Get ready to laugh. Get ready to bust your sides for it is sure a funny story. It's about a hick. It's about a red-neck, like you all, if you please. Yeah, like you. He grew up like any other mother's son on the dirt roads and gully washes of a north-state farm. He knew all about being a hick. He knew what it was to get up before day and get cow dung between his toes and feed and slop and milk before breakfast so he could set off by sunup to walk six miles to a one-room, slab-sided schoolhouse. He knew what it was to pay high taxes for that windy shack of a schoolhouse and those gully-washed red-clay roads to walk over—or to break his wagon axle or string-halt his mules on.

"Oh, he knew what it was to be a hick, summer and winter. He figured if he wanted to do anything he had to do it himself. So he sat up nights and studied books and studied law so maybe he could do something about changing things. He didn't study that law in any man's school or college. He studied it nights after a hard day's work in the field. So he could change things some. For himself and for folks like him. I am not lying to you. He didn't start out thinking about all the other hicks and how he was going to do wonderful things for them. He started out thinking of number one, but something came to him on the way. How he could not do something for himself and not for other folks or for himself without the help of other folks. It was going to be all together or none. That came to him.

"And it came to him with the powerful force of God's own lightning on a tragic time back in his own home county two years ago when the first brick schoolhouse ever built in his county collapsed because it was built of politics-rotten brick, and it killed and mangled a dozen poor little scholars. Oh, you know that story. He had fought the politics back of building that schoolhouse of rotten brick but he lost and it fell. But it started him thinking. Next time would be different.

"People were his friends because he had fought that rotten brick. And some of the public leaders down in the city knew that and they rode up to his pappy's place in a big fine car and said how they wanted him to run for Governor."

I plucked Sadie's arm. "You think he's going to—"

"Shut up," she said savagely.

I looked toward Duffy up there on the platform back of Willie. Duffy's face was worried. It was red and round and sweating, and it was worried.

"Oh, they told him," Willie was saying, "and that hick swallowed it. He looked in his heart and thought he might try to change things. In all humility he thought how he might try. He was just a human, country boy, who believed like we have always believed back here in the hills that even the plainest, poorest fellow can be Governor if his fellow citizens find he has got the stuff and the character for the job.

"Those fellows in the striped pants saw the hick and they took him in. They said how MacMurfee was a limber-back and a dead-head and how Joe Harrison was the tool of the city machine, and how they wanted that hick to step in and try to give some honest government. They told him that. But—" Willie stopped, and lifted his right hand clutching the manuscript to high heaven—"do you know who they were? They were Joe Harrison's hired hands and lickspittles and they wanted to get a hick to run to split MacMurfee's hick vote. Did I guess this? I did not. No, for I heard their sweet talk. And I wouldn't know the truth this minute if that woman right there—" and he pointed down at Sadie—"if that woman right there—"

I nudged Sadie and said, "Sister, you are out of a job."

"—if that fine woman right there hadn't been honest enough and decent enough to tell the foul truth which stinks in the nostrils of the Most High!"

Duffy was on his feet, edging uncertainly toward the front of the platform. He kept looking desperately toward the band as though he might signal them to burst into music and then at the crowd as though he were trying to think of something to say. Then he edged toward Willie and said something to him.

But the words, whatever they were, were scarcely out of his mouth before Willie had turned on him. "There!" Willie roared. "There!" And he waved his right hand, the hand clutching the manuscript of his speech. "There is the Judas Iscariot, the lick-spittle, the nose-wiper!"

And Willie waved his right arm at Duffy, clutching the manuscript which he had not read. Duffy was trying to say something to him, but Willie wasn't hearing it, for he was waving the manuscript under Duffy's retreating nose and shouting, "Look at him! Look at him!"

Duffy, still retreating, looked toward the band and waved his arms at them and shouted, "Play, play! Play the 'Star-Spangled Banner'!"

But the band didn't play. And just then as Duffy turned back to Willie, Willie made a more than usually energetic pass of the fluttering manuscript under Duffy's nose and shouted, "Look at him, Joe Harrison's dummy!"

Duffy shouted, "It's a lie!" and stepped back from the accusing arm.

I don't know whether Willie meant to do it. But anyway, he did it. He didn't exactly shove Duffy off the platform. He just started Duffy doing a dance along the edge, a kind of delicate, feather-toed, bemused, slow-motion adagio accompanied by arms pinwheeling around a face which was like a surprised custard pie with a hole scooped in the middle of the meringue, and the hole was Duffy's mouth, but no sound came out of it. There wasn't a sound over that five-acre tract of sweating humanity. They just watched Duffy do his dance.

Then he danced right off the platform. He broke his fall and half lay, half sat, propped against the bottom of the platform with his mouth still open. No sound came out of it now, for there wasn't any breath to make a sound.

All of that, and me without a camera.

Willie hadn't even bothered to look over the edge. "Let the hog lie!" he shouted. "Let the hog lie, and listen to me, you hicks. Yeah, you're hicks, too, and they've fooled you, too, a thousand times, just like they fooled me. For that's what they think we're for. To fool. Well, this time I'm going to fool somebody. I'm getting out of this race. You know why?"

He paused and wiped the sweat off his face with his left hand, a flat scouring motion.

"Not because my little feelings are hurt. They aren't hurt, I never felt better in my life, because now I know the truth. What I ought to known long back. Whatever a hick wants he's got to do for himself. Nobody in a fine automobile and sweet-talking is going to do it for him. When I come back to run for Governor again, I'm coming on my own and I'm coming for blood. But I'm getting out now.

"I'm resigning in favor of MacMurfee. By God, everything I've said about MacMurfee stands and I'll say it again, but I'm going to stump this state for him. Me and the other hicks, we are going to kill Joe Harrison so dead he'll never even run for dogcatcher in this state. Then we'll see what MacMurfee does. This is his last chance. The time has come. The truth is going to be told and I'm going to tell it. I'm going to tell it over this state from one end to the other if I have to ride the rods or steal me a mule to do it, and no man, Joe Harrison or any other man, can stop me. For I got me a gospel and I—"

I leaned to Sadie. "Listen," I said, "I've got to get on a telephone. I'm starting to town or the first telephone I hit. I got to telephone this in. You stay here and for God's sake remember what happens."

"All right," she said, not paying much mind to me.

"And nab Willie when it's over and bring him to town. It's a sure thing Duffy won't ask you to ride with him. You nab the sap, and—"

"Sap, hell," she said. And added, "You go on."

I went. I worked around the edge of the grandstand, through the crowd, with the sound of Willie's voice hammering on the

93

eardrums and shaking dead leaves off the oak trees. As I rounded the end of the grandstand, I looked back and there was Willie flinging the sheets of his manuscript from him so they swirled about his feet and beating on his chest and shouting how the truth was there and didn't need writing down. There he was, with the papers about his feet and one arm up, the coat sleeve jammed elbow high, face red as a bruised beet and the sweat sluicing, hair over his forehead, eyes bugged out and shining, drunk as a hoot owl, and behind him the bunting, red-white-and-blue, and over him God's bright, brassy, incandescent sky.

I walked down the gravel road a piece and hitched a ride on a truck to town.

That night when all was still and the train bearing Duffy back to the city (to report, no doubt, to Joe Harrison) was puffing across the sage country under the stars and Willie had been in bed for hours sleeping off the fumes, I reached for the bottle on the writing table in my room at the hotel in Upton and said to Sadie, "How about a little more of the stuff that let the bars down and kicked the boards loose?"

"What?" she asked.

"You would not understand that to which I so grammatically refer," I said, and poured the drink for her.

"Oh, I forgot," she said, "you're the fellow who went to college."

Yes, I was the fellow who had gone so grammatically to college where I had not learned, I decided, all there was to know.

Willie kept his word. He stumped the state for MacMurfee. He didn't ride the rods or buy him a mule or steal him one. But he drove the pants off his pretty good secondhand car over the washboard and through the hub-deep dust and got mired in the black gumbo when a rain came and sat in his car waiting for the span of mules to come and pull him out. He stood on schoolhouse steps, and on the top of boxes borrowed from the dry-goods store and on the seats of farm wagons and on the porches of crossroads stores, and talked. "Friends, red-necks, suckers, and fellow hicks," he would say, leaning forward, leaning at them, looking at them. And he would pause, letting the words sink in. And in the quiet the crowd would be restless and resentful under these words, the words they knew people called them but the words nobody ever got up and called them to their face. "Yeah," he would say, "yeah," and twist his mouth on the word, "that's what you are, and you needn't get mad at me for telling you. Well, get mad, but I'm telling you. That's what you are. And me—I'm one, too. Oh, I'm a red-neck, for the sun has beat down on me. Oh, I'm a sucker, for I fell for that sweet-

94

talking fellow in the fine automobile. Oh, I took the sugar tit and hushed my crying. Oh, I'm a hick and I am the hick they were going to try to use and split the hick vote. But I'm standing here on my own hind legs, for even a dog can learn to do that, give him time. I learned. It took me a time but I learned, and here I am on my own hind legs." And he would lean at them. And demand, "Are you, are you on your hind legs? Have you learned that much yet? You think you can learn that much?"

He told them things they didn't like. He called them the names they didn't like to be called, but always, almost always, the restlessness and resentment died and he leaned at them with his eyes bugging and his face glistening in the hot sunlight or the red light of a gasoline flare. They listened while he told them to stand on their own hind legs. Go and vote, he told them. Vote for MacMurfee this time, he told them, for he is all you have got to vote for. But vote strong, strong enough to show what you can do. Vote him in and then if he doesn't deliver, nail up his hide. "Yeah," he would say, leaning, "yeah, nail him up if he don't deliver. Hand me the hammer and I'll nail him." Vote, he told them. Put MacMurfee on the spot, he told them.

He leaned at them and said, "Listen to me, you hicks. Listen here and lift up your eyes and look on the God's blessed and unflyblown truth. If you've got the brain of a sapsucker left and can recognize the truth when you see it. This is the truth; you are a hick and nobody ever helped a hick but the hick himself. Up there in town they won't help you. It is up to you and God, and God helps those who help themselves!"

He gave them that, and they stood there in front of him, with a thumb hooked in the overall strap, and the eyes under the pulled down hat brim squinting at him as though he were something spied across a valley or cove, something they weren't quite easy in the mind about, too far away to make out good, or a sudden movement in the brush seen way off yonder across the valley or across the field and something might pop out of the brush, and under the eyes the jaw revolving worked the quid with a slow, punctilious, immitigable motion, like historical process. And Time is nothing to a hog, or to History, either. They watched him, and if you watched close you might be able to see something beginning to happen. They stand so quiet, they don't even shift from one foot to the other—they've got a talent for being quiet, you can see them stand on the street corner when they come to town, not moving or talking, or see one of them squatting on his heels by the road, just looking off where the road drops over the hill—and their squinched eyes don't flicker off the man up there in front of them. They've got a talent for being quiet. But sometimes the quietness stops. It snaps all of a sudden, like a piece of string pulled tight. One of them sits quiet on the bench, at the brush-arbor revival, listening, and all of a sudden he jumps up and lifts up his arms and yells, "Oh, Jesus! I have seen His name!" Or one of them presses his finger on the trigger, and the sound of the gun surprises even him.

Willie is up there. In the sun, or in the red light of the gasoline flare. "You ask me what my program is. Here it is, you hicks. And don't you forget it. Nail 'em up! Nail up Joe Harrison. Nail up anybody who stands in your way. Nail up MacMurfee if he don't deliver. Nail up anybody who stands in your way. You hand me the hammer and I'll do it with my own hand. Nail 'em up on the barn door! And don't fan away the bluebottles with any turkey wing!"

It was Willie, all right. It was the fellow with the same name.

MacMurfee was elected. Willie had something to do with it, for the biggest vote was polled in the sections Willie had worked that they had any record of. But all the time MacMurfee didn't quite know what to make of Willie. He shied off him at first, for Willie had said some pretty hard things about him, and then when it did look as though Willie would make an impression, he shilly-shallied. And in the end Willie got up on his hind legs and said how the MacMurfee people were offering to pay his expenses but he was on his own, he wasn't MacMurfee's man, even if he was saying to vote for MacMurfee. He was paying his way, he said, even if he had to put another mortgage on his pappy's farm and the last one it would hold. Yes, and if there was anybody who couldn't afford two dollars to pay his poll tax and came to him and said it straight out, he, Willie Stark, would pay that tax out of money he had got by mortgaging his pappy's farm. That was how much he believed in what he was saying.

MacMurfee was in, and Willie went back to Mason City and practiced law. He must have dragged on for a year or so, handling chicken-stealing cases and stray-hog cases and cutting scrapes (which are part of the entertainment at Saturday-night square dances in Mason County). Then a gang of workmen got hurt when some of the rig collapsed on a bridge the state was building over the Ackamulgee River, and two or three got killed. A lot of the workmen were from Mason County and they got Willie for their lawyer. He got all over the papers for that. And he won the case. Then they struck oil just west of Mason County over in Ackamulgee County, and in that section Willie got mixed up in the litigation between an oil company and some independent leaseholders. Willie's side won, and he saw folding money for the first time in his life. He saw quite a lot of it.

During all that time I didn't see Willie. I didn't see him again until he announced in the Democratic primary in 1930. But it wasn't a primary. It was hell among the yearlings and the

Charge of the Light Brigade and Saturday night in the back room of Casey's saloon rolled into one, and when the smoke cleared away not a picture still hung on the walls. And there wasn't any Democratic party. There was just Willie, with his hair in his eyes and his shirt sticking to his stomach with sweat. And he had a meat ax in his hand and was screaming for blood. In the background of the picture, under a purplish tumbled sky flecked with sinister white like driven foam, flanking Willie, one on each side, were two figures, Sadie Burke and a tallish, stooped, slow-spoken man with a sad, tanned face and what they call the eyes of a dreamer. The man was Hugh Miller, Harvard Law School, Lafayette Escadrille, Croix de Guerre, clean hands, pure heart, and no political past. He was a fellow who had sat still for years, and then somebody (Willie Stark) handed him a baseball bat and he felt his fingers close on the tape. He was a man and was Attorney General. And Sadie Burke was just Sadie Burke.

Over the brow of the hill, there were, of course, some other people. There were, for instance, certain gentlemen who had once been devoted to Joe Harrison, but who, when they discovered that there wasn't going to be any more Joe Harrison politically speaking, had had to hunt up a new friend. The new friend happened to be Willie. He was the only place for them to go. They figured they would sign on with Willie and grow up with the country. Willie signed them on, all right, and as a result got quite a few votes not of the wool-hat and cocklebur variety. After a while, Willie even signed on Tiny Duffy, who became Highway Commissioner and, later, Lieutenant Governor in Willie's last term. I used to wonder why Willie kept him around. Sometimes I used to ask the Boss, "What do you keep that lunk-head for?" Sometimes he would just laugh and say nothing. Sometimes he would say, "Hell, somebody's got to be Lieutenant Governor, and they all look alike." But once he said: "I keep him because he reminds me of something."

"What?"

"Something I don't ever want to forget," he said.

"What's that?"

"That when they come to you sweet talking you better not listen to anything they say. I don't aim to forget that."

So that was it. Tiny was the fellow who had come in a big automobile and had talked sweet to Willie back when Willie was a little country lawyer.

But was that it? Or rather, was that all of it? I figured there was another reason. The Boss must have taken a kind of pride in the fact that he could make Tiny Duffy a success. He had busted Tiny Duffy and then he had picked up the pieces and put him back together again as his own creation. He must have taken a lot of pleasure in looking at Tiny's glittering rig and

97

diamond ring, and thinking that it was all hollow, that it was a sham, that if he should crook his little finger Tiny Duffy would disappear like a whiff of smoke. In a way, the very success which the Boss laid on Tiny was his revenge on Tiny, for every time the Boss put his meditative, sleepy, distant gaze on Tiny, Tiny would know, with a cold clutch at his fat heart, that if the Boss should crook a finger there wouldn't be anything but the whiff of smoke. In a way, Tiny's success was a final index of the Boss's own success.

But was that it? In the end, I decided that there was one more reason behind the other reasons. This: Tiny Duffy became, in a crazy kind of way, the other self of Willie Stark, and all the contempt and insult which Willie Stark was to heap on Tiny Duffy was nothing but what one self of Willie Stark did to the other self because of a blind, inward necessity. But I came to that conclusion only at the very end, a long time afterwards.

But now Willie had just become Governor and nobody knew what would come afterwards.

And meanwhile—while the campaign was on—I was out of a job.

My job had been political reporting for the *Chronicle*. I had a column, too. I was a pundit.

One day Jim Madison had me in to stand on the Kelly-green carpet which surrounded his desk like a pasture. "Jack," he said, "you know what the *Chronicle* line is in this election."

"Sure," I replied, "it wants to elect Sam MacMurfee again because of his brilliant record as an administrator and his high integrity as a statesman."

He grinned a little sourly and said, "It wants to elect Sam MacMurfee."

"I'm sorry I forgot we were in the bosom of the family. I thought I was writing my column."

The grin went off his face. He played with a pencil on his desk. "It's about the column I wanted to see you," he said.

"O.K.," I replied.

"Can't you put some more steam in it? This is an election and not a meeting of the Epworth League."

"It is an election, all right."

"Can't you give it a little more?"

"When what you got to work with is Sam MacMurfee," I said, "you haven't even got a sow's ear to make a silk purse out of. I'm doing what I can."

He brooded over that for a minute. Then he began, "Now just because that Stark happens to be a friend of yours, you—"

"He's no friend of mine," I snapped. "I didn't even see him between last election and this one. Personally, I don't care who is ever Governor of this state or how big a son-of-a-bitch he is. But I am a hired hand, and I do my best to suppress in my column my burning conviction that Sam MacMurfee is one of the fanciest sons-of—"

"You know the *Chonicle* line," Jim Madison said heavily and studied the spit-slick, chewed butt of his cigar.

It was a hot day, and the breeze from the electric fan was all on Jim Madison and not on me, and there was a little thread of acid, yellow-feeling saliva down in my throat, the kind you get when your stomach is sour, and my head felt like a dried gourd with a couple of seeds rattling around in it. So I looked at Jim Madison, and said, "All right."

"What do you mean?" he asked.

"I mean it the way I said it," I said, and started for the door.

"Look here, Jack, I'm—" he began, and laid the cigar butt down on the ash tray.

"I know," I said, "you've got a wife and kids and your boy's in Princeton."

I said that and kept on walking.

There was a water cooler outside the door, in the hall, and I stopped by it and took one of the little cone-shaped cups and drank about ten of them full of ice water to wash the yellow thing out of my throat. Then I stood there in the hall with my stomach full of the water like a cold bulb inside of me.

I could sleep late, and then wake up and not move, just watching the hot, melted-butter colored sunlight pour through the cracks in the shade, for my hotel was not the best in town and my room was not the best in the hotel. As my chest rose and fell with my breathing, the sheet would stick damply to my bare hide, for that is the way you sleep there in the summertime. I could hear the streetcars and the blatting of automobile horns off yonder, not too loud but variegated and unremitting, a kind of coarse, hoarse tweedy mixture of sounds to your nerve ends, and occasionally the clatter of dishes, for my room gave on the kitchen area. And now and then a nigger would sing a snatch down there.

I could lie there as long as I wanted, and let all the pictures of things a man might want run through my head, coffee, a girl, money, a drink, white sand and blue water, and let them all slide off, one after another, like a deck of cards slewing slowly off your hand. Maybe the things you want are like cards. You don't want them for themselves, really, though you think you do. You don't want a card because you want the card, but because in a perfectly arbitrary system of rules and values and in a special combination of which you already hold a part the card has meaning. But suppose you aren't sitting in a game. Then, even if you do know the rules, a card doesn't mean a thing. They all look alike.

So I could lie there, though I knew that I would get up after a spell—not deciding to get up but just all at once finding myself standing in the middle of the floor just as later on I would find myself, with a mild shock of recognition, taking coffee, changing a bill, handling a girl, drawing on a drink, floating in the water. Like an amnesia case playing solitaire in a hospital. I would get up and deal myself a hand, all right. Later on. But for the present I would lie there and know I didn't have to get up, and feel the holy emptiness and blessed fatigue of a saint after the dark night of the soul. For God and Nothing have a lot in common. You look either one of Them straight in the eye for a second and the immediate effect on the human constitution is the same.

Lots of nights I would go to bed early, too. Sometimes sleep gets to be a serious and complete thing. You stop going to sleep in order that you may be able to get up, but get up in order that you may be able to go back to sleep. You get so during the day you catch yourself suddenly standing still and waiting and listening. You are like a little boy at the railroad station, ready to go away on the train, which hasn't come yet. You look way up the track, but can't see the little patch of black smoke yet. You fidget around, but all at once you stop in the middle of your fidgeting, and listen. You can't hear it yet. Then you go and kneel down in your Sunday clothes in the cinders, for which your mother is going to snatch you bald-headed, and put your ear to the rail and listen for the first soundless rustle which will come in the rail long before the little black patch begins to grow on the sky. You get so you listen for night, long before it comes over the horizon, and long, long before it comes charging and stewing and thundering to you like a big black locomotive and the black cars grind to a momentary stop and the porter with the black, shining face helps you up the steps, and says, "Yassuh, little boss, yassuh."

You don't dream in that kind of sleep, but you are aware of it every minute you are asleep, as though you were having a long dream of sleep itself, and in that sleep you were dreaming of sleep, sleeping and dreaming of sleep infinitely inward into the center.

That was the way it was for a while after I didn't have any job. It wasn't new. It had been like that before, twice before. I had even given a name to it—The Great Sleep. The time before I quit the University, just a few months before I was supposed to finish my dissertation for the Ph.D in American History. It was almost finished, and they said it was O.K. The sheets of typed-on paper were stacked up on the table by the typewriter. The boxes of cards were there. I would get up late in the morning and see them there, the top sheet of paper beginning to curl up around the paperweight. And I'd see them there when I came in after supper to go to bed. Finally, one morning I got up late and went out the door and didn't come back and left them there. And the other time the Great Sleep had come was the time before I walked out of the apartment and Lois started to get the divorce.

But this time there wasn't any American History and there wasn't any Lois. But there was the Great Sleep.

When I did get up I just piddled around. I went to movies and hung around speak-easies and went swimming or went out to the country club and lay on the grass and watched a couple of hot bastards swing rackets at a little white ball that flashed in the sun. Or perhaps one of the players would be a girl and the short white skirt would swirl and whip about her brown thighs, and flash in the sun, too.

A few times I went to see Adam Stanton at his apartment, the fellow I had grown up with at Burden's Landing. He was a hot-shot surgeon now, with more folks screaming for him to cut on them that he had time to cut on, and a professor at the University Medical School, and busy grinding out the papers he published in the scientific journals or took off to read at meetings in New York and Baltimore and London. He wasn't married. He didn't have time, he said. He didn't have time for anything. But he'd take a little time to let me sit in a shabby overstuffed chair in his shabby apartment, where papers were stacked around and the colored girl had streaked the dust on the furniture. I used to wonder why he lived the way he did when he must have been having quite a handsome take, but I finally got it through my head that he didn't ask anything from a lot of the folks he cut on. He had the name of a softy in the trade. And after he got money, people took him for it if they had a story that would halfway wash. The only thing in his apartment that was worth a plugged nickel was the piano, and it was the best money could buy.

Most of the time when I was at Adam's apartment he would be at the piano. I have heard it said that he was pretty good, but I wouldn't know. But I didn't mind listening, not if the chair was good and comfortable. Adam must have heard me say one time or another that music didn't mean much to me, but I suppose that he'd forgotten it or couldn't believe that it was true for anybody. Anyway, he would turn his head at me and say, "This—now listen to this—my God, this now is sure a—" But his voice would trail off and the words which were going to tell what the thing sure and eternally was in its blessed truth would not ever get said. He would just leave the sentence hanging and twisting slowly in the air like a piece of frayed rope, and would look at me out of his clear, deep-set, ice-water-blue, abstract eyes—the kind of eyes and the kind of look your conscience has about three o'clock in the morning—and then, unlike your conscience, he would begin to smile, not much, just a sort of tentative, almost apologetic smile that took the curse off that straight mouth and square jaw, and seemed to say, "Hell, I can't help it if I look at you that way, buddy, it's just the way I look at things." Then the smile would be gone, and he would turn his face to the piano and set his hands to the keys.

Sooner or later he would get enough of the music and would drop into one of the other shabby chairs. Or he might remember to get me a drink, or might even take one himself, paler than winter sunlight and about as strong. We'd sit there, not talking, sipping slow, his eyes burning cold and blue in his head, bluer because of the swarthiness of the skin, which was drawn back taut over the bones of the face. It was like when we used to go fishing, when we were kids, back at Burden's Landing. We used to sit in the boat, under the hot sun, hour after hour, and never a word. Or lie on the beach. Or go camping together and after supper lie by a little smudge fire for the mosquitoes, and never say a word.

Perhaps Adam didn't mind taking a little time out for me because I made him think back to Burden's Landing and the other days. Not that he talked about it. But once he did. He was sitting in the chair, looking down at the eyewash in the glass which his long, hard-looking, nervous fingers were slowly revolving. Then he looked up at me, and said, "We used to have a pretty good time, didn't we? When we were kids."

"Yeah," I said.

"You and me and Anne," he said.

"Yeah," I said, and thought of Anne. Then I said, "Don't you have a good time now?"

He seemed to take the question under advisement for a half minute, as though I had asked him a real question, which maybe it was. Then he said, "Well, I don't suppose I ever thought about it." Then, "No, I don't suppose I ever thought about it."

"Don't you have a good time?" I asked. "And you a big-shot. Don't you have a good time being a big-shot?" I didn't let go. I knew it was a question you haven't got any right to ask anybody, not with the tone of voice I heard coming out of my mouth, but I couldn't let go. You grow up with somebody, and he is a success, a big-shot, and you're a failure, but he treats you just the way he always did and hasn't changed a bit. But that is what drives you to it, no matter what names you call yourself while you try to stick the knife in. There is a kind of snobbery of failure. It's a club, it's the old school, it's Skull and Bones, and there is no nasty supercilious twist to a mouth like the twist the drunk gets when he hangs over the bar beside the old pal who has turned out to be a big-shot and who hasn't changed a bit, or when the old pal takes him home to dinner and introduces him to the pretty little clear-eyed woman and the healthy kids. There wasn't any pretty little woman in Adam's shabby apartment, but he was a big-shot, and I let him have it.

But it didn't register on him. He simply turned on me the candid, blue gaze, slightly shaded by thought now, and said, "It just isn't something I ever thought about." Then the smile did the trick to the mouth which under ordinary circumstances looked like a nice, clean, decisive surgical wound, well healed and no pucker.

So I tried to make what amends I could for being what I was, and pulled out the soft-and-sweet stop, and said, "Yeah, we did have a good time when we were kids, you and Anne and me."

Yes, Adam Stanton, Anne Stanton, and Jack Burden, back in Burden's Landing, had a good time when they were children by the sea. A squall might, and did, pile in off the Gulf, and the sky blacked out with the rain and the palm trees heaved in distraction and then leaned steady with the vanes gleaming like wet tin in the last turgid, bilious, tattered light, but it didn't chill us or kill us in the kingdom by the sea, for we were safe inside a white house, their house or my house, and stood by the window to watch the surf pile up beyond the sea wall like whipped cream. And back in the room behind us would be Governor Stanton or Mr. Ellis Burden, or both, for they were friends, or Judge Irwin, for he was a friend, too, and there wasn't a wind that would ever have the nerve to bother Governor Stanton or Mr. Ellis Burden or Judge Irwin.

"You and Anne and me," Adam Stanton had said to me, and I had said it to him. So one morning, after I had managed to get out of bed, I called Anne up, and said, "I hadn't thought about you in a long time, but the other night I saw Adam and he said you and he and I used to have a good time when we were kids. So how about having dinner with me? Even if we are on crutches now." She said she would. She certainly wasn't on crutches, but we didn't have any fun.

She asked me what I was doing, and I told her, "Not a blessed thing. Just waiting for my cash to run out." She didn't tell me I ought to do something, and didn't even look it. Which was something. So I asked her what she was doing, and she laughed and said, "Not a blessed thing." Which I knew was a lie, for she was always fooling around with orphans and half-wits and blind niggers, and not even getting paid for it. And looking at her you could know it was all a waste of something and the something wasn't money. So I said, "Well, I hope you're doing it in pleasant company."

"Not particularly," she said.

I looked at her close and saw what I knew I would see and what I had seen a good many times when she wasn't sitting across from me. I saw Anne Stanton, who was not exactly a beauty maybe but who was Anne Stanton. Anne Stanton: the brown-toned, golden-lighted face, not as dark as Adam's, with a hint of the positive structure beneath the skin, which was drawn over the bone with something, a suggestion, of the tension which was in Adam's face, as though the fabricator of the job hadn't wanted to waste any material in softnesses and slacknesses and had stylized the product pretty cleanly. The dark hair drawn smoothly, almost tautly, away from the accurate part. The blue eyes which looked at you like Adam's eyes, with the same directness, but in which the clear, abstract, ice-blue was replaced by a deeper, coiling, troubled blue. Sometimes, anyway. They looked alike, Adam and Anne. They might have been twins. They even had the same smile. But the mouth it came on was, in Anne's case, different. It didn't carry any suggestion of the nice, clean, decisive, well-healed surgical wound. The fabricator had, on this item, allowed himself the luxury of a little extra material. Not too much. But enough.

That was Anne Stanton, and I saw what I knew I would see.

She sat there before me, very erect, with her head held high and straight on the fine, round stalk of her neck above the small, squarish shoulders, and with her rather small but roundly modeled bare arms laid close to her sides in mathematical accuracy. And looking at her, I thought how, below the level of the table, her small legs would be laid accurately together, thigh to thigh, knee to knee, ankle to ankle. There was, in fact, always something a little stylized about her—something of the effect one observes in certain Egyptian bas-reliefs and statuettes of princesses of a late period, forms in which grace and softness, without being the less grace or softness, are caught in mathematical formality. Anne Stanton always looked level at you, and you had the feeling that she was looking at something far away. She always held her head high, and you had the feeling that she was waiting for a voice which you wouldn't be able to hear. She always stood so trim and erect, and you had the feeling that all her grace and softness was caught in the rigor of an idea which you could not define.

I said, "You planning on being an old maid?"

She laughed, and said, "I'm not planning on anything. I quit making plans a long time back."

We danced in the handkerchief-big space between the speakeasy tables, on which stood the plates of half-eaten spaghetti or chicken bones and the bottles of Dago red. For about five minutes the dancing had some value in itself, then it became very much like acting out some complicated and portentous business in a dream which seems to have a meaning but whose meaning you can't figure out. Then the music was over, and stopping dancing was like waking up from the dream, being glad to wake up and escape and yet distressed because now you won't ever know what it had been all about.

She must have felt the same way about it, for when, later, I asked her to dance again, she said that she didn't feel like it, she'd rather talk. We talked, quite a lot, but it was a little bit like the dancing. You can't keep on talking forever about what a hell of a good time you had when you were kids.

I took her to her apartment building, which was quite a few cuts above Adam's joint, for Governor Stanton hadn't died exactly a pauper, and left her in the lobby. She said good night, and, "Be a good boy, Jack."

"Will you have dinner with me again?" I asked her.

"Any time you want," she said, "any time in the world. You know that."

Yes, I knew it.

And she did have dinner with me again, several times. The last time she said: "I've seen your father."

"Yeah," I said in an unencouraging way.

"Don't be like that," she said.

"Like what?"

"Oh, you know what I mean," she said. "Don't you even want to know how he is?"

"I know how he is," I said. "He's sitting in that hole he lives in down there or he's helping round that mission with his bums, or writing those damn-fool little leaflets they pass out to you on the street, all about Mark 4:6, and Job 7:5, and his specs are down on the end of his nose and the dandruff is like a snowstorm in the Dakotas down on his black coat collar."

She didn't say anything for a minute, then said: "I saw him on the street and he didn't look well. He looked sick. I didn't recognize him at first."

"Trying to pass you some of that junk?" I asked.

"Yes," she said. "He held out a piece of paper to me, and I was in a hurry, so I just automatically put out my hand for it. Then I realized he was staring right in my face. I didn't recognize him at first." She paused a little. "That was about two weeks back."

"I haven't seen him in nearly a year," I said.

"Oh, Jack," she said, "you oughtn't do that! You ought to see him."

"Look here, what can I say to him? And God knows, he hasn't got anything to tell me. Nobody made him live like that. Nobody made him walk out of his law office, either, and not even bother to shut the door behind him."

"But, Jack," she said, "you—"

"He's doing what he wants to do. And besides if he was fool enough to do what he did just because he couldn't get along with a woman—especially a woman like my mother. If he couldn't give her what she wanted, whatever the hell it was she wanted and he couldn't give her, then—"

105

"Don't talk like that," she said sharply.

"Look here," I said, "just because your old man was Governor once and died in a mahogany tester bed with a couple of high-priced doctors leaning over him and adding up the bill in their heads and because you think he was Jesus Christ in a black string tie, you needn't try to talk to me like an old woman. I'm not talking about your family, I'm talking about mine, and I can't help seeing the plain unvarnished truth. And if you—"

"Well, you don't have to talk to me about it," she said. "Or anybody."

"It's the truth."

"Oh, the truth," she exclaimed, and clenched her right hand on the tablecloth. "How do you know it's the truth? You don't know anything about it. You don't know what made them do what they did."

"I know the truth. I know what my mother is like. And you do, too. And I know my father was a fool to let her get him down."

"Don't be so bitter!" she said, and reached out to seize my forearm and set her sharp fingers in it, through the coat, and shake it a little.

"I'm not bitter. I don't give a damn what they did. Or do. Or why."

"Oh, Jack," she said, still clutching my forearm, but not hard now, "can't you love them a little, or forgive them, or just not think about them, or something? Something different from the way you are?"

"I could go for the rest of my life and not think about them," I said. Then I noticed that she was shaking her head ever so little from side to side, and that her eyes were as dark a blue as they ever got and too bright, and that she had drawn in the edge of her lower lip and had set her teeth to it. I reached my right hand over and took her hand off my left forearm and laid it down flat, palm down, on the tablecloth, and covered it with my hand. "I'm sorry," I said.

"You're not, Jack," she said, "you're not sorry. Not really. You aren't ever sorry about anything. Or glad, either. You're just—oh, I don't know what."

"I am sorry," I said.

"Oh, you just think you are sorry. Or glad. You aren't really."

"If you think you are sorry, who in the hell can tell you that you aren't?" I demanded, for I was a brass-bound Idealist then, as I have stated, and was not going to call for a plebiscite on whether I was sorry or not.

"That sounds all right," she said, "but it isn't. I don't know why—oh, yes, I do—if you've never been sorry or glad then you haven't got any way to know the next time whether you are or not."

106

"All right," I said, "but can I tell you this: something is happening inside me which I choose to call sorry?"

"You can say it, but you don't know." Then, snatching her hand from under my hand, "Oh, you start to feel sorry or glad or something but it just doesn't come to anything."

"You mean like a little green apple that's got a worm in it and falls off the tree before it ever gets ripe?"

She laughed, and answered, "Yes, like little green apples with worms in them."

"Well," I said, "here's a little green apple with a worm in it: I'm sorry."

I was sorry, or what went for sorry in my lexicon. I was sorry that I had ruined the evening. But candor compelled me to admit that there hadn't been much of an evening to ruin.

I didn't ask her to go to dinner with me again, at least not that time while I was out of a job and doing the sleeping. I had hunted up Adam and heard him play the piano. And I had sat across the spaghetti and the Dago red and looked at Anne Stanton. And as a result of what Anne said to me, I had gone down to the slums and seen the old man, the not very tall man who had once been stocky but whose face now drooped in puffy gray folds beneath the gray hair, with the steel-rimmed spectacles hanging on the end of the nose, and whose shoulders, thin now and snowed with dandruff, sagged down as with the pull of the apparently disjunctive, careful belly which made the vest of his black suit pop up above the belt and the slack-hanging pants. And in every case I had found what I had known I was going to find, because they had happened and nothing was going to change what had happened. I had been sinking down in the sleep like a drowning man in water, and they had flashed across my eyes again the way people say the past flashes across the eyes of the drowning man.

Well, I could go back to sleep now. Till my cash ran out, anyway. I could be Rip Van Winkle. Only I thought that the Rip Van Winkle story was all wrong. You went to sleep for a long time, and when you woke up nothing whatsoever had changed. No matter how long you slept, it was the same.

But I didn't get to do much sleeping. I got a job. Or rather, the job got me. The telephone got me out of bed one morning. It was Sadie Burke, who said, "Get down here to the Capitol at ten o'clock. The Boss wants to see you."

"The who?" I said.

"The Boss," she said, "Willie Stark, Governor Stark, or don't you read the papers?"

"No, but somebody told me in the barbershop."

"It's true," she said, "and the Boss said for you to get down here at ten." And she hung up the phone.

Well, I said to myself, maybe things do change while you

sleep. But I didn't believe it then, and didn't really believe it when I went into the big room with the black oak paneling and padded across the long red carpet under the eyes of all the genuine oil paintings of all the bewhiskered old men toward the man who wasn't very old and wasn't bewhiskered and who sat behind a desk in front of the high windows and who got up as I approached. *Hell,* I thought, *it's just Willie.*

It was just Willie, even though he was wearing something different from the country blue serge he had had on back at Upton. But he just had the thing flung on him anyhow, with his tie loose and to one side and the collar unbuttoned. And his hair hung down over his forehead, the way it used to. I thought for a second that maybe the meaty lips were laid together firmer than they used to be, but before I could be sure, he was grinning and had come around to the front of the desk. So I thought again it was just Willie.

He put out his hand, and said, "Hello, Jack."

"Congratulations," I said.

"I hear they fired you."

"You heard wrong," I said. "I quit."

"You were smart," he said, "because when I get through with that outfit they wouldn't be able to pay you. They won't be able to pay the nigger washes the spittoons."

"That will suit me," I allowed.

"Want a job?" he asked.

"I'd consider a proposition."

"Three hundred a month," he said, "and traveling expenses. When you travel."

"Who do I work for? The state?"

"Hell, no. Me."

"It looks like you'd be working for me," I said. "This Governorship doesn't pay but five thousand."

"All right," he said, and laughed, "I'll be working for you then."

Then I recollected how he'd done right well in his law practice.

"I'll give it a try," I said.

"Fine," he said. Then, "Lucy's wanting to see you. Come to dinner tomorrow night at the house."

"You mean the Mansion?"

"What the hell you think I mean? A tourist home? A boarding house? Sure, the Mansion."

Yes, the Mansion. He was going to treat me just like old times and take me home to dinner and introduce me to the pretty little woman and the healthy kid.

"Boy," he was saying, "we sure do rattle around in that place, Lucy and Tom and me."

"What am I supposed to do?" I asked him.

"Eat," he said. "Come at six-thirty and eat hearty. Call up Lucy and tell her what you want to eat."

"I mean, what do I do for the job?"

"Hell, I don't know," he said. "Something will turn up." He was right about that.

Chapter Three

It was always the same way when I came home and saw my mother. I would be surprised that it was the way it was but I knew at the same time that I had known it would be this way. I would come home with the firm conviction that she didn't really care a thing about me, that I was just another man whom she wanted to have around because she was the kind of woman who had to have men around and had to make them dance to her tune. But as soon as I saw her I would forget all that. Sometimes I forgot it even before I saw her. Anyway, when I forgot it, I would wonder why we couldn't get along. I would wonder even though I knew what would happen, even though I would always know that the scene into which I was about to step and in which I was about to say the words I would say, had happened before, or had never stopped happening, and that I would always just be entering the wide, white, high-ceilinged hall to see across the distance of the floor, which gleamed like dark ice, my mother, who stood in a doorway, beyond her the flicker of firelight in the shadowy room, and smiled at me with a sudden and innocent happiness, like a girl. Then she would come toward me, with a brittle, excited clatter of heels and a quick, throaty laugh, and stop before me and seize a little bunch of my coat between the thumb and forefinger of each hand, in a way that was childlike and both weak and demanding, and lift her face up to me, turning it somewhat to one side so that I could put the expected kiss upon her cheek. The texture of her cheek would be firm and smooth, quite cool, and I would breathe the scent which she always used, and as I kissed her I would see the plucked accuracy of the eyebrow, the delicate lines at the corner of the eye toward me, and note the crinkled, shadowed texture of the eyelid, which would flicker sharply over the blue eye. The eye, very slightly protruding, would be fixed glitteringly on some point beyond me.

That was the way it had always been—when I had come home from school, when I had come back from camps, when I had come back from college, when I had come back from jobs—and that was the way it was that late rainy afternoon, on the borderline between winter and spring, back in 1933, when I came back home again, after not coming home for a long time. It had been six or eight months since my last visit. That time we had had a row about my working for Governor Stark.

We always sooner or later got into a row about something, and in the two and a half years that I had been working for Willie it usually in the end came round to Willie. And if his name wasn't even mentioned, he stood there like a shadow behind us. Not that it mattered much what we rowed about. There was a shadow taller and darker than the shadow of Willie standing behind us. But I always came back, and I had come back this time. I would find myself drawn back. It was that way, and, as always, it seemed to be a fresh start, a wiping out of all the things which I knew could not be wiped out.

"Leave the bags in your car," she said, "the boy will get them." And she drew me toward the open door of the living room, where the firelight was, and down the length of the room to the long couch. I saw the bowl of ice, the siphon of soda, the Scotch on the glass-topped table, all the items sparkling in the firelight.

"Sit down," she said, "sit down, Son," and put the fingers of her right hand against my chest to give a little shove. It wasn't much of a shove, it didn't put me off my balance, but I sat down, and sank back into the couch. I watched her mix me a drink, and then a sort of excuse of a drink for herself, for she never took much. She held the glass out to me, and laughed that quick, throaty laugh again. "Take it," she said, and her face seemed to proclaim that she was offering me something which was absolutely special, something which was so precious that it couldn't be tied on God's green globe.

There's a lot of likker in the world, even Scotch, but I took it and gave a pull, feeling too that it was something special.

She sank down on the couch with an easy motion, vaguely suggestive of a flutter and preening as when a bird touches a bough, and took a sip, and lifted her head as if to let the liquor trickle into her throat. She had drawn one leg up beneath her and the other hung over with the sharp tip of the gray suède pump stretched forward to just touch the floor, with the precision of a dancer. She turned cleanly from the erect waist to look straight at me, twisting the gray cloth of the dress. The firelight defined her small, poised features, one side bright, one side in shadow, and emphasized the slight, famished, haunting hollow beneath the cheekbones (I always figured, after I got old enough to do any kind of figuring, that it was that—the hollow beneath the cheekbone—that got them) and the careful swooping lift of her piled-up hair. Her hair was yellowish, like metal, with gray in it now, but the gray was metallic, too, like spun metal woven and coiled into the yellow. It looked as though that was the way it had been intended from the very first to be, and a damned expensive job. Every detail.

I looked at her and thought: *Well, she's pushing fifty-five but I'll hand it to her.* And suddenly I felt old, and the thirty-five years I had been living suddenly seemed to stretch back forever. But I had to hand it to her.

She kept on looking at me, not saying anything, with that look which always said, "You've got something I want, something I need, something I've got to have," and said, too, "I've got something for you, I won't tell you what, not yet, but I've got something for you, too." The hollow in the cheeks: the hungry business. The glittering eyes: the promising business. And both at the same time. It was quite a trick.

I took the last of the drink, and held the glass in my hand. She reached out and took it, still watching me, and reached out to set it on the little table. Then she said, "Oh, Son, you look tired."

"I'm not," I said, and felt the stubbornness in me.

"You are," she said, and took me by the sleeve of the forearm and drew me toward her. I didn't come at first. I just let her pull the arm. She didn't pull hard, but she kept on looking straight at me.

I let myself go, and keeled over toward her. I lay on my back, with my head on her lap, the way I had known I would do. She let her left hand lie on my chest, the thumb and forefinger holding, and revolving back and forth, a button on my shirt, and her right hand on my forehead. Then she put it over my eyes, and moved it slowly upward over my forehead. Her hands were always cool. It was one of the first things I remembered ever knowing.

For a long time she didn't talk any. She just moved the hand over my eyes and forehead. I had known how it would be, and knew how it had been before and how it would be after. But she had the trick of making a little island right in the middle of time, and of your knowing, which is what time does to you.

Then she said, "You're tired, Son."

Well, I wasn't tired, but I wasn't not tired, either, and tiredness didn't have anything to do with the way things were.

Then, after a while, "Are you working hard, Son?"

I said, "So-so, I reckon."

Then, after another while, "That man—that man you work for—"

"What about it?" I said. The hand stopped on my forehead, and I knew it was my voice that stopped it.

"Nothing," she said. "Only you don't have to work for that man. Theodore could get you a—"

"I don't want any job Theodore would get for me," I said, and tried to heave myself up, but have you ever tried to heave yourself up when you're flat on your back on a deep couch and somebody has a hand on your forehead?

She held her hand firm on my forehead and leaned over and

said, "Don't now, don't. Theodore is my husband, he's your stepfather, don't talk that way, he'd like to—"

"Look here," I said, "I told you I—"

But she said, "Hush, Son, hush," and put her hand over my eyes, and began to move it again upward over my forehead.

She didn't say anything else. But she had already said what she had said, and she had to start the island trick all over again. Perhaps she had said it just so she could start over again, just to prove that she could do it. Anyway, she did it, all over again, and it worked.

Until the front door banged, and there were steps in the hall. I knew that it was Theodore Murrell, and started to heave up again. But even now, just for the last instant, she pressed her palm down on my forehead, and didn't let go until the sound of Theodore's steps had entered the room.

I got to my feet, feeling my coat crawling up around my neck and my tie under one ear, and looked across at Theodore, who had a beautiful blond mustache and apple cheeks and pale hair laid like taffy on a round skull and a hint of dignity at the belly (bend over, you bastard, bend over one hundred times every morning and touch the floor, you bastard, or Mrs. Murrell won't like you, and then where would you be?) and a slightly adenoidal lisp, like too much hot porridge, when he opened the aperture under the beautiful blond mustache.

My mother approached him with that bright stride and her shoulders well back, and stopped right before the Young Executive. The Young Executive put his right arm about her shoulder, and kissed her with the aperture under the beautiful blond mustache, and she seized him by the sleeve and drew him over toward me, and he said, "Well, well, old boy, it's fine to see you. How's tricks, how's the old politician?"

"Fine," I said, "but I'm not a politician, I'm a hired hand."

"Oho," he said, "don't try to kid me. They say you and the Governor are just like this." And he held up two not thin, very clean, perfectly manicured fingers for me to admire.

"You don't know the Governor," I replied, "for the only thing the Governor is just like this with—" and I held up two not very clean and quite imperfectly manicured fingers—"is the Governor, and now and then God-Almighty when he needs somebody to hold the hog while he cuts the throat."

"Well, the way he's going—" Theodore began.

"Sit down, you all," my mother told us, and we sat down, and took the glasses she handed us. She turned on a light.

I leaned back in my chair, and said "Yes" and said "No," and looked down the long room, which I knew better than any room in the world and which I always came back to, no matter what I said. I noticed that there was a new piece in it. A tall Sheraton break-front desk, in the place where the kidney desk had been. Well, the kidney desk would be in the attic now, in the second-string museum, while we sat in the first-string museum and while Bowman and Heatherford, Ltd., London, wrote a large figure in the black column of the ledger. There was always a change in the room. When I came home I'd always look around and wonder what it would be, for there had been a long procession of choice examples through that room, spinets, desks, tables, chairs, each more choice than the last, each in turn finding its way to the attic to make way for a new perfection. Well, the room had come a long way from the way I first remembered it, moving toward some ideal perfection which was in my mother's head, or in the head of a dealer in New Orleans, or New York, or London, and maybe, just before she died, the room would achieve its ideal perfection, and she would sit in it, a trim old lady, with piled-up white hair, and silky skin sagging off a fine jawbone, and blue eyes blinking rapidly, and would take a cup of tea to celebrate the ideal.

The furniture changed, but the people in it changed, too. Way back, there had been the thick-set, strong man, not tall, with a shock of tangled black hair on his head and steel-rimmed glasses on his nose and a habit of buttoning his vest up wrong, and a big gold watch-chain, which I liked to pull at. Then he wasn't there, and my mother pressed my head against her breast and said, "Your Daddy isn't coming back any more, Son."

"Is he dead?" I asked, "will he have a funeral?"

"No," she said, "he isn't dead. He has gone away, but you can think of him like he was dead, Son."

"Why did he go away?"

"Because he didn't love Mother. That's why he went away."

"I love you, Mother," I said, "I'll love you always."

"Yes, Son, yes, you love your mother," she said, and held me tight against her breast.

So the Scholarly Attorney was gone. I was about six years old then.

Then there was the Tycoon, who was gaunt and bald and wheezed on the stair. "Why does Daddy Ross puff going up-stairs?" I said.

"Hush," my mother said, "hush, Son."

"Why, Mother?"

"Because Daddy Ross isn't well, Son."

Then the Tycoon was dead. He had not lasted long.

So my mother put me in a school in Connecticut and left me to go across the ocean. When she came back there was another man, who was tall and slender and wore white suits and smoked long thin cigars, and had a thin black mustache. He was the Count, and my mother was a Countess. The Count sat in the room with people and smiled a great deal and didn't say much. People looked sideways at him, but he looked straight at them and smiled to show the whitest teeth in the world under the thin, accurate black mustache. When nobody was there he played the piano all day, and then went out wearing black boots and tight white trousers and rode a horse and made it jump over gates and gallop along the beach till its sides were flecked with lather and were pumping fit to die. Then the Count came into the house and drank *wis-kee* and held a Persian cat on his knee and stroked it with a hand which was not big but which was so strong that he could make men frown when he shook hands with them. And once I saw four blue-black parallel marks on my mother's upper right arm. "Mother," I said, "look! What happened?"

"Nothing," she said, "I just hurt myself." And she pulled the scarf down over her arm.

The Count's name was Covelli. People said, "That Count fellow is a son-of-a-bitch, but he can evermore ride a horse."

Then he was gone. I was sorry, for I had liked the Count. I had liked to watch him ride a horse.

Then there was quite a while when there was nobody.

Then there was the Young Executive, who had been a Young Executive from the day his mother gave the last push and would be a Young Executive until the day they drained out the blood and pumped in the embalming fluid. But that would be a long time off, because he was just forty-four, and sitting at the desk at the oil company where he earned the pin money to supplement his allowance wasn't breaking him down fast.

Well, I'd sat in that room with all of them, the Scholarly Attorney and the Tycoon and the Count and the Young Executive, and had watched the furniture change. So now I sat and looked at Theodore and at the new Sheraton break-front desk, and wondered how permanent they were.

I had come home. I was the thing that always came back.

It kept on raining that night. I lay in a big fine old family bed, which had come from somebody else's family (a long time ago there had been a white iron bed in my room standing on the floor matting, and the big fine old mahogany Burden family bed, which hadn't been fine enough and which was now in the attic, had been in my mother's room) and listened to the rain hiss on the live-oak and magnolia leaves. In the morning it had stopped raining, and there was sun. I went out and saw the thin pools of water standing on the black ground, like sheets of isinglass. Around the japonicas, the white and red and coral petals, which had been shattered from the blossoms, floated on the blackly gleaming pools. Some of them floated with the curled edges upward, like boats, and around them other petals floated upside down or had shipped water, making

115

a gay carnage as though a battleship had fired a couple of salvos into a fleet of carnival barges and gondolas in some giddy, happy, far-off land.

There was a massive japonica tree by the steps. I leaned over to scoop up some petals in my hand. The water was very cold. I held the petals in my hand, and walked down the curving drive to the gate. I stood there, pressing the petals in the palm and looking out at the bay, which was very bright beyond the strip of whitish sand streaked with drift.

But before noon it began to rain again, a long drizzle and drip from the spongy sky that lasted two days. That afternoon, and the next morning, and the next afternoon, I put on a raincoat belonging to the Young Executive and walked in the drizzle. Not that I was a walker who just has to have his lungs flushed out with ozone. But walking seemed to be the thing to do. The first afternoon I walked down the beach, past the Stanton place, which was cold and hollow-looking beyond the dripping leaves, and on out to the Irwin place, where Judge Irwin put me in a chair with my heels to the fire and opened a bottle of his choice old Maryland rye to give me a drink, and invited me to dinner the next night. But I took one drink and left, and walked on where there weren't any more houses, just brush and oak tangles with here and there a pine rising, and occasionally an open patch of ground with a gray shack.

And the next day I walked up the bay, through the streets of the town, and on beyond till I came to the little half-moon-shaped cove off the bay, where the pine grove came down close to the white sand. I walked just under the shelter of the pines, my heels deep in the needles, then I came out on the sand. There was a place where a half-charred log lay, very black with the wetness and around it the sodden ashes and black butts of driftwood, blacker for the white sand. People still came here for picnics. Well, I had come here for picnics, too. I knew what picnics were like.

I knew what a picnic was like, all right.

Anne and Adam and I had come here years before when we were kids, but it was not raining that day. Not till the end. It was very hot and very still. You could look down the bay, beyond the cove, toward the Gulf, and see the water lifting up into the light as though the horizon had ceased to exist. We swam, and ate our lunch, lying on the sand, then fished some more. But we didn't have any luck. By that time clouds had begun to pile, working in over the whole sky, except toward the west, beyond the pines, where the light struck through the break. The water was very still, and suddenly dark with the darkness of the sky, and away across the bay the line of woods looked black now, not green, above the whiteness of the line which was the beach way over there. A boat, a catboat, was becalmed over in that direction, nearly a mile away, and under the sky and over the dark water and against the black line of the woods, you never saw anything so heart-breakingly white as the sharp sail.

"We better get in," Adam said. "It's going to blow."

"Not quick," Anne said, "let's swim again."

"Better not." Adam hesitated and looked off at the sky.

"Let's," she insisted, and pulled at his arm. He didn't respond, still scanning the sky. All at once she dropped his arm and laughed and began to run toward the water. She didn't run directly to the water, but up the beach, toward a little spit, with her bobbed hair back loose on the air. I watched her run. She ran with her arms not quite outspread, crooked at the elbows, and with a motion of her legs which was graceful and free, and somehow awkward at the same time, as though she hadn't quite forgotten one kind of running, the child's running, and hadn't quite learned another kind of running, the woman's running. The legs seemed to be hung too loose, somewhat uncertainly, from the little hips, which weren't quite rounded yet. I watched her and noticed that her legs were long. Which I had never noticed before.

It wasn't a noise, but, instead, a stillness that made me turn suddenly to Adam. He was staring at me. When I met his eyes, his face flushed, and he jerked his eyes off me, as though embarrassed. Then he said, "I'll race you," huskily, and ran after her. I ran too, and his feet threw the sand back at me.

Anne was out in the water swimming now. Adam plunged in after her and swam hard and straight, outdistancing me. He passed right by Anne, and kept on swimming. He was a powerful swimmer. He hadn't wanted to swim but now he would swim straight out, hard and fast.

I came up to Anne, and slowed down, and said, "Hello." She lifted her head high for an instant, with the gracile motion a seal has, and smiled, then curled over forward in a clean surface dive. Her sharp small heels, side by side, flickered for a second above the water, then drew under. I caught up with her, and she did it again. Every time I caught up with her she would lift her head, and smile, and dive again. The fifth time I caught up, she didn't dive. She rolled over with a light, lounging twist of her body, and floated on her back, looking up at the sky, her arms spread wide. So I turned over, too, and floated, about five or six feet from her, and looked up at the sky.

The sky was darker now, with a purplish, greenish cast. The color of a turning grape. But it still looked high, with worlds of air under it. A gull crossed, very high, directly above me. Against the sky it was whiter even than the sail had been. It passed clear across all the sky I could see. I wondered if Anne

117

had seen the gull. When I looked at her, her eyes were closed. Her arms were still spread out wide, and her hair wavered out free on the water from around her head. Her head was far back, her chin lifted. Her face looked very smooth, as though she were asleep. As I lay in the water, I could see her profile sharp against the far-off black trees.

All at once, she turned, in the direction away from me, as though I hadn't been there, and began to swim in. She swam with a slow stroke now that seemed retarded and yet effortless. Her thin arms rose and sank with a languid and bemused and fastidious punctuality, like your own effortless motion in a dream.

Before we got to the beach, the rain had begun, big, spaced, heavy, independent drops that prickled the yet glossy surface of the water. Then it was a driving gust of rain, and the surface of the water was gone.

We rose out of the water and stood on the sand, with the rain whipping our skin, and looked out at Adam, who was coming in. He still had a long way to come. Down the bay beyond him, to the south, the lightning kept forking out of the dark sky, with steady thunder. Now and then Adam seemed, for a moment, to be lost in a driving sheet of rain which would rake over the water. Watching him, Anne stood there with her head bowed forward a little, almost pensively, and her shoulders hunched and her arms crossed over her insignificant breasts, hugging herself as though she were just about to shiver, and her knees tight together and slightly bent.

Adam came in, we gathered up our stuff, put on our sopping sandals, and passed through the pine grove, where the black masses heaved above us and the boughs made a stridor which you caught now and then coming out of the roar. We reached our car and went home. That summer I was seventeen, Adam was about my age, and Anne was four years younger, or about that. That was back before the World War, or rather, before we got into it.

That was a picnic I never forgot.

I suppose that that day I first saw Anne and Adam as separate, individual people, whose ways of acting were special, mysterious, and important. And perhaps, too, that day I first saw myself as a person. But that is not what I am talking about. What happened was this: I got an image in my head that never got out. We see a great many things and can remember a great many things, but that is different. We get very few of the true images in our heads of the kind I am talking about, the kind which become more and more vivid for us as if the passage of the years did not obscure their reality but, year by year, drew off another veil to expose a meaning which we had only dimly surmised at first. Very probably the last veil will not be removed, for there are not enough years, but the brightness of the image increases and our conviction increases that the brightness is meaning, or the legend of meaning, and without the image our lives would be nothing except an old piece of film rolled on a spool and thrown into a desk drawer among the unanswered letters.

The image I got in my head that day was the image of her face lying in the water, very smooth, with the eyes closed, under the dark greenish-purple sky, with the white gull passing over.

This is not to say that I fell in love with Anne that day. She was a kid then. That came later. But the image would have been there if I had never fallen in love with her, or had never seen her again, or had grown to detest her. There were times afterwards when I was not in love with Anne. Anne told me she wouldn't marry me, and after a while I married Lois who was a better-looking girl than Anne, the kind they turn around on the street to see, and I was in love with Lois. But the image was there all the time, growing brighter as the veils were withdrawn and making the promise of a greater brightness.

So when I stepped out of the pine grove, that drizzly early-spring afternoon a long time afterward, and saw the charred log on the white sand where a picnic had been, I remembered the picnic back in the summer of 1915, the last picnic we had before I left home to go to college.

I wasn't going such a hell of a long way to college. Just up to the State University.

"Oh, Son," my mother said, "why don't you be sensible and go to Harvard or Princeton." For a woman out of the scrub country of Arkansas, my mother had certainly learned a lot by that time about our better educational institutions. "Or even Williams," she said. "They say it's a nice refined place."

"I went to school where you wanted," I said, "and it was sure refined."

"Or even Virginia," she went on, looking brightly at my face and not hearing a word I said. "Your father went to the University of Virginia."

"That shouldn't be such a big recommendation to you," I said, and thought how smart I was to get that one off. I had got in the habit in arguments with her of making some reference to his leaving.

But she didn't hear that, either. She just went on, "If you were East, then it would be easier for you to come over for the summer and see me."

"They're fighting a war over there now," I said.

"They'll stop before long," she said, "then it will be easier."

"Yeah, and it would be easier for you to tell somebody I was in Harvard than in a place they never heard of like State.

119

They wouldn't even have heard of the name of the state it was in."

"It's just I want you to go to a nice place, Son, where you'll make nice friends. And like I said, it would be easier for you to come over to see me in the summer."

(She was talking about going to Europe again, and was very annoyed at the war. The Count had been gone quite a spell, since just before the war, and she was going back across. She did go back across, after the war, but she didn't get any more counts. Maybe she figured it was too expensive to marry them. She didn't marry again until the Young Executive.)

Well, I told her I didn't want to go to a nice place and didn't want any nice friends and wasn't going to Europe and wasn't going to take any money from her. That last part about the money just slipped out in the heat of the moment. It seemed a big manly thing to say, but the effect was so much superior to anything I had expected that I couldn't renege and spoil the drama. It knocked her breath out. It almost floored her. I suppose that she wasn't accustomed to hear anything in pants talk like that. Not that she didn't try to persuade me, but I got on my high horse and was stubborn. A thousand times in the next four years I thought what a damned fool I was. I would be hashing or typing or even, in the last year, doing part-time newspaper work, and would think how I had thrown away about five thousand dollars, just because I had read something in a book about its being manly to work your way through college. Not that my mother didn't send me money. On Christmas and birthdays. And I took that and had me a blowout, a real one with trimmings for days, and then went back to hashing or whatever it was. They didn't take me in the Army. Bad feet.

When he got back from the war, he was full of beans about it. He had been a colonel of artillery and had had himself a wonderful time. He had got there early enough to fire off a lot of iron at the Germans and to dodge a lot of their stuff in reply. In the Spanish-American War he hadn't got farther than a case of flux in Florida. But now his happiness was complete. He felt that all the years he had been making maps of Caesar's campaigns and making working models of catapults and ballistas and scorpions and wild asses and battering rams along ancient and medieval lines hadn't been wasted. Well, they hadn't been wasted as far as I was concerned, for I used to help him make them when I was a kid, and the tricks were wonderful little gadgets. For a kid, anyway. And the war hadn't been wasted, either, for he had made a visit to Alise-Ste-Reine, which was where Caesar beat Vercingetorix, and toward the end of the summer after he got back he had Foch and Caesar and Pershing and Haig and Vercingetorix and Critognatus and

120

Vercassivellaunus and Ludendorff and Edith Cavell pretty well mixed up in his mind. And he got out all the catapults and scorpions we had made and dusted them off. But he had been a good officer, they said, and a brave man. He had a medal to prove it.

I suppose that for a long time I took a snotty tone about the Judge as hero because it was a fashion for a while to take such a tone about heroes and I grew up in that fashion. Or perhaps it was because I had bad feet and never got into the Army, or even the S.A.T.C. when I was in college, and therefore had the case of sour grapes that the wallflower always has. Perhaps if I had been in the Army everything would have been different. But the Judge was a brave man, even if he did have a medal to prove it. He had proved it before he ever got the medal. And he was to prove it again. There was, for instance, the time a fellow he had sent up to the pen stopped him in the street down at the Landing and told him he was going to kill him. The Judge just laughed and turned his back and walked away. The fellow took out a pistol then and called to the Judge, two or three times. Finally the Judge looked around. When he saw the man had a pistol and had it pointing at him, the Judge turned right there and walked straight at the man, not saying a word. He got right up to the man and took the pistol away from him. What he did in the war, I never knew.

The night my mother and the Young Executive and I went to dinner at his place, nearly fifteen years later, he dug up some of the junk again. There were the Pattons, a couple who lived down the Row, and a girl named Dumonde, whose presence I took to be tribute to me, and Judge Irwin, and us. Digging up the ballista was, I suppose, a tribute to me, too, though he always had shown a tendency to instruct his guests in the art of war of the pregunpowder epochs. All during the meal it had been old times, which was another tribute to me, for you come back to the place you have been and they always start chewing over that bone: old times. Old times, just before dessert, worked around to how I used to make models with him. So he got up and went into the library and came back with a ballista, about twenty inches long, and shoved his dessert to one side and set it up there on the table. Then he cocked it, using the little crank on the draw drum to wind back the carriage, just as though he hadn't been strong enough to do it with a finger or two all at once. Then he didn't have anything to shoot. So he rang for the black boy and got a roll. He broke open the roll and removed a little hunk of the soft bread and tried to make a pellet of it. It didn't make a very good pellet, so he dipped it in water to make it stick. He put it in the carriage, "Now," he said, "it works like this," and tipped the trigger.

It worked. The pellet was heavy with a good soaking and the

zip hadn't gone out of the ballista with the passage of the years, for the next thing I knew there was an explosion in the chandelier and Mrs. Patton screamed and spewed mint ice over her black velvet and bits of glass showered down over the tablecloth and the big bowl of japonicas. The Judge had made it dead center on an electric-light bulb. He had also fetched down one of the crystal bangles of the chandelier.

The Judge said he was very sorry about Mrs. Patton. He said that he was a very stupid old man in his second childhood to be playing with toys and then sat up very straight in his chair to show what a chest and pair of shoulders he still had. Mrs. Patton ate the rest of the mint ice, punctuating her activity with distrustful glances at the disgraceful ballista. Then we all went back into the Judge's library to wait for the coffee and the brandy bottle.

But I loitered behind in the dining room for a moment. I have said that the zip hadn't gone out of the ballista with the passage of the years. But that was a misstatement of fact. It hadn't had a chance to. I went over to examine the thing, with a motive more sentimental than scientific. But then I noticed the twists, which gave it its zip. There are two twists of fiber on all those things, ballistas, some types of catapults, scorpions, and wild asses, through each of which the butt of a propelling arm is adjusted to make, as it were, half of the bow and a kind of supercrossbow. We used to cheat by mixing in catgut and fine steel wire with the string of the twists on our models to give more force. Now, as I looked at the thing, I realized that the twists weren't the old twists which I had put in back in the dear dead days. Not by a damned sight. They were practically new.

And all at once I had the sight of Judge Irwin sitting up nights, back in the library, with catgut and steel wire and string and pliers and scissors on the desk beside him, and with his high old red-thatched head bent over, the yellow eyes gimleted upon the task. And seeing that picture in my head, I felt sad and embarrassed. I had never felt anything, one way or the other, about the Judge's making those things in the first place, years back. When I was a kid it seemed natural that anybody in his right mind would want to make them, and read books about them, and make maps and models. And it had kept on seeming all right that the Judge *had* made them. But the picture I now had in my head was different. I felt sad and embarrassed and, somehow, defrauded.

So I joined the guests in the library and left a piece of Jack Burden in the dining room, with the ballista, for good and all.

They were having coffee. All except the Judge, who was opening up a bottle of brandy. He looked up as I came in, and said, "Been looking at our old peashooter, huh?" He put the slightest emphasis upon *our*.

"Yes," I said.

The yellow eyes bored right into me for a second, and I knew he knew what I'd found out. "I fixed it up," he said, and laughed the most candid and disarming laugh in the world. "The other day. You know, an old fellow with nothing to do and nobody to talk to. You can't read law and history and Dickens all the time. Or fish."

I grinned a grin which I somehow felt I had to grin as a tribute to something, not specified in my mind. But I knew that the grin was about as convincing as cold chicken broth in a boarding house.

Then I went over and sat beside the Dumonde girl, who had been provided for my delight. She was a prettyish, dark girl, well got-up but lacking something, too brittle and vivacious, with a trick of lassoing you with her anxious brown eyes and fluttering the eyelids as she cinched the rope and then saying what her mother had told her ten years before to say. "Oh, Mr. Burden, they say you're in politics, oh, it must be just fascinating!" No doubt, her mother had taught her that. Well, she was pushing thirty and it hadn't worked yet. But the eyelids were still busy.

"No, I'm not in politics," I said. "I've just got a job."

"Tell me about your job, Mr. Burden."

"I'm an office boy," I said.

"Oh, they say you're very important, Mr. Burden. They say you're very influential. Oh, it must be fascinating. To be influential, Mr. Burden!"

"It's news to me," I said, and discovered that they were all looking at me as though it had just dawned on them that I was sitting there buck-naked on the couch beside Miss Dumonde, with a demi-tasse on my knee. It's the human fate. Every time some dame like Miss Dumonde snags you and you have to start talking the way you have to talk to dames like Miss Dumonde, the whole world starts listening in. I saw the Judge smiling with what I took to be a vengeful relish.

Then he said, "Don't let him kid you, Miss Dumonde. Jack is very influential."

"I knew it," Miss Dumonde said. "It must be fascinating."

"All right," I said, "I'm influential. You got any pals in the pen you want me to get a pardon for?" Then I thought: *Wonderful manners you got, Jack. You might at least smile if you've got to say that.* So I smiled.

"Well, there's going to be somebody in the pen," old Mr. Patton said, "before it's over. What's going on up there in the city. All these—"

"George," his wife breathed at him, but it didn't do any

123

good, for Mr. Patton was the bluff, burly type, with lots of money and a manly candor. He kept right on: "—yes, sir, all these wild goings-on. Why, that fellow is giving this state away. Free this and free that and free other. Every wool-hat jackass thinking the world is free. Who's going to pay? That's what I want to know? What does he say to that, Jack?"

"I never asked him," I said.

"Well, you ask him," Mr. Patton said. "And ask him, too, how much grabbing there is. All that money flowing, and don't tell me there's not a grab. And ask him what he's going to do when they impeach him? Tell him there's a constitution in this state, or was before he blew it to hell. Tell him that."

"I'll tell him," I said, and laughed, and then laughed again when I thought how Willie would look if I did tell him.

"George," the Judge said, "you're an old fogy. Government is committed these days to give services we never heard of when we were growing up. The world's changing."

"It's changed so much a fellow can step in and grab the whole state. Give him another few years and nothing can blast him out. He'll have half the state on a pay roll and the other half will be afraid to vote. Strong-arm, blackmail, God knows what."

"He's a hard man," the Judge said. "He's played it hard and close. But there's one principle he's grasped: you don't make omelettes without breaking eggs. And precedents. He's broken plenty of eggs and he may make his omelettes. And remember, the Supreme Court has backed him up on every issue raised to date."

"Yeah, and it's *his* court. Since he got Armstrong on, and Talbott. And the issues raised. But what about the issues that haven't been raised? That people have been afraid to raise?"

"There's a great deal of talk," the Judge said calmly, "but we don't really know much."

"I know he's going to tax this state to death," Mr. Patton said, and shifted his big hams, and glared. "And drive business out of this state. Raising royalty on the state coal land. On the oil land. On—"

"Yes, George," the Judge laughed, "and he slammed an income tax on you and me, too."

"On the oil situation, now," the Young Executive began, for the sacred name of oil had been mentioned, "as I see it, the situation—"

Well, Miss Dumonde had certainly opened the corral gate when she mentioned politics, and it was thunder of hoofs and swirl of dust from then on, and I was sitting on the bare ground in the middle of it. For a while it didn't occur to me that there was anything peculiar about the scene. Then it did occur to me. After all, I did work for the fellow who had the tail and the

124

cloven hoof and this was, or had started out to be, a social occasion. I suddenly remembered that fact and decided that the developments were peculiar. Then I realized that they weren't so peculiar, after all. Mr. Patton, and the Young Executive, and Mrs. Patton, for she had begun putting her oar in, and even the Judge, they all assumed that even though I did work for Willie my heart was with them. I was just picking up a little, or maybe a lot, of change with Willie, but my heart was in Burden's Landing and they had no secrets from me and they knew they couldn't hurt my feelings. Maybe they were right. Maybe my heart was in Burden's Landing. Maybe they couldn't hurt my feelings. But I just broke in, after an hour of sitting quiet and drinking in Miss Dumonde's subtle scent, and said something. I don't recall what I interrupted, but it all amounted to the same thing anyway. I said, "Doesn't it all boil down to this? If the government of this state for quite a long time back had been doing anything for the folks in it, would Stark have been able to get out there with his bare hands and bust the boys? And would he be having to make up so many short cuts to get something done to make up for the time lost all these years in not getting something done? I'd just like to submit that question for the sake of argument."

There wasn't a sound for half a minute. Mr. Patton's granite visage seemed to lean toward me like a monument about to fall, and the satchel under Mrs. Patton's chin quivered like a tow sack full of kittens, and the sound of the Young Executive's adenoids was plainly audible, and the Judge just sat, with his yellow eyes working over the crowd, and my mother's hands turned in her lap. Then she said, "Why, Son, I didn't know you—you felt that—that way!"

"Why—er—no," Mr. Patton said, "I didn't realize you —er—"

"I didn't say I felt that way," I said. "I just offered a proposition for the sake of argument."

"Argument! Argument!" burst out Mr. Patton, himself again. "It doesn't matter what kind of government this state's had in the past. They never had this kind. Nobody ever tried to grab the whole damned state. Nobody ever—"

"It's a very interesting proposition," the Judge said, and sipped his brandy.

And they were at it again, all except my mother, whose hands kept turning slow in her lap, with the firelight exploding in the big diamond which never came from the Scholarly Attorney. They kept at it steady until it was time to go.

"Who is that Miss Dumonde?" I asked my mother late the next afternoon, sitting in front of the fire.

"Mr. Orton's sister's child," she said, "and she'll inherit his money."

"Well," I said, "somebody ought to wait till she gets the dough and then marry her and drown her in the bathtub."

"Dont talk that way," my mother was saying.

"Don't worry," I said. "I'd like to drown her but I don't want her money. I'm not interested in money. If I wanted to I could reach out any day and knock off ten thousand. Twenty thousand. I—"

"Oh, Son—what Mr. Patton said—those people you're with —Son, now don't get mixed up in any graft, now—"

"Graft is what he calls it when the fellows do it who don't know which fork to use."

"It's the same thing, Son—those people—"

"I don't know what those people, as you call them, do. I'm very careful not to ever know what anybody anywhere does any time."

"Now, Son, don't you, please don't—"

"Don't what?"

"Don't get mixed up in—in anything."

"All I said was I *could* reach out and knock off ten thousand. And not graft. Information. Information is money. But I told you I'm not interested in money. Not the slightest. Willie isn't either."

"Willie?" she asked.

"The Boss. The Boss isn't interested in money."

"What's he interested in, then?"

"He's interested in Willie. Quite simply and directly. And when anybody is interested in himself quite simply and directly the way Willie is interested in Willie you call it genius. It's only the half-baked people like Mr. Patton who are interested in money. Even the big boys who make a real lot of money aren't interested in money. Henry Ford isn't interested in money. He's interested in Henry Ford and therefore he is a genius."

She reached over and took my hand, and spoke earnestly to me. "Don't, Son, don't talk that way," she said.

"What way?"

"When you talk that way I don't know what to think. I just don't know." And she looked imploringly at me, with the firelight striking across her cheek to make the hollow there hollower and hungrier. She laid her free hand on the hand of mine she held, and when a woman makes that kind of a sandwich out of one of your hands it is always a prelude to something. Which, in this case, was: "Why don't you, Son—why don't you—settle down—why don't you marry some nice girl and—"

"I tried that," I offered. "And if you tried to rig anything for me with that Dumonde you sure rang the lemons."

She was looking at me with a growing, searching, discovering look from her too bright eyes, like somebody puzzling something out of distance. Then she said, "Son—Son, you were sort of funny last night—you didn't enter into things—then the tone you took—"

"All right," I said.

"You weren't like yourself, like you used to be, you—"

"If I'm ever like I used to be I'll shoot myself," I said, "and if I embarrassed you before those half-wit Pattons and that half-wit Dumonde, Im sorry."

"Judge Irwin—" she began.

"Leave him out of it," I said. "He's different."

"Oh, Son," she exclaimed, "what makes you be that way? You didn't embarrass me, but what makes you that way? It's those people—what you do—why don't you settle down—get a decent job—Judge Irwin, Theodore, they could get you a—"

I snatched my hand out of the sandwich she had made, and said, "I don't want anything in God's world out of them. Or anybody. And I don't want to settle down, and I don't want to get married, and I don't want any other job, and as for money—"

"Son—Son—" she said, and turned her hands together on her lap.

"And as for money, I don't want any more than I've got. And besides I don't have to worry about that. You've got enough—" I got up from the couch and lighted a cigarette and flung the match stub into the fire—"enough to leave both Theodore and me pretty well fixed."

She didn't move or say anything. She just looked up at me, and I saw that her eyes had tears coming into them, and that she loved me, for I was her son. And that Time didn't mean anything, but that the lifted face with the bright, too large eyes was an old face. The skin lanked down from the cheek hollows under the bright eyes.

"Not that I want your money," I said.

She reached out with one hand, in a tentative, humble way, and took my right hand, not by my hand itself but just by the fingers, crumpling them together.

"Son," she said, "you know whatever I've got is yours. Don't you know that?"

I didn't say anything.

"Don't you know that?" she said, and swung on to my fingers as though they were the end of a rope somebody had tossed in the water to her.

"All right," I heard my voice say, and felt my fingers twitching to get away, but at the same time I felt my heart suddenly go soft and fluid in my chest like a melting snowball you squash in your hand. "I'm sorry I talked that way," I said, "but, damn

127

it, why can't we just stop talking? Why can't I just come home for a day or two and us not talk, not open our mouths?"

She didn't answer, but kept on holding my fingers. So I released my fingers, and said, "I'm going up and take a bath before dinner," and started toward the door. I knew that she didn't turn her head to watch me go out of the room, but as I crossed the room I felt as though they had forgotten to ring down the curtain at the end of something and a thousand eyes were on my back and the clapping hadn't started. Maybe the bastards didn't know it was over. Maybe they didn't know it was time to clap.

I went upstairs and lay in the bathtub with the hot water up to my ears and knew that it was over. It was over again. I would get in my car, right after dinner, and drive like hell toward town over the new concrete slab between the black, mist-streaked fields, and get to town about midnight and go up to my hotel room where nothing was mine and nothing knew my name and nothing had a thing to say to me about anything that had ever happened.

I lay in the tub and heard a car drive up and knew that it was the Young Executive and knew that he would come in the front door and that the woman on the couch would get up and with a quick step and small, squared, gallant shoulders carry the old face to him like a present.

And, by God, he'd better look grateful.

Two hours later I was in my car and Burden's Landing was behind me, and the bay, and the windshield wipers were making their busy little gasp and click like something inside you which had better not stop. For it was raining again. The drops swung and swayed down out of the dark into my headlights like a bead portiere of bright metal beads which the car kept shouldering through.

There is nothing more alone than being in a car at night in the rain. I was in the car. And I was glad of it. Between one point on the map and another point on the map, there was the being alone in the car in the rain. They say you are not you except in terms of relation to other people. If there weren't any other people there wouldn't be any you because what you do, which is what you are, only has meaning in relation to other people. That is a very comforting thought when you are in the car in the rain at night alone, for then you aren't you, and not being you or anything, you can really lie back and get some rest. It is a vacation from being you. There is only the flow of the motor under your foot spinning that frail thread of sound out of its metal gut like a spider, that filament, that nexus, which isn't really there, between the you which you have just left in

128

one place and the you which you will be when you get to the other place.

You ought to invite those two you's to the same party, some time. Or you might have a family reunion for all the you's with barbecue under the trees. It would be amusing to know what they would say to each other.

But meanwhile, there isn't either one of them, and I am in the car in the rain at night.

This is why I am in the car: Thirty-seven years before, about 1896, the stocky, sober, fortyish man, with the steel-rimmed spectacles and the dark suit, who was the Scholarly Attorney, had gone up to a lumber town in south Arkansas to interview witnesses and conduct an investigation for a big timberland litigation. It was not much of a town, I guess. Shacks, a boarding house for the bosses and engineers, a post office, a company commissary—all rising out of the red mud—and around them the stumps stretching off, and off yonder a cow standing among the stumps, and the scream of saws like a violated nerve in the center of your head, and in the air and in your nostrils the damp, sweet-sick smell of sawn timber.

I have not seen the town. I have never even set foot inside the State of Arkansas. But I have seen the town in my head. And standing on the steps of the commissary is a girl with yellow hair hanging in two heavy braids and with large blue eyes and with the hint of a delicate, famished hollow in each cheek. Let us say that she is wearing a lettuce-green gingham dress, for lettuce-green is a nice, fresh color for a blond girl to be wearing as she stands in the morning sunlight on the commissary steps and listens to the saws scream and watches a stocky man in a dark suit come picking his way soberly through the red mud left by the last big spring rain.

The girl is standing on the commissary steps because her father clerks in the commissary for the company. That is what I know about her father.

The man in the dark suit stays in the town for two months transacting his legal business. In the evening, toward sunset, he and the girl walk down the street of the town, now dusty, and move out beyond the houses, where the stumps are. I can see them standing in the middle of the ruined land, against the background of the brass-and-blood-colored summer sunset of Arkansas. I cannot make out what they say to each other.

When the man has finished his business and leaves the town, he takes the girl with him. He is a kind, innocent, shy man, and as he sits beside the girl on the red plush of the train seat, he holds her hand in his, stiffly and carefully as though he might drop and break something valuable.

He puts her in a big white house, which his grandfather had built. In front of it is the sea. That is new to her. Every day

129

she spends a great deal of time looking at it. Sometimes she goes down to the beach and stands there, alone, looking out at the lift of the horizon.

I know that that is true, the business of looking at the sea, for my mother once, years later when I was a big boy, said to me, "When I first came here I used to stand down at the gate and just look out over the water. I spent hours doing it, and didn't know why. But it wore off. It wore off a long time before you were born, Son."

The Scholarly Attorney went to Arkansas and the girl was on the steps of the commissary, and that is why I was in the car, in the rain, at night.

I entered the lobby of my hotel just about midnight. The clerk saw me enter, beckoned to me, and gave me a number to call. "They been giving the operator prostration," he said. I didn't recognize the number. "Said ask for a party named Miss Burke," the clerk added.

So I didn't bother to go upstairs before calling, but stepped into one of the hotel lobby booths. "Markheim Hotel," the crisp voice answered, and I asked for Miss Burke, and there was Sadie's voice saying, "Well, by God, it's time you got here. I called Burden's Landing God knows when and they said you'd left. What did you do, walk?"

"I'm not Sugar-Boy," I said.

"Well, get on over here. Suite 905. Hell has popped."

I hung the receiver up very deliberately, walked over to the desk and asked the clerk to give my bag to a bellhop, got a drink out of the lobby cooler, bought a couple of packs of cigarettes from the sleepy sister at the lobby stand, opened a package and lighted myself one, and stood there to take a long drag and look at the blank lobby, as though there weren't any place in the world where I had to go.

But there was such a place. And I went there. Quick, once I started.

Sadie was sitting in the outside room of Suite 905, over by the telephone stand, with a tray full of cigarette butts in front of her and a coronal of smoke revolving slowly about her head of hacked-off black hair.

"Well," she said in the tone of the matron of a home for wayward girls from inside the smoke screen, but I didn't answer. I walked straight over to her, past the form of Sugar-Boy, who snored in a chair, and grabbed a handful of that wild black Irish hair to steady her head and kissed her smack on the forehead before she could God-damn me.

Which she did.

"You have no idea why I did that," I said.

"I don't care, just so it isn't a habit."

130

"It was nothing personal," I said. "It was just because your name is not Dumonde."

"Your name is going to be mud if you don't get on in there," she said, and twitched her head in the direction of a door.

"Maybe I'll resign," I said in my whimsey, then for a split second, with a surprising flash in my head like the flash of a photographer's bulb, I thought maybe I would.

Sadie was just about to say something, when the telephone rang and she sprang at it as though she'd strangle it with her bare hands, and snatched up the receiver. As I walked toward the inner door, I heard her saying, "So you got him. All right, get him to town here. . . . To hell with his wife. Tell him he'll be sicker'n she is if he don't come. . . . Yeah, tell him—"

Then I knocked on the inner door, heard a voice, and went in.

I saw the Boss in shirt sleeves, cocked back in an easy chair with his sock-feet propped on a straight chair in front of him, and his tie askew, and his eyes bugging out and a forefinger out in the air in front of him as though it were the stock of a bull whip. Then I saw what the snapper of the bull whip would have been flicking the flies off of it that forefinger of the Boss had been the stock of a bull whip: it was Mr. Byram B. White, State Auditor, and his long bony paraffin-colored face was oozing a few painful drops of moisture and his eyes reached out and grabbed me like the last hope.

I took in the fact that I was intruding.

"Excuse me," I said, and started to back out of the door.

"Shut the door and sit down," the Boss said, and his voice moved right on without any punctuation to something it had been saying before my entrance, and the forefinger snapped, "—and you can just damned well remember you aren't supposed to get rich. A fellow like you, fifty years old and gut-shot and teeth gone and never had a dime, if God-Almighty had ever intended you to be rich he'd done it long back. Look at yourself, damn it! You to figure you're supposed to be rich, it is plain blasphemy. Look at yourself. Ain't it a fact?" And the forefinger leveled at Mr. Byram B. White.

But Mr. White did not answer. He just stood there in his unhappiness and looked at the finger.

"God damn it, has the cat got your tongue?" the Boss demanded. "Can't you answer a civil question?"

"Yes," Mr. White managed with gray lips that scarcely moved.

"Speak up, don't mumble, say, 'It's a fact, it's a blasphemous fact,' " the Boss insisted, still pointing the finger.

Mr. White's lips went grayer, and the voice was less than loud and clear, but he said it. Every word.

"All right, that's better," the Boss said. "Now you know

what you're supposed to do. You're supposed to stay pore and take orders. I don't care about your chastity, which from the looks of you you don't have any trouble keeping plenty of, but I mean it's poverty and obedience and don't you forget it. Especially the last. There'll be a little something coming to you now and then in the way of sweetening, but Duffy'll tend to that. Don't you go setting up on your own any more. There just aren't going to be any one-man bonanzas. You got that? Speak up!"

"Yes," Mr. White said.

"Louder! And say, 'I got that.' "

He said it. Louder.

"All right," the Boss said, "I'm going to stop this impeachment business for you. But don't go and get the notion it's because I love you. It's just because those fellows can't get the idea they can just up and knock off somebody. Are my motives clear?"

"Yes," Mr. White said.

"All right, then sit down over there at that desk." And the Boss pointed at the little desk with the pen tray and telephone. "Get a sheet of plain paper out of the drawer and take your pen in hand." He waited until Mr. White had glided spectrally across the room and settled himself at the desk, making himself remarkably small, like the genie getting ready to go back into the bottle, drawing himself into a hunch as though he wanted to assume the prenatal position and be little and warm and safe in the dark. But the Boss was saying, "Now write what I say." Then he began to dictate: "Dear Governor Stark,—because of ill health—which renders it difficult for me to attend conscientiously—" The Boss interrupted himself, saying, "Be sure you put that *conscientiously* in now, you wouldn't want to leave that out," and then continued in the business voice—"to the duties of my position as Auditor—I wish to offer my resignation—to take effect as soon after the above date—as you can relieve me." He eyed the hunched figure, and added, "Respectfully yours."

There was silence, and the pen scratched across the paper, then stopped. But Mr. White's tall, bald, narrow head remained bent over close to the paper, as though he were nearsighted, or praying, or had lost whatever it is in the back of a neck that keeps a head up straight.

The Boss studied the back of the bent head. Then he demanded, "Did you sign it?"

"No," the voice said.

"Well, God damn it, sign!" Then when the pen had again stopped scratching across the paper, "Don't put any date on it. I can fill that in when I want."

Mr. White's head did not lift. From where I sat I could see

132

that his hand still held the pen staff, the point still touching the paper at the end of the last letter of his name.

"Bring it here," the Boss said.

Mr. White rose and turned, and I looked at his still bent-over face to see what I could see. His eyes didn't have any appeal in them now as he swung them past me. They didn't have anything in them. They were as numb and expressionless as a brace of gray oysters on the half shell.

He held out the sheet to the Boss, who read it, folded it, tossed it over to the foot of the bed near which he sat. "Yeah," he said, "I'll fill in the date when I need to. If I need to. It all depends on you. But you know, Byram—why I didn't get one of those undated resignations from you from the start I don't know. I got a stack of 'em. But I just misjudged you. I just took one look at you, and said, 'Shucks, there ain't any harm in the old bugger.' I figured you were so beat down you'd know the good Lord never meant for you to be rich. I figured you never would try to pull any shines. Shucks, I figured you didn't have any more initiative than a wet washrag dropped on the bathroom floor in a rooming house for old maids. I was wrong, Byram, I am free to confess. Fifty years old and all that time just waiting your one big chance. Waiting for your ship to come in. Saving up one little twitch and try like a one-nut for his wedding night. Waiting for the big chance, and this was it, and everything was going to be different. But—" and he whipped the forefinger at Mr. White again—"you were wrong, Byram. This was not your chance. And there never will be one. Not for the likes of you. Now get out!"

Mr. White got out. One second he was there, and the next second he wasn't there, and there had been scarcely a sound for his passing. There was just the empty space which had been occupied by the empty space which went by the name of Mr. Byram B. White.

"Well," I said to the Boss, "you gave yourself a good time."

"Damn it," he said, "it's just something in their eyes makes you do it. This fellow now, he'd lick spit, and you can see that, and it makes you do it."

"Yeah," I said, "it looks like he's a long worm with no turning, all right."

"I gave him every chance," the Boss said glumly. "Every chance. He didn't have to say what I told him to say. He didn't have to listen to me. He could have just walked out the door and kept on walking. He could have put a date on that resignation and handed it to me. He could have done a dozen things. But did he? Hell, no. Not Byram, and he just stands there and his eyes blink right quick like a dog's do when he leans up against your leg before you hit him, and, by God, you have the

133

feeling if you don't do it you won't be doing God's will. You do it because you are helping Byram fulfill his nature."

"Not that it's any of my business," I said, "but what's all the shouting about?"

"Didn't you read the paper?"

"No, I was on vacation."

"And Sadie didn't tell you?"

"Just got here," I said.

"Well, Byram rigged him up a nice little scheme to get rich. Got himself a tie-in with a realty outfit and fixed things up with Hamill in the Tax Lands Bureau. Pretty, only they wanted it all to themselves and somebody got sore at not being cut in, and squawked to the MacMurfee boys in the Legislature. And if I get my hands on who it was—"

"Was what?"

"Squawked to the MacMurfee outfit. Ought to taken it up with Duffy. Everybody knows he's supposed to handle complaints. And now we got this impeachment business."

"Of who?"

"Byram."

"What's happened to Hamill?"

"He's moved to Cuba. You know, better climate. And, from reports, he moved fast. Duffy went around this morning, and Hamill caught a train. But we got to handle this impeachment."

"I don't think they could put it through."

"They ain't even going to try. You let a thing like that get started and no telling what'll happen. The time to stomp 'em is now. I've got boys out picking up soreheads and wobblies and getting 'em to town. Sadie's been on the phone all day taking the news. Some of the birds are hiding out, for the word must have got round by this time, but the boys are running 'em down. Brought in three this afternoon, and we gave 'em what it took. But we had something ready on them all. You ought to've seen Jeff Hopkins's face when he found out I knew about his pappy selling likker out of that little one-horse drugstore he's got over in Talmadge and then forging prescriptions for the record. Or Martten's when he found out I knew how the bank over in Okaloosa holds a mortgage on his place falling due in about five weeks. Well—" and he wriggled his toes comfortably inside of the socks—"I quieted their nerves. It's the old tonic, but it still soothes."

"What am I supposed to do?"

"Get over to Harmonville tomorrow and see if you can beat some sense into Sim Harmon's head."

"That all?"

Before he could answer Sadie popped her head in the door, and said the boys had brought in Witherspoon, who was a representative from the north tip of the state.

"Put him in the other room," the Boss said, "and let him stew." Then, as Sadie popped out again, he turned to me and answered my question. "All, except get me together all you have on Al Coyle before you leave town. The boys are trying to run him down and I want to be heeled when they book him."

"O.K.," I said, and stood up.

He looked at me as though he were about to say something. For a second I had the notion that he was working himself up to it, and I stood in front of my chair, waiting. But Sadie stuck her head in. "Mr. Miller would like to see you," she said to the Boss, and didn't give the impression of glad tidings.

"Send him in," the Boss ordered, and I could tell that, no matter what he had on his mind to say to me a second before, he had something else on it now. He had Hugh Miller, Harvard Law School, Lafayette Escadrille, Croix de Guerre, clean hands, pure heart, Attorney General, on his mind.

"He won't like it," I said.

"No," he said, "he won't."

And then in the doorway stood the tall, lean, somewhat stooped man, with swarthy face and unkempt dark hair and sad eyes under black brows, and with a Phi Beta Kappa key slung across his untidy blue serge. He stood there for a second, blinking the sad eyes, as though he had come out of darkness into a sudden light, or had stumbled into the wrong room. He looked like the wrong thing to be coming through that door, all right.

The Boss had stood up and padded across in his sock-feet, holding out his hand, saying, "Hello, Hugh."

Hugh Miller shook hands, and stepped into the room, and I started to edge out the door. Then I caught the Boss's eye, and he nodded, quick, toward my chair. So I shook hands with Hugh Miller, too, and sat back down.

"Have a seat," the Boss said to Hugh Miller.

"No, thanks, Willie," Hugh Miller replied in his slow solemn way. "But you sit down, Willie."

The Boss dropped back into his chair, cocked his feet up again, and demanded, "What's on your mind?"

"I reckon you know," Hugh Miller said.

"I reckon I do," the Boss said.

"You are saving White's hide, aren't you?"

"I don't give a damn about White's hide," the Boss said. "I'm saving something else."

"He's guilty."

"As hell," the Boss agreed cheerfully. "If the category of guilt and innocence can be said to have any relevance to something like Byram B. White."

"He's guilty," Hugh Miller said.

"My God, you talk like Byram was human! He's a thing! You don't prosecute an adding machine if a spring goes bust
135

and makes a mistake. You fix it. Well, I fixed Byram. I fixed him so his unborn great-grandchildren will wet their pants on this anniversary and not know why. Boy, it will be the shock in the genes. Hell, Byram is just something you use, and he'll sure be useful from now on."

"That sounds fine, Willie, but it just boils down to the fact you're saving White's hide."

"White's hide be damned," the Boss said, "I'm saving something else. You let that gang of MacMurfee's boys in the Legislature get the notion they can pull something like this and there's no telling where they'd stop. Do you think they like anything that's been done? The extraction tax? Raising the royalty rate on state land? The income tax? The highway program? The Public Health Bill?"

"No, they don't," Hugh Miller admitted. "Or rather, the people behind MacMurfee don't like it."

"Do you like it?"

"Yes," Hugh Miller said, "I like *it*. But I can't say I like some of the stuff around it."

"Hugh," the Boss said, and grinned, "the trouble with you is you are a lawyer. You are a damned fine lawyer."

"You're a lawyer," Hugh Miller said.

"No," the Boss corrected, "I'm not a lawyer. I know some law. In fact, I know a lot of law. And I made me some money out of law. But I'm not a lawyer. That's why I can see what the law is like. It's like a single-bed blanket on a double bed and three folks in the bed and a cold night. There ain't ever enough blanket to cover the case, no matter how much pulling and hauling, and somebody is always going to nigh catch pneumonia. Hell, the law is like the pants you bought last year for a growing boy, but it is always this year and the seams are popped and the shankbone's to the breeze. The law is always too short and too tight for growing humankind. The best you can do is do something and then make up some law to fit and by the time that law gets on the books you would have done something different. Do you think half the things I've done were clear, distinct, and simple in the constitution of this state?"

"The Supreme Court has ruled—" Hugh Miller began.

"Yeah, and they ruled because I put 'em there to rule it, and they saw what had to be done. Half the things *weren't* in the constitution but they are now, by God. And how did they get there? Simply because somebody did 'em."

The blood began to climb up in Hugh Miller's face, and he shook his head just a little, just barely, the way a slow animal does when a fly skims by. Then he said, "There's nothing in the constitution says that Byram B. White can commit a felony with impunity."

"Hugh," the Boss began, soft, "don't you see that Byram
136

doesn't mean a thing? Not in this situation. What they're after is to break the administration. They don't care about Byram, except so far as it's human nature to hate to think somebody else is getting something when you aren't. What they care about is undoing what this administration has done. And now is the time to stomp 'em. And when you start out to do something—" he sat up straight in the chair now, with his hands on the over-stuffed sides, and thrust his head forward at Hugh Miller—"you got to use what you've got. You got to use fellows like Byram, and Tiny Duffy, and that scum down in the Legislature. You can't make bricks without straw, and most of the time all the straw you got is secondhand straw from the cowpen. And if you think you can make it any different, you're crazy as a hoot owl."

Hugh Miller straightened his shoulders a little. He did not look at the Boss but at the wall beyond the Boss. "I am offering my resignation as Attorney General," he said. "You will have it in writing, by messenger, in the morning."

"You took a long time to do it," the Boss said softly. "A long time. Hugh. What made you take such a long time?"

Hugh Miller didn't answer, but he did move his gaze from the wall to the Boss's face.

"I'll tell you, Hugh," the Boss said. "You sat in your law office fifteen years and watched the sons-of-bitches warm chairs in this state and not do a thing, and the rich get richer and the pore get porer. Then I came along and slipped a Louisville Slugger in your hand and whispered low, 'You want to step in there and lay round you a little?' And you did. You had a wonderful time. You made the fur fly and you put nine tin-horn grafters in the pen. But you never touched what was behind 'em. The law isn't made for that. All you can do about that is take the damned government away from the behind guys and keep it away from 'em. Whatever way you can. You know that down in your heart. You want to keep your Harvard hands clean, but way down in your heart you know I'm telling the truth, and you're asking the benefit of somebody getting his little panties potty-black. You know you're welching if you pull out. That," he said, softer than ever, and leaned toward Hugh Miller, peering up at him, "is why it took you so long to do it. To pull out."

Hugh Miller looked down at him a half minute, down into the beefy upturned face and the steady protruding eyes. There was a shadowed, puzzled expression on Hugh Miller's face, as though he were trying to read something in a bad light, or in a foreign language he didn't know very well. Then he said, "My mind is made up."

"I know your mind's made up," the Boss said. "I know I couldn't change your mind, Hugh." He stood up in front of his chair, hitched his trousers up, the way a fellow has to who is putting it on some around the middle, and sock-footed over to

Hugh Miller. "Too bad," he said. "You and me make quite a team. Your brains and my brawn."

Hugh Miller gave something which resembled an incipient smile.

"No hard feelings?" the Boss said, and stuck out his hand. Hugh Miller took it.

"If you don't give up likker, you might drop in and have a drink with me some time," the Boss said. "I won't talk politics."

"All right," Hugh Miller said, and turned toward the door.

He had just about made the door, when the Boss said, "Hugh." Hugh Miller stopped and looked back.

"You're leaving me all alone," the Boss said, in semicomic woe, "with the sons-of-bitches. Mine and the other fellow's."

Hugh Miller smiled in a stiff, embarrassed way, shook his head, said, "Hell—Willie—" let his voice trail off without ever saying what he had started to say, and then Harvard Law School, Lafayette Escadrille, Croix de Guerre, clean hands and pure heart, was with us no longer.

The Boss sank down on the foot of the bed, heaved his left ankle up over his right knee; and while he meditatively scratched the left foot, the way a farmer does when he takes off his shoes at night, he stared at the closed door.

"With the sons-of-bitches," he said, and let the foot slip off the knee and plop to the floor, while he still stared at the door.

I stood up again. It was my third try for getting out of the place and getting back to my hotel for some sleep. The Boss could sit up all night, night after night, and never show it, and that fact was sure hell on his associates. I edged toward the door again, but the Boss swung his stare to me and I knew something was coming. So I just stopped and waited for it, while the stare worked over my face and tried to probe around in the gray stuff inside my head, like a pair of forceps.

Then he said, "You think I ought to thrown White to the wolves?"

'It's a hell of a time to be asking that question," I said.

"You think I ought?"

"*Ought* is a funny word," I said. "If you mean, to win, then time will tell. If you mean, to do right, then nobody will ever be able to tell you."

"What do you think?"

"Thinking is not my line," I said, "and I'd advise you to stop thinking about it because you know damned well what you are going to do. You are going to do what you are doing."

"Lucy is figuring on leaving," he said calmly, as though that answered something I had said.

"Well, I'm damned," I said, in genuine surprise, for I had Lucy figured as the long-suffering type on whose bosom repentant tears always eventually fall. Very eventually. Then my glance strayed to the closed door, beyond which Sadie Burke sat in front of the telephone with that pair of black bituminous eyes in the middle of the pocked face and cigarette smoke tangled in that wild black hacked-off Irish hair like morning mist in a pine thicket.

He caught my glance at the door. "No," he said, "it's not that."

"Well, that would be enough by ordinary standards," I said.

"She didn't know. Not that I know of."

"She's a woman," I said, "and they can smell it."

"That wasn't it," he said. "She said if I took care of Byram White she would leave me."

"Looks like everybody is trying to run your business for you."

"God damn it!" he said, and came up off the bed, and paced savagely across the carpet for four paces, and swung, and paced again, and seeing that motion and the heavy sway of the head when he turned, I thought back to the nights when I had heard the pacing in the next room in those jerkwater hotels over the state, back in the days when the Boss had been Willie Stark, and Willie Stark had been the sucker with the high-school-debater speech full of facts and figures and the kick-me sign on his coattails.

Well, I was seeing it now—the lunging, taut motion that had then been on the other side of the wall, in the dry-goods-box little hotel room. Well, it was out of that room now. It was prowling the veldt.

"God damn it!" he said again, "they don't know a thing about it, they don't know how it is, and you can't tell 'em."

He paced back and forth a couple of times more, then said, "They don't know."

He swung again, paced, and stopped, his head thrust out toward me. "You know what I'm going to do? Soon as I bust the tar out of that gang?"

"No," I said, "I don't know."

"I'm going to build me the God-damnedest, biggest, chromium-platedest, formaldehyde-stinkingest free hospital and health center the All-Father ever let live. Boy, I tell you, I'm going to have a cage of canaries in every room that can sing Italian grand opera and there ain't going to be a nurse hasn't won a beauty contest at Atlantic City and every bedpan will be eighteen-carat gold and by God, every bedpan will have a Swiss music-box attachment to play 'Turkey in the Straw' or 'The Sextet from Lucia,' take your choice."

"That will be swell," I said.

"I'll do it," he said. "You don't believe me, but I'm going to do it."

"I believe every word of it," I said.

I was dead for sleep. I stood there, rocking on my heels, and through the haze I watched him pace and swing and lunge, and sway his big head, with the hair coming down to his eyes.

I supposed then that it was a wonder that Lucy Stark hadn't packed her suitcase a long time before. I didn't see how she didn't know about something which could scarcely be called a secret. When it began I never knew. But it was already full blown when I found out about it. The Boss went up to Chicago on a little piece of private business, about six or eight months after he got to be Governor, and took me with him. Up there a fellow named Josh Conklin did us the town, and he was the man to do it, a big, burly fellow, with prematurely white hair and a red face and black, beetling eyebrows and a dress suit that fitted him like a corset and a trick apartment like a movie set and an address book an inch thick. He wasn't the real thing, but he sure was a good imitation of it, which is frequently better than the real thing, for the real thing can relax but the imitation can't afford to and has to spend all the time being just one cut more real than the real thing, with money no object. He took us to a night club where they rolled out a sheet of honest-to-God ice on the floor and a bevy of "Nordic Nymphs" in silver gee-strings and silver brassières came skating out on real skates to whirl and fandango and cavort and sway to the music under the housebroke aurora borealis with the skates flashing and the white knees flashing and white arms serpentining in the blue light, and the little twin, hard-soft columns of muscle and flesh up the backbones of the bare backs swaying and working in a beautiful reciprocal motion, and what was business under the silver brassières vibrating to music, and the long unbound un-snooded silver innocent Swedish hair trailing and floating and whipping in the air.

It took the boy from Mason City, who had never seen any ice except the skim-ice on the horse trough. "Jesus," the boy from Mason City said, in unabashed admiration. And then, "Jesus." And he kept swallowing hard, as though he had a sizable chunk of dry corn pone stuck in his throat.

It was over, and Josh Conklin said politely, "How did you like that, Governor?"

"They sure can skate," the Governor said.

Then one of the Swedish-haired nymphs came out of the dressing room with her skates off and a silver cloak draped over her bare shoulders, and came over to our table. She was a friend of Josh Conklin's, and a very nice friend to have even if the hair had not come from Sweden but from the drugstore. Well, she had a friend in the act, so she got her friend, who quickly made friends with the Governor, who, for the rest of the stay in Chicago, practically dropped out of my life except for the period every night when the skating was going on. Then he'd be

140

sitting there watching the gyrating, and swallowing on the chunk of dry corn pone stuck in his throat. Then when the last act was over he'd say, "Good night, Jack," and he and the friend of the friend of Josh Conklin would head off into the night.

I don't know that Lucy ever knew about the skating rink, but Sadie did. For Sadie had channels of information closed to the home-maker type. When the Boss and I got back home, and the Nordic Nymphs were but a fond memory, a soft sweet spot in the heart like the bruised place in a muskmelon, it was Sadie who raised the seven varieties of Hibernian hell. The very morning the Boss and I hit town, I heard rumblings from inside the Boss's office as I stood in the outer room chatting with the girl who was the receptionist and catching up with the gossip. I noticed the racket inside, a noise like somebody slamming a book on a desk and then a voice, Sadie's voice. "What's going on?" I asked the girl.

"Yeah, you tell me what went on in Chicago," the girl said.

"Oh," exclaimed I in my innocence, "so that is it."

"Oh," she exclaimed, mimicking me, "that was it, and how!"

I retired to the door of my cubbyhole, which opened off the outside room. I was standing just inside, with my door wide open, when Sadie burst out of the Boss's door about the way one of the big cats, no doubt, used to bounce out of the hutch at the far end of the arena and head for the Christian martyr. Her hair was flying with distinct life and her face was chalk-white with the pock marks making it look like riddled plaster, like, say, a plaster-of-Paris mask of Medusa which some kid has been using as a target for a BB gun. But in the middle of the plaster-of-Paris mask was an event which had nothing whatsoever to do with plaster of Paris: her eyes, and they were a twin disaster, they were a black explosion, they were a conflagration. She was running a head of steam to bust the rivets, and the way she snatched across the floor you could hear the seams pop in her skirt.

Then she caught sight of me, and without change of pace swung straight into my room and slammed the door behind her.

"The son-of-a-bitch," she said, and stood there panting and glaring at me.

"You needn't blame me," I said.

"The son-of-a-bitch," she iterated, glaring, "I'll kill him, I swear to God I'll kill him."

"You set a high valuation on something," I said.

"I'll ruin him, I'll drive him out of this state, I swear to God. The son-of-a-bitch to two-time me after all I've done for him. Listen—" she said, and grabbed a handful of my lapels in each of her strong hands and shook me. (Her hands were squarish

141

and strong and hard like a man's.) "Listen—" she repeated.

"You needn't choke me," I protested peevishly, "and I don't want to listen. I know too God-damned much now." And I wasn't joking. I didn't want to listen. The world was full of things I didn't want to know.

"Listen—" and she shook me—"who made that son-of-a-bitch what he is today? Who made him Governor? Who took him when he was the Sap of the Year and put him in big time? Who gave it to him, play by play so he couldn't lose?"

"I reckon you mean for me to say you did."

"And it's the truth," she said, "and he goes and two-times me, the—"

"No," I said, trying to get loose from the grip on my lapels, "he was two-timing Lucy, so you need some other kind of arithmetic for what he was doing to you. But I don't know whether you multiply or divide in a case like this."

"Lucy!" she burst out from lips that coiled and contorted. "Lucy—she's a fool. She had her way and he'd be in Mason City slopping the hogs right now, and he knows it. He knows what she'd do for him. If he listened to her. She had her chance, she—" She simply stopped for breath, but you could see the words still blazing on in her head while she gasped for air.

"I see you seem to think Lucy is on the way out," I said.

"Lucy—" she said, and stopped, but the tone said everything there was to say about Lucy, who was a country girl, and had gone to a hick Baptist college where they believed in God, and had taught the little towheaded snots in Mason County school, and had married Willie Stark and given him a kid, and had missed her chance. Then she added, suddenly quiet, in a grim matter-of-factness, "Give him time—he'll ditch her, the son-of-a-bitch."

"You ought to know," I said, simply because I couldn't resist the logic of the proposition, but I hadn't got it out before she slapped me. Which is what you ask for when you start mixing into affairs, public or private.

"It's the wrong guy," I said, fingering my cheek and backing off a step from the heat, for she was about to blaze, "I'm not the hero of the piece."

Then she wasn't about to blaze, at all. She stood there in a kind of heavy numbness inside the sagging clothes. I saw a tear gather at the inner corner of each eye, gather very slowly and swollenly and then run down with the precision of a tiny mechanical toy, one on each side of the slightly pitted nose, until they simultaneously arrived at the smear of dark lipstick, and spread. I saw the tongue come out and fastidiously touch the upper lip as though to sample the salt.

She was looking straight at me all the time as though if she looked hard enough she might see the answer to something.

142

Then she went past me to the wall, where a mirror hung, and stared into the mirror, putting her face up close to the mirror and turning it a little from side to side, slowly. I couldn't see what was in the mirror, just the back of her head.

"What was she like?" she asked, distantly and dispassionately.

"Who?" I asked, and it was an honest question.

"In Chicago," she said.

"She was just a little tart," I said, "with fake Swedish hair on her head and skates on her feet and practically nothing on in between."

"Was she pretty?" the distant and dispassionate voice asked.

"Hell," I said, "if I met her on the street tomorrow I wouldn't recognize her."

"Was she pretty?" the voice said.

"How do I know?" I demanded, peevish again. "The condition she earned her living in you didn't get around to noticing her face."

"Was she pretty?"

"For Christ's sake, forget it," I said.

She turned around, and came toward me, holding her hands up at about the level of the chin, one on each side, the fingers together and slightly bent, not touching her face. She came up close to me and stopped. "Forget it?" she repeated, as though she had just heard my words.

Then she lifted her hands a little, and touched the white riddled plaster-of-Paris mask, touching it on each side, just barely prodding the surface as though it were swollen and painful. "Look," she commanded.

She held it there for me to look at. "Look!" she commanded vindictively, and jabbed her fingers into the flesh, hard. For it was flesh, it wasn't plaster of Paris at all.

"Yes, look," she said, "and we lay up there in that God-for-saken shack—both of us, my brother and me—we were kids—and it was the smallpox—and my father was a drunk no-good —he was off drunk, crying and drinking in a saloon if he could beg a dime—crying and telling how the kiddies, the sweet little angel kiddies, was sick—oh, he was a drunk lousy warm-hearted kid-beating crying Irishman—and my brother died—and he ought to have lived—it wouldn't have mattered to him—not to a man—but me, I didn't die—I didn't die, and I got well—and my father, he would look at me and grab me and start kissing me all over the face, all over the holes, slobbering and crying and stinking of whisky—or he'd look at me and say, 'Jeez,' and slap me in the face—and it was all the same—it was all the same, for I wasn't the one that died—I didn't die—I—"

It was all a breathless monotony, suddenly cut off. She had groped out for me and had seized the cloth of my coat in her hands and had stuck her bowed head up against my chest. So I

143

stood there with my right arm around her shoulder, patting her, patting and making a kind of smoothing-out motion with my hand on the back that shook soundlessly with what I took to be sobs.

Then, not lifting her head, she was saying, "It's going to be like that—it's always been that way, and it'll keep on—being like that—"

It, I thought, and thought she was talking about the face.

But she wasn't, for she was saying, "—it'll keep on—they'll kiss it and slobber—then they'll slap you in the face—no matter what you do, do anything for them, make them what they are—take them out of the gutter and make something out of them —and they'll slap you in the face—the first chance—because you had smallpox—they'll see some naked slut on skates—and they'll slap you in the face—they'll kick up dirt in your face—"

I kept on patting and making the smoothing-out motion, for there wasn't anything else to do.

"—that's the way it'll be—always some slut on skates—some—"

"Look here," I said, still patting, "you make out. What do you care what he does?"

She jerked her head up. "What do you know, what the hell do you know?" she demanded, and dug her fingers into my coat and shook me.

"If it's all this grief," I said, "let him go."

"Let him go! Let him go! I'll kill him first, I swear it," she said, glaring at me out of the now red eyes. "Let him go? Listen here—" and she shook me again—"if he does run after some slut, he'll come back. He's got to come back, do you hear? He's got to. Because he can't do without me. And he knows it. He can do without any of those sluts, but he can't do without me. Not without Sadie Burke, and he knows it."

And she lifted her face up, high, almost thrusting it at me, as though she were showing me something I ought damned well to be proud to look at.

"He'll always come back," she asserted grimly.

And she was right. He always came back. The world was full of sluts on skates, even if some of them weren't on skates. Some of them wore grass skirts and some of them pounded typewriters and some of them checked hats and some of them were married to legislators, but he always came back. Not necessarily to be greeted with open arms and a tender smile, however. Sometimes it was a cold silence like the arctic night. Sometimes it was delirium for every seismograph on the continent. Sometimes it was a single well-chosen epithet. For instance, the time the Boss and I had to do a little trip up to the north of the state. The afternoon we got back we walked into the Capitol and there, in the stately lobby, under the great bronze dome, was Sadie. We

144

approached her. She waited until we had arrived, then said, without preliminary, quite simply, "You bastard."

"Gee, Sadie," the Boss said, and grinned his grin of the wayward, attractive boy, "you don't even wait to find out anything."

"You just can't keep buttoned up, you bastard," she said, still simply, and walked away.

"Gee," the Boss said ruefully to me, "I didn't do a thing this trip, and look what happens."

What did Lucy Stark know? I don't know. As far as you could tell, she didn't know anything. Even when she told the Boss she was going to pack her bag, it was, so he said, because he hadn't thrown Byram B. White to the wolves.

But she didn't pack the bag, even then.

She didn't pack it because she was too honorable, or too generous, or too something, to hit him when she thought he was down. Or about to go down. She wasn't going to add the weight of her thumb to what closely resembled a tidy package of disaster lying on the scales with the blood seeping through the brown paper. For the impeachment of Byram B. White had become a minor issue. They had uncorked the real stuff: the impeachment of Willie Stark.

I don't know whether or not they had planned it that way. Or whether they were forced into it before they planned when they figured the Boss was turning on too much heat and it was their only chance to get back on the offensive. Or whether they figured that the Lord had delivered the enemy into their hands, that they could get him dead to rights on the business of attempting to corrupt, coerce, and blackmail the Legislature, in addition to the other little charges of malfeasance and nonfeasance. Maybe they had some heroes lined up from among the ranks to testify that they had had the heat put on them. It would have taken a hero, too (or sound inducements), for nobody but a half-wit would have believed, in the light of the record, that the Boss was bluffing. But apparently they figured they had found, or bought, some heroes.

Anyway, they tried it, and for a brief interval life was a blur for speed. I gravely doubt that the Boss did any sleeping for two weeks. That is, bed sleeping. No doubt, he snatched something in the back of automobiles roaring down highways at night, or in a chair between the time one fellow went out the door and the next came in. He roared across the state at eighty miles an hour, the horn screaming, from town to town, crossroads to crossroads, five, or six, or seven, or eight speakings in a day. He would come out on the platform, almost slouching out, lounging out, as though all the time in the world were before him and all the time were his. He would begin, easy, "Folks, there's going to be a leetle mite of trouble back in town. Between me and that Legislature-ful of hyena-headed, feist-faced, belly-

145

dragging sons of slack-gutted she-wolves. If you know what I mean. Well, I been looking at them and their kind so long, I just figured I'd take me a little trip and see what human folks looked like in the face before I clean forgot. Well, you all look human. More or less. And sensible. In spite of what they're saying back in that Legislature and getting paid five dollars a day of your tax money for saying it. They're saying you didn't have bat sense or goose gumption when you cast your sacred ballot to elect me Governor of this state. Maybe you didn't have bat sense. Don't ask me, I'm prejudiced. But—" and now he wouldn't be lounging with his head cocked a little on one side in that easy sizing-up way, looking out from under the eyelids that drooped a little, for now he'd thrust, all at once, the heavy head forward, and the eyes, red from sleeplessness, would bulge—"I'll ask you a question. And I want an answer. I want an answer before God and under the awful hand of the Most High. Answer me: Have I disappointed you? Have I?" Then, leaning sharply, he would lift his right hand while the question was still ringing in the air, and say, "Stop! Don't answer until you look into the depth of your heart to see the truth. For there is where truth is. Not in a book. Not in a lawyer's book. Not on any scrap of paper. In your heart." Then, in the long pause, he would swing his gaze slowly over the crowd of faces. Then, "Answer me!"

I would wait for the roar. You can't help it. I knew it would come, but I would wait for it, and every time it would seem intolerably long before it came. It was like a deep dive. You start up toward the light but you know you can't breathe yet, not yet, and all you are aware of is the blood beating in your own head in the intolerable timelessness. Then the roar would come and I would feel the way you do when you pop out of the water from a deep dive and the air bursts out of your lungs and everything reels in the light. There is nothing like the roar of a crowd when it swells up, all of a sudden at the same time, out of the thing which is in every man in the crowd but is not himself. The roar would swell and rise and fall and swell again, with the Boss standing with his right arm raised straight to Heaven and his red eyes bulging.

And when the roar fell away, he said, with his arm up, "I have looked in your faces!"

And they would yell.

And he said, "O Lord, and I have seen a sign!"

And they would yell again.

And he said, "I have seen dew on the fleece and the ground dry!"

Then the yell.

Then, "I have seen blood on the moon!" Then, "Buckets of blood, and boy! I know whose blood it will be." Then, leaning

146

forward, grabbing out with his right hand as though to seize something in the air before him, "Gimme that meat ax!"

It was always that way, or like that. And charging across the state with the horn screaming and blatting, and Sugar-Boy shaving the gasoline truck on the highway and the spit flying from his mouth while the lips worked soundlessly and words piled up inside him before he could get them out, "The b-b-b-bas-tud!" And the Boss standing up on something with his arm against the sky (it might be raining, it might be bright sun, it might be night and the red light from sizzling gasoline flares set on the porch of a country store), and the crowd yelling. And me so light-headed from no sleep that my head felt big as the sky and when I walked I seemed to be tiptoeing on clouds of cotton batting.

All of that.

But this too: the Boss sitting in the Cadillac, all lights off, in the side street by a house, the time long past midnight. Or in the country, by a gate. The Boss leaning to a man, Sugar-Boy or one of Sugar-Boy's pals, Heavy Harris or Al Perkins, saying low and fast, "Tell him to come out. I know he's there. Tell him he better come out and talk to me. If he won't come, just say you're a friend of Ella Lou. That'll bring him." Or, "Ask him if he ever heard of Slick Wilson." Or something of the kind. And then there would be a man standing there with pajama tops stuck in pants, shivering, his face white in the darkness.

And this: the Boss sitting in a room full of smoke, a pot of coffee on the floor, or a bottle, saying, "Bring the bastard in. Bring him in."

And when they had brought the bastard in, the Boss would look him over low, from head to foot, and then he would say, "This is your last chance." He would say that slow and easy. Then he would lean suddenly forward, at the man, and say, not slow and easy now, "God damn you, do you know what I can do to you?"

And he could do it, too. For he had the goods.

On the afternoon of the fourth of April, 1933, the streets leading to the Capitol were full of people, and they weren't the kind of people you usually saw on those streets. Not in those numbers, anyway. The *Chronicle* that night referred to the rumor of a march on the Capitol, but affirmed that justice would not be intimidated. Before noon on the fifth of April there were a lot more wool-hats and red-necks and Mother Hubbards and crepe-de-Chine dresses with red-clay dust about the uneven bottom hem, and a lot of clothes and faces which weren't cocklebur and crossroads, but county-seat and filling-station. The crowd moved up toward the Capitol, not singing or yelling, and spread out over the big lawn where the statues were.

Men with tripods and cameras were scurrying about on the edges of the crowd, setting up their rigs on the Capitol steps, climbing on the bases of the frock-coated statues to get shots. Here and there around the edge of the crowd you could see the blue coat of a mounted cop up above the crowd, and in the open space of lawn between the crowd and the Capitol there were more cops, just standing, and a few highway patrolmen, very slick and businesslike in their bright-green uniforms and black boots and black Sam Browne belts and dangling holsters.

The crowd began chanting, "Willie, Willie, Willie—We want Willie!"

I looked out of a window on the second floor and saw it. I wondered if the sound carried into the Chamber of Representatives, where they were yammering and arguing and orating. Outside it was very simple, out there on the lawn, under the bright spring sky. No arguing. Very simple. "We want Willie—Willie, Willie, Willie!" In a long rhythm, with a hoarse undertone, like surf.

Then I saw a big black car pull slowly into the drive before the Capitol, and stop. A man got out, waved his hand to the cops, and walked to the bandstand there on the edge of the lawn. It was a fat man. Tiny Duffy.

Then he was speaking to the crowd. I could not hear his words, but I knew what he was saying. He was saying that Willie Stark asked him to go peaceably into the city, to wait until dark, to be back on the lawn before the Capitol by eight o'clock, when he would have something to tell them.

I knew what he would tell them. I knew that he would stand up before them and say that he was still Governor of the state.

I knew that, because early the previous evening, around seven-thirty, he had called me in and given me a big brown manila envelope. "Lowdan is down at the Haskell Hotel," he said. "I know he's in his room now. Go down there and let him take a peep at that but don't let him get his hands on it and tell him to call his dogs off. Not that it matters whether he does or not, for they've changed their minds." (Lowdan was the kingpin of the MacMurfee boys in the House.)

I had gone down to the Haskell and to Mr. Lowdan's room without sending my name. I knocked on the door, and when I heard the voice, said, "Message." He opened the door, a big jovial-looking man with a fine manner, in a flowered dressing gown. He didn't recognize me at first, just seeing a big brown envelope and some sort of face above it. But I withdrew the brown envelope just as his hand reached for it, and stepped over the sill. Then he must have looked at the face. "Why, howdy-do, Mr. Burden," he said, "they say you've been right busy lately."

"Loafing," I said, "just plain loafing. And I was just loafing by and thought I'd stop and show you something a fellow gave me." I took the long sheet out of the envelope, and held it up for him to look at. "No, don't touch, burn-y, burn-y," I said.

He didn't touch but he looked, hard. I saw his Adam's apple jerk a couple of times; then he removed his cigar from his mouth (a good cigar, two-bit at least, by the smell) and said, "Fake."

"The signatures are supposed to be genuine," I said, "but if you aren't sure you might ring up one of your boys whose name you see on here and ask him man to man."

He pondered that thought a moment, and the Adam's apple worked again, harder now, but he was taking it like a soldier. Or he still thought it was a fake. Then he said, "I'll call your bluff on that," and walked over to the telephone.

Waiting for his number, he looked up and said, "Have a seat, won't you?"

"No, thanks," I said, for I didn't regard the event as social.

Then he had the number.

"Monty," he said into the phone, "I've got a statement here to the effect that the undersigned hold that the impeachment proceedings are unjustified and will vote against them despite all pressure. That's what it says—'all pressure.' Your name's on the list. How about it?"

There was a long wait, then Mr. Lowdan said, "For God's sake, quit mumbling and blubbering and speak up!"

There was another wait, then Mr. Lowdan yelled, "You— you—" But words failed him, and he slammed the telephone to the cradle, and swung the big, recently jovial-looking face toward me. He was making a gasping motion with his mouth, but no sound.

"Well," I said, "you want to try another one?"

"It's blackmail," he said, very quietly, but huskily as though he didn't have the breath to spare. Then, seeming to get a little more breath, "It's blackmail. It's coercion. Bribery, it's bribery. I tell you, you've blackmailed and bribed those men and I—"

"I don't know why anybody signed this statement," I said, "but if what you charge should happen to be true then the moral strikes me as this: MacMurfee ought not to elect legislators who can be bribed or who have done things they can get blackmailed for."

"MacMurfee—" he began, then fell into a deep silence, his flowered bulk brooding over the telephone stand. He'd have his own troubles with Mr. MacMurfee, no doubt.

"A small detail," I said, "but it would probably be less embarrassing to you, and especially to the signers of this document, if the impeachment proceedings were killed before coming to a vote. You might try to see about getting that done by late tomorrow. That should give you time to make your arrangements, and to figure out as graceful a way as possible. Of course, it would be more effective politically for the Governor to let the matter come to a vote, but he was willing to let you do it the easy way, particularly since there's a good deal of unrest in the city about the matter."

He wasn't paying any attention to me, as far as I could tell. I went to the door, opened it, and looked back. "Ultimately," I said, "it is immaterial to the Governor how you manage the matter."

Then I closed the door and went down the hall.

That had been the night of the fourth of April. I was almost sorry, the next day as I looked out the high window at the mass of people filling the streets and the wide sweep of lawn beyond the statues in front of the Capitol, that I knew what I knew. If I hadn't known, I could have stood there in the full excitement of the possibilities of the moment. But I knew how the play would come out. This was like a dress rehearsal after the show has closed down. I stood there and felt like God-Almighty brooding on History.

Which must be a dull business for God-Almighty, Who knows how it is going to come out. Who knew, in fact, how it was going to come out even before He knew there was going to be any History. Which is complete nonsense, for that involves Time and He is out of Time, for God is Fullness of Being and in Him the End is the Beginning. Which is what you can read in the little tracts written and handed out on the street corners by the fat, grubby, dandruff-sprinkled old man, with the metal-rimmed spectacles, who used to be the Scholarly Attorney and who married the girl with the gold braids and the clear, famished-looking cheeks, up in Arkansas. But those tracts he wrote were crazy, I thought back then. I thought God cannot be Fullness of Being. For Life is Motion.

(I use the capital letters as the old man did in the tracts. I had sat across the table from him, with the foul unwashed dishes on one end of it and the papers and books piled on the other end, in the room over across the railroad tracks, and he had talked and I had heard the capital letters in his voice. He had said, "God is Fullness of Being." And I had said, "You've got the wrong end of the stick. For Life is Motion. For——"

(For Life is Motion toward Knowledge. If God is Complete Knowledge then He is Complete Non-Motion, which is Non-Life, which is Death. Therefore, if there is such a God of Fullness of Being, we would worship Death, the Father. That was what I said to the old man, who had looked at me across the papers and fouled dishes, and his red-streaked eyes had blinked above the metal-rimmed spectacles, which had hung down on the end of his nose. He had shaken his head and a flake or two of dandruff had sifted down from the sparse white hair ends which fringed the skull within which the words had been taking shape from the electric twitches in the tangled and spongy blood-soaked darkness. He had said then, "I am the Resurrection and the Life." And I had said, "You've got the wrong end of the stick."

(For Life is a fire burning along a piece of string—or is it a fuse to a powder keg which we call God?—and the string is what we don't know, our Ignorance, and the trail of ash, which, if a gust of wind does not come, keeps the structure of the string, is History, man's Knowledge, but it is dead, and when the fire has burned up all the string, then man's Knowledge will be equal to God's Knowledge and there won't be any fire, which is Life. Or if the string leads to a powder keg, then there will be a terrific blast of fire, and even the trail of ash will be blown completely away. So I had said to the old man.

(But he had replied, "You think in Finite terms." And I had said, "I'm not thinking at all, I'm just drawing a picture." He had said, "Ha!" The way I remembered he had done a long time back when he played chess with Judge Irwin in the long room in the white house looking toward the sea. I had said, "I'll draw you another picture. It is a picture of a man trying to paint a picture of a sunset. But before he can dip his brush the color always changes and the shape. Let us give a name to the picture which he is trying to paint: Knowledge. Therefore if the object which a man looks at changes constantly so that Knowledge of it is constantly untrue and is therefore Non-Knowledge, then Eternal Motion is possible. And Eternal Life. Therefore we can believe in Eternal Life only if we deny God, Who is Complete Knowledge."

(The old man had said, "I will pray for your soul.")

But even if I didn't believe in the old man's god, that morning as I stood at the window of the Capitol and looked down on the crowd, I felt like God, because I had the knowledge of what was to come. I felt like God brooding on History, for as I stood there I could see a little chunk of History right there in front. There were the bronze statues on their pedestals, on the lawn, in frock coats, with the right hand inserted under the coat, just over the heart, in military uniforms with a hand on the sword hilt, even one in buckskin with the right hand grasping the barrel of a grounded long rifle. They were already History, and the grass around their pedestals was shaved close and the flowers were planted in stars and circles and crescents. Then over beyond the statues, there were the people who weren't History yet. Not quite. But to me they looked like History, because I knew the end of the event of which they were a part. Or thought I knew the end.

I knew, too, how the newspapers would regard that crowd of people, as soon as they knew the end of the event. They would

151

regard that crowd as cause. "A shameful display of cowardice on the part of the Legislature . . . allow themselves to be intimidated by . . . deplorable lack of leadership . . ." You could look at the crowd out there and hear that undertone in its cry, hoarse like surf, and think that the crowd there could cause the event. But no, it could be said, Willie Stark caused the event by corrupting and blackmailing the Legislature. But no, in turn it could be replied that Willie Stark merely gave the Legislature the opportunity to behave in the way appropriate to its nature and that MacMurfee, who sponsored the election of those men, thinking to use their fear and greed for his own ends, was truly responsible. But no, to that it could be replied that the responsibility belonged, after all, to that crowd of people, indirectly in so far as it had allowed MacMurfee to elect such men, and directly in so far as it had, despite MacMurfee, elected Willie Stark. But why had they elected Willie Stark? Because of a complex of forces which had made them what they were, or because Willie Stark could lean toward them with bulging eyes and right arm raised to Heaven?

One thing was certain: The sound of that chant hoarsely rising and falling was to be the cause of nothing, nothing at all. I stood in the window of the Capitol and hugged that knowledge like a precious and thorny secret, and did not think anything.

I watched the fat man get out of the black limousine and mount the bandstand. I saw the crowd shift and curdle and thin and dissolve. I looked across beyond the now lonely and occupationless policemen, beyond the statues—frock coats, uniforms, buckskin—to the great lawn, which was empty and bright in the spring sunshine. I spewed out the last smoke from my cigarette and flicked the butt out the open window and watched it spin over and over to the stone steps far below.

Willie Stark was to stand on those steps at eight o'clock that night, in a flood of light, looking small at the top of the great steps with the mountainous heave of the building behind him.

That night the people pressed up to the very steps, filling all the shadow beyond the sharply defined area of light. (Lighting apparatus had been mounted on the pedestals of two of the statues, one buckskin, one frock coat.) They called and chanted, "Willie—Willie—Willie," pressing at the cordon of police at the foot of the steps. Then, after a while, out of the tall doorway of the Capitol, he appeared. Then, as he stood there, blinking in the light, the words of the chant disappeared, and there was a moment of stillness, and then there was only the roar. It seemed a long time before he lifted his hand to stop it. Then the roar seemed to die away, slowly, under the downward pressure of his hand.

I stood down in the crowd with Adam Stanton and Anne Stanton and watched him come out on the steps of the Capitol. When it was over—when he had said what he had to say to the crowd and had gone back inside leaving the new, unchecked roar of voices behind him—I told Anne and Adam good night and went to meet the Boss.

I rode with him back to the Mansion. He hadn't said a word when I joined him at the car. Sugar-Boy worked through the back streets, while behind us we could still hear the roaring and shouting and the protracted blatting of automobile horns. Then Sugar-Boy shook himself free into a quiet little street where the houses sat back from the pavement, lights on inside them now and people in the lighted rooms, and where the budding boughs interlaced above us. At the corners where the street lamps were you could catch the hint of actual green on the boughs.

Sugar-Boy drove up to the rear entrance of the Mansion. The Boss got out and went into the door. I followed him. He walked down the back hall, where we met nobody, and then into the big hall. He paced right across the hall, under the chandeliers and mirrors, past the sweep of the stairway, looked into the drawing room, crossed the hall again to look into the back sitting room, then again to look into the library. I caught on, and quit following him. I just stood in the middle of the big hall and waited. He hadn't said he wanted me, but he hadn't said he didn't. In fact, he hadn't said anything. Not a word.

When he turned from the library into the hall again, a white-coated Negro boy came out of the dining room. "Boy," the Boss asked, "you seen Mrs. Stark?"

"Yassuh."

"Where, dammit?" the Boss snapped. "You think I'm asking for my health?"

"Naw, suh, I didn't think nuthin, I—"

"Where?" the Boss demanded in a tone to set the chandelier tingling.

After the first paralysis, the lips began to work in the black face. In the beginning without effect. Then a sound was detectable. "Upstairs—she done gone upstairs—I reckin she done gone to bed—she—"

The Boss had headed up the stairs.

He came back almost immediately, walked past me without a word, and back to the library. I trailed along. He flung himself down on the big leather couch, heaved his feet off the floor to the leather, and said, "Shut the God-damned door."

I shut the door, and he leaned back on the cushions, at about a thirty-degree angle from horizontal, and glumly studied his knuckles. "You would have thought she might wait up for me tonight," he said finally, still studying the knuckles. Then, looking at me, "She's gone to bed. Gone to bed and locked her door. Said she had a headache. I go upstairs and there is Tom sitting in the room across from her room doing his schoolwork. Before I lay hand to the knob of her door, he comes out and says, 'She don't want to be bothered.' Like I was a delivery boy. 'I'm not going to bother her,' I said to him, 'I'm just going to tell her what happened.' He looked at me and said, 'She's got a headache, and she don't want to be bothered.' " He hesitated, looked at the knuckles again, then back to me, and said with a hint of defensiveness in his tone, "All I was going to do was tell her how it came out tonight."

"She wanted you to throw Byram to the wolves," I said. "Did she want you to throw yourself to the wolves?"

"I don't know what the hell she wants," he said. "I don't know what the hell any of 'em want. A man can't tell. But you can tell this, if any man tried to run things the way they want him to half the time, he'd end up sleeping on the bare ground. And how would she like that?"

"I imagine Lucy could take it," I said.

"Lucy—" he said, and looked sort of surprised, as though I had introduced a new topic of conversation. Then I recollected that Lucy's name hadn't been mentioned. Sure, he had been talking about Lucy Stark, he knew that and I knew that. But as soon as the name *Lucy* was mentioned, to take the place of that *she,* somehow it was different. It was as though she had walked into the room, and looked at us.

"Lucy—" he repeated. Then, "All right—Lucy. She could take it. Lucy could sleep on the bare ground and eat red beans, but it wouldn't change the world a damned bit. But can Lucy understand that? No, Lucy cannot." He was, apparently, taking a relish in using the name now, in saying *Lucy* instead of *she,* as though he proved something about something, or about her, or about himself, by saying it, by being able to say it. "Lucy," he was saying, "she could sleep on the bare ground. And that's exactly what she's going to raise Tom to do, too, if she has her way. She'd have him so the six-year kids will be plugging him with nigger-shooters, and then not bothering to run. He's a good stout boy—plays a good game of football, bet he makes the team when he gets to college—but she's going to ruin him. Make him a sissy. Looks like I say a word to the boy and you can just see her face freeze. I called up here tonight to get Tom to come down and see the crowd. Was going to send Sugar-Boy to get him because I wasn't going to have time to get home. But would she let him go? No, sir. Said he had to stay home and study. Study," he said. Then, "Didn't want him down there, that was it. Me and the crowd."

"Take it easy," I said. "That's the way all women treat their kids. Besides, you got to be a big-shot by hitting your books."

"He's smart, smart enough without being a sissy," he said.

"He makes good grades in school, and, by God, he better. Sure, I want him to study. And he better, but what I don't get is—"

There was a racket out in the hall, voices, then a knock at the door.

"See who it is," the Boss said.

I opened the door and in stormed the familiar faces, somewhat flushed, Tiny Duffy's in the lead. They ringed round the Boss and wheezed and shoved and chortled. "We fixed 'em!—We damned well fixed 'em!—You're telling it, we stopped that clock!—It'll be a long time till next time!" While the Boss lay back on the cushions at his thirty-degree angle, with his feet propped on the leather, and his eyes flickering around from face to face, under the half-lowered lids, you got the notion he was spying through a peephole. He hadn't said a word.

"Champagne," one of the boys was saying, "real champagne! A case and it is honest-to-God stuff. French, from France. Out in the kitchen, and Sambo is icing up. Boss, it's a celebration!"

The Boss didn't say anything.

"Celebrate, it's a celebration, ain't you gonna celebrate, Boss."

"Duffy," the Boss said, not loud, "if you aren't too drunk you can see I don't want this assing around in here. Take your rabble over to the other side of the house and stay out from under foot." Then in the silence of his pause his eyes flickered over the faces again, to come back to Duffy. To whom he said, "You think you grasp the idea?"

Tiny Duffy did grasp the idea. But the others grasped it, too, and I thought that I detected a slight competition among the brothers of the lodge to be among the first out.

The Boss regarded the fine paneling of the closed door for a couple of minutes. Then he said, "You know what Lincoln said?"

"What?" I asked.

"He said a house divided against itself cannot stand. Well, he was wrong."

"Yeah?"

"Yeah," the Boss said, "for this government is sure half slave and half son-of-a-bitch, and it is standing."

"Which is which?" I asked.

"Slaves down at the Legislature, and the sons-of-bitches up here," he said. And added, "Only sometimes they overlap."

But Lucy Stark did not leave the Boss after the settlement of the impeachment trouble. Nor even after the next election, when the Boss came in for a second term in 1934. (A Governor can succeed himself in our state, and the Boss succeeded himself with a vengeance. There never had been a vote like it.) I suppose Tom was the reason she hung on. When she did leave him, there wasn't any noise. Health. She went to Florida for a long pull. When she got back, she stayed out of town at a little place her sister had, a poultry farm and hatchery just out of town. Tom used to spend a lot of his time out with her, but I imagined that by that time she figured he wasn't Mamma's Boy any more. By that time he was a strapping fellow, cocky and fast on his feet, a natural-born quarterback, and he had discovered that something besides pasteurized milk came in bottles and that approximately half the human race belonged to a sex interestingly different from his own. Lucy probably figured that she could do something to hold Tom down, and so there wasn't any absolute break with Willie. Now and then, but not often, she would appear in public with him. For instance, on that trip up to Mason City—the time the Boss and I made the midnight visit on Judge Irwin—Lucy came along. That was in 1936, and by that time Lucy had been staying out at her sister's poultry farm for going on a year.

The Boss himself used to go out to the poultry farm occasionally, to keep up appearances. Two or three times the papers —the administration papers, that is—ran photographs of him standing with his wife and kid in front of a hen yard or incubator house. The hens didn't do any harm, either. They gave a nice, homey atmosphere. They inspired confidence.

Chapter Four

THAT night when the Boss and I called on Judge Irwin in the middle of the night and when, burning the road back to Mason City in the dark, the car hurtled between the back fields, he said to me, "There is always something."

And I said, "Maybe not on the Judge."

And he said, "Man is conceived in sin and born in corruption and he passeth from the stink of the didie to the stench of the shroud. There is always something."

And he told me to dig it out, dig it up, the dead cat with patches of fur still clinging to the tight, swollen, dove-gray hide. It was the proper job for me, for, as I have said, I was once a student of history. A student of history does not care what he digs out of the ash pile, the midden, the sublunary dung heap, which is the human past. He doesn't care whether it is the dead pussy or the Kohinoor diamond. So it was a proper assignment for me, an excursion into the past.

It was to be my second excursion into the past, more interesting and sensational than the first, and much more successful. In fact, this second excursion into the past was to be perfectly successful. But the first one had not been successful. It had not been successful because in the midst of the process I tried to discover the truth and not the facts. Then, when the truth was not to be discovered, or discovered could not be understood by me, I could not bear to live with the cold-eyed reproach of the facts. So I walked out of a room, the room where the facts lived in a big box of three-by-five-inch note cards, and kept on walking until I walked into my second job of historical research, the job which should be known as the "Case of the Upright Judge."

But I must tell about the first excursion into the enchantments of the past. Not that the first excursion has anything directly to do with the story of Willie Stark, but it has a great deal to do with the story of Jack Burden, and the story of Willie Stark and the story of Jack Burden are, in one sense, one story.

Long ago Jack Burden was a graduate student, working for his Ph.D. in American History, in the State University of his native state. This Jack Burden (of whom the present Jack Burden, *Me,* is a legal, biological, and perhaps even metaphysical continuator) lived in a slatternly apartment with two other graduate students, one industrious, stupid, unlucky, and alcoholic and the other idle, intelligent, lucky, and alcoholic.

At least, they were alcoholic for a period after the first of the month, when they recived the miserable check paid them by the University for their miserable work as assistant teachers. The industry and ill luck of one canceled out against the idleness and luck of the other and they both amounted to the same thing, and they drank what they could get when they could get it. They drank because they didn't really have the slightest interest in what they were doing now, and didn't have the slightest hope for the future. They could not even bear the thought of pushing on to finish their degrees, for that would mean leaving the University (leaving the first-of-the-month drunks, the yammer about "work" and the "ideas" in smoke-blind rooms, the girls who staggered slightly and giggled indiscreetly on the dark stairs leading to the apartment) to go to some normal school on a sun-baked crossroads or a junior college long on Jesus and short on funds, to go to face the stark reality of drudgery and dry rot and prying eyes and the slow withering of the green wisp of dream which had, like some window plant in an invalid's room, grown out of a bottle. Only the bottle hadn't had water in it. It had had something which looked like water, smelled like kerosene, and tasted like carbolic acid: one-run corn whisky.

Jack Burden lived with them, in the slatternly apartment among the unwashed dishes in the sink and on the table, the odor of stale tobacco smoke, the dirty shirts and underwear piled in corners. He even took a relish in the squalor, in the privilege of letting a last crust of buttered toast fall to the floor to be undisturbed until the random heel should grind it into the mud-colored carpet, in the spectacle of the fat roach moving across the cracked linoleum of the bathroom floor while he steamed in the tub. Once he had brought his mother to the apartment for tea, and she had sat on the edge of the overstuffed chair, holding a cracked cup and talking with a brittle and calculated charm out of a face which was obviously being held in shape by a profound exercise of will. She saw a roach venture out from the kitchen door. She saw one of Jack Burden's friends crush an ant on the inner lip of the sugar bowl and flick the carcass from his finger. The nail of the finger itself was not very clean. But she kept right on delivering the charm, out of the rigid face. He had to say that for her.

But afterward, as they walked down the street, she had said, "Why do you live like that?"

"It's what I'm built for, I reckon," Jack Burden said.

"With those people," she said.

"They're all right," he said, and wondered if they were, and wondered if he was.

His mother didn't say anything for a minute, making a sharp, bright clicking on the pavement with her heels as she walked along, holding her small shoulders trimly back, carrying her

158

famished-cheeked, blue-eyed, absolutely innocent face slightly lifted to the pulsing sunset world of April like a very expensive present the world ought to be glad even to have a look at.

Walking along beside him, she said meditatively, "That dark-haired one—if he'd get cleaned up—he wouldn't be bad looking."

"That's what a lot of other women think," Jack Burden said, and suddenly felt a nauseated hatred of the dark-haired one, the one who had killed the ant on the sugar bowl, who had the dirty nails. But he had to go on, something in him made him go on, "Yes, and a lot of them don't even care about cleaning him up. They'll take him like he is. He's the great lover of the apartment. He put the sag in the springs of that divan we got."

"Don't be vulgar," she said, because she definitely did not like what is known as vulgarity in conversation.

"It's the truth," he said.

She didn't answer, and her heels did the bright clicking. Then she said, "If he'd throw those awful clothes away—and get something decent."

"Yeah," Jack Burden said, "on his seventy-five dollars a month."

She looked at him now, down at his clothes. "Yours are pretty awful, too," she said.

"Are they?" Jack Burden demanded.

"I'll send you money for some decent clothes," she said.

A few days later the check came and a note telling him to get a "couple of decent suits and accessories." The check was for two hundred and fifty dollars. He did not even buy a necktie. But he and the two other men in the apartment had a wonderful blowout, which lasted for five days, and as a result of which the industrious and unlucky one lost his job and the idle and lucky one got too sociable, and, despite his luck, contracted a social disease. But nothing happened to Jack Burden, for nothing ever happened to Jack Burden, who was invulnerable. Perhaps that was the curse of Jack Burden: he was invulnerable.

So Jack Burden lived in the slatternly apartment with the two other graduate students, for even after being fired the unlucky, industrious one still lived in the apartment. He simply stopped paying anything but he stayed. He borrowed money for cigarettes. He sullenly ate the food the others brought in and cooked. He lay around during the day, for there was no reason to be industrious any more, ever again. Once at night, Jack Burden woke up and thought he heard the sound of sobs from the living room, where the unlucky, industrious one slept on a wall bed. Then one day the unlucky, industrious one was not there. They never did know where he had gone, and they never heard from him again.

But before that they lived in the apartment, in an atmosphere of brotherhood and mutual understanding. They had this in common: they were all hiding. The difference was in what they were hiding from. The two others were hiding from the future, from the day when they would get degrees and leave the University. Jack Burden, however, was hiding from the present. The other two took refuge in the present. Jack Burden took refuge in the past. The other two sat in the living room and argued and drank or played cards or read, but Jack Burden was sitting, as like as not, back in his bedroom before a little pine table, with the notes and papers and books before him, scarcely hearing the voices. He might come out and take a drink or take a hand of cards or argue or do any of the other things they did, but what was real was back in that bedroom on the pine table.

What was back in the bedroom on the pine table?

A large packet of letters, eight tattered, black-bound account books tied together with faded red tape, a photograph, about five by eight inches, mounted on cardboard and stained in its lower half by water, and a plain gold ring, man-sized, with some engraving in it, on a loop of string. The past. Or that part of the past which had gone by the name of Cass Mastern.

Cass Mastern was one of the two maternal uncles of Ellis Burden, the Scholarly Attorney, a brother of his mother, Lavinia Mastern. The other uncle was named Gilbert Mastern, who died in 1914, at the age of ninety-four or -five, rich, a builder of railroads, a sitter on boards of directors, and left the packet of letters, the black account books, and the photograph, and a great deal of money to a grandson (and not a penny to Jack Burden). Some ten years later the heir of Gilbert Mastern, recollecting that Jack Burden, with whom he had no personal acquaintance, was a student of history, or something of the sort, sent him the packet of letters, the account books, and the photograph, asking if he, Jack Burden, thought that the enclosures were of any "financial interest" since he, the heir, had heard that libraries sometimes would pay a "fair sum for old papers and antebellum relics and keepsakes." Jack Burden replied that since Cass Mastern had been of no historical importance as an individual, it was doubtful that any library would pay more than a few dollars, if anything, for the material, and asked for instructions as to the disposition of the parcel. The heir replied that under the circumstances Jack Burden might keep the things for "sentimental reasons."

So Jack Burden made the acquaintance of Cass Mastern, who had died in 1864 at a military hospital in Atlanta, who had been only a heard but forgotten name to him, and who was the pair of dark, wide-set, deep eyes which burned out of the photograph, through the dinginess and dust and across more than fifty years. The eyes, which were Cass Mastern, stared out of a long, bony face, but a young face with full lips above a rather thin, curly black beard. The lips did not seem to belong to that bony face and the burning eyes.

The young man in the picture, standing, visible from the thighs up, wore a loose-fitting, shapeless jacket, too large in the collar, short in the sleeves to show strong wrists and bony hands clasped at the waist. The thick dark hair, combed sweepingly back from the high brow, came down long and square-cut, after the fashion of time, place, and class, almost to brush the collar of the coarse, hand-me-down-looking jacket, which was the jacket of an infantryman in the Confederate Army.

But everything in the picture in contrast with the dark, burning eyes, seemed accidental. That jacket, however, was not accidental. It was worn as the result of calculation and anguish, in pride and self-humiliation, in the conviction that it would be worn in death. But the death was not to be that quick and easy. It was to come slow and hard, in a stinking hospital in Atlanta. The last letter in the packet was not in Cass Mastern's hand. Lying in the hospital with his rotting wound, he dictated his farewell letter to his brother, Gilbert Mastern. The letter, and the last of the account books in which Cass Mastern's journal was kept, were eventually sent back home to Mississippi, and Cass Mastern was buried somewhere in Atlanta, nobody had ever known where.

It was, in a sense, proper that Cass Mastern—in the gray jacket, sweat-stiffened, and prickly like a hair shirt, which it was for him at the same time that it was the insignia of a begrudged glory—should have gone back to Georgia to rot slowly to death. For he had been born in Georgia, he and Gilbert Mastern and Lavinia Mastern, in the red hills up toward Tennessee. "I was born," the first page of the first volume of the journal said, "in a log cabin in north Georgia, in circumstances of poverty, and if in later years I have lain soft and supped from silver, may the Lord not let die in my heart the knowledge of frost and of coarse diet. For all men come naked into the world, and in prosperity 'man is prone to evil as the sparks fly upward.'" The lines were written when Cass was a student at Transylvania College, up in Kentucky, after what he called his "darkness and trouble" had given place to the peace of God. For the journal began with an account of the "darkness and trouble"—which was a perfectly real trouble, with a dead man and a live woman and long nail scratches down Cass Mastern's bony face. "I write this down," he said in the journal, "with what truthfulness a sinner may attain unto, that if ever pride is in me, of flesh or spirit, I can peruse these pages and know with shame what evil has been in me, and may be in me, for who knows what breeze may blow upon the charred log and fan up flame again?"

The impulse to write the journal sprang from the "darkness and trouble," but Cass Mastern apparently had a systematic mind, and so he went back to the beginning, to the log cabin in the red hills of Georgia. It was the older brother, Gilbert, some fifteen years older than Cass, who lifted the family from the log cabin. Gilbert, who had run away from home when a boy and gone west to Mississippi, was well on the way to being "a cotton snob" by the time he was in his thirties, that is, by 1850. The penniless and no doubt hungry boy walking barefoot onto the black soil of Mississippi was to become, ten or twelve years later, the master sitting the spirited roan stallion (its name was Powhatan—that from the journal) in front of the white veranda. How did Gilbert make his first dollar? Did he cut the throat of a traveler in the canebrake? Did he black boots at an inn? It is not recorded. But he made his fortune, and sat on the white veranda and voted Whig. After the war when the white veranda was a pile of ashes and the fortune was gone, it was not surprising that Gilbert, who had made one fortune with his bare hands, out of the very air, could now, with all his experience and cunning and hardness (the hardness harder now for the four years of riding and short rations and disappointment), snatch another one, much greater than the first. If in later years he ever remembered his brother Cass and took out the last letter, the one dictated in the hospital in Atlanta, he must have mused over it with a tolerant irony. For it said: "Remember me, but without grief. If one of us is lucky, it is I. I shall have rest and I hope in the mercy of the Everlasting and in His blessed election. But you, my dear brother, are condemned to eat bread in bitterness and build on the place where the charred embers and ashes are and to make bricks without straw and to suffer in the ruin and guilt of our dear Land and in the common guilt of man. In the next bed to me there is a young man from Ohio. He is dying. His moans and curses and prayers are not different from any others to be heard in this tabernacle of pain. He marched hither in his guilt as I in mine. And in the guilt of his Land. May a common Salvation lift us both from the dust. And, dear brother, I pray God to give you strength for what is to come." Gilbert must have smiled, looking back, for he had eaten little bread in bitterness. He had had his own kind of strength. By 1870 he was again well off. By 1875 or '76 he was rich. By 1880 he had a fortune, was living in New York, was a name, a thick, burly man, slow of movement, with a head like a block of bare granite. He had lived out of one world into another. Perhaps he was even more at home in the new than in the old. Or perhaps the Gilbert Masterns are always at home in any world. As the Cass Masterns are never at home in any world.

But to return: Jack Burden came into possession of the papers from the grandson of Gilbert Mastern. When the time came for him to select a subject for his dissertation for his Ph.D., his professor suggested that he edit the journal and letters of Cass Mastern, and write a biographical essay, a social study based on those and other materials. So Jack Burden began his first journey into the past.

It seemed easy at first. It was easy to reconstruct the life of the log cabin in the red hills. There were the first letters back from Gilbert after he had begun his rise (Jack Burden managed to get possession of the other Gilbert Mastern papers of the period before the Civil War). There was the known pattern of that life, gradually altered toward comfort as Gilbert's affluence was felt at that distance. Then, in one season, the mother and father died, and Gilbert returned to burst, no doubt, upon Cass and Lavinia as an unbelievable vision, a splendid imposter in black broadcloth, varnished boots, white linen, heavy gold ring. He put Lavinia in a school in Atlanta, bought her trunks of dresses, and kissed her good-bye. ("Could you not have taken me with you, dear Brother Gilbert? I would have been ever so dutiful and affectionate a sister," so she wrote to him in the copybook hand, in brown ink, in a language not her own, a language of schoolroom propriety. "May I not come to you now? Is there no little task which I—" But Gilbert had other plans. When the time came for her to appear at his house she would be ready.) But he took Cass with him, a hobbledehoy now wearing black and mounted on a blooded mare.

At the end of three years Cass was not a hobbledehoy. He had spent three years of monastic rigor at Valhalla, Gilbert's house, under the tuition of a Mr. Lawson and of Gilbert himself. From Gilbert he learned the routine of plantation management. From Mr. Lawson, a tubercular and vague young man from Princeton, New Jersey, he learned some geometry, some Latin, and a great deal of Presbyterian theology. He liked the books, and once Gilbert (so the journal said) stood in the doorway and watched him bent over the table and then said, "At least you may be good for *that*."

But he was good for more than that. When Gilbert gave him a small plantation, he managed it for two years with such astuteness (and such luck, for both season and market conspired in his behalf) that at the end of the time he could repay Gilbert a substantial part of the purchase price. Then he went, or was sent, to Transylvania. It was Gilbert's idea. He came into the house on Cass's plantation one night to find Cass at his books. He walked across the room to the table where the books lay, by which Cass now stood. Gilbert stretched out his arm and tapped the open book with his riding crop. "You might make something out of that," he said. The journal reported that, but it did not report what book it was that Gilbert's riding crop tapped. It is not important what book it was. Or perhaps it is important, for something in our mind, in our imagination, wants to know that fact. We see the red, square, strong hand ("my brother is strong-made and florid") protruding from the white cuff, grasping the crop which in that grasp looks fragile like a twig. We see the flick of the little leather loop on the open page, a flick brisk, not quite contemptuous, but we cannot make out the page.

In any case, it probably was not a book on theology, for it seems doubtful that Gilbert, in such a case, would have used the phrase "make something out of that." It might have been a page of the Latin poets, however, for Gilbert would have discovered that, in small doses, they went well with politics or the law. So Transylvania College it was to be—suggested, it developed, by Gilbert's neighbor and friend, Mr. Davis, Mr. Jefferson Davis, who had once been a student there. Mr. Davis had studied Greek.

At Transylvania, in Lexington, Cass discovered pleasure. "I discovered that there is an education for vice as well as for virtue, and I learned what was to be learned from the gaming table, the bottle, and the racecourse and from the illict sweetness of the flesh." He had come out of the poverty of the cabin and the monastic regime of Valhalla and the responsibilities of his own little plantation; and he was tall and strong, and to judge from the photographs, well favored, with the burning dark eyes. It was no wonder that he "discovered pleasure"—or that pleasure discovered him. For, though the journal does not say so, in the events leading up to the "darkness and trouble," Cass seems to have been, in the beginning at least, the pursued rather than the pursuer.

The pursuer is referred to in the journal as "she" and "her." But Jack Burden learned the name. "She" was Annabelle Trice, Mrs. Duncan Trice, and Mr. Duncan Trice was a prosperous young banker of Lexington, Kentucky, who was an intimate of Cass Mastern and apparently one of those who led him into the paths of pleasure. Jack Burden learned the name by going back to the files of the Lexington newspapers for the middle 1850's to locate the story of a death. It was the death of Mr. Duncan Trice. In the newspaper it was reported as an accident. Duncan Trice had shot himself by accident, the newspaper said, while cleaning a pair of pistols. One of the pistols, already cleaned, lay on the couch where he had been sitting, in his library, at the time of the accident. The other, the lethal instrument, had fallen to the floor. Jack Burden had known, from the journal, the nature of the case, and so when he had located the special circumstances, he had learned the identity of "she." Mr. Trice, the newspaper said, was survived by his widow, nee Annabelle Puckett, of Washington, D.C.

Shortly after Cass had come to Lexington, Annabelle Trice met him. Duncan Trice brought him home, for he had received a letter from Mr. Davis, recommending the brother of his good friend and neighbor, Mr. Gilbert Mastern. (Duncan Trice had come to Lexington from southern Kentucky, where his own father had been a friend of Samuel Davis, the father of Jefferson, when Samuel lived at Fairview and bred racers.) So Duncan Trice brought the tall boy home, who was no longer a hobbledehoy, and set him on a sofa and thrust a glass into his hand and called in his pretty, husky-voiced wife, of whom he was so proud, to greet the stranger. "When she first entered the room, in which the shades of approaching twilight were gathering though the hour for the candles to be lit had scarcely come, I thought that her eyes were black, and the effect was most striking, her hair being of such a fairness. I noticed, too, how softly she trod and with a gliding motion which, though she was perhaps of a little less than moderate stature, gave an impression of regal dignity—

> *et avertens rosea cervice refulsit*
> *Ambrosiaeque comae divinum vertice odorem*
> *Spiravere, pedes vestis defluxit ad imos,*
> *Et vera incessu patuit Dea.*

So the Mantuan said, when Venus appeared and the true goddess was revealed by her gait. She came into the room and was the true goddess as revealed in her movement, and was, but for Divine Grace (if such be granted to a parcel of corruption such as I), my true damnation. She gave me her hand and spoke with a tingling huskiness which made me think of rubbing my hand upon a soft deep-piled cloth, like velvet, or upon a fur. It would not have been called a musical voice such as is generally admired. I know that, but I can only set down what effect it worked upon my own organs of hearing."

Cass set down a very conscientious description of every feature and proportion, a kind of tortured inventory, as though in the midst of the "darkness and trouble," at the very moment of his agony and repudiation, he had to take one last backward look even at the risk of being turned into the pillar of salt. "Her face was not large though a little given to fullness. Her mouth was strong but the lips were red and moist and seemed to be slightly parted or about to part themselves. The chin was short and firmly moulded. Her skin was of a great whiteness, it seemed then before the candles were lit, but afterwards I was to see that it had a bloom of color upon it. Her hair, which was in a remarkable abundance and of great fairness, was drawn back from her face and worn in large coils low down to the neck. Her waist was very small and her breasts, which seemed natu-

165

rally high and round and full, were the higher for the corsetting. Her dress, of a dark blue silk I remember, was cut low to the very downward curve of the shoulders, and in the front showed how the breasts were lifted like twin orbs."

Cass described her that way. He admitted that her face was not beautiful. "Though agreeable in its proportions," he added. But the hair was beautiful, and "of an astonishing softness, upon your hand softer and finer than your thought of silk." So even in that moment, in the midst of the "darkness and trouble," the recollection intrudes into the journal of how that abundant, fair hair had slipped across his fingers. "But," he added, "her beauty was her eyes."

He had remarked how, when she first came in, into the shadowy room, her eyes had seemed black. But he had been mistaken, he was to discover, and that discovery was the first step toward his undoing. After the greeting ("she greeted me with great simplicity and courtesy and bade me again take my seat"), she remarked on how dark the room was and how the autumn always came to take one unawares. Then she touched a bellpull and a Negro boy entered. "She commanded him to bring light and to mend the fire, which was sunk to ash, or near so. He came back presently with a seven-branched candlestick which he put upon the table back of the couch on which I sat. He struck a lucifer but she said, 'Let me light the candles.' I remember it as if it were only yesterday when I sat on that couch. I had turned my head idly to watch her light the candles. The little table was between us. She leaned over the candles and applied the lucifer to the wicks, one after another. She was leaning over, and I saw how the corset lifted her breasts together, but because she was leaning the eyelids shaded her eyes from my sight. Then she raised her head a little and looked straight at me over the new candle flames, and I saw all at once that her eyes were not black. They were blue, but a blue so deep that I can only compare it to the color of the night sky in autumn when the weather is clear and there is no moon and the stars have just well come out. And I had not known how large they were. I remember saying that to myself with perfect clearness, 'I had not known how large they were,' several times, slowly, like a man marvelling. Then I knew that I was blushing and I felt my tongue dry like ashes in my mouth and I was in the manly state.

"I can see perfectly clearly the expression on her face even now, but I cannot interpret it. Sometimes I have thought of it as having a smiling hidden in it, but I cannot be sure. (I am only sure of this: that man is never safe and damnation is ever at hand, O God and my Redeemer!) I sat there, one hand clenched upon my knee and the other holding an empty glass, and I felt that I could not breathe. Then she said to her husband, who stood in the room behind me, 'Duncan, do you see that Mr. Mastern is in need of refreshment?' "

The year passed. Cass, who was a good deal younger than Duncan Trice, and as a matter of fact several years younger than Annabelle Trice, became a close companion of Duncan Trice and learned much from him, for Duncan Trice was rich, fashionable, clever, and high-spirited ("much given to laughter and full-blooded"). Duncan Trice led Cass to the bottle, the gaming table and the racecourse, but not to the "illicit sweetness of the flesh." Duncan Trice was passionately and singlemindedly devoted to his wife. ("When she came into a room, his eyes would fix upon her without shame, and I have seen her avert her face and blush for the boldness of his glance when company was present. But I think that it was done by him unawares, his partiality for her was so great.") No, the other young men, members of the Trice circle, led Cass first to the "illicit sweetness." But despite the new interests and gratifications, Cass could work at his books. There was even time for that, for he had great strength and endurance.

So the year passed. He had been much in the Trice house, but no word beyond the "words of merriment and civility" had passed between him and Annabelle Trice. In June, there was a dancing party at the house of some friend of Duncan Trice. Duncan Trice, his wife, and Cass happened to stroll at some moment into the garden and to sit in a little arbor, which was covered with a jasmine vine. Duncan Trice returned to the house to get punch for the three of them, leaving Annabelle and Cass seated side by side in the arbor. Cass commented on the sweetness of the scent of jasmine. All at once, she burst out ("her voice low-pitched and with its huskiness, but in a vehemence which astonished me"), "Yes, yes, it is too sweet. It is suffocating. I shall suffocate." And she laid her right hand, with the fingers spread, across the bare swell of her bosom above the pressure of the corset.

"Thinking her taken by some sudden illness," Cass recorded in the journal, "I asked if she were faint. She said, No, in a very low, husky voice. Nevertheless I rose, with the expressed intention of getting a glass of water for her. Suddenly she said, quite harshly and to my amazement, because of her excellent courtesy, 'Sit down, sit down, I don't want water!' So somewhat distressed in mind that unwittingly I might have offended, I sat down. I looked across the garden where in the light of the moon several couples promenaded down the paths between the low hedges. I could hear the sound of her breathing beside me. It was disturbed and irregular. All at once she said, 'How old are you, Mr. Mastern?' I said twenty-two. Then she said, 'I am twenty-nine.' I stammered something, in my surprise. She laughed as though at my confusion, and said, 'Yes, I am seven
167

years older than you, Mr. Mastern. Does that surprise you, Mr. Mastern?' I replied in the affirmative. Then she said, 'Seven years is a long time. Seven years ago you were a child, Mr. Mastern.' Then she laughed, with a sudden sharpness, but quickly stopped herself to add, 'But I wasn't a child. Not seven years ago, Mr. Mastern.' I did not answer her, for there was no thought clear in my head. I sat there in confusion, but in the middle of my confusion I was trying to see what she would have looked like as a child. I could call up no image. Then her husband returned from the house."

A few days later Cass went back to Mississippi to devote some months to his plantation, and, under the guidance of Gilbert, to go once to Jackson, the capital, and once to Vicksburg. It was a busy summer. Now Cass could see clearly what Gilbert intended: to make him rich and to put him into politics. It was a flattering and glittering prospect, and one not beyond reasonable expectation for a young man whose brother was Gilbert Mastern. ("My brother is a man of great taciturnity and strong mind, and when he speaks, though he practices no graces and ingratiations, all men, especially those of the sober sort who have responsibility and power, weigh his words with respect.") So the summer passed, under the strong hand and cold eye of Gilbert. But toward the end of the season, when already Cass was beginning to give thought to his return to Transylvania, an envelope came addressed to him from Lexington, in an unfamiliar script. When Cass unfolded the single sheet of paper a small pressed blossom, or what he discovered to be such, slipped out. For a moment he could not think what it was, or why it was in his hand. Then he put it to his nostrils. The odor, now faint and dusty, was the odor of jasmine.

The sheet of paper had been folded twice, to make four equal sections. In one section, in a clean, strong, not large script, he read: "Oh, Cass!" That was all.

It was enough.

One drizzly autumn afternoon, just after his return to Lexington, Cass called at the Trice house to pay his respects. Duncan Trice was not there, having sent word that he had been urgently detained in the town and would be home for a late dinner. Of that afternoon, Cass wrote: "I found myself in the room alone with her. There were shadows, as there had been that afternoon, almost a year before, when I first saw her in that room, and when I had thought that her eyes were black. She greeted me civilly, and I replied and stepped back after having shaken her hand. Then I realized that she was looking at me fixedly, as I at her. Suddenly, her lips parted slightly and gave a short exhalation, like a sigh or suppressed moan. As of one accord, we moved toward each other and embraced. No words passed between us as we stood there. We stood there for a long

168

time, or so it seemed. I held her body close to me in a strong embrace, but we did not exchange a kiss, which upon recollection has since seemed strange. But was it strange? Was it strange that some remnant of shame should forbid us to look each other in the face? I felt and heard my heart racing within my bosom, with a loose feeling as though it were unmoored and were leaping at random in a great cavity within me, but at the same time I scarcely accepted the fact of my situation. I was somehow possessed by incredulity, even as to my identity, as I stood there and my nostrils were filled with the fragrance of her hair. It was not to be believed that I was Cass Mastern, who stood thus in the house of a friend and benefactor. There was no remorse or horror at the turpitude of the act, but only the incredulity which I have referred to. (One feels incredulity at the first breaking of a habit, but horror at the violation of a principle. Therefore what virtue and honor I had known in the past had been an accident of habit and not the fruit of will. Or can virtue be the fruit of human will? The thought is pride.)

"As I have said, we stood there for a long time in a strong embrace, but with her face lowered against my chest, and my own eyes staring across the room and out a window into the deepening obscurity of the evening. When she finally raised her face, I saw that she had been silently weeping. Why was she weeping? I have asked myself that question. Was it because even on the verge of committing an irremediable wrong she could weep at the consequence of an act which she felt powerless to avoid? Was it because the man who held her was much younger than she and his embrace gave her the reproach of youth and seven years? Was it because he had come seven years too late and could not come in innocence? It does not matter what the cause. If it was the first, then the tears can only prove that sentiment is no substitue for obligation, if the second, then they only prove that pity of the self is no substitute for wisdom. But she shed the tears and finally lifted her face to mine with those tears bright in her large eyes, and even now, though those tears were my ruin, I cannot wish them unshed, for they testify to the warmth of her heart and prove that whatever her sin (and mine) she did not step to it with a gay foot and with the eyes hard with lust and fleshly cupidity.

"The tears were my ruin, for when she lifted her face to me some streak of tenderness was mixed into my feelings, and my heart seemed to flood itself into my bosom to fill that great cavity wherein it had been leaping. She said, 'Cass'—the first time she had ever addressed me by my Christian name. 'Yes,' I replied. 'Kiss me,' she said very simply, 'you can do it now.' So I kissed her. And thereupon in the blindness of our mortal blood and in the appetite of our hearts we performed the act. There in that very room with the servants walking with soft feet somewhere in the house and with the door to the room open and with her husband expected, and not yet in the room the darkness of evening. But we were secure in our very recklessness, as though the lustful heart could give forth a cloud of darkness in which we were shrouded, even as Venus once shrouded Aeneas in a cloud so that he passed unspied among men to approach the city of Dido. In such cases as ours the very recklessness gives security as the strength of the desire seems to give the sanction of justice and righteousness.

"Though she had wept and had seemed to perform the act in a sadness and desperation, immediately afterward she spoke cheerfully to me. She stood in the middle of the room pressing her hair into place, and I stumblingly ventured some remark about our future, a remark very vague for my being was still confused, but she responded, 'Oh, let us not think about it now,' as though I had broached a subject of no consequence. She promptly summoned a servant and asked for lights. They were brought and thereupon I inspected her face to find it fresh and unmarked. When her husband came, she greeted him familiarly and affectionately, and as I witnessed it my own heart was wrenched, but not, I must confess, with compunction. Rather with a violent jealousy. When he spoke to me and took my hand, so great was my disturbance that I was sure that my face could not but betray it."

So began the second phase of the story of Cass Mastern. All that year, as before, he was often in the house of Duncan Trice, and as before he was often with him in field sports, gambling, drinking, and racegoing. He learned, he says, to "wear his brow unwrinkled," to accept the condition of things. As for Annabelle Trice, he says that sometimes looking back, he could scarcely persuade himself that "she had shed tears." She was, he says, "of a warm nature, reckless and passionate of disposition, hating all mention of the future (she would never let me mention times to come), agile, resourceful, and cheerful in devising to gratify our appetites, but with a womanly tenderness such as any man might prize at a sanctified hearth-side." She must indeed have been agile and resourceful, for to carry on such a liaison undetected in that age and place must have been a problem. There was a kind of summerhouse at the foot of the Trice garden, which one could enter unobserved from an alley. Some of their meetings occurred there. A half-sister of Annabelle Trice, who lived in Lexington, apparently assisted the lovers or winked at their relationship, but, it seems, only after some pressure by Annabelle, for Cass mentions "a stormy scene." So some of the meetings were there. But now and then Duncan Trice had to be out of town on business, and on those occasions Cass would be admitted, late at night, to the house, even during a period when Annabelle's mother and father were staying there; so he actually lay in the very bed belonging to Duncan Trice.

There were, however, other meetings, unplanned and unpredictable moments snatched when they found themselves left alone together. "Scarce a corner, cranny, or protected nook or angle of my friend's trusting house did we not at one time or another defile, and that even in the full and shameless light of day," Cass wrote in the journal, and when Jack Burden, the student of history, went to Lexington and went to see the old Trice house he remembered the sentence. The town had grown up around the house, and the gardens, except for a patch of lawn, were gone. But the house was well maintained (some people named Miller lived there and by and large respected the place) and Jack Burden was permitted to inspect the premises. He wandered about the room where the first meeting had taken place and she had raised her eyes to Cass Mastern above the newly lighted candles and where, a year later, she had uttered the sigh, or suppressed moan, and stepped to his arms; and out into the hall, which was finely proportioned and with a graceful stair; and into a small, shadowy library; and to a kind of back hall, which was a well "protected nook or angle" and had, as a matter of fact, furniture adequate to the occasion. Jack Burden stood in the main hall, which was cool and dim, with dully glittering floors, and, in the silence of the house, recalled that period, some seventy years before, of the covert glances, the guarded whispers, the abrupt rustling of silk in the silence (the costume of the period certainly had not been designed to encourage casual vice), the sharp breath, the reckless sighs. Well, all of that had been a long time before, and Annabelle Trice and Cass Mastern were long since deader than mackerel, and Mrs. Miller, who came down to give Jack Burden a cup of tea (she was flattered by the "historical" interest in her house, though she didn't guess the exact nature of the case), certainly was not "agile" and didn't look "resourceful" and probably had used up all her energy in the Ladies Altar Guild of St. Luke's Episcopal Church and in the D.A.R.

The period of the intrigue, the second phase of the story of Cass Mastern, lasted all of one academic year, part of the summer (for Cass was compelled to go back to Mississippi for his plantation affairs and to attend the wedding of his sister Lavinia, who married a well-connected young man named Willis Burden), and well through the next winter, when Cass was back in Lexington. Then, on March 19, 1854, Duncan Trice died, in his library (which was a "protected nook or angle" of his house), with a lead slug nearly the size of a man's thumb in his chest. It was quite obviously an accident.

The widow sat in church, upright and immobile. When she once raised her veil to touch at her eyes with a handkerchief,

171

Cass Mastern saw that the cheek was "pale as marble but for a single flushed spot, like the flush of fever." But even when the veil was lowered he detected the fixed, bright eyes glittring "within that artificial shadow."

Cass Mastern, with five other young men of Lexington, cronies and boon companions of the dead man, carried the coffin. "The coffin which I carried seemed to have no weight, although my friend had been of large frame and had inclined to stoutness. As we proceeded with it, I marvelled at the fact of its lightness, and once the fancy flitted into my mind that he was not in the coffin at all, that it was empty, and that all the affair was a masquerade or mock show carried to ludicrous and blasphemous length, for no purpose, as in a dream. Or to deceive me, the fancy came. I was the object of the deception, and all the other people were in league and conspiracy against me. But when that thought came, I suddenly felt a sense of great cunning and a wild exhilaration. I had been too sharp to be caught so. I had penetrated the deception. I had the impulse to hurl the coffin to the ground and see its emptiness burst open and to laugh in triumph. But I did not, and I saw the coffin sink beneath the level of the earth on which we stood and receive the first clods upon it.

"As soon as the sound of the first clods striking the coffin came to me, I felt a great relief, and then a most overmastering desire. I looked toward her. She was kneeling at the foot of the grave, with what thoughts I could not know. Her head was inclined slightly and the veil was over her face. The bright sun poured over her black-clad figure. I could not take my eyes from the sight. The posture seemed to accentuate the charms of her person and to suggest to my inflamed senses the suppleness of her members. Even the funereal tint of her costume seemed to add to the provocation. The sunshine was hot upon my neck and could be felt through the stuff of my coat upon my shoulders. It was preternaturally bright so that I was blinded by it and my eyes were blinded and my senses warm. But all the while I could hear, as from a great distance, the scraping of the blades upon the piled earth and the muffled sound of earth falling into the excavation."

That evening Cass went to the summerhouse in the garden. It was not by appointment, simply on impulse. He waited there a long time, but she finally appeared, dressed in black "which was scarce darker than the night." He did not speak, or make any sign as she approached, "gliding like a shadow among shadows," but remained standing where he had been, in the deepest obscurity of the summerhouse. Even when she entered, he did not betray his presence. "I can not be certain that any premeditation was in my silence. It was prompted by an over-powering impulse which gripped me and sealed my throat and froze my limbs. Before that moment, and afterwards, I knew that it is dishonorable to spy upon another, but at the moment no such considerations presented themselves. I had to keep my eyes fixed upon her as she stood there thinking herself alone in the darkness of the structure. I had the fancy that since she thought herself alone I might penetrate into her being, that I might learn what change, what effect, had been wrought by the death of her husband. The passion which had seized me to the very extent of paroxysm that afternoon at the brink of my friend's grave was gone. I was perfectly cold now. But I had to know, to try to know. It was as though I might know myself by knowing her. (It is human defect—to try to know oneself by the self of another. One can only know oneself in God and in His great eye.)

"She entered the summerhouse and sank upon one of the benches, not more than a few feet from my own location. For a long time I stood there, peering at her. She sat perfectly upright and rigid. At last I whispered her name, as low as might be. If she heard it, she gave no sign. So I repeated her name, in the same fashion, and again. Upon the third utterance, she whispered, 'Yes,' but she did not change her posture or turn her head. Then I spoke more loudly, again uttering her name, and instantly, with a motion of wild alarm she rose, with a strangled cry and her hands lifted toward her face. She reeled, and it seemed that she would collapse to the floor, but she gained control of herself and stood there staring at me. Stammeringly, I made my apology, saying that I had not wanted to startle her, that I had understood her to answer yes to my whisper before I spoke, and I asked her, 'Did you not answer to my whisper?'

"She replied that she had.

" 'Then why were you distressed when I spoke again?' I asked her.

" 'Because I did not know that you were here,' she said.

" 'But,' I said, 'you say that you had just heard my whisper and had answered to it, and now you say that you did not know I was here.'

" 'I did not know that you were here,' she repeated, in a low voice, and the import of what she was saying dawned upon me.

" 'Listen,' I said, 'when you heard the whisper—did you recognize it as my voice?'

"She stared at me, not answering.

" 'Answer me,' I demanded, for I had to know.

"She continued to stare, and finally replied hesitantly, 'I do not know.'

" 'You thought it was—' I began, but before I could utter the words she had flung herself upon me, clasping me in desperation like a person frantic with drowning, and ejaculat-

173

ing, 'No, no, it does not matter what I thought, you are here, you are here!' And she drew my face down and pressed her lips against mine to stop my words. Her lips were cold, but they hung upon mine.

"I too was perfectly cold, as of a mortal chill. And the coldness was the final horror of the act which we performed, as though two dolls should parody the shame and filth of man to make it doubly shameful.

"After, she said to me, 'Had I not found you here tonight, it could never have been between us again.'

" 'Why?' I demanded.

" 'It was a sign,' she said.

" 'A sign?' I demanded.

" 'A sign that we cannot escape, that we—' and she interrupted herself, to resume, whispering fiercely in the dark—'I do not want to escape—it is a sign—whatever I have done is done.' She grew quiet for a moment, then she said, 'Give me your hand.'

"I gave her my right hand. She grasped it, dropped it, and said, 'The other, the other hand.'

"I held it out, across my own body, for I was sitting on her left. She seized it with her own left hand, bringing her hand upward from below to press my hand flat against her bosom. Then, fumbling, she slipped a ring upon my finger, the finger next to the smallest.

" 'What is that?' I asked.

" 'A ring,' she answered, paused, and added, 'It is his ring.'

"Then I recalled that he, my friend, had always worn a wedding ring, and I felt the metal cold upon my flesh. 'Did you take it off of his finger?' I asked, and the thought shook me.

" 'No,' she said.

" 'No?' I questioned.

" 'No,' she said, 'he took it off. It was the only time he ever took it off.'

"I sat beside her, waiting for what, I did not know, while she held my hand pressed against her bosom. I could feel it rise and fall. I could say nothing.

"Then she said, 'Do you want to know how—how he took it off?'

" 'Yes,' I said in the dark, and waiting for her to speak, I moved my tongue out upon my dry lips.

" 'Listen,' she commanded me in an imperious whisper, 'that evening after—after it happened—after the house was quiet again, I sat in my room, in the little chair by the dressing table, where I always sit for Phebe to let down my hair. I had sat there out of habit, I suppose, for I was numb all over. I watched Phebe preparing the bed for the night.' (Phebe was her waiting maid, a comely yellow wench somewhat given to

174

the fits and sulls.) 'I saw Phebe remove the bolster and then look down at a spot where the bolster had lain, on my side of the bed. She picked something up and came toward me. She stared at me—and her eyes, they are yellow, you look into them and you can't see what is in them—she stared at me—a long time—and then she held out her hand, clenched shut and she watched me—and then—slow, so slow—she opened up the fingers—and there lay the ring on the palm of her hand—and I knew it was his ring but all I thought was, it is gold and it is lying in a gold hand. For Phebe's hand was gold—I had never noticed how her hand is the color of pure gold. Then I looked up and she was still staring at me, and her eyes were gold, too, and bright and hard like gold. And I knew that she knew.'

" 'Knew?' I echoed, like a question, but I knew, too, now. My friend had learned the truth—from the coldness of his wife, from the gossip of servants—and had drawn the gold ring from his finger and carried it to the bed where he had lain with her and had put it beneath her pillow and had gone down and shot himself but under such circumstances that no one save his wife would ever guess it to be more than an accident. But he had made one fault of calculation. The yellow wench had found the ring.

" 'She knows,' she whispered, pressing my hand hard against her bosom, which heaved and palpitated with a new wildness. 'She knows—and she looks at me—she will always look at me.' Then suddenly her voice dropped, and a wailing intonation came into it: 'She will tell. All of them will know. All of them in the house will look at me and know—when they hand me the dish—when they come into the room—and their feet don't make any noise!' She rose abruptly, dropping my hand. I remained seated, and she stood there beside me, her back toward me, the whiteness of her face and hands no longer visible, and to my sight the blackness of her costume faded into the shadow, even in such proximity. Suddenly, in a voice which I did not recognize for its hardness, she said in the darkness above me, 'I will not abide it, I will not abide it!' Then she turned, and with a swooping motion leaned to kiss me upon the mouth. Then she was gone from my side and I heard her feet running up the gravel of the path. I sat there in the darkness for a time longer, turning the ring upon my finger."

After that meeting in the summerhouse, Cass did not see Annabelle Trice for some days. He learned that she had gone to Louisville, where, he recalled, she had close friends. She had, as was natural, taken Phebe with her. Then he heard that she had returned, and that night, late, went to the summerhouse in the garden. She was there, sitting in the dark. She greeted him. She seemed, he wrote later, peculiarly cut off, remote, and vague in manner, like a somnambulist or a person drugged. He asked about her trip to Louisville, and she replied briefly that she had been down the river to Paducah. He remarked that he had not known that she had friends in Paducah, and she said that she had none there. Then, all at once, she turned on him, the vagueness changing to violence, and burst out, "You are prying—you are prying into my affairs—and I will not tolerate it." Cass stammered out some excuse before she cut in to say, "But if you must know, I'll tell you. I took her there."

For a moment Cass was genuinely confused.

"Her?" he questioned.

"Phebe," she replied, "I took her to Paducah, and she's gone."

"Gone—gone where?"

"Down the river," she answered, repeated, "down the river," and laughed abruptly, and added, "and she won't look at me any more like that."

"You sold her?"

"Yes, I sold her. In Paducah, to a man who was making up a coffle of Negroes for New Orleans. And nobody knows me in Paducah, nobody knew I was there, nobody knows I sold her, for I shall say she ran away into Illinois. But I sold her. For thirteen hundred dollars."

"You got a good price," Cass said, "even for a yellow girl as sprightly as Phebe." And, as he reports in the journal, he laughed with some "bitterness and rudeness," though he does not say why.

"Yes," she replied, "I got a good price. I made him pay every penny she was worth. And then do you know what I did with the money, do you?"

"No."

"When I came off the boat at Louisville, there was an old man, a nigger, sitting on the landing stage, and he was blind and picking on a guitar and singing 'Old Dan Tucker.' I took the money out of my bag and walked to him and laid it in his old hat."

"If you were going to give the money away—if you felt the money was defiled—why didn't you free her?" Cass asked.

"She'd stay right here, she wouldn't go away, she would stay right here and look at me. Oh, no, she wouldn't go away, for she's the wife of a man the Motleys have, their coachman. Oh, she'd stay right here and look at me and tell, tell what she knows, and I'll not abide it!"

Then Cass said, "If you had spoken to me I would have bought the man from Mr. Motley and set him free, too."

"He wouldn't have sold," she said, "the Motleys won't sell a servant."

"Even to be freed?" Cass continued, but she cut in, "I tell you I won't have you interfering with my affairs, do you understand that?" And she rose from his side and stood in the middle of the summerhouse, and he saw the glimmer of her face in the shadow and heard her agitated breathing. "I thought you were fond of her," Cass said.

"I was," she said, "until—until she looked at me like that."

"You know why you got that price for her?" Cass asked, and without waiting for an answer, went on, "Because she's yellow and comely and well-made. Oh, the drovers wouldn't take her down chained in a coffle. They wouldn't wear her down. They'll take her down the river soft. And you know why?"

"Yes, I know why," she said, "and what is it to you? Are you so charmed by her?"

"That is unfair," Cass said.

"Oh, I see, Mr. Mastern," she said, "oh, I see, you are concerned for the honor of a black coachman. It is a very delicate sentiment, Mr. Mastern. Why—" and she came to stand above him as he still sat on the bench—"why did you not show some such delicate concern for the honor of your friend? Who is now dead."

According to the journal, there was, at this moment, "a tempest of feeling" in his breast. He wrote: "Thus I heard put into words for the first time the accusation which has ever in all climes been that most calculated to make wince a man of proper nurture or natural rectitude. What the hardened man can bear to hear from the still small voice within, may yet be when spoken by any eternal tongue an accusation dire enough to drain his very cheeks of blood. But it was not only that accusation in itself, for in very truth I had supped full of that horror and made it my long familiar. It was not merely the betrayal of my friend. It was not merely the death of my friend, at whose breast I had levelled the weapon. I could have managed somehow to live with those facts. But I suddenly felt that the world outside of me was shifting and the substance of things, and that the process had only begun of a general disintegration of which I was the center. At that moment of perturbation, when the cold sweat broke on my brow, I did not frame any sentence distinctly to my mind. But I have looked back and wrestled to know the truth. It was not the fact that a slave woman was being sold away from the house where she had had protection and kindness and away from the arms of her husband into debauchery. I knew that such things had happened in fact, and I was no child for after my arrival in Lexington and my acquaintance with the looser sort

177

of companions, the sportsmen and the followers of the races, I had myself enjoyed such diversions. It was not only the fact that the woman for whom I had sacrificed my friend's life and my honor could, in her own suffering, turn on me with a cold rage and the language of insult so that I did not recognize her. It was, instead, the fact that all of these things—the death of my friend, the betrayal of Phebe, the suffering and rage and great change of the woman I had loved—all had come from my single act of sin and perfidy, as the boughs from the bole and the leaves from the bough. Or to figure the matter differently, it was as though the vibration set up in the whole fabric of the world by my act had spread infinitely and with ever increasing power and no man could know the end. I did not put it into words in such fashion, but I stood there shaken by a tempest of feeling."

When Cass had somewhat controlled his agitation, he said, "To whom did you sell the girl?"

"What's it to you?" she answered.

"To whom did you sell the girl?" he repeated.

"I'll not tell you," she said.

"I will find out," he said. "I will go to Paducah and find out."

She grasped him by the arm, driving her fingers deep into the flesh, "like talons," and demanded, "Why—why are you going?"

"To find her," he said. "To find her and buy her and set her free." He had not premeditated this. He heard the words, he wrote in the journal, and knew that that was his intention. "To find her and buy her and set her free," he said, and felt the grasp on his arm released and then in the dark suddenly felt the rake of her nails down his cheek, and heard her voice in a kind of "wild sibilance" saying, "if you do—if you do—oh, I'll not abide it—I will not!"

She flung herself from his side and to the bench. He heard her gasp, and sob, "a hard dry sob like a man's." He did not move. Then he heard her voice, "If you do—if you do—she looked at me that way, and I'll not abide it—if you do—" Then after a pause, very quietly, "If you do, I shall never see you again."

He made no reply. He stood there for some minutes, he did not know how long, then left the summerhouse, where she still sat, and walked down the alley.

The next morning he left for Paducah. He learned the name of the trader, but he also learned that the trader had sold Phebe (a yellow wench who answered to Phebe's description) to a "private party" who happened to be in Paducah at the time but who had gone on downriver. His name was unkown in Paducah. The trader had presumably sold Phebe so that he would

178

be free to accompany his coffle when it had been made up. He had now headed, it was said, into South Kentucky, with a few bucks and wenches, to pick up more. As Cass had predicted, he had not wanted to wear Phebe down by taking her in the coffle. So getting a good figure of profit in Paducah, he had sold her there. Cass went south as far as Bowling Green, but lost track of his man there. So rather hopelessly, he wrote a letter to the trader, in care of the market at New Orleans, asking for the name of the purchaser and any information about him. Then he swung back north to Lexington.

At Lexington he went down to West Short Street, to the Lewis C. Robards barracoon, which Mr. Robards had converted from the old Lexington Theatre a few years earlier. He had a notion that Mr. Robards, the leading trader of the section, might be able, through his downriver connections, to locate Phebe, if enough of a commission was in sight. At the barracoon there was no one in the office except a boy, who said that Mr. Robards was downriver but that Mr. Simms was "holding things down" and was over at the "house" at an "inspection." So Cass went next door to the house. (When Jack Burden was in Lexington investigating the life of Cass Mastern, he saw the "house" still standing, a two-story brick building of the traditional residential type, roof running lengthwise, door in center of front, window on each side, chimney at each end, lean-to in back. Robards had kept his "choice stock" there and not in the coops, to wait for "inspection.")

Cass found the main door unlocked at the house, entered the hall, saw no one, but heard laughter from above. He mounted the stairs and discovered, at the end of the hall, a small group of men gathered at an open door. He recognized a couple of them, young hangers-on he had seen about town and at the track. He approached and asked if Mr. Simms was about. "Inside," one of the men said, "showing." Over the heads, Cass could see into the room. First he saw a short, strongly made man, a varnished-looking man, with black hair, black neckcloth, large bright black eyes, and black coat, with a crop in his hand. Cass knew immediately that he was a French "speculator," who was buying "fancies" for Louisiana. The Frenchman was staring at something beyond Cass's range of vision. Cass moved farther and could see within.

There he saw the man whom he took to be Mr. Simms, a nondescript fellow in a plug hat, and beyond him the figure of a woman. She was a very young woman, some twenty years old perhaps, rather slender, with skin slightly darker than ivory, probably an octaroon, and hair crisp rather than kinky, and deep dark liquid eyes, slightly bloodshot, which stared at a spot above and beyond the Frenchman. She did not wear the ordinary plaid Osnaburg and kerchief of the female slave

179

up for sale, but a white, loosely cut dress, with elbow-length sleeves, and skirts to the floor and no kerchief, only a band to her hair. Beyond her, in the neatly furnished room ("quite genteel," the journal called it, while noting the barred windows), Cass saw a rocking chair and little table, and on the table a sewing basket with a piece of fancy needlework lying there with the needle stuck in it, "as though some respectable young lady or householder had dropped it casually aside upon rising to greet a guest." Cass recorded that somehow he found himself staring at the needlework.

"Yeah," Mr. Simms was saying, "yeah." And grasped the girl by the shoulder to swing her slowly around for a complete view. Then he seized one of her wrists and lifted the arm to shoulder level and worked it back and forth a couple of times to show the supple articulation, saying, "Yeah." That done, he drew the arm forward, holding it toward the Frenchman, the hand hanging limply from the wrist which he held. (The hand was, according to the journal, "well moulded, and the fingers tapered.") "Yeah," Mr. Simms said, "look at that-air hand. Ain't no lady got a littler, teensier hand. And round and soft, yeah?"

"Ain't she got nuthen else round and soft?" one of the men at the door called, and the others laughed.

"Yeah," Mr. Simms said, and leaned to take the hem of her dress, which with a delicate flirting motion he lifted higher than her waist, while he reached out with his other hand to wad the cloth and draw it into a kind of "awkward girdle" about her waist. Still holding the wad of cloth he walked around her, forcing her to turn (she turned "without resistance and as though in a trance") with his motion until her small buttocks were toward the door. "Round and soft, boys," Mr. Simms said, and gave her a good whack on the near buttock to make the flesh tremble. "Ever git yore hand on anything rounder ner softer, boys?" he demanded. "Hit's a cushion, I declare. And shake like sweet jelly."

"God-a-Mighty and got on stockings," one of the men said.

While the other men laughed, the Frenchman stepped to the side of the girl, reached out to lay the tip of his riding crop at the little depression just above the beginning of the swell of the buttocks. He held the tip delicately there for a moment, then flattened the crop across the back and moved it down slowly, evenly across each buttock, to trace the fullness of the curve. "Turn her," he said in his foreign voice.

Mr. Simms obediently carried the wad around, and the body followed in the half revolution. One of the men at the door whistled. The Frenchman laid his crop across the woman's belly as though he were a "carpenter measuring something or as to demonstrate its flatness," and moved it down as before,

180

tracing the structure, until it came to rest across the thighs, below the triangle. Then he let his hand fall to his side, with the crop. "Open your mouth," he said to the girl.

She did so, and he peered earnestly at her teeth. Then he leaned and whiffed her breath. "It is a good breath," he admitted, as though grudgingly.

"Yeah," Mr. Simms said, "yeah, you ain't a-finden no better breath."

"Have you any others?" the Frenchman demanded. "On hand?"

"We got 'em," Mr. Simms said.

"Let me see," the Frenchman said, and moved toward the door with, apparently, the "insolent expectation" that the group there would dissolve before him. He went out into the hall, Mr. Simms following. While Mr. Simms locked the door, Cass said to him, "I wish to speak to you, if you are Mr. Simms."

"Huh?" Mr. Simms said ("grunted" according to the journal), but looking at Cass became suddenly civil for he could know from dress and bearing that Cass was not one of the casual hangers-on. So Mr. Simms admitted the Frenchman to the next room to inspect its occupant, and returned to Cass. Cass remarked in the journal that trouble might have been avoided if he had been more careful to speak in private, but he wrote that at the time the matter was so much upon his mind that the men who stood about were as shadows to him.

He explained his wish to Mr. Simms, described Phebe as well as possible, gave the name of the trader in Paducah, and offered a liberal commission. Mr. Simms seemed dubious, promised to do what he could, and then said, "But nine outa ten you won't git her, Mister. And we got sumthen here better. You done seen Delphy, and she's nigh white as airy woman, and a sight more juicy, and that gal you talk about is nuthen but yaller. Now Delphy—"

"But the young gemmun got a hankeren fer yaller," one of the hangers-on said, and laughed, and the others laughed too.

Cass struck him across the mouth. "I struck him with the side of my fist," Cass wrote, "to bring blood. I struck him without thought, and I recollect the surprise which visited me when I saw the blood on his chin and saw him draw a bowie from his shirt front. I attempted to avoid his first blow, but received it upon my left shoulder. Before he could withdraw, I had grasped his wrist in my right hand, forced it down so that I could also use my left hand, which still had some strength left at that moment, and with a turning motion of my body I broke his arm across my right hip, and then knocked him to the floor. I recovered the bowie from the floor, and with it faced the man who seemed to be the friend of the man who was now prostrate. He had a knife in his hand, but he seemed disinclined to pursue the discussion."

Cass declined the assistance of Mr. Simms, pressed a handkerchief over his wound, walked out of the building and toward his lodgings, and collapsed on West Short Street. He was carried home. The next day he was better. He learned that Mrs. Trice had left the city, presumably for Washington. A couple of days later his wound infected, and for some time he lay in delirium between life and death. His recovery was slow, presumably retarded by what he termed in the journal his "will toward darkness." But his constitution was stronger than his will, and he recovered, to know himself as the "chief of sinners and a plague spot on the body of the human world." He would have committed suicide except for the fear of damnation for that act, for though "hopeless of Grace I yet clung to the hope of Grace." But sometimes the very fact of damnation because of suicide seemed to be the very reason for suicide: he had brought his friend to suicide and the friend, by that act, was eternally damned; therefore he, Cass Mastern, should, in justice, insure his own damnation by the same act. "But the Lord preserved me from self-slaughter for ends which are His and beyond my knowledge."

Mrs. Trice did not come back to Lexington.

He returned to Mississippi. For two years he operated his plantation, read the Bible, prayed, and, strangely enough, prospered greatly, almost as though against his will. In the end he repaid Gilbert his debt, and set free his slaves. He had some notion of operating the plantation with the same force on a wage basis. "You fool," Gilbert said to him, "be a private fool if you must, but in God's name don't be a public one. Do you think you can work them and free them? One day work, one day loaf. Do you think you can have a passel of free niggers next door to a plantation with slaves? If you did have to set them free, you don't have to spend the rest of your natural life nursing them. Get them out of this country, and take up law or medicine. Or preach the Gospel and at least make a living out of all this praying." Cass tried for more than a year to operate the plantation with his free Negroes, but was compelled to confess that the project was a failure. "Get them out of the country," Gilbert said to him. "And why don't you go with them. Why don't you go North?"

"I belong here," Cass replied.

"Well, why don't you preach Abolition right here?" Gilbert demanded. "Do something, do anything, but stop making a fool of yourself trying to raise cotton with free niggers."

"Perhaps I shall preach Abolition," Cass said, "some day. Even here. But not now. I am not worthy to instruct others.

182

Not now. But meanwhile there is my example. If it is good, it is not lost. Nothing is ever lost."

"Except your mind," Gilbert said, and flung heavily from the room.

There was a sense of trouble in the air. Only Gilbert's great wealth and prestige and scarcely concealed humorous contempt for Cass saved Cass from ostracism, or worse. ("His contempt for me is a shield," Cass wrote. "He treats me like a wayward and silly child who may learn better and who does not have to be taken seriously. Therefore my neighbors do not take me seriously.") But trouble did come. One of Cass's Negroes had a broad-wife on a plantation near by. After she had had some minor trouble with the overseer, the husband stole her from the plantation and ran away. Toward the Tennessee border the pair were taken. The man, resisting officers, was shot; the woman was brought back. "See," Gilbert said, "all you have managed to do is get one nigger killed and one nigger whipped. I offer my congratulations." So Cass put his free Negroes on a boat bound upriver, and never heard of them again.

"I saw the boat head out into the channel, and watched the wheels churn against the strong current, and my spirit was troubled. I knew that the Negroes were passing from one misery to another, and that the hopes they now carried would be blighted. They had kissed my hands and wept for joy, but I could take no part in their rejoicing. I had not flattered myself that I had done anything for them. What I had done I had done for myself, to relieve my spirit of a burden, the burden of their misery and their eyes upon me. The wife of my dead friend had found the eyes of the girl Phebe upon her and had gone wild and had ceased to be herself and had sold the girl into misery. I had found their eyes upon me and had freed them into misery, lest I should do worse. For many cannot bear their eyes upon them, and enter into evil and cruel ways in their desperation. There was in Lexington a decade and more before my stay in that city, a wealthy lawyer named Fielding L. Turner, who had married a lady of position from Boston. This lady Caroline Turner, who had never had blacks around her and who had been nurtured in sentiments opposed to the institution of human servitude, quickly became notorious for her abominable cruelties performed in her fits of passion. All persons of the community reprehended her floggings, which she performed with her own hands, uttering meanwhile little cries in her throat, according to report. Once while she was engaged in flogging a servant in an apartment on the second floor of her palatial home, a small Negro boy entered the room and began to whimper. She seized him and bodily hurled him through the window of the apartment so that he fell upon stone below and broke his back to become a cripple for his

183

days. To protect her from the process of law and the wrath of the community, Judge Turner committed her to a lunatic asylum. But later the physicians said her to be of sound mind and released her. Her husband in his will left her no slaves, for to do so would, the will said, be to doom them to misery in life and a speedy death. But she procured slaves, among them a yellow coachman named Richard, mild of manner, sensible, and plausible disposition. One day she had him chained and proceeded to flog him. But he tore himself from the chains that held him to the wall and seized the woman by the throat and strangled her. Later he was captured and hanged for murder, though many wished that his escape had been contrived. This story was told me in Lexington. One lady said to me, 'Mrs. Turner did not understand Negroes.' And another, 'Mrs. Turner did it because she was from Boston where the Abolitionists are.' But I did not understand. Then, much later, I began to understand. I understood that Mrs. Turner flogged her Negroes for the same reason that the wife of my friend sold Phebe down the river: she could not bear their eyes upon her. I understand, for I can no longer bear their eyes upon me. Perhaps only a man like my brother Gilbert can in the midst of evil retain enough of innocence and strength to bear their eyes upon him and to do a little justice in the terms of the great injustice."

So Cass, who had a plantation with no one to work it, went to Jackson, the capital of the state, and applied himself to the law. Before he left, Gilbert came to him and offered to take over the plantation and work it with a force of his people from his own great place on a share basis. Apparently he was still trying to make Cass rich. But Cass declined, and Gilbert said, "You object to my working it with slaves, is that it? Well, let me tell you, if you sell it, it will be worked with slaves. It is black land and will be watered with black sweat. Does it make any difference then, which black sweat falls on it?" And Cass replied that he was not going to sell the plantation. Then Gilbert, in an apoplectic rage, bellowed, "My God, man, it is land, don't you understand, it is land, and land cries out for man's hand!" But Cass did not sell. He installed a caretaker in the house, and rented a little land to a neighbor for pasture.

He went to Jackson, sat late with his books, and watched trouble gathering over the land. For it was the autumn of 1858 when he went to Jackson. On January 9, 1861, Mississippi passed the ordinance of secession. Gilbert had opposed secession, writing to Cass: "The fools, there is not a factory for arms in the state. Fools not to have prepared themselves if they have foreseen the trouble. Fools, if they have not foreseen it, to act thus in the face of facts. Fools not to temporize now and, if they must, prepare themselves to strike a blow. I have told responsible men to prepare. All fools." To which Cass replied: "I pray much for peace." But later, he wrote: "I have talked with Mr. French, who is, as you know, the Chief of Ordnance, and he says that they have only old muskets for troops, and those but flintlocks. The agents have scraped the state for shotguns, at the behest of Governor Pettus. Shotguns, Mr. French said, and curled his lips. And what shotguns, he added, and then told me of a weapon contributed to the cause, an old musket barrel strapped with metal to a piece of cypress rail crooked at one end. An old slave gave his treasure to the cause, and does one laugh or weep?" After Jefferson Davis had come back to Mississippi, having resigned from the Senate, and had accepted the command of the troops of Mississippi with the rank of Major General, Cass called upon him, at the request of Gilbert. He wrote to Gilbert: "The General says that they have given him 10,000 men, but not a stand of modern rifles. But the General also said, they have given me a very fine coat with fourteen brass buttons in front and a black velvet collar. Perhaps we can use the buttons in our shotguns, he said, and smiled."

Cass saw Mr. Davis once more, for he was with Gilbert on the steamboat *Natchez* which carried the new President of the Confederacy on the first stage of his journey from his plantation, Brierfield, to Montgomery. "We were on old Mr. Tom Leather's boat," Cass wrote in the journal, "which had been supposed to pick up the President at a landing a few miles below Brierfield. But Mr. Davis was delayed in leaving his house and was rowed out to us. I leaned on the rail and saw the little black skiff proceeding toward us over the red water. A man waved from the skiff to us. The captain of the *Natchez* observed the signal, and gave a great blast of his boat's whistle which made our ears tingle and shivered out over the expanse of waters. The boat stopped and the skiff approached. Mr. Davis was received on board. As the steamboat moved on, Mr. Davis looked back and lifted his hand in salute to the Negro servant (Isaiah Montgomery, whom I had known at Brierfield) who stood in the skiff, which rocked in the wash of the steamboat, and waved his farewell. Later, as we proceeded upriver toward the bluffs of Vicksburg, he approached my brother, with whom I was standing on the deck. We had previously greeted him. My brother again, and more intimately, congratulated Mr. Davis, who replied that he could take no pleasure in the honor. 'I have,' he said, 'always looked upon the Union with a superstitious reverence and have freely risked my life for its dear flag on more than one battlefield, and you, gentlemen, can conceive the sentiment now in me that the object of my attachment for many years has been withdrawn from me.' And he continued, 'I have in the present moment only the melancholy pleasure of an easy conscience.' Then he smiled, as he did rarely. Thereupon he took his leave of us and retired within. I had observed how worn to emaciation was his face by illness and care, and how thin the skin lay over the bone. I remarked to my brother that Mr. Davis did not look well. He replied, 'A sick man, it is a fine how-de-do to have a sick man for a president.' I responded that there might be no war, that Mr. Davis hoped for peace. But my brother said, 'Make no mistake, the Yankees will fight and they will fight well and Mr. Davis is a fool to hope for peace.' I replied, 'All good men hope for peace.' At this my brother uttered an indistinguishable exclamation, and said, 'What we want now they've got into this is not a good man but a man who can win, and I am not interested in the luxury of Mr. Davis's conscience.' Then my brother and I continued our promenade in silence, and I reflected that Mr. Davis was a good man. But the world is full of good men, I now reflect as I write these lines down, and yet the world drives hard into darkness and the blindness of blood, even as now late at night I sit in this hotel room in Vicksburg, and I am moved to ask the meaning of our virtue. May God hear our prayer!"

Gilbert received a commission as colonel in a cavalry regiment. Cass enlisted as a private in the Mississippi Rifles. "You could be a captain," Gilbert said, "or a major. You've got brains enough for that. And," he added, "damned few of them have." Cass replied that he preferred to be a private soldier, "marching with other men." But he could not tell his brother why, or tell his brother that, though he would march with other men and would carry a weapon in his hand, he would never take the life of an enemy. "I must march with these men who march," he wrote in the journal, "for they are my people and I must partake with them of all bitterness, and that more fully. But I cannot take the life of another man. How can I who have taken the life of my friend, take the life of an enemy, for I have used up my right to blood." So Cass marched away to war, carrying the musket which was, for him, but a meaningless burden, and wearing on a string, against the flesh of his chest, beneath the fabric of the gray jacket, the ring which had once been Duncan Trice's wedding ring and which Annabelle Trice, that night in the summerhouse, had slipped onto his finger as his hand lay on her bosom.

Cass marched to Shiloh, between the fresh fields, for it was early April, and then into the woods that screened the river. (Dogwood and redbud would have been out then.) He marched into the woods, heard the lead whistle by his head, saw the dead men on the ground, and the next day came out of the woods and moved in the sullen withdrawal toward Corinth.

He had been sure that he would not survive the battle. But he had survived, and moved down the crowded road "as in a dream." And he wrote: "And I felt that henceforward I should live in that dream." The dream took him into Tennessee again—Chickamauga, Knoxville, Chattanooga, and the nameless skirmishes, and the bullet for which he waited did not find him. At Chickamauga, when his company wavered in the enemy fire and seemed about to break in its attack, he moved steadily up the slope and could not understand his own inviolability. And the men regrouped, and followed. "It seemed strange to me," he wrote, "that I who in God's will sought death and could not find it, should in my seeking lead men to it who did not seek." When Colonel Hickman congratulated him, he could "find no words" for answer.

But if he had put on the gray jacket in anguish of spirit and in hope of expiation, he came to wear it in pride, for it was a jacket like those worn by the men with whom he marched. "I have seen men do brave things," he wrote, "and they ask for nothing." And he added, "It is not hard to love men for the things they endure and for the words they do not speak." More and more, too, there crept into the journal the comments of the professional soldier, between the prayers and the scruples—criticism of command (of Bragg after Chickamauga), satisfaction and an impersonal pride in maneuver or gunnery ("the practice of Marlowe's battery excellent"), and finally the admiration for the feints and delays executed by Johnston's virtuosity on the approaches to Atlanta, at Buzzard's Roost, Snake Creek Gap, New Hope Church, Kenesaw Mountain ("there is always a kind of glory, however strained or obscured, in whatever man's hand does well, and General Johnston does well").

Then, outside Atlanta, the bullet found him. He lay in the hospital and rotted slowly to death. But even before the infection set in, when the wound in the leg seemed scarcely serious, he knew that he would die. "I shall die," he wrote in the journal, "and shall be spared the end and the last bitterness of war. I have lived to do no man good, and have seen others suffer for my sin. I do not question the Justice of God, that others have suffered for my sin, for it may be that only by the suffering of the innocent does God affirm that men are brothers, and brothers in His Holy Name. And in this room with me now, men suffer for sins not theirs, as for their own. It is a comfort to know that I suffer only for my own." He knew not only that he was to die, but that the war was over. "It is over. It is all over but the dying, which will yet go on. Though the boil has come to a head and has burst, yet must the pus flow. Men shall come together yet and die in the common guilt of man and in the guilt that sent them hither from far places and distant firesides.

187

But God in His Mercy has spared me the end. Blessed be His Name."

There was no more in the journal. There was only the letter to Gilbert, written in the strange hand, dictated by Cass after he had grown too weak to write. "Remember me, but without grief. If one of us is lucky, it is I . . ."

Atlanta fell. In the last confusion, the grave of Cass Mastern was not marked. Someone at the hospital, a certain Albert Calloway, kept Cass's papers and the ring which he had carried on the cord around his neck, and much later, after the war in fact, sent them to Gilbert Mastern with a courteous note. Gilbert preserved the journal, the letters from Cass, the picture of Cass, and the ring on its cord, and after Gilbert's death, the heir finally sent the packet to Jack Burden, the student of history. So they came to rest on the little pine table in Jack Burden's bedroom in the slatternly apartment which he occupied with the two other graduate students, the unlucky, industrious, and alcoholic one, and the lucky, idle, and alcoholic one.

Jack Burden lived with the Mastern papers for a year and a half. He wanted to know all of the facts of the world in which Cass and Gilbert Mastern had lived, and he did know many of the facts. And he felt that he knew Gilbert Mastern. Gilbert Mastern had kept no journal, but Jack Burden felt that he knew him, the man with the head like the block of bare granite, who had lived through one world into another and had been at home in both. But the day came when Jack Burden sat down at the pine table and realized that he did not know Cass Mastern. He did not have to know Cass Mastern to get the degree; he only had to know the facts about Cass Mastern's world. But without knowing Cass Mastern, he could not put down the facts about Cass Mastern's world. Not that Jack Burden said that to himself. He simply sat there at the pine table, night after night, staring at the photograph, and writing nothing. Then he would get up to get a drink of water, and would stand in the dark kitchen, holding an old jelly glass in his hand, waiting for the water to run cold from the tap.

I have said that Jack Burden could not put down the facts about Cass Mastern's world because he did not know Cass Mastern. Jack Burden did not say definitely to himself why he did not know Cass Mastern. But I (who am what Jack Burden became) look back now, years later, and try to say why.

Cass Mastern lived for a few years and in that time he learned that the world is all of one piece. He learned that the world is like an enormous spider web and if you touch it, however lightly, at any point, the vibration ripples to the remotest perimeter and the drowsy spider feels the tingle and is drowsy no more but springs out to fling the gossamer coils about you who have touched the web and then inject the black, numbing

188

poison under your hide. It does not matter whether or not you meant to brush the web of things. Your happy foot or your gay wing may have brushed it ever so lightly, but what happens always happens and there is the spider, bearded black and with his great faceted eyes glittering like mirrors in the sun, or like God's eye, and the fangs dripping.

But how could Jack Burden, being what he was, understand that? He could read the words written many years before in the lonely plantation house after Cass Mastern had freed his slaves or in the lawyer's room in Jackson, Mississippi, or by candle-light in the hotel room in Vicksburg after the conversation with Jefferson Davis or by the dying campfire in some bivouac while the forms of men lay stretched on the ground in the night around and the night was filled with a slow, sad, susurrous rus-tle, like the wind fingering the pines, which was not, however, the sound of wind in the pines but the breath of thousands of sleeping men. Jack Burden could read those words, but how could he be expected to understand them? They could only be words to him, for to him the world then was simply an ac-cumlation of items, odds and ends of things like the broken and misused and dust-shrouded things gathered in a garret. Or it was a flux of things before his eyes (or behind his eyes) and one thing had nothing to do, in the end, with anything else.

Or perhaps he laid aside the journal of Cass Mastern not be-cause he could not understand, but because he was afraid to understand for what might be understood there was a reproach to him.

In any case, he laid aside the journal and entered upon one of the periods of the Great Sleep. He would come home in the evening, and because he knew that he could not work he would go to bed immediately. He would sleep twelve hours, fourteen hours, fifteen hours, feeling himself, while asleep, plunge deeper and deeper into sleep like a diver groping downward into dark water feeling for something which may be there and which would glitter if there were any light in the depth, but there isn't any light. Then in the morning he would lie in bed, not wanting anything, not even hungry, hearing the small sounds of the world sneaking and seeping back into the room, under the door, through the glass, through the cracks in the wall, through the very pores of the wood and plaster. Then he would think: *If I don't get up I can't go back to bed.* And he would get up and go out into a world which seemed very unfamiliar, but with a tantalizing unfamiliarity like the world of boyhood to which an old man returns.

Then one morning he went out into that world and did not come back to the room and the pine table. The black books, in which the journal was written, the ring, the photograph, the packet of letters were left there, beside the thick stack of manuscript, the complete works of Jack Burden, which was already beginning to curl at the edges under the paperweight.

Some weeks later, the landlady of the apartment sent him a big parcel, collect, containing the stuff he had left on the little pine table. The parcel, unopened, traveled around with him from furnished room to furnished room, to the apartment where he lived for a while with his beautiful wife Lois until the time came when he just walked out the door and didn't come back; to the other furnished rooms and hotel rooms, a big squarish parcel with the brown paper turning yellow and the cords sagging, and the name *Mr. Jack Burden* fading slowly.

Chapter Five

THAT was the end of my first journey into the enchantments of the past, my first job of historical research. It was, as I have indicated, not a success. But the second job was a sensational success. It was the "Case of the Upright Judge" and I had every reason to congratulate myself on a job well done. It was a perfect research job, marred in its technical perfection by only one thing: it meant something.

It all began, as I have said, when the Boss, sitting in the black Cadillac which sped through the night, said to me (to Me who was what Jack Burden, the student of history, had grown up to be), "There is always something."

And I said, "Maybe not on the Judge."

And he said, "Man is conceived in sin and born in corruption and he passeth from the stink of the didie to the stench of the shroud. There is always something."

The black Cadillac made its humming sound through the night and the tires sang on the slab and the black fields streaked with mist swept by. Sugar-Boy was hunched over the wheel, which looked too big for him, and the Boss sat straight up, up there in the front seat. I could see the black mass of his head against the tunnel of light down which we raced. Then I dozed off.

It was the stopping of the car that woke me up. I realized that we were back at the Stark place. I crawled out of the car. The Boss was already out, standing in the yard, just inside the gate in the starlight; Sugar-Boy was locking the car doors.

When I went into the yard, the Boss said, "Sugar-Boy is going to sleep on the couch downstairs, but there's a cot made up for you upstairs, second door on the left at the head of the stairs. You better get some shut-eye, for tomorrow you start digging for what the judge dropped."

"It will be a long dig," I said.

"Look here," he said, "if you don't want to do it you don't have to. I can always pay somebody else. Or do you want a raise?"

"No, I don't want a raise," I said.

"I am raising you a hundred a month, whether you want it or not."

"Give it to the church," I said. "If I wanted money, I could think of easier ways to make it than the way I make it with you."

"So you work for me because you love me," the Boss said.

"I don't know why I work for you, but it's not because I love you. And not for money."

"No," he said, standing there in the dark, "you don't know why you work for me. But I know," he said, and laughed.

Sugar-Boy came into the yard, said good night, and went on to the house.

"Why?" I asked.

"Boy," he said, "you work for me because I'm the way I am and you're the way you are. It is an arrangement founded on the nature of things."

"That's a hell of a fine explanation."

"It's not an explanation," he said, and laughed again. "There ain't any explanations. Not of anything. All you can do is point at the nature of things. If you are smart enough to see 'em."

"I'm not smart enough," I said.

"You're smart enough to dig up whatever it is on the Judge."

"There may not be anything."

"Nuts," he said. "Go to bed."

"Aren't you coming to bed?"

"No," he said, and I left him walking across the yard in the dark, with his head bowed a little, and his hands clasped behind him, walking casually as though he had come out to stroll through the park on Sunday afternoon. But it was not afternoon: it was 3:15 A. M.

I lay on the cot upstairs, but I didn't go right to sleep. I thought about Judge Irwin. About the way he had looked at me that very night from his tall old head, the way the yellow eyes had glittered and the lip curled over the strong old yellow teeth as he said, "I'm dining with your mother this week. Shall I tell her you still like your work?" But that didn't last, and I saw him sitting in the long room in the white house by the sea, leaning over a chessboard, facing the Scholarly Attorney, and he wasn't an old man, he was a young man, and the high aquiline florid face was brooding over the board. But that didn't last, and the face leaned toward me among the stems of the tall gray marsh grass, in the damp gray wintry dawn, and said. "You ought to have led that duck more, Jack. You got to lead a duck, son. But, son, I'll make a duck hunter out of you yet." And the face smiled. And I wanted to speak out and demand, "Is there anything, Judge? Will I find anything?" But the face only smiled, and I went to sleep. Before it could say anything, I went to sleep in the middle of the smile.

Then it was another day, and I set out to dig up the dead cat, to excavate the maggot from the cheese, to locate the canker in the rose, to find the deceased fly among the raisins in the rice pudding.

I found it.

But not all at once. You do not find it all at once if you are hunting for it. It is buried under the sad detritus of time, where, no doubt, it belongs. And you do not want to find it all at once, not if you are a student of history. If you found it all at once, there would be no opportunity to use your technique. But I had an opportunity to use my technique.

I took the first step the next afternoon while I sat in a beer parlor in the city, surrounded by a barricade of empty beer bottles. I lighted a fresh cigarette from the butt of the last one and asked myself the following question: "For what reason, barring Original Sin, is a man most likely to step over the line?"

I answered: "Ambition, love, fear, money."

I asked: "Is the Judge ambitious?"

I answered: "No. An ambitious man is a man who wants other people to think he is great. The Judge knows he is great and doesn't care what other people think."

I asked: "What about love?"

I was perfectly sure that the Judge had had his innings, but I was also perfectly sure that nobody around the Landing had anything on him in that respect. For if anybody in a small town has anything on anybody it isn't long before everybody knows it.

I asked: "Is the Judge a man to scare easy?"

I answered: "He does not scare easy."

That left money.

So I asked: "Does the Judge love money?"

"All the money the Judge wants is just enough money to make the Judge happy."

I asked: "Was there ever a time when the Judge didn't have enough money to make the Judge happy?" But naturally that wouldn't be chicken feed.

I lighted another cigarette and turned that question over in my mind. I did not know the answer. Some voice out of my childhood whispered, but I could not catch what it said. I had the vague sense, rising from a depth of time, and of myself, of being a child, of entering the room where the grown people were, of knowing that they had just that instant stopped talking because I had come into the room and was not supposed to know what they were talking about. Had I overheard what they had been talking about? I listened for the voice whispering out of my childhood, but that voice was a long way off. It could not give me the answer. So I rose from the table, and left the empty beer bottles and the cigarette butts, and went out into the street, which still steamed from the late afternoon shower like a Turkish bath, and where now the tires of automobiles hissed hotly through the film of moisture on the asphalt. If we were lucky there might be a breeze off the Gulf later. If we were lucky.

I got a taxi finally, and said, "Corner South Fifth and Saint-

Etienne Street," and fell back on the leather to listen to the tires hiss through the wetness like something frying in a skillet. I was riding to the answer about the Judge. If the man who had the answer would tell me.

The man was the man who had been the Judge's close friend for many a year, his other self, his Damon, his Jonathan, his brother. That man was the man who had been the Scholarly Attorney. He would know.

I stood on the pavement, in front of the Mexican restaurant, where the juke box made the jellylike air palpitate, and paid my taxi and turned to look up at the third floor of the building which vibrated around the juke box. The signs were still up there, hung by wire from the little iron balcony, nailed to the wall, wooden boards painted different colors, some white, some red, some black, some green, with lettering in contrasted colors. A big sign hanging from the balcony said: *God is not mocked.* Another sign said: *Now is the Day of Salvation.*

Yeah, I said to myself, *he still lives here.* He lived there above a spick restaurant, and nigger children played naked in the next block among starving cats, and nigger women sat on the steps after the sun got low and fanned right slow with palm-leaf fans. I reached for a cigarette as I prepared to enter the doorway of the stairs, but found I had none. So I went into the restaurant, where the juke box was grinding to a halt.

To the old woman who stood behind the beer bar squatly like a keg and whose eyebrows were very thorny and white against the brown Mexican skin and black *rebozo,* I said, *"Cigarrillos?"*

"Que tipo?" she asked.

"Lucky," I said, and as she laid them before me, I pointed upward, and asked, "The old man, is he upstairs?" But she looked blank, so I said, *"Esta arriba el viejo?"* And felt pleased with myself for getting it off.

"Quien sabe?" she replied. *"Viene y va."*

So he came and went. Upon the Lord's business.

Then a voice said in tolerable English, from the shadows at the end of the bar, "The old man has gone out."

"Thank you," I replied to the old man, a Mexican, who was propped there in a chair. I turned back to the old woman, and said, "Give me a beer," and pointed at the spigot.

While I drank the beer I looked up above the counter and saw another one of the signs, painted on a big slab of plywood, or something of the sort, hanging from a nail. The background of the sign was bright red, there were blue scrolls of flowers in relief in the upper corners, the lettering was in black, high-lighted in white. It said: *Repent ye; for the Kingdom of Heaven is at hand. Matt., iii, 2.*

I pointed to the sign. *"De el?"* I asked. "The old man's huh?"
194

"*Si, señor,*" the old woman said. Then added irrelevantly, "*Es como un santito.*"

"He may be a saint," I agreed, "but he is also nuts."

"Nutz?"

"*Es loco,*" I explained, "*es nuts.*"

She said nothing to that, and I continued with the beer until the old Mexican at the end of the bar suddenly said, "Look, here comes the old one!"

Turning, I saw the black-clothed figure through the dingy glass of the door; then the door pushed open and he entered, older than I remembered, the white patches of hair hanging damply from under the old Panama hat, the steel-rimmed spectacles dangerously loose on the nose and the pale eyes behind, the shoulders stooped and drawn together as though pulled by the obscene, disjunctive, careful weight of the belly, as though it were the heavy tray, or satchel, worn by some hawker on a street corner. The black coat did not button across the belly.

He stood there, blinking gravely at me, apparently not recognizing me, for he had come from the last sunshine into the dimness of the restaurant.

"Good evening, *señor,*" the old Mexican said to the Scholarly Attorney.

"*Buenas tardes,*" the woman said.

The Scholarly Attorney took off his Panama and turned to the woman, and bowed slightly, with a motion of the head which stirred suddenly in my mind the picture of the long room in the white house by the sea, the picture of a man, the same but different, younger, the hair not gray, in that room. "Good evening," he said to the woman, and then turning to the old Mexican, repeated, "Good evening, sir."

The old Mexican pointed at me, and said, "He waits."

At that the Scholarly Attorney first, I believe, really observed me. But he did not recognize me, blinking at me in the dimness. Certainly he had no reason to expect to find me there.

"Hello," I said, "don't you know me?"

"Yes," he said, and continued to peer at me. He offered me his hand, and I took it. It was clammy in my grasp.

"Let's get out of here," I said.

"Do you want the bread?" the old Mexican asked.

The Scholarly Attorney turned to him. "Yes, thank you. If it is convenient."

The Mexican rose, went to the end of the counter, and took a largish brown paper bag full of something, and handed it to the other.

"Thank you," the Scholarly Attorney said, "thank you very much, sir."

"*De nada,*" the Mexican said, bowing.

"I wish you a good evening," the Scholarly Attorney said,

and bowed to the man, then to the woman, with an inclination of the head which again twitched the old recollection in me of the room in the white house by the sea.

Then I followed him out of the restaurant, into the street. Across the street lay the little park of trampled brown grass, now glistening with moisture, where the bums sat on benches and the pigeons cooed softly like an easy conscience and defecated in delicate little lime-white pinches on the cement around the fountain. I looked at the pigeons, then at the bulged-open bag, which, I observed, was full of bread crusts. "Are you going to feed the pigeons?" I asked.

"No, it is for George," he said, moving toward the doorway that led above.

"You keeping a dog?"

"No," he said, and led the way into the vestibule, and up the wooden stairs.

"What is George, then? A parrot?"

"No," he said, wheezily, for the stairs were steep, "George is an unfortunate."

That meant, I remembered, a bum. An unfortunate is a bum who is fortunate enough to get his foot inside a softy's door and stay there. If he gets a good berth he is promoted from bum to unfortunate. The Scholarly Attorney had, on several occasions before, taken in unfortunates. One unfortunate had popped the organist down at the mission where the Scholarly Attorney operated. Another unfortunate had lifted his watch and Phi Beta Kappa key.

So George was another unfortunate. I looked at the bread, and said, "Well, he must be pretty unfortunate if that's what he's got to eat."

"He eats some of it," the Scholarly Attorney said, "but that is almost accidental. He uses it in his work. But some of it slips down, I am sure, and that is why he is never hungry. Except for sweets," he added.

"How in God's name does he use bread crusts in his work and the bread crusts slip down his throat?"

"Do not take the name of the Lord in vain," he said. And added, "George's work, it's very clever. And artistic. You will see."

I saw. We got to the top of the second flight, turned in the narrow hall under the cracked skylight, and entered a door. There was what I took to be George, in one corner of the big, sparsely furnished room, sitting tailor-fashion on a piece of old blanket, with a couple of big mixing bowls in front of him, and a big piece of plywood about two feet by four lying on the floor by him.

George looked up when we came in and said, "I ain't got any more bread."

196

"Here it is," the Scholarly Attorney said, and took the brown bag to him.

George emptied the crusts into one of the bowls, then stuck a piece into his mouth and began to chew, soberly and purposively. He was a fair-sized, muscular man, with a hell of a strong-looking neck, and the tendons in his neck worked and pulled slickly while he chewed. He had yellow hair, almost gone, and a smooth, flat face with blue eyes. While he chewed he just looked straight ahead at a spot across the room.

"What does he do that for?" I asked.

"He's making an angel."

"Well," I said. And just then George leaned forward over one of the bowls and let the thoroughly masticated bread drop from his mouth into the bowl. Then he put another crust into his mouth.

"There is one he has finished," the Scholarly Attorney said, and pointed at another corner of the room, where another piece of plywood was propped up. I went to examine it. At one end, the figure of an angel, with wings and flowing drapery, had been executed in bas-relief in what looked like putty. "That one is just drying," the Scholarly Attorney said. "When it gets good and dry, he'll color it. Then he'll shellac it. Then the board will be painted and a motto put on it."

"Very pretty," I said.

"He makes statues of angels, too. See," and he went to a kitchen safe, and opened it, to expose a shelf of dishes and pots and another with an array of gaudy angels.

I examined the angels. While I did so, the Scholarly Attorney took a can of soup, a loaf of bread, and some soft butter out of the safe, put them on the table in the center of the room, and lighted one of the burners on the two-burner plate in the corner. "Will you join me in my supper?" he asked.

"No, thanks," I said, and continued to stare at the angels.

"He sometimes sells them on the street," he said, pouring out his soup into a stewpan, "but he can't bear to sell the best ones."

"Are these the best ones?" I asked.

"Yes," the Scholarly Attorney replied. And added, "They are pretty good, aren't they?"

I said, "Yes," for there wasn't anything else to say. Then, looking at the artist, asked, "Doesn't he make anything but angels? What about Kewpie dolls and bulldogs?"

"He makes angels. Because of what happened."

"What happened?"

"His wife," the Scholarly Attorney said, stirring the soup in the stewpan. "On account of her he makes angels. They were in a circus, you know."

"No, I didn't know."

"Yes, they were what you call aerialists. She did the angel act. She had large white wings, George said."

"White wings," George said through the bread, but it was a sound like *wite whungs,* and he fluttered his big hands like wings, and smiled.

"She fell down a long way with white wings which fluttered as though she were flying," the Scholarly Attorney continued, explaining patiently.

"And one day the rope broke," I affirmed.

"Something went wrong with the apparatus. It affected George very deeply."

"How about the way it affected her?"

The old man ignored my wit, and said, "He got so he could not perform his act."

"What was his act?"

"He was the man who got hanged."

"Oh," I said, and looked at George. That accounted for the big neck, no doubt. Then, "Did the apparatus go wrong with him and choke him or something?"

"No," the Scholarly Attorney said, "the whole matter simply grew distasteful to him."

"Distasteful?" I said.

"Yes, distasteful. Matters came to such a pass that he could not perform happily in his chosen profession. He dreamed of falling every time he went to sleep. And he would wet his bed like a child."

"Falling, falling," George said through the bread, with a sound like *fawing, fawing*, but still smiled brightly in the midst of the chewing.

"One day when he got up on his platform with the loop around his neck, he could not jump. In fact, he could not move at all. He sank down on the platform and crouched there weeping. They had to remove him bodily, and bring him down," the Scholarly Attorney said. "Then for some time he was completely paralyzed."

"It sounds," I said, "like that hanging act must have got pretty distasteful to him. As you so quaintly put it."

"He was completely paralyzed," he repeated, ignoring my wit. "Through no physical cause—if—" he paused—"anything ever comes to pass from a physical cause. For the physical world, though it exists and its existence cannot be denied without blasphemy, is never cause, it is only result, only symptom, it is the clay under the thumb of the potter and we—" He stopped, the gleam which had started up fitfully in the pale eyes flickered out, the hands which had lifted to gesticulate sank. He leaned above the gas plate and stirred the soup. He resumed, "The trouble was here," and he laid a finger to his own forehead. "It was his spirit. Spirit is always cause—I tell you—"

He stopped, shook his head, and peered at me before he said sadly, "But you do not understand."

"I reckon not," I agreed.

"He recovered from the paralysis," he said. "But George is not exactly a well man. He cannot bear high places. He will not look out the window. He covers his eyes with his hands when I lead him downstairs to go on the street to sell his artistic work. So I take him down only rarely now. He will not sit on a chair or sleep in a bed. He must always be on the floor. He does not like to stand. His legs simply collapse and he begins to cry. It is fortunate he had always had this artistic bent. It helps him to take his mind off things. And he prays a good deal. I taught him to pray. That helps. I get up and pray and he says the prayers after me. When he wakes at night with the dreams and cannot sleep."

"Does he still wet the bed?" I asked.

"Sometimes," the Scholarly Attorney replied gravely.

I looked at George. He was weeping silently, the tears running down his smooth, flat cheeks, but his jawbone was not missing a beat on the bread. "Look at him," I said.

The Scholarly Attorney looked at him. "Stupid, stupid," he muttered fretfully, shaking his head, so that an additional flake or two of dandruff floated down to the black serge collar, "stupid of me to be talking that way with him listening. Stupid—I'm an old man and I forget—" and clucking and muttering and shaking his head in that same fretful fashion he poured some soup into a bowl, took a spoon, and went to George. "Look, look," he said, leaning, with a spoon of soup thrust toward George's face, "good, it's good soup—soup—take some soup."

But the tears continued to flow out of George's eyes, and he didn't open his mouth. But the jaws weren't working on the bread now. They were just shut tight.

The old man set the bowl on the floor, and with one hand still holding the spoon to George's mouth, with the other he patted George on the back soothingly, all the while clucking with that distraught, henlike, maternal little noise. All of a sudden he looked up at me, the spectacles hanging over, and said, peevishly like a mother, "I just don't know what to do—he just won't take soup—he won't eat much of anything but candy—chocolate candy—I just don't know—" His voice trailed off.

"Maybe you spoil him," I said.

He put the spoon back into the bowl, which was on the floor beside him, then began to fumble in his pockets. He fished out, finally, a bar of chocolate, somewhat wilted from the heat, and began to peel back the sticky tinfoil. The last tears were running down George's cheeks, while he watched the process, with his mouth open in damp and happy expectation. But he did not grab with his chubby little mitts.

Then the old man broke off a piece of chocolate and placed it between the expectant lips, and peered into George's face while taste buds, no doubt, glowed incandescent in the inner dark and glands with a tired, sweet, happy sigh released their juices, and George's face took on an expression of slow, deep, inward, germinal bliss, like that of a saint.

Well, I almost said to the old man, *you said the physical was never cause, but a chocolate bar is physical and look what it's causing, for to look at that face you might think it was a bite of Jesus and not a slug of Hershey's had done it. And how you going to tell the difference, huh?*

But I didn't say it, for I was looking there at the old man, who was leaning over with his spectacles hanging and his coat hanging and his belly hanging from the leaning, and who was holding out another morsel of chocolate and who was clucking soft, and whose own face was happy, for that was the word for what his face was, and as I looked at him I suddenly saw the man in the long white room by the sea, the same man but a different man, and the rain of the squall driving in off the sea in the early dark lashed the windowpanes but it was a happy sound and safe because the fire danced on the hearth and on the windowpanes where the rain ran down to thread the night-black glass with silver, to mix the silver with the flames caught there, too, and the man leaned and held out something and said, "Here's what Daddy brought tonight, but just one bite now—" and the man broke off a piece and held it out—"just one bite, for your supper's near ready now—but after supper—"

I looked at the old man over there and my guts went warm and a big lump seemed to dissolve in my chest—as though I had carried a big lump around in there for so long I had got used to it and didn't realize it had been there until suddenly it was gone and the breath came easy. "Father," I said. "Father—"

The old man looked up at me and said querulously, "What— what did you say?"

Oh, father, father! but he wasn't in the long white room by the sea any more and never would be, for he had walked out of it—why? why? because he wasn't enough of a man to run his own house, because he was a fool, because—and he had walked a long way and up the steps to this room where an old man leaned with the chocolate in his hand and happiness—if that was what it was—momentarily on his face. Only it wasn't on his face now. There was just the faint peevishness of an old person who hasn't quite understood something said.

But I had come a long way, too, from that long white room by the sea, I had got up off that hearthrug before the fire, where I had sat with my tin circus wagon and my colored crayons and paper, listening to the squall-driven rain on the glass, and where Daddy had leaned to say, "Here's what Daddy brought tonight," and I had come to this room where Jack Burden leaned against the wall with a cigarette in his mouth. Nobody was leaning over him to give him chocolate.

So, looking into the old man's face, answering his querulous questions, I said, "Oh, nothing." For that was what it was. Whatever it had been was nothing now. For whatever was is not now, and whatever is will not be, and the foam that looks so sun-bright when the wind is kicking up the breakers lies streaked on the hard sand after the tide is out and looks like scum off the dishwater.

But there was something: scum left on the hard sand. So I said, "Yeah, there was something."

"What?"

"Tell me about Judge Irwin," I said.

He straightened up to face me, blinking palely behind the spectacles as he had blinked at me upon coming from light into the darkness of the Mexican restaurant below.

"Judge Irwin," I repeated, "you know—your old bosom pal."

"That was another time," he croaked, staring at me, holding the broken chocolate in his hand.

"Sure, it was," I said, and looking at him now, thought, *It sure-God was*. And said, "Sure, but you remember."

"That time is dead," he said.

"Yeah, but you aren't."

"The sinful man I was who reached for vanity and corruption is dead. If I sin now it is in weakness and not in will. I have put away foulness."

"Listen," I said, "it's just a simple question. Just one question."

"I have put it away, that time," he said, and made a pushing gesture with his hands.

"Just one question," I insisted.

He looked at me without speaking.

"Listen," I said, "was Irwin ever broke, did he ever really need money? Bad?"

He stared at me from a long way off, across the distance, beyond the bowl of soup on the floor, over the chocolate in his hand, through time. Then he demanded, "Why—why do you want to know?"

"To tell the truth," I burst out without meaning to, "I don't. But somebody does, and that somebody pays me the first of the month. It is Governor Stark."

"Foulness," he said, staring across whatever it was between us, "foulness."

"Was Irwin ever broke?" I said.

"Foulness," he affirmed.

201

"Listen," I said, "I don't reckon Governor Stark—if that is what all this foulness stuff is about—takes it to the Lord in prayer, but did you ever stop to think what a mess your fine, God-damned, plug-hatted, church-going, Horace-quoting friends like Stanton and Irwin left this state in? At least the Boss does something, but they—they sat on their asses—they—"

"All foulness!" the old man uttered, and swept his right arm wildly before him, the hand clutching the chocolate hard enough to squash it. A part of the chocolate fell to the floor. Baby got it.

"If you meant to imply," I said, "that politics, including that of your erstwhile pals, is not exactly like Easter Week in a nunnery, you are right. But I will beat you to the metaphysical draw this time. Politics is action and all action is but a flaw in the perfection of inaction, which is peace, just as all being is but a flaw in the perfection of nonbeing. Which is God. For if God is perfection and the only perfection is in nonbeing, then God is nonbeing. Then God is nothing. Nothing can give no basis for the criticism of Thing in its thingness. Then where do you get anything to say? Then where do you get off?"

"Foolishness, foolishness," he said, "foolishness and foulness!"

"I guess you are right," I said. "It is foolishness. But it is no more foolish than all that kind of talk. Always words."

"You speak foulness."

"No, just words," I said, "and all words are alike."

"God is not mocked," he said, and I saw that his head was quivering on his neck.

I stepped quickly toward him, stopping just in front of him. "Was Irwin ever broke?" I demanded.

He seemed about to say something, his lips opening. Then they closed.

"Was he?" I demanded.

"I will not touch the world of foulness again," he said, his pale eyes looking steadily upward into my face, "that my hand shall come away with the stink on my fingers."

I felt like grabbing him and shaking him till his teeth rattled. I felt like shaking it out of him. But you can't grab an old man and do that. I had gone at the whole thing wrong. I ought to have led up to it and tried to trick him. I ought to have wheedled him. But I always got so keyed up and on edge when I got around him that I couldn't think of anything but getting away from him. And then when I had left I always felt worse until I got him out of my mind. I had muffed it.

That was all I got. As I was going out, I looked back to see Baby, who had finished the piece of chocolate dropped by the old man, meditatively moving his hand about on the floor to locate any stray crumbs. Then the old man leaned slowly and heavily toward him, again.

Going down the stairs, I decided that even if I had tried to wheedle the old man I would probably have learned nothing. It wasn't that I had gone at it wrong. It wasn't that I burst out about Governor Stark. What did he know or care about Governor Stark? It was that I had asked him about the world of the past, which he had walked away from. That world and all the world was foulness, he had said, and he was not going to touch it. He was not going to talk about it, and I couldn't have made him.

But I got one thing. I was sure that he had known something. Which meant that there was something to know. Well, I would know it. Sooner or later. So I left the Scholarly Attorney and the world of the past and returned to the world of the present.

Which was:

An oblong field where white lines mathematically gridded the turf which was arsenical green under the light from the great batteries of floodlamps fixed high on the parapet of the massive arena. Above the field the swollen palpitating tangle of light frayed and thinned out into hot darkness, but the thirty thousand pairs of eyes hanging on the inner slopes of the arena did not look up into the dark but stared down into the pit of light, where men in red silky-glittering shorts and gold helmets hurled themselves against men in blue silky-glittering shorts and gold helmets and spilled and tumbled on the bright arsenical-green turf like spilled dolls, and a whistle sliced chillingly through the thick air like that scimitar through a sofa cushion.

Which was:

The band blaring, the roaring like the sea, the screams like agony, the silence, then one woman-scream, silver and soprano, spangling the silence like the cry of a lost soul, and the roar again so that the hot air seemed to heave. For out of the shock and tangle and glitter on the green a red fragment had exploded outward, flung off from the mass tangentially to spin across the green, turn and wheel and race, yet slow in the out-of-timeness of the moment, under the awful responsibility of the roar.

Which was:

A man pounding me on the back and screaming—a man with a heavy face and coarse dark hair hanging over his forehead—screaming, "That's my boy! That's Tom—Tom—Tom! That's him—and he's won—they won't have time for a touchdown now—he's won—his first varsity game and it's Tom won —it's my boy!" And the man pounded me on the back and grappled me to him with both arms, powerful arms, and hugged me like his brother, his true love, his son, while tears came into his eyes and tears and sweat ran down the heavy cheeks, and he screamed, "He's my boy—and there's not any like him

—he'll be All American—and Lucy wants me to stop him playing—my wife wants him to stop—says it's ruining him—ruining him, hell—he'll be All American—boy, did you see him—fast—fast—he's a fast son-of-a-bitch! Ain't he, ain't he?"

"Yes," I said, and it was true.

He was fast and he was a son-of-a-bitch. At least, if he wasn't a son-of-a-bitch yet, he had shown some very convincing talent in that line. You couldn't much blame Lucy for wanting to stop the football—his name always on the sporting page—the pictures—the Freshman Whiz—the Sophomore Thunderbolt—the cheers—the big fat hands always slapping his shoulder—Tiny Duffy's hand on his shoulder—yeah, Boss, he's a chip off the old block—the roadhouses—the thin-legged, tight-breasted little girls squealing. Oh, Tom, oh, Tom—the bottles and the tourist cabins—the sea-roar of the crowd and always the single woman-scream spangling the sudden silence like damnation.

But Lucy did not have a chance. For he was going to be All American. All American quarterback on anybody's team. If bottle and bed didn't manage to slow down too soon something inside that one hundred and eighty pounds of split-second, hair-trigger, Swiss-watch beautiful mechanism which was Tom Stark, the Boss's boy, the Sophomore Thunderbolt, Daddy's Darling, who stood that night in the middle of a hotel room, with a piece of court plaster across his nose and a cocky grin on his fine, clean, boyish face—for it was fine and clean and boyish—while all the hands of Papa's pals pawed at him and beat his shoulders, while Tiny Duffy slapped him on the shoulder, and Sadie Burke, who sat a little outside the general excitement in her own private fog of cigarette smoke and whisky fumes, a not entirely unambiguous expression on her riddled, handsome face, said, "Yeah, Tom, somebody was telling me you played a football game tonight."

But her irony was not the sort of thing Tom Stark would hear or understand, for he stood there in the midst of his own gleaming golden private fog of just being Tom Stark, who had played in a football game.

Until the Boss said, "Now you go on and get to bed, Son. Get your sleep, Son. Get ready to pour it on 'em next Saturday." And he laid his arm across the boy's shoulder, and said, "We're all mighty proud of you, boy."

And I said to myself: *If he gets his eyes starry with tears again I am going to puke.*

"Go on to bed, Son," the Boss said.

And Tom Stark said, "Sure," almost out of the side of his mouth, and went out the door.

And I stood there in what was the present.

But there was the past. There was the question. There was the dead kitty buried in the ash heap.

So I stood, later, in the embrasure of a big bay window and looked out as the last light ceased to gleam from the metallic leaves of magnolias and the creamy wash of the sea beyond dulled in the thickening dusk. Behind me was a room not very different from that other long white room giving on the sea —where now, at this moment perhaps, my mother would be lifting to the taffy-haired Young Executive that face which was still like a damned expensive present and which he had damned well better admire. But in the room behind me, scarcely lighted by the stub of a candle on the mounted shelf, the furniture was shrouded in white cloth, and the grandfather's clock in the corner was as severely mute as grandfather. But I knew that when I turned around there would also be, in the midst of the sepulchral sheetings and the out-of-time silence, a woman kneeling before the cold blackness of the wide fireplace to put pine cones and bits of light-wood beneath the logs there. She had said, "No, let me do it. It's my house, you know, and I ought to light the fire when I come back like this. You know, a ritual. I want to. Adam always lets me do it. When we come back."

For the woman was Anne Stanton, and this was the house of Governor Stanton, whose face, marmoreal and unperturbed and high, above black square beard and black frock coat, gazed down in the candlelight from the massy gold frame above the fireplace, where his daughter crouched, as though at his feet, rasping a match to light a fire there. Well, I had been in this room when the Governor had not been the marmoreal brow in the massy gold frame but a tall man sitting with his feet on the hearthrug with a little girl, a child, on a hassock at his feet, leaning her head against his knee and gazing into the fire while his large man hand toyed deliciously with the loose, silken hair. But I was here now because Anne Stanton, no longer a little girl, had said, "Come on out to the Landing, we're just going back for Saturday night and Sunday, just to build a fire and eat something out of a can and sleep under the roof again. It's all the time Adam can spare. And he can't spare that much often now." So I had come, carrying my question.

I heard the match rasp, and turned from the sea, which was dark now. The flame had caught the fat of the light-wood and was leaping up and spewing little stars like Christmas sparklers, and the light danced warmly on Anne Stanton's leaning face and then on her throat and cheek as, still crouching, she looked up at me when I approached the hearth. Her eyes were glittering like the eyes of a child when you give a nice surprise, and she laughed in a sudden throaty, tingling way. It is the way a woman laughs for happiness. They never laugh that way just when they are being polite or at a joke. A woman only laughs that way a few times in her life. A woman only laughs that way when something has touched her way down in the very quick of her being and the happiness just wells out as natural as breath and the first jonquils and mountain brooks. When a woman laughs that way it always does something to you. It does not matter what kind of a face she has got either. You hear that laugh and feel that you have grasped a clean and beautiful truth. You feel that way because that laugh is a revelation. It is a great impersonal sincerity. It is a spray of dewy blossom from the great central stalk of All Being, and the woman's name and address hasn't got a damn thing to do with it. Therefore, that laugh cannot be faked. If a woman could learn to fake it she would make Nell Gwyn and Pompadour look like a couple of Campfire Girls wearing bifocals and ground-gripper shoes and with bands on their teeth. She could set all society by the ears. For all any man really wants is to hear a woman laugh like that.

So Anne looked up at me with the glittering eyes and laughed that way while the firelight glowed on her cheek. Then I laughed, too, looking down at her. She reached up her hand to me, and I took it and helped her as she rose easy and supple—God, how I hate a woman who scrambles up off things—and I still held her hand as she swayed at the instant of reaching her full height. She was very close to me, with the laughter still on her face—and echoing somehow deep inside me—and I was holding her hand, as I had held it a long time back, fifteen years back, twenty years back, to help her up to stand swaying for an instant in front of me before I could put my arm around her and feel her waist surrender supplely to the cup of my hand. It had been that way. So now I must have leaned toward her and for an instant the trace of the laughter was still on her face, and her head dropped a little back the way a girl's head does when she expects you to put your arm around her and doesn't care if you do.

But all at once the laughter was gone. It was as though someone had pulled a shade down in front of her face. I felt as you do when you pass down a dark street and look up to see a lighted window and in the bright room people talking and singing and laughing with the firelight splashing and undulating over them and the sound of the music drifts out to the street while you watch; and then a hand, you will never know whose hand, pulls down the shade. And there you are, outside.

And there I was, outside.

Maybe I should have done it anyway, put my arm around her. But I didn't. She had looked up at me and had laughed that way. But not for me. Because she was happy to be there again in the room which held the past time—of which I had been a part, indeed, but was no longer a part—and to be kneeling on the hearth with the new heat of the fire laid on her face like a hand.

It had not been meant for me. So I dropped her hand which I had been holding and stepped back and asked, "Was Judge Irwin ever broke—bad broke?"

I asked it quick and sharp, for if you ask something quick and sharp out of a clear sky you may get an answer you never would get otherwise. If the person you ask has forgotten the thing, the quick, sharp question may spear it up from the deep mud, and if the person has not forgotten but does not want to tell you, the quick, sharp question may surprise the answer out of him before he thinks.

But it didn't work. Either she didn't know or she wasn't to be surprised out of herself. I ought to have guessed that a person like her—a person who you could tell had a deep inner certitude of self which comes from being all of one piece, of not being shreds and patches and old cogwheels held together with pieces of rusty barbed wire and spit and bits of string, like most of us—I ought to have guessed that that kind of a person would not be surprised into answering a question she didn't want to answer. Even if she did know the answer. But maybe she didn't.

But she was surprised a little. "What?" she asked.

So I said it again.

She turned her back to me and went to sit on the couch, to light a cigarette and face me again, looking levelly at me. "Why do you want to know?" she asked.

I looked right back at her and said, "I don't want to know. It is a pal wants to know. He is my best pal. He hands it to me on the first of the month."

"Oh, Jack—" she cried, and flung her newly lit cigarette across to the hearth, and stood up from the couch. "Oh, why do you have to spoil everything! We had that time back there. But you want to spoil it. We—"

"We?" I said.

"—had something then and you want to spoil it, you want to help him spoil it—that man—he—"

"We?" I said again.

"—wants to do something bad—"

"We," I said, "if we had such a damned fine time why was it you turned me down?"

"That hasn't anything to do with it. What I mean is—"

"What you mean is that it was a fine, beautiful time back then, but I mean that if it was such a God-damned fine, beautiful time, why did it turn into this time which is not so damned fine and beautiful if there wasn't something in that time which wasn't fine and beautiful? Answer that one."

"Hush," she said, "hush, Jack!"

"Yeah, answer me that one. For you certainly aren't going to say this time is fine and beautiful. This time came out of that time, and now you're near thirty-five years old and you creep out here as a special treat to yourself and sit in the middle of a lot of sheet-wrapped, dust-catching furniture in a house with the electricity cut off, and Adam—he's got a hell of a life, cutting on people all day till he can't stand up, and him tied up in knots himself inside and—"

"Leave Adam out of it, leave him out—" she said, and thrust her hands, palms out as though to press me off, but I wasn't in ten feet of her—"he does something anyway—something—"

"—and Irwin down there playing with his toys, and my mother up there with that Theodore, and me—"

"Yes, you," she said, "you."

"All right," I said, "me."

"Yes, you. With that man."

"That man, that man," I mimicked, "that's what all the people round here call him, what that Patton calls him, all those people who got pushed out of the trough. Well, he does something. He does as much as Adam. More. He's going to build a medical center will take care of this state. He's—"

"I know," she said, wearily, not looking at me now, and sank down on the couch, which was covered by a sheet.

"You know, but you take the same snobbish attitude all the rest take. You're like the rest."

"All right," she said, still not looking at me. "I'm snobbish, I'm so snobbish I had lunch with him last week."

Well, if grandfather's clock in the corner hadn't been stopped already, that would have stopped it. It stopped me. I heard the flame hum on the logs, gnawing in. Then the hum stopped and there wasn't anything.

Then I said, "For Christ's sake." And the absorbent silence sucked up the words like blotting paper.

"All right," she said, "for Christ's sake."

"My, my," I said, "but the picture of the daughter of Governor Stanton at lunch with Governor Stark would certainly throw the society editor of the *Chronicle* into a tizzy. Your frock, my dear—what frock did you wear? And flowers? Did you drink champagne cocktails? Did—"

"I drank a Coca Cola, and I ate a cheese sandwich. In the cafeteria in the basement of the Capitol."

"Pardon my curiosity, but—"

"—but you want to know how I got there. I'll tell you. I

went to see Governor Stark about getting state money for the Children's Home. And I—"

"Does Adam know?" I asked.

"—and I'm going to get it, too. I'm to prepare a detailed report and—"

"Does Adam know?"

"It doesn't matter whether Adam knows or not—and I'm to take the report back to—"

"I can imagine what Adam would say," I remarked grimly.

"I guess I can manage my own affairs," she said with some heat.

"Gee," I said, and noticed that the blood had mounted a little in her cheeks, "I thought you and Adam were always just like that." And I held my right hand up with forefinger and the next one side by side.

"We are," she said, "but I don't care what—"

"—and you don't care what *he*—" and I jerked a thumb toward the high, unperturbed, marmoreal face which gazed from the massy gold frame in the shadow—"would say about it either, huh?"

"Oh, Jack—" and she rose from the couch, almost fretful in her motion, which wasn't like her—"what makes you talk like that? Can't you see? I'm just getting the money for the Home. It's a piece of business. Just business." She jerked her chin up with a look that was supposed to settle the matter, but succeeded in unsettling me.

"Listen," I said, and felt myself getting hot under the collar, "business is not, it's worth your reputation to be caught running round with—"

"Running round, running round!" she exclaimed. "Don't be a fool. I had lunch with him. On business."

"Business or not, it's worth your reputation, and—"

"Reputation," she said. "I'm old enough to take care of my reputation. You just told me I was nearly senile."

"I said you were nearly thirty-five," I said, factually.

"Oh, Jack," she said, "I am, and I haven't done anything. I don't do anything. Not anything worth anything." She wavered there and with a hint of distraction lifted her hands to touch her hair. "Not anything. I don't want to play bridge all the time. And what little I do—that Home, the playground thing—"

"There's always the Junior League," I said. But she ignored it.

"—that's not enough. Why didn't I do something—study something? Be a doctor, a nurse. I could have been Adam's assistant. I could have studied landscape gardening. I could have—"

"You could make lampshades," I said.

"I could have done something—something—"

"You could have got married," I said. "You could have married me."

"Oh, I don't mean just getting married, I mean—"

"You don't know what you mean," I said.

"Oh, Jack," she said, and reached out and took my hand and hung on to it, "maybe I don't. I don't know what's wrong with me tonight. When I come out here sometimes—I'm happy when I come, I truly am, but then—"

She didn't say any more about it. By this time she had sunk her head to my chest, and I had given her a few comforting pats on the shoulder, and she had said in a muffled sort of way that I had to be her friend, and I had said, "Sure," and had caught some good whiffs of the way her hair smelled. It smelled just the way it always had, a good, clean, well-washed, little-girl-ready-for-a-party smell. But she wasn't a little girl and this wasn't a party. It definitely was not a party. With pink ice cream and devil's-food cake and horns to blow and we all played clap-in-and-clap-out and the game in which you sang about King William being King James's son and down on this carpet you must kneel sure as the grass grows in the field and choose the one you love best.

She stood there for a minute or two with her head on my chest, and you could have seen daylight between her and her friend, if there had been any daylight, while her friend gave her the impersonal and therapeutic pats on the shoulder. Then she walked away from him and stood by the hearth, looking down at the fire, which was doing fine now and making the room look what is called real homey.

Then the front door swung open and the wind off the cold sea whipped into the room like a great dog shaking itself and the fire leaped. It was Adam Stanton coming into that homey atmosphere. He had an armful of packages, for he had been down into the Landing to get our provisions.

"Hello," he said over the packages, and smiled out of that wide, thin, firm mouth which in repose looked like a clean, well-healed surgical wound but which when he smiled—if he smiled—surprised you and made you feel warm.

"Look here," I said quick, "way back yonder, any time, was Judge Irwin ever broke? Bad broke?"

"Why, no—I don't know—" he began, his face shading.

Anne swung round to look at him, and then sharply at me. I thought for an instant she was about to say something. But she didn't.

"Why, yes!" Adam said, standing there, still hugging the parcels.

I had speared it up from the deep mud.

"Why, yes," he repeated, with the pleased bright look on

210

his face which people get when they dredge up any lost thing from the past, "yes, let me see—I was just a kid—about 1913 or 1914—I remember father saying something about it to Uncle John or somebody, before he remembered I was in the room—then the Judge was here and he and father—I thought they were having a row, their voices got so high—they were talking about money."

"Thanks," I said.

"Welcome," he said, with a slightly puzzled smile on his face, and moved to the couch to let the parcels cascade to the safe softness.

"Well," Anne said, looking at me, "you might at least have the grace to tell him why you asked the question."

"Sure," I said. And I turned to Adam: "I wanted to find out for Governor Stark."

"Politics," he said, and the jaw closed like a trap.

"Yes, politics," Anne said, smiling a little sourly.

"Well, thank God, I don't have to mess with 'em," Adam said. "Nowadays, anyway." But he said it almost lightly. Which surprised me. Then added, "What the hell if Stark knows about the Judge being broke. It was more than twenty years ago. And there's no law against being broke. What the hell."

"Yeah, what the hell," Anne said, and looking at me, gave that not unsour smile.

"And what the hell are you doing?" Adam demanded laughing, and grabbed her by the arm and shook her. "Standing there when the grub needs cooking. Get the lead out, Sourpuss, and get going!" He shoved her toward the couch, where the packages were heaped.

She bent to scoop up a lot of packages, and he whacked her across the backsides, and said, "Get going!" And laughed. And she laughed, too, with pleasure, and everything was forgotten, for it wasn't often that Adam opened up and laughed a lot, and then he could be free and gay, and you knew you would have a wonderful time.

We had a wonderful time. While Anne cooked, and I fixed drinks and set the table, Adam snatched the sheet off the piano (they kept the thing in tune out there and it wasn't a bad one even yet) and beat hell out of it till the house bulged and rocked. He even took three good highballs before dinner instead of one. Then we ate, and he beat on the piano some more, playing stuff like "Roses Are Blooming in Picardy" and "Three O'Clock in the Morning," while Anne and I danced and cavorted, or he would mush it up and Anne would hum in my ear and we would sway sweet and slow like young poplars in the slightest breeze. Then he jumped up from the piano bench and whistling "Beautiful Lady," snatched her out

211

of my arms and swung her wide in a barrel-house waltz while she leaned back on his arm with her head back and eyes closed for a swoon, and with right arm outstretched, held delicately the hem of her fluttering skirt.

But Adam was a good dancer, even clowning. It was because he was a natural, for he never got any practice any more. And never had taken his share. Not of anything except work. And he could have had them crawling to him and asking for it. And once in about five years he would break out in a kind of wild, free, exuberant gaiety like a levee break streaming out to snatch the trees and brush up by the roots, and you would be the trees and brush. You and everybody around him. His eyes would gleam wild and he would gesture wide with an excess of energy bursting from deep inside. You would think of a great turbine or dynamo making a million revs a minute and boiling out the power and about to jump loose from its moorings. When he gestured with those strong, long, supple white hands, it was a mixture of Svengali and an atom-busting machine. You expected to see blue sparks. When he got like that they wouldn't have had the strength to crawl to him and ask for it. They would just be ready to fall back and roll over where they were. Only it didn't do them any good.

But that didn't come often. And didn't last long. The cold would settle down and the lid would go on right quick.

Adam didn't have the power on that night. He was just ready to smile and laugh and joke and beat the piano and swing his sister in the barrel-house waltz while the fire leaped on the big hearth and the high face gazed down from the massy gold frame and the wind moved in off the sea and in the dark outside clashed the magnolia leaves.

Not that in that room, with the fire crackling and the music, we heard the tiny clashing of the magnolia leaves the wind made. I heard it later, in bed upstairs in the dark, through the open window, the tiny dry clashing of the leaves, and thought, *Were we happy tonight because we were happy or because once, a long time back, we had been happy? Was our happiness tonight like the light of the moon, which does not come from the moon, for the moon is cold and has no light of its own, but is reflected light from far away?* I turned that notion around in my head and tried to make a nice tidy little metaphor out of it, but the metaphor wouldn't work out, for you have to be the cold, dead, wandering moon, and you have to have been the sun, too, way back, and how the hell can you be both the sun and the moon? It was not consistent. It was not tidy. *To hell with it,* I thought, listening to the leaves.

Then thought, *Well, anyway, I know now Irwin was broke.* I had dug that much up out of the past, and tomorrow I

212

would leave Burden's Landing and the past, and go back to the present. So I went back to the present.

Which was:

Tiny Duffy sitting in a great soft leather chair with his great soft hams flowing over the leather, and his great soft belly flowing over his great soft hams, and a long cigarette holder with a burning cigarette stuck jauntily out from one side of his face (the cigarette holder was a recent innovation, imitated from a gentleman who was the most prominent member of the political party to which Tiny Duffy gave his allegiance) and his great soft face flowing down over his collar, and a diamond ring on his finger, big as a walnut—for all of that was Tiny Duffy, who was not credible but true and who had obviously consulted the cartoons by *Harper's Weekly* in the files of the 'nineties to discover exactly what the successful politician should be, do, and wear.

Which was:

Tiny Duffy saying, "Jesus, and the Boss gonna put six million bucks in a hospital—six million bucks." And lying back in the chair, eyes dreamily on the coffered ceiling, head wreathed in the baby-blue smoke from the cigarette, murmuring dreamily, "Six million bucks."

And Sadie Burke saying, "Yeah, six million bucks, and he ain't planning for you to get your fingers on a penny of it."

"I could fix it up for him in the Fourth District. Mac-Murfee still got it sewed up down there. Him and Gummy Larson. But throw that hospital contract to Gummy and—"

"And Gummy would sell out MacMurfee. Is that it?"

"Well, now—I wouldn't put it that way. Gummy'd sort of talk reason into MacMurfee, you might say."

"And would sort of slip you a slice, Is that it, Tiny?"

"I ain't talking about me. I'm talking about Gummy. He'd handle MacMurfeee for the Boss."

"The Boss don't need anybody to handle MacMurfee. He'll handle MacMurfee when the time comes and it will be permament. For God's sake, Tiny, you known the Boss as long as you have and you still don't know him. Don't you know he'd rather bust a man than buy him? Wouldn't he, Jack?"

"How do I know?" I said. But I did know.

At least, I knew that the Boss was out to bust a man named Judge Irwin. And I was elected to do the digging.

So I went back to the digging.

But the next day, before I got back at the digging, a call came from Anne Stanton. "Smarty," she said, "smarty, you thought you were smart!"

I heard her laughing, way off somewhere at the end of the line, but the tingling came over the wire, and I thought of her face laughing.

"Yes, smarty! you found out from Adam how Judge Irwin was broke a long time ago, but I've found out something too!"

"Yeah?" I said.

"Yeah, smarty! I went to see old Cousin Mathilde, who knows everything about everybody for a hundred years back. I just got to talking about Judge Irwin and she began to talk. You just mention something and it is like putting a nickel in a music box. Yes, Judge Irwin was broke, or near it, then, but—and the joke's on you, Jackie-boy, it's on you, smarty-boy! And on your Boss!" And there was the laughter again, coming from far away, coming out of the little black tube in my hand.

"Yeah?" I said.

"Then he got married!" she said.

"Who?" I said.

"Who are we talking about, smarty? Judge Irwin got married."

"Sure, he was married. Everybody knew he was married, but what the hell has that—"

"He married money. Cousin Mathilde says so, and she knows everything. He was broke but he married money. Now, smarty, put that in your pipe and smoke it!"

"Thanks," I said. But before it was out of my mouth, I heard a clicking sound and she had hung up.

I lighted a cigarette and leaned back in the swivel chair, and swung my feet up to the desk. Sure, everybody knew, or had known, that Judge Irwin was married. Judge Irwin, in fact, had been married twice. The first woman, the woman he was married to when I was a little boy, had been thrown from a horse and couldn't do more than lie up in bed and stare at the ceiling or, on her good days, out the window. But she had died when I was just a kid, and I scarcely remembered her. But you almost forgot the other wife, too. She was from far away—I tried to remember how she looked. I had seen her several times, all right. But a kid of fifteen or so doesn't pay much attention to a grown woman. I called up an image of a dark, thin woman, with big dark eyes, wearing a long white dress and carrying a white parasol. Maybe it wasn't the right image at all. Maybe it was somebody else who had been married to Judge Irwin, and had come to Burden's Landing, and had received all the curious, smiling ladies in Judge Irwin's long white house, and had been aware of the eyes and the sudden silence for attention and then the new sibilance as she walked own the aisle in St. Matthew's just before the services began, and had fallen sick and had lived with a Negro nurse in an upstairs room for so long that people forgot about her very existence and were surprised when the funeral came to remind them of the fact that she had existed. But after the funeral there was nothing to remind them, for the body had gone back to whatever place it was she came from, and not even a chiseled name was left in the Irwin plot in the St. Matthew's graveyard, under the oaks and the sad poetic festoons of Spanish moss, which were garlanded on the boughs as though to prepare for the festivities of ghosts.

The Judge had had bad luck with his wives, and people felt sorry for him. Both of them sickly for a long time and then had died on his hands. He got a lot of sympathy for that.

But his second wife, I was told, was rich. That explained why the face I called up was not pretty—not the kind of face you would expect to find on Judge Irwin's wife—but a sallowish, thin face, not even young, with only the big dark eyes to recommend it.

So she had been rich, and that disposed of my notion that back in 1913 or 1914 the Judge had been broke and had stepped over the line. And that made Anne Stanton happy. Happy because now Adam hadn't played, even unwittingly, stool pigeon to the Boss. Well, if it made her happy, it made me happy too, I reckoned. And maybe she was happy to think, too, that Judge Irwin was innocent. Well, that would have made me happy too. All I was doing was trying to prove Judge Irwin innocent. I would be able, sooner or later, to go to the Boss and say, "No sale, Boss. He is washed in the Blood."

"The son-of-a-bitch is washed in whitewash," the Boss would say. But he'd have to take my word. For he knew I was thorough. I was a very thorough and well-trained research student. And truth was what I sought, without fear or favor. And let the chips fly.

Anyway, I could cross 1913 off the ticket. Anne Stanton had settled that.

Or had she?

When you are looking for the lost will in the old mansion, you tap, inch by inch, along the beautiful mahogany wainscoting, or along the massive stonework of the cellarage, and listen for the hollow sound. Then upon hearing it, you seek the secret button or insert the crowbar. I had tapped and had heard something hollow. Judge Irwin had been broke. "But, oh, no," Anne Stanton had said, "there is no secret hiding place there, that's just where the dumb-waiter goes."

But I tapped again. Just to listen to that hollow sound, even if it were just the place where the dumb-waiter went.

I asked myself: If a man needs money, where does he get it? And the answer is easy: He borrows it. And if he borrows it, he has to give security. What would Judge Irwin have given as security? Most likely his house in Burden's Landing or his plantation up the river.

If it was big dough he needed, it would be the plantation.

So I got in my car and headed up the river for Mortonville, which is the county seat of La Salle County, a big chunk of which is the old Irwin plantation where the cotton grows white as whipped cream and the happy darkies sing all day, like Al Jolson.

In the court house at Mortonville, I got hold of the abstract on the Irwin place. There it was, from the eighteenth-century Spanish grant to the present moment. And in 1907, there was the entry: *Mortgage, Montague Irwin to Mortonville Mercantile Bank, $42,000, due January 1, 1910.* Late in January, 1910, a chunk had been paid, about $12,000 and the mortgage redrawn. By the middle of 1912, interest payments were being passed. In March, 1914, foreclosure proceedings had been instituted. But the Judge had been saved by the bell. In early May there was an entry for the satisfaction of the mortgage in full. No further entries were on the abstract.

I had tapped again, and there was the hollow sound. When a man is broke there is always a hollow sound, like the tomb.

But he had married a rich wife.

But was she rich?

I had only the word of old Cousin Mathilde for that. And the evidence of Mrs. Irwin's sallow face. I decided to put in the crowbar.

I would check the date of marriage with the dates on the abstract. That might tell something. But whatever that said, I would put in the crowbar.

I knew nothing about Mrs. Irwin, not the date of her marriage, not even her name or where she came from. But that was easy. An hour in the newspaper files of the public library back in the city, looking at the society pages, which after more then twenty years were yellow and crumbling and somewhat less than gay or grand, and I came out again into the light of day with my collar wilted and my hands begrimed but with the words scribbled on the back of an envelope in my inside coat pocket: *Mabel Carruthers, only child of Le Moyne Carruthers, Savannah, Georgia. Married, January 12, 1914.*

The date of marriage didn't tell me much. True, the foreclosure proceedings had been instituted after the marriage, but that didn't prove that Mabel wasn't rich: it might have taken the Judge all the honeymoon to work around to the gross subject of the long green. The Judge would not have been crude. So she might have been rich as goose grease. But nevertheless, that night I was on the train for Savannah.

Twenty-five years is not a long time in the eye of God, but it damned near takes the eye of God to spy much about the inside story of even a leading citizen like Le Moyne Carruthers who has been dead twenty-five years. I didn't have the eye of God. I had to poke and pry and work newspaper files and pump the broken-down old bird who was city editor and cultivate the society of a fellow I had once known who was now a local hot-shot in the insurance game and get to know his friends. I ate roast duck stuffed with oysters and yams and that wonderful curry they make in Savannah, which tastes good even to a man like me who loathes food, and drank rye whisky, and walked down those beautiful streets General Oglethorpe laid out, and stared at the beautiful severe fronts of the houses, which were more severe than ever now, for the last leaves were off the arching trees of the streets and it was the season when the wind blows great chunks of gray sky in off the Atlantic which come dragging in so low their bellies brush the masts and chimney pots, like gravid sows crossing a stubble field.

I saw the Le Moyne Carruthers house. The old boy must have been rich, all right. And when he died in 1904 he had been rich, according to the probate of the will. But it was nine years between 1904 and 1913, and a lot can happen. Mabel Carruthers had lived high. That was the story. But they all said she could afford it. And, according to what I could pick up, there was no reason to believe that the uncle in New York, who was the executor of the will, hadn't known his business about handling Mabel's investments.

It looked absolutely level. But there is one thing you must never forget: the judgment docket book in the courthouse.

I did not forget it. And there I found the name of Mabel Carruthers. People had had some trouble getting money out of Mabel. But this didn't prove anything. Lots of rich girls are so rich they are just above paying bills and you have to pinch them to make them disgorge. But I noticed one thing. Mabel didn't get the bad habit until 1911. In other words, she had paid her bills all right for the first seven years she had had her money. Now, I argued, if this amiable failing had been merely the result of temperament and not of necessity, why did it come on her all at once? It had come on her all at once, and in a flock. Not that it was the corner grocer by himself. He had some fast company, for Mabel didn't like to pay Le Clerc in New York for a diamond pendant, and didn't like to pay her dressmaker, and didn't like to pay a local vintner for some pretty impressive stuff. Mabel had lived high, all right.

The last judgment was to the Seaboard Bank for a loan, amounting to $750. Small change for Mabel. Now there was no Seaboard Bank in Savannah. The telephone directory told me that. But an old fellow sitting in a split-bottom chair in the courthouse told me that the Seaboard Bank had been bought out by the Georgia Fidelity back about 1920. Down at the Georgia Fidelity, they told me, Yes, back in 1920. Who was president of the Seaboard then? Why, just a minute, and they'd find out. Mr. Percy Poindexter had been. Was he in Savannah? Well, they couldn't say for sure, times changed so fast. But Mr. Pettis would know, Mr. Charles Pettis, who was his son-in-law. Oh, you are welcome, sir. Quite welcome.

Mr. Percy Poindexter was not in Savannah now, and scarcely in this world, for after the exhalation of each breath you waited and waited for that delicate little contraption of matchwood and transparent parchment and filigree of blue veins to gather strength enough for one more effort. Mr. Poindexter reclined in his wheel chair, his transparent hands lying on the wine-colored silk of his dressing gown, his pale-blue eyes fixed on the metaphysical distance, and breathed each breath, saying, "Yes, young man—you have lied to me, of course—but I do not care—care why you want to know—it could not matter now—not to anyone—for they are all dead—Le Moyne Carruthers is dead—he was my friend—my dearest friend—but that was very long ago and I do not clearly recollect his face —and his daughter Mabel—I did what I could for her—even after her financial reverse she would have had enough to live decently—even in modest luxury—but no, she threw money away—always more—I loaned her a great deal at the bank— some of it I shamed her into paying—two or three notes I paid myself—for the memory of Le Moyne—and sent them canceled to her to shame her to discretion—but no—but she would come back to me without shame and stare at me out of her big eyes—they were dark and sullen and hot-looking like a fever—and would say, I want money—and at last I brought a note to judgment—to shame her—to frighten her —for her own good—for she spent money like water—she spent it in a fever to give balls and parties—to adorn herself, and she was plain—but she got a husband—from the West somewhere, a wealthy man, they said—he married her quickly and took her away—she died and was brought back here— the burial—it was a bad day and few came—not even in respect to Le Moyne—not even his friends, some of them—dead twelve years and they had forgotten him—people forget—"

The breath gave out, and for a long moment I thought there would not be any more. But some more came, and he said, "But—that—doesn't matter—either."

I thanked him, and shook his hand, which was like cold wax and left a chill in my palm, and went out and got into my rented car and drove back to the city, where I got a drink, not to celebrate but to take the ice out of my marrow, which not the weather but the old man had put there.

I had found out that Mabel Carruthers had been broke, but had married a rich man from the West. Or rather what in Savannah they called "the West." Well, that was a joke. No doubt the rich man from the West had married her for her money, too. There must have been some gay times as the truth emerged. I left Savannah the next day, but not before I had gone out to the cemetery to look at the Carruthers vault, where moss encroached upon the great name and the angel lacked one arm. But that didn't matter, for all the Carrutherses were inside now.

I had knocked and the sound had been very, very hollow. I sunk the crowbar in deeper. Judge Irwin had not paid off his mortgage in 1914 with his wife's money. What had he been doing in 1914 to get money? He had been running a plantation, and he had been, under Governor Stanton, the state's Attorney General. Well, you don't clear $44,000 a season off a cotton plantation (it was that amount he had paid, for the $12,000 he had paid in 1910 had come from a mortgage on the house in the Landing, I discovered, which he cleared at the same time as the plantation). And his salary as Attorney General had been $3,400. You don't get rich being an Attorney General in a Southern state. At least, you aren't supposed to.

But in March of 1915 the Judge had a good job, a very good job. He resigned as Attorney General to become counsel and vice-president for the American Electric Power Company, at a very good figure, $20,000 a year. There was no reason why they shouldn't have hired Judge Irwin, who was a good lawyer. But you could have hired a lot of good lawyers for a lot less then $20,000 a year. But a job in 1915 doesn't pay off the bailiff in 1914. When I knocked, it still sounded hollow.

So I took my one plunge in the stock market. One share of common stock of the American Electric Power Company, and it was cheap as dirt in the middle of the Depression. But it turned out to be a very expensive piece of paper. For a lot of people.

I was a coupon-clipper now, and I wanted to know how they were going to take care of my investment. So I took advantage of the stockholder's right. I went down to look at the stock records of the American Electric Power Company. From the literal dust of time, I dug up certain facts: In May, 1914, Montague M. Irwin had sold five hundred shares of common stock, at par, to Wilbur Satterfield and Alex Cantor, who were, I was to discover later, officials in the company. That meant Irwin had plenty in his pocket in late May to pay off the mortgages and have some change left over. But when had he got hold of the stock? That was easy. In March, 1914, the company had been reorganized and a big chunk of new stock issued. Irwin's stock was part of the new chunk. The boys had passed it to Irwin (or had he bought it?) and some of the other boys had bought it back. (Irwin must have kicked himself about selling it, for it began to climb shortly and kept on climbing for quite a spell. Had Messrs. Satterfield and

219

Cantor taken Irwin? They were old hands, on the inside. But Irwin had had to sell, and quick. There was the mortgage.)

Irwin had had the stock, and had sold it to Messrs. Satterfield and Cantor. So far, so good. But how had Irwin got the stock? Had they just given it to him out of the blue? Not likely. But why do people give you great big chunks of nice new stock issues with gold seals? The answer is simple: Because you are nice to them.

The job, then, was to find out if Judge Irwin—then state's Attorney General—had been nice to the American Electric Power Company. And that meant a long dig. With exactly nothing in the bottom of the hole. For the entire period when Judge Irwin was Attorney General, the American Electric Power Company had been an exemplary citizen. It had looked every man in the eye and had asked no favors. There was nothing in the hole.

Well, how had Judge Irwin spent his time as Attorney General?

The usual odds and ends, it developed. But there had almost been a case. The suit to recover royalties from the Southern Belle Fuel Company, which had operated, under lease, the state coal lands. There had been some hullabaloo about it, a little stir in the Legislature, and some editorials, and some speechmaking, but it was only the ghost of a whisper now. I was probably the only person in the state who knew about it now.

Unless Judge Irwin knew, and woke up in the night and lay in the dark.

It was all about the interpretation of a royalty contract between the state and the company. It was a very ambiguous contract. Perhaps it had been designed to be that way. In any case, by one reading, the state stood to gain about $150,000 in back royalties and God knew how much before the end of the contract period. But it was a very ambiguous contract. It was so ambiguous that, just as the shooting was about to start, the Attorney General decided that there was no case. "We feel, however," he said in his public statement, "that it is most reprehensible that those responsible for this agreement should have been so lax in their protection of the public interest as to accept the figures of this contract by which the state has sold for a song one of her richest assets. But we also feel that, since the contract exists and is susceptible of only one reasonable interpretation, this state, which wishes to encourage industry and enterprise within her borders, cannot do otherwise than bow to an arrangement which, though obviously unjust in its working, is binding in the law. And we must remember, even in circumstances such as this, that it is by law that justice herself lives."

220

I read that in the old *Times-Chronicle* of February 26, 1914, which was dated a couple of weeks before the foreclosure proceedings were instituted against the Irwin plantation. And about three weeks before the final reorganization of the American Electric and the issue of the new stock. The relationship was a relationship in time.

But is any relationship a relationship in time and only in time? I eat a persimmon and the teeth of a tinker in Tibet are put on edge. The flower-in-the-crannied-wall theory. We have to accept it because so often our teeth are on edge from persimmons we didn't eat. So I plucked the flower out of its cranny and discovered an astonishing botanical fact. I discovered that its delicate little root, with many loops and kinks, ran all the way to New York City, where it tapped the lush dung heap called the Madison Corporation. The flower in the cranny was the Southern Belle Fuel Company. So I plucked another little flower called the American Electric Power Company, and discovered that its delicate little root tapped the same dung heap.

I was not prepared to say that I knew what God and man are, but I was getting ready to make a shrewd guess about a particular man. But just a guess.

It was just a guess for a long time. For I had reached the stage in my problem where there was nothing to do but pray. That stage always comes. You do all you can, and you pray till you can't pray, and then you go to sleep and hope to see it all in the dream, by grace. "Kubla Khan," the benzine ring, Caedmon's song—they all came in the dream.

It came to me. Just as I fell asleep one night. It was only a name. A funny name. *Mortimer L. Littlepaugh.* The name drifted around inside my head, and I thought how funny it was and went to sleep. But when I woke up in the morning, my first thought was: *Mortimer L. Littlepaugh.* Then walking down the street that day, I bought a newspaper and as I looked at it I saw the name *Mortimer L. Littlepaugh.* Only it was not in the newspaper I had just bought. It was on a yellow, crumbling, old-cheese-smelling sheet, which I saw, suddenly, in my mind's eye. *Mortimer L. Littlepaugh's Death Accident, Coroner's Jury Decides.* That was it. Then, wavering slowly up, like a chunk of waterlogged wood stirred loose from the depth, the phrase came: *Counsel for the American Electric Power Company.* That was it.

I went back to the files, and found the story. Mortimer had fallen out of a hotel window, or rather, off the little iron-railed balcony outside the window. He had fallen from the fifth floor, and that was the end of Mortimer. At the inquest his sister, who lived with him, said he had recently been in ill health and had complained of fits of dizziness. There had been some theory of suicide, for Mortimer's affairs were in a tangled condition, it

221

developed, and the railing was high for an accidental fall. And there was a little mystery about a letter a bellhop swore Mortimer had given him the evening before his death, with a four-bit tip and instructions to go out and mail it immediately. The bellhop swore it had been addressed to Miss Littlepaugh. Miss Littlepaugh swore that she had received no letter. Well, Mortimer had been dizzy.

He had also been a lawyer for the American Electric. He had, I learned, been let out not long before Irwin came in. It did not sound too promising, but one more dead end wouldn't matter. There had been plenty of dead ends in the six or eight months I had been on the job.

But this was not a dead end. There was Miss Lily Mae Littlepaugh, whom, after five weeks, I tracked down to a dark, foul, fox-smelling lair in a rooming house on the edge of the slums, in Memphis. She was a gaunt old woman, wearing black spotted and stained with old food, almost past the pretense of gentility, blinking slowly at me from weak red eyes set in the age-crusted face, sitting there in the near-dark room, exuding her old-fox smell, which mixed with the smell of oriental incense and candle wax. There were holy pictures on the walls on every spare space, and in one corner of the room, on a little table, a sort of shrine, with a curtain of faded wine-colored velvet hanging above it, and inside not a Madonna or crucifix as you would expect from the other pictures, but a big image made of felt and mounted on a board which I at first took to be a sunflower pincushion swollen to an impractical size, but then realized was an image of the sun and its rays. The Life-Giver. And in that room. Before it, on the table, a candle burned fatly as though fed not merely from the wax but from the substance of the greasy air.

In the middle of the room was a table with a wine-colored velvet cover, and on the table a dish of poisonously colored hard candies, a glass of water, and a couple of long narrow horns or trumpets apparently made of pewter. I sat well back from the table. On the other side, Miss Littlepaugh studied me from the red eyes, then said, in a voice surprisingly strong, "Shall we begin?"

She continued to study me, then said, half as though to herself, "If Mrs. Dalzell sent you, I reckon—"

"She sent me." She had sent me. It had cost me twenty-five dollars.

"I reckon it's all right."

"It's all right," I said.

She got up and went to the candle on the little table, watching me all the while as though, in the last flicker of the light before she blew it out, I might turn out to be distinctly not all right.

Then she blew out the candle and made her way back to her chair.

After that, there were wheezings and moanings for a bit, the chink of metal which I took to be from one of the trumpets, some conversation, not very enlightening or edifying, from Princess Spotted Deer, who was Miss Littlepaugh's control, and some even more unenlightening remarks, given in a husky guttural, from somebody on the Other Side who claimed to be named Jimmy and to have been a friend of my youth. Meanwhile, the radiator against the wall at my back thumped and churned, and I inhaled the pitch darkness and sweated. Jimmy was saying that I was going to take a trip.

I leaned forward in the dark and said, "Ask for Mortimer. I want to ask Mortimer a question."

One of the trumpets chinked softly again, and the Princess made a remark I didn't catch.

"It's Mortimer L. I want," I said.

There was some huskiness in the trumpet, very indistinct.

"He is trying to come through," Miss Littlepaugh's voice said, "but the vibrations are bad."

"I want to ask him a question," I said. "Get Mortimer. You know Mortimer L. The L. is for Lonzo."

The vibrations were still bad.

"I want to ask him about the suicide."

The vibrations must have been very bad, for there wasn't a sound now.

"Get Mortimer," I said. "I want to ask him about the insurance. I want to ask him about the last letter he wrote."

The vibrations must have been terrific, for a trumpet banged on the table and bounced off to the floor, and there was a racket and rustling across the table, and when the electric light came suddenly on, there was Miss Littlepaugh standing by the door with her hand on the switch, staring at me out of the red eyes, while her breath hissed quite audibly over old teeth.

"You lied," she said, "you lied to me!"

"No, I didn't lie to you," I said. "My name is Jack Burden, and Mrs. Dalzell sent me."

"She's a fool," she hissed, "a fool to send you—you—"

"She thought I was all right. And she wasn't a fool to want twenty-five dollars."

I took out my wallet, removed some bills, and held them in my hand. "I may not be all right," I said, "but this stuff always is."

"What do you want?" she demanded, her eyes snatching from my face to the green sheaf and back to my face.

"What I said," I said. "I want to talk to Mortimer Lonzo Littlepaugh. If you can get him on the wire."

"What do you want from him?"

"What I said I wanted. I wanted to ask him about the suicide."

"It was an accident," she said dully.

I detached a bill and held it up. "See that," I said. "That is one hundred bucks." I laid it on the table, at the end toward her. "Look at it good," I said. "It is yours. Pick it up."

She looked fearfully at the bill.

I held up two more bills. "Two more," I said, "just like it. Three hundred dollars. If you could put me in touch with Mortimer, the money would be yours."

"The vibrations," she muttered, "sometimes the vibrations—"

"Yeah," I said, "the vibrations. But a hundred bucks will do a lot for the vibrations. Pick up that bill. It is yours."

"No," she said quickly and huskily, "no."

I took one of the two bills in my hand and laid it on top of the other one on the table.

"Pick it up," I said, "and to hell with the vibrations. Don't you like money? Don't you need money? When did you get a square meal? Pick it up and start talking."

"No," she whispered, cringing back against the wall, with a hand now on the doorknob as though she might flee, staring at the money. Then she stared at me, thrusting her head out suddenly, saying, "I know—I know you—you're trying to trick me—you're from the insurance company!"

"Wrong number," I said. "But I know about Mortimer's insurance policy. Suicide clause. That's why you—"

"He—" she hissed, and her gaunt face gathered itself into a contortion which might have been grief, or rage, or despair, you couldn't tell for sure—"he borrowed on his insurance—nearly all—and didn't tell me—he—"

"So you lied for almost nothing," I said. "You collected the insurance, all right, but there wasn't much left to collect."

"No," she said, "there wasn't. He left me—that way—he didn't tell me—he left me with nothing—and this——this—" She looked about the room, the broken furniture, the foulness, and seemed to shudder and shrink from it as though she had just entered and perceived it. "This—" she said, "this."

"Three hundred would help," I said, and nodded toward the two bills on the velvet.

"This—this—" she said, "he left me—he was a coward—oh, it was easy for him—easy—all he had to do was—"

"Was to jump," I finished.

That quieted her. She looked at me heavily for a long moment, then said, "He didn't jump."

"My dear Miss Littlepaugh," I said in the tone usually described as "not unkindly," "why don't you admit it? Your brother has been dead a long time and it will do him no harm.

The insurance company has forgotten about the business. Nobody would blame you for lying—you had to live. And—"

"It wasn't the money," she said. "It was the disgrace. I wanted him buried from the church. I wanted—" She stopped suddenly.

"Ah," I said, and glanced at the holy pictures around the wall.

"I was a believer then," she said, paused, corrected herself, "I believe now in God, but it is different."

"Yes, yes," I said soothingly, and looked at the one trumpet left on the table. "And, of course, it is stupid to think of it as a disgrace. When your brother did it—"

"It was an accident," she said.

"Now, Miss Littlepaugh, you just admitted the fact a second ago."

"It was an accident," she repeated, drawing back into herself.

"No," I said, "he did it, but it was not his fault. He was driven to it." I watched her face. "He had given years to that company, then they threw him out. To make room for a man who had done a wicked thing. Who drove your brother to his death. Isn't that true?" I got up, and took a step toward her. "Isn't that true?"

She looked at me steadily, then broke. "He did! He drove him to it, he killed him, he was hired because it was a bribe—my brother knew that—he told them he knew it—but they threw him out—they said he couldn't prove it, and threw him out—"

"Could he prove it?" I said.

"Oh, he knew, all right. He knew all about that coal business —he knew long before but he didn't know what they were going to do to him—they treated him fine then and knew all the time they would throw him out—but he went to the Governor and said—"

"What," I demanded, "what did you say?" And stepped toward her.

"To the Governor, he—"

"Who?"

"To Governor Stanton, and the Governor wouldn't listen, he just—"

I grasped the old woman's arm and held it tight. "Listen," I said, "you are telling me that your brother went to Governor Stanton and told him?"

"Yes, and Governor Stanton wouldn't listen. He wouldn't listen. He told him he couldn't prove anything, he wouldn't investigate, and that—"

"Are you lying?" I demanded, and shook the matchwood arm.

"It's true, true to God!" she exclaimed quivering in my grasp. "And that killed my brother. The Governor killed him. He went to the hotel and wrote the letter to me and told me, and that night—"

"The letter," I said, "what happened to the letter?"

"—that night—just before day—but waiting all night in that room—and just before day—"

"The letter," I demanded, "what happened to the letter?"

I shook her again, as she repeated, whispering, "Just before day—" But she came up out of the depth of the thought she was in, looked at me, and answered, "I have it."

I released my grip on her arm, thrust a bill into her clammy hand, and crushed her fingers upon it. "It's a hundred dollars," I said. "Give me the letter, and you can have the rest—three hundred dollars!"

"No," she said, "no, you want to get rid of the letter. Because it tells the truth. You're that man's friend." She stared into my face, prying into it, blinking, like an old person prying with feeble fingers to open a box. She gave up, and asked helplessly, "Are you his friend?"

"If he could see me right now," I said, "I don't imagine he would think so."

"You aren't his friend?"

"No," I said. She looked at me dubiously. "No," I said, "I'm not his friend. Give me the letter. If it is ever used it will be used against him. I swear it."

"I'm afraid," she said, but I could feel her fingers under my arm slowly working the bill I had thrust there.

"Don't be afraid of the insurance company. That was long back."

"When I went to the Governor—" she began.

"Did you go to the Governor, too?"

"After it happened—after everything—I wanted to hurt that man—I went to the Governor—"

"My God," I said.

"—and asked him to punish him—because he had taken a br'be—because he had killed my brother—but he said I had no proof, that that man was his friend and I had no proof."

"The letter, did you show him the letter?"

"Yes, I had the letter."

"Did you show Governor Stanton the letter?"

"Yes—yes—and he stood there and said, 'Miss Littlepaugh, you have sworn that you did not receive that letter, you have sworn to a lie, and that is perjury and the penalty for perjury ιs severe, and if that letter becomes known you will be prosecuted to the full extent of the law.'"

"What did you do?" I asked.

The head, which was nothing but gray hair and yellow skin stuck on bone, and old memories, wavered on its thin stalk of a neck, lightly and dryly as though touched by a breeze. "Do,"

226

she echoed, "do," shaking her head. "I was a poor woman, alone. My brother, he had gone away. What could I do?"

"You kept the letter," I affirmed, and she nodded.

"Get it," I said, "get it. Nobody will bother you now. I swear it."

She got it. She clawed into the mass of yellow and acid-smelling papers, and old ribbons and crumpled cloth in a tin trunk in the corner, while I leaned over her and fretted at the palsied incompetence of the fingers. Then she had it.

I snatched the envelope from her hand and shook the paper out. It was a sheet of hotel stationery—the Hotel Moncastello—dated August 3, 1915. I read:

Dear Sister:

I have been this afternoon to see Governor Stanton and told him how I have been thrown out of my job like a dog after all these years because that man Irwin was bribed to let up on the suit against the Southern Belle Fuel people and how he now has my place at a salary they never paid me and I gave them my heart's blood all these years. And they call him vice-president, too. They lied to me and they cheated me and they make him vice-president for taking a bribe. But Governor Stanton would not listen to me. He asked me for my proof and I told him what Mr. Satterfield told me months ago how the case had been fixed and how in our company they'd take care of Irwin. Now Satterfield denies it. He denies he ever told me, and looks me in the eye. So I have no proof, and Governor Stanton will not investigate.

I can do no more. I went as you know to the people who are against Governor Stanton in politics but they would not listen to me. Because that blackguard and infidel McCall who is their kingpin is tied up with Southern Belle. At first they were interested but now they laugh at me. What can I do? I am old and not well. I will never be any good again. I will be a drag on you and not a help. What can I do, Sister?

You have been good to me. I thank you. Forgive me for what I am going to do, but I am going to join our sainted Mother and our dear Father who were kind and good to us and who will meet me on the Other Shore, and dry every tear.

Good-bye until the happy day when we shall meet again in Light.

MORTIMER

P.S. I have borrowed against my insurance a good bit. On account of bad investments. But there is something left and if they know I have done what I am going to do they will not pay you.

P.S. Give my watch which was Father's to Julian, who will respect it even if he is only a cousin.

P.S. I could do what I am going to do easier if I were not trying to get the insurance for you. I have paid for the insurance and you ought to have it.

So the poor bastard had gone to the Other Shore, where Mother and Father would dry away every tear, immediately after having instructed his sister how to defraud the insurance company. There it all was—all of Mortimer Lonzo—the confusion, weakness, piety, self-pity, small-time sharpness, vindictiveness, all of it in the neat, spidery, old-fashioned bookkeeper's sort of hand a little shakier than ordinary perhaps, but with all the t's crossed and the i's dotted.

I replaced it in the envelope and put it in my pocket. "I am going to have it photostated," I said, "and you may have it back. I'll have the photostat certified. But you must make a statement before a notary about your visit to Governor Stanton. And—" I went over to the table and picked up the two bills and handed them to her—"there will be another one coming to you after you make your statement. Get your hat."

So I had it after all the months. For nothing is lost, nothing is ever lost. There is always the clue, the canceled check, the smear of lipstick, the footprint in the canna bed, the condon on the park path, the twitch in the old wound, the baby shoes dipped in bronze, the taint in the blood stream. And all times are one time, and all those dead in the past never lived before our definition gives them life, and out of the shadow their eyes implore us.

That is what all of us historical researchers believe.

And we love truth.

Chapter Six

IT WAS late March in 1937 when I went to see Miss Little-paugh in the foul, fox-smelling lair in Memphis, and came to the end of my researches. I had been on the job almost seven months. But other things had happened during that period besides my researches. Tom Stark, a sophomore, had made quarterback on the mythical All Southern Eleven and had cele-brated by wrapping an expensive yellow sport job around a culvert on one of the numerous new speedways which bore his father's name. Fortunately, a Highway Patrol car, and not some garrulous citizen, discovered the wreck, and the half-empty bottle of evidence was, no doubt, flung into the night to fall in the dark waters of the swamp. Beside the unconscious form of the Sophomore Thunderbolt lay another form, con-scious but badly battered, for in the big yellow expensive sport job Tom had had with him a somewhat less expensive yellow-headed sport job, named, it turned out, Caresse Jones. So Caresse wound up in the operating room of the hospital and not in the swamp. She obligingly did not die, though in the future she never would be much of an asset in a roadster. But her father was less obliging. He stamped and swore that he was going to have blood, and breathed indictments, jail, pub-licity, and lawsuits. His fires, however, were pretty soon banked. Not that it didn't cost some nice change. But in the end the whole transaction was conducted without noise. Mr. Jones was in the trucking business, and somebody pointed out to him that trucks ran on state roads and that truckers had a lot of contacts with certain state departments.

Tom wasn't hurt a bit, though he lay up in the hospital un-conscious for three hours while the Boss, pale as a starched sheet, and with his hair hanging and his eyes wild and sweat running down his cheeks, paced the floor of the waiting room and ground one fist into the palm of the other hand while his breath made a labored sound like the breath of his son in the room beyond. Then Lucy Stark got there—it was about four in the morning then—her eyes red but tearless and a stunned look on her face. They had quite a row. But that was after the word had come out that Tom was all right. Up till then he had paced the floor breathing hard, and she had sat and stared straight into the blackness. But when the word came, she got

229

rp and went over to stand before him, and say, "You must stop him." Her voice was scarcely above a whisper.

He stood there staring heavily, uncomprehendingly into her face, then put one hand out to touch her, like a bear touching something with a clumsy exploratory paw, and said, through dry lips, "He's—he's going to be all right, Lucy. He's all right."

She shook her head. "No," she said, "he's not all right."

"The doctor—" he took a lurching step toward her—"the doctor said—"

"No, he's not all right," she repeated. "And won't be. Unless you make him."

The blood suddenly flushed heavily into his cheeks. "Now look here, if you mean stopping football—if you—" That was an old story between them.

"Oh, it's not just football. That's bad enough, thinking he's a hero, that there's nothing else in the world—but it's everything that goes with it—he's wild and selfish and idle and—"

"No boy of mine's going to be a sissy, now. That's what you want!"

"I would rather see him dead at my feet than what your vanity will make him."

"Don't be a fool!"

"You will ruin him." Her voice was quiet and even.

"Hell, let him be a man. I never had any fun growing up. Let him have some fun! I want him to have some fun. I used to see people having fun and never had any. I want him to—"

"You will ruin him," she said, with her voice as quiet and even as doom.

"God damn it!—look here—" he began, but by that time I had sneaked out the door and had closed it softly behind me.

But Tom's accident wasn't all that happened that winter.

There was Anne Stanton's project of getting state money for the Children's Home. She got a good handout, and was pleased as punch with herself. She claimed she was about to get a two-year grant, which was badly needed, she said, and was probably right, for the springs of private charity had nigh dried up about 1929 and weren't running more than a trickle even seven years or so later.

There were stirrings down in the Fourth District, where MacMurfee still had things by the short ones. His representative got up in Congress in Washington, which was far off but not as far off as the moon, and aired his views about the Boss and made headlines over the country; so the Boss bought himself a big wad of radio time and aired his views of Congressman Petit and treated the nation to a detailed biography, in several installments, of Congressman Petit, who, it developed from the work of the Boss's research department, had thrown a grenade in a glass house. The Boss didn't answer anything

Petit had said, he simply took care of the sayer. The Boss knew all about the so-called fallacy of the *argumentum ad hominem.* "It may be a fallacy," he said, "but it is shore-God useful. If you use the right kind of *argumentum* you can always scare the *hominem* into a laundry bill he didn't expect."

Petit didn't come off too well, but you had to hand it to MacMurfee, he never quit trying. Tiny Duffy didn't quit trying, either. He was hell-bent on selling the Boss on the idea of throwing the basic contract for the hospital to Gummy Larson, who was a power in the Fourth District and would no doubt persuade MacMurfee, or, to speak more plainly, would sell him out. The Boss would listen to Tiny about as attentively as you listen to rain on the roof, and say, "Sure, Tiny, sure, we'll talk about it some time," or "God damn it, Tiny, change your record." Or he might say nothing in reply, but would look at Tiny in a massive, deep-eyed, detached, calculating way, as though he were measuring him for something, and not say a word, till Tiny's voice would trail off into a silence so absolute you could hear both men's breathing, Tiny's breath sibilant, quick, and shallow for all his bulk, the Boss's steady and deep.

The Boss, meanwhile, was making that hospital his chief waking thought. He took trips up East to see all the finest, biggest ones, the Massachusetts General, the Presbyterian in New York, the Philadelphia General, and a lot more. "By God," he would say, "I don't care how fine they are, mine's gonna be finer, and I don't care how big they are, mine's gonna be bigger, and any poor bugger in this state can go there and get the best there is and not cost him a dime." When he was off on his trips he spent his time with doctors and architects and hospital superintendents, and never a torch singer or a bookmaker. And when he was back home, his office was nothing but a pile of blueprints and notebooks full of his scribbling and books on architecture and heating systems and dietetics and hospital management. You would come in, and he would look up at you and begin talking right in the middle of a beat as though you had been there all the time, "Now up at the Massachusetts General they've got—" It was his baby, all right.

But Tiny wouldn't give up.

One night I came into the Mansion, saw Sugar-Boy, who was lounging in the high, chastely proportioned hall with a sheet of newspaper across his knee, a dismantled .38 in his hand, and a can of gun oil on the floor, asked him where the Boss was, watched him while his lips tortured themselves to speak and the spit flew, realized from the jerk of his head that the Boss was back in the library, and went on back to knock on the big door. As soon as I opened the door I ran right into the Boss's eyes like running into the business end of a double-barreled 10-gauge shotgun at three paces, and halted. "Look!"

he commanded, heaving his bulk up erect on the big leather couch where he had been propped, "look!"

And he swung the double-barrel round to cover Tiny, who stood at the hearthrug before him and seemed to be melting the tallow down faster than even the log fire on the bricks would have warranted.

"Look," he said to me, "this bastard tried to trick me, tried to smuggle that Gummy Larson in here to talk to me, gets him all the way up here from Duboisville and thinks I'll be polite. But the hell I was polite." He swung to Tiny again. "Was I, was I polite?"

Tiny did not manage to utter a sound.

"Was I, God damn it?" the Boss demanded.

"No," Tiny said, as from the bottom of a deep well.

"I was not," the Boss said. "I didn't let him get across that doorsill." He pointed at the closed door beyond me. "I told him if I ever wanted to see him I'd send for him, and to get the hell out. But you——" and he snapped out a forefinger at Tiny—"you——"

"I thought——"

"You thought you'd trick me—trick me into buying him. Well, I'm not buying him. I'm going to bust him. I've bought too many sons-of-bitches already. Bust 'em and they'll stay busted, but buy 'em and you can't tell how long they'll stay bought. I bought too many already. I made a mistake not busting you. But I figured you'd stay bought. You're scared not to."

"Now, Boss," Tiny said, "now, Boss, that ain't fair, you know how all us boys feel about you. And all. It ain't being scared, it's——"

"You damned well better be scared," the Boss said, and his voice was suddenly sweet and low. Like a mother whispering to her child in the crib.

But there was new sweat on Tiny.

"Now get out!" the Boss said in a more positive tone.

I looked at the door after it had been closed upon the retreating form, and said, "You certainly do woo your constituency."

"Christ," he said, and sank back on the leather of the couch and shoved some of the blueprints aside. He reached up and tried to unbutton his collar, fumbled, got impatient and snapped off the button and jerked the tie loose. He twisted his heavy head a little from side to side, as though the collar had been choking him.

"Christ," he said, almost pettishly, "can't he understand I don't want him messing round with this thing?" And he shoved at the blueprints again.

"What do you expect?" I asked. "There's six million dollars

involved. Did you ever see the flies stay away from the churn at churning time?"

"He better stay away from this churn."

"He's just being logical. Obviously, Larson is ready to sell out MacMurfee. For a contract. He is a competent builder. He—"

He lunged up to a sitting position, stared at me and demanded, "Are you in on this?"

"It is nothing to me," I said, and shrugged. "You can build it with your bare hands for all of me. I merely said that, given his premises, Tiny is logical."

"Can't you understand?" he demanded, searching my face. "Damn it, can't you understand either?"

"I understand what I understand."

"Can't you understand?" he demanded, and heaved up from the couch, and the instant he was on his feet, from the slight sway of his posture, I knew he had been drinking. He stepped to me and seized my lapel, and shook me a little, fixing his eyes upon my face—now close to him, I could see that they were bloodshot—and saying, "Can't you understand either? I'm building that place, the best in the country, the best in the world, and a bugger like Tiny is not going to mess with it, and I'm going to call it the Willie Stark Hospital and it will be there a long time after I'm dead and gone and you are dead and gone and all those sons-of-bitches are dead and gone, and anybody, no matter he hasn't got a dime, can go there—"

"And will vote for you," I said.

"I'll be dead," he said, "and you'll be dead, and I don't care whether he votes for me or not, he can go there and—"

"And bless your name," I said.

"Damn it!" he shook me hard, crumpling my lapel in his big hand, "you stand there grinning like that—get that grin off your face—get it off or I'll—"

"Listen," I said, "I'm not any of your scum, and I'm still grinning when I please."

"Jack—hell, Jack—you know I don't mean that—it's just you stand there and grin. Damn it, can't you understand? Can't you?" He held the lapel and thrust the big face at me, his eyes gouging into mine, saying, "Can't you? Can't you see I'm not going to let those bastards muck with it? The Willie Stark Hospital? Can't you see? And I'm going to get me the damned best man there is to run it. Yes, sir! The best there is. Yes, sir, up in New York they told me to get him, he was the man. And, Jack, you—"

"Yeah?" I asked.

"You're going to get him."

I disengaged myself from the grasp on my lapel, straightened it, and dropped into a chair. "Get who?" I asked.

"Dr. Stanton," he said, "Dr. Adam Stanton."

I almost bounced right out of the chair. The ash off my cigarette fell down my shirt front. "How long have you been having these symptoms?" I asked. "You been seeing any pink elephants?"

"You get Stanton," he said.

"You are hearing voices," I said.

"You get him," he repeated dourly.

"Boss," I said, "Adam is an old pal of mine. I know him like a brother. And I know he hates your guts."

"I'm not asking him to love me. I'm asking him to run my hospital. I'm not asking anybody to love me. Not even you."

"We all love you," I mimicked Tiny, "you know how all us boys feel."

"Get him," he said.

I stood up, stretched, yawned, moved toward the door. "I am leaving," I declared. "Tomorrow, when you are in possession of your faculties, I'll hear what you've got to say."

And I shut the door behind me.

Tomorrow, when he was in full possession of his faculties, I heard what he had to say, and it was: "Get Stanton."

So I went to the shabby little monastic apartment where the grand piano glittered like a sneer in the midst of near-squalor and the books and papers piled on chairs and the old coffee cup with dried dregs inside which the colored girl had forgotten to pick up, and where the friend of my youth received me as though he were not a Success and I were not a Failure (both spelled with capital letters), laid his hand on my shoulder, pronounced my name, looked at me from the ice-water-blue, abstract eyes which were a reproach to all uncertain, twisted, and clouded things and were as unwavering as conscience. But the smile on his face, unsealing almost tentatively the firm suture of the mouth, put a warmth in you, a shy warmth like you discover with surprise in the winter sunshine in late February. That smile was his apology for being what he was, for looking at you the way he did, for seeing what he saw. It did not so much forgive you, and the world, as ask forgiveness for himself for the crime of looking straight at whatever was before him, which might be you. But he didn't smile often. He smiled at me not because I was what I was but because I was the Friend of His Youth.

The Friend of Your Youth is the only friend you will ever have, for he does not really see you. He sees in his mind a face which does not exist any more, speaks a name—Spike, Bud, Snip, Red, Rusty, Jack, Dave—which belongs to that now nonexistent face but which by some inane and doddering confusion of the universe is for the moment attached to a not too happily met and boring stranger. But he humors the drooling doddering confusion of the universe and continues to address politely that dull stranger by the name which properly belongs to the boy face and to the time when the boy voice called thinly across the late afternoon water or murmured by a campfire at night or in the middle of a crowded street said, "Gee, listen to this—'On Wenlock Edge the wood's in trouble; His forest fleece the Wrekin heaves—' " the Friend of Your Youth is your friend because he does not see you any more.

And perhaps he never saw you. What he saw was simply part of the furniture of the wonderful opening world. Friendship was something he suddenly discovered and had to give away as a recognition of and payment for the breathlessly opening world which momently divulged itself like a moonflower. It didn't matter a damn to whom he gave it, for the fact of giving was what mattered, and if you happened to be handy you were automatically endowed with all the appropriate attributes of a friend and forever after your reality is irrelevant. The Friend of Your Youth is the only friend you will ever have, for he hasn't the slightest concern with calculating his interest or your virtue. He doesn't give a damn, for the moment, about Getting Ahead or Needs Must Admiring the Best, the two official criteria in adult friendships, and when the boring stranger appears, he puts out his hand and smiles (not really seeing your face) and speaks your name (which doesn't really belong to your face), saying, "Well, Jack, damned glad you came, come on in, boy!"

So I sat in one of his broken-down easy chairs, after he had cleared the books out, and drank his whisky, and waited for the moment when I was going to say, "Now, listen here, I'm going to tell you something and don't you start yelling till I finish."

He didn't yell till I had finished. Not that I took long to finish. I said, "Governor Stark wants you to be director of the new hospital and medical center."

He didn't, to be precise, yell then. He didn't make a sound. He looked at me for nearly a minute, with an unsmiling clinical eye as though my symptoms merited special attention; then he slowly shook his head. "Better think it over," I said, "maybe it's not as bad as it sounds, there may be some angles—" But I let my voice trail off, watching him shake his head again and smile now with the smile which did not forgive me but humbly asked me to forgive him for not being like me, for not being like everybody else, for not being like the world.

If he had not smiled. If he had smiled but had smiled a confident to-hell-with-you, satirical smile. Or even a smile forgiving me. If he had not smiled the smile which humbly, but with dignity, begged me to forgive him, then things might have been different. But he smiled that way out of the fullness of whatever

235

it was he had, out of the depth of the idea he lived by—whatever the hell it was or whyever the hell he lived that way—and things were the way they turned out to be. Giving that smile, he was like a man who stops to give a beggar a buck and in opening his wallet lets the beggar catch sight of the big roll. If the beggar hadn't seen the big roll he would never have followed the man down the street, waiting for the block without the street lamp. Not so much because he wants the roll as because he now cannot endure the man who has it and gave him a buck.

For as he smiled and said, "But I'm not interested in the angles," I did not feel that shy warmth as of the winter sunshine which I had always felt before when he smiled, but suddenly felt something else, which I didn't have a name for but which was like the winter itself and not the winter sunshine, like the stab of an icicle through the heart. And I thought: *All right, you smile like that—you smile like that—*

So, even as the thought vanished—if a thought can ever be said to vanish, for it rises out of you and sinks back into you—so I said, "But you don't know what the angles are. For instance, the Boss expects you to write your ticket."

"The Boss," he repeated, and on the word his upper lip curled more than customary to expose the teeth, and the sibilance seemed exaggerated, "need not expect to buy me. I have—" he looked about the room at the clutter and near-squalor—"everything I want."

"The Boss isn't any fool. You don't think he was trying to buy you?"

"He couldn't," he said.

"What do you think he was trying to do?"

"Threaten me. That would be next."

"No," I nodded, "not that. He couldn't scare you."

"That is what he seems to depend on. The bribe or the threat."

"Guess again," I said.

He rose from his chair, took a couple of restless paces across the frayed green carpet, then swung to face me. "He needn't think he can flatter me," he said, fiercely.

"Nobody could flatter you," I said, softly, "nobody in the world. And do you know why?"

"Why?"

"Listen, pal, there was a man named Dante, who said that the truly proud man who knew his own worth could never commit the sin of envy, for he could believe that there was no one for him to envy. He might just as well have said that the proud man who knew his own worth would not be susceptible to flattery, for he would believe that there was nothing anybody else

236

could tell him about his own worth he didn't know already. No, you couldn't be flattered."

"Not by him, anyway," Adam said grimly.

"Not by anybody," I said. "And he knows it."

"What does he try for, then? Does he think I—"

"Guess again," I said.

He stood there in the middle of the frayed green carpet and stared at me, head slightly lowered, with the slightest shade—not of doubt or perturbation—over the fine abstract blue of the eyes. It was just the shade of question, of puzzlement.

But that is something. Not much, but something. It is not the left to the jaw and it does not rock them on their heels. It does not make the breath come sharp. It is just the tap on the nose, the scrape across with the rough heel of the glove. Nothing lethal, just a moment's pause. But it is an advantage. Push it.

So I repeated, "Guess again."

He did not answer, looking at me, with the shade deeper like a cloud passing suddenly over blue water.

"All right," I said, "I'll tell you. He knows you are the best around, but you don't cash in on it. So obviously, you don't want money, or you would charge folks something like the others in the trade or would hang on to what you do take. You don't want fun, or you would get some, for you are famous, relatively young, and not crippled. You don't want comfort, or you would quit working yourself like a navvy and wouldn't live in this slum. But he knows what you want."

"I don't want anything he can give me," Adam affirmed.

"Are you sure, Adam?" I said. "Are you sure?"

'Damn it—" he began, and the blood was up in his cheeks.

"He knows what you want," I cut in. "I can put it in a word, Adam."

"What?"

"You want to do good," I said.

That stopped him. His mouth was open like a fish's gaping for air.

"Sure," I said, "that's it. He knows your secret."

"I don't see what—" he began, fiercely again.

But I cut in, saying, "Easy now, it's no disgrace. It's just eccentric. That you can't see somebody sick without having to put your hands on him. That you can't see somebody with something broken without wanting to fix it. Somebody with something rotten inside him without wanting to take a knife in your strong, white, and damned well-educated fingers, pal, and cut it out. It is merely eccentric, pal. Or maybe it is a kind of super-sickness you've got yourself."

"There's a hell of a lot of sick people," he said glumly, "but I don't see—"

"Pain is evil," I said, cheerfully.

237

"Pain is *an* evil," he said, "but it is not evil—it is not evil in itself," and took a step toward me, looking at me like an enemy.

"That's the kind of question I don't debate when I've got the toothache," I retorted, "but the fact remains that you are the way you are. And the Boss—" I delicately emphasized the word *Boss*—"knows it. He knows what you want. He knows your weakness, pal. You want to do good, and he is going to let you do good in wholesale lots."

"Good," he said, wolfishly, and twisted his long, thin upper lip, "good—that's a hell of a word to use around where he is."

"Is it?" I asked casually.

"A thing does not grow except in its proper climate, and you know what kind of a climate that man creates. Or ought to know."

I shrugged. "A thing is good in itself—if it is good. A guy gets ants in his pants and writes a sonnet. Is the sonnet less of a good—if it is good, which I doubt—because the dame he got the ants over happened to be married to somebody else, so that his passion, as they say, was illicit? Is the rose less of a rose because—"

"You are completely irrelevant," he said.

"So I am irrelevant," I said, and got out of the chair. "That's what you always used to say when I got you in a corner in an argument a thousand years ago when we were boys and argued all night. Could a first-class boxer whip a first-class wrestler? Could a lion whip a tiger? Is Keats better than Shelley? The good, the true, and the beautiful. Is there A God? We argued all night and I always won, but you—you bastard—" and I slapped him on the shoulder—"you always said I was irrelevant. But little Jackie is never irrelevant. Nor is he immaterial, and —" I looked around, scooped up my hat and coat—"I am going to leave you with that thought and—"

"A hell of a thought it is," he said, but he was grinning now, he was my pal now, he was the Friend of My Youth.

But I ignored him anyway, saying—"You can't say I don't put the cards on the table, me and the Boss, but I'm hauling out, for I catch the midnight to Memphis, where I am going to interview a medium."

"A medium?" he echoed.

"An accomplished medium named Miss Littlepaugh, and she is going to give me word from the Other Shore that the Boss's hospital is going to have a dark, handsome, famous, son-of-a-bich of a director named Stanton." And with that I slammed his door and was running and stumbling down the dark stairs, for it was the kind of apartment house where the bulb burns out and nobody ever puts a new one in and there is always a kiddie car left on a landing and the carpet is worn to ribbons and the air smells dankly of dogs, diapers, cabbage, old women, burnt grease, and the eternal fate of man.

I stood in the dark street and looked back at the building. The shade of a window was up and I looked in where a heavy, bald man in shirt sleeves sat at a table in what is called a "dinette" and slumped above a plate like a sack propped in a chair, while a child stood at his elbow, plucking at him, and a woman in a slack colorless dress and hair stringing down brought a steaming saucepan from the stove, for Poppa had come home late as usual with his bunion hurting, and the rent was past due and Johnnie needed shoes and Susie's report card wasn't any good and Susie stood at his elbow, plucking at him feebly, and staring at him with her imbecilic eyes and breathing through her adenoids, and the Maxfield Parrish picture was askew on the wall with its blues all having the savage tint of copper sulphate in the glaring light from the unshaded bulb hanging from the ceiling. And somewhere else in the building a dog barked, somewhere else a baby was crying in automatic gasps. And that was Life and Adam Stanton lived in the middle of it, as close as he could get to it; he snuggled up to Life, breathing the cabbage smell, stumbling on the kiddie car, bowing to the young just-married, gum-chewing, hand-holding couple in the hall, hearing through the thin partition the sounds made by the old woman who would be dead (it was cancer he had told me) before summer, pacing the frayed green carpet among the books and broken-down chairs. He snuggled up to Life, to keep warm perhaps, for he didn't have any life of his own—just the office, the knife, the monastic room. Or perhaps he didn't snuggle to keep warm. Perhaps he leaned over Life with his hand on the pulse, watching from the deep-set, abstract, blue, clinical eyes, slightly shadowed, leaning ready to pop in the pill, pour the potion, apply the knife. Perhaps he had to be close in order to keep a reason for the things he did. To make the things he did be themselves Life. And not merely a delightful exercise of technical skill which man had been able to achieve because he, of all the animals, had a fine thumb.

Which is nonsense, for whatever you live is Life. That is something to remember when you meet the old classmate who says, "Well, now on our last expedition up the Congo—" or the one who says, "Gee, I got the sweetest little wife and three of the swellest kids ever—" You must remember it when you sit in hotel lobbies or lean over bars to talk to the bartender or stand in a dark street at night, in early March, and stare into a lighted window. And remember little Susie in there has adenoids and the bread is probably burned, and turn up the street, for the time has come to hand me down that walking cane, for I got to catch that midnight train, for all my sin is taken away. For whatever you live is Life.

As I turned away, there was the wild burst of music from up in the building, louder than the baby's crying, shaking the mortar out of the old brickwork. It was Adam's piano.

I caught the train for Memphis, stayed three days, had my séance with Miss Littlepaugh, and returned. With some photostats and an affidavit in my brief case.

Upon my return I found the call in my box. It was Anne's number, then Anne's voice on the wire, and, as always, the little leap and plunk in my heart like a frog jumping into a lily pool. With the ripples spreading round.

It was her voice saying she had to see me. I told her that was easy, she could see me all the rest of her life. But she ignored that little joke, as no doubt it deserved, and said for me to meet her right away. "At the Crescent Cove," I suggested, and she agreed. The Crescent Cove was Slade's place.

I was there first, and had a drink with Slade himself in the midst of soft lights and sweet music and the gleam of chromium, and looked at Slade's yellow-ivory bullet head and expensive tailoring and at the reigning blond at the cash register, and remembered wistfully the morning long ago in Prohibition, when in the back room of his fly-bitten speakeasy Slade, with hair on his head then and not a dime in his pocket, had refused to fall in with Duffy's attempt to force beer on Cousin Willie from the country, who was, it turned out, Willie Stark, and who wanted orange pop. That had fixed Slade up forever. So now I had my drink, and looking at him, marveled how little is required for a man to be lost or saved.

And I looked up into the mirror of the bar and saw Anne Stanton come in the door. Or rather, her image come through the image of the door. For the moment I did not turn to face the reality. Instead, I looked at the image which hung there in the glass like a recollection caught in the ice of the mind—you have seen, in winter in the clear ice of a frozen stream, some clean bright gold and red leaf embedded to make you think suddenly of the time when all the bright gold and red leaves had been on the trees like a party and the sunshine had poured down over them as though it would never stop. But it wasn't a recollection, it was Anne Stanton herself, who stood there in the cool room of the looking glass, above the bar barricade of bright bottles and siphons across some distance of blue carpet, a girl—well, not exactly a girl any more, a young woman about five-feet-four with the trimmest pair of nervous ankles and smallish hips which, however, looked as round as though they had been turned on a lathe, and a waist just the width to make you wonder if you could span it with your hand, and all of this done up in a swatch of gray flannel which pretended to a severe

240

mannish cut but actually did nothing but scream for attention to some very unmannish arrangements within.

She was standing there, not quite ready to start patting the blue carpet with an impatient toe, turning her smooth, cool face (under a light-blue felt hat) slowly from one side to the other to survey the room. I caught the flash of blue in her eyes as she glanced about.

Then she spotted my back by the bar and came my way. I did not look around and did not meet her eyes in the mirror. When she was just behind me, she said, "Jack."

I didn't look round. "Slade," I said, "this strange woman keeps following me round, and I thought you ran a respectable place. What the hell are you going to do about it?"

Slade had swung round to look at the strange woman, whose face was all at once chalk-white and whose eyes were uttering sparks like a couple of arc lights. "Lady," Slade said, "now look here, lady——"

Then the lady suddenly overcame the paralysis which had frozen her tongue and the blood hit her cheeks. "Jack Burden!" she said, "if you don't——"

"She knows your name," Slade said.

I turned around to face the reality which was not something caught in the ice of the mind but was something now flushed, feline, lethal, and electric and about to blow a fuse. "Well, I declare," I said, "if it isn't my fiancée! Say, Slade, I want you to meet Anne Stanton. We're going to get married."

"Gee," Slade said, his pan as dead as something in the sink next morning, "I'm glad ter——"

"We're getting married in twenty-hundred-and-fifty," I said. "It will be a June wedding, with——"

"It will be a March murder," Anne said, "right now." Then she smiled, and the blood subsided in her cheeks, and she put out her hand to Slade.

"Glad ter meetcha," Slade said, and though the face which he exhibited might well have belonged to a wooden Indian, the eyes in it didn't miss any of the details suggested by the coat suit. "How about a drink?" he asked.

"Thank you," Anne said, and settled on a Martini.

After the drink, she said, "Jack, we've got to go," thanked Slade again, and led me away into the night full of neon lights, gasoline fumes, the odor of roasted coffee, and the honk of taxis.

"You have a wonderful sense of humor," she said.

"Where are we going?" I sidestepped her remark.

"You are such a smart aleck."

"Where are we going?"

"Aren't you ever going to grow up?"

"Where are we going?"

241

We were walking aimlessly down the side street past the swinging doors of bars and oyster joints and past newsstands and old women selling flowers. I bought some gardenias, gave them to her, and said, "I reckon I am a smart aleck, but it is just a way to pass the time."

We walked on another half block, threading through the crowd that drifted and eddied in and out of the swinging doors.

"Where are we going?"

"I wouldn't be going anywhere with you," she said, "if I didn't have to talk to you."

We were passing another old woman selling flowers. So I took another bunch of gardenias, laid down my four bits, and shoved the blossoms at Anne Stanton. "If you can't be civil," I said, "I'm going to smother you in these damned things."

"All right," she said, and laughed, "all right, I'll be good." And she swung onto my arm and matched her step to mine, holding the flowers in her free hand, her bag tucked under the off elbow.

We kept step, not talking for a half block. I looked down, watching her feet flick out, one-two, one-two. She was wearing black suède shoes, very severe, very mannish, and she clicked the pavement with authority, but they were small and the fine ankles flickered, one-two, one-two, hypnotically.

Then I said, "Where are we going?"

"To walk," she said, "just walk. I'm too restless to be still."

We walked on, down toward the river.

"I had to talk to you," she said.

"Well, talk then. Sing. Spill."

"Not now," she said soberly and looked up at me and I saw in the light of the street lamp that her face was very serious, even worried. The flesh seemed smoothed back, even painfully taut over the wonderful perfection of the bone structure of her face. There wasn't any waste material in that face, and always there was a hint in it of a trained-down, keyed-up intensity, though an intensity kept under the smooth surface of calm, like a flame behind glass. But the intensity was keyed up more than usual, I could see. And I had the feeling that if you turned the wick up a fraction the glass might crack.

I didn't reply, and we took a few more paces. Then she said, "Later. Now just walk."

So we walked. We had left the streets where the bars and poolrooms and restaurants were, and the blare or whimper of music from beyond the swinging doors. We passed down a grubby, dark street where a couple of boys scurried along by the walls of the houses, uttering short, lost-sounding, hollow calls, like marsh birds. The shutters were all closed on these houses, with here and there a tiny clink of light showing, or perhaps the faint sound of voices Later in the spring, when the weather turned, people would be sitting out on the sidewalk stoops here in the evenings, talking back and forth, and now and then, if you were a man passing, one of the women would say in a conversational tone, "Hey, bud, you want it?" For this was the edge of the crib section, and some of these houses were cribs. But at this season, at night, whatever kinds of life were in these houses—the good life and the bad life—were still withdrawn deep inside the old husks of damp, crumbling brick or flaking wood. A month from now, in early April, at the time when far away, outside the city, the water hyacinths would be covering every inch of bayou, lagoon, creek, and backwater with a spiritual-mauve to obscene-purple, violent, vulgar, fleshy, solid, throttling mass of bloom over the black water, and the first heartbreaking, misty green, like girlhood dreams, on the old cypresses would have settled down to be leaf and not a damned thing else, and the arm-thick, mud-colored, slime-slick mocassins would heave out of the swamp and try to cross the highway and your front tire hitting one would give a slight bump and make a sound like *kerwhush* and a tinny thump when he slapped heavily up against the underside of the fender, and the insects would come boiling out of the swamps and day and night the whole air would vibrate with them with a sound like an electric fan, and if it was night the owls back in the swamps would be *whoo*-ing and moaning like love and death and damnation, or one would sail out of the pitch dark into the rays of your headlights and plunge against the radiator to explode like a ripped feather bolster, and the fields would be deep in that rank, hairy or slick, juicy, sticky grass which the cattle gorge on and never gets flesh over their ribs for that grass is in that black soil and no matter how far the roots could ever go, if the roots were God knows how deep, there would never be anything but that black, grease-clotted soil and no stone down there to put calcium into that grass—well, a month from now, in early April, when all those things would be happening beyond the suburbs, the husks of the old houses in the street where Anne Stanton and I were walking would, if it were evening, crack and spill out onto the stoops and into the street all that life which was now sealed up within.

But now the street was blank, and dim, with a leaning lamp-post at the end of the block, and the cobbles oily-greasy-glimmering in its rays and the houses shuttered, and the whole thing looked like a set for a play. You expected to see the heroine saunter up, lean against the lamppost and light a cigarette. She didn't come, however, and Anne Stanton and I walked straight through the set, which you knew was cardboard until you put out your hand to touch the damp, furry brick or spongy stucco. We walked on through without talking. Perhaps for the reason that if you are in a place like that which looks like a cardboard stage set and is so damned *q-u-a-i-n-t,* whatever you say will sound as though it had been written by some lop-haired, swivel-hipped fellow who lived in one of those cardboard houses in an upstairs apartment (overlooking the patio—Oh, Jesus, yes, overlooking the patio) and wrote a play for the Little Theater which began with the heroine sauntering into a dim street between rows of cardboard houses and leaning against an askew lamppost to light a cigarette. But Anne Stanton was not that heroine, so she didn't lean against the lamppost and didn't say a word, and we kept on walking.

We walked on down till we came to the river, where the warehouses were and the docks fingered out into the water. The metal roofs of the docks glimmered dully in the rays of the street lamps. Above the pilings of the docks a thick tangle of mist coiled and drifted, broken here and there to show the sleek, velvety, motionless water, which glimmered darkly like the metal of the roofs, or like a seal's black, water-slick fur. A few docks down, the stubby masts of freighters were barely visible against the dark sky. Somewhere downstream a horn was hooting and moaning. We moved along beside the docks, looking out into the river, which was tufted and matted over the blackness with the scraggly, cirrus, cottony mist. But the mist stayed close to the surface of the river, and to look out over it made you think of being on a mountain at night and looking for miles out over clouds below. There were a few lights over on the far shore.

We came to an open pier which I remembered as the place where excursion boats picked up their crowds on summer afternoons for the moonlight ride up the river—big, jostling, yelling, baby-carrying, pop-and-likker-drinking, sweating crowds. But there wasn't any big side-wheeler there now, white as a wedding cake, cranky and improbable, with red and gilt decorations, and no calliope was playing "Dixie" and no whistles blowing. The place was as still as a tomb and as blank as Gobi on a moonless night. We walked out to the end of the pier, leaned on the railing, and looked across the river.

"All right," I said.

She didn't answer.

"All right," I repeated, "I thought you wanted to talk."

"It's Adam," she said.

"What about Adam?" I asked, evenly.

"You know—you know perfectly well—you went there and—"

"Look here," I said, and I felt my blood getting up and my voice taking on an edge, "I went there and made him a proposition. He's a grown man and if he doesn't like it he doesn't have to take it. There's no use blaming me and—"

"I'm not blaming you," she said.

244

"You just started to jump me," I said, "but if Adam can't make up his own mind and can't take care of himself, you needn't blame me."

"I'm not blaming you, Jack. You're so jumpy and touchy, Jack." She laid her hand on my arm, on the rail, and patted me, and I felt the head of steam in me drop a few pounds of pressure.

"If he can't take care of himself, then you—" I began.

But she cut in, quick and sharp, "He can't. That's the trouble."

"Now, look here, all I did was to offer him a proposition."

Her hand, which had been laid on my forearm to soothe me and pat down the steam pressure, suddenly clamped on me, driving the fingers damned near to the bone. I jumped, and even as I jumped, I heard her say, in a low, tense voice, almost a whisper, "You can make him take it."

"He's a grown man and he—" I began.

But she cut in again, "You've got to make him—you've got to!"

"For God's sake!" I said.

"You've got to," she repeated, in that same voice, and I was sure that the fingers clenched on my arm were bringing blood.

"You were just now giving me hell because I merely offered him the proposition," I said, "and now you say I've got to make him take it."

"I want him to take it," she said, and her fingers fell away from their grip.

"Well, I'm damned," I observed in the direction of the great interstellar darkness, and then peered into her face. There wasn't much light—I could see the face, an unnatural chalk-white, and the eyes were just dark gleams—but I could tell that she meant what she said. "So you want him to take it?" I said slowly. "And you're Governor Stanton's daughter and Adam Stanton's sister, and you want him to take it?"

"He's got to," she said, and I saw her small gloved hands clench on the railing, and felt sorry for the railing. She stared out over the coiling carpet of river mist, as from the mountain out over the clouds hiding the dark world.

"Why?" I asked.

"I went up there," she said, still looking out over the river, "to talk to him about it. I wasn't sure he ought to when I went up. I wasn't sure then, but when I saw him I was."

Something about what she was saying disturbed me, like an offstage noise or something caught out of the tail of your eye or an itch that comes when your hands are full and you can't scratch. I was listening to what she was saying, and it wasn't that. It was something else. But I couldn't catch what. So I

245

shoved it onto the back of the stove, and listened to what she was saying.

"When I saw how he was," she was saying, "I knew. I just knew. Oh, Jack, he was all worked up—it wasn't natural—just because he had been asked. He has cut himself off from everything—from everybody. Even from me. Not really, but it's not like it used to be."

"He's awful busy," I objected lamely.

"Busy," she echoed, "busy—yes, he's busy. Ever since he was in medical school, he has worked like a slave. There's just something driving him—driving him. It's not money and it's not reputation and it's not—I just don't know what—" Her voice drifted off.

"It is very simple," I said. "He wants to do good."

"Good," she echoed. Then, "I used to think so—oh, he does good—but—"

"But what?"

"Oh, I don't know—and I shouldn't say it—I shouldn't—but I almost think that the work—even the doing good—everything is just a way to cut himself off. Even from me—even me—"

Then she said, "Oh, Jack, we had an awful row. It was awful. I went home and cried all night. You know how we've always been. And to have a terrible row. You know how we've been? You know?" She insisted, and clutched my arm, as though to make me agree, to make me tell her how they had been.

"Yes," I said, "I know." I looked at her and was afraid for a second she was going to cry again, but she didn't, and I should have known it, for she was the kind that did her crying on the midnight pillow. If she did any.

"I told him," she was saying, "I told him that if he wanted to do any good—really do any good—here was the time. And the way. To see that the Medical Center was run right. And even expanded. And all that. But he just froze up and said he wouldn't touch the thing. And I accused him of being selfish—of being selfish and proud—of putting his pride before everything. Before doing good—before his duty. Then he just glared at me, and grabbed me by the wrist and said I couldn't understand anything, that a man owed himself something. I said it was his pride, just his pride, and he said he was proud not to touch filth, and if I wanted him to do that I could just—" She stopped, took a breath and, I guessed, a new grip on her nerve to say what she was about to say. "Well, what he was going to say was that I could get out. But he didn't say it. I'm glad—" she paused again—"I'm glad he didn't say it. At least, he didn't say it."

"He didn't mean it," I said.

"I don't know—I don't know. If you had seen his eyes blazing and his face all white and drawn. Oh, Jack——" she grabbed my arm again, and shook me as though I were holding back an answer——"why won't he do it? Why is he this way? Doesn't he see he ought to? That he's the man and he's got to? Why, Jack? Why?"

"To be perfectly brutal," I said, "it is because he is Adam Stanton, the son of Governor Stanton and the grandson of Judge Peyton Stanton and the great-grandson of General Morgan Stanton, and he has lived all his life in the idea that there was a time a long time back when everything was run by high-minded, handsome men wearing knee breeches and silver buckles or Continental blue or frock coats, or even buckskin and coonskin caps, as the case may be——for Adam Stanton isn't any snob——who sat around a table and candidly debated the good of the public thing. It is because he is a romantic, and he has a picture of the world in his head, and when the world doesn't conform in any respect to the picture, he wants to throw the world away. Even if that means throwing out the baby with the bath. Which," I added, "it always does mean."

That held her for a moment. She turned her face from me and looked out over the misty river again. Then she murmured, "He ought to take it."

"Well," I said, "if you want him to do it, you've got to change the picture of the world inside his head. If I know Adam Stanton." And I did know Adam Stanton, and at that moment I could see his face with the skin drawn back tight over the bone and the strong mouth like the neatly healed wound and the deep-set blue eyes blazing like pale ice.

She hadn't answered me.

"That's the only way," I said, "and you might as well settle for that."

"He ought to do it," she whispered, looking over the river.

"How much do you want him to?"

She swung to me, and I peered into her face. Then she said, "As much as I want anything."

"You mean that?" I said.

"I mean it. He's got to. To save himself." She grabbed my arm again. "For himself. As much as for everybody else. For himself."

"Are you sure?"

"Sure," she said, fiercely.

"I mean sure that you want him to do it? More than anything?"

"Yes," she said.

I studied her face. It was a beautiful face——or if not beautiful, better than beautiful, a tense, smooth, spare-modeled, finished face, and it was chalk-white in the shadow and the eyes were dark gleams. I studied her face, and for the moment just

247

did that and let all the questions just slide away, like something dropped into the mist and water below us to slide away in the oily silence of the current.

"Yes," she repeated, whispering.

But I kept on peering into her face, really looking at it for the first time, after all the years, for the close, true look at a thing can only be one snatched outside of time and the questions.

"Yes," she whispered, and laid her hand on my arm, lightly this time.

And at the touch I came out of what I had been sunk in.

"All right," I said, shaking myself, "but you don't know what you are asking for."

"It doesn't matter," she said. "Can you make him?"

"I can," I said.

"Well, why didn't you—why did you wait—why—"

"I don't think—" I said slowly—"I don't think I would have ever done it—at least, not this way—if you, you yourself, hadn't asked me."

"How can you do it?" she demanded, and the fingers closed on my arm.

"It is easy," I said. "I can change that picture of the world he carries around in his head."

"How?"

"I can give him a history lesson."

"A history lesson?"

"Yes, I am a student of history, don't you remember? And what we students of history always learn is that the human being is a very complicated contraption and that they are not good or bad but are good and bad and the good comes out of bad and the bad out of good, and the devil take the hindmost. But Adam, he is a scientist, and everything is tidy for him, and one molecule of oxygen always behaves the same way when it gets around two molecules of hydrogen, and a thing is always what it is, and so when Adam the romantic makes a picture of the world in his head, it is just like the picture of the world Adam the scientist works with. All tidy. All neat. The molecule of good always behaves the same way. The molecule of bad always behaves the same way. There are—"

"Stop it," she ordered, "stop it, and tell me. You are trying not to tell me. You are talking so you won't tell me. Now, tell me."

"All right," I said. "You remember I asked you about Judge Irwin being broke? Well, he was. His wife wasn't rich, either. He just thought she was. And he took a bribe."

"Judge Irwin?" she echoed. "A bribe?"

"Yes," I said. "And I can prove it."

"He—he was father's friend, he was—" She paused, straightened herself, swung her face from me and looked out over the river, then, after a moment, in a sturdy voice, as though not to me but to the whole wide world over there beyond the mist: "Well, that doesn't prove anything. Judge Irwin."

I didn't reply. I, too, stared out over the coiling mist, in the dark.

I was aware, though I didn't look, when she turned toward me again.

"Well, say something," she said, and I heard the tension in her voice.

But I didn't say anything. I stood there waiting; and waiting, I could hear, in the silence, the tiny suck and lapping about the piles down in the mist.

Then she said, "Jack—was my—was my father—was—"

I didn't answer.

"You coward!" she said, "you coward, you won't tell me."

"Yes," I said.

"Did he take a bribe? Did he? Did he?" She had grabbed my arm and was shaking me, hard.

"Not that bad," I said.

"Not that bad, not that bad," she mimicked, and burst out laughing, hanging on my arm. Then she suddenly released me, thrust my arm from her as though it were foul, and shrank back. "I don't believe it," she announced.

"It's true," I said. "He knew about Irwin and protected him. I can prove it. I have documents. I'm sorry, but it's true."

"Oh, you're sorry! You're so sorry. You dug it all up, all the lies—for that man—for that Stark—for him—and you—you're so sorry." And she began to laugh again, and swung away, and was running down the pier, laughing and stumbling as she ran.

I ran after her.

I was just about to grab her, at the end of the pier, when the cop stepped out of the shadow of the warehouse, and said, "Hey, buddy!"

Just then, Anne stumbled and I grabbed her by the arm. She swayed in my grasp.

The cop approached. "What's up?" he demanded. "What you runnen that dame fer?"

"She's hysterical," I said, talking fast, "I'm just trying to take care of her, she's had a few drinks, just a couple, and she's hysterical, she's had a great shock, a grief—"

The cop, heavy, squat, hairy, took one waddling stride toward us, then leaned and whiffed her breath.

"—she's had a shock, and it has upset her so she took a drink, and she's hysterical. I'm trying to get her home."

His beefy, black-jowled face swung toward me. "I'll get you home," he allowed, "in the wagon. If you ain't careful."

He was just talking. I knew he was just talking to hear himself, for it was late and he was bored and dull. I knew that, and should have said, respectfully, that I would be careful, or have said, laughing and perhaps winking, that sure, Captain, I'd get her home. But I didn't say either thing. I was all keyed up, and she was swaying in my clutch, making a kind of sharp, broken noise with her breathing, and his God-damned beefy, black-jowled face was there in front of me. So I said, "The hell you will."

His eyes bugged out a little at that, the jowls swelled with black blood, and he lunged one step closer, fingering his stick, saying, "The hell I won't, I'm gonna right now, both of you, by God!"

Then he said, "Come on," prodded me with the stick, and repeated, "Come on," herding me toward the end of the pier, where, no doubt, the box was he would use to call.

I took two or three steps forward, feeling the prod of the stick in the small of my back, dragging Anne, who hadn't said a word. Then I remembered, "Listen here, if you want to be on the force in the morning, you better listen to me."

"Listen, hell," he rejoined and jabbed my kidney a little harder.

"If it weren't for the lady," I said, "I'd let you go on and bust yourself. I don't mind a ride to headquarters. But I'll give you a chance."

"Chance," he echoed, and spat from the side of his mouth, and jabbed again.

"I'm going to reach into my pocket," I said, "not for a gun, just for my wallet, so I can show you something. Did you ever hear of Willie Stark?"

"Sure," he said. And jabbed.

"You ever hear of Jack Burden," I asked, "that newspaper fellow who is a sort of secretary to Willie?"

He reflected a moment, still prodding me on. "Yeah," he said then, grudgingly.

"Then maybe you'd like my card," I said, and reached for the wallet.

"Naw, you don't," he said, and let the weight of the stick lie across my lifted forearm, "naw, you don't, I'm gitten it myself."

He reached in for the wallet, took it, and started to open it. As a matter of principle.

"You open that," I said, "and I'll bust you anyway, call the wagon or not. Give it here."

He passed it over to me. I drew out a card, and handed it to him.

He studied it in the bad light. "Jeez," he said, with a slight hissing sound like the air escaping from a child's balloon, "how wuz I to know you wuz on the payroll?"

"You damned well better find out next time," I said, "before you get gay. Now call me a cab."

"Yes, sir," he said, hating me with the pig's eyes out of the swollen face. "Yes, sir," he said, and went to the box.

Suddenly Anne pulled herself loose from me, and I thought she was going to run. So I grabbed her again. "Oh, you're so wonderful," she said, in a harsh whisper, "so wonderful—you're grand—you bully the bullies—you cop the cops—you're wonderful—"

I stood there holding her, not listening, aware only of a weight in my middle like a cold stone.

"—you're so wonderful—and clean—everything is so wonderful and clean—"

I didn't say anything.

"—you're so damned wonderful—and clean and strong—oh, you're a hero—"

"I'm sorry I acted like a son-of-a-bitch," I said.

"I can't imagine to what particular thing you are referring," she whispered in mock sweetness, underscoring the *particular*, setting it meticulously in my hide like a banderilla. Then she swung her face from me, and wouldn't look at me, and the arm I clutched might as well have belonged to a dummy in a show window, and the cold stone in my stomach was a stone in a deep well covered with slime, and the pig's eyes in the swollen, black-jowled face came back and hated me in the dull, mist-streaked night, and a horn moaned down the river, and in the cab Anne Stanton sat back in one corner, very straight and as far from me as possible, and the light from street lamps we passed would flicker across her white face. She would not speak to me. Until we came to a street with a car track on it. Then she said, "Get out. You can catch some car here. I don't want you to take me home."

So I got out.

Five nights later I heard Anne Stanton's voice on the telephone.

It said, "Those things—those papers you said you had—send them to me."

I said, "I'll bring them."

It said, "No. Send them."

I said, "All right. I've got extra photostats of one thing. Tomorrow I'll get a photostat of the other paper and send them together."

It said, "A photostat. So you don't trust me."

I said, "I'll send them tomorrow."

Then there was the click, in the little black tube. Then the tiny, windy, humming sound which is the sound of space falling away from you, and of infinity, and of absolute nothingness.

Every night when I came into my room, I would look at the

telephone. I would say to myself: *It is going to ring*. Once, even, I was sure that it had rung, for the tingle and stab of its ringing was in all my nerves. But it hadn't rung. I had merely fallen asleep. Once I picked up the thing and held it to my ear, listening to the tiny, humming sound which is the sound of the various things I have already mentioned.

Every night, at the desk in the lobby, I asked if there had been any numbers left for me. Yes, sometimes there were numbers. But never the right number.

Then I would go up to my room, where the telephone was and the brief case with the photostat and the affidavit from Memphis. I hadn't given that to the Boss yet. I hadn't even told him about not giving it to him. I would give it to him. That was in the cards. But not yet. Not quite yet. After the telephone had rung.

But it didn't ring.

Instead, after about a week, one night as I turned the corner of the corridor, I saw a woman sitting on the bench down beyond my door. I fumbled for my key, inserted it in the lock, and was about to enter when I was aware that the woman stood beside me. I swung toward her. It was Anne Stanton.

She had made no sound on the deep carpet. Not with her light foot.

"You gave me heart failure," I said, and swung the door wide, and added, "Come in."

"I thought you were so careful about my reputation," she said. "At least you claimed to be. Once."

"I remember," I said, "but come in anyway."

She walked into the room and stood in the middle of the floor with her back to me while I shut the door. I noticed that she had a brown manila envelope in her hand, with her bag.

Not turning to me, she stepped to the desk by the wall and flung down the envelope. "There it is," she said. "The photostats. I brought them back. But I would have brought back the originals if you had trusted me with them."

"I know it," I said.

"It was awful," she said, still not turning to me.

I went across to her and touched her shoulder. "I'm sorry," I said.

"It was awful. You don't know."

I didn't know how awful. So I stood there just behind her and didn't dare to touch her again, even with the weight of my finger.

"You don't know," she said.

"No," I said, "I don't."

"It was awful." Then she turned to put her wide eyes on me, and I had the impression of stumbling into a well. "It was awful," she said. "I gave them to him—those things—and he

252

read them and then he just stood there—he didn't move—he didn't make a sound—and his face was white as a sheet and I could hear him breathing. Then I touched him—and he looked at me—he looked at me a long time. Then he said—he looked at me and said, 'You.' that was what he said, 'You.' Looking at me."

"God damn it," I said, "God damn it, what's he blaming you for, why doesn't he blame Governor Stanton?"

"He does," she said. "Oh, he blames him. That is what is so awful. The way he blames him. His father. You remember—you remember, Jack—" she reached out and laid her hand on my forearm—"you remember—our father—how he was—how he used to read to us—how he loved us—how he taught Adam and how proud he was of him—how he took all that time to teach Adam himself—oh, Jack, he sat there in front of the fire and I was a little girl and he would read to us and I put my head against his knee—oh, Jack—you remember?"

"I remember," I said.

"Yes," she said, "yes—and mother was dead and father did all he could—he was so proud of Adam—and now Adam—and now—" She released my arm, and stepped back and lifted her hands, putting her fingers to her forehead in a distracted gesture. "Oh, Jack, what have I done?" she whispered.

"You did what you thought you ought to do," I said firmly.

"Yes," she whispered, "yes, that was it."

"It's done now," I said.

"Yes, it is done," she said, out loud, and her jaw closed with an expression which suddenly made her look like Adam, the mouth firm and sealed, the skin drawn and tight on the flesh, and she lifted her head to stare the world down, and I felt like bursting into tears. If that had been my habit.

"Yes," I said, "it's done."

"He'll do it," she said.

And I almost demanded, What, do what? For, for the moment, I had forgotten the reason that I had told Anne the facts, the reason that I had given her the photostats, the reason that she had shown them to her brother. I had forgotten that there was a reason. But I remembered now, and questioned, "You persuaded him?"

"No," she shook her head slowly, "no, I didn't say anything. I gave those things to him. He knew."

"What happened?"

"What I told you. He looked at me hard, and said 'You.' Just like that. Then I said, 'Adam, don't say it that way, you mustn't, Adam, you mustn't!' And he said, 'Why?' And I said, 'Because I love you, because I love him, love Father.' And he kept on looking at me, then said, 'Love him!' Then, 'Damn his soul to hell!' I called out, 'Adam, Adam,' but he turned his

253

back on me, and walked across the room to his bedroom door and went in and shut the door. Then I went out and walked by myself, in the dark, for a long time. So I could sleep. For three days I didn't hear from him. Then he asked me to come to see him. I went, and he gave me back those things." She pointed to the manila envelope. "He told me to tell you that he would do it. To arrange it. That was all."

"That was a good deal," I said.

"Yes," she said, and moved past me toward the door. She put her hand to the knob, turned it, and drew the door ajar. She looked back at me, and said, "Yes, it was a good deal."

And went out.

But she stood with her hand on the doorjamb. "One thing," she said.

"What?" I asked.

"A favor," she said, "to me. Before you ever use those things, those papers, show them to Judge Irwin. Give him a chance. At least, a chance."

I agreed to that.

The big black Cadillac, the hood glistening dully under the street lamps—as I could see even from the back seat—eased down the street, making its expensive whisper under the boughs which had new leaves on them, for it was early April now. Then we got to a street where there were not any nice trees arching over.

"Here," I said, "that place on the right, just beyond that grocery."

Sugar-Boy put the Cadillac up to the curb, like a mother laying Little Precious down with a last kiss. Then he ran around to open the door for the Boss, but the Boss was already on the curb. I uncoiled myself and stood beside him. "This is the joint," I remarked, and started in.

For we were going to see Adam Stanton.

When I told the Boss that Adam Stanton would take the job and that he had sent me a message to arrange things, the Boss had said, "Well." Then he had looked at me from toe to crown, and said, "You must be Svengali."

"Yeah," I had said, "I am Svengali."

"I want to see him," the Boss had said.

"I'll try to get him up here."

"Get him up here?" the Boss had said. "I'll go there. Hell, he's doing me a favor."

"Well, you're the Governor, aren't you?"

"You're damned right I am," the Boss had said, "but he is Doc Stanton. When do we go?"

I had told him it would have to be at night, that you never could catch him except at night.

254

So here we were, at night, entering the door of the crummy apartment house, climbing the dark stairs, stumbling over the kiddie car, inhaling the odor of cabbage and diapers. "He sure picked himself a place to live," the Boss said.

"Yeah," I agreed, "and lots of folks can't figure out why."

"I reckon I can," the Boss said.

And as I wondered whether he could or not, we reached the door, and I knocked, entered, and confronted the level eyes of Adam Stanton.

For a half moment, while Sugar-Boy was easing in, and I was shutting the door, Adam and the Boss simply took each other in, without a word. Then I turned and said, "Governor Stark, this is Dr. Stanton."

The Boss took a step forward and put out his right hand. Perhaps I imagined it, but I thought I noticed a shade of hesitation before Adam took it. And the Boss must have noticed it, too, for when Adam did put out his hand, the Boss, in the middle of the shake, before any other word had been spoken, grinned suddenly, and said, "See, boy, it's not as bad as you thought, it won't kill you."

Then, by God, Adam grinned, too.

Then I said, "And this is Mr. O'Shean," and Sugar-Boy lurched forward and put out one of his stubby arms with a hand hanging on the end of it like a stuffed glove, and twisted his face and began, "I'm pl-pl-pl-pl—"

"I'm glad to know you," Adam said. Then I saw his glance pick up the bulge under Sugar-Boy's left armpit. He turned to the Boss. "So this is one of your gunmen I've heard about?" he said, definitely not grinning now.

"Hell," the Boss said, "Sugar-Boy just carries that for fun. Sugar-Boy is just a pal. Ain't anybody can drive a car like Sugar-Boy."

Sugar-Boy was looking at him like a dog you've just scratched on the head.

Adam stood there, and didn't reply. For a second I thought the deal was about to blow up. Then Adam said, very formally, "Won't you gentlemen have seats?"

We did.

Sugar-Boy sneaked one of his lumps of sugar out of the side pocket of his coat, put it into his mouth, and began to suck it, with his fey Irish cheeks drawn in and his eyes blurred with bliss.

Adam waited, sitting straight up in his chair.

The Boss, leaning back in one of the overstuffed wrecks, didn't seem to be in any hurry. But he finally said, "Well, Doc, what do you think of it?"

"Of what?" Adam demanded.

"Of my hospital?"

"I think it will do the people of the state some good," he said. Then added, "And get you some votes."

"You can forget about the vote side of it," the Boss said. "There are lots of ways to get votes, son."

"So I understand," Adam said. Then he handed the Boss another big chunk of silence to admire.

The Boss admired it awhile, then said, "Yeah, it'll do some good. But not too much unless you take over."

"I won't stand any interference," Adam said, and bit the sentence off.

"Don't worry," the Boss laughed. "I might fire you, boy, but I won't interfere."

"If that is a threat," Adam said, and the pale-blue blaze flickered up in his eyes, "you have wasted your time by coming here. You know my opinions of this administration. They have been no secret. And they will be no secret in the future. You understand that?"

"Doc," the Boss said, "Doc, you just don't understand politics. I'll be frank with you. I could run this state and ten more like it with you howling on every street corner like a hound with a sore tail. No offense. But you just don't understand."

"I understand some things," Adam said grimly, and the jaw set.

"And some you don't, just like I don't, but one thing I understand and you don't is what makes the mare go. I can make the mare go. And one more thing, now we are taking down our hair—" The Boss suddenly stopped, cocked his head, leered at Adam, then demanded, "Or are we?"

"You said there was one more thing," Adam replied, ignoring the question, sitting straight in his chair.

"Yeah, one more thing. But look here, Doc—you know Hugh Miller?"

"Yes," Adam said, "yes, I know him."

"Well, he was in with me—yeah, Attorney General—and he resigned. And you know why?" But he went on without waiting for the answer. "He resigned because he wanted to keep his little hands clean. He wanted the bricks but he just didn't know somebody has to paddle in the mud to make 'em. He was like somebody that just loves beefsteak but just can't bear to go to a slaughter pen because there are some bad, rough men down there who aren't animal lovers and who ought to be reported to the S.P.C.A. Well, he resigned."

I watched Adam's face. It was white and stony, as though carved out of some slick stone. He was like a man braced to hear what the jury foreman was going to say. Or what the doctor was going to say. Adam must have seen a lot of faces like that in his time. He must have had to look into them and tell them what he had to tell.

"Yeah," the Boss said, "he resigned. He was one of those guys wants everything and wants everything two ways at once. You know the kind, Doc?"

He flicked a look over at Adam, like a man flicking a fly over by the willows in the trout stream. But there wasn't any strike.

"Yeah, old Hugh—he never learned that you can't have everything. That you can have mighty little. And you never have anything you don't make. Just because he inherited a little money and the name Miller he thought you could have everything. Yeah, and he wanted the one last damned thing you can't inherit. And you know what it is?" He stared at Adam's face.

"What?" Adam said, after a long pause.

"Goodness. Yeah, just plain, simple goodness. Well you can't inherit that from anybody. You got to make it, Doc. If you want it. And you got to make it out of badness. Badness. And you know why, Doc?" He raised his bulk up in the broken-down wreck of an overstuffed chair he was in, and leaned forward, his hands on his knees, his elbows cocked out, his head outthrust and the hair coming down to his eyes, and stared into Adam's face. "Out of badness," he repeated. "And you know why? Because there isn't anything else to make it out of." Then, sinking back into the wreck, he asked softly, "Did you know that, Doc?"

Adam didn't say a word.

Then the Boss asked, softer still, almost whispering, "Did you know that, Doc?"

Adam wet his lips and said, "There is one question I should like to ask you. It is this. If, as you say, there is only the bad to start with, and the good must be made from the bad, then how do you ever know what the good is? How do you even recognize the good? Assuming you have made it from the bad. Answer me that."

"Easy, Doc, easy," the Boss said.

"Well, answer it."

"You just make it up as you go along."

"Make up what?"

"The good," the Boss said, "What the hell else are we talking about. Good with a capital G."

"So you make it up as you go along?" Adam repeated gently.

"What the hell else you think folks been doing for a million years, Doc? When your great-great-grandpappy climbed down out of the tree, he didn't have any more notion of good or bad, or right and wrong, than the hoot owl that stayed up in the tree. Well, he climbed down and he began to make Good up as he went along. He made up what he needed to do business, Doc. And what he made up and got everybody to mirate on as good and right was always just a couple of jumps behind what he

257

needed to do business on. That's why things change, Doc. Because what folks claim is right is always just a couple of jumps short of what they need to do business. Now an individual, one fellow, he will stop doing business because he's got a notion of what is right, and he is a hero. But folks in general, which is society, Doc, is never going to stop doing business. Society is just going to cook up a new notion of what is right. Society is sure not ever going to commit suicide. At least, not that way and of a purpose. And that is a fact. Now ain't it?"

"It is?" Adam said.

"You're damned right it is, Doc. And right is a lid you put on something and some of the things under the lid look just like some of the things not under the lid, and there never was any notion of what was right if you put it down on folks in general that a lot of them didn't start squalling because they just couldn't do any human business under that kind of right. Hell, look at when folks couldn't get a divorce. Look at all the good women got beat and the good men got nagged and couldn't do any human damned thing about it. Then, all of a sudden, a divorce got to be right. What next, you don't know. Nor me. But I do know this." He stopped, leaned forward again, the elbows again cocked out.

"What?" Adam demanded.

"This. I'm not denying there's got to be a notion of right to get business done, but by God, any particular notion at any particular time will sooner or later get to be just like a stopper put tight in a bottle of water and thrown in a hot stove the way we kids used to do at school to hear the bang. The steam that blows the bottle and scares the teacher to wet her drawers is just the human business that is going to get done, and it will blow anything you put it in if you seal it tight, but you put it in the right place and let it get out in a certain way and it will run a freight engine." He sank back again into the chair, his eyelids sagging now, but the eyes watchful, and the hair down over his forehead like an ambush.

Adam got up suddenly, and walked across the room. He stopped in front of the dead fireplace, with old ashes still in it, and some half-burned paper, though spring was on us, and there hadn't been any fire for a time. The window was up, and the night air came into the room, with a smell different from the diaper-and-cabbage smell, a smell of damp grass and the leaves hanging down from the arched trees in the dark, a smell that definitely did not belong there in that room. And all of a sudden I remembered once how into a room where I was sitting one night, a big pale apple-green moth, big as a bullbat and soft and silent as a dream—a Luna moth, the name is, and it is a wonderful name—came flying in. Somebody had left the screen door open, and the moth drifted in over the tables and chairs like a big pale-green, silky, live leaf, drifting and dancing along without any word under the electric light where a Luna moth certainly did not belong. The night air coming into the room now was like that.

Adam leaned an elbow on the wooden mantelpiece where you could write your name in the dust and the books were stacked and the old, dregs-crusted coffee cup sat. He stood there as though he were all by himself.

The Boss was watching him.

"Yeah," the Boss said, watchful, "it will run a freight engine and—"

But Adam broke in, "What are you trying to convince me of? You don't have to convince me of anything. I've told you I'd take the job. That's all!" He glared at the bulky man in the big chair, and said, "That's all! And my reasons are my own."

The Boss gave a slow smile, shifted his weight in the chair, and said, "Yeah, your reasons are your own, Doc. But I just thought you might want to know something about mine. Since we're going to do business together."

"I am going to run the hospital," Adam said, and added with curling lip, "If you call that doing business together."

The Boss laughed out loud. Then he got up from the chair. "Doc," he said, "just don't you worry. I'll keep your little mitts clean. I'll keep you clean all over, Doc. I'll put you in that beautiful, antiseptic, sterile, six-million-dollar hospital, and wrap you in cellophane, untouched by human hands." He stepped to Adam, and slapped him on the shoulder. "Don't you worry, Doc," he said.

"I can take care of myself," Adam affirmed, and looked down at the hand on his shoulder.

"Sure you can, Doc," the Boss said. He removed his hand from the shoulder. Then his tone changed, suddenly business-like and calm. "You will no doubt want to see all the plans which have been drawn up. They are subject to your revision after you consult with the architects. Mr. Todd, of Todd and Waters, will come to see you about it. And you can start picking your staff. It is all your baby."

He turned away and picked up his hat from the piano top. He swung back toward Adam and gave him a summarizing look, from top to toe and back. "You're a great boy, Doc," he said, "and don't let 'em tell you different."

Then he wheeled to the door, and went out before Adam could say a word. If there was any word he had to say.

Sugar-Boy and I followed. We didn't stop to say good night and thanks for the hospitality. That just didn't seem to be in the cards. At the door, however, I looked back and said, "So long, boy," but Adam didn't answer.

Down in the street, the Boss hesitated on the curb, beside the

259

car. Then he said, "You all go on. I'm walking." He turned up the street, toward town, past the crummy apartment house and the little grocery and the boarding houses and the shotgun bungalows.

Just as I climbed in beside Sugar-Boy, in the place the Boss always took, I heard the burst of music from the apartment house. The window was open and the music was very loud. Adam was beating the hell out of that expensive piano, and filling the night air with racket like Niagara Falls.

We rolled down the street, and passed the Boss, who, walking along with his head down, didn't pay us any mind. We pulled on into one of the good streets with the trees arching overhead and the new leaves looking black against the sky, or pale, almost whitish, where the rays of a street lamp struck them. We were beyond the sound of Adam's music now.

I lay back and closed my eyes and took the sway and dip of the car, which was soft and easy, and thought of the Boss and Adam Stanton facing each other across that room. I had never expected to see that. But it had happened.

I had found the truth, I had dug the truth up out of the ash pile, the garbage heap, the kitchen midden, the bone yard, and had sent that little piece of truth to Adam Stanton. I couldn't cut the truth to match his ideas. Well, he'd have to make his ideas match the truth. That is what all of us historical researchers believe. The truth shall make you free.

So I lay back and thought of Adam and the truth. And of the Boss and what he had said the truth was. The good was. The right was. And lying there, lulled in the Cadillac, I wondered if he believed what he had said. He had said that you have to make the good out of the bad because that is all you have got to make it out of. Well, he had made some good out of some bad. The hospital. The Willie Stark Hospital, which was going to be there when Willie Stark was dead and gone. As Willie Stark had said. Now if Willie Stark believed that you always had to make the good out of the bad, why did he get so excited when Tiny just wanted to make a logical little deal with the hospital contract? Why did he get so heated up just because Tiny's brand of Bad might get mixed in the raw materials from which he was going to make some Good? "Can't you understand?" the Boss had demanded of me, grabbing my lapel. "Can't you understand, either? I'm building that place, the best in the country, the best in the world, and a bugger like Tiny is not going to mess with it, and I'm going to call it the Willie Stark Hospital and it will be there a long time after I'm dead and gone and you are dead and gone and all those sons-of-bitches are dead and gone—" That was scarcely consistent. It was not at all consistent. I would have to ask the Boss about it sometime.

I had asked the Boss about something else once. The night after the impeachment blew up. The night when the great crowd that had poured into town stood on the lawn of the Capitol, trampling the flower beds beneath the great frock-coated and buckskin-clad and sword-bearing bronze statues which were History. When out of the tall dark doorway of the Capitol, under the blue glares of the spotlights Willie Stark walked out to stand at the top of the high steps, heavy and slow-looking, blinking in the light. He stood there, the only person up there on the wide expanse of stone, seeming to be lonely and lost against the mass of stone which reared behind him, standing there blinking. The long chant of "Willie—Willie—we want Willie," which had swelled up from the crowd, stopped as he came out. For an instant as he waited, there wasn't a sound. Then suddenly there was the great roar from the crowd, without any words. It was a long time before he lifted his hand to stop it. Then the roar died away as though under the pressure of his slowly descending hand.

Then he said, "They tried to ruin me, but they are ruined."

And the roar came again, and died away, under the hand.

He said, "They tried to ruin me because they did not like what I have done. Do you like what I have done?"

The roar came, and died.

He said, "I tell you what I am going to do. I am going to build a hospital. The biggest and the finest money can buy. It will belong to you. Any man or woman or child who is sick or in pain can go in those doors and know that all will be done that man can do. To heal sickness. To ease pain. Free. Not as charity. But as a right. It is your right. Do you hear? It is your right!"

The roar came.

He said, "And it is your right that every child shall have a complete education. That no person aged and infirm shall want or beg for bread. That the man who produces something shall be able to carry it to market without miring to the hub, without toll. That no poor man's house or land shall be taxed. That the rich man and the great companies that draw wealth from this state shall pay this state a fair share. That you shall not be deprived of hope!"

The roar came. As it died away, Anne Stanton, who had her arm through mine and was pressed close by the weight of the crowd, asked, "Does he mean that, Jack? Really?"

"He's done a great deal of it already," I said.

"Yes," Adam Stanton said, and his lips curled back with the words, "yes—that's his bribe."

I didn't answer—and I didn't know what my answer would have been—for Willie Stark, up there on the high steps, was saying, "I will do those things. So help me God. I shall live in

261

your will and your right. And if any man tries to stop me in the fulfilling of that right and that will I'll break him. I'll break him like that!" He spread his arms far apart, shoulder-high, and crashed the right first into the left palm. "Like that! I'll smite him. Hip and thigh, shinbone and neckbone, kidney punch, rabbit punch, uppercut, and solar plexus. And I don't care what I hit him with. Or how!"

Then, in the midst of the roar, I leaned toward Anne's ear and yelled, "He damned well means that."

I didn't know whether or not Anne heard me. She was watching the man up there on the steps, who was leaning forward toward the crowd, with bulging eyes, saying, "I'll hit him. I'll hit him with that meat ax!"

Then he suddenly stretched his arms above his head, the coat sleeves drawn tight to expose the shirt sleeves, the hands spread and clutching. He screamed, "Gimme that meat ax!"

And the crowd roared.

He brought both hands slowly down, for silence.

Then said, "Your will is my strength."

And after a moment of silence said, "Your need is my justice."

Then, "That is all."

He turned and walked slowly back into the tall doorway of the Capitol, into the darkness there, and disappeared. The roar was swelling and heaving in the air now, louder than ever, and I felt it inside of me, too, swelling like blood and victory. I stared into the darkness of the great doorway of the Capitol, where he had gone, while the roar kept on.

Anne Stanton was tugging at my arm. She asked me, "Does he mean that, Jack?"

"Hell," I said, and heard the savage tone in my own voice, "hell, how the hell do I know?"

Adam Stanton's lip curled and he said, "Justice! He used that word."

And suddenly, for the flicker of an instant, I hated Adam Stanton.

I told them I had to go, which was true, and worked my way around through the edge of the crowd, to the police cordon. Then I went around to the back of the Capitol, where I joined the Boss.

Late that night, back at the Mansion, after he had thrown Tiny and his rabble out of the study, I asked him the question. I asked, "Did you mean what you said?"

Propped back on the big leather couch, he stared at me, and demanded, "What?"

"What you said," I replied, "tonight. You said your strength was their will. You said your justice was their need. All of that."

262

He kept on staring at me, his eyes bulging, his stare grappling and probing into me.

"You said that," I said.

"God damn it," he exclaimed, violently, still staring at me, "God damn it—" he clenched his right fist and struck himself twice on the chest—"God damn it, there's something inside you—there's something inside you—"

He left the words hanging there. He turned his eyes from me and stared moodily into the fire. I didn't press my question.

Well, that was how it had been when I asked him a question, a long time back. Now I had a new question to ask him: If he believed that you had to make the good out of the bad because there wasn't anything else to make it out of, why did he stir up such a fuss about keeping Tiny's hands off the Willie Stark Hospital?

There was another little question. One I would have to ask Anne Stanton. It had come to me that night down on the pier at the mist-streaked river when Anne said that she had gone up to Adam Stanton's apartment "to talk to him about it"—about the offer of the directorship of the Willie Stark Hospital. She had said that to me, and at the moment, it had disturbed like an itch that comes when your hands are full and you can't scratch. I hadn't, in the press of the moment, defined what was disturbing, what was the question. I had simply pushed the whole pot to the back of the stove and left it to simmer. And there it simmered for weeks. But one day, all at once, it boiled over and I knew what the question was: How had Anne Stanton known about the hospital offer?

One thing was a cinch. I hadn't told her.

Perhaps Adam had told her, and then she had gone up there "to talk to him about it." So I went to see Adam, who was furiously deep in work, his usual practice and teaching, and in addition, the work on the hospital plans, who hadn't been able, he said, to touch the piano in almost a month, whose eyes fixed on me glacially out of a face now thin from sleeplessness, and who treated me with a curtesy too chromium-plated to be given to the friend of your youth. It took some doing, on my part, in the face of that courtesy, to get my nerve up to ask him the question. But I finally asked it. I said, "Adam, that first time Anne came up to talk to you about—about the job—you know, the hospital—had you told—"

And he said, with a voice like a scalpel, "I don't want to discuss it."

But I had to know. So I said, "Had you told her about the proposition?"

"No," he said, "and I said I didn't want to discuss it."

"O.K.," I heard myself saying, in a flat voice which wasn't quite my own. "O.K."

He looked sharply at me, then rose from his chair and took a step toward me. "I'm sorry," he said, "I'm sorry, Jack. I'm on edge." He shook his head slightly like a man trying to shake the fog of sleep out. "Not been getting enough shut-eye," he said. He took another step to me—I was leaning against the mantel—and looked into my face again and laid his hand on my arm, saying, "I'm really sorry, Jack—talking that way—but I didn't tell Anne anything—and I'm sorry."

"Forget it," I said.

"I'll forget it," he agreed, smiling wintrily, tapping my arm, "if you will."

"Sure," I said, "sure, I'll forget it. Yeah, I'll forget it. It didn't amount to anything anyway. Who told her. I guess I told her myself. It just slipped my mind that—"

"I mean forget about the way I acted," he corrected me, "blowing off the way I did."

"Oh," I said, "oh, that. Sure, I'll forget it."

Then he was peering into my face, with a question darkening his eyes. He didn't say anything for a moment. Then, "What did you want to know for?"

"Nothing," I replied, "nothing. Just idle curiosity. But I recollect now. I told her myself. Yeah, and I guess maybe I shouldn't. I didn't mean to get her into it. Just let it slip. I didn't mean to cause any ruckus. I didn't think—" And all the while that cold, unloving part of the mind—that maiden aunt, that washroom mirror the drunk stares into, that still small voice, that maggot in the cheese of your self-esteem, that commentator on the ether nightmare, that death's-head of lipless rationality at your every feast—all that while that part of the mind was saying: *You're making it worse, your lying is just making it worse, can't you shut up, you blabbermouth!*

And Adam, with whitening face, was saying, "There wasn't any ruckus. As you call it."

But I couldn't stop, as when your car comes to the glare ice over the brow of the hill and hits it before you can get on the brake, and you feel the beautiful free glide and spin of the skid and almost burst out laughing, it is so fine and free, like boyhood. I was saying, "—not any ruckus exactly—just I'm sorry I sicked her on you—I didn't want to cause any trouble—it was just that—"

"I don't want to discuss it," he said, and the jaw snapped shut, and he swung from me and went to stand on the other side of the room, very stiff and military.

So I took my leave, and the chromium-plated courtesy was so bright and cold that my, "Be seeing you, boy," stuck in my throat, like old corn bread.

But he hadn't told Anne Stanton. And I hadn't told her. Who had told her? And at that point I could see no answer except that there had been some loose talk, some leak, and the news had got around. I guess I took that answer—if I really took it—because it was the easiest answer for me to take. But I knew, deep down, that the Boss wasn't given to loose talk except when he wanted to talk loose, and he would have known that one sure way to ruin the chance of ever getting Adam Stanton would be to let the gossip mill start grinding on the topic. I knew that all right, but my mind just closed up like a clam when that shadow came floating over. A clam has to live, hasn't it?

But I did find out who had told Anne Stanton.

It was a beautiful morning in middle May, and just that morning, at that hour, about nine-thirty, there was still some last touch of spring—by that time you had almost forgotten there had been a spring—a kind of milkiness in the air, and way off yonder, from my window, I could see a little white haze on the river, milky too. The season was like the fine big-breasted daughter of some poor spavined share-cropper, a girl popping her calico but still having a waist, with pink cheeks and bright eyes and just a little perspiration at the edge of her tow hair (which would be platinum blond in some circles), but you see her and know that before long she will be a bag of bone and gristle with a hag face like a rusted brush hook. But she looks good enough to scare you now, if you really look at her, and that morning the season still had that look and feel even if you did know that by the end of June everything would be bone and gristle and hag face and a sweat-sticky sheet to wake up on and a taste in your mouth like old brass. But now the leaves on the trees hung down thick and fleshy and had not begun to curl yet. I could look down from my office window on the great bolls and tufts and swollen globes of green which were the trees of the Capitol grounds seen from the height of my window, and think of the deep inner maze of green in one of the big trees and of the hollow shadowy chambers near the trunk, where maybe a big cantankerous jay would be perched for a moment like a barbarous potentate staring with black, glittering, beady eyes into the green tangle. Then he would dive soundlessly off the bough and break through the green screen and be gone into the bright sunshine where suddenly he would be screaming his damned head off. I could look down and think of myself inside that hollow inner chamber, in the aqueous green light, inside the great globe of the tree, and not even a jaybird in there with me now, for he had gone, and no chance of seeing anything beyond the green leaves, they were so thick, and no sound except, way off, the faint mumble of traffic, like the ocean chewing its gums.

It was a fine, peaceful, beautiful thought and I took my eyes off the green below and lay back in my swivel chair, with my heels on the desk, and shut my eyes and thought of swooping down and bursting through the green to the sudden green quietness inside. I lay back with my eyes closed and listened to the electric fan, which was humming like a dream, and could almost feel the wonderful swoop and then the poise inside. It was a fine idea. If you had wings.

Then I heard the racket outside in the reception room, and opened my eyes. Somebody had slammed a door. Then I caught the whir of a passage and Sadie Burke swung into my ken, making a great curve through my open door, and, all in one motion, slamming it behind her and charging on in my direction. She stood in front of my desk and fought for air enough to say what she had to say.

It was just like old times. I hadn't seen her worked up that much since the morning when she had found out about the Nordic Nymph who had skated her way into the Boss's bed up in Chicago a long time back. That morning she had exploded out of the Boss's door, and had described a parabola into my office, with her black chopped-off hair wild and her face like a riddled plaster-of-Paris mask of Medusa except for the hot bituminous eyes, which were in full blaze with a bellows pumping the flame.

Well, since that morning there had, no doubt, been plenty of occasions when Sadie and the Boss had not seen exactly eye to eye. The Boss had had everything from the Nordic Nymph to the household-hints columnist on the *Chronicle* in his life, and Sadie hadn't been exactly condoning—for Sadie did not have a condoning nature—but a peculiar accommodation had finally been reached. "Damn him," Sadie had said to me, "let him have his sluts, let him have them. But he'll always come back to me. He knows he can't get along without me. He knows he can't." And she had added grimly, "And he better not try." So, with her fury and her *God-damns* and her satire and her tongue-lashings—and she had a tongue like a cat-o'-nine tails—and even with her rare bursts of dry-eyed grief, she seemed to take a kind of pleasure, wry and twisted enough God knows, in watching the development of the pattern in each new-old case, in watching the slut get bounced and the Boss come back to stand before her, grinning and heavy and sure and patient, to take his tongue-lashing. A long time back she herself had probably ceased to believe in the tongue-lashing or even to think what she was saying. The juicy epithets had long since lost their fine savor and a strident mechanical quality had crept into the rendering of the scene. Like a stuck phonograph record or a chicken-hungry preacher getting over the doxology. The words came but her mind wasn't on them.

But it was different that fine May morning. It was like old times, all right, with her bosom heaving and the needle of the steam gauge pricking deep into the red on the dial. Then she blew the plug.

"He's done it," she blew, "he's done it again—and I swear—"

"Done what?" I demanded, though I knew perfectly well what he had done. He had another slut.

"He's two-timing me," she said.

I lay back in my swivel chair and looked at her. The bright morning light was hitting her face square and without pity, but the eyes were magnificent.

"The bastard," she said, "he's two-timing me!"

"Now, Sadie," I said, lying back in my chair and sighting at her over the toes of my shoes crossed on the desk, "we went into that arithmetic a long time back. He's not two-timing you. He's two-timing Lucy. He may be one-timing you, or four-timing you. But it can't be two-timing." I was watching her eyes, and just saying that to see if it was possible to put a little more snap into them. It was.

For she said, "You—you—" Then words failed her.

"Me what?" I defended myself.

"You—you and your high-toned friends—what do they know—what do they know about anything—and you've got to mix them in."

"What are you talking about?"

"I may not be high-toned and maybe I did live in a shack but it hadn't been for me he wouldn't be Governor this minute and he knows it and she better not get gay, for high-toned or not, I'll show her. By God, I'll show her!"

"What the hell are you talking about?"

"You know what I'm talking about," she affirmed, and leaned over the desk top toward me, shaking her finger at me, "and you sit there and smile that way and think you are so high-toned. If you were a man you'd get up and go in there and knock hell out of him. I thought she was yours. Or maybe he's fixed you up, too. Maybe he's fixed you up like he fixed up that doctor." She leaned farther toward me. "Maybe he's making you director of a hospital. Yeah, what's he making you director of?"

Under the flood of words and the savage finger and the snapping eyes, I jerked myself forward, dropped my feet to the floor with a crash, and lunged up to stand before her, while the blood pounded in my head to make me dizzy, as it does when you rise suddenly, and little red flecks danced before me and the words kept on. Then the words stopped on her question.

"Are you saying," I began firmly, "that—that—" I had been about to pronounce the name of Anne Stanton, for the name itself had been quite clearly in my mind, as though spelled out on a billboard, but all at once the name stuck in my throat and

267

with surprise I discovered that I could not say it. So I continued, "—that she—she—"

But Sadie Burke was looking straight into my mind—at least, I had that feeling—and quick as a boxer she jabbed that name at me, "Yeah, she, she, that Stanton girl, Anne Stanton!"

I looked at Sadie in the face for a moment and felt so sorry for her I could cry. That was what surprised me. I felt so sorry for Sadie. Then I didn't feel anything. I didn't even feel sorry for myself. I felt as wooden as a wooden Indian, and I remember being surprised to discover that my legs worked perfectly even if they were wooden, and were walking directly toward the hatrack, where my right arm, even if it was wooden, reached out to pick up the old Panama which hung there and put it on my head, and my legs then walked straight out the door and across the long reception room over the carpet which was deep and soft as the turf of a shaven lawn in spring and walked on out the door across the ringing marble slabs.

And out into a world which seemed bigger than it had ever seemed before. It seemed forever down the length of white, sun-glittering concrete which curled and swooped among the bronze statues and brilliant flower beds shaped like stars and crescents, and forever across the green lawn to the great swollen bulbs of green which were the trees, and forever up into the sky, where the sun poured down billows and surges of heat like crystalline lava to engulf you, for the last breath of spring was gone now and gone for good, the fine, big-breasted girl popping the calico, with the face like peaches and cream and the tiny, dewy drop of perspiration at the edge of the tow head of hair, she was gone for good, too, and everything from now on out was bone and gristle and the hag face like a rusty brush hook, and green scum on the shrunk pool around which the exposed earth cracks and scales like a gray scab.

It was a source of perpetual surprise to find how well the legs worked carrying me down the white concrete of the drive, and how even if it was forever down the drive and past the trees I was finally past them and moving down the street as though sustained in a runnel of crystalline lava. I looked with the greatest curiosity at the faces which I saw but found nothing beautiful or remarkable in them and was not assured of their reality. For it takes the greatest effort to believe in their reality and to believe in their reality you must believe in your own, but to believe in your own you must believe in theirs, but to believe in theirs you must believe in your own—one-two, one-two, one-two, like feet marching. But if you have no feet to march with. Or if they are wooden. But I looked down at them and they were marching, one-two, one-two.

They marched a long time. But at the end of forever they brought me to a door. Then the door opened, and there, with the cool, white-shadowy room behind her, wearing a pale-blue, cool-crisp linen dress, her bare white long small arms hanging straight down against the pale blue, was Anne Stanton. I knew that it was Anne Stanton, though I had not looked into her face. I had looked into the other faces—all the faces I had met—I had looked into them with the greatest frankness and curiosity. But now I did not look into hers.

Then I looked into her face. She met my gaze quite steadily. I did not say anything. And I did not need to. For, looking at me, she slowly nodded.

Chapter Seven

AFTER MY visit to Anne Stanton's apartment that morning in late May, I was out of town for a while, about eight days. I left her apartment that morning and went down to the bank and drew out some money and got my car out of the garage and packed a bag and was headed out. I was headed out down a long bone-white road, straight as a string and smooth as glass and glittering and wavering in the heat and humming under the tires like a plucked nerve. I was doing seventy-five but I never seemed to catch up with the pool which seemed to be over the road just this side of the horizon. Then, after a while, the sun was in my eyes, for I was driving west. So I pulled the sun screen down and squinted and put the throttle to the floor. And kept on moving west. For West is where we all plan to go some day. It is where you go when the land gives out and the old-field pines encroach. It is where you go when you get the letter saying: *Flee, all is discovered*. It is where you go when you look down at the blade in your hand and see the blood on it. It is where you go when you are told that you are a bubble on the tide of empire. It is where you go when you hear that thar's gold in them-thar hills. It is where you go to grow up with the country. It is where you go to spend your old age. Or it is just where you go.

It was just where I went.

The second day I was in Texas. I was traveling through the part where the flat-footed, bilious, frog-sticker-toting Baptist biscuit-eaters live. Then I was traveling through the part where the crook-legged, high-heeled, gun-wearing, spick-killing, callous-rumped sons of the range live and crowd the drugstore on Saturday night and then all go round the corner to see episode three of "Vengeance on Vinegar Creek," starring Gene Autry as Borax Pete. But over both parts, the sky was tall hot brass by day and black velvet by night, and Coca Cola is all a man needs to live on. Then I was traveling through New Mexico, which is a land of total and magnificent emptiness with a little white filling station flung down on the sand like a sun-bleached cow skull by the trail, with far to the north a valiant remnant of the heroes of the Battle of Montmartre in a last bivouac wearing huaraches and hammered silver and trying to strike up conversations with Hopis on street corners. Then Arizona, which is grandeur and the slow incredulous stare of sheep, until you hit the Mojave. You cross the Mojave at night and even at night your breath rasps your gullet as though you were a sword swallower who had got hold of a hack-saw blade by mistake, and in the darkness the hunched rock and towering cactus loom at you with the shapes of a visceral, Freudian nightmare.

Then California.

Then Long Beach, which is the essence of California. I know because I have never seen any of California except Long Beach and so am not distracted by competing claims. I was in Long Beach thirty-six hours, and spent all of that time in a hotel room, except for forty minutes in a barbershop off the lobby of the hotel.

I had had a puncture in the morning and so didn't hit Long Beach till about evening. I drank a milk shake, bought a bottle of bourbon, and went up to my room. I hadn't had a drop the whole trip. I hadn't wanted a drop. I hadn't wanted anything, except the hum of the motor and the lull of the car and I had had that. But now I knew that if I didn't drink that bourbon, as soon as I shut my eyes to go to sleep the whole hot and heaving continent would begin charging at me out of the dark. So I took some, took a bath, and then lay on the bed, with my light off, watching the neon sign across the street flare on and off to the time of my heartbeat, and drinking out of the bottle, which, between times, I set on the floor by the bed.

I got a good sleep out of it. I didn't wake up till noon the next day. Then I had breakfast sent up and a pile of newspapers, for it was Sunday. I read the papers, which proved that California was just like any place else, or wanted to think the same things about itself, and then I listened to the radio till the neon sign began to flare on and off again to the time of my heartbeat, and then I ordered up some food, ate it, and put myself to sleep again.

The next morning I headed back.

I was headed back and was no longer remembering the things which I had remembered coming out.

For example. But I cannot give you an example. It was not so much any one example, any one event, which I recollected which was important, but the flow, the texture of the events, for meaning is never in the event but in the motion through event. Otherwise we could isolate an instant in the event and say that this is the event itself. The meaning. But we cannot do that. For it is the motion which is important. And I was moving. I was moving West at seventy-five miles an hour, through a blur of million-dollar landscape and heroic history, and I was moving back through time into my memory. They say the drowning man relives his life as he drowns. Well, I was not drowning in water, but I was drowning in West. I drowned westward through the hot brass days and black velvet nights.

It took me seventy-eight hours to drown. For my body to sink down to the very bottom of West and lie in the motionless ooze of History, naked on a hotel bed in Long Beach, California.

To the hum and lull of the car the past unrolled in my head like a film. It was like a showing of a family movie, the kind the advertisements tell you to keep so that you will have a record of the day Susie took her first little toddle and the day Johnny went off to kindergarten and the day you went up Pike's Peak and the day of the picnic on the old home farm and the day you were made chief sales manager and bought your first Buick. The picture on the advertisement always shows a dignified, gray-haired, kindly old gent, the kind you find on the whisky ad (or a gray-haired, kindly, sweet-faced old biddy), looking at the home movie and dreaming gently back over the years. Well, I was not gray-haired or dignified or kindly or sweet-faced, but I did have a showing of my home movie and dreamed gently back over the years. Therefore, if you have any home movies, I earnestly advise you to burn them and to be baptized to get born again.

I dreamed gently back over the years. And the stocky man with the black coat and spectacles leaned over me as I sat with my colored crayons on the rug before the fire and he held me the candy and said, "Just one bite, now, for supper's almost ready." And the woman with the pale hair and the blue eyes and the famished cheeks leaned over me and kissed me good night and left the sweet smell in the dark after the light was out. And Judge Irwin leaned at me in the gray dawn light, saying, "You ought to have led that duck more, Jack. You got to lead a duck, son." And Count Covelli sat straight in an expensive chair in the long white room and smiled from under his clipped black mustache and in one hand—the smallish, strong hand which could make a man wince at its clasp—held the glass and with the other stroked the big cat on his knee. And there was the Young Executive with his hair laid on his round skull like taffy. And Adam Stanton and I drifted in the yawl, far out, while the white sails hung limp in the breathless air and the sea was like hot glass and the sun burned like a barn on the western horizon. And always there was Anne Stanton.

Little girls wear white dresses with skirts that flare out to show their funny little knees, and they wear round-toed black patent-leather slippers held by a one-button strap, and their white socks are held up by a dab of soap, and their hair hangs down the back in a braid with a blue ribbon on it. That was Anne Stanton and it was Sunday and she was going to church to sit still as a mouse and rub her tonguetip pensively at the place where she had just lost the tooth. And little girls sit on hassocks and lean their cheeks pensively against the dear father's knee while his hand toys with the silken locks and his voice reads beautiful words. That was Anne Stanton. And little girls are fraidy-cats and try the surf with one toe that first day in spring, and when the surf makes a surprising leap and splashes their thighs with the tingle and cold they squeal and jump up and down on thin little legs like stilts. That was Anne Stanton. Little girls get a smudge of soot on the end of the nose when they roast wieners over the campfire and you—for you are a big boy and do not get soot on your nose—point your finger and sing, "Dirty-Face, Dirty-Face, you are so dirty you are a disgrace!" And then one day when you sing it, the little girl doesn't say a thing back the way she always had, but turns her big eyes on you, out of the thin little smooth face, and her lips quiver an instant so that you think she might cry even though she is too big for that now, and as the eyes keep fixed on you, the grin dries up on your face and you turn quickly away and pretend to be getting some more wood. That was Anne Stanton.

All the bright days by the water with the gulls flashing high were Anne Stanton. But I didn't know it. And all the not bright days with the eaves dripping or the squall driving in from the sea and with the fire on the hearth were Anne Stanton, too. But I didn't know that, either. Then there came a time when the nights were Anne Stanton. But I knew that.

That began the summer when I was twenty-one and Anne Stanton was seventeen. I was back from the University for vacation and I was a grown man who had been around. I got back from the University late in the afternoon, had a quick swim, ate my dinner, and bolted off to the Stanton house to see Adam. I saw him sitting out on the galley reading a book (Gibbon, I remember) in the long twilight. And I saw Anne. I was sitting in the swing with Adam, when she came out the door. I looked at her and knew that it had been a thousand years since I had last seen her back at Christmas when she had been back at the Landing on vacation from Miss Pound's School. She certainly was not now a little girl wearing round-toed, black patent-leather, flat-heeled slippers held on by a one-button strap and white socks held up by a dab of soap. She was wearing a white linen dress, cut very straight, and the straightness of the cut and the stiffness of the linen did nothing in the world but suggest by a kind of teasing paradox the curves and softnesses sheathed by the cloth. She had her hair in a knot on the nape of her neck, and a little white ribbon around her head, and she was smiling at me with a smile which I had known all my life but which was entirely new, and saying, "Hello, Jack," while I held her strong narrow hand in mine and knew that summer had come.

It had come. And it was not like any summer which ever had been or was to be again. During the day I would be with Adam

273

a lot, like always, and a lot of the time she would tag along, for that was the way it had been before, she'd tag along for she and Adam were very close. That summer Adam and I would play tennis in the early morning before the sun got high and hot, and she would come to the court with us and sit in the dappled shade of the mimosas and myrtles and watch Adam beat the tar out of me as usual and laugh like bird song and mountain brooks when I got my feet tangled up in my own racket. Then she might play me some, for she was pretty good and I was pretty bad. She was pretty good, all right, for a light-built girl, and had a lot of power in those small round arms, which flashed in the morning sun like wings. She was fast on her feet, too, and there would be the whipping skirt like a dancer's, and the flicker of white shoes. But of those mornings I chiefly remember her far over yonder across the court, tiptoe, poised to serve, at the moment when the racket is back of her ribbon-bound head, with the pull of the arm lifting the right breast, and the left hand, from which the ball has just risen, still up, as though to pluck something out of the air, the face lifted gravely and intensely to the bright light and the wide sky and the absolute little white ball hung there like the spinning world in the middle of brilliance. Well, that is the classic pose, and it is too bad the Greeks didn't play tennis, for if they had played tennis they would have put Anne Stanton on a Greek vase. But on second thought, I guess they would not have done it. That is the moment which, for all its poise, is too airy, too tiptoe, too keyed up. It is the moment just before the stroke, before the explosion, and the Greeks didn't put that kind of moment on a vase. So that moment is not on a vase in a museum, but is inside my head, where nobody else can see it but me. For it was the moment before the explosion, and it did explode. The racket smacked and the sheep gut whanged and the white ball came steaming across at me, and I missed it as like as not, and the game was over, and the set was over, and we all went home, through the motionless heat, for the dew was off the grass now and the morning land breeze had died.

But back then there was always the afternoon. In the afternoon we always went swimming, or sailing and then swimming afterward, all three of us, and sometimes some of the other boys and girls whose folks lived down the Row from the Landing or who were visiting there. Then after dinner we would get together again and sit in the shadow on their gallery or mine, or go to a movie, or take a moonlight swim. But one night when I went down, Adam wasn't there—he had had to drive his father somewhere—and so I asked Anne to go down to the Landing to a movie. On the way back, we stopped the car—I had the roadster, for my mother had gone off somewhere with a gang in her big one—and looked at the moonlight on the bay beyond Hardin Point. The moonlight lay on the slightly ruffling water like a swath of brilliant white, cold fire. You expected to see that white fire start eating out over the whole ocean the way fire in a sage field spreads. But it lay there glittering and flickering in a broad nervous swath reaching out yonder to the bright horizon blur.

We sat there in the car, arguing about the movie we had just seen and looking up the swath of light. Then the talking died away. She had slid down a little in the seat, with her head lying on the top of the back cushion so that now she wasn't looking out toward the horizon but up into the sky—for the top of the roadster was down—with the moonlight pouring down on her face to make it look smooth as marble. I slid down a little, too, and looked up at the sky, and the moonlight poured down over my face, such as it was. I kept thinking that now in a minute I would reach over and take hold. I stole a look sidewise and saw how her face was smooth as marble in the moonlight. And how her hands lay supine on her lap, the fingers curling a little as though to receive a gift. It would be perfectly easy to reach over and take her hand and get started and see where we wound up. For I was thinking in language like that, the stale impersonal language of the College Boy who thinks he's such a God-damned big man.

But I didn't reach over. It seemed a thousand miles across that little patch of leather to where she lay with her head back and her hands in her lap and the moonlight over her face. I didn't know why I didn't reach over. I kept assuring myself that I wasn't timid, wasn't afraid, I said to myself, hell, she was just a kid, what the hell was I hanging back for, all she could do would be to get sore and I could stop if she got sore. Hell, I told myself, she wouldn't get sore anyway, she knew what was up, she knew you didn't sit in parked cars with boys to play checkers in the moonlight, and she had probably been worked over plenty, somebody had probably run the scales on her piano. I played with that thought a second, and then all at once I was both hot and angry. I started up in the seat, a sudden tumult of something in my chest. "Anne," I said, "Anne—"and didn't know what I was going to say.

She turned her face toward me, not lifting her head from the back of the seat, just rolling it on the leather cushion. She lifted a finger to her lip, and said, "Sh, sh!" Then she took the finger away, and smiled directly and simply across the thousand miles of leather cushion between us.

I sank back. We lay there for quite a time, with that space between us, looking up at the moon-drenched sky and hearing the faintest whisper as the water lipped the shingle along the point. The longer we lay there, the bigger the sky seemed. After a long while I stole another sidewise look at Anne. Her eyes were closed, and when I thought that she wasn't looking up into that expanding sky, too, I suddenly felt alone and abandoned. But she opened her eyes—I was spying and saw that happen—and again was looking up into the sky. I lay there and looked up and didn't think of anything in the world.

Back then there was a train that passed the crossing just out of Burden's Landing at eleven-forty-five at night. The train always blew for the crossing. It blew that night, and I knew that it was eleven-forty-five. And time to go. So I sat up, touched the starter, turned the car around, and headed home. We hadn't said a word and we didn't say a word, until we pulled up in front of the Stanton house. Then Anne slipped out of the car, quick as a wink, poised there a moment on the shell drive, said, "Good night, Jack," in a low voice and with a last flicker of the smile she had smiled at me across the thousand miles of leather cushion two hours back, and ran up the steps of her house, light as a bird. All of this before I had half a chance to begin to collect myself.

I gaped at the blackness of the doorway back in the shadow of the gallery—she hadn't turned on a light when she entered—and listened hard as though I were waiting for a signal. But there wasn't a sound except that nameless stir of the night which comes even when there isn't a breath of wind and you are too far from the beach to get the whisper and riffle that is always there, even when the sea is quietest.

Then, after a few minutes, I switched on the motor again, and exploded off the Stanton property with a grind of tires that must have scattered the shells of the drive like spray. On the road down the Row I just pushed the accelerator to the floor board and let all those drowsy bastards up in those white houses have the works. I was letting that cutout snatch them bolt upright in bed like a cannon. I roared on out about ten miles till I hit the pine woods where there wasn't anybody to snatch up except hoot owls and some stray malarial squatter who would be lying off yonder as God's gift to the anopheles in his shack on the edge of the tidelands. So I turned the roadster around and eased on back with the throttle cut down to nothing, just drifting along in the roadster, lying back on the leather, like a boat drifting on a slow current.

At home, as soon as I lay back on my bed, I suddenly remembered—I didn't remember, I saw—Anne's face lying back, with the eyes closed and the moonlight pouring over it, and I remembered that day of the picnic long back—the day when we had swum out in the bay, under the storm clouds, when she had floated on the water, her face turned up to the purple-green darkening sky, her eyes closed, and the white gull passing over, very high. I hadn't thought of that since it happened, I guess, or if I had thought of it, it hadn't meant a thing, but all at once,

276

lying there, I had the feeling of being on the teetering verge of a most tremendous discovery. I saw that the moment tonight was just an extension of the moment long back, on the picnic, that this moment tonight had been in that moment all the time, and I hadn't known it, I had dropped it aside or thrown it away, but it had been like a seed you throw away to find, when you come back that way again, that the plant is tall and covered with bloom, or it had been like a little dirt-colored stick you throw into the fire with the other trash, but the thing is dynamite and there is an awful bang.

There was an awful bang. I popped up in bed like those drowsy bastards when I gave them the cutout. But this was more so. I sat up in bed and was absolutely filled with rapture. It wasn't like anything that had ever happened to me. It stopped my breath and I could feel my veins swelling to burst as when you take your deepest dive and think you'll never come up. I felt that I was right on the verge of knowing the real and absolute truth about everything. Just one instant and I would know it. Then I got my breath. "Jesus," I said out loud, "Jesus!" I stretched my arms out as wide as I could, as though I could grab the whole empty air.

Then I thought of the image of the face on the water, under the purple-green darkening sky, with the white gull flying over. It was almost a shock to remember that, to have the image come back, for the thing which had, apparently, provoked the rapture had itself been lost and forgotten in the rapture which had exploded out into the whole universe. Anyway, now I saw the image again, and all at once the rapture was gone, and I experienced a great tenderness, a tenderness shot through and veined with sadness, as though the tenderness were the very flesh of my body and the sadness the veins and nerves of it. That sounds absurd, but that was the way it was. And for a fact.

Then I thought, quite objectively as though I were observing the symptoms of a total stranger: *You are in love.*

I was, for a moment, bemused by that thought. That I was in love. And that it wasn't a bit like the way I had thought it would be. I was surprised, and a little bit awed by the fact, like a person who learns unexpectedly that he has inherited a million dollars, all lying up there in the bank for him to draw on, or who learns that the little stitch in the side is cancer and that he is carrying around inside himself that mysterious, apocalyptic, burgeoning thing which is part of himself but is, at the same time, not part of himself but the enemy. I got out of bed, very carefully, handling myself with awe-struck care as though I were a basket of eggs, and went to the window and stared out into the moon-drenched night.

So the College Boy, who had thought he was such a God-damned big man and knew everything and who had, that evening, looked across the little space of leather cushion and had thought the stale impersonal thoughts almost as a kind of duty to the definition of what he considered himself to be—so he hadn't reached out his hand across that little space and now as a result of that fact stood buck-naked in a shadowy room before an open window and stared out into enormous moon-soaked, sea-glittering night while off yonder in the myrtle hedge a mocking bird hysterically commented on the total beauty and justice of the universe.

That was how the nights became Anne Stanton, too. For that night in the roadster, Anne Stanton had done her trick very well. It was a wordless and handless trick, but it didn't need words or hands. She had rolled her head on the leather seat back, and touched her finger to her lips to say, "Sh, sh," and smiled. And had sunk her harpoon deeper than ever. Queequeg sunk it, through four feet of blubber to the very quick, but I hadn't really known it until the line played out and the barb jerked in the red meat which was the Me inside of all the blubber of what I had thought I was. And might continue to think I was.

Anne Stanton was the nights, all right. And the days, too, but in the days she was not the total substance, rather the flavor, the distillate, the climate, the breath, without which the rest wouldn't be anything at all. There would be Adam with us often, and sometimes the other people, with books, sandwiches, and a blanket in the pine woods, on the beach, at the tennis courts, on the shadowy gallery with a phonograph going, in the boat, at the movies. But sometimes she would let her book slide down to the blanket and lie back staring up into the high arch and tangle of the pine boughs, and I would begin to spy on her until, in a minute, it would be as though Adam weren't there. Or on the gallery she would be laughing and jabbering with all the others while the phonograph worked away, and then I would catch sight of her suddenly still and pensive, just for a moment it might be, with her eyes fixed off beyond the gallery and the yard, and again, just for that moment, it would be as though Adam and the others weren't there.

Or we would go down the hotel, where there was a high-dive tower, a good high one because the hotel was pretty swank and had exhibitions and races there now and then. Anne was crazy about diving that summer. She would go up high—she worked up higher and higher, day by day—and stand up there in the sunlight poised there at the very verge. Then, when she lifted her arms, I would feel that something was about to snap in me. Then down she would fly, a beautiful swan dive, with her arms wide to emphasize her trim breasts and her narrow back arched and her long legs close and sweet together. She would come flying down in the sunlight, and as I watched her it would be as though nobody else were there. I would hold my breath till whatever was going to snap inside me snapped. Then she would knife into the water, and her twin heels would draw through the wreath of ripple and the flicker of spray, and be gone. Adam sometimes got sore as hell at her for going up so high, "Oh, Adam," she'd say, "oh, Adam, it'll be all right, and it's wonderful!" And up the ladder she'd go. Up and plunge. Up and plunge. Up and plunge. Over and over again. I used to wonder what her face was like just at the moment when she entered the water. What expression was on it.

But sometimes in the day we would be quite literally alone. Sometimes she and I would slip off and go to the pine woods and walk on the soundless matting of needles, holding hands. And then there was a little diving float, with just a single low board, anchored about a hundred yards off the beach, near the Stanton slip. Sometimes we would swim out there when other people were pranking on the beach, or when nobody was there, and lie flat on our backs on the float, with our eyes closed, and just the fingertips touching and tingling as though they were peeled skinless with the nerves laid bare, so that every bit of my being was focused there.

At night we were alone pretty often. It had always been Adam and I, with Anne tagging along, and then, all at once, it was Anne and I, and Adam tagging along or, more likely, back up at his house reading Gibbon or Tacitus, for he was great on Rome back then. The change came more easily than I had expected. The day after that night in the roadster I played tennis with them in the morning as usual, and in the afternoon went swimming with them. I found myself watching Anne all the time, but that was the only difference. I couldn't see any change in her. I began to doubt that anything had happened, that I had even taken her to the movie the night before. But I had to see her that night.

I went up to their house just about dusk. She was on the gallery, in the swing. Adam, it turned out, was upstairs writing a letter he had to get off. He would be down in a few minutes, she said. It was something for their father, she said. I didn't sit down, though she asked me. I stood at the top of the steps, very uneasy, just inside the screen door, trying to think up what I would say. Then I blurted out, "Let's go out on the slip, let's walk." And added lamely, "Till Adam comes down."

Without a word, she got up, came to me, gave me her hand—that was her own doing and the fact set blaring and bonging all the fire bells and calliopes and burglar alarms in my system —and walked down the steps with me, down the path, across the road, and toward the slip. We stayed out on the slip a long time. Adam could have written a dozen letters in that time. But nothing happened out on the slip, except that we sat on the end,

279

our feet dangling over, and held hands, and looked over the bay.

On the side of the road toward the bay, just opposite the Stanton house, there was a big thicket of myrtle. When we got there, going hand in hand on our way back to the house, I stopped there in the protection of the shadow, drew her to me a little clumsily and abruptly, I guess, for I had had to key myself up to the act, plotting it all the way up the slip—and kissed her. She didn't put up any protest when I did it, just letting her arms hang limp, but she didn't return the kiss, just taking it submissively like a good little girl doing what she's told. I looked her in the face, after the kiss, and its smoothness was shaded by a reflective, inward expression, the kind of expression you see sometimes on a child's face when it is trying to decide whether or not it likes a new food it has just tasted. And I thought, my God, she probably hadn't been kissed before, even if she was seventeen, or almost, and I almost burst out laughing, the expression on her face was so funny and I was so happy. So I kissed her again. This time she returned the kiss, timidly and tentatively, but she returned it. "Anne," I said, with my heart bursting and my head reeling, "Anne, I love you, I'm crazy about you."

She was clutching my coat, a hand on each side of my chest, just under the shoulder, crumpling up the seersucker and hanging on, with her head, a little to one side and down, pressed weakly against me, as though she were asking pardon for a piece of misbehavior. She didn't answer what I said, and when I tried to lift her face up, she pressed it harder against me and clutched the seersucker tighter. So I stood there and ran my hand over her hair and breathed in the clean odor it had.

Then, after a while which may have been long or short, she disengaged herself from me, and stepped back. "Adam—" she said, "he's waiting—we've got to go."

I followed her across the road and into the gateway of the Stanton drive. A few paces up the drive she hesitated for me to come abreast of her. Then she took my hand, and that way, hand in hand, we proceeded toward the gallery where back in the shadow Adam would be sitting.

Yes, he was sitting there, for I caught the glow of a cigarette, the sudden intensification as the smoker took a deep pull, and then the fading.

Still holding my hand, tighter now as though executing a decision, she mounted the steps of the gallery, opened the screen with her free hand, and entered, drawing me behind her. We stood there for a moment, hand in hand. Then she said, "Hello, Adam," and I said, "Hello, Adam."

"Hello," he said.

We continued to stand there, as though waiting for something. Then she released my hand. "I'm going upstairs," she announced. "Good night, you all." And she was gone with the quick, muted patter of her rubber soles across the boards of her gallery floor and down the hall inside.

I still stood there.

Till Adam said, "Why the hell don't you sit down?"

So I sat down at the other end of the swing from Adam. He tossed a pack of cigarettes my way. I took one, and fumbled in my pockets for a match, but didn't find one. He leaned toward me, struck a match, and held it for my cigarette. As the flame flared there in front of my face while the cigarette caught, I had the feeling that he had put the light there for a purpose, to spy on my face while his own was back out of the direct days. I had the crazy impulse to jerk back and wipe my hand across my mouth to see if there was any lipstick there.

But the cigarette caught, and I drew my head back from the light and said, "Thanks."

"You're welcome," he replied, and that about wound up the conversation for the evening. There was something for us to say. He could ask me the question which I knew was in his mind. Or I could answer it without his asking it. But neither of us said what was to say. I was afraid he would ask me, for with all my saying to myself that he could go to hell, that it wasn't his business, I had the feeling of guilt as though I had robbed him of something. But at the same time I sat there keyed up and wanting him to ask me, for I wanted to tell somebody that Anne Stanton was wonderful and that I was in love. It was as though the condition of being in love were not completed until I could say to somebody, "Look here, I'm in love, be damned if I'm not." At the moment it seemed to require the telling for its fulfillment just as much as it would later require the hot, moist contact of bodies. So I sat there in the swing, in the dark, absorbed with the fact that I was in love, wanting to say it to complete it, and not, for the moment, missing Anne, the object of my love, who had gone upstairs to her room. I was so absorbed at the time with the fact of what had happened to me that I did not even wonder why she had gone upstairs. Later I decided that she had gone because, having served notice to Adam by standing there before him holding my hand, she wanted to leave him alone with that fact, to let him accustom himself to the new structure of our little crystal, our little world.

But maybe, I decided later, much later, years later when it didn't seem that it would ever matter again, she had gone up because she had to be alone, to sit by the window in the un-lighted room, looking out on the night, or lying on the bed watching the dark ceiling, to accustom herself to her new self, to see if she could breathe the new air, or sustain herself in the new element or dive and lounge in the new tide of feeling. Maybe she went up there to be alone, absorbed in herself the way a child is absorbed in watching a cocoon gradually part in the dusk to divulge the beautiful moth—the Luna moth again, with its delicate green and silver damp and crumpled but gradually spreading in the dusk, defining itself, slowly fanning the air to make a breeze so light that you would not be able to feel it on your eyeball were you to lean that close to peer. So maybe she was up in the room trying to discover what her new self was, for when you get in love you are made all over again. The person who loves you has picked you out of the great mass of uncreated clay which is humanity to make something out of, and the poor lumpish clay which is you wants to find out what it has been made into. But at the same time, you, in the act of loving somebody, become real, cease to be a part of the continuum of the uncreated clay and get the breath of life in you and rise up. So you create yourself by creating another person, who, however, has also created you, picked up the you-chunk of clay out of the mass. So there are two you's, the one you yourself create by loving and the one the beloved creates by loving you. The farther those two you's are apart the more the world grinds and grudges on its axis. But if you loved and were loved perfectly then there wouldn't be any difference between the two you's or any distance between them. They would coincide perfectly, there would be a perfect focus, as when a stereoscope gets the twin images on the card into perfect alignment.

Anyway, Anne Stanton, age seventeen, had probably gone upstairs to be alone because she was, all of a sudden, in love. She was in love with a rather tall, somewhat gangly, slightly stooped youth of twenty-one, with a bony horse face, a big almost askew hook of a nose, dark, unkempt hair, dark eyes (not burning and deep like the eyes of Cass Mastern, but frequently vague or veiled, bloodshot in the mornings, brightening only with excitement), big hands that worked and twisted slowly on his lap, plucking at each other, and twisted big feet that were inclined to shamble—a youth not beautiful, not brilliant, not industrious, not good, not kind, not even ambitious, given to excesses and confusions, thrown between melancholy and random violence, between the cold mire and the hot flame, between curiosity and apathy, between humility and self-love, between yesterday and tomorrow. What she had succeeded in creating out of that unpromising lump of clay scooped up from the general earth, nobody was ever to know.

But in any case, in her loving she was also re-creating herself, and she had gone upstairs to be in the dark and try to learn what that new self was. While downstairs Adam and I sat in the swing on the gallery, not saying a word. That was the evening Adam got counted out for all the other evenings, and out you go, you dirty dishrag, you.

Everybody else got counted out, too, for even on those evenings when a crowd would get together on the Stanton gallery, or my mother's, to play a phonograph and dance (with some of the boys—some of them veterans back from France—slipping off to take a drink from a bottle hidden out there in the crotch of a live oak), Anne and I would count them out. For organdie and seersucker are pretty thin materials, and the only person in the world I ever danced decently with was Anne Stanton and the nights were warm, and I wasn't so much taller than Anne that I could not inhale the full scent of her hair while our music-locked limbs paced out the pattern of our hypnosis and our breathing kept time together, till, after a while, I would pass from an acute awareness of body to a sense of being damned near disembodied, of floating as light as a feather or as light as a big empty-headed balloon held captive to the ground by a single thread, and waiting for a puff of breeze.

Or we would get into the roadster and drive out of the Landing and pull the cutout and tear along, hell-for-leather, or as much hell-for-leather as was possible on the roads and with the mechanism of those days, out beyond the houses between the pines and the tidelands, with her head leaned against my shoulder and her hair puffed with the wind and tendrils whipping against my cheek. She would lean there and laugh out loud and say, "Oh, Jackie, Jackie, it's a wonderful night, it's a wonderful night, it's a wonderful night, say it's a wonderful night, Jackie-boy, say it, say it!" Till I had to say it after her, like a lesson I was learning. Or she would hum or sing a song, one of those off the phonograph—God, what were they then? I don't remember. And maybe let the humming die off, and be perfectly still, with her eyes closed, until I stopped the car at some place where the breeze off the Gulf was enough to blow the mosquitoes away. (On nights when there wasn't any breeze, you simply didn't do any stopping.) Sometimes then, when I stopped the car she wouldn't even open her eyes till I had leaned over to kiss her, and I might have to kiss her enough to stop her breath. Or again, she would wait till just the instant before the kiss, then open her eyes wide, all at once, and say, "Boo!" and laugh. Then she'd be all knees and sharp elbows and little short laughs and giggles and serpentine evasions and strategy worthy of a jujitsu expert when I tried to capture her for a kiss. It was remarkable then how that little seat of a roadster gave as much room for deployment and maneuver as the classic plains of Flanders and how a creature who could lie in your clutch as lissome as willow and soft as silk and cuddly as a kitten could suddenly develop that appalling number of cunning, needle-pointed elbows and astute knees. While beyond the elbows and knees and sharp fingers, the eyes gleamed in the moonlight, or starlight, through the hair that had worked down loose, and the parted lips emitted the little bursts of breathless laughter, between the chanted words—"I don't—love—Jackie-Boy—nobody loves Jackie-Bird—I don't—love—Jackie-Boy—nobody loves—Jackie-Bird—" Till she would collapse laughing and exhausted into my arms and take her kiss and sigh and whisper, "I love Jackie-Boy," and rub a finger lightly over my face, and repeat, "I love Jackie-Boy—even with his ugly nose!" Then she would give the nose a sound tweak. And I would fondle that hooked, askew, cartilaginous monstrosity, pretending great pain but proud as Punch of the thing simply because she had put her fingers on it.

You never could tell whether it was going to be the long kiss or the furious swirl of elbows and giggles. And it didn't matter much, for it always came to the same thing in the end, for she would lean back with her head on my shoulder and look up at the sky. Between kisses we might not talk at all, or I might quote her poetry—for in those days I used to read some of it and thought I liked it—or we would talk about what we would do after we were married. I had never proposed to her. We simply assumed that we were going to be married and be together always in a world composed of sunlit beaches and moonlit pines by the sea and trips to Europe (where neither of us had ever been) and a house in an oak grove and the leather cushions of a roadster and somewhere a handful of delightful children who remained very vague in my imagination though very vivid in hers, and whose names, in moments when other topics of conversation failed, we would decide on with great debate and solemnity. All of them would have to have Stanton for a middle name. And one of the boys would be named Joel Stanton for the Governor. Of course, the oldest would be named Jack, for me. "Because you are the oldest thing in the world, Jackie-Boy," Anne would say, "The oldest will be named Jackie for you, because you are the oldest thing in the world, you are older than the ocean, you are older than the sky, you are older than the ground, you are older than the trees, and I always loved you and I always pulled your nose because you are an old, old mess, Jackie-Boy, Jackie-Bird, and I love you." So she would pull my nose.

Only once, toward the end of the summer, did she ask me what I was going to do for a living. Lying quietly on my arm, after a long silence, she suddenly said, "Jack, what are you going to do?"

I didn't know what the hell she was talking about. So I said, "What am I going to do? I am going to blow in your ear." And did it.

"What are you going to do? Do for a living?" she asked, again.

"Going to blow in your ear for a living," I said.

284

She didn't smile. "I mean it," she said.

I didn't answer for a minute. Then I said, "I've been thinking I might study law."

She was quiet for a little, then said, "You just thought of that this minute. You just said it."

I had just said it. The subject of my future, as a matter of fact, was one on which I had never cared to dwell. I simply didn't care. I would think that I'd get a job, any kind of a job, and do it and collect my pay and spend the pay and go back to the job on Monday morning, and that would be all. I had no ambitions. But I couldn't sit there and say to Anne, "Oh, I'll just get some kind of job." I had to give the impression of being farsighted and purposeful and competent.

I had played hell giving that impression.

She had seen right through me, like a piece of glass, and there wasn't anything to answer except to say that she was very wrong, that I was indeed going to study law, and what was wrong with studying law, please?

"You just made it up," she repeated stubbornly.

"Hell," I said, "I won't let you starve, I'll give you everything you've got. If you've got to have a big house and a lot of dresses and parties, well, I'll—"

But I didn't get to finish that.

"You know perfectly well, Jack Burden," she interrupted, "I don't have to have anything like that. You're just being mean. You're trying to put me in wrong. I don't want anything like that. You know I don't. You know I love you and I'll live in a shack and eat red beans if you've got to live that way because what you want to do doesn't make any money. But if you don't want to do anything—even if you do just sort of get a job and have plenty of money—oh, you know what I mean—you know the way some people are." She sat up very straight on the seat of the roadster and her eyes, ever in nothing but starlight, flashed that fine seventeen-year-old scorn. Then she fixed the gleam on me very steadily and said in a serious way that made her a funny mixture of a really grown-up woman and a little girl play-acting, probably with mother's loose clip-clopping high-heeled shoes and a feather boa, a serious way that made her both older and younger than she was—she said, "You know I love you, Jack Burden, and I believe in you, Jack Burden, and you are not going to be like those people, Jack Burden."

I laughed, it was so funny, and tried to kiss her, but she wouldn't let me and became suddenly all sharp elbows and knees working like a mowing machine and in dead earnest and I was the hay crop. I couldn't soothe her. I couldn't even lay a finger on her. She made me take her home, and wouldn't even kiss me good night.

That was the last I heard of it, except for one sentence. The next day, when she and I were lying out on the diving float, she said, all of a sudden, after a long sun-baked silence, "You remember last night?"

I said I did.

"Well," she said, "I meant it. I really did." Then she took her hand out of mine, slipped off the float, and swam away to keep me from making any answer.

I didn't hear any more about the business. And didn't think anything more about it. Anne was just like before, and I fell back into the full flood of the summer, into the full tide of feeling in which we drifted in a kind of breathless ease, like a strong, massive, deep current which didn't hurry but which had an irresistible weight of water behind it, and over which the days and nights passed like flickers of light and shade. It was drifting, all right, but not drifting in any nasty pejorative sense, like a waterlogged old skiff drifting in a horsepond or a cake of soap in the gray water before you pull the plug in the bathtub. No, it was a fine, conscious surrender which was a participation in and a willing of the flood itself, and not a surrender at all but an affirmation and all that, like the surrender of the mystic to God, which isn't a surrendering to God any more than it is also a creating of God, for if he loves God he has willed the being of God. Well, in my very surrender I willed and mastered that great current in which I drifted, and over which the days and nights flickered, and in which I didn't have to lift a hand to hurry myself, for the current knew its own pace and own time, and would take me with it.

I never tried to hurry anything all summer. Not in the porch swing, or in the pine woods, or on the float at night when we swam out, or in the roadster. Everything that happened came to happen as simply and as naturally and as gradually as a season coming on or a plant unrolling a leaf or a kitten waking up. And there was a kind of luxuriousness in not rushing things, in not driving toward the hot grip and awkward tussle and the leer for the boys back in the dormitory when you got in, a new sensuality in waiting for the massive current to take you where you belonged and would go in the end. She was young—she seemed younger to me then than she did later on looking back, for that summer I was so sure that I was old and jaded—and she was timid and sensitive and shy, but it wasn't any squealing, squeaking, pullet-squawking, teasing, twitching, oh-that's-not-nice-and-I-never-let-anybody-do-that-before-oh kind of shyness. Perhaps shyness is the wrong word for it, after all. Certainly it is wrong if back behind that word there is any implication or color of shame or fear or desire to be "nice." For in one way, she seemed to be detached from her very slender, compactly made, tight-muscled, soft-fleshed, golden-shouldered body, as though it were an elaborate and cunning mechanism in which she and I shared ownership, which had suddenly dropped to us out of the blue, and which, in our ignorance, we had to study with the greatest patience and most reverent attention lest we miss some minute, scholarly detail without knowledge of which everything would be wasted. So it was a period of the most delicate discrimination and subtle investigations, with her seriousness mixed with a graceful gaiety ("Oh, Jackie-Boy, oh, Jackie-Bird, it's a wonderful night, a wonderful night, his eyes are not bad but his nose is a fright"), a gaiety to which the words didn't mean much but the tune meant everything, a tune which seemed to come from the very air as though it were full of invisible strings and she simply reached out at random in the dark to pluck them with an idle familiar finger. And beyond the serious investigations was a kind of level-eyed affection, as natural and simple as the air you breathe, which sometimes didn't seem to belong with our hot-lipped and shallow-breathed occupations, which seemed to be something I had always had and not something connected with the new, mysterious body which now fascinated both her and me. She would sit and cup my head in both her hands and press it against her breast and sing, with the words just a whisper, the rhymes she made up as she went along ("Poor Jackie-Bird, he is a pest, but I'll rock him to sleep in a soft warm nest, and I'll sing a song to Jackie-Bird, the sweetest song he ever heard, poor Jackie-Bird, poor Jackie-Bird"), and after a while the words would just die away until there was only the little crooning sound, with the whisper now and then, "Poor Jackie-Bird, I'll never let anything hurt poor Jackie-Bird." Then after a while I would turn my face a little, toward her body, and kiss it through the light summer cloth and breathe through the cloth, upon it.

We went quite a long way, that summer, and there were times when I was perfectly sure I could have gone farther. When I could have gone the limit. For that fine, slender, compactly made, tight-muscled, soft-fleshed, golden-shouldered mechanism which fascinated Anne Stanton and me, which had dropped to us out of the blue, was a very sensitive and beautifully tuned-up contraption. But maybe I was wrong in that surmise, and maybe I could not have hurried the massive deliberation of that current in which we were caught and suspended, or hurried Anne Stanton's pensive and scholarly assimilation of each minute variation which had to be slowly absorbed into the body of our experience before another could be permitted. It was as though she was aware of a rhythm, a tune, a compulsion, outside of herself, and devoutly followed it in its subtle and winding progression. But wrong or not, I did not put my surmise to the test, for if I myself was not truly aware of that rhythm and compulsion which bemused her, I was aware of her devotion to it, and could find every moment with her full enough. Paradoxically enough, it was when I was away from her, when I was withdrawn from her context, back in my room at night or in the hot early afternoon, after lunch, that I was savagely impatient of the delays and discriminations. This would be especially true at those times when she wouldn't see me for a day, the times which seemed to mark, I came to understand, some stage, some milepost, we had passed. She would simply withdraw herself from me, as she had done that night after we first kissed, and leave me, at first, confused and guilty, but later, as I came to grasp the pattern of things, merely impatient for the next day when she would appear at the court, swinging her racket, her face so smooth, young, healthy and apparently disinterested, though comradely, that I could not equate it with the face I remembered with the eyelids drooping and the damp, starlight-or-moonlight-glistening lips parted for the quick, shallow breath or the unashamed sigh.

But once, late in the summer, I didn't see her for two days. The night before, which was windless, with a full moon and an atmosphere that scarcely cooled or stirred with the coming on of evening, Anne and I had swum down to the hotel diving tower, late enough for everybody else to be out of the water. We lay on the big float for a while, not doing any talking, not touching each other, just lying on our backs and looking up at the sky. After a while she got up and began to climb the tower. I rolled over on my side to watch her. She went up to the twenty-foot board, poised a moment, and did a swan dive, a nice one. Then she went up to the next board. I don't know how many dives she made, but it was a lot. I drowsily watched them, watched her climb up, very slow, rung by rung, the moonlight on the wet fabric of the dark bathing suit making it look like metal, or lacquer, watched her poise at the verge, lift her arms out to the tingling extreme, rise on her toes, leave the board, and seem to hang there an instant, a dully gleaming form so slender and high up it blotted out only a star or two, just an instant before the heady swoop and the clean swishing rip into the water as though she had dived through a great circus hoop covered with black silk spangled with silver.

It happened when she took the highest dive I had ever seen her take, perhaps the highest she was ever to take in her life. I saw her climbing up, slow, then pass the board she had been using, the twenty-foot board, and go on up. I called to her, but she didn't even look down at me. I knew she had heard me. I also knew that she would go on where she was going, no matter what I said now, now that she had started. I didn't call again.

She made the dive. I knew it was a good one from the very instant she left the board, but I jumped to my feet, just the same, and stood at the edge of the float, holding my breath, my eyes fixed on her flight. Just as she entered the water, clean as a whistle, I plunged in, too, diving deep and drawing down with my stroke. I saw the silvery tangle and trail of bubbles and the glimmer of her legs and arms in the dark water when she turned. She had gone down deep. Not that she had to go down deep, for she could whisk out shallow if she wanted. But that time—and other times—she went in deep, as if to continue the flight as long as possible through the denser medium. I pulled deep and met her as she began to rise. I put my arms around her waist and drew her to me and put our lips together. She let her arms trail down, loose, not making a motion, while I held her body to me and pressed her face back and our legs trailed down together as we rose slowly and waveringly through the blackness of the water and the silver of ascending bubbles. We rose very slowly, or at least it seemed very slowly, and I was holding my breath so long there was a pain in my chest and a whirling dizziness in my head, but the pain and the dizziness had passed the line over into a rapture like that I had had in my room the night I had first taken her to a movie and had stopped on the way home. I thought we would never reach the surface, we rose so slowly.

Then we were there, with the moonlight brittle and fractured on the water all about our eyes. We hung there together, still not breathing, for another moment, then I released her and we fell apart to float on our backs and gaspingly draw the air in and stare up at the high, whirling, star-stung sky.

After a little while I realized that she was swimming away. I thought that she would be taking a few strokes to the float. But when I did finally roll over and swim to the float, she was already at the beach. I saw her pick up her robe, wrap it around her, and stoop to put on her sandals. I called to her. She waved back, then shaking her hair loose out of the cap, began to run up the beach toward home. I swam in, but by the time I reached the beach she was near her house. I knew I couldn't catch her. So I walked on up the beach, taking my time.

I didn't see her for two days after that. Then she appeared at the tennis court, swinging her racket, friendly and cool, getting ready to beat the hell out of me as soon as Adam had given me his lacing.

We were in September then. In a few days Anne was to leave to go back up East to Miss Pound's School. Her father was going to take her a few days early and stop with her in Washington and then in New York before sending her on to Boston, where Miss Pound would get her hooks in. Anne hadn't seemed particularly excited about the trip, or about getting back to Miss Pound. She liked the school fine, she had told me, but I hadn't been overwhelmed by tales of midnight snacks and memory books and that darling teacher of French, and her vocabulary wasn't slimed up with offensive bits of esoteric finishing-school slang. Back in August she had mentioned the plan, the date of departure, but without pleasure or displeasure, as though it were something completely irrelevant to us, the way a young person mentions death. When she mentioned it, I had felt a sudden twinge, but I had managed to put the thought aside, for even though the calendar said it was August I had not been able to believe that the summer, and the world, would ever end. But that morning when Anne reappeared at the tennis court, my first thought was that she would be going soon. It really came over me then. I went up to her, not even saying hello, and took her hand, feeling a kind of unformulated desperation and urgency.

She looked at me with an expression of mild surprise.

"Don't you love me?" I demanded, angrily.

She burst out laughing, and fixed her eyes on me, with the laughter making innocent, mocking crinkles at the outer corners of the absolutely clear eyes. "Sure," she said, laughing, the idle racket swinging in her free hand, "sure, I love you, Jackie-Boy, Jackie-Bird, who said I didn't love poor old Jackie-Bird?"

"Don't be silly," I said, for the language of all our nights in the roadster and in the porch swing suddenly seemed, in the glare of morning and with the desperation in me, fatuous and loathsome. "Don't be silly," I repeated, "and don't call me Jackie-Bird."

"But you *are* Jackie-Bird," she replied gravely, but with the crinkles still at the corners of the eyes.

"Don't you love me?" I demanded, ignoring what she had said.

"I love Jackie-Bird," she said, "poor Jackie-Bird."

"God damn it," I said, "don't you love me?"

She studied me a moment, with the crinkles entirely gone low. "Yes," she said then, "I do," and pulled her hand out of mine and walked across the court, with a kind of finality in the stride as though she had made up her mind to go somewhere and it was quite a way and she had better start walking. She only walked across the court, to sit on the bench in the feathery shade of the mimosa, but I watched her as though the court were as wide as the Sahara and she were dwindling into distance.

Then Adam came, and we played tennis.

She had come back that morning, but it was not to be as it had been before. She had come back, all right, but not all of her. She was with me as much as before, but she seemed to be wrapped in her own thoughts, and when I caressed her she seemed to submit out of a sense of duty or at the best out of a kindness which wasn't quite contemptuous. That was the way it was for the last week, while the days stayed hot and breathless, and clouds piled up in the late afternoons as though promising a squall but the squall didn't come, and the nights were as heavy and blunt as a big black silver-dusted grape ready to burst.

Two nights before she was supposed to leave we went in to the Landing to a movie. It was raining when we came out of the movie. We had intended to go for a swim after the show, but we didn't. We had taken lots of swims in the rain, that summer and the summers before when Adam had been with us. We would no doubt have gone that night too, if the rain had been a different kind of rain, if it had been a light sweet rain, falling out of a high sky, the kind that barely whispers with a silky sound on the surface of the water you are swimming in, or if it had been a driven, needle-pointed, cold, cathartic rain to make you want to run along the beach and yell before you took refuge in the sea, or even if it had been a torrent, the kind you get on the Gulf that is like nothing so much as what happens when the bottom finally bursts out of a big paper bag suspended full of water. But it wasn't like any of those kinds of rain. It was as though the sky had sagged down as low as possible and there were a universal leaking of bilge down through the black, gummy, dispirited air.

So we put the top up on the roadster, getting well wet doing it, got in, and drove toward home. The light was blazing in my mother's place and on the gallery, and so we decided to go in there and make some coffee and sandwiches. It was still early, about nine-thirty. My mother, I remembered, had gone down the Row to play bridge with the Pattons and some fellow who was visiting them and was stuck on her. We wheeled up the drive and ground to a stop with a great crunching and spraying of shells and rain water. We ran up the right-hand sweep of the twin flights of steps leading to the gallery, then safe under the gallery roof began to stamp and shake the water from us like dogs. The running and stamping and the wet had made Anne's hair come loose. It was hanging down her back, with some odd wet strands plastered across her brow and one over her cheek to make her look like a child coming out of a bath. She laughed as she cocked her head to one side and shook it, the way girls do, to make the hair fall free. She ran her spread fingers through the hair like a big comb to catch the stray hairpins. A couple of them fell to the gallery floor. "I'm a fright," she said, "I'm an awful fright," and kept on cocking her head over and laughing and looking up at me sidewise with bright eyes. She was more like she had been before.

I said, yes, she was a fright, and we went on into the house.

I switched the light off in the big hall, but let the gallery lights stay on, then led the way back to the kitchen, through the dining room and pantry, off to the right of the hall. I put the coffee on to make, and got some food out of the icebox (that was back yonder before electric refrigerators or my mother would have had a brace of them big as a log cabin and surrounded at midnight by ladies with bare shoulders and tipsy men in dinner jackets, just like the ads). While I did the scullery work, Anne was braiding her hair. Apparently she was planning a pigtail on each side, for one was well under way by the time I had the grub laid out on the kitchen table. "Why don't you make the sandwiches and stop primping?" I said.

"All right," she said, "and you'll have to fix the hair."

So while she sat at the table and fixed the sandwiches, I finished the first pigtail. "There ought to be a ribbon on it to hold it together," I said, "or something." I was pressing the end between my fingers to keep it from coming unplaited. Then my eyes fell on a clean dish towel on the rack. I dropped the braid and went over to the towel and tore with the aid of a pocket knife two strips off the end. The dish towel was white with a red border. I came back, repaired the damage to the braid, and tied up the end with the piece of towel in a bow-knot. "You'll look like a pickaninny," I said. She giggled and kept on spreading peanut butter.

I saw that the coffee was made, and turned off the gas. Then I began to work on the second pigtail. I leaned over and ran the silky stuff through my fingers, which were all tingling thumbs as rough as sandpaper, separated it into three skeins, and while I folded them over into place, one after another, breathed in the fresh meadowy smell the hair had because it was damp. I was thus occupied when the telephone rang. "Take this," I ordered Anne, "or it'll unravel," and thrust the end of the pigtail at her. Then I went out to the hall.

It was my mother. She and the Pattons and the fellow who was stuck on her, and God knew who else, were going to pile into the car and drive forty miles to La Grange, a joint in the next county, on the road to the city, where there were a few dice tables and a couple of roulette wheels and where the best people rubbed shoulders with the worst and inhaled a communal blue fog of throat-lacerating tobacco smoke and illicit alcohol fumes. She said she didn't know when she'd be in, but to leave the door open, for she'd forgotten her key. She didn't have to tell me to leave the door open, for nobody ever locked up in the Landing, anyway. She said not to worry, for she felt lucky, and laughed and hung up. Well, she needn't have told me not to worry, either. Not about her luck. She was lucky, all right. She got everything she wanted.

I hung up the receiver and looked up to see, in the light that came to the hall from the door to the back passage, Anne standing a few feet from me, just tying the bow to the end of the second long pigtail. "It was my mother," I explained.

"She and the Pattons are going to La Grange." Then added, "She won't be back till late."

As I said that last, I was suddenly aware of the emptiness of the house, the dark rooms around us, the weight of darkness stored above us, stuffing the rooms and the attic, spilling thickly but weightlessly down the stairs, and aware of the darkness outside. As I looked into Anne's face there wasn't a sound in the house. Outside there was the drip on leaves and on the roof, now subsiding. Then my heart took a big knock, and I felt the new blood coursing through me as though somebody had opened a sluice gate.

I was looking right into Anne's face, and doing so, I knew, and knew that she knew, that this was the moment the great current of the summer had been steadily moving toward all the time. I turned around and moved slowly up the hall toward the foot of the stairs. I couldn't tell at first whether she was following or not. Then I knew she was. I climbed the stairs, and knew she was following about four steps behind me.

At the head of the stairs, in the upstairs hall, I didn't even pause or look around. I moved up the hall, which was pitch dark, toward the door of my room. My hand touched the knob in the dark, and I pushed the door open and entered. There was a little light in the room, for the night had, apparently, cleared for the moment, and too, the glare of the gallery light below was reflected up from the wet leaves. I stood to one side, with my hand still on the knob of the door, while she walked into the room. She didn't even glance at me as she came in. She took about three steps into the room and stopped. I closed the door and moved toward the white-clothed narrow figure; but she did not turn around. I stood behind her, drawing her shoulders back against me and folding my forearms over her bosom and putting my dry lips down against her hair. Meanwhile her arms hung loosely at her sides. We stood that way for a couple of minutes, like lovers in an advertisement watching a dramatic sunset or the ocean or Niagara Falls. But we weren't watching anything. We were standing in the middle of a bare, shadowy room (iron bed, old dresser, pine table, trunks and books and male gear—for I hadn't let my mother turn that room into a museum) and staring across the room out into the dark tops of trees which all at once began to stir with a wind off the Gulf and rattle in an increase of rain.

Then Anne lifted her arms and folded them before her so that one of her hands was on each of mine. "Jackie," she said in a low voice, which wasn't, however, a whisper, "Jackie-Bird, I came up here."

She had come, all right.

I began to undo the hooks and eyes down the back of the white dress. She stood absolutely still, as though good and obedient, with a pigtail hanging back over each shoulder. The fact that the light cloth was damp and clingy didn't make things any easier. I kept fumbling the God-damned hooks and eyes. Then I came to the sash. It was tied in a bow on the left side, I remember. I got that free, and it fell to the floor, and I began again on the dress. She was as patient, standing there with her arms at her side, as though I were a dressmaker and she were having a fitting. She didn't say anything except when I, in my clumsiness and confusion, tried to pull the dress down over her hips. "No," she said then, in the same low voice as before, "no, this way," and lifted her bare arms above her head. I noticed, even then, that she didn't let the fingers fall loose in the natural way, but held them together on each hand, and almost straight, as though she were lifting her arms for a dive and had stopped just before completing the preliminary posture. I drew the dress over her head and stood there with it clutched foolishly in my hands before I got the wit to lay it across a chair.

She was standing with her arms still up, and I took that as a sign the slip was to come off the same way the dress had. It came off the same way, and with my clumsy, nervous meticulousness I laid it across a chair, as though it might break. She lowered her arms to her sides and stood with the same passivity while I finished the task. While I unhooked the brassière, and lifted it forward so that it would fall down her motionless arms, and released the drawers and drew them down her legs, kneeling on the floor beside her, I was somehow so careful that my fingers never even brushed her skin. My breath was quick and the constriction in my throat and chest was like a knot, but my mind kept flying off to peculiar things—to a book I had started and never finished, to wondering whether I would go back to the dormitory that fall or take a room out, to an algebraic formula I remembered which kept running through my head, to a scene, just the corner of a field with a broken stile, which I tried desperately to locate out of my past. My mind would just take those crazy wild leaps and centrifugal plunges like an animal with one foot in a trap or a June bug on a string.

As I crouched there beside her, just as I had let the batiste drop about her feet, she slipped one foot from its pump—you know how girls do, pressing the heels together a little so that the feet can be drawn out—then the other. I rose to stand beside her, and experienced a kind of shock to find how small she was, standing flat on the floor without her heels. I had seen her that way a thousand times, in a bathing suit, standing barefooted on the sand or float. But it struck me now.

She stood there, as I rose, with her arms hanging loose as before, then she folded them across her breast and hunched her

294

shoulders a little and gave a slight shiver, and I saw how with the drawing forward of the shoulders the shoulder blades suddenly seemed sharp and frail, with a pigtail hanging down across each one.

It was raining hard outside now, with violent gusts. I noticed that.

Her head was slightly inclined forward, and she apparently saw, or remembered, that she still had on her stockings. Turning from me a little, she leaned forward, and balancing herself on one foot and then the other, drew them off and let them fall with the sash and the little wispy pile of stuff there before her. Then she stood as before, hunched slightly forward, perhaps shivering, her knees slightly bent and pressed together.

While I stood there fumbling with the buttons on my shirt, tearing one loose because I couldn't seem to get it through the buttonhole (in a momentary lull of the wind and rain, it made a single *tick* when it struck the uncarpeted floor), and while my mind made the crazy June-bug leaps and plunges, she walked across to the iron bed and sat down, tentatively, close to the edge, her feet and knees pressed close, her arms still folded and her shoulders slightly hunched as before. She was looking up at me across the space, with a question, or appeal, in her eyes—I couldn't read them in the dimness.

Then, letting one hand drop to the bed for support, she leaned a little sideways, lifted her feet from the floor, still together, and with a gentle, curling motion, lay back on the white counterpane, then punctiliously straightened out and again folded her hands across her bosom, and closed her eyes.

And at the instant when she closed her eyes, as I stared at her, my mind took one of the crazy leaps and I saw her floating in the water, that day of the picnic three years before, with her eyes closed and the violent sky above and the white gull flashing high over, and that face and this face and that scene and this scene seemed to fuse, like superimposed photographs, each keeping its identity but without denying the other. And at that instant, as I stood there with the constriction in my throat that made me swallow hard and with my body tumescent, I looked at her there on the iron bed, then looked suddenly around the big, bare, shadowy room and heard the gusty rain and knew that everything was wrong, completely wrong, how I didn't know, didn't try to know, and that this was somehow not what the summer had been driving toward. That I wasn't going to do it. "Anne," I said, hoarsely, "Anne—"

She didn't answer, but she opened her eyes, and looked at me.

"We oughtn't," I began, "we oughtn't—it wouldn't—it wouldn't be—it wouldn't be right." So I used the word *right*, which came to my lips to surprise me, for I hadn't ever thought of anything I had done with Anne Stanton or with any other woman or girl as being right or wrong, but as just something that happened, and hadn't ever thought about right or wrong very much in connection with anything but had simply done the things people do and not done the things people don't do. Which are the things people do and don't do. And I remember now the surprise I felt when I heard that word there in the air, like the echo of a word spoken by somebody else God knows how many years before, and now unfrozen like a word in Baron Munchausen's tale. I couldn't any more have touched her then than if she had been my little sister.

She didn't answer then, but kept on looking at me, with an expression I could not fathom, and as I looked at her I was overwhelmed by a great, warm pity, like a flood in my bosom, and burst out, "Anne—oh, Anne—" and felt the impulse to fling myself to my knees beside the bed and seize her hand.

Now if I had done that, things might have developed differently and more in the normal pattern, for it is probable that when a half-clothed and healthy young man kneels beside a bed and seizes the hand of an entirely unclothed and good-looking young girl, developments will follow the normal pattern sooner or later. And if I had once touched her in the process of undressing her, or even if she had spoken to me to say anything, to call me Jackie-Boy or tell me she loved me, or had giggled or seemed gay, or had even answered me, saying anything whatsoever, when I looked at her lying there on the bed and first cried out her name—if any of those things had happened things might have been different then and forever afterward. But none of those things had happened, and I was not to follow the wild impulse to throw myself on my knees by the bed and take her hand to make the first trifling contact of flesh with flesh, which would probably have been enough. For just as I burst out, "Anne—oh, Anne—" there was the sound of tires on the drive, then the creaking of brakes.

"They've come back, they've come back!" I exclaimed, and Anne rose abruptly to a sitting position on the bed and looked wildly at me.

"Grab your stuff," I ordered, "grab your stuff, and get to the bathroom—you could have been in the bathroom!" I was cramming my shirt in and was trying to buckle my belt all at once and was going toward the door. "I'll be in the kitchen," I said, "I'll be fixing something to eat!"

Then I bolted from the room, and ran down the hall, trying to run on tiptoe, and ran down the back stairs to the back passage and then into the kitchen, where I put a match to the gas under the coffeepot with trembling fingers just as the front screen door slammed and people entered the hall. I sat down at the table and began to make sandwiches, waiting for my heart to stop pounding before I confronted my mother and the Pattons and whatever bastards they had with them.

When my mother came on back to the kitchen, right away, followed by her gang, there I was and there was a nice pile of toothsome sandwiches and they weren't going to La Grange because of the storm and kidded me about being a mind reader and having the sandwiches and coffee all ready for them, and I was charming and gracious to them all. Then Anne came down (she had done a good circumstantial job and flushed the toilet twice to advertise her whereabouts) and they kidded her about her pigtails and her pickaninny hair ribbons, and she didn't say anything but smiled shyly the way a nice well-bred young girl should when the grownups take amiable notice of her, and then she sat quietly and ate a sandwich and I couldn't read a thing from her face, not a thing.

Well, that was the way the summer ended. True, there was the rest of the night, with me lying on the iron bed and hearing the leaves drip and cursing myself for a fool and cursing my luck and trying to figure out what Anne had thought and trying to plan how I would get her off alone the next day—the last day. But then I would think how if I had gone on, it would have been worse, with my mother coming back and going upstairs with the ladies (as she had done), and with Anne and me trapped there in my room. And as that thought scared me into a cold sweat, I suddenly had the feeling of great wisdom: I had acted rightly and wisely. Therefore we had been saved. And so my luck became my wisdom (as the luck of the damned human race becomes its wisdom and gets into the books and is taught in schools), and then later my wisdom became my nobility, for in the end, a long time after, I got the notion that I had acted out of nobility. Not that I used that word to myself, but I skirted all around its edges and frequently, late at night or after a few drinks, thought better of myself for remembering my behavior on that occasion.

And as my home movie unrolled, as I drove west, I could not help but reflect that if I hadn't been so noble—if it was nobility—everything would have been different. For certainly if Anne and I had been trapped in that room, my mother and Governor Stanton would have set us up in matrimony, even if grimly and grudgingly. And then whatever else might have happened, the thing that had happened to send me west would never have happened. So, I observed, my nobility (or whatever it was) had had in my world almost as dire a consequence as Cass Mastern's sin had had in his. Which may tell something about the two worlds.

There was, as I was saying, the rest of the night after Anne had gone home. But there was also the next day. Anne, however, was busy packing and doing errands in the Landing during the day. I hung around her house, and tried to talk with her, but we never got more than a few words together, except when I drove her down to town. I tried to make her marry me right away, just to go home and get a bag and tear out. She was under age, and all that, but I figured we could get by—in so far as I figured anything. Then let the Governor and my mother raise hell. She only said, "Jackie-Boy, you know I'm going to marry you. Of course, I'm going to marry you forever and ever. But not today." When I kept pestering her, she said, "You go on back to State and finish up and I'll marry you. Even before you get your law degree."

When she said "law degree," I didn't really remember right off what she was talking about. But I remembered in time not to express any surprise and had to be satisfied with that.

I helped her with the errands, took her home, and then went to my house for dinner. After dinner I went to see her early, going in the roadster with the hope, despite the lowering gusty weather, that we could take a ride. But it was no soap. Some of the boys and girls we had played round with that summer were there to tell Anne good-bye, and some parents, two couples, were there, too, to see the Governor (who wasn't Governor any more, but to the Landing would always be the "Governor") and give him a stirrup cup. The young people played a phonograph on the gallery, and the old people, who looked old to us anyway, sat inside and drank gin and tonic. The best I could do was to dance with Anne, who was sweet to me but who, when I kept asking her to slip out with me, said she couldn't just then, she couldn't because of the guests and she'd try to later. But then another storm blew up, for it was right at the equinox, and the parents came out to say they had better go home, and told their particular young ones in a loud voice that they ought to come too and let Anne get some sleep for the trip.

I hung around, but it didn't do any good. Governor Stanton sat in the living room and had another drink by himself and looked over the evening paper. We clung together in the porch swing, and listened to his paper rattle when he turned the page, and whispered that we loved each other. Then we just clung without talking, for the words began to lose their meaning, and listened to the rain beat the trees.

When a little break came in the rain, I got up, went inside, and shook hands with the Governor, then came out, kissed Anne good-bye, and left. It was a stiff cold-lipped kiss, as though the summer never had been at all, or hadn't been what it had been.

I went on back to State. I felt that I couldn't wait for Christmas when she would come home. We wrote every day, but the letters began to seem like checks drawn on the summer's capital. There had been a lot in the bank, but it is never good business practice to live on your capital, and I had the feeling, somehow, of living on the capital and watching something dwindle. At the same time, I was wild to see her.

I saw her Christmas, for ten days. It wasn't like the summer. She told me she loved me and was going to marry me, and she let me go pretty far. But she wouldn't marry me then, and she wouldn't go the limit. We had a row about that just before she left. She had been willing to in September, but now she wouldn't. It seemed that she was, in a way, breaking a promise, and so I got pretty mad. I told her she didn't love me. She said she did. I wanted to know why she wouldn't go on, then. "It's not because I'm afraid and it's not beause I don't love you. Oh, I do love you, Jackie, I do," she said, "and it's not because I'm a nasty old nicey-pants. It's because you are the way you are, Jackie."

"Yeah," I sneered, "you mean you don't trust me, you think I wouldn't marry you and then you'd be the ruined maid."

"I know you'd marry me," she said, "it's just because you're the way you are."

But she wouldn't say any more. So we had an awful row. I went back to State a nervous wreck.

She didn't write to me for a month. I held out about two weeks, and then began to apologize. So the letters began again, and far off somewhere in the great bookkeeping system of the universe somebody punched some red buttons every day on a posting machine and some red figures went on the ledger sheet.

She was back at the Landing in June for a few days. But the Governor was not well and before long the doctors packed him off to Maine to get him out of the heat. He took Anne with him. Before she left, it was just like Christmas, and not like the summer before. It was even worse than Christmas, for I had my B.A. now and it was time for me to get into the Law School. We had a row about that. Or was it about that? She said something about law and I blew up. We made it up, by letter, after she had been in Maine six weeks, and the letters began again and the red figures fell like bloody little bird tracks on that ledger leaf bearing my name in the sky, and I lay around Judge Irwin's house and read American history, not for school, not because I had to, but because I had, by accident, stepped through the thin, crackly crust of the present, and felt the first pull of the quicksand about my ankles. When she came back for a week or so in the fall, with her father, before she went off to some refined female college in Virginia, we spent a lot of time in the bay and in the roadster, and made all the motions we had made before. She flew down from the diving tower like a bird. She lay in my arms in the moonlight, when there was moonlight. But it was not the way it had been.

For one thing, there was the incident of the new kiss. About the second or third time we were together that fall, she kissed me in a new way, a way she had never used before. And she didn't do it in the discriminating, experimental way she had done things the summer before. She just did it, in the heat of the moment, you might say. I knew right away she had picked it up from some man up in Maine that summer, some summer bastard in white flannel pants with vowels that clicked like dominoes. I told her I knew she'd been fooling with some fellows in Maine. She didn't deny it, not even for an instant. She just said, "Yes," as cool as could be, and asked me how I knew. I told her. Then she said, "Oh, of course," and I got pretty mad and pulled away from her. She had kept her arm around my neck the whole time.

She just looked at me, still cool, and said, "Jack, I did kiss a man up in Maine. He was a nice boy, Jack, and I liked him a lot and he was fun to be with. But I didn't love him. And if you and I hadn't had that row and I hadn't felt that the world had sort of come to an end and I wouldn't be with you again, I wouldn't have done it. Maybe I wanted to fall in love with him. To fill up the empty place you left, Jackie.—Oh, Jackie, there was a place, an awful big place—" And with a simple unthinking gesture she laid her right hand on her heart. "But I couldn't," she said. "I couldn't fall in love with him. And I quit kissing him. Even before we made up, you and I." She reached out and laid her right hand on one of my hands, and leaned toward me. "For we did make up, you and I," she asked, "didn't we, Jackie-Bird?" She laughed a quick laugh that welled up in her throat, then asked, "Didn't we, Jackie-Boy? Didn't we? And I'm happy again!"

"Yeah," I said, "we did."

"Aren't you happy?" she asked, leaning.

"Sure," I said, and was as happy, I suppose, as I deserved to be. But the thing was there all the time, breathing back there in the dark of my mind and waiting to pounce. Even though I forgot it was there. Then, the next night when she didn't kiss me in the new way, I felt the thing stir. And the next night. Because she didn't kiss that new way I was even angrier than I had been when she had. So I kissed her the way that man in Maine had done. She drew back from me immediately and said, quite quietly, "I know why you did that."

"You liked it well enough up in Maine," I said.

"Oh, Jackie," she said, "there isn't any place called Maine and never was, there just isn't anything but you and you are all forty-eight states together and I loved you all the time. Now will you be good? And kiss me our way?"

So I did that, but the world is a great snowball rolling downhill and it never rolls uphill to unwind itself back to nothing at all and nonhappening.

Even though the summer just past had not been like the summer before, I went on to State again and got my job back hashing and did some newspaper reporting and entered the Law School and loathed it. Meanwhile I wrote letters to Anne at the very refined female college in Virginia, and the capital on which those checks were drawn dwindled and dwindled. Till Christmas, when I came home and Anne came home, I told her I simply loathed the Law School, and expected (and, in a twisted way, wanted) hell to pop. But hell did not pop. She merely reached over and patted my hand. (We were sitting on the couch in the Stanton living room, where we had clutched and clung until we had finally fallen apart from each other, she in a kind of withdrawn melancholy, and I in the fatigue and irritation of desire too long protracted and frustrated.) She patted my hand, and said, "Well, don't study law, then. You don't have to study law."

"What do you want me to do then?"

"Jackie, I never wanted you to study law. It was your idea."

"Oh, was it?" I asked.

"Yes," she said, and patted my hand again. "Do what you want to, Jackie. I want you to do what you want. And I don't care if you don't make money. I told you long back I'd live on red beans with you."

I got up from the couch. For one reason so she couldn't pat my hand in that way which suddenly reminded me of the way a nurse pats the hand of a patient, a sort of impersonal pat intended to be soothing. I stood well back from her, and spoke firmly. "All right, you'll eat red beans with me. Let's get married. Tomorrow. Tonight. We've fooled around long enough. You say you love me. All right, I love you."

She didn't say anything, but sat there on the couch with her hands lying loose in her lap, and lifted her face, which suddenly was tired and drawn, and looked up at me from eyes which gradually brightened with unshed tears.

"You do love me?" I demanded.

She nodded slowly.

"And you know I love you?" I demanded.

She nodded again.

"All right, then?"

"Jack," she said, then stopped for a moment. "Jack, I do love you. I guess I feel sometimes that I might just kiss you and hold you tight and close my eyes and jump off a cliff with you. Or like that time when you dived down to me and we kissed in the water and it seemed like we'd never come up. Do you remember, Jack?"

"Yes," I said.

"I loved you like that then, Jack."

"Now?" I demanded, "what about now?"

"Now, too, Jack, I guess I could do it now, too. But it's different, too."

"Different?"

"Oh, Jack," she exclaimed, and for the first time, at least the first time I ever remembered, made the gesture of lifting her hands to her temples, that gesture to control distraction which was never to become characteristic but which I was to see again. "Oh, Jack," she said again, "things have happened, so much has happened. Since then."

"What has happened?"

"Oh, it's just that getting married isn't like jumping off a cliff. Love isn't either, isn't like jumping off a cliff. Or getting drowned. It's—it's—oh, I don't know how to say it—it's trying to live, it's having a way to live."

"Money," I said, "if it's money you—"

"It's not money," she interrupted, "I don't mean money—oh, Jack, if you only could see what I mean!"

"Well, I'm not going to get a job with Patton or anybody round here. Or have them get me a job. Not even Irwin. I'll get a job, I don't care what kind, but not with them."

"Darling," she said tiredly, "I'm not trying to make you come here. Or get a job with Patton. Or anybody. I want you to do what you want. Just so it is something. Even if you don't make money. I told you I'd live in a shack."

So I went back to the Law School and by dint of consistent effort succeeded in busting out before the end of the year. It took a lot of attention to get busted out, for a man just can't achieve that by the ordinary means at State. He has to work at it. I could have simply resigned, of course, but if you simply drop out or resign, you might be able to come back. So I busted out. Then while I was celebrating my busting out and was pretty sure Anne would be sore and throw me over, I got involved with a pal of mine and two girls and there was a small scandal, which got into the papers. I was an ex-student then, and so the University couldn't do anything about it. Anne didn't do anything either, for I guess I was an ex-Jackie-Bird by that time.

So Anne went her way and I went mine. My way was to work for a newspaper and hang around the lower part of the city and read books on American history. Finally I was taking courses at the University again, just spare time at first, then seriously. I was entering the enchantments of the past. For a while it looked as though Anne and I had made it up, but somehow a gear slipped and it was like before. I didn't finish the Ph.D. So I went back to the *Chronicle*, where I was a reporter and a damned good one. I even got married. To Lois, who was damned good looking, a lot better looking, I suppose, than Anne, and juicy while Anne was inclined to bone and muscle under flesh. Lois looked edible, and you knew it was tender all the way through, a kind of mystic combination of filet mignon and a Georgia peach aching for the tongue and ready to bleed gold. Lois married me for reasons best known to herself. But one was, I am sure, that my name was Burden. I am forced to this conclusion by the process of elimination. It could not have been my beauty, grace, charm, wit, intellect, and learning, for, in the first place, my beauty, grace, and charm, were not great, and in the second place Lois didn't have the slightest interest in wit, intellect, and learning. Even if I had had them. It could not have been my mother's money, for Lois's own widowed mother had plenty of money, which Lois's father had made from a lucky war contract for gravel, a little too late to give those things called advantages to his daughter at her most impressionable age. So it must have been the name of Burden.

Unless it was that Lois was in love with me. I put this possibility in the list merely for logical and schematic completeness, for I am quite sure that the only things Lois knew about love was how to spell the word and how to make the physiological adjustments traditionally associated with the idea. She did not spell very well, but she made those adjustments with great skill and relish. The relish was nature, but the skill was art, and *ars longa est*. I knew this despite the very expert and sustained histrionics of which Lois was capable. I knew it, but I succeeded in burying it out in the back yard of my mind, like a rat that has been caught in the pantry gnawing the cheese. I didn't really care, I suppose, so long as nothing happened to make me have to face the fact. And once in my arms, Mrs. Burden was very faithful or very discreet, for nothing ever happened. And the arrangement was perfect.

"Jack and I are perfectly adjusted sexually," Lois used to say primly, for she was very advanced in what with her passed for thought and was very sophisticated in her language. She would look around at the faces of the guests in the very slick modernistic apartment (her taste ran that way and not to balconies overlooking charming old patios, and her money paid the rent), and would tell them how perfectly adjusted she and I were, and in telling would add about two extra chocolate-cream-puff syllables to the word *sexually*. For a while I didn't mind her telling the guests about how well adjusted we were. It even flatttered my ego, for nobody would mind having his name coupled with that of Lois or having his picture taken with her in a public place. So I would beam modestly around the little group, while Lois told them about that perfect adjustment. But later it began to annoy me.

As long as I regarded Lois as a beautiful, juicy, soft, vibrant, sweet-smelling, sweet-breathed machine for provoking and satisfying the appetite (and that was the Lois I had married), all was well. But as soon as I began to regard her as a person, trouble began. All would have been well, perhaps, had Lois been struck dumb at puberty. Then no man could have withstood her. But she could talk, and when something talks you sooner or later begin to listen to the sound it makes and begin, even in the face of all other evidence, to regard it as a person. You begin to apply human standards to it, and the human element infects your innocent Eden pleasure in the juicy, sweet-breathed machine. I had loved Lois the machine, the way you love the filet mignon or the Georgia peach, but I definitely was not in love with Lois the person. In fact, as the realization grew that the machine-Lois belonged to, and was the instrument of, the person-Lois (or at least to the thing which could talk), the machine-Lois which I had innocently loved began to resemble a beautiful luscious bivalve open and pulsing in the glimmering deep and I some small speck of marine life being drawn remorselessly. Or it resembled the butt of wine in which the duke was drowned, and I was sure-God the Duke of Clarence. Or it resembled a greedy, avid, delicious quagmire which would swallow up the lost, benighted traveler with a last tired, liquid, contented sigh. Yes, in that greedy, delicious quagmire, the solemn temples, the gorgeous palaces, towers, battlements, libraries, museums, huts, hospitals, houses, cities, and all the works of man might be swallowed up, with that last luxurious sigh. Or so, I recall, it seemed. But the paradox is that as long as Lois was merely the machine-Lois, as long as she was simply a well-dressed animal, as long as she was really a part of innocent nonhuman nature, as long as I hadn't begun to notice that the sounds she made were words, there was no harm in her and no harm in the really extraordinary pleasure she could provide. It was only when I observed that this Lois was mixed up with the other Lois, with certain human traits, that I began to feel that all the works of man might be swallowed up in the quagmire. It is a delicate paradox.

I did not make a decision not to be swallowed up. The instinct for self-preservation is more deep-seated than decision. A man doesn't make a decision to swim when he falls into the creek. He starts kicking. I simply began to wriggle and squirm and kick. First, I recall, there was the matter of Lois's friends (no friends of mine ever set foot in the slick apartment, if as a matter of fact, the people I knew in the city room and the speak-easy and the press club could be called friends). I began to take a distaste to the friends Lois had. There was nothing particularly wrong with them. They were just the ordinary garden variety of human garbage. There were some who had what Lois, who was not too well informed on the subject, regarded as "position" but who didn't have much money and liked Lois's free likker. There were some who didn't have any "position" but who had more money than Lois and knew which fork to use. And there were some who didn't have very much of either position or money, but who had some credit at the better clothing stores and who could be bullied by Lois. They all read *Vanity Fair* or *Harper's Bazaar* (according to sex, and some read both) and *Smart Set,* and they quoted Dorothy Parker, and those who had been merely to Chicago licked the spittle of those who had been to New York, and those who had been merely to New York licked the spittle of those who had been to Paris. As I say, there was nothing particularly wrong with those people, many of whom were quite agreeable and attractive. The only thing I found wrong with them, I admit as I look back, was that they were Lois's friends. First, I developed a certain reserve in my dealings with them, then I developed an attitude which Lois defined as snotty. After one of my exhibitions Lois would try to discipline me by withholding the sweets of her gender.

That was the matter of Lois's friends. But there was, second, the matter of Lois's apartment. I took a distaste for the apartment. I told Lois I didn't want to live there. That we would get a place on which I could afford to pay the rent out of my salary. We had some rows on that point, rows which I didn't expect to win. Then the sweets would be withheld.

That was the matter of the apartment. But there was, third, the matter of my clothes and what Lois loved to call my "grooming." I was accustomed to thirty-dollar suits, shirts that had been worn two days, a bimonthly haircut, unpolished shoes, a hat with a brim that looped and sagged, and fingernails always broken and sometimes dirty. And I regarded the habit of pressing pants as something which had not come to stay. In the early days when I looked on Lois as merely the luscious machine, I had allowed certain scarcely perceptible changes to be made in my appearance. But as I began to realize that the noises she made with her mouth resembled human speech and were more than rudimentary demands for, or expressions of gratification at, food or copulation, a certain resistance began to grow in me. And as the pressure to improve my grooming increased, so the resistance increased, too. More and more often, accustomed objects of my wardrobe disappeared, to be replaced by proclaimed or surreptitious gifts. Originally I had interpreted these gifts as springing from a misguided and love-inspired attempt to give me pleasure. In the end I understood that my pleasure was the last consideration involved. The crisis came when I polished a shoe with a new tie. A row ensued, the first of many occasioned by the divergence of our tastes in haberdashery. And the sweets would be withheld on that count.

They were withheld on many counts. But never for very long at a stretch. Sometimes I would capitulate and apologize. My early apologies were sometimes sad and, for the moment, even sincere, though sometimes sincere with a kind of self-pity. Then later, they became masterpieces of irony, *double-entendre,* and histrionics, and I would lie in bed, uttering them, aware that my face in the dark was twisted into a mask of self-congratulatory cunning, bitterness, and loathing. But I wasn't always the one to crack first, for sometimes the juicy machine-Lois got the upper hand over the dry and brittle person-Lois. She might utter an invitation in a low voice tense with hatred, and then in the subsequent process avert her face from me, or if she did look at me, she would glare like a cornered animal. Or if she did not invite me, she might collapse in the heat of a scuffle which she had undertaken against me in all seriousness but which had proved too much for the dry and brittle person-Lois and had given the other Lois the upper hand. In any case, whether she cracked or I, we demonstrated, in the midst of tangled bedclothes, unspoken loathing, and the wreckage of somebody's self-respect, that we were, as Lois had affirmed to her guests, perfectly adjusted sexually. And we were.

The fact that the adjustment was so perfect merely meant that in the end, with the deep-seated instinct for self-preservation, I was consorting with common whores. I was at that time on the evening edition, and finished my stint about two in the afternoon. After a couple of drinks and a late lunch in a speak-easy, then a couple more drinks and a game of billiards at the press club, I might call on one of my friends. Then at dinner, if I managed to get home to dinner, and in the evening I would study Lois with a clinical detachment and a sense of mystic regeneration. It even got so that almost at will I could produce an optical illusion. I could look at Lois in a certain way and find that she seemed to be withdrawing steadily, the whole room elongating with her, until it would be as though I were staring at her through the wrong end of a pair of binoculars. By this practice I gained great spiritual refreshment. I finally grew so adept at it that I could hear her voice, if it was one of her vituperative and not sullen evenings, as though it were coming from a great distance and were not, as a matter of fact, even addressed to me.

Then came the final phase, the phase of the Great Sleep. Immediately after dinner every evening, I went to bed and slept soundly, with the sweet feeling of ever falling toward the center of delicious blackness, until the last possible moment the next morning. Sometimes I did not even wait for dinner and the pleasure of observing Lois. I would just go to bed. I remember that this became almost a habit in the late spring. I would come in from my afternoon's occupation and draw the shade in the bedroom and go to bed, with the mild light oozing in from around the shade and birds twittering and caroling in the trees of the little park next the apartment building and children calling musically from the playground in the park. Going to bed in the late spring afternoon or just at the beginning of twilight, with those sounds in your ears, gives you a wonderful sense of peace, a peace which must resemble the peace of old age after a well-spent life.

But of course there was Lois. Sometimes she would come into my bedroom—by this time I had moved into the guest room for my serious sleeping—and sit on the edge of the bed and give me long descriptions of myself, rather monotonous descriptions, as a matter of fact, for Lois had little gift of phrase and had to fall back on the three or four classic terms. Sometimes she would beat me with her clenched fists. She had a feeble, female way of using her little white fists. I could sleep through the descriptions, and almost through the beating of the clenched fists on my side or back. Sometimes she would cry and give vent to a great deal of self-pity. Once or twice she even snuggled into bed with me. Sometimes she would open the door to my room and turn up the phonograph in the living room until the joint shook. But no soap. I could sleep through anything, or just about.

Then the morning came when I opened my eyes and felt the finger of Fate upon me; I knew the time had come. I got up and packed my suitcase and walked out the door and didn't come back. To the slick apartment and to Lois who was beautiful and to whom I was so perfectly adjusted.

I never saw her again, but I know what she looks like now when cocktails, bonbons, late hours, and nearly forty years have done their work on the peach bloom of cheeks, the pearly, ripe but vigorous bosom, the supple midriff, the brooding, black, velvety-liquid eyes, the bee-stung lips, the luxurious thighs. She sits on a divan somewhere, held more of less in shape by the vigor of a masseuse and the bands of lastex which secretly sheathe her like a mummy, but bloated with the entire universe she has ingurgitated with a long delicious sigh. And now with a hand on which the pointed nails are as red as though she had just used them to rip greedily the guts from a yet living sacrificial fowl, she reaches out to a silver dish to pick up a chocolate. And while the chocolate is yet mid-air, the lower lip drops open and beyond the purplish tint of the microscopically scaling veneer of lipstick, one sees the damp, paler red, expectant membranes of the mouth, and the faint glitter of a gold filling in the dark, hot orifice.

Good-bye, Lois, and I forgive you for everything I did to you.

As for the way Anne Stanton went meanwhile, the story is short. After two years at the refined female college in Virginia she came home. Adam by this time was in medical school up East. Anne spent a year going to parties in the city, and got engaged. But nothing came of it. He was a decent, intelligent, prosperous fellow, too. After a while there was another engagement, but something happened again. By this time Governor Stanton was nearly an invalid, and Adam was studying abroad. Anne quit going to parties, except an occasional party at the Landing in the summer. She stayed at home with her father, giving him his medicine, patting his pillow, assisting the nurse, reading to him hour by hour, holding his hand in the summer twilights or in the winter evenings when the house shook to the blasts off the sea. It took him seven years to die. After the Governor had died in the big tester bed with a lot of expensive medical talent leaning over him, Anne Stanton lived in the house fronting the sea, with only the company of Aunt Sophonisba, a feeble, grumbling, garrulous, and incompetent old colored woman, who combined benevolence and a vengeful tyranny in the ambiguous way known only to old colored women who have spent their lives in affectionate service, in prying, wheedling, and chicanery, in short-lived rebelliousness and long irony, and in secondhand clothes. Then Aunt Sophonisba died, too, and Adam came back from abroad, loaded with academic distinctions and fanatically devoted to his work. Shortly after his return, Anne moved to the city to be near him. By this time she was pushing thirty.

She lived alone in a small apartment in the city. Occasionally she had lunch with some woman who had been a friend of her girlhood but who now inhabited another world. Occasionally she went to a party, at the house of one of the women or at the country club. She became engaged for a third time, this time to a man seventeen or eighteen years older than she, a widower with several children, a substantial lawyer, a pillar of society. He was a good man. He was still vigorous and rather handsome. He even had a sense of humor. But she did not marry him. More and more, as the years passed, she devoted herself to sporadic reading—biography (Daniel Boone or Marie Antoinette), what is called "good fiction," books on social betterment—and to work without pay for a settlement house and an orphanage. She kept her looks very well and continued, in a rather severe way, to pay attention to her dress. There were moments now when her laugh sounded a little hollow and brittle, the laughter of nerves not of mirth or good spirits. Occasionally in a conversation she seemed to lose track and fall into a self-absorption, to start up overwhelmed by embarrassment and unspoken remorse. Occasionally, too, she practiced the gesture of lifting her hands to her brow, one on each side, the fingers just touching the skin or lifting back the hair, the gesture of a delicate distraction. She was pushing thirty-five. But she could still be good company.

That was the Anne Stanton whom Willie Stark had picked out, who had finally betrayed me, or rather, had betrayed an idea of mine which had had more importance for me than I had ever realized.

That was why I had got into my car and headed west, because when you don't like it where you are you always go west. We have always gone west.

That was why I drowned in West and relived my life like a home movie.

That was why I came to lie on a bed in a hotel in Long Beach, California, on the last coast amid the grandeurs of nature. For that is where you come, after you have crossed oceans and eaten stale biscuits while prisoned forty days and nights in a stormy-tossed rat-trap, after you have sweated in the greenery and heard the savage whoop, after you have built cabins and cities and bridged rivers, after you have lain with women and scattered children like millet seed in a high wind, after you have composed resonant documents, made noble speeches, and bathed your arms in blood to the elbows, after you have shaken with malaria in the marshes and in the icy wind across the high plains. That is where you come, to lie alone on a bed in a hotel room in Long Beach, California. Where I lay, while outside my window a neon sign flickered on and off to the time of my heart, systole and diastole, flushing and flushing again the gray sea mist with a tint like blood.

I lay there, having drowned in West, my body having drifted down to lie there in the comforting, subliminal ooze on the sea floor of History. Lying there, I had what I thought then was a fine perspective on my own history, and saw that the girl I had known that summer a long time back hadn't been beautiful and charming but had merely been smooth-faced and healthy, and though she had sung songs to Jackie-Bird while she cradled his head on her breast, she hadn't loved him, but had merely had a mysterious itch in the blood and he was handy and the word *love* was a word for the mysterious itch. And that she had been tormented by the mysterious itch and torn between its impulse and fear, and that all her withholdments and hesitations had not been prompted by some dream of making "love mean something" and making me understand that dream but that they had been prompted by all the fears which the leaning, sibilant, sour-breathed old dough-faces of conventional society had whispered into her ear like fairy godmothers while she lay in her cradle, and that those withholdments and hesitions were no better or worse than the hottest surrender nor better or worse than those withholdments practiced by Lois for other ends. And in the end you could not tell Anne Stanton from Lois Seager, for they were alike, and though the mad poet William Blake wrote a poem to tell the Adversary who is Prince of This World that He could not ever change Kate into Nan, the mad poet was quite wrong, for anybody could change Kate into Nan, or if indeed the Prince couldn't change Kate into Nan it was only because Kate and Nan were exactly alike to begin with and were, in fact, the same with only the illusory difference of name, which meant nothing, for names meant nothing and all the words we speak meant nothing and there was only the pulse in the blood and the twitch of the nerve, like a dead frog's leg in the experiment when the electric current goes through. So when I lay there on the bed in Long Beach, and shut my eyes, I saw in the inward darkness as in mire the vast heave and contortion of numberless bodies, and limbs detached from bodies, sweating and perhaps bleeding from inexhaustible wounds. But finally this spectacle, which I could summon up by the mere act of closing my eyes, seemed merely funny to me. So I laughed out loud.

I laughed out loud, and then after watching for some time the rhythmic flushing of the sea mist by the neon sign, I went to sleep. When I woke up I made ready to go back to the place and the things I had come from.

Years before, a young girl had lain there naked on the iron bed in my room with her eyes closed and her hands folded over her breast, and I had been so struck by the pathos of her submissiveness and her trust in me and of the moment which would plunge her into the full, dark stream of the world that I had hesitated before laying my hands upon her and had, without understanding myself, called out her name. At that time I had had no words for what I felt, and now, too, it is difficult to find them. But lying there, she had seemed to be again the little girl who had, on the day of the picnic, floated on the waters of the bay, with her eyes closed under the stormy and grape-purple sky and the single white gull pasing over, very high. As she lay there the image came into my head, and I had wanted to call her name, to tell her something—what, I did not know. She trusted me, but perhaps for that moment of hesitation I did not trust myself, and looked back upon the past as something precious about to be snatched away from us and was afraid of the future. I had not understood then what I think I have now come to understand: that we can keep the past only by having the future, for they are forever tied together. Therefore I lacked some essential confidence in the world and in myself. She came, as time passed, to suspect this fact about me. I do not know that she had words to describe the fact to herself. Or she only had the easy words people gave her: wanting to have a job, studying law, doing something.

We went different ways in the world, as I have said, but I had with me always that image of the little girl on the waters of the bay, all innocence and trustfulness, under the stormy sky. Then, there came the day when that image was taken from me. I learned that Anne Stanton had become the mistress of Willie Stark, that somehow by an obscure and necessary logic I had handed her over to him. That fact was too horrible to face, for it robbed me of something out of the past by which, unwittingly until that moment, I had been living.

So I fled west from the fact, and in the West, at the end of History, the Last Man on that Last Coast, on my hotel bed, I had discovered the dream. That dream was the dream that all life is but the dark heave of blood and the twitch of the nerve. When you flee as far as you can flee, you will always find that dream, which is the dream of our age. At first, it is always a nightmare and horrible, but in the end it may be, in a special way, rather bracing and tonic. At least, it was so for me for a certain time. It was bracing because after the dream I felt that, in a way, Anne Stanton did not exist. The words *Anne Stanton* were simply a name for a peculiarly complicated piece of mechanism which should mean nothing whatsoever to Jack Burden, who himself was simply another rather complicated piece of mechanism. At that time, when I first discovered that view of things—really discovered, in my own way and not from any book—I felt that I had discovered the secret source of all strength and all endurance. That dream solves all problems.

At first it was, as I have said, rather bracing and tonic. For after the dream there is no reason why you should not go back and face the fact which you have fled from (even if the fact seems to be that you have, by digging up the truth about the past, handed over Anne Stanton to Willie Stark), for any place to which you may flee will now be like the place from which you have fled, and you might as well go back, after all, to the place where you belong, for nothing was your fault or anybody's fault, for things are always as they are. And you can go back in good spirits, for you will have learned two very great truths. First, that you cannot lose what you have never had. Second, that you are never guilty of a crime which you did not commit. So there is innocence and a new start in the West, after all.

If you believe the dream you dream when you go there.

Chapter Eight

So HAVING lain on the bed in Long Beach, California, and seen what I had seen, I rose, much refreshed, and headed back with the morning sun in my face. It threw in my direction the shadows of white or pink or baby-blue stucco bungalows (Spanish mission, Moorish, or American-cute in style), the shadows of filling stations resembling the gingerbread house of fairy tale or Anne Hathaway's cottage or an Eskimo igloo, the shadows of palaces gleaming on hills among the arrogant traceries of eucalyptus, the shadows of leonine hunched mountains, the shadow of a boxcar forgotten on a lonely siding, and the shadow of a man walking toward me on a white road out of the distance which glittered like quartz. It threw the beautiful purple shadow of the whole world in my direction, as I headed back, but I kept right on going, at high speed, for if you really been to Long Beach, California, and have had your dream on the hotel bed, then there is no reason why you should not return with a new confidence to wherever you came from, for now you know, and knowledge is power.

You can put your throttle to the floor and let the sixty-horse-power mystery whine like a wolfhound straining on leash.

I passed the man who was walking toward me, and his face whirled away like a scrap of paper in a gale or boyhood hopes. And I laughed out loud.

I saw the people walking in the plaza of little towns in the desert. I saw the waitress in the restaurant wave in feeble protest at the fly while the electric fan needled the air which was as thin and hot as the breath of a blast furnace. I saw the traveling salesman who stood at the hotel desk just ahead of me and said, "You call this a hotel, bud, and me wiring for a room and bath and you ain't held it. It's a wonder you got a room and bath in a burg like this." I saw the sheepherder standing alone on an enormous mesa. I saw the Indian woman with eyes the color of blackstrap molasses looking at me over a pile of pottery decorated with the tribal symbols of life and fertility and eminently designed for the five-and-ten-cent-store trade. As I looked at all these people I felt great strength in my secret knowledge.

I remembered how once, long back when Willie Stark had been the dummy and the sap, at the time when he was Cousin Willie from the country and was running for governor the first time, I had gone over to the flea-bitten west part of the state to cover the barbecue and speaking at Upton. I had gone on the local, which had yawed and puffed for hours across the cotton fields and then across the sagebrush. At one little town where it stopped, I had looked out of the window and thought how the board or wire fences around the little board houses were inadequate to keep out the openness of the humped and sage-furred country which seemed ready to slide in and eat up the houses. I had thought how the houses didn't look as though they belonged there, improvised, flung down, ready to be abandoned, with the scraps of washing still on the line, for there wouldn't be time to grab it off when the people finally realized they had to go and go quick. I had had that thought, but just as the train was pulling out, a woman had come to the back door of one of the nearest houses to fling out a pan of water. She flings the water out, then looks a moment at the train drawing away, then deliberately enters the house. She is not going to run away. She is going into the house to some secret which is there, some knowledge. And as the train pulled away, I had had the notion that I was the one running away and had better run fast for it was going to be dark soon. I had thought of that woman as having a secret knowledge, and had envied her. I had often envied people. People I had seen fleetingly, or some people I had known a long time, a man driving a long, straight furrow across a black field in April, or Adam Stanton. I had, at moments, envied the people who seemed to have a secret knowledge.

But now, as I whirled eastward, over desert, under the shadow of mountains, by mesas, across plateaus, and saw the people in that magnificent empty country, I did not think that I would ever have to envy anybody again, for I was sure that now I had the secret knowledge, and with knowledge you can face up to anything, for knowledge is power.

In a settlement named Don Jon, New Mexico, I talked to a man propped against the shady side of the filling station, enjoying the only patch of shade in a hundred miles due east. He was an old fellow, seventy-five if a day, with a face like sun-brittled leather and pale-blue eyes under the brim of a felt hat which had once been black. The only thing remarkable about him was the fact that while you looked into the sun-brittled leather of the face, which seemed as stiff and devitalized as the hide on a mummy's jaw, you would suddenly see a twitch in the left cheek, up toward the pale-blue eye. You would think he was going to wink, but he wasn't going to wink. The twitch was simply an independent phenomenon, unrelated to the face or to what was behind the face or to anything in the whole tissue of phenomena which is the world we are lost in. It was remarkable, in that face, the twitch which lived that

313

little life all its own. I squatted by his side, where he sat on a bundle of rags from which the handle of a tin skillet protruded, and listened to him talk. But the words were not alive. What was alive was the twitch, of which he was no longer aware.

After my tank had been filled, I continued to watch that twitch, with glances stolen from the highway, as we sat side by side in the car and hurtled eastward. He was going east, too, going back. That was back in the days when the dust storms were blowing half the country away and folks headed west like the lemmings on a rampage. Only, the folks who got there lacked the fine ecstasy of the lemmings. They did not start swimming in teeming, obsessed hordes straight out to the middle of the blue Pacific. That would have been the logical thing for them to do, just start swimming, pa and ma, grandpa and grandma, and Baby Rosebud with the running sore on her little chin, the whole kit and kaboodle of 'em, flailing the water to a froth and heading out. But, no, they were not like the lemmings, and so they just sat down and starved slowly in California. But this old fellow didn't. He was going back to north Arkansas to starve where he had come from. "Californy," he said, "hit is jes lak the rest of the world, only it is more of hit."

"Yeah," I replied, "that is a fact."

"You been thar?" he demanded.

I told him I had been there.

"You goen back home?" he asked.

I told him I was going home.

We rode across Texas to Shreveport, Louisiana, where he left me to try for north Arkansas. I did not ask him if he had learned the truth in California. His face had learned it anyway, and wore the final wisdom under the left eye. The face knew that the twitch was the live thing. Was all. But, having left that otherwise unremarkable man, it occurred to me, as I reflected upon the thing which made him remarkable, that if the twitch was all, what was it that could know that the twitch was all? Did the leg of the dead frog in the laboratory know that the twitch was all when you put the electric current through it? Did the man's face know about the twitch, and how it was all? And if I was all twitch how did the twitch which was me know that the twitch was all? Ah, I decided, that is the mystery. That is the secret knowledge. That is what you have to go to California to have a mystic vision to find out. That the twitch can know that the twitch is all. Then, having found that out, in the mystic vision, you feel clean and free. You are at one with the Great Twitch.

So I kept on riding east, and after long enough I was home.

I got back, late at night, and went to bed. The next morning I turned up at the office, well rested and well shaved, and strolled in to say howdy-do to the Boss. I had a great desire to see him, to observe him closely and find if there was anything in his make-up which I had previously missed. I had to look at him very closely, for he was the man who had everything now, and I had nothing. Or rather, I corrected myself, he had everything, except the thing I had, the great thing, the secret. So I corrected myself, and in much the mood of a priest who looks down with benign pity on the sweat and striving, I entered the Governor's office, and walked past the receptionist and, with a perfunctory knock, into the inside.

There he was, and he hadn't changed a bit.

"Hello, Jack," he said, and swiped the forelock out of his eyes and swung his feet off the desk and came toward me, putting out his hand, "where the hell you been, boy?"

"Out West," I said, with elaborate casualness, taking the proffered hand. "Just drove out West. I got sort of fed up round here, so I took me a little vacation."

"Have a good time?"

"I had a wonderful time," I said.

"Fine," he said.

"How you been making out?" I asked.

"Fine," he said, "everything is fine."

And so I had come home to the place where everything was fine. Everything was fine just the way it had been before I left, except that now I knew the secret. And my secret knowledge cut me off. If you have the secret, you cannot really communicate any more with somebody who has not got it, any more than you can really communicate with a bustling vitamin-crammed brat who is busy with his building blocks or a tin drum. And you can't take somebody off to one side and tell him the secret. If you do that, then the fellow, or female, you are trying to tell the truth to thinks you are feeling sorry for yourself and asking for sympathy, when the real case is that you are not asking for sympathy but for congratulations. So I did my daily tasks and ate my daily bread and saw the old familiar faces, and smiled benignly like a priest.

It was June, and hot. Every night, except those nights when I went to sit in an air-conditioned movie, I went to my room after dinner and stripped buck-naked and lay on the bed, with an electric fan burring and burrowing away into my brain, and read a book until the time when I would become aware that the sound of the city had sunk off to almost nothing but the single hoot of a taxi far off or the single lost clang and grind of a streetcar, an owl car heading out. Then I would reach up and switch off the light and roll over and go to sleep with the fan still burring and burrowing.

I did see Adam a few times in June. He was more deeply involved than before in the work of the medical center, more

315

grimly and icily driving himself. There was, of course, some letup in the work at the University with the end of term, but whatever relief was there, was more than made up for by an increase in his private practice and work at the clinic. He said he was glad to see me when I went to his apartment, and maybe he was, but he didn't have much to say, and as I sat there he would seem to be drawing deeper and deeper into himself until I had the feeling that I was trying to talk to somebody down a well and had better holler if I wanted to be understood. The only time he perked up was one night when, after he had remarked on the fact that he was to perform an operation the next morning, I asked about the case.

It was a case of catatonic schizophrenia, he said.

"You mean he is a nut?" I asked.

Adam grinned and allowed that that wasn't too far wrong.

"I didn't know you cut on folks for being nutty," I said. "I thought you just humored them and gave them cold baths and let them make raffia baskets and got them to tell you their dreams."

"No," he said, "you can cut on them." Then he added, almost apologetically, "A prefrontal lobectomy."

"What's that?"

"You remove a piece of the frontal lobe of the brain on each side," he said.

I asked would the fellow live. He said you never could tell for sure, but if he did live he would be different.

I asked how did he mean, different.

"Oh, a different personality," he replied.

"Like after you get converted and baptized?"

"That doesn't give you a different personality," he said. "When you get converted you still have the same personality. You merely exercise it in terms of a different set of values."

"But this fellow will have a different personality?"

"Yes," Adam said. "The way he is now he simply sits on a chair or lies on his back on a bed and stares into space. His brow is creased and furrowed. Occasionally he utters a low moan or an exclamation. In some such cases we discover the presence of delusions of persecution. But always the patient seems to experience a numbing, grinding misery. But after we are through with him he will be different. He will be relaxed and cheerful and friendly. He will smooth his brow. He will sleep well and eat well and will love to hang over the back fence and compliment the neighbors on their nasturtiums and cabbages. He will be perfectly happy."

"If you can guarantee results like that," I said, "you ought to do a land-office business. As soon as the news gets round."

"You can't ever guarantee anything," Adam said.

"What happens if it doesn't come out according to Hoyle?"

"Well," he said, "there have been cases—not mine, thank God—where the patient didn't become cheerfully extroverted but became completely and cheerfully amoral."

"You mean he would throw the nurses down right on the floor in broad daylight?"

"About that," Adam said. "If you'd let him. All the ordinary inhibitions disappeared."

"Well, if your guy tomorrow comes out like that he will certainly be an asset to society."

Adam grinned sourly, and said. "He won't be any worse than a lot of other people who haven't been cut on."

"Can I see the cutting?" I asked. I felt all of a sudden that I had to see it. I had never seen an operation. As a newspaperman, I had seen three hangings and one electrocution, but they are different. In a hanging you do not change a man's personality. You just change the length of his neck and give him a quizzical expression, and in an electrocution you just cook some bouncing meat in a wholesale lot. But this operation was going to be more radical even than what happened to Saul on the road to Damascus. So I asked could I see the operation.

"Why?" Adam asked, studying my face.

I told him it was plain curiosity.

He said, all right, but it wouldn't be pretty.

"It would be as pretty as a hanging, I guess," I replied.

Then he started to tell me about the case. He drew me pictures and he got down books. He perked up considerably and almost talked my ear off. He was so interesting that I forgot to ask him a question which had flitted through my mind earlier in our conversation. He had said that in the case of a religious conversion the personality does not change, that it is merely exercised in terms of a different set of values. Well, I had meant to ask him how, if there was no change in personality, how did the person get a different set of values to exercise his personality in terms of? But it slipped my mind at the time.

Anyway, I saw the operation.

Adam got me rigged up so I could go right down in the pit with him. They brought in the patient and put him on the table. He was a hook-nosed, sour-faced, gaunt individual who reminded me vaguely of Andrew Jackson or a back-country evangelist despite the white turban on his head made out of sterile towels. But that turban was pushed pretty far back at a jaunty angle, for the front part of his head was exposed. It had been shaved. They put the mask on him and knocked him out. Then Adam took a scalpel and cut a neat little cut across the top of the head and down at each temple, and then just peeled the skin off the bone in a neat flap forward. He did a job that would have made a Comanche brave look like a tyro with a

317

scalping knife. Meanwhile, they were sopping up the blood, which was considerable.

Then Adam settled down to the real business. He had a contraption like a brace and bit. With that he drilled five or six holes—burr holes they call them in the trade—on each side of the skull. Then he started to work with what he had told me earlier was a Gigli saw, a thing which looked like a coarse wire. With that he sawed on the bone till he had a flap loose on each side of the front of the head and could bend the flap down and get at the real mechanism inside. Or could as soon as he had cut the pale little membrane which they call the meninges.

By that time it had been more than an hour, or so it seemed to me, and my feet hurt. It was hot in there, too, but I didn't get upset, even with the blood. For one thing, the man there on the table didn't seem real. I forgot that he was a man at all, and kept watching the high-grade carpenter work which was going on. I didn't pay much attention to the features of the process which did indicate that the thing on the table was a man. For instance, the nurse kept on taking blood-pressure readings and now and then she would mess with the transfusion apparatus—for they were giving the patient a transfusion all the time out of a bottle rigged up on a stand with a tube coming down.

I did fine until they started the burning. For taking out the chunks of brain they use an electric gadget which is nothing but a little metal rod stuck in a handle with an electric cord coming out of the handle. The whole thing looks like an electric curling iron. In fact, all the way through I was struck by the notion that all the expensive apparatus was so logical and simple and homey, and reminded me so completely of the stuff around any well-equipped household. By ransacking the kitchen and your wife's dressing table you can get together in five minutes enough of a kit to set up in business for yourself.

Well, in the process of electrocautery this little rod does the trick of cutting, or rather burning. And there is some smoke and quite a lot of odor. At least, it seemed like a lot to me. At first it wasn't so bad, but then I knew where I had smelled an odor like that before. It was the night, long back when I was a kid, when the old livery stable had burned down at the Landing and they hadn't managed to get all the horses out. The smell of the cooking horses was on the still, damp, ripe night air and you couldn't forget it, even after you didn't hear any more the shrieks the horses had made. As soon as I realized that the burning brain had a smell like the burning horses, I didn't feel good.

But I stuck it out. It took a long time, hours more, for they can't cut but a little bit of brain at a time, and have to keep working deeper and deeper. I stuck it out until Adam had sewed up the meninges and had pulled the skull flaps back into place and had drawn up the flap of skin and laced it down all ship-shape.

Then the little pieces of brain which had been cut out were put away to think their little thoughts quietly somewhere among the garbage, and what was left inside the split-open skull of the gaunt individual was sealed back up and left to think up an entirely new personality.

When Adam and I went out, and he was washing up and we were getting our white nightshirts off, I said to him, "Well, you forgot to baptize him."

"Baptize him?" Adam asked, sliding out of the white night-shirt.

"Yeah," I said, "for he is born again and not of woman. I baptize thee in the name of the Big Twitch, the Little Twitch, and the Holy Ghost. Who, no doubt, is a Twitch, too."

"What the hell are you talking about?" he demanded.

"Nothing," I said, "I was just trying to be funny."

Adam put on a faint, indulgent smile, but he didn't seem to think it was very funny. And looking back on it, I can't find it very funny myself. But I thought it was funny at the time. I thought it would bust a gut. But that summer from the height of my Olympian wisdom, I seemed to find a great many things funny which now do not appear quite as funny.

After the operation I did not see anything of Adam for quite a while. He went out of town, up East, on business, on some of the hospital business, I supposed. Then, shortly after he got back, the thing happened which just about left the Boss in the position of having to hunt up a new director.

What happened was simple and predictable. One night Adam and Anne, who had had dinner together, mounted the stairs of the crummy apartment house to spy, on the landing before the door, a tall, thin, white-clad figure with a white Panama hat on its head, a cigar glowing in the shadow out of one side of the place where the mouth would be and putting out an expensive aroma to compete with the cabbage. The fellow took the white hat off, tucked it lightly under an elbow, and asked if Adam was Dr. Stanton. Adam said he was. So the fellow said his name was Coffee (the name is Hubert Coffee) and asked if he could come in for a minute.

Adam and Anne went in, and Adam asked the fellow what he wanted. He stood there in his white, well-pressed suit and two-color shoes with, no doubt, intricate stitchings and ventila-tors in the leather (for I have found Hubert to be quite a dude —two white suits a day, and white silk shorts with red mono-grams, they say, and red silk socks and trick shoes), and hum-med and hawed out of his knobby, long, squash-yellow face, and coughed discreetly, and significantly rolled his brown eyes (which are the color and texture of used motor oil) in the

319

direction of Anne. Anne told me later, for she is my authority for the event, that she thought he was coming about being sick, so she excused herself and went back to the kitchen to put into the electric icebox a little carton of ice cream she had picked up at the corner drugstore. She was planning on a quiet little evening with Adam. (Though her quiet little visits with Adam that summer must have been less than restful for her. She must have always had in the back of her mind the question about what would happen when Adam found out how she was spending some of her other evenings. Or was she able to lock off that part of her mind, the way you lock off some of the rooms of a big house, and just sit in the cozy, or perhaps not now so cozy, parlor? And sitting there, did she listen always for the creak of floor or the ceaseless tread of feet in the locked-off rooms upstairs?)

After she had put the ice cream away, she noticed that some dirty dishes were piled up in the sink. So to keep out from under foot in the apartment while the men conferred she set about washing the dishes. She had about wound up the dishes, when suddenly the incomprehensible drone of voices stopped. The sudden silence was what she noticed. Then there was a dry thump (that was the way she described it), and her brother's voice saying, "Get out!" Then there was the sound of rapid motion and the slamming of the apartment door.

She went into the living room to find Adam standing in the middle of the floor, very white in the face, nursing his right hand in his left across his stomach, and staring at the door. When Anne came in, he turned his head slowly to her and said, "I hit him. I didn't mean to hit him. I never hit anybody before."

He must have hit Hubert pretty hard, too, for his knuckle was split and swelling. Adam had a good weight of shoulder even if he was slender. Anyway he stood there nursing his split knuckle and wearing an expression of blank incredulity on his face. The incredulity, apparently, was at his own behavior.

Anne, very much agitated, asked him what was the trouble.

The trouble was, as I have suggested, simple and predictable. Gummy Larson had sent Hubert Coffee, who, on account of his white suits and silk monogrammed drawers, was supposed to have finesse and the gentlemanly approach, to try to persuade Dr. Stanton to use his influence to get the Boss to throw the basic medical-center contract to Larson. Adam didn't know all of this, for we can be quite sure that Hubert had not named the behind-guy in the exploratory stages of the interview. But as soon as I heard the name Coffee I knew that it was Larson. Hubert never got past the exploratory stages of the interview. But, apparently, he handled those stages rather broadly. At first, Adam didn't get what he was driving at, and Hubert must have decided that any of his high-priced subtlety would be wasted on this dumb cluck and moved pretty directly to the point. He got as far as the idea that there would be some candy in it for Adam, before he finally touched the button which set off the explosion.

Still caught in the incredulity and nursing the numbed hand, Adam stood there and in a distant voice told Anne what had happened. Then, having finished he leaned down to pick up, with the good left hand, the cigar stub, which was slowly burning a hole in the old green carpet. He walked across the carpet, holding the stinking stub out at some length, and flung it into the fireplace, which still had in it (as I had noticed on my visits) the ashes of the last fire of spring and bits of paper and orange peel from the summer. Then he walked back across the carpet, and ground his foot on the smoldering place, probably with a kind of symbolic savagery. At least, I could imagine that picture.

He went to his desk, sat down, took out pen and paper, and began to write. When he had finished, he swung round to Anne, and announced that he had just written his resignation. She didn't say anything. Not a word. She knew, she told me, that there wasn't any use trying to argue with him, to point out to him that it wasn't the fault of Governor Stark or the fault of the job that some crook had come and tried to bribe him. She knew from looking at his face that there wasn't any use in talking. In other words, he must have been in the grip of an instinctive withdrawal, which took the form of moral indignation and moral revulsion, but which, no doubt, was different from either, and more deep-seated than either, and finally irrational. He got up from the chair, and took a few strides about the room, apparently in great excitement. He seemed almost gay, Anne said, as though he were about to burst out laughing. He seemed happy that the whole thing had happened. Then he picked up the letter and stamped it.

Anne was afraid that he would go out immediately to mail it, for he stood there in the middle of the floor, fingering it as though debating the issue. But he did not go out. Instead, he propped it on the mantelpiece, took a few more turns about the apartment, then flung himself down on the piano bench and started to beat out the music. He sat there and beat it for more than two hours in a breathless July night, and the sweat ran down his face. Anne sat there, afraid, she told me, and not knowing what she was afraid of.

When he got through, and turned his sweat-streaked white face toward her, she fetched the ice cream and they had a jolly little family party. Then she went out and got into her car and drove home.

She telephoned me. I met her at an all-night drugstore, and across the imitation-marble top of the table in the booth, I saw her for the first time since the morning in May when she had stood at the door of her apartment and had read the question in my face and had slowly and wordlessly nodded the answer. When I heard her voice on the telephone that night, my heart took the little leap and *kerplunk,* like the frog into the lily pond, just as it had before, and for the moment what had happened might as well not have happened. But it had happened, and what I had now as my cab wheeled me down-town to the all-night drugstore, was the wry and bilious satisfaction that I was being called on for some special reason the other fellow couldn't be expected to answer. But the satisfaction forgot even to be wry and bilious and was, for the moment, just simple satisfaction when I stepped out of the cab and saw her standing inside the glass doors of the drugstore, a trim erect figure in a light-green polka-dot dress with some kind of a white jacket hung across one of her bare arms. I tried to make out the expression on her face, but before I could discover what it was, she spied me and smiled.

It was a tentative, apologetic sort of smile, which said *please* and *thank you* and at the same time expressed an innocent and absolute confidence that your better nature would triumph. I walked across the hot pavement toward that smile and the green polka-dot figure which stood there behind the glass like something put in a showcase for you to admire but not touch. Then I laid my hand on the glass of the door, and pushed, and left the street, where the air was hot and sticky like a Turkish bath and where the smell of gasoline fumes mixed with the brackish, dead-sweet smell of the river which crept into the city on still nights in summer, and entered the bright, crisp, anti-septic, cool world behind the glass where the smile was, for there is nothing brighter, crisper, more antiseptic, and cooler than a really first-rate corner drugstore on a hot summer night. If Anne Stanton is inside the door and the air conditioning is working.

The smile was on me and the eyes looked straight at me and she put out her hand. I took it, thought how cool and small and firm it was, as though I were just discovering the fact, and heard her say, "It looks like I'm always calling you up, Jack."

"Oh, that's O.K.," I said, and released the hand.

It couldn't have been more than an instant we stood there then without saying anything, but it seemed a long and painfully embarrassed time, as if neither of us knew what to say, before she said, "Let's sit down."

I started to move back toward the booths. Out of the tail of my eye, I noticed that she made a motion, quickly suppressed, to hang on to my arm. As I noticed that fact, the satisfaction which had been for the moment simple satisfaction, was again merely the wry and bilious satisfaction with which I had started out. And it stayed that kind, as I sat in the booth and looked at her face which was not smiling now and was showing the tensions and the tightness of the skin over the fine bone and showing, I suppose, the years that had gone by since the summer when we sat in the roadster and she sang to Jackie-Bird, and promised never to let anybody hurt poor Jackie-Bird. Well, she had kept her promise, all right, for Jackie-Bird had flown away that summer, before the fall came, to some place with a better climate where nobody would ever hurt him, and he had never come back. At least, I had never seen him since.

Now she sat in the booth and told me, over our glasses of Coca Cola, what had happened in Adam's apartment.

"What do you want me to do?" I asked, when she got through.

"You know," she said.

"You want me to make him stick to it?"

"Yes," she said.

"It'll be hard."

She nodded.

"It'll be hard," I said, "because he is acting perfectly crazy. The only thing I can prove to him is that if this Coffee bastard tried to bribe him it only indicates that the job is on the level as long as Adam wants to keep it that way. It only indicates, furthermore, that somebody farther up the line had declined to take a bribe, too. It even indicates that Tiny Duffy is an honest man. Or," I added, "hasn't been able to deliver the goods."

"You will try?" she asked.

"I'll try," I said, "but don't get your hopes up. I can only prove to Adam what he would already know if he hadn't gone crazy. He just has the high cantankerous moral shrinks. He does not like to play with the rough boys. He is afraid they might dirty his Lord Fauntleroy suit."

"That's not fair," she burst out.

I shrugged, then said, "Well, I'll try, anyway."

"What will you do?"

"There is only one thing to do. I'll go to Governor Stark, get him to agree to arrest Coffee on the grounds of attempted bribery of an official—Adam is an official, you know—and call on Adam to swear to the charges. If he'll swear to them. That ought to make him see how things line up. That ought to show him the Boss will protect him. And—" to that point I had only been thinking of the Adam end but now my mind got to work on the possibilities of the situation—"it wouldn't do the Boss any harm to hang a rap on Coffee. Particularly if he will squeal on the behind-guy. He might bust up Larson. And with Larson out, MacMurfee wouldn't mean much. He might hang it on Coffee, too, if you—" And I stopped dead.

"If I what?" she demanded.

"Nothing," I said, and felt the way you do when you are driving merrily across the drawbridge, and all at once the span starts up.

"What?" she demanded.

I looked into her level eyes and saw the way her jaw was set, and knew that I might as well say it. She would work on me till she had it. So I said it. "If you will testify," I said.

"I'll do it," she said without hesitation.

I shook my head. "No," I said.

"I'll do it."

"No, it won't wash."

"Why?"

"It just won't. After all, you didn't see anything."

"I was there."

"It would just be hearsay testimony. Absolutely that. It would never stand up."

"I don't know," she said. "I don't know about those things. But I know this. I know that isn't the reason you changed your mind. What made you change your mind?"

"You never have been on a witness stand. You don't know what it is to have a mean, smart lawyer saw at you while you sweat."

"I'll do it," she said.

"No."

"I don't mind."

"Listen here," I said, and shut my eyes and took the plunge off the end of the open drawbridge, "if you think Coffee's lawyer wouldn't have plenty on the ball you are crazy as Adam. He would be mean and he would be smart and he would not have one damned bit of fine old Southern chivalry."

"You mean—" she began, and I knew from her face that she had caught the point.

"Exactly," I said. "Nobody may know anything now, but when the fun started they would know everything."

"I don't care," she affirmed, and lifted her chin up a couple of notches. I saw the little creases in the flesh of her neck, just the tiniest little creases, and little mark left day after day by that absolutely infinitesimal gossamer cord of thuggee which time throws around the prettiest neck every day to garrote it. The cord is so gossamer that it breaks every day, but the marks get there finally, and finally one day the gossamer cord doesn't break and is enough. I looked at the marks when Anne lifted her chin, and realized that I had never noticed them before and would always notice them again. I suddenly felt awful— literally sick, as though I had been socked in the stomach, or as though I had met a hideous betrayal. Then before I knew it, the way I felt changed into anger, and I lashed out.

"Yeah," I said, "you don't care, but you forget one thing. You forget that Adam will be sitting right there looking at little sister."

Her face was white as a sheet.

Then she lowered her head a little and was looking at her hands, which were clenched together now around the empty Coca Cola glass. Her head was low enough so that I could not see her eyes, only the lids coming down over them.

"My dear, my dear," I murmured. Then as I seized her hands pressed around the glass, the words wrenched out of me, "Oh, Anne, why did you do it?"

It was the one question I had never meant to ask.

For a moment she did not answer. Then, without raising her eyes, she said in a low voice, "He wasn't like anybody else. Not anybody else I'd ever known. And I love him. I love him, I guess. I guess that is the reason."

I sat there and reckoned I had asked for that one.

She said, "Then you told me—you told me about my father. There wasn't any reason why not then. After you told me."

I reckoned I had asked for that one, too.

She said, "He wants to marry me."

"Are you going to?"

"Not now. It would hurt him. A divorce would hurt him. Not now."

"Are you going to?"

"Perhaps. Later. After he goes to the Senate. Next year."

One part of my mind was busy ticketing that away: *The Senate next year. That means he won't let old Scoggan go back. Funny he hadn't told me.* But the other part of my mind which was not the nice, cool, steel filing cabinet with alphabetical cards was boiling like a kettle of pitch. A big bubble heaved up and exploded out of the pitch, and it was my voice saying, "Well, I suppose you know what you are up to."

"You don't know him," she said, her voice even lower than before. "You've known him all these years and you don't know him at all." Then she had lifted her head and was looking straight into my eyes. "I'm not sorry," she said, quite distinctly. "Not for anything that's happened."

I walked down the street in the hot darkness toward my hotel under a magnificent throbbing sky, breathing the old gasoline fumes the day had left and the sweet, marshy smell of the river at low water which the night brought up into the streets, and thinking, yes, I knew why she had done it.

The answer was in all the years before, and the things in them and not in them.

The answer was in me, for I had told her.

I only told her the truth, I said savagely to myself, *and she can't blame me for the truth!*

But was there some fatal appropriateness inherent in the very nature of the world and of me that I should be the one to tell her that truth? I had to ask myself that question, too. And I couldn't be sure of the answer. So I walked on down the street, turning that question over and over in my mind without any answer until the question lost meaning and dropped from my mind as something heavy drops from numb fingers. I would have faced the responsibility and the guilt, I was ready to do that, if I could know. But who is going to tell you?

So I walked on, and after a while I remembered how she had said I had never known him. And the *him* was Willie Stark, whom I had known for the many years since Cousin Willie from the country, the Boy with the Christmas Tie, had walked into the back room of Slade's old place. Sure, I knew him. Like a book. I had known him a long time.

Too long. I thought then, *too long to know him.* For maybe the time had blinded me, or rather I had not been aware of the passing of time and always the round face of Cousin Willie had come between me and the other face so that I had never really seen the other face. Except perhaps in those moments when it had leaned forward to the crowds and the forelock had fallen and the eyes had bulged, and the crowd had roared and I had felt the surge in me and had felt that I was on the verge of the truth. But always the face of Cousin Willie above the Christmas tie had come again.

But it did not come now. I saw the face. Enormous. Bigger than a billboard. The forelock shagged down like a mane. The big jaw. The heavy lips laid together like masonry. The eyes burning and bulging powerfully.

Funny, I had never seen it before. Not really.

That night I telephoned the Boss, told him what had happened and how Anne had told me, and made my suggestion about getting Adam to swear out a warrant for Coffee. He said to do it. To do anything that would nail Adam. So I went to the hotel, where I lay on my bed under the electric fan until the desk called me to get up at about six o'clock. Then by seven I was on Adam's doorstep, with a single cup of java sloshing about in my insides and a fresh razor cut on my chin and sleep like sand under my eyelids.

I worked it. It was a hard little job I had cut out for me. First, I had to enlist Adam on the side of righteousness by getting him to agree to swear out a warrant for Coffee. My method was to assume, of course, that he was aching for the opportunity to nail Coffee, and to indicate that the Boss was cheering on the glorious exploit. Then I had to lead him to the discovery, which had to be all his own, that this would involve Anne as a witness. Then I had to play the half-wit and imply that this had never occurred to me before. The danger was, with a fellow like Adam, that he would get so set on seeing justice done that he would let Anne testify, hell and high water. He almost did that, but I painted a gory picture of the courtroom scene (but not as gory by half as it would have been in truth), refused to be party to the business, hinted that he was an un-natural brother, and wound up with a vague notion of another way to get Coffee for a similar attempt in another quarter—a vague notion of laying myself open for Coffee to approach me. I could put out a feeler for him, and all that. So Adam dropped the idea of the charge, but retained the implied idea that he and the Boss had teamed up to keep things clean for the hospital.

Just as we were ready to walk out of the apartment, he stepped to the mantelpiece and picked up the stamped letters waiting there to be mailed. I had spotted the top envelope already, the one addressed to the Boss. So as he turned around with the letters in his hand, I simply lifted that one out of his grasp, said with my best smile, "Hell, you haven't got any use for this in the daylight," and tore it across and put the pieces into my pocket.

Then we went out back and got into his car. I rode with him all the way to his office. I would have sat with him all day to keep an eye on him if it had been possible. Anyway, I chatted briskly all the way down-town to keep his mind clear. My chatter was as gay and sprightly as bird song.

So the summer moved on, swelling slowly like a great fruit, and everything was as it had been before. I went to my office. I went back to my hotel and sometimes ate a meal and sometimes did not and lay under the fan and read till late. I saw the same faces, Duffy, the Boss, Sadie Burke, all the faces I had known for a long time and saw so often I didn't notice the changes in them. But I did not see Adam and Anne for a while. And I had not seen Lucy Stark for a long time. She was living out in the country now. The Boss would still go out to see her now and then, to keep up appearances, and have his picture taken among the white leghorns. Sometimes Tom Stark would stand there with him and, perhaps, Lucy, with the white leghorns in the foreground and a wire fence behind. *Governor Willie Stark and Family,* the caption would read.

Yes, those pictures were an asset to the Boss. Half the people in the state knew that the Boss had been tom-catting around for years, but the pictures of the family and the white leghorns gave the voters a nice warm glow, it made them feel solid, sub-stantial, and virtuous, it made them think of gingerbread and nice cold buttermilk, and if somewhere not too far in the wings

327

there was a flicker of a black-lace negligee and a whiff of musky perfume, then, "Well, you cain't blame him a-taken hit, they put hit up to him." It only meant that the Boss was having it both ways, and that seemed a mark of the chosen and superior. It was what the voter did when he shook loose and came up to town to the furniture dealers' convention and gave the bellhop a couple of bucks to get him a girl up to the room. Or if he wasn't doing it classy, he rode into town with his truckload of hogs and for two bucks got the whole works down at a crib. But either way, classy or crib, the voter knew what it meant, and he wanted both Mom's gingerbread and the black-lace negligee and didn't hold it against the Boss for having both. What he would have held against the Boss was a divorce. Anne was right about that. It would have hurt even the Boss. That would have been very different, and would have robbed the voter of something he valued, the nice warm glow of complacency, the picture that flattered him and his own fat or thin wife standing in front of the henhouse.

Meanwhile, if the voter knew that the Boss had been tom-catting for years, and could name the names of half of the ladies involved, he didn't know about Anne Stanton. Sadie had found out, but that was no miracle. But as far as I could detect, nobody else knew, not even Duffy with his wheezing, ele-phantine wit and leer. Maybe Sugar-Boy knew, but he could be depended upon. He knew everything. The Boss didn't mind telling anything in front of Sugar-Boy, or close to it—any-thing, that is, that he would tell. Which probably left a lot un-told, at that. Once Congressman Randall was in the Boss's library with him, Sugar-Boy, and me, pacing up and down the floor, and the Boss was giving him play-by-play instructions on how to conduct himself when the Milton-Broderick Bill was presented to Congress. The instructions were pretty frank, and the Congressman kept looking nervously at Sugar-Boy. The Boss noticed him. "God damn it," the Boss said, "you afraid Sugar-Boy's finding out something? Well, you're right, he's finding out something. Well, Sugar-Boy has found out plenty. He knows more about this state than you do. And I trust him a hell of a lot farther than I'd trust you. You're my pal, ain't you, Sugar-Boy?"

Sugar-Boy's face darkened with the rush of pleasurable, embarrassed blood and his lips began to work and the spit to fly as he prepared to speak.

"Yeah, Sugar's my pal, ain't you, Sugar-Boy?" he said, and slapped Sugar-Boy on the shoulder, and then swung again toward the Congressman while Sugar-Boy finally was managing to say, "I'm—y-y-y-your pal—and—I—ain't ta-ta-ta-talking—none."

Yes, Sugar-Boy probably knew, but he was dependable.

328

And Sadie was dependable, too. She had told me, but that was in the flush of her first fine rage and I (I thought of this with a certain grim humor) was, you might say, in the family. She wouldn't tell anybody else. Sadie Burke didn't have any confidant, for she didn't trust anybody. She didn't ask any sympathy, for the world she had grown up in didn't have any. So she would keep her mouth shut. And she had plenty of patience. She knew he'd come back. Meanwhile, she could hack him into a rage, or could try to for it was hard to do, and she herself would get into one, and you would think that they would be ready to fly at each other in the frenzy they could build up. By that time, too, you wouldn't be able to tell whether it was a frenzy of love or hate that coiled and tangled them together. And after all the years it had been going on, it probably didn't matter which it was. Her eyes would blaze black out of her chalk-white, pocked face and her wild black hair would seem to lift electrically off her scalp and her hands would flay out in a gesture of rending and tearing. While the flood of her language poured over him, his head would rock massively but almost imperceptibly from side to side and his eyes would follow her every motion, at first drowsily, then raptly, until he would heave himself up, the big veins in his temples pumping and his right fist raised. Then the raised fist would crash into the palm of the other hand, and he would burst out, "God damn, God damn it, Sadie!"

Or for weeks there wouldn't be any shenanigans. Sadie would treat the Boss with an icy decorum, meeting him only and strictly in the course of business, standing quietly before him while he talked. She would stand there before him and study him out of the black eyes, in which the blaze was banked now. Well, despite all the shenanigans, Sadie knew how to wait. She had learned that a long time back. She had had to wait for everything she had ever got out of the world.

So the summer went on, and we all lived in it. It was a way to live, and when you have lived one way for a while you forget that there was ever any other way and that there may be another way again. Even when the change came, it didn't at first seem like a change but like more of the same, an extension and repetition.

It came through Tom Stark.

Given the elements, it was perfectly predictable. On one hand there was the Boss, and on the other hand there was Mac-Murfee. MacMurfee didn't have any choice. He had to keep fighting the Boss, for the Boss wouldn't deal with him, and if (and it looked more like *when* than *if*) the Boss ever broke MacMurfee in the Fourth District, Mac was a goner. So he had no choice, and he would use anything he could lay his hands on.

What he laid his hands on was a fellow named Marvin Frey,

previously unknown to fame. Frey had a daughter named Sibyl, also unknown to fame, but not, Mr. Frey said, unknown to Tom Stark. It was simple, not a new turn to the plot, not a new line in the script. An old home remedy. Simple. Simple and sordid.

The outraged father, accompanied by a friend, for witness and protector no doubt, called on the Boss and stated his case. He got out, white in the face and obviously shaken, but he had the strength to walk. He walked across the long stretch of carpet from the Boss's door to the door to the corridor, getting inadequate support from the friend, whose own legs seemed to have lost some of their stiffening, and went out.

Then the buzzer on my desk went wild, the little red light which meant headquarters flashed, and when I switched on the voice box, the Boss's voice said, "Jack, get the hell in here." When I got the hell in there, he succinctly outlined the case to me, and gave me two assignments: first, get hold of Tom Stark, and second, find all there was about Marvin Frey.

It took all day and the efforts of half of the Highway Patrol to locate Tom Stark, who was, it developed, at a fishing lodge on Bigger's Bay with several cronies and some girls and a lot of wet glasses and dry fishing tackle. It was near six o'clock before they fetched him in. I was out in the reception room when he came in. "Hi, Jack," he said, "what's eating on him now?" And he cocked his head toward the Boss's door.

"He'll tell you," I said, and watched him head toward the door, a wonderfully set-up fellow in dirty white duck trousers, sandals, and a pale-blue short-sleeved silky sport shirt that stuck to the damp pectoral muscles and almost popped over the brown biceps. His head, with a white gob cap stuck on it, was thrust forward just a little bit, and had the slightest roll when he walked, and his arms hung slightly crooked with the elbows a little out. Watching the arms hanging that way, you got the impression that they were like weapons just loosened and riding easy and ready in the scabbards. He didn't knock, but walked straight into the Boss's office. I retreated to my own office and waited for the dust to settle. Whatever it was, Tom was not going to stand and take it, not even from the Boss.

A half hour later Tom came out, slamming the door so that the heavy gold-framed paintings of the former governors hung around the paneled walls of the big reception room shivered like autumn leaves in a blast. He stalked across the room, not even giving a look in the direction of my open door, and went out. At first, he had, the Boss told me later, denied everything. Then he had admitted everything, looking the Boss in the eye, with a what-the-hell's-it-to-you expression. The Boss was fit to be tied when I saw him a few minutes after Tom's departure. He had only one small comfort—that from the legal point of view, Tom had been just one of a platoon of Sibyl's friends, according to Tom himself. But, aside from the legal point of view, that fact just made the Boss madder, Tom's being one of a platoon. It would be convenient in any discussion of the paternity of Sibyl's alleged child, but it seemed to hurt the Boss's pride.

I had found Tom and brought him in as one of my assignments. The second one took a little longer. Finding out about Marvin Frey. There wasn't much to find out, it appeared. He was a barber in the only hotel in a fair-sized town, Duboisville, over in the Fourth District. He was a sporting barber, with knife-edged creases in his striped pants, ointment on his thinning hair, hands like inflated white rubber gloves, a *Racing Form* in his hip pocket, the shapeless soft nose with the broken veins like tiny purple vines, and breath sweetly flavored with Sen-Sen and red-eye. He was a widower, living with his two daughters. You don't have to find out much about a fellow like that. You know it all already. Sure, he has an immortal soul which is individual and precious in God's eye, and he is that unique agglomeration of atomic energy known as Marvin Frey, but you know all about him. You know his jokes, you know the insinuative *hee-hee* through his nose with which he prefaces them, you know how the gray tongue licks luxuriously over his lips at the conclusion, you know how he fawns and drools over the inert mass with the face covered with steaming towels which happens to be the local banker or the local gambling-house proprietor or the local congressman, you know how he kids the hotel chippies and tries to talk them out of something, you know how he gets in debt because of his bad hunches on the horses and bad luck with the dice, you know how he wakes up in the morning and sits on the edge of the bed with his bare feet on the cold floor and a taste like brass on the back of his tongue and experiences his nameless despair. You know that, with the combination of poverty, fear, and vanity, he is perfectly designed to be robbed of his last pride and last shame and be used by MacMurfee. Or by somebody else.

But it happened to be MacMurfee. This angle had not appeared in Marvin's first interview. It appeared a few days later. One of MacMurfee's boys called on the Boss, said MacMurfee had heard how a fellow named Frey had a daughter named Sibyl who had something on Tom Stark, but MacMurfee had always liked football and sure liked the way Tom carried the ball, and didn't want to see the boy get mixed up in anything unpleasant. Frey, the fellow said, was not in any frame of mind to be reasonable. He was going to make Tom marry the daughter. (The Boss's face must have been something to see at that point.) But Frey lived over in MacMurfee's district, and MacMurfee knew him a little, and maybe Mac-

Murfee could put some reasonableness into Frey's head. It would cost something, of course, to do it that way, but there wouldn't be any publicity, and Tom would still be a bachelor.

What would it cost? Well, some money for Sibyl. Folding money.

But this meant that MacMurfee was simply acting out of a deep heart and generous nature.

What would it cost? Well, MacMurfee was thinking he might run for Senator.

So that was it.

But the Boss, as Anne Stanton had told me, was figuring on going to the Senate himself. He had it in the sack. He had the state in a sack. Except for MacMurfee. MacMurfee and Marvin Frey. But still, he wasn't in any mood to dicker with Mac-Murfee. He didn't dicker, but he stalled.

There was one reason he could take the chance and stall. If Marvin and MacMurfee had had it sewed up absolutely tight, and could have ruined the Boss, they would have done it without further ado. They wouldn't have bothered to dicker. They had some cards, all right, but it wasn't necessarily a straight flush, and they had to take their gamble, too. They had to wait, while the Boss did his thinking, and hope that he wouldn't think up anything unpleasant in his turn.

While the Boss did his thinking, I saw Lucy Stark. She wrote me a note and asked me to come to see her. I knew what she wanted. She wanted to talk about Tom. Obviously, she wasn't finding out anything from Tom himself, or at least, what she considered to be the truth and the whole truth, and she wasn't talking it over with the Boss for on the matter of Tom she and the Boss had never agreed. So she was going to ask me questions, and I was going to sit and sweat on the red plush upholstery in the parlor of the farmhouse where she was living. But that had to be. Long back, I had made up my mind that when Lucy Stark asked me to do something I was going to do it. It was not exactly that I felt I owed Lucy Stark a debt, or had to make restitution, or do penance. At least, if there was a debt, it was not to Lucy Stark, and if there was restitution to be made it was not to be made to her. If there was a debt, it was, perhaps, due to me, from me. And if restitution was to be made, it was to be made to me, by me. And as for penance, there had been no crime for which I should do it. My only crime was being a man and living in the world of men, and you don't have to do special penance for that. The crime and the penance, in that case, coincide perfectly. They are identical.

If you have ever been down toward the Gulf, you know the kind of house. White frame, but with the glitter long gone. One story, a wide gallery across the front with spindly posts supporting the shed over it. A tin roof, with faint streaks of rust showing red in the channel joints. The whole thing set high on brick pillars, to make a cool cobweb-draped cloister underneath, screened on the front side by rank ligustrums and canna beds, for hens to congregate and fluff in the dust and an old shepherd dog to lie and pant in the hot days. It sits pretty well back from the road, in a lawn gone sparse and rusty in the late season. On each side of an anachronistic patch of concrete walk, which dies blankly at the gate where the earth of the highway shoulder shows raw, there are two round flower beds made by laying an old automobile tire on the ground and filling it with wood earth. There are a few zinnias in each, hairy like an animal, brilliant in the dazzling sun. At each end of the house is a live oak, not grand ones. Beyond the house, flanking it on each side are the chicken houses and barns, unpainted. But the faded-white decent house itself, sitting there in the middle of the late-summer afternoon, in the absolute quiet of that time of day and year, with the sparse lawn and tidy flower beds and the prideful patch of concrete walk in front, the oaks at each side, is like nothing so much as a respectable, middle-aged woman, in a clean gray gingham dress, with white stockings and black kid shoes, the pepper-and-salt hair coiled on her head, sitting in her rocker with her hands folded across her stomach to take a little ease, now the day's work is done and the menfolks are in the field and it's not yet time to think about supper and strain the evening milk.

I stepped gingerly up that patch of concrete walk, as though I were treading on dozens of eggs laid by all those white leghorns back in the chicken run.

Lucy led me into the parlor, which was just the place I had known it would be, the carved black-walnut furniture upholstered in red plush, with a few tassels still left hanging here and there, the Bible and the stereoscope and the neat pile of cards for the stereoscope on the carved black-walnut table, a flowered carpet, with little rag rugs laid over the places most worn, the big walnut and gilt frames on the wall enclosing the stern, malarial, Calvinistic faces whose eyes fixed you with little sympathy. The windows of the room were closed, and the curtains drawn to give a shadowy, aqueous light in which we sat silently for a minute as though at a funeral. The palm of my hand laid down on the plush prickled drily.

She sat there as though I hadn't come, not looking at me but down at a floral figure in the carpet. The abundant dark-brown hair which, when I first met Lucy out at the Stark place, had been massacred off at the neck and marcelled by the beauty operator of Mason City, had long since grown back to its proper length. The auburn luster was still in it, maybe, but I couldn't see it in the dim light of the parlor. I had, however, noticed the few touches of gray, when I met her at the door.

333

She sat across from me on the red plush seat of a stiff, carved, walnut chair, with her still good angles crossed in front of her, and her waist, not so little now, still straight, and her bosom full but not shapeless under the blue summer cloth. The soft soothing contours of her face weren't girlish any more, as they had been on that first evening back in Old Man Stark's house, for now there was a hint of weight, of the infinitesimal downward drag, in the flesh, the early curse and certain end of those soft, soothing faces which, especially when very young, appeal to all our natural goodness and make us think of the sanctity of motherhood. Yes, that is the kind of face you would put on the United States Madonna if you were going to paint her. But you aren't, and meanwhile it is the kind of face they try to put on advertisements of ready-mix cake flour and patented diapers and whole-wheat bread—good, honest, wholesome, trusting, courageous, tender, and with the glow of youth. The glow of youth wasn't on the particular face any more, but when Lucy Stark lifted her head to speak, I saw that the large, deep-brown eyes hadn't changed much. Time and trouble had shaded and deepened them some, but that was all.

She said, "It's about Tom."

"Yes," I said.

She said, "I know something is wrong."

I nodded.

She said, "Tell me."

I inhaled the dry air and the faint closed-parlor odor of furniture polish, which is the odor of decency and care and modest hopes, and squirmed on my seat while the red plush prickled my pressed-down palm like a nettle.

She said, "Jack, tell me the truth. I've got to know the truth, Jack. You will tell me the truth. You've always been a good friend. You were a good friend to Willie and me—back yonder—back yonder—when—"

Her voice trailed off.

So I told her the truth. About Marvin Frey's visit.

Her hands twisted in her lap while I spoke, and then clenched and lay still. Then she said, "There's just one thing for him to do."

"There might be a—a settlement—you know, a—"

But she broke in. "There's just one right thing," she said.

I waited.

"He'll—he'll marry her," she said, and held her head up very straight.

I squirmed a little, then said, "Well—well, you see—it looks like—like there might have been—some others—other friends of Sibyl—others who—"

"Oh, God," she breathed so softly I could scarcely tell it was more than a breath she uttered, and I saw the hands clench and unclench on her lap again.

"And," I went on, now I was in it, "there's another angle to it, too. There's some politics mixed up, too. You see Mac-Murfee wants—"

"Oh, God," she breathed again, and rose abruptly from the chair, and pressed her clenched hands together in front of her bosom. "Oh, God, politics," she whispered, and took a distracted step or two away from me, and said again, "Politics." Then she swung toward me, and said, out loud now, "Oh, God, in this too."

"Yes," I nodded, "like most things."

She went to one of the windows, where she stood with her back to me and the parlor and peered through a crack between the curtains out into the hot, sun-dazzled world outside, where everything happened.

After a minute she said, "Go on, tell me what you were going to tell."

So not even looking at her as she peered out the crack into the world but looking at the empty chair where she had been sitting, I told her about the MacMurfee proposition and how things were.

My voice stopped. Then there was another minute of silence. Then, I heard her voice back over by the window, "It had to be this way, I guess. I have tried to do right but it had to be this way, I guess. Oh, Jack—" I heard the rustle as she turned from the window, and swung my head toward her, as she said —"Oh, Jack, I tried to do right. I loved my boy and tried to raise him right. I loved my husband and tried to do my duty. And they love me. I think they love me. After everything. I have to think that, Jack. I have to."

I sat there and sweated on the red plush, while the large, deep-brown eyes fixed on me in a mixture of appeal and affirmation.

Then she said, very quietly now, "I have to think that. And think that it will be all right in the end."

"Listen," I said, "the Boss stalled them off, he'll think of something, it'll be all right."

"Oh, I didn't mean that, I meant—" but she stopped.

But I knew what she had meant, even as her voice, lower and steadier now, and at the same time more resigned, resumed to say, "Yes, he'll think of something. It will be all right."

There wasn't any use to hang round longer. I got up, rescued my old Panama off the carved walnut table, where the Bible and stereoscope were, walked across to Lucy, put out my hand to her, and said, "It'll be all right."

She looked at my hand as though she didn't know why it was there. Then she looked at me. "It's just a baby," she almost whispered. "It's just a little baby. It's a little baby in the dark. It's not even born yet, and it doesn't know about what's happened. About money and politics and somebody wanting to be a senator. It doesn't know about anything—about how it came to be—about what that girl did—or why—or why the father —why he—" She stopped, and the large brown eyes kept looking at me with appeal and what might have been accusation. Then she said, "Oh, Jack, it's a little baby, and nothing's its fault."

I almost burst out that it wasn't my fault, either, but I didn't.

Then she added, "It may be my grandbaby. It may be my boy's baby."

Then, after a moment, "I would love it."

Her hands, which had been clenched into fists and pressed together at the level of her breast, opened slowly at the words, and reached out, supine and slightly cupped, but with the wrists still against her own body as though expectation were humble or hopeless.

She noticed me looking down at the hands, then quickly let them drop.

"Good-bye," I said, and moved toward the door.

"Thank you, Jack," she said, but didn't follow me. Which ᵗuited me down to the ground, for I was really on my way out.

I walked out into the dazzling world and down the prideful ⱼatch of concrete and got into my car and headed back to town, ᵛhere, no doubt, I belonged.

The Boss did think up something.

First, he thought that it might be a good idea to get in touch ʳⁱth Marvin Frey, directly and not through MacMurfee, to .eel out the situation there. But MacMurfee was too smart for ᵗhat. He didn't trust Frey or the Boss, either, and Marvin had been whisked off, nobody knew where exactly. But, as it developed later, Marvin and Sibyl had been carried off into Arkansas, which was probably the last place they wanted to be, on a farm up in Arkansas, where the only horses were mules and the brightest light came from a patented gasoline pressure lamp on the parlor table and there weren't any fast cars and people went to bed to sleep at eight-thirty and got up at dawn. Of course, they had some company along, and could play three-handed poker and rummy, for MacMurfee had sent along one of his boys, who, I was to learn, kept the car keys in his pants pocket by day and under his pillow by night, and practically stood outside the door of the backhouse, leaning on the trellis of honeysuckle, with a derby on the side of his head, when one of them went there, just to be sure there weren't any shenanigans like cutting across the back lot in the direction of the railroad ten miles off. He was also the one who thumbed through the mail first, for Marvin and Sibyl weren't supposed to be getting any mail. Nobody was supposed to know where they were. And we didn't find out. Not until a long time after.

Second, the Boss thought about Judge Irwin. If MacMurfee would listen to sense at all, he would listen to sense from Judge Irwin. He owed Irwin a lot, and there weren't so many legs left to MacMurfee's stool he could afford to lose one. So, the Boss thought, there was Judge Irwin.

He called me in and said, "I told you to dig on Irwin. What did you get?"

"I got something," I said.

"What?"

"Boss," I said, "I'm going to give Irwin a break. If he can prove to me it isn't true, I won't spill it."

"God damn it," he began, "I told you—"

"I'm giving Irwin a break," I said. "I promised two people I would do it."

"Who?"

"Well, I promised myself, for one. The other doesn't matter."

"You promised yourself, huh?" He looked hard at me.

"Yeah, I did."

"O.K.," he said. "Do it your way. If it'll stick, you know what I want." He surveyed me glumly, then added, "And it better stick."

"Boss," I said, "I'm afraid it will."

"Afraid?" he said.

"Yeah."

"Who you working for? Him or me?"

"Well, I'm not framing Judge Irwin."

He kept on studying me. "Boy," he said then, "I'm not asking you to frame him. I never asked you to frame anybody. Did I?"

"No."

"I never did ask you to frame anybody. And you know why?"

"No."

"Because it ain't never necessary. You don't ever have to frame anybody, because the truth is always sufficient."

"You sure take a high view of human nature," I said.

"Boy," he said, "I went to a Presbyterian Sunday school back in the days when they still had some theology, and that much of it stuck. And—" he grinned suddenly—"I have found it very valuable."

So our conversation ended, and I got into my car and headed for Burden's Landing.

The next morning, as soon as I had my breakfast, which I

ate alone, for the Young Executive had left for town and my mother wouldn't get up till pushing noon, I strolled down the beach. It was a fine morning, but not as hot as usual. The beach was deserted at that hour, except for some kids playing in the bright shallows a quarter of a mile off, thin-legged little kids like sandpipers. I wandered on down past them, and as I passed they paused an instant in their leaping and splashing and gyration to favor me with an indifferent stare from their brown, water-slick faces. But it was only for an instant, for I obviously belonged to that dull and purblind race which wears shoes and trousers, and you do not leap up and down in the bright shallows in shoes and trousers. You do not even walk on the sand and get sand in your shoes if you can avoid it. But at least I was walking on the sand and getting it liberally into my shoes. I wasn't too old for that. I reflected on that with satisfaction, and moved on toward the cluster of pines and the big oak and the mimosas and myrtles, just back from the beach, where the tennis courts were. There were some benches there in the shade, and I had the unread morning paper in my hand. After I had read the paper, I would begin to think about what would happen later on in the day. But I wasn't even thinking about it yet.

I found the bench near the vacant court and lighted my cigarette and began to read. I read the front page, every word, with the mechanical devotion of a padre working over the missal, and didn't even think of all the news which I knew and which wasn't on the front page. I was well into the third page, when I heard voices and looked up to see the pair of players, a boy and girl, approaching on the other side of the courts. After an idle glance at me, they took possession of the farther court, and began to beat the little white ball back and forth, just idly to loosen up their muscles.

You could tell by the first exchange that they knew what they were about. And you could tell that their muscles didn't need much loosening up. He was of medium height, perhaps a shade under, with a deep chest and big arms and nothing extra around the waist. His red hair had a crew cut, crinkly red hair showed on his chest above the underwear vest he was wearing instead of a shirt, and his skin was an even baby-pink except for the big blotches of brown freckles on his face and shoulders. In the middle of the freckles his face was all white-toothed grin and the glint of blue eyes. She was a brown lively girl, short brown hair that snapped when she pirouetted, and brown arms and shoulders above the white halter tied over her breasts, and brown legs flashing above white shoes and socks, and a little brown flat tummy between the white shorts and the white halter. They were both pretty young.

They began the game right quick, and I watched them over

338

my newspaper. Maybe the red-headed fellow wasn't trying his hardest, but she was handing them back to him well enough and could make him move around the court. She was even taking a game from him now and then. She was a pretty thing to watch, so light and springy and serious-faced and flashy-legged. But not as pretty as Anne Stanton had been, I decided. I even meditated on the superior beauty of a white skirt which could flow and whip with the player's motion as compared to shorts. But shorts were good. They were good on the lively brown girl. I had to admit that.

And I had to admit, as I watched, that I had a knot in my stomach. Because I wasn't out there on the court. With Anne Stanton. It was a terrific and fundamental injustice that I wasn't out there. What was that red-faced, crop-headed fellow doing there? What was that girl doing there? I suddenly didn't like them. I felt like going over there and stopping the game and saying, "You think you'll be here playing tennis forever, don't you? Well, you won't."

"Why, no," the girl would say, "not forever."

"Hell, no," the fellow would say, "we're going swimming this afternoon, then tonight we're—"

"You don't get it," I would say. "Sure, I know you're going swimming, and you're going out somewhere tonight and you'll stop the car on the way home. But you think you'll be here this way forever."

"Hell, no," he would say, "I'm going back to college next week."

"I'm going off to school," she would say, "but Thanksgiving I'll see Al, won't I, Al—and you'll take me to the big game—won't you, Al?"

They wouldn't get it worth a damn. There was no use in giving them the benefit of my wisdom. Not even of the great big piece of wisdom which I had learned on my trip to California. They didn't know the wisdom of the Great Twitch, but they would have to find it out for themselves, for there was no use to tell them. They might listen politely, but they wouldn't believe a word of it. And watching the brown girl dance and flash over there against the myrtles and the brilliant sea, I wasn't so sure for the moment that I believed it myself.

But I did believe it, of course, for I had had my trip to California.

I didn't see out the first set. The score was five to two when I left, but it seemed that she might make it five-three, for the crop-headed fellow was feeding them to her, not too obviously, and grinning out of the freckles when she'd whang them back.

I went to the house, changed, and took a swim. I idled out a long way, and floated around in the bay, which is a corner of the Gulf of Mexico, which is a corner of the great, salt, unplumbed waters of the world, and got back in time for lunch.

My mother had lunch with me. She kept giving me a chance to tell her why I had come down, but I just skirted round the subject till we got to the dessert. Then I asked her if Judge Irwin was at the Landing. I hadn't asked that yet. I could have found out the night before. But I hadn't asked. I had postponed finding out.

He was at the Landing, all right.

My mother and I went out on the side gallery and had coffee and cigarettes. After a while I went upstairs to lie down for a spell and digest. I lay up there in my old room for an hour or so. Then I figured I had better get on with my work. I eased downstairs and started out the front door.

But my mother was in the living room and called to me. It was a strange place for her to be at that time of day, but there she was. She had waited to waylay me, I decided. I stepped inside and leaned against the wall, waiting for her to speak.

"You're going down to the Judge's?" she asked.

I said, yes, I was.

She was holding up her right hand, the back to her, the fingers spread, to inspect the polish on her red nails. Then with her brow ruffled as though the inspection were not satisfactory, she asked, "Oh, politics, I suppose?"

"Sort of," I said.

"Why don't you go later on?" she asked. "He hates to be bothered this time of day."

"There isn't any time, day or night, when he wouldn't hate to hear what I'm going to tell him."

She looked sharply at me, her hand with the spread fingers forgotten in the air.

Then she said, "He's not very well. Why do you have to bother him? He isn't at all well now."

"I can't help that," I said, feeling the stubbornness grow inside me.

"He's not well."

"I can't help it."

"You at least might wait till later."

"No, I'm not waiting," I said. I felt that I couldn't wait. I had to go on and get it done. The obstacle, the resistance, had confirmed me in that. I had to know. Quick.

"I wish you wouldn't," she said, and lowered that hand which she had held up, forgotten, in the air the time we had been talking.

"I can't help it."

"I wish you wouldn't get mixed up in—in things," she complained.

"I'm not the one mixed up in this something."

340

"What do you mean?"

"I'll know when I've put it up to Irwin," I told her, and went out of the room, and the house, and walked up the Row toward the Irwin place. At least, I would walk, hot as it was, and that would give the old bugger a little extra time before I popped the question to him. He deserved the extra few minutes, I reckoned.

The old bugger was upstairs lying down when I got there.

That was what the black boy in the white coat said. "The Jedge, he upstairs layen on the baid, he resten," he said, and seemed to think that that settled something.

"All right," I said, "I'll wait till he comes down." And without invitation I drew open the screen door, and entered into the shadowy gracious coolness of the hall, like the perfect depth of time, where the mirrors and the great hurricane glasses glittered like ice, and my image was caught as noiselessly as velvet or recollection in all the reflecting surfaces.

"The Jedge, he—" the black boy began again to protest.

I walked right past him saying, "I'll sit in the library. Till he comes down."

So I walked past the eyes of which the whites were like peeled hard-boiled eggs and past the sad big mouth which didn't know what to say now and just hung open to show the pink, and walked on back to the library, and entered into the deep, shuttered shadow which depended from the high ceiling and the walls of books laid close like stone and which lay on the deep-red Turkey carpet like a great dog asleep and scarcely breathing. I sat down in one of the big leather chairs, dropped by the chair the big manila envelope I had brought, and lay back. I got the notion that all the books were staring meaninglessly down at me like sculptured stone closed eyes, in a gallery. I noticed, as before, that all the old calf-bound law books there gave the room the faint odor of cheese.

After a while, there was some movement upstairs, then the tinkle of a bell in the back of the house. I guessed that the Judge had rung for the boy. A moment later I heard the boy's soft feet padding in the hall, and guessed that he was headed upstairs.

In about ten minutes the Judge came down. His firm tread came toward the library door. He paused an instant at the threshold, a tall head above a black bowtie and white coat, as though to adjust his eyes to the shadow, then moved toward me with his hand out. "Hello, Jack," he was saying, in the voice I had always known, "damned glad you came by. I didn't know you were at the Landing. Just get in?"

"Last night," I said briefly, and rose to take the hand.

He gave me a firm grasp, then waved me back into the chair. "Damned glad you came by," he repeated, and smiled out of the high, tired, rust-colored old hawk's head up there in the shadow. "How long you been in the house? Why didn't you make that rascal rout me out instead of letting me sleep all afternoon? It's a long time since I've seen you, Jack."

"Yes," I agreed, "it is."

It had been a long time. The last time had been in the middle of the night. With the Boss. And in the silence after my remark I knew that he was remembering, too. He was remembering, but after he had said it. Then I knew that he had put the memory away. He was denying the memory. "Well, it is a long time," he said as he settled himself, as though he had remembered nothing, "but don't let it be as long next time. Aren't you ever coming to see the old fellow? We old ones like a little attention."

He smiled, and there wasn't anything I could say into the face of that smile.

"Damn it," he said, popping up out of his chair without any audible creaking of joints, "look at me forgetting hospitality. I bet you are dry as Andy Jackson's powder. Little early in the day perhaps for the real thing, but a touch of gin and tonic never hurt anybody. Not you and me, anyway. We're indestructible, aren't we, you and me?"

He was halfway across to the bellpull before I managed to say anything.

"No, thanks," I said.

He looked down at me, the faintest shade of disappointment on his face. Then the smile came back, a good, honest, dog-toothed, manly smile, and he said, "Aw, come on, and have a little one. This is a celebration. I want to celebrate your coming to see me!"

He got in another step toward the bellpull before I said, "No, thanks."

For a moment he stood there looking down at me again, with his arm lifted for the pull. Then he let his arm drop and turned again toward his own chair, with the slightest slackening visible—or I imagined it—in his frame. "Well," he said offering something which wasn't quite the smile, "I'm not going to drink by myself. I'll get my stimulation out of your conversation. What's on your mind?"

"Nothing much," I said.

I looked at him over there in the shadow and saw that something was keeping the old shoulders straight and the old head up. I wondered what it was. I wondered if what I had dug up were true. I looked across at him, and didn't want it to be true. With all my heart, I discovered, I didn't want it to be true. And I had the sudden thought that I might have his drink of gin and tonic, and talk with him and never tell him, and go back to town and tell the Boss that I was convinced it was

342

not true. The Boss would have to take that. He would pitch and roar, but he would know it was my show. Besides by that time I would have destroyed the stuff from Miss Littlepaugh. I could do that.

But I had to know. Even as the thought of going away without knowing came through my head, I knew that I had to know the truth. For the truth is a terrible thing. You dabble your foot in it and it is nothing. But you walk a little farther and you feel it pull you like an undertow or a whirlpool. First there is the slow pull so steady and gradual you scarcely notice it, then the acceleration, then the dizzy whirl and plunge to blackness. For there is a blackness of truth, too. They say it is a terrible thing to fall into the Grace of God. I am prepared to believe that.

So I looked across at Judge Irwin, and liked him suddenly in a way I hadn't liked him in years, his old shoulders were so straight and the dog-toothed smile so true. But I knew I had to know.

So, as he studied me—for my face must have been something then to invite a reading—I met his gaze.

"I said there wasn't much," I said. "But there is something."

"Out with it," he said.

"Judge," I began, "you know who I work for."

"I know, Jack," he said, "but let's just sit here and forget it. I can't say I approve of Stark, but I'm not like most of our friends down the Row. I can respect a man, and he's a man. I was almost for him at one time. He was breaking the window-panes out and letting in a little fresh air. But—" he shook his head sadly, and smiled—"I began to worry about him knocking down the house, too. And some of his methods. So—" He didn't finish the sentence, but gave his shoulders the slightest shrug.

"So," I finished it for him, "you threw in with MacMurfee."

"Jack," he said, "politics is always a matter of choices, and a man doesn't set up the choices himself. And there is always a price to make a choice. You know that. You've made a choice, and you know how much it cost you. There is always a price."

"Yes, but—"

"Jack, I'm not criticizing you," he said. "I trust you. Time will show which of us is wrong. And meanwhile, Jack, let's don't let it come between us. If I lost my temper that night, I apologize. From my heart. It has cost me some pain."

"You say you don't like Stark's methods," I said. "Well, I'll tell you something about MacMurfee's methods. Listen, here is what MacMurfee is up to—" And I lurched and ground on like a runaway streetcar charging downhill and the brakes busted. I told him what MacMurfee was up to.

He sat and took it.

Then I asked him, "Is that pretty?"

"No," he said, and shook his head.

"It is not pretty." I said. "And you can stop it."

"Me?" he demanded.

"MacMurfee will listen to you. He's got to listen to you, for you are one of the few friends he's got left, and he knows the Boss's breath is hot on his neck. If he really had anything of more than nuisance value, he would go on and try to bust the Boss and not haggle. But he knows he hasn't got anything. And I'll tell you that if it comes to a pinch the Boss will fight in the courts. This Sibyl Frey is a homemade tart, and we can damned well prove it. We'll have an entire football squad in there, plus a track team, and all the truckers who run Highway 69 past her pappy's house. If you talk MacMurfee into sense, there might be some chance of saving his shirt when the time comes. But mind you, I can't promise a thing. Not now."

There was nothing but shadow and silence and the faint odor like old cheese for a spell, while what I had just said all went through the hopper inside that handsome old head. Then he shook the head slowly. "No," he said.

"Look here," I said, "there'll be something in it for Sibyl, the tart. We can take care of that side of it, unless she's got ideas of grandeur. She'll have to sign a little statement, of course. And I won't conceal from you that our side will have a few affidavits from her other boy-friends salted away just in case she ever gets gay again. If you think Sibyl isn't getting a square deal, I can reassure you on that point."

"It isn't that," he said.

"Judge," I said, and caught the tone of pleading in my own voice, "what the hell is it?"

"It's MacMurfee's affair. He may be making a mistake. I think he is. But it is his affair. It is the sort of thing I am not mixing in."

"Judge," I begged, "you think it over. Take a little time to think it over."

He shook his head.

I got up. "I've got to run," I said. "You think it over. I'll be back tomorrow and we can talk about it then. Give me your answer then."

He put the yellow agates on me and shook his head again. "Come to see me tomorrow, Jack. Tomorrow and every other day. But I'm giving you my answer now."

"I'm asking you, Judge, as a favor to me. Wait till tomorrow to make up your mind."

"You talk like I didn't know my own mind, Jack. That's about the only thing I've learned out of my three score and ten. That I know when I know my own mind. But you come back tomorrow, anyway. And we won't talk politics." He made a sudden gesture as though sweeping off the top of a table with his arm. "Damn politics anyway!" he exclaimed humorously.

I looked at him, and even with the wry, humorous expression on his face and the arm flung out at the end of its gesture, knew that this was it. It wasn't the dabble of the foot in the water, or even the steady deep pull of the undertow or the peripheral drag of the whirlpool. It was the heady race and plunge of the vortex. I ought to have known it would be this way.

Looking at him, I said, almost whispering, "I asked you, Judge. I near begged you, Judge."

A mild question came on his face.

"I tried," I said. "I begged you."

"What?" he demanded.

"Did you ever hear," I asked, my voice still not much more than a whisper, "of a man named Littlepaugh?"

"Littlepaugh?" he queried, and his brow wrinkled in the effort of memory.

"Mortimer L. Littlepaugh," I said, "don't you remember?"

The flesh of the forehead drew more positively together to make the deep vertical mark like a cranky exclamation point between the heavy, rust-colored eyebrows. "No," he said, and shook his head, "I don't remember."

And he didn't. I was sure he didn't. He didn't even remember Mortimer L. Littlepaugh.

"Well," I questioned, "do you remember the American Electric Power Company?"

"Of course. Why wouldn't I? I was their counsel for ten years." There wasn't a flicker.

"Do you remember how you got the job?"

"Let me see—" he began, and I knew that he didn't for the moment remember, that he was in truth reaching back into the past, trying to remember. Then, straightening himself, he said, "Yes, of course, I remember. It was through a Mr. Satterfield."

But there had been the flicker. The barb had found meat, and I knew it.

I waited a long minute, looking at him, and he looked straight back at me, very straight in his chair.

"Judge," I asked softly, "you won't change your mind? About MacMurfee?"

"I told you," he said.

Then I could hear his breathing, and I wanted more than anything to know what was in his head, why he was sitting there straight and looking at me, while the barb bled into him.

I stepped to the chair which I had occupied and leaned down to pick up the manila envelope on the floor beside it. Then I move to his chair, and laid the envelope in his lap.

He looked at the envelope, without touching it. Then he looked up at me, a hard straight look out of the yellow agates, with no question in them. Then, without saying a word, he opened the envelope and read the papers there. The light was bad, but he did not lean forward. He held the papers, one by one up to his face. He read them very deliberately. Then he laid the last, deliberately, on his lap.

"Littlepaugh," he said musingly, and waited. "You know," he said marveling, "you know, I didn't even remember his name. I swear, I didn't even remember his name."

He waited again.

"Don't you think it remarkable," he asked, "that I didn't even remember his name?"

"Maybe so," I said.

"You know," he said, still marveling, "for weeks—for months sometimes—I don't even remember any of—" he touched the papers lightly with his strong, swollen right finger —"of this."

He waited, drawn into himself.

Then he said, "You know, sometimes—for a long time at a stretch—it's like it hadn't happened. Not to me. Maybe to somebody else, but not to me. Then I remember, and when I first remember I say, No, it could not have happened to me."

Then he looked up at me, straight in the eye. "But it did," he said.

"Yes," I said, "it did."

"Yes," he nodded, "but it is difficult for me to believe."

"It is for me, too," I said.

"Thanks for that much, Jack," he said, and smiled crookedly.

"I guess you know the next move," I said.

"I guess so. Your employer is trying to put pressure on me. To blackmail me."

"*Pressure* is a prettier word," I averred.

"I don't care much about pretty words any more. You live with words a long time. Then all at once you are old, and there are the things and the words don't matter any more."

I shrugged my shoulders, "Suit yourself," I replied, "but you get the idea."

"Don't you know—your employer ought to know, since he claims to be a lawyer, that this stuff," he tapped the papers again with the forefinger, "wouldn't stick? Not for one minute. In a court of law. Why, it happened almost twenty-five years ago. And you wouldn't get any testimony, anyway. Except from this Littlepaugh woman. Which would be worthless. Everybody is dead."

"Except you, Judge," I said.

"It wouldn't stick in court."

"But you don't live in a court. You aren't dead, and you live in the world and people think you are a certain kind of man. You aren't the kind of man who could bear for them to think different, Judge."

"They couldn't think it!" he burst out, leaning forward. "By God, they haven't any right to think it. I've done right, I've done my duty, I've—"

I took my gaze from his face and directed it to the papers on his lap. He saw me do that, and looked down, too. The words stopped, and his fingers touched the papers, tentatively as though to verify their reality. Quite slowly, he raised his eyes back to me. "You're right," he said. "I did this, too."

"Yes," I said, "you did."

"Does Stark know it?"

I tried to make out what was behind that question, but I couldn't read him.

"No, he doesn't," I replied. "I told him I wouldn't tell him till I'd seen you. I had to be sure, you see, Judge."

"You have a tender sensibility," he said. "For a blackmailer."

"We won't start calling names. All I'll say is that you're trying to protect a blackmailer."

"No, Jack," he said quietly, "I'm not trying to protect Mac-Murfee. Maybe—" he hesitated—"I'm trying to protect myself."

"You know how to do it, then. And I'll never tell Stark."

"Maybe you'll never tell him, anyway."

He said that even more quietly, and for the instant I thought he might be ready to reach for a weapon—the desk was near him—or ready to spring at me. He might be old but he would still be a customer.

He must have guessed the thought, for he shook his head, smiled, and said, "No, don't worry. You needn't be afraid."

"Look here—" I began angrily.

"I wouldn't hurt you," he said. Then, reflectively, added. "But I could stop you."

"By stopping MacMurfee," I said.

"A lot easier than that."

"How?"

"A lot easier than that," he repeated.

"How?"

"I could just—" he began, "I could just say to you—I could just tell you something—" He stopped, then suddenly rose to his feet, spilling the papers off his knees. "But I won't," he said cheerfully, and smiled directly at me.

"Won't tell me what?"

"Forget it," he said, still smiling, and waved his hand in a gay dismissal of the subject.

I stood there irresolutely for a moment. Things were not making sense. He was not supposed to be standing there, brisk

347

and confident and cheerful, with the incriminating papers at his feet. But he was.

I stooped to pick up the papers, and he watched me from his height.

"Judge," I said, "I'll be back tomorrow. You think it over, and make up your mind tomorrow."

"Why, it's made up."

"You'll—"

"No, Jack."

I went to the hall door. "I'll be back tomorrow," I said.

"Sure, sure. You come back. But my mind is made up."

I walked down the hall without saying good-bye. I had my hand lifted to the front door when I heard his voice calling my name. I turned and took a few steps toward him. He had come out into the hall. "I just wanted to tell you," he said, "that I did learn something new from those interesting documents. I learned that my old friend Governor Stanton impaired his honor to protect me. I do not know whether to be more glad or sorry, at the fact. At the knowledge of his attachment or the knowledge of the pain it cost him. He had never told me. That was the pitch of his generosity. Wasn't it? Not ever telling me."

I mumbled something to the effect that I supposed it was.

"I just wanted you to know about the Governor. That his failing was a defect of his virtue. The virtue of affection for a friend."

I didn't mumble anything to that.

"I just wanted you to know that about the Governor," he said.

"All right," I said, and went to the front door, feeling his yellow gaze and calm smile upon me, and out into the blaze of light.

It was still hotter than hell's hinges as I walked up the Row toward home. I debated a swim or getting in my car and heading back to town to tell the Boss that Judge Irwin wouldn't budge. Then I decided that I might wait over another day. I might wait on just the chance that the Judge would change his mind. But I wouldn't swim till later. It was too hot even to swim now. I would take a shower when I got in and lie down till it had cooled off enough for a swim.

I took my shower and lay down on my bed and went to sleep.

I came out of the sleep and popped straight up in the bed. I was wide awake. The sound that had awakened me was still ringing in my ears. I knew that it had been a scream. Then it came again. A bright, beautiful, silvery soprano scream.

I bounced off the bed and started for the door, realized that I was buck-naked, grabbed a robe, and ran out. There was a

348

noise down the hall from my mother's room, a sound like moaning. The door was open and I ran in.

She was sitting on the edge of her bed, wearing a negligee, clutching the white bedside telephone in her hand, staring at me with wide, wild eyes, and moaning in a spaced, automatic fashion. I went toward her. She dropped the telephone to the floor with a clatter, and pointed her finger at me and cried out, "You did it, you did, you killed him!"

"What?" I demanded, "what?"

"You killed him!"

"Killed who?"

"You killed him!" She began to laugh hysterically.

I was holding her by the shoulders now, shaking her, trying to make her stop laughing, but she kept clawing and pushing at me. She stopped laughing an instant to gasp for breath, and in that interval I heard the dry, clicking signal the telephone was making to call attention to the fact it was not on its rack. Then her laughter drowned out the sound.

"Shut up, shut up!" I commanded, and she suddenly stared at me as though just discovering my presence.

Then, not loud now but with intensity, she said, "You killed him, you killed him."

"Killed who?" I demanded, shaking her.

"Your father," she said, "your father and oh! you killed him."

That was how I found out. At the moment the finding out simply numbed me. When a heavy-caliber slug hits you, you may spin around but you don't feel a thing. Not at first. Anyway, I was busy. My mother was in bad shape. By this time there were a couple of black faces at the door, the cook and the maid, and I was damning them to get Dr. Bland and stop gawking. Then I raked the clicking telephone up off the floor so they could use the one downstairs, and let my mother go long enough to slam the door to keep those all-seeing, all-knowing eyes off what was happening.

My mother was talking between her moans and laughing. She was saying how she had loved him and how he was the only person she had ever loved and how I had killed him and had killed my own father and a lot of stuff like that. She was still carrying on when Dr. Bland arrived and gave her the hypodermic. Across her form on the bed, from which the moans and the mutterings were now subsiding, he turned his gray, gray-bearded owlish face and said, "Jack, I'm sending a nurse up here. A very trustworthy woman. Nobody else is to come in here. Do you understand?"

"Yes," I told him, for I understood, and understood that he

had understood perfectly well what my mother's wild talking had meant.

"You stay here till the nurse arrives," he said, "and don't let anybody in. And the nurse isn't supposed to let anybody in until I get back to see if your mother is normal. Not anybody."

I nodded, and followed him to the door of the room.

After he had said his good-bye, I detained him a moment. "Doctor," I asked, "what about the Judge? I didn't get it straight from my mother. Was it a stroke?"

"No," he said, and inspected my face.

"Well, what was it?"

"He shot himself this afternoon," he replied, still inspecting my face. But then he added quite matter-of-factly, "It was undoubtedly a question of health. His health was failing. A very active man—a sportsman—very often—" he was even more dry and detached in his tone—"very often such a man doesn't want to face the last years of limited activity. Yes, I am sure that was the reason."

I didn't answer.

"Good day, sir," the doctor said, and took his eyes off me and started down the hall.

He was almost to the head of the stairs before I called, "Doctor!" and ran after him.

I came up to him and said, "Doctor, where did he shoot himself? What part of the body, I mean? Not the head?"

"Straight through the heart," he said. And added, "A .38 automatic. A very clean wound."

Then he went off down the stairs. I stood there and thought how the dead man was shot through the heart, a very clean wound, and not through the head with the muzzle of the weapon put into the mouth to blaze into the soft membranes to scorch them and the top of the skull exploding off like an egg to make an awful mess. I stood there, and was greatly relieved to think of the nice clean wound.

I went to my own room, snatched up some clothes, and then went back to my mother's room, and shut the door. I dressed and sat by the side of the big magnificent tester bed in which the lace-filmed form looked so small. I noticed how the bosom looked slack and the face sunken and grayish. The mouth was somewhat open and the breath through it heavy. I scarcely recognized the face. Certainly it was not the face of the girl in the lettuce-green dress and with the golden hair who had stood by the stocky, dark-suited man on the steps of a company commissary in a lumber town in Arkansas, forty years before, while the scream of saws filled the air and the head like a violated nerve and the red earth between the fields of stumps curdled with pale green and steamed in the spring sun. It was not the famish-cheeked, glowing face that, back in those years, had looked up eagerly and desperately to the hawk-headed, hot-eyed man in alleys of myrtle or in secret pine groves or in shuttered rooms. No, it was an old face now. And I felt very sorry for it. I reached across to take one of the unconscious hands which lay loose on the sheet.

I held the hand and tried to imagine how things would have been if it had not been the Scholarly Attorney but his friend who had gone to the little lumber town in Arkansas. No, that wouldn't have helped much, I decided, remembering that at that time Monty Irwin had been married to an invalid wife, the first wife, who had been crippled by being thrown from a horse and who had had lain in bed for some years and had then died quietly and sunk from our sight and thought at the Landing. No doubt Monty Irwin had been held by some notion of obligation to that invalid wife: he hadn't been able to divorce her and marry the other woman. No doubt that was why he had not married the famish-cheeked girl, why he had not gone to his friend the Scholarly Attorney and told him, "I love your wife," or why, after the husband had learned the truth, as he must have done to make him walk out of the house and away to all the years in the slum garrets, he had not then married her. He still had his own wife then, to whom, because she was an invalid, he must have felt bound with a kind of twisted honor. Then my mother had married again. There must have been bitterness and dire quarrels all along mixed with the stolen satisfactions and ardors. Then the invalid had died. Why hadn't they married then? Perhaps my mother wouldn't then, to punish him for his own earlier refusals. Or perhaps their life was by this time set into a pattern they couldn't break. Anyway, he had married the woman from Savannah, the woman who hadn't brought him anything, neither money nor happiness, but who had, after a certain time, died. Why hadn't they married then?

I dismissed the question finally. Perhaps the only answer, I thought then, was that by the time we understand the pattern we are in, the definition we are making for ourselves, it is too late to break out of the box. We can only live in terms of the definition, like the prisoner in the cage in which he cannot lie or stand or sit, hung up in justice to be viewed by the populace. Yet the definition we have made of ourselves is ourselves. To break out of it, we must make a new self. But how can the self make a new self when the selfness which it is, is the only substance from which the new self can be made? At least that was the way I argued the case back then.

As I say, I dismissed the question, and dismissed the answer I had tried to give to it, and simply held the lax hand between my own, and listened to the heavy breathing from the sunken face, and thought how in the scream which had snatched me from sleep that afternoon there had been the bright, beautiful, silver purity of feeling. It had been, I decided, the true cry of the buried soul which had managed, for one instant after all the years, to utter itself again. Well, she had loved Monty Irwin, I supposed. I had thought that she had never loved anybody. So now, as I held the hand, I felt not only pity for her but something like love, too, because she had loved somebody.

After a while the nurse came and released me from the room. Then Mrs. Daniell, who was a neighbor of Judge Irwin, came by to see my mother. It had been her telephone call which brought the news to my mother. Mrs. Daniell had heard the shot in the afternoon but had thought nothing about it until the colored boy at the Irwin place ran out into the yard and began yelling. She had gone back into the house with the boy, and had seen the Judge sitting in one of the big leather chairs in his library with the pistol on his knee, his head canted over on one shoulder, and the blood spreading out over the left side of the white coat. She had plenty to tell, and she was working down the Row in a systematic fashion. She told me her story, pried unsuccessfully into my visit there of the afternoon and into my mother's indisposition (she had, of course, heard the screams on the telephone), and then took her leave without much to add to her basic narrative at the next port of call.

The Young Executive came in about seven o'clock. He already knew about the death of Judge Irwin, but I had to tell him about my mother. I made it damned plain and without trimmings that he was to stay out of her room. Then he and I went out on the side gallery and had a silent drink together. I didn't mind his presence more than a shadow.

Two days later Judge Irwin was buried in the churchyard under the ghostly, moss-garlanded oak. Earlier, in his house, I had filed past the coffin with everybody else and had locked down at the dead face. The hawk nose seemed to be paper thin and almost transparent. The usual strong color of the flesh was gone and on the cheeks there was only the coy tint of the mortician's art. But the coarse rufous hair, thinner than ever, seemed to stand up electrically and individually from the high-domed skull. The people filed past, looked down, murmured to each other, and went to stand at the end of the drawing room near the potted palms imported for the occasion. Thus the fact of his death was absorbed effortlessly into the life of the community, like a single tiny drop of stain dropped into a glass of clear water. It would spread outward and outward from the point of vindictive concentration, raveling and thinning away, drawing away the central fact of the stain until nothing at all was visible.

I stood then in the churchyard, while the process was being completed, and the earth, a mixture of sand and the black surface humus, was being shoveled into the hole where Judge Irwin lay. I thought how he had forgotten the name of Mortimer L. Littlepaugh, had forgotten that he had ever existed, but how Mortimer had never forgotten him. Mortimer had been dead more than a score of years but he had never forgotten Judge Irwin. Remembering the letter in his sister's trunk, he had worn his fleshless grin and soundless chuckle and waited. Judge Irwin had killed Mortimer L. Littlepaugh. But Mortimer had killed Judge Irwin in the end. Or had it been Mortimer? Perhaps I had done it. That was one way of looking at it. I turned that thought over and speculated upon my responsibility. It would be quite possible to say that I had none, no more than Mortimer had. Mortimer had killed Judge Irwin because Judge Irwin had killed him, and I had killed Judge Irwin because Judge Irwin had created me, and looking at matters in that light one could say that Mortimer and I were merely the twin instruments of Judge Irwin's protracted and ineluctable self-destruction. For either killing or creating may be a crime punishable by death, and the death always comes by the criminal's own hand and every man is a suicide. If a man knew how to live he would never die.

They filled up the hole and rounded off a neat mound on which they placed a carpet of artificial grass, savagely green, in the churchyard where, under the dense shade of moss and boughs and under the mat of trodden leaves, no natural grass ever sprang. Then following the decorous crowd, I left the dead man under that green grass of the mortician's fancy which spared all tender sensibilities the sight of raw earth and proclaimed that nothing whatsoever had happened and veiled, as it were, all significance of life and death.

So I left my father, and walked down the Row. I had by this time grown accustomed to think of him as my father. But this meant that I had disaccustomed myself to thinking of the man who had been the Scholarly Attorney as my father. There was a kind of relief in knowing that that man was not my father. I had always felt some curse of his weakness upon me, or what I had felt to be that. He had had a beautiful and eager young wife and another man had taken her away from him and had fathered his child, and all he had done was to walk away, leaving her in possession of everything he owned, and crawl into a hole in the slums and lie there like a wounded animal and let his intellect bleed away into pious drivel and his strength bleed away into weakness. And he had been good. But his goodness had told me nothing except that I could not live by it. My new father, however, had not been good. He had cuckolded a friend, betrayed a wife, taken a bride, driven a man, though unwittingly, to death. But he had done good. He had been a just judge. And he had carried his head high. That last afternoon of his life

353

he had done that. He hadn't said, "Look here, Jack, you can't do it—you can't—you see, you see—I am your father."

Well, I had swapped the good, weak father for the evil, strong one. I didn't feel bad about it. I felt sorry for the Judge as I walked down the Row by the sea, but as far as I myself was concerned I didn't feel dissatisfied with the swap. Then I thought of the other old man leaning over the half-wit acrobat in the grubby room and holding out the bit of chocolate to the tear-stained face, and I thought of the child on the rug before the fire and the stocky black-coated man leaning to him and saying, "Here, Son, just one bite before supper." Then I wasn't so sure what I felt.

So I quit trying to decide. There was no use trying to probe my feelings about them, for I had lost both of them. Most people lose one father, but I was peculiarly situated, I had lost two at the same instant. I had dug up the truth and the truth always kills the father, the good and weak one or the bad and strong one, and you are left alone with yourself and the truth, and can never ask Dad, who didn't know anyway and who is deader than mackerel.

The next day, after I was back in town, I got a call from the Landing. It was a Mr. Pettus, who, it turned out, was the Judge's executor. According to what he said, I was, except for a few minor bequests to servants, the sole heir. I was the sole heir to the estate which Judge Irwin had saved, years before, by his single act of dishonesty, the act for which I, as the blameless instrument of justice, had put the pistol to his heart.

The whole arrangement seemed so crazy and so logical that after I had hung up the phone I burst out laughing and could scarcely stop. Before I stopped, as a matter of fact, I found that I was not laughing at all but was weeping and saying over and over again, "The poor old bugger, the poor old bugger." It was like the ice breaking up after a long winter. And the winter had been long.

Chapter Nine

AFTER a great blow, or crisis, after the first shock and then after the nerves have stopped screaming and twitching, you settle down to the new condition of things and feel that all possibility of change has been used up. You adjust yourself, and are sure that the new equilibrium is for eternity. After the death of Judge Irwin, after I got back to the city, I felt that way. I felt that a story was over, that what had been begun a long time back had been played out, that the lemon had been squeezed dry. But if anything is certain it is that no story is ever over, for the story which we think is over is only a chapter in a story which will not be over, and it isn't the game that is over, it is just an inning, and that game has a lot more than nine innings. When the game stops it will be called on account of darkness. But it is a long day.

The little game the Boss was playing was not over. But I had nearly forgotten all about it. I had forgotten that the story of Judge Irwin, which seemed so complete in itself, was only a chapter in the longer story of the Boss, which was not over and which was itself merely a chapter in another bigger story.

The Boss looked across the desk at me as I walked in, and said, "God damn it, so the bastard crawled out on me."

I didn't say anything.

"I didn't tell you to scare him to death, I just told you to scare him."

"He wasn't scared," I said.

"What the hell did he do it for then?"

"I told you a long time back when the mess started he wouldn't scare."

"Well, why did he do it?"

"I don't want to discuss it."

"Well, why did he do it?"

"God damn it," I said, "didn't I tell you I didn't want to discuss it?"

He looked at me with some surprise, got up from his chair and came around the desk. "I'm sorry," he said, and put his heavy hand on my shoulder.

I moved out from under the hand.

"I'm sorry," he repeated. "He had been quite a pal of yours at one time, hadn't he?"

"Yeah," I said.

He sat back on the desk and raised one big knee to clasp his hands around it.

"There is still MacMurfee," he said reflectively.

"Yes, there is MacMurfee, but if you want any blackmailing done, get somebody else to do it."

"Even on MacMurfee?" he asked, with a hint of jocularity, to which I didn't respond.

"Even on MacMurfee," I said.

"Hey," he demanded, "you aren't quitting me?"

"No, I'm just quitting certain things."

"Well, it was true, wasn't it?"

"What?"

"What the Judge did, whatever the hell it was."

I couldn't deny that. I had to say yes. So I nodded and said, "Yes, he did it."

"Well?" he demanded.

"I said what I said."

He was studying me drowsily from under the shagged-down forelock. "Boy," he said then, soberly, "we been together a long time. I hope we'll be in it together all the way. We been in it up to the ears, both of us, you and me, boy."

I didn't answer.

He continued to study me. Then he said, "Don't you worry. It'll all come out all right."

"Yeah," I said sourly, "you'll be Senator."

"I didn't mean that. I could be Senator right now if that was all."

"What did you mean?"

He didn't answer for a moment, not even looking at me but down at the hands clasped around the crooked knee. "Hell," he said suddenly, "forget it." Suddenly, he released the knee, the leg dropped, the foot struck the floor heavily, and he lunged off the desk. "But nobody had better forget—MacMurfee and nobody else—that I'll do what I've got to do. By God, I'll do it if I've got to break their bones with my bare hands." And he held the hands before him with spread fingers, crooked and tense as though to seize.

He sank back against the support of the desk then, and said, half as though to himself, "That Frey, now. That Frey."

Then he fell into a brooding silence, which had Frey been able to see it, would have made him very happy to be way off there on the Arkansas farm with no forwarding address left behind.

So the story of the Boss and MacMurfee, of which the story of Judge Irwin had been but a part, went on, but I had no hand in it. I went back to my own innocent little chores and sat in my office as the fall drew imperceptibly on and the earth leaned on its axis and shouldered the spot I occupied a little out of the direct, billowing, crystalline, consuming blaze of the enormous sun. The leaves rattled dryly on the live oaks when a breeze sprang up in the evenings, the matted jungles of sugar cane in the country beyond the concrete walks and trolley lines were felled now by the heavy knife and in the evenings the great high-wheeled carts groaned along the rutted tracks, piled high with the fetid-sweet burden, and far off across the flat black fields laid bare by the knife, under the saffron sky, some nigger sang sadly about the transaction between him and Jesus. Out at the University, on the practice field, the toe of some long-legged, slug-footed, box-shouldered lad kept smacking the leather, over and over, and farther away scrimmage surged and heaved to the sound of shouts and peremptory whistles. On Saturday nights under the glare of the battery of lights, the stadium echoed to the roar of "Tom!—Tom!—Tom!—yea, Tom!" For Tom Stark carried the ball, Tom Stark wheeled the end, Tom Stark knifed the line, and it was Tom, Tom, Tom.

The sports writers said he was better than ever. Meanwhile he was making his old man sweat. The Boss was dour as a tee-totaling Scot, and the office force walked on tiptoe and girls suddenly burst out crying over their typewriters after they had been in to take dictation and state officials coming out of the inner room laid a handkerchief to the pallid brow with one hand and with the other groped across the long room under the painted eyes of all the gilt-framed dead governors. Only Sadie suffered no change. She bit her syllables off the way a seam-stress snaps off the thread, and looked at the Boss with her dark, unquenched glance, like the spirit of the future meditating on your hopeful plans.

The only times the Boss got the black dog off his shoulder those days were at the games. I went with him a couple of times, and when Tom uncorked his stuff the Boss was a changed man. His eyes would bug and gleam, and he would slap me on the back and grab me like a bear. There might be a flicker of that left the next morning when he opened the Sunday sporting page, but it certainly didn't last out the week. And Tom was not doing a thing to make up to the old man for the trouble he had caused. They had high words once or twice because Tom would slack off on his training and had had a row with Billie Martin, the coach. "What the hell's it to you?" Tom demanded, standing there in the middle of the hotel room, his feet apart as though he were on a swaying deck and his head wreathed in the cigar smoke of the place. "What the hell's it to you, or Martin either, so long as I can put 'em across? And I can put 'em across, see. I can still put 'em across, and what the hell else do you want? I can put 'em across and you can big-shot around about it. That's what you want, isn't it?"

357

And with those remarks, Tom Stark went out and slammed the door, probably leaving the Boss paralyzed with the rush of blood to his head.

"That's what he said to me," the Boss told me, "by God, that's what he said, and I ought to slapped him down." But he was shaken. You could see that, all right.

Meanwhile the Boss had handled the Sibyl Frey business. I had, as I said, no part in it. What happened was, however, simple and predictable. There had been two ways to get at Mac-Murfee: Judge Irwin and Gummy Larson. The Boss had tried to scare the Judge, and that had failed. So now he had to buy Gummy. He could buy Gummy because Gummy was a businessman. Strictly business. He would sell anything for the proper figure, immortal soul or mother's sainted bones, and his old friend MacMurfee was neither. If Gummy told MacMurfee to lay off, that he wasn't going to be Senator, MacMurfee would lay off, because without Gummy, MacMurfee was nothing.

The Boss had no choice. He had to buy. He might have dealt directly with MacMurfee, and have let MacMurfee go to the Senate, with the intention of following up himself when the next senatorial election rolled around. But there were two arguments against that. First, the timing would have been bad. Now was the time for the Boss to step out. Later on he would be just another Senator getting on toward fifty. Now he would be a boy wonder breathing brimstone. He would have a future. Second, if he let MacMurfee climb back on the gravy train, a lot of people on whose brows the cold sweat would break now if even in the privacy of the boudoir the mere thought of crossing the Boss should dawn on them would figure that you could buck the Boss and get away with it. They would begin to make friends and swap cigars with friends of MacMurfee. They would even begin to get ideas of their own. But there was a third argument, too, against doing business with MacMurfee. It was, rather, not an argument; it was simply a fact. The fact was that the Boss was the way he was. If MacMurfee had forced him into a compromise, at least MacMurfee shouldn't be the one to profit by it. So he did business with Gummy Larson.

The figure was not cheap. It was not peanuts. It was the medical-center contract, the general contract. It would be arranged that Larson would get the contract.

But I had nothing to do with the arranging. Duffy did that, for he had been pulling all along for such an arrangement, and I suppose that he must have got some sort of private kickback or sweetening from Larson. Well, I don't begrudge him that. He had worked for it. He had cringed and sweated and felt the baleful speculative stare of the Boss on him in the long silence after he had tried to sell the idea of Gummy Larson. It wasn't his fault that an accident now made the deal possible and not his own conscientious efforts. So I don't begrudge him his sweetening.

All of this went on behind my back, or perhaps even under my eyes, for in those days as fall came on I felt as though I were gradually withdrawing from the world around me. It could go its way and I would go mine. Or I would have gone my way if I had known what it was. I toyed with the thought of going away, of saying to the Boss, "Boss, I'm getting the hell away from here and never coming back." I could afford to do it, I thought. I didn't have to lift a finger for my morning sinker and Java. Maybe I wouldn't be rich-rich, but I figured I was going to be rich in a nice, genteel, Southern way. Nobody down here ever wants to be rich-rich, for that, of course, would be crass and vulgar. So I was going to be just genteel rich. As soon as they wound up the Judge's estate. (If they ever did, for his affairs were complicated and it was going to take some time.)

I was going to be genteel rich, for I had inherited the fruit of the Judge's crime, just as some day I would inherit from my mother the fruit of the Scholarly Attorney's weakness, the money he had left with her when he learned the truth and just walked away. On the proceeds of the Judge's old crime I would be able to go away and lead a nice, clean, blameless life in some place where you sit under a striped awning beside a marble-topped table and drink vermouth, cassis and soda and look out over the wimpling, dimpling, famous sunlit blue of the sea. But I didn't go. True, since I had lost both my fathers, I felt as though I could float effortlessly away like a balloon when the last cord is cut. But I would have to go on the money from Judge Irwin. And that particular money, which would have made the trip possible, was at the same time, paradoxically enough, a bond that held me here. To change the image, it was a long cable to an anchor, and the anchor flukes clung and bit away down there in the seaweed and ooze of a long time past. Perhaps I was a fool to feel that way about my little inheritance. Perhaps it was no different from any other inheritance anybody had. Perhaps the Emperor Vespasian was right when, jingling in his jeans the money which had been derived from a tax on urinals, he wittily remarked: *"Pecunia non olet."*

I didn't go away, but I was out of the swim of things, and sat in my office or out at the University library and read books and monographs on taxation, for I now had a nice clean assignment to work on: a tax bill. I knew so little of what was going on that it wasn't until the arrangement was an accomplished fact that I knew anything about it.

I went up to the Mansion one night with my brief case full of notes and charts to have a session with the Boss. The Boss was not alone. Back there in the library with him were Tiny Duffy, Sugar-Boy, and, to my surprise, Gummy Larson. Sugar-

Boy sat over in a corner, hunched in a chair and holding a glass between both hands, the way a child holds a glass. Out of the glass he would take little finicking sips, after each sip lifting his head up the way a chicken does when it drinks. Sugar-Boy wasn't a drinker. He was afraid, he said, it might make him "n-n-n-n-ner-ner-vous." It would have been awful if Sugar-Boy got so nervous he couldn't bust jelly glasses every shot when you threw them up in the air for him or couldn't wipe a mule's nose with the rear fender of the black Cadillac. Duffy, of course, was a drinker, but he wasn't drinking that night. He obviously was not in any mood for drinking, even if in fleeting glimpses one caught a glimmer of triumph mixed with the acute discomfort he was experiencing as he stood in the open space in front of the big leather couch. The discomfort was due, in part at least, to the fact that the Boss was, very definitely, drinking. For when the Boss really drank, what tender inhibitions ordinarily shackled up his tongue were absolutely removed. And now he was drinking all right. It looked like the first fine flush of a three-day blow and the barometer falling. He was cocked back on the leather couch with a pitcher of water, a bottle, and a bowl of ice on the floor beside his crumpled coat and empty shoes. When the Boss really got the works, he usually took off his shoes. He was sock-feet drunk now. The bottle was a long way down.

Mr. Larson stood back from the foot of the couch, a middle-sized, middle-aged, compact, gray-faced, gray-suited unimaginative-looking man. He did not drink. He had once been a gambling-house operator and had found that it did not pay to drink. Gummy was strictly business and he didn't do anything unless it paid.

As I entered and took in the layout, the Boss put his already red-rimmed gaze on me, but didn't say a word until I approached the open space in front of the couch. Then he flung out an arm to indicate Tiny, who stood in the middle of that unprotected open space, with a wan smile on his tallow. "Look!" the Boss said to me, pointing. "He was the one going to fiix it up with Larson, and what did I tell him? I told him, hell, no. Hell, no. I told him, I'd be damned first. And what happened?"

I took that as rhetorical question and said nothing. I could see that the tax bill was out for the evening, and started sidling back the way I had come.

"And what happened?" the Boss bellowed at me.

"How do I know?" I asked, but with that cast present I had begun to have a fair notion of the nature of the drama.

The Boss swung his head toward Tiny. "Tell him," he commanded, "tell him, and tell him how puking smart you feel!"

Tiny didn't manage it. All he managed was the wan smile like
360

a winter dawn above the expanse of expensive black tailoring and the white-piped waistcoat and diamond pin.

"Tell him!"

Tiny licked his lips and glanced shyly as a bride at the impassive, gray-faced Gummy, but he didn't manage it.

"Well, I'll tell you," the Boss said, "Gummy Larson is going to build my hospital and Tiny fixed it up like he has been trying to do and everybody is happy."

"That's fine," I said.

"Yeah, everybody is happy," the Boss said. "Except me. Except me," he repeated, and struck himself heavily on the chest. "For I'm the one said to Tiny, Hell, no. I won't deal with Larson. For I'm the one wouldn't let Larson come in this room when Tiny got him here. For I'm the one ought to driven him out of this state long ago. And where is he now? Where is he now?"

I looked over at Gummy Larson, whose gray face didn't show a thing. Way back in the old days, when I had first known Gummy and he had been a gambling-house operator, the police had beat him up one time. Probably because he got behind in his protection money. They had worked over his face until it looked like uncooked hamburger. But that had healed up now. He had known it would heal up and had taken the beating without opening his trap because it always paid to keep your trap shut. It had paid him in the end. Eventually he was a rich contractor and not a gambling-house operator. He was a rich contractor because he had finally made the right connections in the City Hall and because he knew how to keep his mouth shut. Now he stood there on the floor and took everything the Boss was throwing at him. Because it paid. Gummy had the instincts of a businessman, all right.

"I'll tell you where he is," the Boss said. "Look, there he is. Right in this room. Standing right there, and look at him. He is a beauty, ain't he? Know what he has just done? He has just sold out his best pal. He has just sold out MacMurfee."

Larson might have been standing in church, waiting for the benediction, for all his face showed.

"Oh, but that isn't anything. Not a thing. Not for Gummy." Who didn't twitch a muscle.

"Oh, not for Gummy. The only difference between him and Judas Iscariot is that Gummy would have got some boot with that thirty pieces of silver. Oh, Gummy would sell out anything. He sold out his best pal, and I—and I—" he struck himself savagely on the chest with a hollow sound like a thump on a barrel—"and I—I had to buy, the sons-of-bitches made me buy!"

He relapsed into silence, glowered across at Gummy, then reached down for the bottle. He poured a lot into the glass, and sloshed in some water. He wasn't bothering with ice now. He was nearly down to essentials. Before long the water would go.

Gummy, from the vast distance of sobriety and victory and the moral certainty which comes from an accurate knowledge of exactly to the penny what everything in the whole world is worth, surveyed the figure on the couch, and when the pitcher had been set back down, said, "If we've got our business arranged, Governor, I think I'll be on my way."

"Yeah," the Boss said, "yeah," and swung his sock-feet to the floor, "yeah, it's arranged, by God. But—" he stood up, clutching the glass in one hand, and shook himself like a big dog, so that some of the liquor sloshed from the glass—"listen here!" He started across to Larson, sock-feet heavy on the rug, head thrust out.

Tiny Duffy wasn't exactly in the way, but he didn't give back fully enough or perhaps with enough alacrity. Anyway, the Boss nearly brushed him in passing, or perhaps did brush him. At that instant, without even looking at his target, the Boss flung the liquid in his glass full in Duffy's face. And in one motion simply let the glass fall to the floor. It bounced on the rug, not breaking.

I could see Duffy's face at the moment of contact, the big pie face of surprise which reminded me of the time years before when the Boss had scared Duffy off the platform at Upton at the barbecue, and Duffy had fallen over the edge. Now, after the surprise, there was the flash of fury, then the merely humble and aggrieved expression and the placating whine, "What made you go and do that now, Boss, what made you go and do that?"

And the Boss, who had passed him, turned at that, looked at Duffy, and said, "I ought to done it long ago. I ought to done it long ago."

Then he moved to Larson, who, unperturbed by the goings-on, had picked up his coat and hat and stood waiting for the dust to settle. The Boss stood directly in front of him, the bodies almost touching. Then he seized Larson by the lapels and thrust his own flushed face down to the gray one. "Arranged," he said, "yeah, it's arranged, but you—you leave one window latch off, you leave one piece of iron out of that concrete, you put in one extra teaspoon of sand, you chip one piece of marble, and by God—by God—I'll rip you open. I'll—" And still clutching the lapels, he jerked his hands apart sideways. A button from Larson's coat, which had been buttoned up, spun across the room and bounced on the hearth with a little click.

"For it's mine," the Boss said, "you hear—that's my hospital—it's mine!"

Then there wasn't any other sound, but the Boss's breathing.

Duffy, the damp handkerchief with which he had sponged himself still clutched in his hand, regarded the scene, with awe and horror on his face. Sugar-Boy wasn't paying the slightest attention.

Meanwhile, Larson stood there, the Boss's hands still gripping the lapels and didn't blink an eye. I had to hand it to Gummy. He didn't quiver. He had ice water in his veins. Nothing fazed him, not insult or anger or violence or getting his face beat into a hamburger. He was a true businessman. He knew the value of everything.

He stood there under the heavy, flushed face, no doubt feeling the hot, alcoholic breath rasp on his own face, and waited. Then the Boss released his hold. He simply opened his hands in mid-air, fingers spread, and stepped back. He turned his back and walked away from the spot as though it were vacant. His sock-feet made no sound, and his head swayed ever so little as he moved.

He sat on the couch and leaned forward with his elbows on his spread knees, the forearms hanging forward, and stared into the embers on the hearth as though he were absolutely alone.

Larson, without a word, walked to the door, opened it, and went out, leaving it ajar. Tiny Duffy, with the peculiar impression of lightness, the lightness of a drowned bloated body swaying slowly upward on the ninth day, which a fat man can give when he tiptoes, moved toward the door, too. Once there, with his hand on the knob, he looked back. As his eyes rested on the unregarding Boss, the fury flashed again into the face, and just for that instant I thought, *By God, he's human.* Then he caught my gaze on him, and looked back at me with a kind of suffering, mute appeal which asked to be forgiven for everything, asked for my understanding and sympathy, asked for everybody to think well of poor old Tiny Duffy, who had done what he could according to his lights and then they threw stuff in his face. Didn't he have his rights? Didn't poor old Tiny have his feelings?

Then he followed Larson off into the night. He managed to close the door without a sound.

I looked at the Boss, who hadn't stirred. "Glad I got here for the last act," I said, "but I got to toddle now." There certainly wouldn't be any talk about the tax bill.

"Wait," he said.

He reached down for the bottle and took a drag out of it. He was down to essentials now.

"I told him," he said, glaring up at me, "I told him, I said, if you leave off a window latch, I said if you leave one iron out of the concrete, I said if you—"

"Yeah," I said, "I heard you."

—"if you put one extra teaspoon of sand, you do a thing, a single thing, and I'll rip you wide open, I'll rip you!" He got up

363

and came toward me. He stood very close to me. "I'll rip him," he said, and breathed heavily.

"So you said," I agreed.

"I told him I would, and I will. Let him do one thing wrong."

"All right."

"I'll rip him anyway. By God—" he flung his arms out wide —"I'll rip him anyway. I'll rip all of 'em. All of 'em who put their dirty hands on it. They do the job and when it's over I'll rip 'em. Every one. I'll rip 'em and ruin 'em. By God, I will! Putting their dirty hands on it. For they made me, they made me do it."

"Tom Stark had something to do with it," I said.

That stopped him, as far gone as he was. He stared at me with a look that made me think he was about to lay hands on me. Then he turned from me, and moved back toward the couch. But he didn't sit down. He leaned over for the bottle, did it some direct damage, stared at me again, and said, indistinctly, "He's just a boy."

I didn't say anything to that. He took another try at the bottle.

"He's just a boy," he repeated, dully.

"All right," I said.

"But the others," he burst out, swinging his arms wide again, "the others—they made me do it—I'll rip 'em—I'll ruin 'em!"

He had quite a lot to say along that line before he took his dive into the sofa. After he got there he made a few more muffled remarks along the same line and about how Tom Stark was just a boy. Then the one-sided conversation died away, and there wasn't anything but the heavy draw and puff of his breathing.

I stood there and looked down at him and thought about the first time, God knows how many years before, when he got drunk in my hotel room at Upton and passed out. He had come a long way. And it wasn't the chubby boy face of Cousin Willie I looked down into now. Everything was changed now. It sure God was.

Sugar-Boy, who had sat quiet all that time over in the shadow with his short legs barely reaching the floor, got off his chair and came over to the couch. He looked down at the Boss.

"He is out deader than a mackerel," I said to him.

He nodded, still looking down at the burly form. The Boss was lying on his back. One leg was off the couch, dragging on the floor. Sugar-Boy leaned to pick it up and adjust it on the couch. Then he saw the discarded coat on the floor. He picked that up and spread it over the Boss's sock-feet. He looked at me, and explained, almost apologetically, "He mi-mi-mi-might catch c-c-c-cold."

I gathered up my brief case and topcoat, and moved toward the door. I looked back at the scene of carnage. Sugar-Boy had gone back to his chair in the shadow. I must have had some trace of question in my look, for he said. "I'll s-s-s-s-set up and s-s-s-s-see no-no-no-body bothers him."

So I left them together.

As I drove down the night street on my way home, I wondered what Adam Stanton would have to say if he ever learned about how the hospital was going to be built. I knew what the Boss would say, however, if the question about Adam were put up to him. He would say, "Hell, I said I would build it, and I'm building it. That's the main thing, I'm building it. Let him stay in it and keep his own little patties sterile as hell." Which was exactly what he did say when I asked him the question.

And as I drove down the night street, I wondered what Anne Stanton would have to say if she had been there in that room and had seen the Boss piled up there, out blind on the couch. I took some sardonic pleasure in that speculation. If she had taken up with him because he was so big and tough and knew his own mind and was willing to pay the price for anything, well she ought to see him piled up there like a bull that's got tangled up in the lead rope and is down on its knees and can't budge and can't even lift its head any more on account of the ring in the nose. She ought to see that.

Then I thought that maybe that was what she was waiting for. There is nothing women love so much as the drunkard, the hellion, the roarer, the reprobate. They love him because they—women, I mean—are like the bees in Samson's parable in the Bible: they like to build their honeycomb in the carcass of a dead lion.

Out of the strong shall come forth sweetness.

Tom Stark may have been just a boy, as the Boss said, but he had had a good deal to do with the way things were going. But, then, the Boss had had a good deal to do, I suppose, with making Tom what Tom was. So there was a circle in the proof, and the son was merely an extension of the father, and when they glared at each other it was like a mirror looking into a mirror. As a matter of fact they did look alike, the same cock to the head on the shoulders, the same forward thrust of the head, the same sudden gestures. Tom was a trained-down, slick-faced, confident, barbered version of what the Boss had been a long time back when I first knew him. The big difference was this: Back in those days the Boss had been blundering and groping his unwitting way toward the discovery of himself, of his great gift, wearing his overalls that bagged down about the seat, or the blue serge suit with the tight, shiny pants, nursing some blind

365

and undefined compulsion within him like fate or a disease. Now Tom wasn't blundering and groping toward anything, and certainly not toward a discovery of himself. For he knew that he was the damnedest, hottest thing there was. Tom Stark, All American, and there were no flies on him. And no overalls bagged down about his snake hips and pile-driver knees. No, he would stand in his rubber-soled saddle shoes in the middle of the floor with a boxer's stance, the gray-striped sport coat draped over his shoulders, the top button of his heavy-weave white shirt unbuttoned, the red wool tie tied in a loose hanging knot as big as your fist under his bronze-looking throat, jerked over to one side though, and his confident eyes would rove slowly over the joint and his slick, strong, brown jaw would move idly over the athlete's chewing gum. You know how athletes chew gum. Oh, he was the hero, all right, and he wasn't blundering or groping. He knew what he was.

He knew he was good. So he didn't have to bother to keep all the rules. Not even the training rules. He could deliver anyway, he told his father, so what the hell? But he did it once too often. He and Thad Mellon, who was a substitute tackle, and Gup Lawson, who was a regular guard, did themselves proud one Saturday night after the game out at a roadhouse. They might have managed very well, if they hadn't got into a fight with some yokels who didn't know or care much about football and who resented having their girls fooled with. Gup Lawson took quite a beating from the yokels and went to the hospital and was out of football for several weeks. Tom and Thad didn't get more than a few punches before the crowd broke up the fight. But the breach of rules was dumped rather dramatically into the lap of Coach Billie Martin. It got into one of the papers. He suspended Tom Stark and Thad Mellon. That definitely changed the betting odds for the Georgia game for the following Saturday, for Georgia was good that year, and Tom Stark was the local edge.

The Boss took it like a man. No kicking and screaming even when Georgia wound up the half with the score seven to nothing. As soon as the whistle blew he was on his feet. "Come on," he said to me, and I knew he was on his way to the field house. I trailed him down there, and leaned against the doorjamb and watched it. Back off on the field there was the band music now. The band would be parading around with the sunshine (for this was the first of the afternoon games, now that the season was cooling off) glittering on the brass and on the whirling gold baton of the leader. Then the band, way off there, began to tell Dear Old State how we loved her, how we'd fight, fight, fight for her, how we'd die for her, how she was the mother of heroes. Meanwhile the heroes, pretty grimy and winded, lay around and got worked over.

366

The Boss didn't say a word at first. He just walked into the place, and looked slowly around over the relaxed forms. The atmosphere would have reminded you of a morgue. You could have heard a pin drop. There wasn't a sound except once the scrape of a cleat on the concrete when somebody supreptitiously moved his foot, once or twice the creak of harness when somebody shifted his position. Coach Billie Martin, standing over across the room with his hat jammed down to his eyes, looked glum and chewed an unlit cigar. The Boss worked his eyes over them all, one by one, while the band made its promises and the old grads in the stands stood up in the beautiful autumn light with their hats over their hearts and felt high and pure.

The Boss's eyes came to rest on Jimmy Hardwich, who was sitting on a bench. Jimmy was a second-string end. He had been put in at the second quarter because the regular at left end had been performing like a constipated dowager. It was going to be Jimmy's big chance. The chance came. It was a pass. And he dropped it. So now when the Boss's eyes fixed on Jimmy, Jimmy stared sullenly back. Then, when the Boss's eyes lingered a moment, Jimmy burst out, "God damn it—God damn it—go on and say it!"

But the Boss didn't say it. He didn't say anything. He just moved slowly over to stand in front of Jimmy. Then, very deliberately, he reached out and laid his right hand on Jimmy's shoulder. He didn't pat the shoulder. He just laid it there, the way some men can do to gentle a nervous horse.

He wasn't looking at Jimmy now, but swept his glance around over all the others. "Boys," he said, "I just came down to tell you I know you did your best."

He stood there, with his hand still lying on Jimmy's shoulder, and let that sink in. Jimmy began to cry.

Then he said, "And I know you will do your best. For I know the stuff you got in you."

He waited again. Then he took his hand off Jimmy's shoulder, and turned slowly and moved toward the door. There he paused, and again swept his glance over the room. "I want to tell you I won't forget you," he said, and walked out the door.

Jimmy was really crying now.

I followed the Boss back outside, where the band was now playing some brassy march.

When the second half opened up, the boys came out for blood. They made a touchdown early in the third quarter, and kicked the point. The Boss felt pretty good, in a grim way, about that. In the fourth quarter Georgia drove down to the danger zone, was held, then kicked a field goal. That was the way it ended, ten to seven.

But we still had a shot at the Conference. If we took everything else in the season. The next Saturday Tom Stark was back out. He was out because the Boss had put the heat on Billie Martin. That was why, all right, for the Boss told me so himself.

"How did Martin take it?" I asked.

"He didn't," the Boss said. "I crammed it down his throat."

I didn't say anything to that, and didn't even know I was looking anything. But the Boss thrust his head at me and said, "Now look here, I wasn't going to let him throw it away. We got a chance for the Conference, and the bastard would throw it away."

I still didn't say anything.

"It's not Tom, it's the championship, by God," he said. "It's not Tom. If it weren't anything but Tom, I wouldn't say a word. And if he breaks training again, I'll pound his head on the floor. I'll beat him with my own hands. I swear it."

"He's a pretty good-sized boy," I remarked.

He swore again he would do it. So the next Saturday Tom Stark was back out, and he carried the ball, and he was a cross between a ballerina and a locomotive, and the stands cheered, Yea, Tom, Tom, Tom, for he was their darling, and the score was twenty to nothing, and State had the sights back on the championship. There were two more games. There was an easy one with Tech, and then the Thanksgiving pay-off.

Tech was easy. In the third quarter, when State already had a lead, the coach sent Tom in just to give him a canter. Tom put on a little show for the stands. It was casual and beautiful and insolent. There was nothing to it, the way he did his stuff, it looked so easy. But once after he had knifed through for seven yards and had been nailed by the secondary, he didn't get up right away.

"Just got the breath knocked out," the Boss said.

And Tiny Duffy, who was with us in the Governor's box, said, "Sure, but it won't faze old Tom."

"Hell, no," the Boss agreed.

But Tom didn't get up at all. They picked him up and carried him to the field house.

"They sure knocked it out of him," the Boss said, as though he were commenting on the weather. Then, "Look, they're putting in Axton. Axton's pretty good. Give him another season."

"He's good, but he ain't Tom Stark. That Tom Stark is my boy," Duffy proclaimed.

"They'll pass now, I bet," the Boss said judicially, but all the time he was sneaking a look at the procession making for the field house.

"Axton for Stark," the loud-speaker up above the stands bellowed, and the cheerleader called for the stuff for Stark. They gave Tom his cheer, and the leader and the assistant leaders cart-wheeled and cavorted and flung up their megaphones.

The ball went back into play. It was a pass, just as the Boss had predicted. Nine yards, and first down. "First down on Tech's twenty-four-yard line," the loud-speaker announced. Then added, "Tom Stark, who was stunned on the previous play, shows signs of regaining consciousness."

"Stunned, huh?" Tiny Duffy echoed. Then he slapped the Boss on the shoulder (he loved to slap the Boss on the shoulder in public to show what buddies they were), and said, "They can't stun our old Tom, huh?"

The Boss's face darkened for a moment, but he said nothing.

"Not for long," Tiny asseverated. "That boy, he is too tough for 'em."

"He's tough," the Boss agreed. Then he gave his attention with the greatest devotion to the game.

The game was dull, but the duller it got, the more devoutly the Boss followed every play, and the more anxious he was to cheer. State ground out the touchdowns like a butcher's machine making hamburger. There was about as much sporting chance in the process as in betting on whether or not water runs downhill. But the Boss cheered every time we made three yards. He had just cheered a pass which had put State on the six-yard line, when a fellow appeared in front of our box and took off his hat, and said, "Governor Stark—Governor Stark."

"Yeah?" the Boss asked.

"The doc—over at the field house—he says can you come over a minute?" the man said.

"Thanks," the Boss said, "you tell him I'll be over in a minute. Soon as I see the boys run this one over." And he put his attention on the game.

"Hell," Tiny began, "I know it ain't nothing. Not old Tom, he—"

"Shut up," the Boss commanded, "can't you see I'm watching the game!"

And when the touchdown had been driven over and the point had been kicked, the Boss turned and said to me, "It's getting on to quitting time here. You let Sugar-Boy drive you to the office and wait for me there. I want to see you and Swinton, if you can get him. I'll take a cab down. Probably beat you there." And he vaulted over the railing to the green, and went toward the field house. But he stopped by the bench for a moment to kid the boys. Then with his hat jammed down over the heavy, outthrust head, he went on toward the field house.

The rest of us in the box didn't wait for the last whistle. We worked out before the rush started, and headed for town. Duffy got off at the Athletic Club, where he kept his wind in condition by blowing the froth off beer and bending over pool tables, and I went on to the Capitol.

I could tell even before I put my key to the lock that there wasn't any light in the big reception room. The girls had shut up shop and gone home for Saturday afternoon, off to their movies and bridge games and dates and steaks on sizzling platters at Ye Olde Wagon Wheel roadhouse or dancing at the Dream of Paris where the lights were blue and the saxophone made a sound like the slow, sweet regurgitation of sorghum molasses, off to all the chatter and jabber and giggles and whispers and gasps, off to all the things called having a good time.

For a moment, as I stood there in the big darkened room in the unaccustomed stillness of the place, a kind of sneer flickered along the edge of my mind as I thought of all the particular good times they would be having, the places they would be having the good times in (Ye Olde Wagon Wheel, Dream of Paris, Capitol City Movie Palace, parked cars, darkened vestibules), the people they would be having the good times with (the college boy with his cocksureness and scarcely concealed air of being on a slumming expedition, the drug clerk with nine hundred dollars saved up in the bank and his hope of buying into the business next year and his notion of getting him a little woman and settling down, the middle-aged sport with hair plastered thinly over the big skull veined like agate and big, damp, brutally manicured hands the color of uncooked pork fat and an odor of bay rum and peppermint chewing gum).

Then as I stood there, the thought changed. But the sneer remained flickering along the edge of the mind, like a little flame nibbling at the edge of a piece of damp paper. Only now it was for myself. What right had I to sneer at them, I demanded. I had had all those good times too. If I wasn't having one tonight it wasn't because I had passed beyond it into a state of beatitude. Perhaps it was something had passed out of me. Virtue by defect. Abstinence by nausea. When they give you the cure, they put something in your likker to make you puke, and after they have puked you enough you begin to take a distaste to your likker. You are like Pavlov's dog whose saliva starts every time he hears the bell. Only with you the reflex works so that every time you catch a whiff of likker or even think of it, your stomach turns upside down. Somebody must have slipped the stuff into my good times, for now I just didn't want any more good time. Not now, anyway. But I could pinch out that sneer that flickered along the edge of my mind. I didn't have to be proud because a good time wouldn't stay on my stomach.

So I would go into my office and, after sitting there a couple of minutes in the dusk, would flick on the light and get out the tax figures and work on them. I thought of the figures with a sense of cleansing and relief.

But as I thought of the figures and resumed my passage across the big room to the door of my office, I heard, or thought I heard, a noise from one of the offices on the other side. I looked over there. There wasn't any light showing under either of the doors. Then I heard the noise again. It was a perfectly real noise. Nobody—certainly nobody without a light—was supposed to be in there. So I went across the room, my feet noiseless on the thick carpet, and pushed open the door.

It was Sadie Burke. She sat in the chair before her desk (it must have been the creaking of the chair I had heard), her arms were laid on the desk, the forearms bent together, and I knew that she had, just that instant, raised her head from them. Not that Sadie had been crying. But she had been sitting in the dusk, in the abandoned office, on Saturday evening when everybody else was out having a hell of a good time, with her head laid on her arms on the desk.

"Hello, Sadie," I said.

She eyed me for a moment. Her back was toward what little light seeped in from the window, on which the Venetian blind was closed, and so I could not make out the expression of her face, just the gleam of the eyes. Then she demanded, "What do you want?"

"Nothing," I said.

"Well, you needn't wait."

I went across to a chair and sat down and looked at her.

"You heard what I said," she commented.

"I heard it."

"Well, you'll hear it again: you needn't wait."

"I find it quite restful here," I replied, making no motion to rise. "Because, Sadie, we've got so much in common. You and me."

"I hope you don't mean that as a compliment," she said.

"No, just a scientific observation."

"Well, it don't make you any Einstein."

"You mean because it is not true that we have a lot in common or because it is so obviously true that it doesn't take Einstein's brain to figure it out?"

"I mean I don't give a damn," she said sourly. And added, "And I don't give a damn about having you in here either."

I stayed in the chair and studied her. "It's Saturday night," I said. "Why aren't you out painting the town?"

"To hell with this town." She fished a cigarette out of the desk and lighted it. The flare of the match jerked the face out of shadow. She whipped the match flame out with a snapping motion of her arm, then spewed the first gulp of smoke out over the full, curled-down lower lip. That done, she looked at me, and said, "And to hell with you." She swept her damning gaze around the office as though it were full of forms and faces,

371

and spewed the gray smoke out of her lungs and said, "And to hell with all of them. To hell with this place."

Her eyes came back to rest on me, and she said, "I'm going to get out of here."

"Here?" I questioned.

"This whole place," she affirmed, and swung her arm wide with the cigarette tip glowing with the swiftness of the motion, "this place, this town."

"Stick around and you'll get rich," I said.

"I could have been rich a long time back," she said, "paddling in this much. If I had wanted to."

She could have, all right. But she hadn't. At least as far as I knew.

"Yeah—" she jabbed out the cigarette in the tray on the desk—"I'm getting out of here." She lifted her eyes to mine, as though daring me to say something.

I didn't say anything, but I shook my head.

"You think I won't?" she demanded.

"I think you won't."

"I'll show you, damn you."

"No," I said, and shook my head again, "you won't. You've got a talent for this, just like a fish has for swimming. And you can't expect a fish not to swim."

She started to say something, but didn't. We sat there in the dimness for a couple of minutes. "Stop staring at me," she ordered. Then, "Didn't I tell you to get out of here? Why don't you get out and go home?"

"I'm waiting for the Boss," I said matter-of-factly, "he's—" Then I remembered. "Didn't you hear what happened?"

"What?"

"Tom Stark."

"Somebody ought to kick his teeth down his throat."

"Somebody did," I said.

"They ought to done it long back."

"Well, they did a pretty good job this afternoon. The last I heard he was unconscious. They called the Boss over to the field house."

"How bad was it?" she asked. "Was it bad?" She leaned forward at me.

"He was unconscious. That's all I know. I reckon they took him to the hospital."

"Didn't they say how bad? Didn't they tell the Boss?" she demanded, leaning forward.

"What the hell's it to you? You said somebody ought to kick his teeth down his throat, and now they did it you act like you loved him."

"Hah," she said, "that's a laugh."

372

I looked at my watch. "The Boss is late. I reckon he must be at the hospital with the triple threat."

She was silent for a moment, looking down at the desk top again and gnawing the lip. Then, all at once, she got up, went across to the rack, put her coat on and jerked on her hat, and went to the door. I swung my head around to watch her. At the door she hesitated, throwing the latch, and said, "I'm leaving, and I want to lock up. I don't see why you can't sit in your own office, anyway."

I got up and went out into the reception room. She slammed her door, and without a word to me moved, pretty fast, across the place and out into the corridor. I stood there and listened to the rapid, diminishing staccato of her heels on the marble of the corridor.

When it had died away, I went into my own office and sat down by the window and looked down at the river mist which was fingering in over the roofs.

I wasn't, however, looking out over the mist-veiled, romantic, crepuscular city, but was bent over my nice, tidy, comforting tax figures, under a green-shaded light, when the telephone rang. It was Sadie. She said that she was at the University hospital, and that Tom Stark was still unconscious. The Boss was there but she hadn't seen him. But she understood he had asked for me.

So Sadie had gone over there. To lurk in the antiseptic shadows.

I left the tidy, comforting tax figures and went out. I had a sandwich at a hamburger stand and a cup of coffee and drove to the hospital. I found the Boss alone in a waiting room. He was looking a little grim. I asked how Tom was, and learned that he was then in the X-ray room and that they didn't know much. Dr. Stanton was on the case, and some other specialist was flying in by special plane from Baltimore for a consultation.

Then he said, "I want you to go out and get Lucy. She ought to be here. Out there in the country I guess she hasn't seen the paper yet."

I said I would go, and started out the door.

"Jack," he called, and I turned. "Sort of break it to her easy," he said. "You know—sort of build her up for it."

I said I would, and left. It sounded pretty bad if Lucy had to have all that build-up. And as I drove along the highway, against the lights of the Saturday-night incoming traffic, I thought how much fun it was going to be to build Lucy up for the news. And I thought the same thing again as I walked up the anachronistic patch of concrete walk toward the dimly lighted white house. Then as I stood in the parlor surrounded by the walnut and red plush and the cards for the stereoscope and the malarial crayon portrait on the easel, and built Lucy up for the news, it was definitely not fun.

But she took it. It hit her where she lived, but she took it. "Oh, God," she said, not loud, "oh, God." Then, out of the stiff, white face, "Wait a minute. I'll get my coat."

So we got into the car and drove back to town. There wasn't any conversation. Once I heard her say again, "Oh, God," but the remark was not addressed to me. I presumed that she was praying, for she had gone to the little Baptist college way back in the red clay where they had been long on praying, and maybe the habit had stuck.

And it wasn't fun, either, when I led her into the waiting room where the Boss was. He turned his face heavily to her from the midst of the floral design on the chintz-covered, over-stuffed, highbacked chair in which he sat, and looked at her as at a stranger. She stood in the middle of the floor, not going toward him, and asked, "How is he?"

At her question the light flared up in the Boss's eyes, and he rose violently from the chair. "Look here," he said, "he's all right—he's going to be all right. You understand that!"

"How is he?" she repeated.

"I told you—I told you he's going to be all right," he said with a grating voice.

"You say it," she said, "but what do the doctors say?"

The blood apoplectically flushed his face and I heard the snatch of his breathing before he said, "You wanted it this way. You said you did. You said you had rather see him dead at your feet. You wanted it this way. But—" and he stepped toward her—"he'll fool you. He's all right. Do you hear? He will be all right."

"God grant it," she said quietly.

"Grant it, grant it!" he burst out. "He's all right, right now. That boy is tough, he can take it."

She made no answer to that, but stood and looked at him while the blood subsided in his face and his frame seemed to sag with the weight of the flesh on it. Then she asked, "Can I see him?"

Before answering, the Boss stepped back to the chair and sank into it. Then he looked at me. "Take her down to Room 305," he directed. He spoke dully, and apparently without interest now, as though in a railway waiting room answering foolish questions about the schedule for some traveler.

So I took her down to Room 305, where the body lay like a log under the white sheet and the breath labored through the gaping mouth. At first, she did not approach the bed. She stood just inside the door, looking across at it. I thought she was going to keel over, and put my arm out to prop her, but she stayed on her legs. Then she moved to the bed and reached down with a timid motion to touch the body there. She laid her hand on the right leg, just above the ankle, and let it rest there as though she could draw, or communicate, some force by the contact. Meanwhile, the nurse, who stood on the other side of the bed, leaned down to wipe from the brow of the patient the drops of moisture which gathered there. Lucy Stark took a step or two up the bed, and, looking at the nurse, reached out her hand. The nurse put the cloth into it, and Lucy finished the job of wiping the brow and temples. Then she handed the cloth back to the nurse. "Thank you," she whispered. The nurse gave a sort of smile of professional understanding out of her plain, good anonymous, middle-aged face, like a light flicked on momentarily in a comfortable, shabby living room.

But Lucy wasn't looking at that face, but at the sag-jawed face below her where the breath labored in and out. There wasn't any light on there. So after a while—the nurse said Dr. Stanton wouldn't be back for some little time and she would notify us when he did come—we went back to the room where the Boss sat with his heavy head in the middle of the floral design.

Lucy sat in another chintz-covered chair (the waiting room was very cozy and cheerful with potted plants on the window ledge and chintz on the chairs and water colors on the walls in natural-wood frames and a fireplace with artificial logs in it) and looked at her lap or, now and then, across at the Boss, and I sat on the couch over by the wall and thumbed through the picture magazines, from which I gathered that the world outside our cozy little nook was still the world.

About eleven-thirty Adam came in to say that the doctor from Baltimore who was coming for the consultation had been forced down by fog and would fly in as soon as the ceiling lifted.

"Fog!" the Boss exclaimed, and came up out of the chair. "Fog! Telephone him—you telephone him—tell him to come on, fog or no fog."

"A plane can't fly in fog," Adam said.

"Telephone him—that boy in there—that boy in there—my boy—" The voice didn't trail off. It simply stopped with a sound like something of great weight grinding to a stop, and the Boss stared at Adam Stanton with resentment and a profound accusation.

"Dr. Burnham will come when it is possible," Adam said coldly. Then after a moment in which he met the resentment and accusation, he said, "Governor, I think that it would be a good thing for you to lie down. To get some rest."

"No," the Boss said hoarsely, "no."

"You can do no good by not lying down. You will only waste your strength. You can do no good."

"Good," the Boss said, "good," and clenched his hands as though he had tried to grasp some substance which had faded at his touch and dissolved to air.

"I would advise it," Adam said quietly, almost softly. Then he turned an inquiring glance upon Lucy.

She shook her head. "No, doctor," she almost whispered. "I'll wait. Too."

Adam inclined his head in acceptance, and went out. I got up and followed him.

I caught up with Adam down the hall. "What is it like?" I asked.

"Bad," he said.

"How bad?"

"He is unconscious and paralyzed," Adam said. "His extremities are quite limp. The reflexes are quite gone. If you pick up his hand it is like jelly. The X-ray—we took a skull plate—shows a fracture and dislocation of the fifth and sixth cervical vertebrae."

"Where the hell is that?"

Adam reached out and laid a couple of fingers on the back of my neck. "There," he said.

"You mean he's got a broken neck?"

"Yes."

"I thought that killed them."

"It usually does," he said. "Always if the fracture is a little higher."

"Has he got a chance?"

"Yes."

"To just live or to be all right?"

"To be all right. Or almost all right. Just a chance."

"What are you going to do?"

He looked at me directly, and I saw that his own face didn't look much different from the way it would have looked if somebody had kicked him in the head, too. It was white and drawn.

"It is a difficult decision," he said. "I must think. I don't want to talk about it now."

So he turned from me, and squared his shoulders, and went off down the hall, over the polished composition floor, which glittered in the soft light like brown ice.

I went back to the room where Lucy Stark sat across from the Boss, in the midst of the chintz and potted plants and water colors. Now and then she would lift her gaze from her lap, where the hands were clasped together with the veins showing blue, and would look across the intervening distance into her husband's face. He did not meet her gaze, but stared into the heatless illumination of the artificial logs on the hearth.

After one o'clock a nurse came down to the room with the message that the fog had cleared and that Dr. Burnham's plane was on the way again. They would let us know as soon as it came in. Then she went away.

The Boss sat silent for a minute or two, then said to me, "Go down and call up the airport. Ask what the weather is like here. Tell 'em to tell Sugar-Boy I said for him to get here quick. Tell Murphy I said I meant quick. By God! by God——" And the oath was left suspended, directed at nothing.

I went down the corridor and down to the telephone booths on the first floor, to give that crazy message to Sugar-Boy and Murphy. Sugar-Boy would drive like hell anyway, and Murphy—he was the lieutenant in charge of the motorcycle escort—knew he wasn't out there for fun. But I called the port, was told that the weather was lifting—a wind had sprung up—and left the message for Murphy.

When I stepped out of the booth, there was Sadie. She must have been hanging around in the lobby, probably sitting on one of the benches back in the shadow, for I hadn't seen her when I entered.

"Why didn't you say boo and give me real heart failure and finish the job?" I asked.

"How is it?" she demanded, seizing my coat sleeve.

"Bad. He broke his neck."

"Has he got any chance?"

"Dr. Stanton said he did, but he wasn't wreathed in smiles."

"What are they going to do? Operate?"

"There is another big shot doctor coming in from Johns Hopkins for a consultation. After he gets here they will flip a nickel and find out what to do."

"Did he sound like there was a real chance?" Her hand was still clutching my sleeve.

"How do I know?" I was suddenly irritated. I jerked my sleeve out of her grasp.

"If you find out anything—you know, when the doctor comes—will you let me know?" she asked humbly, letting her hand fall.

"Why the hell don't you go home and quit spooking around here in the dark? Why don't you go home?"

She shook her head, still humbly.

"You wanted to kick his teeth down his throat, and now you hang round and lose sleep. Why don't you go home?"

She shook her head slowly. "I'll wait," she said.

"You're a sap," I affirmed.

"Let me know," she said, "when you find out anything."

I didn't even say anything to that, but walked on away, back

377

upstairs, where I rejoined the party. Things hadn't changed in the atmosphere of the room.

After a spell a nurse came back to say that the plane was expected at the port in about thirty or forty minutes. Then a little later she came back to say that there was a telephone call for me.

"Who is it?" I asked the nurse.

"It's a lady," she said, "but she wouldn't give her name."

I figured that one out, and when I got to the phone at the floor desk I found I was right. It was Anne Stanton. She had stood it as long as she could. She didn't seize me by the sleeve, for she was a few miles away in her apartment, but her voice did pretty near the same thing. I told her what I knew, and answered her repetitious questions. She thanked me and apologized for bothering me. She had had to know, she said. She had been calling at my hotel all evening, thinking I would come in, then she had called me at the hospital. There wasn't anybody else she could ask. When she had just called the hospital and had asked for news, they had been noncommittal. "So you see," she said, "so you see I had to call you."

I said I saw, all right, and hung up the phone and went back down the hall. In the room nothing had changed. And nothing did change till toward four o'clock, when the Boss, who had been sunk in the chintz chair with his gaze on the artificial logs, suddenly lifted up his head, the way a drowsing dog does on the hearth to a sound you can't even hear. But the Boss hadn't been drowsing. He had been listening for that sound. One instant he held his head up intently, then swung up to his feet. "There!" he exclaimed raspingly. "There!"

Then I heard it, for the first time, the far-off wail of the siren of the motorcycle escort. The plane had got in.

In a minute a nurse came in and announced that Dr. Burnham was with Dr. Stanton. She could not say how long before they would give an opinion.

The Boss had not sat back down, after the first sound of the siren. He had stood in the middle of the floor, with his head up, hearing the siren wail and fade and wail again and die off, then waiting for the steps in the hall. He did not sit back down now. He began to pace up and down. Over to the window, where he snatched back the chintz curtains to look out on the blackness of the lawn and off across the lawn, where, no doubt, a solitary street light glowed in the mist. Then back to the fireplace, where he would turn with a grinding motion that twisted the rug under his heel. His hands were clasped behind him, and his head, with the forelock down, hung forward sullenly and seemed to sway a little from side to side.

I kept on looking at my picture magazines, but the solid tread, nervous and yet deliberate, stirred something back in

378

my mind. I was irritated, as you are when the memory will not rise and be recognized. Then I knew what it was. It was the sound of a tread, back and forth, back and forth, caged in a room in a country hotel beyond the jerry-built wall. That was it.

He was still pacing when a hand outside was laid on the knob of the door. But at that sound, the first sound of the hand on the knob, he swung his head toward the door and froze in his tracks like a pointer. Adam walked into the room into the clutch of that gaze.

The Boss licked his lower lip, but he controlled the question.

Adam shut the door behind him, and took a few steps forward. "Dr. Burnham has examined the patient," he said, "and studied the X-ray plates. His diagnosis and my own check absolutely. You know what that is." He paused as though expecting some reply.

But there was no reply, not even a sign, and the gaze on him did not relinquish its clutch.

"There are two lines of action possible," he resumed. "One is conservative, the other radical. The conservative line would be to put the patient in traction, in a heavy cast, and wait for some resolution of the situation. The radical line would be to resort to surgical procedure immediately. I want to emphasize that this is a difficult decision, a very technical decision. Therefore I want you to understand the situation as fully as possible." He paused again, but there was no sign, and the gaze did not relax.

"As you know," he began again, and now his tone carried a hint of the lecture room, of academic precision, "the plate showed in lateral view a fracture and dislocation of the fifth and sixth cervical vertebrae. But the X-ray cannot show the condition of soft tissue. Therefore we cannot know at this moment the condition of the spinal cord itself. We can learn that only by surgical action. If upon operating we discover that the cord is crushed, the patient will remain paralyzed for the rest of his life, for the cord has no regenerative power. But it is possible that a displaced segment of bone is merely pressing upon the cord. In that case we can, by performing a laminectomy, relieve the pressure. We cannot predict the degree of benefit from such procedure. We might restore some or we might restore almost all function. Of course, we should not expect too much. Some muscle groups might remain paralyzed. You understand?"

This time, Adam scarcely seemed to expect any response, and his pause was only momentary. "I must emphasize one consideration. This operation is very near the brain. It may be fatal. And the chances of infection are greater with the operation. Dr. Burnham and I have discussed the matter at length and are in agreement. I myself take full responsibility

379

for advising the operation. But I want you to know that it is radical. That it is the outside chance. It is the gambler's chance."

He stopped, and in the silence, the Boss's breath rasped two or three times, in and out. Then he said, gratingly, "Do it."

He had taken the outside chance, the gambler's chance. But that was no surprise to me.

Adam was looking inquiringly at Lucy Stark, as though he wished corroboration from her. She turned her eyes from him and looked at her husband, who had walked over to the window to look out over the black lawn. For a moment, she studied the hunched shoulders, then returned to Adam Stanton. She nodded her head slowly, while her hands worked together on her lap. Then she whispered, "Yes—yes."

"We shall operate immediately," Adam said. "I had ordered arrangements made. It does not have to be done immediately, but in my judgment it is better so."

"Do it," the grating voice over by the window said. But the Boss did not turn around, not even when the door closed behind Adam Stanton.

I went back to my picture magazines, but I turned the pages over with the greatest care as though I couldn't afford to make a sound in the special kind of devouring stillness there was in the room. That stillness lasted a long time, while I kept on looking at the pictures of girls in bathing suits and race horses and scenes of natural beauty and long files of erect, clean-faced youths in some kind of shirt or other lifting their arms in a salute and detective stories acted out in six photographs with the answer on the next page. But I wasn't paying much attention to the pictures, and they were always alike anyway.

Then Lucy Stark got up from her chair. She walked over to the window, where the Boss stood and stared out. She laid her hand on his right arm. He drew away, without even looking at her. But she took him by the forearm and drew him, and after a momentary resistance he followed her. She led him back to the big chintz-covered chair. "Sit down, Willie," she said, very quietly, "sit down and rest."

He sank down into the chair. She turned away and went back to her own chair.

He was looking at her, not at the artificial logs now. Finally, he said, "He'll be all right."

"God grant it," she replied.

He was silent for two or three minutes, still looking at her. Then he said, violently, "He will, he's got to."

"God grant it," she said, and met his gaze until his eyes fell away from hers.

By that time I had had enough of sitting there. I got up and went out and down the hall to the nurse who was on the floor desk. "Any chance of getting some sandwiches and coffee brought up here for the Governor and his wife?" I asked.

She said she would get some brought up, and I told her just to have them brought to her desk, that I would take them in. Then I wandered down to the lobby again. Sadie was still there, spooking in the shadows. I told her about the operation and left her there. I hung around at the floor desk upstairs until the sandwiches arrived, then took the tray down to the waiting room.

The grub and coffee, however, didn't do much to change the atmosphere there. I put a little table by Lucy with a sandwich on a plate and a cup of coffee. She thanked me, and broke off a piece of the sandwich and put it to her mouth two or three times, but I could not see that she was doing it much damage. But she took some coffee. I put some food and coffee handy to the Boss. He looked up out of himself and said, "Thanks, Jack." He did not even make a pretense, however, of eating. He held the cup in his hand for a few minutes, but I didn't notice that he even took a sip. He just held it.

I ate a sandwich and had a cup of coffee. I was pouring myself a second cup, when the Boss reached to set his cup down, sloshingly, on the little table beside him.

"Lucy," he said, "Lucy!"

"Yes?" she answered.

"You know—you know what I'm going to do?" He leaned forward, not waiting for an answer. "I'm going to name the new hospital for him. For Tom. I'm going to call it the Tom Stark Hospital and Medical Center. It'll be named for Tom, it'll—"

She was slowly shaking her head, and his words stopped.

"Those things don't matter," she said. "Oh, Willie, don't you see? Those things don't matter. Having somebody's name cut on a piece of stone. Getting it in the paper. All those things. Oh, Willie, he was my baby boy, he was our baby boy, and those things don't matter, they don't ever matter, don't you see?"

He sank back into his chair, and the silence picked up where it had left off. The silence was still going full blast when I got back from taking the dishes and uneaten food down to the desk. It gave me an excuse for getting out. It was twenty minutes to six when I got back.

At six o'clock Adam came in. He was pretty gray and stony in the face. The Boss got to his feet and stood there looking at Adam, but neither he nor Lucy uttered a sound.

Then Adam said, "He will live."

"Thank God," Lucy breathed, but the Boss still stared into Adam's face.

Adam stared back. Then he said, "The cord was crushed."

I heard a gasp from Lucy, and looked over to see her with her head bowed on her breast.

The Boss didn't show a sign for a moment. Then he lifted his hands, chest-high, with the fingers spread as though to seize on something. "No!" he declared. "No!"

"It was crushed," Adam said. And added, "I am sorry, Governor."

Then he left the room.

The Boss stared at the closed door, then slowly sank back into the chair. He kept on staring at the door, his eyes bulging and the moisture gathering in drops on his forehead. Then he jerked upright and the sound wrenched out of him. It was a formless, agonized sound torn raw right out of the black animal depths inside of the bulk there in the chair. "Oh!" he said. Then, "Oh!"

Lucy Stark was looking across at him. He was still staring at the door.

Then the sound came again: "Oh!"

She rose from her chair and went across to him. She didn't say anything. She simply stood by his chair and laid a hand on his shoulder.

The sound came again, but it was the last time. He sank back, still staring at the door, and breathed heavily. It must have been like that for three or four minutes. Then Lucy said, "Willie."

He looked up at her for the first time.

"Willie," she said, "it's time to go."

He stood up from the chair, and I got their coats off the couch by the wall. I helped Lucy on with hers, and then she picked up the other one and helped him. I didn't interfere.

They started for the door. He had drawn himself erect now and looked straight ahead, but her hand was still on his arm, and if you had seen them you would have got the impression that she was expertly and tactfully guiding a blind man. I opened the door for them, and then went on ahead to tell Sugar-Boy to get the car ready.

I was there when the Boss got into the car and she got in after him. That surprised me a little, but it didn't hurt my feelings if Sugar-Boy drove her home. Despite the coffee, I was ready to drop.

I went back inside and up to Adam's office. He was just about ready to pull out. "What is the story?" I asked.

"What I said," he said. "The cord is crushed. That means paralysis. The prognosis is that for a time the limbs will be absolutely limp. Then the muscle tone will come back. But he will never use arms or legs. The bodily functions will continue but without control. He'll be like a baby. And the skin will be inclined to break down. He will get infections easily. The respiratory control will be impaired, too. Pneumonia will be likely. That's what usually knocks off cases like this sooner or later."

"It sounds to me the sooner the better," I said, and thought of Lucy Stark.

"Maybe so," he said, tiredly. He was sagging now, all right. He slipped on his coat and picked up his bag. "Can I drop you somewhere?" he asked.

"Thanks, I'm in my car," I said. Then my eyes fell on the telephone on his desk. "But I'll make a call, if I may," I said. "I'll pull the door to."

"All right," he said, and went to the door. "Good night," he added, and went out.

I dialed outside, and got Anne's number, and told her the news. She said it was horrible. She kept saying that into the telephone—"It is horrible"—in a low bemused voice, three or four times. Then she thanked me and hung up.

I left the office. I had one more errand to do. I went down to the lobby. Sadie was still there. So I told her. She said it was pretty tough. I agreed.

"It will be tough on the Boss," she said.

"It will be tough as hell on Lucy," I said, "for she is the one who will have to fix the baby. Don't forget that while you're giving out the free samples of sympathy."

She must have been pretty tired or something for that didn't make her mad. So I asked her if I could take her into town. She had her car, too, she said.

"Well, I am going home and sleep forever," I said, and left her in the lobby.

By the time I got out to my car, the sky was curdling blue with dawn.

The accident occurred on Saturday afternoon. The operation was performed just before dawn on Sunday. The big pay-off was on Monday. It was the Monday before Thanksgiving.

That day, there was a gradual piling up of events, then the rush to the conclusion, as when a great weight that has been grinding and slipping suddenly breaks the last mooring and takes the plunge. As I experienced that day, there was at first an impression of the logic of the events, caught flickeringly at moments, but as they massed to the conclusion I was able to grasp, at the time, only the slightest hints as to the pattern that was taking shape. This lack of logic, the sense of people and events driven by impulses which I was not able to define, gave the whole occasion the sense of a dreamlike unreality. It was only after the conclusion, after everything was over, that the sense of reality returned, long after, in fact, when I had been able to gather the pieces of the puzzle up and put them together to see the pattern. This is not remarkable, for, as we know, reality is not a function of the event as event, but of the relationship of that event to past, and future, events. We seem here to have a paradox: that the reality of an event, which is not real in itself, arises from other events which, likewise, in themselves are not real. But this only affirms what we must affirm: that direction is all. And only as we realize this do we live, for our own identity is dependent upon this principle.

Monday morning I got to the office early. I had slept all day Sunday, getting up only in time for a bite of dinner and then some silly movie, and being back in bed by ten-thirty. I came into the office with that sense you get after a lot of sleep of being spiritually pure.

I went back to the Boss's office. He hadn't come in. But while I was there one of the girls came in carrying a big tray piled up with telegrams. "They are all about his boy getting hurt," she said, "and they keep coming in."

"They'll be coming in all day," I said.

That would be true, all right. Every pinfeather politician, county-courthouse janitor, and ambitious lickspittle in the state who hadn't seen the story in the Sunday paper would see it in this morning's paper and get off his telegram. Getting that telegram off would be like praying. You couldn't tell that praying would do any good, but it certainly never did anybody any harm. Those telegrams were part of the system. Like presents for the wedding of a politician's daughter or flowers for a cop's funeral. And it was part of the system, too, for the flowers, now that we are on the subject, to come from Antonio Giusto's flower store. A girl in the flower store kept a record in a special file of all the orders that came in for a cop's funeral, and then Tony just ran through the file after the funeral and checked the names by his master list of perennially bereaved friends and if your name was on the master list it had sure-God better be in the file for Murphy's funeral, and I don't mean any bunch of sweet peas, either. Tony was a good friend of Tiny Duffy.

It was Tiny Duffy who came into the office just as the girl flounced out with a cute little twitch of her skirt. He mooned in with a face full of professional sympathy and mortician's gloom, but as soon as he took in the fact that the Boss was not present he relaxed a little, showed his teeth, and said, "How's tricks?"

I said tricks was O.K.

"You seen the Boss?" he asked.

I shook my head.

"Gee," he said, and the sympathy and gloom appeared magically on his face, "it is sure tough. It is what I always calls tragic. A kid like that. A good clean square-shooting kid like that. It is tragic, and no mistake."

"You needn't practice on me," I said.

"It will be tough on the Boss," he said, and shook his head. "Just save your fire till he gets here."

"Where is he?"

"I don't know."

"I tried to get hold of him yesterday," Tiny said, "but he wasn't at the Mansion. They said they didn't know where he was, he hadn't been home. He was out to the hospital a while, but I missed him there. He wasn't in a hotel, either."

"You seem to have been thorough," I said.

"Yeah," Tiny said, "I wanted to tell him how us boys all felt."

Just then Calvin Sperling, who was Commissioner of Agriculture, came in with a couple of other fellows. They were wearing crepe on their faces, too, till they saw the Boss was not in. Then they eased off and began to snap their bubble gum. "Maybe he won't be coming," Sperling suggested.

"He'll come," Tiny pronounced. "It won't faze him. The Boss is tough."

A couple more of the fellows came by, and then Morrisey, who had followed Hugh Miller a long time back as Attorney General, after Miller's resignation. The cigar smoke began to get thick.

Once Sadie stopped at the door, laid one hand on the jamb, and surveyed the scene.

"Hi, Sadie," one of the boys said.

She did not respond. She continued her survey for a moment longer, then said, "Jesus Christ," and moved on. I heard the door of her own office shut.

I drifted over to the window back of the Boss's desk and looked out over the grounds. It had rained during the night and now in the weak sunlight the grass and the leaves of the live oaks, even the trailing moss, had a faint sheen, and the damp concrete of the curving drives and walks gave off an almost imperceptible, glimmering reflection. The whole world, the bare boles of the other trees, which had lost their leaves now, the roofs of the houses, even the sky itself, had a pale, washed, relieved look, like the look on the face of a person who has been sick a long time and now feels better and thinks maybe he is going to get well.

That wasn't exactly the look on the Boss's face when he came in, but it gives some idea of what that look was. He wasn't really pale, but he was paler than usual, and the flesh seemed to hang a little loose at the jawbone. There were a couple of razor nicks along the bone. Under his eyes were gray circles, as though the flesh had been bruised but was just about well now. But the eyes were clear.

He had come across the reception room without making any noise on the thick carpet, and for an instant he stood in the doorway of the office before anybody noticed his arrival. The chatter didn't die; it was frozen in mid-syllable. Then there was a kind of noiseless scurry and fumble to adjust the funeral faces which had been laid aside. Then, with the faces in place and only a little askew, they crowded around the Boss and shook his hand. They told him they wanted to tell him how they felt. "You know how us boys all feel, Boss," they said. He said, yes, he knew, very quietly. He said, yes, yes, and thank you.

Then he moved toward the desk, the boys falling away from him like water from the prow of a ship when it is first warped out from the pier and the screw makes the first revolutions. He stood before the desk, handling the telegrams, looking at them, letting them drop.

"Boss," somebody said, "Boss—those telegrams—that shows you now—that shows you how folks feel about you."

He said nothing.

Just then the girl came in with another batch of telegrams. She set the tray on the desk in front of him. He fixed her with his glance. Then he laid his hand on the pile of yellow paper and gave it a slight shove and said, in a quiet, matter-of-fact voice, "Get this muck out of here."

The girl got the muck out of there.

The bloom had gone from the occasion. The boys began to drift out of the office and off to the swivel chairs which had not been warmed that morning. As Tiny was leaving, the Boss said, "Tiny, wait a minute. I want to talk to you."

Tiny came back. I was heading out, too, but the Boss called me. "I want you to be in on this," he said. So I sank into one of the chairs over by the wall. Tiny disposed himself in a big green leather chair to one side of the desk, crossed his knees, to the great strain of his hams and of the fabric which covered them, inserted a cigarette in his long holder, lighted it, and waited.

The Boss was in no hurry. He brooded a full minute before he lifted his eyes to Tiny Duffy. But then he came in fast. "There won't be any contract with Larson," he said.

When breath came back, Tiny managed, "Boss—Boss—you can't, Boss."

"Yes, I can," the Boss said, without raising his voice.

"You can't, Boss. It's all fixed up, Boss."

"It isn't too late to unfix it," the Boss said. "It isn't too late."

"Boss—Boss—" the word was almost a wail, and the cigarette ash was falling down the starched white front of the

Duffy shirt, "you can't break your word to old Larson. He's a good guy and you can't. You're a square-shooter, Boss."

"I can break my word to Larson," the Boss said.

"You can't—you can't change your mind, Boss. Not now. You can't change it now."

The Boss rose very abruptly from his chair at the desk. He fixed his eyes on Tiny and said, "I can change a hell of a lot of things."

In the ensuing silence, the Boss came round the desk. "That's all," he said, in a voice not much more than a husky whisper. "And you can tell Larson to do his damnedest."

Tiny got to his feet. He opened his mouth several times, wet his lips, and seemed about to speak, but each time the now gray face closed back up over the expensive bridgework.

The Boss went up to him. "You tell Larson," he said. "Larson is your pal, and you tell him." He punched Tiny's front with a stiff forefinger. "Yeah," he said, "he is your pal, and when you tell him you can put your hand on his shoulder." Then the Boss grinned. I had not expected a grin. But it was a wintry and uncomforting grin. It put the seal on everything that had been said.

Tiny made the door, and was gone. He didn't bother to close it, but kept on going through without a pause, dwindling away over the long green carpet. Then he had disappeared.

But the Boss was not watching his departure. He was staring moodily down at the bare top of his desk. After a moment he said, "Shut the door." I got up and shut it.

I did not sit back down, but stood in the open space between the desk and door, waiting for him to say whatever it was he was going to say. Whatever it was, he didn't say it. He merely looked up at me with a look that was innocent and questioning, and asked, "Well?"

I do not know what it was he wanted me to say or what he expected me to say. Since that time I have thought a good deal about that. That was the time for me to say whatever it was I was ever going to have to say to Willie Stark, who had been Cousin Willie from the country and who was now the Boss. But I did not say it. I shrugged my shoulders, and said, "Well, it doesn't matter if you kick Tiny around some more. He is built for it. But Larson is a different kind of cooky."

He continued to look at me and seemed about to say something, but the question faded off his face. Then he said, "You got to start somewhere."

"Start what?"

He studied me a moment before he said, "Skip it."

I went on back to my own office. That was how that day started. I got to work on a last review of the subsidiary figures for the tax bill. Swinton, who was handling the thing through the Senate, had wanted them Saturday, but I had been running behind on my homework. I had had that date to meet Swinton and the Boss Saturday evening, but things had not fallen out that way. Later in the morning I ran into a kink. I went out into the big room and started for the Boss's door. The girl out there said that he had gone across to Sadie Burke's office. The door there was closed. I hung around a few minutes in the big room, waiting for the Boss to come out, but the door stayed closed. Once I could hear a voice raised beyond the door, but then it dropped.

The ringing of my own telephone bell took me back into my office. It was Swinton saying what the hell, why didn't I get the figures down to him. So I got my papers together and went down to see Swinton and give him the stuff. I was with him about forty minutes. When I came back up to the office, the Boss was gone. "He's gone to the hospital," the girl said. "He'll be back this afternoon."

I looked over toward Sadie's door, thinking maybe she could help me and Swinton. The girl caught my glance. "Miss Burke," she said, "she's gone, too."

"Where did she go?"

"I don't know," the girl replied, "but I can tell you this, Mr. Burden, wherever it is she sure must already be there the way she tore out of here." Then she smiled with that knowing snotty little secret way the hired help always uses to make you think they know more than they are telling, and reached up a nice rounded little red-nailed white hand to tuck in a stray back lock of really beautiful corn-colored hair. Having tucked in the lock, with a motion which raised her breast for Mr. Burden's inspection, she added, "And wherever it is she's gone they probably won't like her getting there, to judge from the look on her face when she left." Then she smiled sweetly to show how happy any place would be to have her arrive there.

I went back into my office and gave some letters until lunch. I had a sandwich down in the basement cafeteria of the Capitol, where eating was like eating in a jolly, sanitary, well-run, marble-glistening morgue. I ran into Swinton, jawed some with him, and went, at his suggestion, up to the Senate when it reconvened after lunch. About four o'clock a page came up to me and handed me a slip of paper. It was a message from upstairs. It read:: "Miss Stanton telephoned to ask you to come right away to her apartment. It is urgent."

I crumpled up the slip, threw it down, and headed up to my office for my coat and hat. I told them in the office to notify Miss Stanton I was on my way. When I got outdoors I discovered that it had begun to rain. The clean, pale sunlight of the morning was gone now.

Anne answered my knock so quickly that I figured she must

388

have been standing by the door. But when the door flung open, I might not have recognized, at the first glance, the face I saw there unless I had known it to be Anne Stanton's. It was white and desperate and ravaged, and past the tears which you could know had been shed. And somehow you could know what kind of tears they had been tardy, sparse and painful, quickly suppressed.

She clutched my arm with both hands, as though to support herself. "Jack," she exclaimed, "Jack!"

"What the hell?" I asked, and shoved the door shut behind me.

"You've got to find him—you've got to find him—find him and tell him—" She was shaking as if with a chill.

"Find who?"

"—tell him how it was—oh, it wasn't that way—not what they said—"

"For Christ's sake, what who said?"

"—they said it was because of me—because of what I did —because—"

"Who said?"

"—oh, you've got to find him, Jack—you've got to find him and tell him and bring him to me and—"

I grabbed her, hard, with a hand on each shoulder, and shook her. "Look here!" I said. "You come out of this. Just stop jabbering a minute and come out of this."

She stopped talking and stood between my hands, in my clutch, and looked up at me with her white face and shivered. Her breathing was shallow, quick, and dry.

After a minute, I said, "Now tell me who you want me to find."

"Adam," she said. "It's Adam."

"Now why do I find him? What's happened?"

"He came here and said it was all because of me. Of what I had done."

"What was because of what you had done?"

"He was made Director because of me. That's what he said. Because of what I had done. That's what he said. And he said —oh, Jack, he said it—"

"Said what?"

"He said he wouldn't be paid pimp to his sister's whore— he said that—he said that, Jack—to me, Jack—and I tried to tell him—tell him how it was—and he pushed me and I fell down on the floor and he ran out—he ran out and you've got to find him, Jack—you've got to and—"

And she was off again on the jabber. I gave her a good shaking. "Stop it," I commanded. "Stop it or I'll shake your teeth out."

When she had quieted down again and was hanging there

between my hands, I said, "Now start slowly from the start and tell me what happened." I led her over to a chair and pushed her down into it. "Now tell me," I said, "but take it easy."

She looked up at me for a moment as though she were afraid to begin.

"Tell me," I said.

"He came up here," she began. "It was about three o'clock. As soon as he came in the door I knew something terrible had happened—something terrible had already happened to me today but I knew this was another terrible thing—and he grabbed me by the arm and stared in my face and didn't say a word. I guess I kept asking him what was the matter, and he held my arm tighter and tighter."

She pushed the sleeve up and showed the bruise marks half-way down the left forearm.

"I kept asking him what was the matter, and all at once he said, 'Matter, matter, you know what's the matter.' Then he said how there had been a telephone call to him, how some-body—a man—that was all he said—had called and told him —told him about me—about me and—"

She didn't seem to be able to go on.

"About you and Governor Stark," I completed it for her. She nodded.

"It was awful," she whispered, not at me, but raptly, to her-self. And repeated, "It was awful."

"Stop that and go ahead," I ordered, and shook her.

She came up out of it, looked at me, and said, "He told him about me and then how that was the only reason he was ever made Director and how now the Governor was going to dis-miss him as Director—because he had paralyzed his son with a bad operation—and how he was going to get rid of me— throw me out—that was what that man said on the telephone, throw me out—because of what Adam did to his son—and Adam heard him and ran right over here because he believed it—he believed it about me—"

"Well," I demanded savagely, "the part about you is true, isn't it?"

"He ought to have asked me," she said, and made a dis-tracted motion with her hands, "he ought to have asked me before he believed it."

"He's not a half-wit," I said, "and it was there ready to be believed. You're damned lucky he didn't guess something long back, for if—"

She seized me by the arm and her fingers dug in. "Hush, hush!" she said, "you mustn't say it—for nothing was that way —and not the way Adam said—oh, he said terrible things—oh, he called me terrible things—he said if everything else was

390

filthy a man didn't have to be—oh, I tried to tell him how things were—how they weren't like he said—but he pushed me so hard I fell down and he said how he wouldn't pimp to his sister's whore and nobody would ever say that about him —and then he ran out the door and you've got to find him. Find him and tell him, Jack. Tell him, Jack."

"Tell him what?"

"Tell him it wasn't like he said. You've got to tell him that. You know why I did everything I did, you know what happened. Oh, Jack—" and she grabbed my sleeve and hung on, "it wasn't like that. It wasn't horrible like that. I tried not to be horrible. Was I, Jack? Was I? Tell me, Jack!"

I looked down at her. "No," I said, "you weren't horrible."

"But it has happened to me. It has all happened to me. And he's gone."

"I'll find him," I said, and detached myself from her, ready to go.

"It won't do any good."

"He'll listen to sense," I said.

"Oh, I don't mean Adam. I mean—".

"Stark?"

She nodded. Then said, "Yes. I went to the place—the place out of town we used to meet in. He called me early this afternoon. I went there and he told me. He is going back to his wife."

"Well, I'll be damned," I said.

Then I pulled myself together, and headed for the door. "I'll get Adam," I said.

"Get him," she said, "get him. For he's all I've got now."

As I stepped out the door of the apartment house into the rain, I reflected that she had Jackie Burden, too. At least, as an errand boy. But I made the reflection without bitterness and quite impersonally.

Finding somebody in a city if you can't call in the cops is quite an undertaking. I had tried it often enough back when I was a reporter, and it takes luck and time. But one rule is always to try the obvious first. So I went to Adam's apartment. When I saw his car sitting out front I figured I had played into the blue ones. I parked my own car, noticed that the driver's door of his car was open and might get swiped off by a passing truck and was certainly letting the seat get wet, slammed it shut as I passed, and went on into the apartment house.

I knocked vigorously on the door. There was no answer. But that didn't mean anything. Even if Adam was there, he might not be willing, under the circumstances, to answer his door. So I tried the knob. The door was locked. I went down to the basement and dug out the Negro janitor and told him some cock-and-bull story about having left some stuff up there in

Adam's place. He had seen me around with Adam a lot, and so he let me in. I prowled through the place, but no Adam. Then I spied his telephone. I called his office, then the hospital, then the medical-school office, then the exchange where the doctors left numbers when they weren't at their unual haunts. It was no go. Nobody knew anything about Adam. Or rather, each one had a pretty good idea where he was, but the idea was never any good. That left all the town wide open.

I went back down into the street. The fact that the car was there was funny. He had abandoned it. Where in the hell did a man go off in the rain, on foot, this time of day? Or night, rather?—for it was dusk now.

I thought of the bars. For it is a tradition that a man, when he has received a great shock, heads for a bar, puts his foot on the rail, orders five straight whiskies in a row, downs them one after another while he stares with uncomprehending eyes at the white, tortured face in the mirror opposite him, and then engages the bartender in a sardonic conversation about Life. But I couldn't see Adam Stanton playing that game. But I went to the bars, anyway.

That is, I went to a lot of them. A lifetime isn't long enough to go to all the bars in our city. I began with Slade's place, had no luck, asked Slade to try to hang on to Dr. Stanton if he came in, and then moved through the other establishments of chromium, glass bricks, morros, colored lights, comfy Old English worm-eaten oak, sporting prints, comic frescoes, or three-piece orchestras. Around seven-thirty I called up Adam's office and then the hospital again. He wasn't at either place. When they told me that at the hospital, I said I was calling for Governor Stark, whose son was there as a patient of Dr. Stanton, and could they please try to dig up something. They came back with the report that Dr. Stanton had been expected well before seven, that he had had an appointment with another doctor to examine some plates, but that he had not come. They had been unable to locate him at his office or at his home. Would I like to leave a message for Dr. Stanton when he came in? I said, yes, to have him get in touch with me at the earliest possible moment, it was important. I would leave word at my own hotel as to my whereabouts.

I went back to my hotel and had a meal in the coffee shop, having left word at the desk to page me if a call came. But none came. So I dawdled in the lobby with the evening papers. The *Chronicle* had a long editorial lauding the courage and sound sense of the handful of men in the Senate who were making a fight against the administration's tax bill, which would throttle business and enterprise in the state. There was a cartoon opposite the editorial. It showed the Boss, or rather, a figure with the Boss's head but a great swollen belly, dressed in a Buster Brown suit with the little pants tight above great hairy thighs. On one knee the monster balanced a big pudding and from the gaping hole in the top had just plucked a squirming little creature. The pudding bore the label *The State* and the squirming little creature the label *Hardworking Citizen*. From the mouth of the Boss's head came one of those balloons of words the comic-strip artists use to indicate the speech of their characters. It said: "Oh, what a good boy am I!" Under the cartoon was the caption: *Little Jack Horner*.

I read on down through the editorial. It said that our state was a poor state, and could not bear the burden thus tyrannically imposed upon it. That was an old one. Every time the Boss had cracked down—income tax, mineral-extraction tax, liquor tax, every time—it had been the same thing. The pocketbook is where it hurts. A man may forget the death of the father, but never the loss of the patrimony, the cold-faced Florentine, who is the founding father of our modern world, said, and he said a mouthful.

This is a poor state, the opposition always screamed. But the Boss said: "There is a passel of pore folks living in it and no mistake, but the state isn't poor. It is just a question of who has got his front feet in the trough when slopping time comes. And I aim to do me some shoving and thump me some snouts." And he had leaned forward to the crowd, with the shagged-down forelock and the bulging eyes, and had lifted his right arm to demand of them and of the hot sky, "Are you with me? Are you with me?" And the roar had come.

More money for graft, the opposition always screamed. "Sure," the Boss had said, lounging easy, "sure, there's some graft, but there's just enough to make the wheels turn without squeaking. And remember this. There never was a machine rigged up by man didn't represent some loss of energy. How much energy do you get out of a lump of coal when you run a steam dynamo or a locomotive compared to what there actually is in that lump of coal? Damned little. Well, we do a hell of a lot better than the best dynamo or locomotive ever invented. Sure, I got a bunch of crooks around here, but they're too lily-livered to get very crooked. I got my eye on 'em. And do I deliver the state something? I damned well do."

The theory of historical costs, you might put it. All change costs something. You have to write off the costs against the gain. Maybe in our state change could only come in the terms in which it was taking place, and it was sure due for some change. The theory of the moral neutrality of history, you might call it. Process as process is neither morally good nor morally bad. We may judge results but not process. The morally bad agent may perform the deed which is good. The morally

393

good agent may perform the deed which is bad. Maybe a man has to sell his soul to get the power to do good.

The theory of historical costs. The theory of the moral neutrality of history. All that was a high historical view from a chilly pinnacle. Maybe it took a genius to see it. To really see it. Maybe you had to get chained to the high pinnacle with the buzzards pecking at your liver and lights before you could see it. Maybe it took a genius to see it. Maybe it took a hero to act on it.

But sitting there in the lobby, waiting for the call which did not come, I was willing to let those speculations rest. I went back to the editorial. That editorial was shadow-boxing, all right. It was shadow-boxing, for at the very minute it was just as likely true as not that the vote was being called up in the Capitol, and it would take the winged hosts to make the vote different from what it was going to be after the MacMurfee boys had talked themselves out and the count was called.

It was around nine o'clock when I was paged. But it wasn't Adam. It was a message from the Capitol saying the Boss was there and wanted me to come up. I left word at the desk that if Dr. Stanton should call me, he was to be asked to call the Capitol, I would leave instructions with the operator on the switchboard there. Then I rang up Anne to give her the news, or rather, the no-news, about my efforts to date. She sounded calm and tired. I went out to my car. It had been raining again, for the gutter by the curb was running with a black stream which gleamed like oil in the lights of the street. But it had let up now.

When I pulled into the Capitol grounds I saw that the place was pretty well lit up. But that wasn't surprising, even at that hour, when the Legislature was in session. And when I got inside, the place was certainly not uninhabited. The solons had broken up shop for the evening and were milling about in the corridors, especially at those strategic points where the big brass spittoons stood. And there were plenty of other people around, too. There were a lot of reporters, and herds of bystanders, those people who love to have the feeling that they are around when something big is happening.

I worked through the place and up to the Boss's office. They told me there that he had gone down with somebody to the Senate.

"There wasn't any hitch about the tax bill passing, was there?" I asked the girl.

"Don't be silly," the girl said.

I started to tell her that I had been around there back when she was lying in the crib sucking her thumb, but didn't do it. Instead, I asked her to take care of the business of Adam's call for me, and went down to the Senate.

At first I didn't spot the Boss. Then I saw him off to one side, with a couple of the Senators and Calvin Sperling and discreetly in the background several other men, just hangers-on who were warming their hands at the blaze of greatness. Over to one side of the Boss, I saw Sugar-Boy lounging against the marble wall, with his cheeks drawn in to suck the sugar cube which, at that moment no doubt, was dissolving its bliss down his gullet. The Boss stood with his hands clasped behind him and his head hanging a little forward. He was listening to something one of the Senators was telling him.

I approached the group and stood back from it, waiting. In a minute I caught the Boss's eye and knew that he had seen me. So I went over to Sugar-Boy and said, "Hello."

He managed to get the word out after several efforts. Then he resumed work on the sugar. I leaned against the wall beside him, and waited.

Four or five minutes passed, and the Boss still stood there with his head hanging forward, listening. He could listen a long time and not say a word, just let the fellow pour it out. The stuff would pour out and pour out, and the Boss would just be waiting to see what was in the bottom of the bucket. Finally, I knew that he had had enough. He knew what was in the bottom of the fellow's bucket or that there wasn't anything there, after all. I knew that he had had enough, for I saw him suddenly lift his head up sharp and look straight at the man. That was the sign. I stopped leaning against the wall. I knew the Boss was ready to go.

He looked at the man and shook his head. "It won't wash," he said in a perfectly amiable fashion. It was loud enough for me to hear. The other fellow had been talking low and fast.

Then the Boss looked over at me and called, "Jack."

I went to him.

"Let's get upstairs," he said to me, "I want to tell you something."

"O.K.," I said, and started toward the door.

He left the men and followed me, catching up with me at the door. Sugar-Boy fell in just on his other side and a little back.

I started to ask the Boss how the boy was, but thought better of it. It was just a question of the kind of badness, and there wasn't any use asking about that. So we moved on through the corridor to the big lobby, where we would take an elevator up to his office. Some of the men lounging along the corridor stepped back a little and said, "Howdy-do, Governor," or "Hi, Boss," but the Boss only bowed his response to the greetings. The other men, those who said nothing, turned their heads to watch the Boss as he passed. There wasn't anything out of the ordinary about all that. He must have passed down that corridor a thousand times, or near that many, with men calling out to him, or saying nothing and following with their eyes his progress over the glittering marble.

We came out into the great lobby, under the dome, where there was a blaze of light over the statues which stood with statesmanlike dignity on pedestals to mark the quarters of the place, and over the people who moved about in the area. We walked along the east wall, toward the inset where the elevators were. Just as we approached the statue of General Moffat (a great Indian fighter, a successful land speculator, the first governor of the state), I noticed a figure leaning against the pedestal.

It was Adam Stanton. I saw that his clothes were soaked and that mud and filth were slopped up his trousers half to the knees. I understood the abandoned car. He had walked away from it, in the rain.

Just as I saw him, he looked in our direction. But his eyes were on the Boss, not on me. "Adam," I said, "Adam!"

He took a step toward us, but still did not look at me.

Then the Boss veered toward Adam, and thrust out his hand in preparation for a handshake. "Howdy-do, Doctor," he began, holding out his hand.

For an instant Adam stood there immobile, as though about to refuse to shake the hand of the man approaching him. Then he put out his hand, and as he did so I felt a surge of relief and thought: *He's shaking hands with him, he's all right now, he's all right.*

Then I saw what was in his hand, and even as I recognized the object, but before the significance of the recognition had time to form itself in my mind and nerves, I saw the two little spurts of pale-orange flame from the muzzle of the weapon.

I did not hear the report, for it was lost and merged with the other more positive staccato series of reports, on my left. With his right arm still extended Adam reeled back a step, swung his reproachful and haggard gaze upon me and fixed it, even as a second burst of firing came and he spun to the floor.

In the astonishing silence, I rushed toward Adam as he fell. Then I heard somewhere in the lobby a woman begin screaming, then a great rush of feet and babble of voices. Adam was bleeding heavily. He was stitched across the chest. The chest was all knocked in. He was already dead.

I looked up to see Sugar-Boy standing there with the smoking automatic in his hand, and off to the right, near the elevator, a highway patrolman with a pistol in his hand.

I didn't see the Boss. And thought: *He didn't hit him.*

But I was wrong. Even as I thought that and looked around, Sugar-Boy dropped his automatic clattering to the marble, and

396

uttering some strangled, animal-like sound, rushed back beyond the statue of Governor Moffat.

I laid Adam's head back on the marble and went beyond the statue. I had to shove the people back now, they were crowding so. Somebody was yelling, "Stand back, stand back, give him air!" But they kept crowding up, running to the spot from all over the lobby and from the corridors.

When I broke through, I saw the Boss sitting on the floor, breathing heavily, staring straight ahead. He had both hands pressed to his body, low on the chest and toward the center. I could see no sign that he was hit. Then I saw a very little ooze of blood between two of the fingers, just a little.

Sugar-Boy was leaning above him, weeping and sputtering, trying to speak. He finally managed to get out the words: "D-d-d-does it hur-hur-hur-hurt much, Boss—does it hur-hur-hur-hurt?"

The Boss did not die there in the lobby under the dome. In fact, he lived quite a while and died on a clean, white, antiseptic bed, with all the benefits of science. For a couple of days it was given out that he would not die at all. He was seriously wounded—there were two little .25-caliber slugs in his body, slugs from a little toy target pistol Adam had had since he was a kid—but an operation was possible, and he was a very strong man.

So there was all over again the business of the waiting room with the potted plants and water colors and artificial logs on the cozy hearth. A sister of Lucy Stark came with Lucy the morning of the operation. Old Man Stark, the Boss's father, was too feeble to leave Mason City. You could see that Lucy's sister, a woman a good deal older than Lucy, dressed in country black with high-laced black kid shoes, was a strong-minded, sensible woman who had been through a lot and knew how to help somebody else through. You could look at her squarish, slightly reddened, coarse-skinned hands, with their square-cut nails, and know that she knew how to take hold. When she entered the waiting room there at the hospital and cast a practiced and critical, not quite scornful, glance over the potted plants and the artificial logs, it was like a pilot mounting to the pilothouse and taking over.

She sat very stiff and severe in a chair, not one of the chintz-covered soft ones. She was going to permit no spilling over of emotion, not in a strange room and at that time of day—the time of day when every day there was breakfast to get and the children to fix and the men to clear out of the house. There would be a proper place and time. After it was over, after she got Lucy home, she would put her to bed in a room with the curtains drawn, and would put a cloth dabbled with vinegar

397

on her forehead, and would sit by the bed and hold her hand, and would say, "Now just you cry if you want to, baby, then you'll feel better, then you lie still and I'll sit here, I won't leave you, baby." But that would come later. Meanwhile Lucy now and then stole a look across at her sister's hewn and eroded face. It wasn't exactly a sympathetic face, but it seemed to have what Lucy was looking for.

I sat over on the couch and looked at the same old picture magazines. I felt definitely that I was out of place. But Lucy had asked me to come. "He would want you to be there," she had said.

"I'll wait down in the lobby," I said.

She shook her head. "Come upstairs," she said.

"I don't want to be underfoot. Your sister will be there, you said."

"I want you to," she had said, and so there I was. And it was better, I decided, even if I was out of place, than being down in the lobby with all the newshawks and politicos and curiosity-seekers.

It didn't take them awfully long. They said the operation was a success. When the nurse who had brought the news said that, Lucy slumped in her chair and uttered a dry, gasping sob. The sister, who herself had seemed to relax a little at the words, looked sharply at Lucy. "Lucy," she said, not loud but with some severity, "Lucy!"

Lucy raised her head, met the sister's reproving gaze, murmured humbly, "I'm sorry, Ellie, I'm sorry. It's just that I've—I've—"

"We must thank God," Ellie announced. Then she rose briskly, as though she were about to step right out and do that before it slipped her mind. But she turned to the nurse. "When can she see her husband?" she asked.

"It will be some time," the nurse said. "I can't tell you exactly, but it will be some time. If you wait here I can let you know." She moved to the door. There she turned, and asked, "Can I get anything for you? Some lemonade? Some coffee?"

"That's right kind and considerate," the sister said, "but we'll just say no thanks this time of morning."

The nurse went out, and I excused myself and followed. I went down to the office of Dr. Simmons, who had performed the operation. I had known him around the place. He was a sort of friend of Adam—about as good a one as Adam had, for he never had chummed up with anybody, that is, anybody except me, and I didn't count, for I was the Friend of His Youth. I had known Dr. Simmons around the place. Adam had introduced us.

Dr. Simmons, a dry, thin, grayish man, was at his desk, writing something on a big card. I told him to finish what he was doing. He said he was about through, the secretary picked up the card and put it into a filing cabinet, and he turned to me. I asked him how the Governor was doing. The operation had been a success, he said.

"You mean you got the bullets out?" I asked.

He smiled in a sort of chilly way, and said he meant a little more than that. "'He's got a chance," he said. "He's a strong man."

"He's that," I agreed.

Dr. Simmons picked up a little envelope from his desk, and emptied the contents into his hand. "No matter how strong they are they can't take much of this diet," he said, and held out his hand, open, to show me the two little pellets resting there. A .25-caliber slug is small, all right, but these looked even smaller and more trivial than I had remembered.

I picked one of them out of his hand and examined it. It was a little misshapen slug of lead. Fingering it, I thought of how a long time back, when we were kids at the Landing, Adam and I used to shoot at a pine board, and how sometimes we had dug the slugs out of the soft wood with a pocketknife. Sometimes the slugs dug out of the wood hadn't been a bit more misshapen than this one, the wood was so soft.

"The son-of-a-bitch," Dr. Simmons said irrelevantly.

I gave the slug back to him and went down to the lobby. It was pretty well cleared out down there now. The politicos had gone. Two or three newspapermen still hung around, waiting for developments.

There weren't any developments that day. Or the next day either. The Boss seemed to be getting on all right. But the third day he took a turn for the worse. An infection had started up. It moved pretty fast. I knew from the way Dr. Simmons looked, even if he wouldn't say much, that he was a gone gosling.

That evening, shortly after I had arrived at the hospital and had gone up to the waiting room to see how Lucy was making out, I got the message that the Boss wanted to see me. He had rallied, they said.

He was a sick-looking customer when I saw him. The flesh had fallen away on his face till the skin sacked off the bone the way it does on an old man's face. He looked like Old Man Stark, up at Mason City. He was white as chalk.

When I first saw the eyes in the white face, they seemed to be filmed and unrecognizing. Then, as I moved toward the bed, they fixed on me and a thin light flickered up in them. His mouth twisted a little in a way which I took to be the feeble shorthand for a grin.

I came over close to the bed. "Hello, Boss," I said, and hung something on my features which I meant to be taken for a grin.

He lifted the forefinger and the next finger of his right hand, which lay prone on the sheet, in an incipient salute, then let them drop. The strength of the muscles which held his mouth twisted gave out, too, and the grin slid off his face and the weight of flesh sagged back.

I stood up close to the bed and looked down at him, and tried to think of something to say. But my brain felt as juiceless as an old sponge left out in the sun a long time.

Then he said, in something a little better than a whisper, "I wanted to see you, Jack."

"I wanted to see you, too, Boss."

For a minute he didn't speak, but his eyes looked up at me, with the light still flickering in them. Then he spoke: "Why did he do it to me?"

"Oh, God damn it," I burst out, very loud, "I don't know." The nurse looked warningly at me.

"I never did anything to him," he said.

"No, you never did."

He was silent again, and the flicker went down in his eyes. Then, "He was all right. The Doc."

I nodded.

I waited, but it began to seem that he wasn't going to say any more. His eyes were on the ceiling and I could scarcely tell that he was breathing. Finally, the eyes turned toward me again, very slowly, and I almost thought that I could hear the tiny painful creak of the balls in their sockets. But the light flickered up again. He said, "It might have been all different, Jack."

I nodded again.

He roused himself more. He even seemed to be straining to lift his head from the pillow. "You got to believe that," he said hoarsely.

The nurse stepped forward and looked significantly at me.

"Yes," I said to the man on the bed.

"You got to," he said again. "You got to believe that."

"All right."

He looked at me, and for a moment it was the old strong, probing, demanding glance. But when the words came this time, they were very weak. "And it might even been different yet," he whispered. "If it hadn't happened, it might—have been different—even yet."

He barely got the last words out, he was so weak.

The nurse was making signals to me.

I reached down and took the hand on the sheet. It felt like a piece of jelly.

"So long, Boss," I said. "I'll be seeing you."

He didn't answer, and I wasn't even sure that there was recognition in the eyes now. I turned away and went out.

He died the next morning, just about day. There was a hell of a big funeral. The city was jam-packed with people, all kinds of people, county-courthouse slickers and red-necks and wool-hat boys and people who had never been on pavement before. And they had their women with them. They filled all the space around the Capitol and spilled and eddied back into the streets beyond, while the drizzle came down and the loud-speakers placed on the trees and poles blared out the words which made you want to puke.

Then after the coffin had been brought down the great steps of the Capitol and loaded into the hearse and after the state patrolmen and the mounted cops had fought out a passage, the procession rolled slowly away to the cemetery. The crowd seethed after it. At the cemetery they surged and swayed over the grass, trampling the graves, breaking down shrubbery. A couple of gravestones were overturned and broken. It was two hours after the burial before the police managed to clear the place.

That was my second funeral within a week. The first one had been very different. It had been the funeral of Adam Stanton, down at Burden's Landing.

Chapter Ten

AFTER the Boss was safe underground, and the pussel-gutted city cops sweating in their blue and lean, natty boys of the State Patrol and the mounted police on glossy, dancing horses whose hoofs sank fetlock deep in the flower beds had driven the crowd sullenly out of the cemetery—but long before the tramped grass began to lift itself or the caretakers came to repair the knocked-over tombstones—I left town and took out for the Landing. There were two reasons. First, I couldn't stand to stay in town. Second, Anne Stanton was at the Landing.

She had been there since Adam's funeral. She had gone down with the body, trailing the sun-glittering, expensive hearse in an undertaker's limousine with a nurse, who proved to be superfluous, and Katy Maynard, an old friend who proved, no doubt, to be superfluous, too. I didn't see her as she sat in the rented limousine which moved at its decorous torturer's pace the near-hundred miles, lifting the miles slowly off the concrete slab, slowly and fastidiously as though you were peeling an endless strip of skin off the live flesh. I didn't see her, but I know how she had been: erect, white in the face, the beautiful bones of her face showing under the taut flesh, her hands clenched in her lap. For that was the way she was when I saw her standing under the moss-garlanded oaks, looking absolutely alone despite the nurse and Katy Maynard and all the people—friends of the family, curiosity-seekers come to gloat and nudge, newspapermen, big-shot doctors from town and from Baltimore and Philadelphia—who stood there while the shovels did their work.

And she was that way when she walked out of the place, not leaning on anybody, with the nurse and Katy Maynard trailing along with that look of embarrassed and false piety which people get on their faces when they are caught in the open with the principal mourner at a funeral.

Even when—just as she was coming out the gate of the cemetery—a newspaperman jammed a camera at her and took her picture, she didn't change the expression on her face.

He was still there when I came up, a squirt with his hat over one eye and the camera hung round his neck and a grin on his squirt face. I thought maybe I had seen him around town, but maybe not, the squirts look so much alike when they grind them out of journalism school. "Hello," I said.

He said hello.

"I saw you get that picture," I said.

He said yeah.

"Well, son," I said, "if you live long enough, you'll find out there are some kinds of a son-of-a-bitch you don't have to be even to be a newspaperman."

He said yeah, out of his squirt face, and looked at me. Then he asked, "You're Burden?"

I nodded.

"Jesus Christ," he exclaimed, "you work for Stark and you call somebody a son-of-a-bitch."

I just looked at him. I'd been over all that ground before. I had been over it a thousand times with a thousand people. Hotel lobbies and dinner tables and club cars and street corners and bedrooms and filling stations. Sometimes they didn't say it just exactly that way and sometimes they didn't say it at all, but it was there. Oh, I'd fixed them, all right. I knew how to roll with that punch and give it right back in the gut. I ought to have known, I'd had plenty of practice.

But you get tired. In a way it is too easy, and so it isn't fun any more. And then you get so you don't get mad any more, it has happened so often. But those aren't the reasons. It is just that those people who say that to you—or don't say it—aren't right and they aren't wrong. If it were absolutely either way, you wouldn't have to think about it, you could just shut your eyes and let them have it in the gut. But the trouble is, they are half right and half wrong, and in the end that is what paralyzes you. Trying to sort out the one from the other. You can't explain it to them, for there isn't ever time and there is always that look on their faces. So you get to a point in the end where you don't even let them have it in the gut. You just look at them, and it is like a dream or something remembered from a long time back or like they weren't there at all.

So I just looked at the squirt face.

There were other people there. They were looking at me. They expected me to say something. Or do something. But somehow I didn't even mind their eyes on me. I didn't even hate them. I didn't feel anything except a kind of numbness and soreness inside, more numbness than soreness. I stood there and looked at him and waited the way you wait for the pain to start after you have been hit. Then, if the pain started, I would give it to him. But it didn't start, and there was just the numbness. So I turned around and walked away. I didn't even mind the eyes that were following me or the snatch of a laugh somebody gave and cut off short because it was a funeral.

I walked on down the street with the numbness and soreness in me. But what had happened at the gate hadn't given it to me. I had had it before I came.

I went on down the Row toward the Stanton house. I didn't imagine she'd want to see me right then, but I intended to leave word that I would be at the hotel down at the Landing till late afternoon. This, of course, if something didn't break about the Boss's condition.

But when I got to the Stanton house I learned that Anne wasn't seeing anybody. Katy Maynard and the nurse weren't superfluous any more. For when Anne entered the house she went into the living room and stood there just inside the door and looked slowly all over the place, at the piano, the furniture piece by piece, the picture above the fireplace, the way a woman looks over a room just before she sails in to redecorate the place and rearrange the furniture (that was Katy Maynard's way of putting it), and then she just gave down. She didn't even reach for the doorjamb, or stagger, or make a sound, they said. She just gave down, now it was over, and was out cold on the floor.

So when I got there, the nurse was upstairs working on her, and Katy Maynard was calling the doctor and taking charge. There wasn't any reason for me to stay. I got in my car and headed back to the city.

But now the Boss was dead, too, and I was back at the Landing. My mother and her Theodore were off on a trip and I had the house to myself. It was as empty and still as a morgue. But even so, it was a bit more cheerful than the hospitals and cemeteries I had been hanging around. What was dead in this house had been dead a long time, and I was accustomed to the fact. I was even becoming accustomed to the fact of the other deaths. They had shoveled it over Judge Irwin, and Adam Stanton, and the Boss.

But there were some of us left. And Anne Stanton was among those left. And I was.

So back at the Landing again, we sat on the gallery side by side, when there was sun—the lemon-pale sun of late autumn —and the afternoon made its shortened arc over the onyx-mottled waters of the bay, which stretched south to the autumn-hazy horizon. Or when there wasn't any sun, and the wind piled the sea up over the beach, even to the road, and the sky seemed to be nothing but gusty rain, we sat side by side in the living room. Either place, we never talked much those days, not because there was nothing to say but because there might be too much and if you once started you would upset the beautiful and perilous equilibrium which we had achieved. It was as though we each sat on the end of a seesaw, beautifully balanced, but not in any tidy little play yard but over God knows what blackness on a seesaw which God had rigged up for us kiddies. And if either of us should lean toward the other, even a fraction of an inch, the balance would be upset and we would both go sliding off into that blackness. But we fooled God, and didn't say a word.

We didn't say a word, but some afternoons I read to Anne. I read the first book I had laid hand to the first afternoon when I found I couldn't sit there any longer in that silence which bulged and creaked with all the unsaid words. It was the first volume of the works of Anthony Trollope. That was a safe bet. Anthony never upset any equilibriums.

In a peculiar way those late-autumn days began to remind me of the summer almost twenty years before when I had fallen in love with Anne. That summer we had been absolutely alone, together, even when people were around, the only inhabitants of the kind of floating island or magic carpet which being in love is. And now we were absolutely alone, but it was a different kind of floating island or magic carpet. That summer we had seemed to be caught in a massive and bemusing tide which knew its own pace and time and would not be hurried even to the happiness which it surely promised. And now again we seemed to be caught in such a tide and couldn't lift a finger in its enormous drift, for it knew its own pace and time. But what it promised we didn't know. I did not even wonder.

Now and then, however, I wondered about something else. Sometimes when I was sitting beside her, reading or not talking, and sometimes when I was away, eating breakfast or walking down the Row or lying awake. There was a question without an answer. When Anne had told me about Adam's last, wild visit to her apartment—how he rushed in and said he wouldn't be pimp for her and all that—she had said that some man had telephoned Adam to tell him about her and Governor Stark.

Who?

In the first days after the event I had really forgotten the fact, but then the question came. At first, even then, the question didn't seem important to me. For nothing seemed very important to me then, in the pervasive soreness and numbness. Or at least what seemed important to me then had nothing to do with the question. What had happened was important, but not the cause of what had happened, in so far as such a cause was not in me myself.

But the question kept coming back. Even when I wasn't thinking of it, I would suddenly be aware of its gnawing like a mouse's tooth stitching away inside the wainscoting of my mind.

For a while I didn't see how I could ask Anne. I couldn't ever say anything to her about what had happened. We would sit forever in our conspiracy of silence, forever bound together in that conspiracy by our awareness of our earlier, unwitting conspiracy to commit Adam Stanton and Willie Stark to each other and to their death. (If we should ever break the conspiracy of silence we might have to face the fact of that other conspiracy and have to look down and see the blood on our hands.) So I said nothing.

Until the day when I had to say it.

I said, "Anne, I'm going to ask you one question. About—about—it. Then I'll never say another word about it to you unless you speak up first."

She looked at me without answering. But I could see in her eyes the recoil of fear and pain, and then the stubborn mustering of what forces she had.

So I plunged on, "You told me—that day when I came to your apartment—that somebody had telephoned Adam—had told him—had told him about—"

"About me," she said, finishing the sentence on which I had, for the moment, wavered. She hadn't waited for the impact. With whatever force she had she was meeting it head-on.

I nodded.

"Well?" she queried.

"Did he say who had telephoned him?"

She thought a minute. You could see her, even as she sat there, lifting the sheet off that moment when Adam had burst in on her, like somebody lifting the sheet off the face of a corpse on a marble slab in a morgue and peering into the face.

Then she shook her head. "No," she said, "he didn't say—" she hesitated—"except that it was a man. I'm sure he said man."

So we resumed our conspiracy of silence, while the seesaw wavered and swayed beneath us and the black clawed up at us and we clung on.

I left the Landing the next day.

I got to town in the late afternoon, and put in a call to Sadie Burke's apartment. There was no answer. So I tried the Capitol, on the off chance that she would be there, but there was no answer on her extension. Off and on during the evening I tried her apartment number, but with no luck. I didn't go around to the Capitol to see her in the morning. I didn't want to see the gang who would be there. I didn't ever want to see them again.

So I telephoned again. Her extension didn't answer. So I asked the switchboard to find out if possible where she was. After two or three minutes the voice said, "She is not here. She is ill. Will that be all, please?" Then before I could put my thoughts in order, I heard the click of being cut off.

I rang again.

"This is Jack Burden," I said, "and I'd like to—"

"Oh—Mr. Burden—" the switchboard said noncommittally, or perhaps in question.

There had been a time and it hadn't been very long back

when the name *Jack Burden* got something done around that joint. But that voice, the tone of that voice, told me that the name *Jack Burden* didn't mean a damned thing but a waste of breath around there any more.

For a second I was sore as hell. Then I remembered that things had changed.

Things had changed out there. When things change in a place like that, things change fast and all the way down, and the voice at the switchboard gets a new tone when it speaks your name. I remembered how much things had changed. Then I wasn't sore any more, for I didn't give a damn.

But I said sweetly, "I wonder if you can tell me how to get in touch with Miss Burke. I'd sure appreciate it."

Then I waited a couple of minutes for her to try to find out. "Miss Burke is at the Millett Sanatorium," the voice then said.

Cemeteries and hospitals: I was back in the swing of things, I thought.

But the Millett place wasn't like the hospital. It didn't look at all like a hospital, I discovered when I turned off the highway twenty-five miles out of the city and tooled gently up the drive under the magnificent groining of the century-old live oaks whose boughs met above the avenue and dripped stalactites of moss to make a green, aqueous gloom like a cavern. Between the regularly spaced oaks stood pedestals on which classical marbles—draped and undraped, male and female, stained by weathers and leaf acid and encroaching lichen, looking as though they had, in fact, sprouted dully out of the clinging black-green humus below them—stared out at the passer-by with the faintly pained, heavy, incurious unamazement of cattle. The gaze of those marble eyes must have been the first stage in the treatment the neurotic got when he came out to the sanatorium. It must have been like smearing a cool unguent of time on the hot pustule and dry itch of the soul.

Then at the end of the avenue the neurotic reached the sanatorium, which graciously promised peace beyond the white columns. For the Millett Sanatorium was what is called a rest home. But it had been built more than a century back for vanity and love by a cotton snob to whom money had been no object, who had bought near a shipload of Empire furniture in Paris for his house and near a shipload of shining marble statues in Rome for his avenue, and who had probably had a face like brutally hewed cedar and not a nerve in his body, and now people who were descended from such people, or who had enough money (made in the administration of Grant or Coolidge) to assume that they were descended from such people, brought their twitches, tics, kinks, and running sores out here and rested in the high-ceilinged rooms and ate crawfish bisque

407

and were soothed by the voice of a psychiatrist in whose wide, unwavering, brown, liquid, depthless eyes one slowly drowned.

I almost drowned in those eyes during the one-minute interview I had in order to get permission to see Sadie. "She is very difficult," he said.

Sadie was lying on a chaise longue by a window which gave over a stretch of lawn sloping down to a bayou. Her chopped-off black hair was wild and her face was chalk-white and the afternoon light striking across it made it look more than ever like the plaster-of-Paris mask of Medusa riddled with BB shot. But it was a mask flung down on a pillow and the eyes that looked out of it belonged to the mask. They did not belong to Sadie Burke. There wasn't anything burning there.

"Hello, Sadie," I said, "I hope you don't mind me coming to see you."

She studied me a moment out of the unburning eyes. "It's O.K. with me," she said.

So I sat down and hitched my chair up closer and lighted a cigarette.

"How you getting on?" I asked.

She turned her head in my direction and gave me another long look. For an instant, there was a flicker in the eyes as when a breath of air touches an ember. "Look here," she said, "I'm getting on all right. Why the hell shouldn't I be getting on all right?"

"That's fine," I said.

"I didn't come out here because there was anything wrong with me. I came because I was tired. I wanted a rest. That's what I said to that God-damned doctor. I said, 'I'm here to get a rest because I'm tired and I don't want you messing around and trying to swap secrets with me and find out if I ever had any dreams about red fire engines,' I said, 'If I ever started swapping secrets with you I'd burn your ears off, but I'm here to rest and I don't want you in my hair.' I said, 'I'm tired of a lot of things and I'm God-damned tired of a lot of people and that goes for you, too, Doc.'"

She pushed herself up on one arm and looked at me. Then said, "And that goes for you, too, Jack Burden."

I didn't say anything to that and I didn't move. So she sank back down, and into herself.

I let my cigarette burn up in my fingers and lighted another one before I said, "Sadie, I reckon I know how you feel and I don't want to be bringing everything up again, but——"

"You don't know a thing about how I feel," she said.

"Some idea—maybe," I said. "But what I came for was to ask you a question."

"I thought you came because you were so damned fond of me."

408

"As a matter of fact," I said, "I am. We've been around a long time together and we always got along. But that's not—"

"Yeah," she interrupted, and again thrust herself up on one arm, "everything and everybody just got along fine. Oh, Jesus, just fine."

I waited while she sank back again and turned her eyes from me across the lawn below toward the bayou. A crow was making its way across the clear air above the tattered cypress tops beyond the bayou. Then the crow was gone, and I said, "Adam Stanton killed the Boss, but he never got that idea by himself. Somebody primed him to do it. Somebody who knew the kind of man Adam was and knew the inside of how he took the job at the medical center and knew—"

She didn't seem to be listening to me. She was watching the clear air above the tattered cypresses where the crow had gone. I hesitated, and then, watching her face, went on. "— and knew about the Boss and Anne Stanton."

I waited again and watched her face as I handed those names to her, but it didn't show a thing. It simply looked tired, tired and not giving a damn.

"I found out one thing," I continued. "A man called up Adam that afternoon and told him about the Boss and his sister. And some more stuff. You can guess what stuff. So he went wild. He went to see his sister and jumped her and she didn't deny it. She isn't the kind of person who could deny it. I guess she was sick of having a secret and she was almost glad not to have it any longer and—"

"Yeah," Sadie said, not turning to me, "tell me how noble and high-toned Anne Stanton is."

"I'm sorry," I said, and felt the blood flushing my face. "I guess I did get off the point."

"I guess you did, all right."

I waited. Then, "That man who called up Adam, do you have any notion who it was?"

She seemed to be turning that question over in her mind. If she had heard it, for I couldn't be sure.

"Do you?" I asked.

"I don't have any notion," she said.

"No?"

"No," she said, still not looking at me, "and I don't have to have any. Because, you see, I know."

"Who?" I demanded. "Who?" And came up out of my chair.

"Duffy," she said.

"I knew it!" I exclaimed, "I ought to have known it! It had to be."

"If you knew it," she said, "what the hell you come messing around me for?"

"I had to be sure. I had to know. Really know. I—" I

stopped and stood there at the foot of the chaise longue and looked down at her averted face, which the sunlight lay across. "You say you know it was Duffy. How do you know?"

"God damn you, Jack Burden, God damn you," she said in a tired voice, and turned her head to look up at me. Then looking at me, she thrust herself up to a sitting position, and burst out in a voice which all at once wasn't tired any more but angry and violent, "God damn you, Jack Burden, what made you come here? What always makes you mess in things? Why can't you leave me alone? Why can't you? Why?"

I stared down into the eyes, which in the pain-contorted face were burning now and wild.

"How do you know?" I demanded softly.

"God damn you, Jack Burden, God damn you," she said like a litany.

"How do you know?" I demanded, more softly than before —I was almost whispering—and leaned down toward her.

"God damn you, Jack Burden," she said.

"How do you know?"

"Because——" she began, hesitated, and tossed her head in a desperate tired way like a fevered child on a pillow.

"Because?" I demanded.

"Because," she said, and let herself fall back on the cushions of the chaise longue, "I told him. I told him to do it."

That was it. That was it, and I hadn't guessed it. My knees gave slowly down, like a pneumatic jack letting down the weight of a car to the floor, and I was back in my chair. There I was and there Sadie Burke was, and I was looking at her as though I had never seen her before.

After a minute, she said, "Stop looking at me." But there wasn't any heat in what she said.

I must have continued to look, for she said, as before, "Stop looking at me."

Then I heard my lips saying, as though to myself, "You killed him."

"All right," she said, "all right, I killed him. He was throwing me over. For good. I knew it was for good that time. For that Lucy. After all I had done. After I made him. I told him I'd fix him, but he turned that new sick smile of his on me like he was practicing to be Jesus and took my hands in his, and asked me to understand—understand, Jesus!—and just then like a flash I knew I'd kill him."

"You killed Adam Stanton," I said.

"Oh, God," she breathed, "oh, God."

"You killed Adam," I repeated.

"Oh," she breathed, "and I killed Willie. I killed him."

"Yes," I agreed, and nodded.

"Oh, God," she said, and lay there staring up at the ceiling.

410

I had found out what I had come to find out. But I kept on sitting there. I didn't even light a cigarette.

After a while she said, "Come over here. Pull your chair over here."

I hitched my chair over by the chaise longue, and waited. She didn't look at me, but she reached out her right hand uncertainly in my direction. I took it and held it while she continued to stare at the ceiling and the afternoon light struck cruelly across her face.

"Jack," she said, finally, still not looking at me.

"Yes?"

"I'm glad I told you," she said. "I knew I had to tell somebody. Sometime. I knew it would come, but there wasn't anybody for me to tell. Till you came. That's why I hated you for coming. As soon as you came in the door, I knew I'd have to tell you. But I'm glad I told. I don't care who knows now. I may not be noble and high-toned like that Stanton woman, but I'm glad I told."

I didn't find much to say to that. So I continued to sit here for quite a while, holding Sadie's hand in the silence which she seemed to want and looking across her down toward the bayou, which coiled under the moss depending from the line of tattered cypresses on the farther bank, the algae-mottled water heavy with the hint and odor of swamp, jungle, and darkness, along the edge of the expanse of clipped lawn.

I had found out that Tiny Duffy, who was now Governor of the state, had killed Willie Stark as surely as though his own hand had held the revolver. I had also found out that Sadie Burke had put the weapon into Duffy's hand and had aimed it for him, that she, too, had killed Willie Stark. And Adam Stanton. But what she had done had been done hot. What Duffy had done had been done cold. And, in the end, Sadie Burke's act had somehow been wiped out. It did not exist for me any more.

And that left Duffy. Duffy had done it. And strangely, there was a great joy and relief in that knowledge. Duffy had done it, and that made everything clear and bright as in frosty sunshine. There, over yonder, was Tiny Duffy with his diamond ring, and over here was Jack Burden. I felt free and clean, as when you suddenly see that, after being paralyzed by ignorance or indecision, you can act. I felt on the verge of the act.

But I did not know what the act was to be.

When I went back out to see Sadie—she had asked me to come back— she told me, without my saying a word on the subject, that she would make a statement if I wanted her to. I told her that that was wonderful, and I felt that it was wonderful for I still felt clean and free, on the verge of the act, and she was putting the thing into my hand. I thanked her.

"Don't thank me," she said, "I'm doing myself a favor. Duffy—Duffy—" she rose to a sitting position on the chaise longue and her eyes had the old flash—"you know what he did?"

Before I could answer she plunged on, "Afterwards—after it had happened—I didn't feel a thing. Not a thing. I knew that night what had happened, and I didn't feel a thing. And next morning Duffy came to me—he was grinning and puffing—and he said, 'Girlie, I'll sure hand it to you, I'll sure hand it to you.' I still didn't feel a thing, not even when I looked in his face. But then he put his hand around my shoulder and sort of patted and rubbed my back between the shoulder blades, and said, 'Girlie, you sure stopped his clock and I ain't forgetting you, girlie, you and me, we might sure get along.' Then it happened. It happened right then. It was like it had all happened that second, right in front of me instead of up at the Capitol. And I clawed at him and jumped away. I ran out of the place. And three days later, after he died, I came here. It was the only place I could come."

"Well, thanks anyway," I said. "I reckon we can stop Duffy's clock."

"It won't stick in law," she said.

"I didn't reckon it would. Whatever you said to him or he said to you doesn't prove a thing. But there are other ways."

She thought awhile. Then, "Any other way, law or not, and I reckon you know it drags that—" she hesitated, and did not say what she was about to say, then revised it—"drags Anne Stanton into it."

"She'll do it," I affirmed. "I know she would."

Sadie shrugged. "You know what you want," she said, "you all."

"I want to get Duffy."

"That suits me," she said, and again shrugged. Suddenly she seemed to have gone tired again. "That suits me," she repeated, "but the world is full of Duffy's. It looks like I been knowing them all my life."

"I'm just thinking about one," I declared.

I was still thinking about that one about a week later (by this time it seemed that the only way was to break the thing through an antiadministration paper), when I got the note from that particular Duffy himself. Would I mind coming to see him, it said. At my convenience.

My convenience was immediately, and I found him imperially and porcinely filling his clothes and the great leather couch in the library at the Mansion where the Boss used to sit. The leather of his shoes creaked as he stepped forward to greet me, but his body swayed with the bloated lightness of a drowned

412

body stirred loose at last from the bottom mud of the river to rise majestically and swayingly to the surface. We shook hands and he smiled. And waved me to a seat as the couch groaned to receive him.

A black boy in a white coat brought the drinks. I took the drink but declined a cigar, and waited.

He said how sad it was about the Boss. I nodded.

He said how the boys all missed the Boss. I nodded to that.

He said how things were getting done though. Just like the Boss would have wanted. I nodded to that.

He said how they sure missed the Boss, though. I nodded to that.

He said, "Jack, the boys sure miss you around here, too."

I nodded modestly and said that I sure missed the boys.

"Yeah," he resumed, "I was saying to myself the other day, just let me get settled into harness and I'm going to get hold of Jack. Yeah, Jack's the kind of fellow I like to have around. The Boss sure thought a lot of him, and what was good enough for the Boss is good enough for old Tiny. Yeah, I said to myself, I'm gonna get old Jack. The kind of guy I need. A square-shooter. A guy you can trust. He'll speak the truth, fear nor favor. His word is his bond."

"Are you referring to me?" I asked.

"I sure am," he replied. "And I'm making you a proposition. I don't exactly know what arrangement you had with the Boss, but you just tell me straight what it was and I'll up it ten per cent."

"I had no complaints about my treatment."

"Now that's talking like a white man, Jack," he said, and added earnestly, "And don't get me wrong, I know you and the Boss was like that." He held up two large, white, glistening episcopal fingers as in benediction. "Like that," he repeated. "And don't get me wrong, I'm not criticizing the Boss. I just want to show you I appreciate you."

"Thanks," I said with some lack of warmth.

The lack of warmth was such, I presume, that he leaned slightly forward and said, "Jack, I'm going to make that twenty per cent."

"That's not enough," I said.

"Jack," he said, "you're right. That's not enough. Twenty-five per cent."

I shook my head.

He showed a slight uneasiness and the couch creaked, but he rallied with a smile. "Jack," he said soothingly, "you just tell me what you think's right, and I'll see how we make out. You tell me what's enough."

"There ain't enough," I said.

"Huh?"

"Listen," I said, "didn't you just tell me that I am the guy whose word is his bond?"

"Yeah, Jack."

"So you'll believe me if I tell you something?"

"Why, yeah, Jack."

"Well, I'm telling you something. You are the stinkingest louse God ever let live."

I relished the moment of profound silence which followed, then plunged on, "And you think you can buy me in. Well, I know why you want to. You don't know how much I know or what. I was thick with the Boss and I know a lot. I'm the joker in the deck. My name is Jack and I'm the wild jack and I'm not one-eyed. You want to deal me to yourself from the bottom of the deck. But it's no sale, Tiny, it's no sale. And it's too damned bad, Tiny. And do you know why?"

"Look here!" he said with authority. "Look here, you can't be——"

"It's too bad because I do know something. I know a lot. I know that you killed the Boss."

"It's a lie!" he exclaimed, and heaved on the couch and the couch creaked.

"It's no lie. And it's no guess. Though I ought to have guessed it. Sadie Burke told me. She——"

"She's in it, she's in it!"

"She *was* in it," I corrected, "but not any more. And she'll tell the world. She doesn't care who knows. She's not afraid."

"She better be. I'll——"

"She's not afraid, because she's tired. She's tired of everything and she's tired of you."

"I'll kill her," he said, and the perspiration exuded delicately on his temples.

"You won't kill anybody," I said, "and this time there's nobody to do it for you. For you're afraid to. You were afraid to kill the Boss and you were afraid not to, but luck helped you out. But you gave luck a little push, Tiny, and I swear, I admire you for it. It opened my eyes. You see, Tiny, all those years I never thought you were real. You were just something off the cartoon page. With your diamond ring. You were just the punching bag the Boss used, and you just grinned your sick grin and took it. You were like the poodle I heard about. You ever hear about the poodle?"

I didn't give him time to answer. I watched his mouth get ready, then I went on. "There was a drunk had a poodle and he took him everywhere with him from bar to bar. And you know why? Was it devotion? It was not devotion. He took that poodle everywhere just so he could spit on him and not get the floor dirty. Well, you were the Boss's poodle. And you liked it. You liked to be spit on. You weren't human. You weren't real. That's what I thought. But I was wrong, Tiny. Somewhere down in you there was something made you human. You resented being spit on. Even for money."

I got up, with my half-empty glass in my hand.

"And now, Tiny," I said, "that I know you are real, I sort of feel sorry for you. You are a funny old fat man, Tiny, with your heart getting bad and your liver nigh gone and sweat running down your face and a mean worry on your mind and a great blackness like water rising in a cellar inside you and I almost feel sorry for you but if you say a word I might stop feeling sorry for you. So now I'm going to drink up your whisky and spit in the glass and go."

So I drank off the whisky, dropped the glass on the floor (on the thick rug it didn't break), and started for the door. I had almost got there, when I heard a croak from the couch. I looked around.

"It—" he croaked, "it won't stand in a court."

I shook my head. "No," I said, "it won't. But you still got plenty to worry about."

I opened the door and walked through and left the door open behind me and walked down the long hall under the great, glittering chandelier, and walked out into the brisk night.

I took a deep drag of fresh air and looked up through the trees at the distinct stars. I felt like a million. I had sure-God brought off that scene. I had hit him where he lived. I was full of beans. I had fire in my belly. I was a hero. I was St. George and the dragon, I was Edwin Booth bowing beyond the gas-lights, I was Jesus Christ with the horsewhip in the temple.

I was the stuff.

And all at once under the stars I was like a man who has done himself the best from soup to nuts and a Corona Corona and feels like a virtuous million and all at once there isn't anything but the yellow, acid taste which has crawled up to the back of the mouth from the old, tired stomach.

Three days later I got the registered letter from Sadie Burke. It read:

Dear Jack:

Just so you won't think I am going to welch on what I said I would do I am enclosing the statement I said I would make. I have got it witnessed and notarized and nailed down as tight as you can nail anything down and you can do anything with it you want for it is yours. I mean this. It is your baby, just like I said.

As for me I am getting out of here. I don't mean just getting out of this cross between an old folks' home and a booby-hatch, but out of this town and out of this state. I can't stand it round here and I'm pulling out. I'll be gone a long way and I'll be gone a long time and maybe somewhere the climate will be better. But my cousin (Mrs. Sill Larkin, 2331 Rousseau Ave.) who is the nearest thing to a relative I got will have some kind of address for me sometime, and if you ever want to contact me just write me care of her. Wherever I am I'll do what you say. I'll come if you say come. I don't want you thinking I am going to welch. I don't care who knows anything. I'll do anything you say about that piece of business.

But if you take my advice about that piece of business you will let it drop. This is not because I love Duffy. I hope you will give him an earful and let him wet his pants. But my advice is to let it drop. First, you cannot do anything in law. Second, if you use it politically the best you can get will be to keep Duffy from being re-elected, and you know as well as I do he will never get nominated even. The boys will never nominate him for they know he is a dummy even by their standards. He was just something the Boss kept around. Springing this stuff won't hurt the gang any. It will just give them an excuse to get rid of Duffy. If you want to get the gang you got to let them dig their own grave like they sure will now the Boss is gone. But third, it is sure going to be rough on that Stanton dame if you break this stuff. She may be so noble and high-toned like you said that she will want you to do it, but you are a sap if you do. She has maybe had plenty to put up with already in her way, and you would be a sap to crucify her just because you got some high-faluting idea you are an Eagle Scout and she is Joan of Arc. You would be a sap to tell her even. Unless you are so blabber mouthed you have done it already. Like you maybe have. I am not going on to say she is my best friend but she has had her troubles like I said and you might give her a break.

Remember I am not welching. I am just giving you my advice.
Keep your tail over the dashboard.

Sincerely yours,

SADIE BURKE

I read through Sadie's statement. It said everything there was to say, and each page was signed and witnessed. Then I folded it up. It was no good to me. Not because of the advice which Sadie had given me. Her letter made sense, all right. That is, the part about Duffy and the gang. But something had happened. To hell with them all, I thought. I was sick of it all.

I looked down at the letter again. So Sadie had called me an Eagle Scout. But that wasn't news, either. I had called myself worse names than that the night after I had seen Duffy and was walking down the street under the stars. But it touched the sore place and made it throb. It throbbed the worse because I knew that it wasn't a secret sore place. Sadie had known about it. She had seen through me. She had read me like a book.

There was only one wry piece of consolation in the thought. At least, I had not had to wait for her to read me. I had read myself to myself that night walking down the street, full of beans and being an Eagle Scout, when the yellow, acid taste had all at once crawled up to the back of my mouth.

What had I read? I had read this: When I found out about Duffy's killing the Boss and Adam I had felt clean and pure, and when I kicked Duffy around I felt like a million because I thought it let me out. Duffy was the villain and I was the avenging hero. I had kicked Duffy around and my head was big as a balloon with grandeur. Then all at once something happened and the yellow taste was in the back of my mouth.

This happened: I suddenly asked myself why Duffy had been so sure I would work for him. And suddenly I saw the eyes of the little squirt-face newspaperman at the cemetery gate on me, and all the eyes that had looked at me that way, and suddenly I knew that I had tried to make Duffy into a scapegoat for me and to set myself off from Duffy, and my million-dollar meal of heroism backfired that yellow taste into my gullet and I felt caught and tangled and mired and stuck like an ox in a bog and a cat in flypaper. It wasn't simply that I again saw myself as party to that conspiracy with Anne Stanton which had committed Willie Stark and Adam Stanton to each other and to their death. It was more than that. It was as though I were caught in a more monstrous conspiracy whose meaning I could not fathom. It was as though the scene through which I had just lived had been a monstrous and comic miming for ends I could not conceive and for an audience I could not see but which I knew was leering from the shadow. It was as though in the midst of the scene Tiny Duffy had slowly and like a brother winked at me with his oyster eye and I had known he knew the nightmare truth, which was that we were twins bound together more intimately and disastrously than the poor freaks of the midway who are bound by the common stitch of flesh and gristle and the seepage of blood. We were bound together forever and I could never hate him without hating myself or love myself without loving him. We were bound together under the unwinking eye of Eternity and by the Holy Grace of the Great Twitch whom we must all adore.

And I heaved and writhed like the ox or the cat, and the acid burned my gullet and that was all there was to it and I hated everything and everybody and myself and Tiny Duffy and Willie Stark and Adam Stanton. To hell with them all, I said impartially under the stars. They all looked alike to me then. And I looked like them.

That was the way it was for quite a while.

I did not go back to the Landing. I did not want to see Anne Stanton. I did not even open a letter she wrote me. It lay on my bureau where I saw it every morning. I did not want to see anybody I knew. I hung around town and sat in my room or sat in bars which I had never frequented and sat in movies in

417

the front row, where I could admire the enormous and distorted shadows which gesticulated and struck or clutched or clung and uttered asseverations which reminded you of everything which you had ever remembered. And I sat for hours in the newspaper room of the public library, the place which like railway stations and missions and public latrines is where the catarrhal old men and bums go and where they sit to thumb the papers which tell about the world in which they live for a certain number of years or to sit and wheeze and stare while the gray rain slides down the big windowpanes above them.

It was in the newspaper room of the library that I saw Sugar-Boy. It was such an improbable place to encounter him that at first I scarcely accepted the evidence of my eyes. But there he was. The rather largish head hung forward as though its weight were too much for the little stem of a neck, and I could see how thin and pink like a baby's the skin was over the skull in the areas where the hair had prematurely gone. His short arms in sleeves of wrinkled blue serge lay symmetrically out before him on the table, like a brace of stuffed sacks of country sausage laid on a butcher's counter. The pale, chubby hands curled innocently on the varnished yellow oak of the table. He was looking at a picture magazine.

Then one of the hands, the right hand, with the quick, flickering motion which I remembered, dropped below the level of the table—to the side pocket of his coat, I presumed—and returned with a cube of sugar which he popped into his mouth. The flickering motion of the hand reminded me, and I wondered if he was still carrying a gun. I looked at the left side toward the shoulder, but I couldn't tell. Sugar-Boy's blue serge coat was always a size too big for him.

It was Sugar-Boy all right, and I didn't want to see him. If he should raise his head he would look right at me. Now while he was sunk in the picture magazine I tried for the door. I edged over to one side easy and was almost past his natural area of vision when he lifted his head and our eyes met. He rose from the chair and came toward me.

I gave an ambiguous nod which might have served merely for recognition, a rather chilly and discouraging recognition, or for a signal to follow me out to the hall where we could talk. He took the latter interpretation, and followed me. I didn't wait just outside the door, but moved some distance across the hall to the steps (those newspaper rooms in public libraries are always in a half basement, next to the men's latrine) which led up to the main lobby. Maybe he would read something into that extra distance. But he didn't. He came padding over to me, with his blue serge trousers bagging down low off his can and the tops crumpling over his black, soft-leather box-toed shoes.

"How-how-how——" he began, and the face began its pained, apologetic contortions, and the spit flew.

"I'm making out," I said. "How're you making out?"

"Aw-aw-aw-right."

We stood there in the dingy, dimly lit basement hall of the public library with the cigarette butts on the cement floor around us and the door of the men's latrine behind us and the air smelling of dry paper and dust and disinfectant. It was eleven-thirty in the morning and outside the gray sky dripped steadily like a sogged old awning. We look at each other. Each one knew the other was there out of the rain because he had no other place to go.

He shuffled his feet on the floor, looked down at the floor, then back up at me. "I-I-I could-a had a-a-a-a job," he declared earnestly.

"Sure," I said, without much interest.

"I-I-I-I just didn't wa-wa-wa-want one. Not yet," he said. "I didn't fee-fee-feel like no job yet."

"Sure," I repeated.

"I-I-I got me some mo-mo-money saved up," he said apologetically.

"Sure."

He looked searchingly at me. "Y-y-y-you got a job?" he asked.

I shook my head, but was about to say in my defense what he had just said, that I could have had one if I had wanted it. I could have been sitting up in a nice office next door to Tiny Duffy's office with my feet on a mahogany desk. If I had wanted. And as that crossed my mind, with the momentary flicker of weary self-irony, I suddenly saw like a blaze of lightning and a clap of thunder what the Lord had put before me. Duffy, I thought, Duffy.

And there was Sugar-Boy standing before me.

"Listen," I said, and leaned toward him in the empty hall, "listen, do you know who killed the Boss?"

The biggish head rolled a little to one side on the little stem of a neck as he looked up at me and the face began its painful twitching. "Yeah," he said, "yeah—the son-of-a-bi-bi-bitch and I-I-I shot him."

"Yeah," I said, "you shot Stanton—" and I thought with an instantaneous stab of Adam Stanton alive a long time back and now dead, and I hated the malformed, sad little creature before me—"yeah, you shot him."

The head rolled slightly and tiredly on the neck, and he repeated, "I-I-I shot him."

"But suppose you don't know," I said, leaning, "suppose there was somebody behind Stanton, somebody who framed him to do it."

I let that sink in, and watched his face twitch while no sound came.

"Suppose," I continued, "suppose I could tell you who—suppose I could prove it—what would you do?"

Suddenly his face wasn't twitching. It was smooth as a baby's and peaceful, but peaceful in the way that intensity can sometimes momentarily make a face look peaceful and pure.

"What would you do?" I demanded.

"I'd kill the son-of-a-bitch," he said. And he had not stuttered at all.

"They'd hang you," I said.

"I'd k-k-k-kill him. They couldn't h-h-h-hang me before I killed him."

"Remember," I whispered, leaning closer, "they'd hang you."

He stared up at me, prying into my face. "Who-who-who is it?"

"They'd hang you. Are you sure you'd kill him?"

"Who-who-who—" he began. Then he clutched my coat. "Y-y-you know—" he said, "y-y-you know something you ain't t-t-t-telling me."

I could tell him. I could say to him, meet me here at three o'clock, I want to show you something. I could bring the stuff from Sadie, the stuff that lay up in my room in a desk, and he would take one look. One look. It would be like touching a trigger.

His hands were clutching and clawing at my coat. "T-t-tell me," he was saying.

One look. It was perfect. I could meet him here in the afternoon. We could step into the latrine and he could take one look, and I would go home and burn the stuff. Hell, why burn it? What had I done? I even warned the little bugger they'd hang him. They had nothing on me.

He was clawing at me, importunately and feebly, saying, "T-t-tell me, you better t-t-tell me now."

It would be too easy. It was perfect. And the perfect mathematical irony of it—the perfect duplication of what Duffy had done—struck me, and I felt like laughing out loud. "Listen here," I said to Sugar-Boy. "Stop clawing me and listen here and I'll—"

He stopped clawing and stood meekly before me.

He would do it. I knew he would do it. And it was such a joke on Duffy I almost laughed out loud. And as the name of Duffy flashed across my mind I saw Duffy's face, large and lunar and sebaceous, nodding at me as at the covert and brotherly appreciation of a joke, and even as I opened my lips to speak the syllables of his name, he winked. He winked right at me like a brother.

I stood there stock-still.

Sugar-Boy's face began to twitch again. He was going to ask again. I stared down at him. "I was kidding," I said.

There was absolute blankness on his face, and then an absolute murderousness. There wasn't any flare of fury. It was a cold and innocent and murderous certainty. It was as though his face had suddenly frozen in a split second in that certainty, and it looked like the face of a man who had been trapped and had died in the snow long ago, centuries ago—back in the ice age, perhaps—and the glacier brings it down all those centuries, inch by inch, and suddenly, with its primitive purity and lethal innocence, it stares at you through the last preserving glaze of ice.

I stood there for what seemed forever. I couldn't move. I was sure I was a goner.

Then the ice face wasn't there. It was just Sugar-Boy's face on a head too big for the neck, and it was saying, "I-I-I durn near d-d-done it."

I ran my tongue over my dry lips. "I know it," I said.

"Y-y-you oughtn't d-d-d-done me that way," he said in humble complaint.

"I'm sorry."

"Y-y-you know h-h-how I feel, and y-y-you oughtn't d-d-done me like that."

"I know how you feel," I said. "And I'm sorry. I really am."

"F-f-fergit it," he said. He stood there, seeming smaller than before, slumped and forlorn as though he were a doll that had lost some of its sawdust.

I studied him. Then I said, as much to myself as to him, I suppose, "You really would have done it."

"It w-w-was the B-B-Boss," he said.

"Even if they'd hang you."

"They w-w-wasn't n-n-nobody like the B-B-Boss. And they k-k-killed him. They h-h-had to go and k-k-kill him."

He shuffled his feet on the cement floor and looked down at them. "He could t-t-talk so good," he half-mumbled with his stuttering. "The B-B-Boss could. Couldn't nobody t-t-talk like him. When a m-m-made a speech and ev-ev-everybody y-y-yelled, it looked l-l-like something was gonna b-b-burst inside y-y-you." He touched his chest with his hand to indicate where something looked like it might bust inside you. Then he looked questioningly at me.

"Sure," I agreed, "he was a great talker."

We stood there for a half minute more without anything to say to each other. He looked at me and then down at his feet. Then back at me, and said, "W-w-well, I reckon I'll b-b-be getting on."

He put out one of his hands to me and I took it and gave it a shake.

"Well, good luck," I said.

And he went up the stairs, bending his knees excessively for the stairs, for his legs were stumpy. When he used to drive the big black Cadillac he always had a couple of flat cushions—the kind you take with you on picnics or in a canoe—to prop behind him so he could properly work the clutch and brake pedals.

So that was the last I saw of Sugar-Boy. He had been born over in Irish Town. He had been the runt the big boys shoved around in the vacant lot. They had played baseball, but he hadn't been good enough to play. "Hey, Sawed-Off," they'd say, "go git me that bat." Or, "Hey, Sawed-Off, go git me a coke." And he had gone to get the bat or the coke. Or they'd say, "Aw, dry up, Mush-Mouth, write me a letter." And he had dried up. But somehow, sometime, he had learned what he could do. Those stubby arms could flip the steering wheel of a car as clean as a bee martin whips round the corner of a barn. Those pale-blue eyes, which didn't have any depth, could look down the barrel of a .38 and see, really see for one frozen and apocalyptic instant, what was over yonder. So he had found himself one day in the big black Cadillac with a couple of tons of expensive machinery pulsing under his fingers and the blue-steel .38 riding in the dark under his left armpit like a tumor. And the Boss was by his side, who could talk so good.

"Well, good luck," I had said to him, but I knew what his luck would be. Some morning I would pick up the paper and see that a certain Robert (or was it Roger?) O'Sheean had been killed in an automobile crash. Or had been shot to death by unidentified assailants while he sat in a car in the shadow outside the Love-Me-and-Leave-Me roadhouse and gambling hell operated by his employer. Or had that morning walked unassisted to the scaffold as a result of having been quicker on the draw than a policeman named, no doubt, Murphy. Or perhaps that was romantic. Perhaps he would live forever and outlive everything and his nerve would go (likker, dope, or just plain time) and he would sit, morning after morning while the gray winter rain sluiced down the high windows, in the newspaper room of the public library, a scrawny bald little old man in greasy tattered clothes bent over a picture magazine.

So perhaps I hadn't done Sugar-Boy any favor after all in not telling him about Duffy and the Boss and allowing him to whang straight to his mark and be finished like a bullet when it strikes in. Perhaps I had robbed Sugar-Boy of the one thing which he had earned out of the years he had lived and which was truly himself, and everything else to come after, no matter what it was, would be waste and accident and the sour and stinking curdle of truth like what you find in the half-full bottle of milk you had left in the ice-box when you went away for your six-week vacation.

Or perhaps Sugar-Boy had had something of which he could never be robbed.

I stood there in the hall after Sugar-Boy had gone, breathing the odor of old papers and disinfectant, and turning these thoughts over in my mind. Then I went back into the newspaper room and sat down and bent over a picture magazine.

It was February when I saw Sugar-Boy in the library. I continued with the way of life which I had adopted, still hugging the aimlessness and the anonymity about me like a blanket. But there was a difference now, in my own mind if not in the circumstances of my life. And in the end, months later, in May, in fact, the difference which my meeting with Sugar-Boy had made in my mind sent me to see Lucy Stark. Now, at least, I can see that such was the case.

I telephoned her out at the farm where she was still staying. She sounded all right on the phone. And she asked me to come out.

So I was back in the parlor in the little white house, among the black-walnut furniture upholstered in red plush, looking down at the flowers in the carpet. Nothing had changed in that room for a long time, or would change for a long time. But Lucy had changed a little. She was fleshier now, with a more positive gray in her hair. She was more like the woman the house had reminded me of the first time I had seen it—a respectable, middle-aged woman, in a clean gray gingham dress, with white stockings and black kid shoes, sitting in her rocker on the porch, with her hands folded across her stomach to take a little ease now the day's work is done and the men-folks are still in the fields and it's not yet time to think about supper or strain the evening milk. She wasn't that woman yet, but give her six or seven more years and she would be.

I sat there with my eyes on a flower in the carpet, or I looked up at her and then again at the flower, and her own glance strayed about the room in that abstracted way a good housewife has of looking around to surprise a speck of dust in the act. We were saying things to each other all the while, but they were strained and difficult things, completely empty.

You meet somebody at the seashore on a vacation and have a wonderful time together. Or in a corner at a party, while the glasses clink and somebody beats on a piano, you talk with a stranger whose mind seems to whet and sharpen your own and with whom a wonderful new vista of ideas is spied. Or you share some intense or painful experience with somebody, and discover a deep communion. Then afterward you are sure that when you meet again, the gay companion will give you the old gaiety, the brilliant stranger will stir your mind from its torpor, the sympathetic friend will solace you with the old communion of spirit. But something happens, or almost always happens, to the gaiety, the brilliance, the communion. You remember the individual words from the old language you spoke together, but you have forgotten the grammar. You remember the steps of the dance, but the music isn't playing any more. So there you are.

So there we sat for a while, and the minutes sifted and wavered down around us, one by one, like leaves dropping in still autumn air. Then, after a space of silence, she excused herself and I was left alone to watch the leaves drift down.

But she came back, carrying now a tray on which was a pitcher of iced tea, two glasses with sprigs of mint stuck in them, and a large devil's-food cake. That is what they give you in the country in a little white house like that when you make a visit, iced tea and devil's food cake. She had made the cake that morning, no doubt, in preparation for my visit.

Well, eating the cake would be something to do. Nobody expects you to talk with your mouth full of cake.

In the end, however, she said something. Perhaps having the cake on the table beside her, seeing somebody eat her cake, which she knew was a good cake, as people had sat on Sunday afternoons and eaten cake in that room for years, made it possible for her to say something.

She said, "You knew Tom was dead."

She said it perfectly matter-of-factly, and that was a comfort.

"Yes," I replied, "I knew it."

I had seen it in the paper, back in February. I hadn't gone to the funeral. I figured I had been to enough funerals. And I hadn't written her a letter. I couldn't very well write a letter and say I was sorry, and I couldn't very well write her a letter of congratulations.

"It was pneumonia," she said.

I remembered Adam's saying that that was what often got such cases.

"He died very quickly," she continued. "Just three days."

"Yes," I said.

She was silent for a moment, then said, "I am resigned now. I am resigned to it all now, Jack. A time comes when you think you cannot bear another thing, but it happens to you, and you can bear it. I am resigned now, by God's help."

I didn't make any answer.

"Then after I was resigned, God gave me something so I could live."

I murmured something inarticulate.

She rose abruptly from her chair, and thinking I was being

dismissed, I rose, too, clumsily, and started to say something by way of a good-bye. I was ready and anxious to go. I had been a fool to come. But she reached to touch my sleeve, and said, "I want to show you something." She moved away, toward the door. "Come with me," she said.

I followed her into the little hall, down it, and into a back room. She went across the room briskly. I didn't take it in at first, but there by the window was a crib and in the crib was a baby.

She was standing on the far side of the crib looking across at me at the instant when I really saw what was there. I guess my face was a study. Anyway, she said, "It's Tom's baby. It's my little grandbaby. It's Tom's baby."

She leaned over the crib, touching the baby here and there the way women do. Then she picked it up, holding it up with one hand behind its head to prop the head. She joggled it slightly and looked directly in its face. The baby's mouth opened in a yawn, and its eyes squinched and unsquinched, and then with the joggling and clucking it was getting it gave a moist and pink and toothless smile, like an advertisement. Lucy Stark's face had exactly the kind of expression on it which you would expect, and that expression said everything there was to say on the subject in hand.

She came around the crib, holding the baby up for my inspection.

"It's a pretty baby," I said, and put out a forefinger for the baby to clutch, the way you are supposed to do.

"It looks like Tom," she said. "Don't you think so?"

Then before I could get an answer ready that wouldn't be too horrendous a lie, she went on, "But that's silly to ask you. You wouldn't know. I mean he looks like Tom when he was a baby." She paused to inspect the baby again. "It looks like Tom," she said, more to herself than to me. Then she looked directly at me. "I know it's Tom's," she declared fiercely to me, "it's got to be Tom's, it looks like him."

I looked critically at the baby, and nodded. "It favors him, all right," I agreed.

"To think," she said, "there was a time I prayed to God it wasn't Tom's baby. So an injustice wouldn't be Tom's." The baby bounced a little in her arms. It was a husky, good-looking baby, all right. She gave the baby an encouraging jiggle, and then looked back at me. "And now," she continued, "I have prayed to God that it is Tom's. And I know now."

I nodded.

"I knew in my heart," she said. "And then, do you think that poor girl—the mother—would have given it to me if she hadn't known it was Tom's? No matter what that girl did—even what they said—don't you think a mother would know? She would just know."

"Yes," I said.

"But I knew, too. In my heart. So I wrote her a letter. I went to see her, I saw the baby. Oh, I knew even more then. As soon as I saw him and held him. I persuaded her to let me adopt him."

"You've got it fixed for a legal adoption?" I asked. "So she won't—" I stopped before I could say, "be bleeding you for years."

"Oh, yes," she said, apparently not reading my mind. "I got a lawyer to go see her and fix everything. I gave her some money, too. The poor girl wanted to go to California and get away. Willie didn't leave much money—he spent almost everything he made—but I gave her what I could. I gave her six thousand dollars."

So Sibyl had made a good thing of it after all, I reflected.

"Don't you want to hold him?" Lucy asked me in an access of generosity, thrusting out the expensive baby in my direction.

"Sure," I said, and took him. I hefted him, while I carefully tried to keep him from falling apart. "How much does he weigh?" I asked, and suddenly realized that I had the tone of a man about to buy something.

"Fifteen pounds and three ounces," she answered promptly; and added, "that is very good for three months."

"Sure," I said, "that's a lot."

She relieved me of the baby, gave him a sort of quick snuggle to her bosom, bending her head down so her face was against the baby's head, and then replaced him in the crib.

"What's his name?" I asked.

She straightened up and came around to my side of the crib. "At first," she said, "I thought I'd name him for Tom. I thought that for quite a while. Then it came to me. I would name him for Willie. His name is Willie—Willie Stark."

She led the way out into the little hall again. We walked up toward the table where my hat lay. Then she turned around and scrutinized my face as though the light weren't very good in the hall.

"You know," she said, "I named him for Willie because—" She was still scrutinizing my face.

"—because," she continued, "because Willie was a great man."

I nodded, I suppose.

"Oh, I know he made mistakes," she said, and lifted up her chin as though facing something, "bad mistakes. Maybe he did bad things, like they say. But inside—in here, deep down—" and she laid her hand to her bosom—"he was a great man."

426

She wasn't bothering with my face any more, with trying to read it. For the moment, she wasn't bothering with me. I might as well not have been there.

"He was a great man," she affirmed again, in a voice nearly a whisper. Then she looked again at me, calmly. "You see, Jack," she said, "I have to believe that."

Yes, Lucy, you have to believe that. You have to believe that to live. I know that you must believe that. And I would not have you believe otherwise. It must be that way, and I understand the fact. For you see, Lucy, I must believe that, too. I must believe that Willie Stark was a great man. What happened to his greatness is not the question. Perhaps he spilled it on the ground the way you spill a liquid when the bottle breaks. Perhaps he piled up his greatness and burnt it in one great blaze in the dark like a bonfire and then there wasn't anything but dark and the embers winking. Perhaps he could not tell his greatness from ungreatness and so mixed them together that what was adulterated was lost. But he had it. I must believe that.

Because I came to believe that, I came back to Burden's Landing. I did not come to believe it at the moment when I watched Sugar-Boy mount the stairs from the basement hall of the public library or when Lucy Stark stood before me in the hall of the little paint-peeling white house in the country. But because of those things—and of all the other things which had happened—I came, in the end, to believe that. And believing that Willie Stark was a great man, I could think better of all other people, and of myself. At the same time that I could more surely condemn myself.

I came back to Burden's Landing in early summer, at the request of my mother. She telephoned me one night and said, "Son, I want you to come here. As soon as you can. Can you come tomorrow?"

When I asked her what she wanted, for I still did not want to go back, she refused to answer me directly. She said she would tell me when I came.

So I went.

She was waiting for me on the gallery when I drove up late the next afternoon. We went around to the screened side gallery and had a drink. She wasn't talking much, and I didn't rush her.

When by near seven o'clock the Young Executive hadn't turned up, I asked her was he coming to dinner.

She shook her head. "Where is he?" I asked.

She turned her empty glass in her hand, lightly clinking the ice left there. Then she said, "I don't know."

"On a trip?" I asked.

"Yes," she answered, clinking the ice. Then she turned to

me. "He has been gone five days," she said. "He won't come back until I have gone. You see—" she set the glass down on the table beside her with an air of finality—"I am leaving him."

"Well," I breathed, "I'm damned."

She continued to look at me, as though expecting something. What, I didn't know.

"Well, I'm damned," I said, still fumbling with the fact which she had presented to me.

"Are you surprised?" she asked me, leaning a little toward me in her chair.

"Sure, I'm surprised."

She examined me intently, and I could detect a curious shifting and shading of feelings on her face, too evanescent and ambiguous for definition.

"Sure, I'm surprised," I repeated.

"Oh," she said, and sank back in her chair, sinking back like somebody who has fallen into deep water and clutches for a rope and seizes it and hangs on a moment and loses the grip and tries again and doesn't make it and knows it's no use to try again. There wasn't anything ambiguous now about her face. It was like what I said. She had missed her grip.

She turned her face away from me, out toward the bay, as though she didn't want me to see what was on it. Then she said, "I thought—I thought maybe you wouldn't be surprised."

I couldn't tell her why I or anybody else would be surprised. I couldn't tell her that when a woman as old as she was getting to be had her hooks in a man not much more than forty years old and not wind-broke it was surprising if she didn't hang on. Even if the woman had money and the man was as big a horse's-ass as the Young Executive. I couldn't tell her that, and so I didn't say anything.

She kept on looking out to the bay. "I thought," she said, hesitated, and resumed, "I thought maybe you'd understand why, Jack."

"Well, I don't," I replied.

She held off awhile, then began again. "It happened last year. I knew when it happened.—Oh, I knew it would be like this."

"When what happened?"

"When you—when you—" Then she stopped, and corrected what she had been about to say. "When Monty—died."

Then she swung back toward me and on her face was a kind of wild appeal. She was making another grab for that rope. "Oh, Jack," she said, "Jack, it was Monty—don't you see?—it was Monty."

I reckoned that I saw, and I said so. I remembered the silvery, pure scream which had jerked me out into the hall that afternoon of Judge Irwin's death, and the face of my mother

428

as she lay on the bed later with the knowledge sinking into her.

"It was Monty," she was saying. "It was always Monty. I didn't really know it. There hadn't been—been anything between us for a long time. But it was always Monty. I knew it when he was dead. I didn't want to know it but I knew it. And I couldn't go on. There came a time I couldn't go on. I couldn't."

She rose abruptly from her chair, like something jerked up by a string.

"I couldn't," she said. "Because everything was a mess. Everything had always been a mess." Her hands twisted and tore the handkerchief she held before her at the level of her waist. "Oh, Jack," she cried out, "it had always been a mess."

She flung down the shredded handkerchief and ran off the gallery. I heard the sound of her heels on the floor inside, but it wasn't the old bright, spirited tattoo. It was a kind of desperate, slovenly clatter, suddenly muted on the rug.

I waited on the gallery for a while. Then I went back to the kitchen. "My mother isn't feeling very well," I told the cook. "You or Jo-Belle might go up a little later and see if she will take some broth and egg or something like that."

Then I went back into the dining room and sat down in the candlelight and they brought me the food and I ate some of it.

After dinner Jo-Belle came to tell me that she had carried a tray up to my mother's room but she wouldn't take it. She hadn't even opened the door at the knock. She had just called to say she didn't want anything.

I sat on the gallery a long time while the sounds died out back in the kitchen. Then the light went out back there. The rectangle of green in the middle of blackness where the light of the window fell on the grass was suddenly black, too.

After a while I went upstairs and stood outside the door of my mother's room. Once or twice I almost knocked to go in. But I decided that even if I went in, there wouldn't be anything to say. There isn't ever anything to say to somebody who has found out the truth about himself, whether it is good or bad.

So I went back down and stood in the garden among the black magnolia trees and the myrtles, and thought how by killing my father I had saved my mother's soul. Then I thought how maybe I had saved my father's soul, too. Both of them had found out what they needed to know to be saved. Then I thought how all knowledge that is worth anything is maybe paid for by blood. Maybe that is the only way you can tell that a certain piece of knowledge is worth anything: it has cost some blood.

My mother left the next day. She was going to Reno. I drove

her down to the station, and arranged all her nice, slick matched bags and valises and cases and hatboxes in a nice row on the cement of the platform to wait for the train. The day was hot and bright, and the cement was hot and gritty under our feet as we stood there in that vacuity which belongs to the period just before parting at a railway station.

We stood there quite a while, looking up the track for the first smudge of smoke on the heat-tingling horizon beyond the tide flats and the clumps of pines. Then my mother suddenly said, "Jack, I want to tell you something."

"Yes?"

"I am letting Theodore have the house."

That took me so by surprise I couldn't say anything. I thought of all the years she had been cramming the place with furniture and silver and glass till it was a museum and she was God's gift to the antique dealers of New Orleans, New York, and London. I was surprised anything could pry her loose from it.

"You see," she said, hurrying on in the tone of explanation, misreading my silence, "it isn't really Theodore's fault and you know how crazy he is about the place and about living on the Row and all that. And I didn't think you'd want it. You see— I thought—I thought you had Monty's place and if you ever lived at the Landing you'd prefer that because—because—"

"Because he was my father," I finished for her, a little grimly.

"Yes," she said, simply. "Because he was your father. So I decided to—"

"Damn it," I burst out, "it is your house and you can do whatever you want to with it. I wouldn't have it. As soon as I get my bag out of there this afternoon I'll never set foot in it again, and that is a fact. I don't want it and I don't care what you do with it or with your money. I don't want that either. I've always told you that."

"There won't be any too much money to worry about," she said. "You know what the last six or seven years have been like."

"You aren't broke?" I asked. "Look here, if you're broke, I'll—"

"I'm not broke," she said. "I'll have enough to get on with. If I go somewhere quiet and am careful. At first I thought I might go to Europe, then I—"

"You better stay out of Europe," I said. "All hell is going to break loose over there and not long either."

"Oh, I'm not going. I'm going to some quiet, cheap place. I don't know where. I'll have to think."

"Well," I said, "don't worry about me and the house. You can be plenty sure I'll never set foot in it again."

She looked up the tracks, east, where there wasn't any smoke yet beyond the pines and the tidelands. She mused for a couple of minutes on the emptiness off there. Then said, as though just picking up my own words, "I ought never set foot in it. I married and I came to it and he was a good man. But I ought to have stayed where I was. I ought never come."

I couldn't very well argue that point with her one way or the other, and so I kept quiet.

But as she stood there in the silence, she seemed to be arguing it with herself, for suddenly she lifted up her head and looked straight at me and said, "Well, I did it. And now I know." And she squared her trim shoulders under her trim blue linen suit and held her face up in the old way like it was a damned expensive present she was making to the world and the world had better appreciate it.

Well, she knew now. As she stood there on the hot cement in the dazzle, she seemed to be musing on what she knew.

But it was on what she didn't know. For after a while she turned to me and said, "Son, tell me something."

"What?"

"It's something I've got to know, Son."

"What is it?"

"When—when it happened—when you went to see Monty—"

That was it. I knew that was it. And in the midst of the dazzle and the heat shimmering off the cement, I was cold as ice and my nerves crawled cold inside me.

"—did he—was there—" she was looking away from me.

"You mean," I said, "had he got into a jam and had to shoot himself? Is that it?"

She nodded, then looked straight at me and waited for what was coming.

I looked into her face and studied it. The light wasn't any too kind to it. Light would never be kind to it again. But she held it up and looked straight at me and waited.

"No," I said, "he wasn't in any jam. We had a little argument about politics. Nothing serious. But he talked about his health. About feeling bad. That was it. He said good-bye to me. I can see now he meant it as the real thing. That was all."

She sagged a little. She didn't have to brace up so stiff any longer.

"Is that the truth?" she demanded.

"Yes," I said. "I swear to God it is."

"Oh," she said softly and let her breath escape in an almost soundless sigh.

So we waited again. There wasn't anything else to say. She had finally, at the last minute, asked what she had been wanting to ask and had been afraid to ask all the time.

Then, after a while, there was the smoke on the horizon. Then we could see, far off, the black smoke moving toward us along the edge of the bright water. Then with the great grind-

431

ing and trampling and hissing and the wreaths of steam, the engine had pulled past us to a stop. A white-coated porter began to gather up the nice matched bags and boxes.

My mother turned to me and took me by the arm. "Good-bye, Son," she said.

"Good-bye," I said.

She stepped toward me and I put my arm around her.

"Write to me, Son," she said. "Write to me. You are all I've got."

I nodded. "Let me know how you make out," I said.

"Yes," she said, "yes."

Then I kissed her good-bye, and as I did so I saw the conductor who was beyond her look at his watch and flick it into his pocket with that contemptuous motion a conductor on a crack train has when he is getting ready to wind up the ninety-second stop at a hick town. I knew he was that very instant going to call, "All aboard!" But it seemed a long time coming. It was like looking at a man across a wide valley and seeing the puff of smoke from his gun and then waiting God knows how long for the tiny report, or like seeing the lightning way off and waiting for the thunder. I stood there with my arm around my mother's shoulder and her cheek against mine (her cheek was wet, I discovered) and waited for the conductor to call, "All aboard!"

Then it came, and she stepped back from me and mounted the steps and turned to wave as the train drew away and the porter slammed the vestibule door.

I looked after the dwindling train that was carrying my mother away until it was nothing but the smudge of smoke to the west, and thought how I had lied to her. Well, I had given that lie to her as a going-away present. Or a kind of wedding present, I thought.

Then I thought how maybe I had lied just to cover up myself.

"Damn it," I said out loud, savagely, "it wasn't for me, it wasn't."

And that was true. It was really true.

I had given my mother a present, which was a lie. But in return she had given me a present, too, which was a truth. She gave me a new picture of herself, and that meant, in the end, a new picture of the world. Or rather, that new picture of herself filled in the blank space which was perhaps the center of the new picture of the world which had been given to me by many people, by Sadie Burke, Lucy Stark, Willie Stark, Sugar-Boy, Adam Stanton. And that meant that my mother gave me back the past. I could now accept the past which I had before felt was tainted and horrible. I could accept the past now because I could accept her and be at peace with her and with myself.

432

For years I had condemned her as a woman without heart, who loved merely power over men and the momentary satisfaction to vanity or flesh which they could give her, who lived in a strange loveless oscillation between calculation and instinct. And my mother, realizing a condemnation of her, but without, perhaps, realizing its nature, had done everything she could to hold me and to throttle the condemnation. What she could do to me was to use the force which she was able to use on other men. I resisted and resented this but I wanted to be loved by her and at the same time I was drawn by the force, for she was a vital and beautiful woman by whom I was drawn and by whom I was repelled, whom I condemned and of whom I was proud. But the change came.

The first hint was in the wild, silvery scream which filled the house when the word of Judge Irwin's death was received. That scream rang in my ears for many months, but it had faded away, lost in the past and the corruption of the past, by the time she called me back to Burden's Landing to tell me that she was going to go away. Then I knew that she was telling the truth. And I felt at peace with her and with myself.

I did not say why to myself at the moment when she told me or even the next day when we stood on the cement platform and waited for the train, or even when I stood there alone and watched the last smudge of smoke fade to the west. Nor did I say why to myself when I sat alone that night in the house which had been Judge Irwin's house but which was now mine. I had closed up my mother's house that afternoon, had put the key under the mat on the gallery, and had left it for good.

Judge Irwin's house had the odor of dust and disuse and close air. In the afternoon I opened all the windows and left them open while I went down to the Landing for some supper. When I got back and turned the lights on, it seemed more like the house which I remembered from all the years. But sitting there in the study, with the damp, sweet-heavy night air coming in through the windows, I did not say to myself why I now felt so fully at peace with myself. I thought of my mother and I felt the peace and the relief and the new sense of the world.

After a while I got up and walked out of the house and down the Row. It was a very calm, clear night with scarcely a sibilance from the water on the shingle of the beach, and the bay was bright under the stars. I walked down the Row until I came to the Stanton house. There was a light on in the little back sitting room, a dim light as though from a reading lamp. I looked at the house for a couple of minutes and then entered the gate and walked up the path.

The screen door of the gallery was latched. But the main door of the hall inside the gallery was open, and looking across the gallery I could see down the hall to the place where a rec-

433

tangle of light was laid on the floor from the open door of the back sitting room. I knocked on the frame of the kitchen door and waited.

In a moment Anne Stanton appeared in the patch of light down the hall.

"Who is it?" she called.

"It's me," I called back.

She came down the hall and across the gallery toward me. Then she was at the door, a thin, white-clad figure in the dimness beyond the screen. I started to say hello, but didn't. And she did not speak, either, as she fumbled with the latch. Then the door was open and I stepped inside.

As I stood there, I caught the trace of the scent she used, and a cold hand compressed my heart.

"I didn't know you'd let me in," I said, trying to make it sound like a joke and trying to see her face in the shadow. I could only see the paleness in shadow and the gleam of her eyes.

"Of course I'd let you in," she said.

"Well, I didn't know," I said, and gave a kind of laugh.

"Why?"

"Oh, the way I've behaved."

We moved over to the swing on the gallery and sat down. The chains creaked, but we sat so still that the thing did not sway a hair's breadth.

"What have you done?" she asked.

I fished for a cigarette, found one, and lighted it. I flicked the match out without looking at her face. "What have I done?" I repeated. "Well, it's what I didn't do. I didn't answer your letter."

"That's all right," she said. Then added reflectively, as though to herself, "That was a long time ago."

"It was a long time back, six months, seven months. But I did worse than not answering it," I said. "I didn't even read it. I just set it up on my bureau and never even opened it."

She didn't say anything to that. I took a few drags on the cigarette and waited but there wasn't a word.

"It came at the wrong time," I said finally. "It came at a time when everything and everybody—even Anne Stanton—looked just alike to me and I didn't give a damn. You know what I mean?"

"Yes," she said.

"Like hell you do," I said.

"Maybe I do," she said quietly.

"Not the way I mean. You couldn't."

"Maybe."

"Well, anyway that was the way it was. Everything and everybody looked alike. I didn't even feel sorry for anybody. I didn't even feel sorry for myself."

434

"I never asked you to feel sorry for me," she said fiercely. "In the letter or anywhere else."

"No," I said slowly, "I don't reckon you did."

"I never asked you that."

"I know," I said, and fell silent for a moment. Then said: "I came up here to tell you I don't feel that way any more. I had to tell somebody—I had to say it out loud—to be sure it's true. But it is true."

I waited in the silence, which remained unbroken until I began again.

"It's my mother," I said. "You know," I said, "how it always was with us. How we didn't get along. How I thought that she—"

"Don't!" Anne burst out. "Don't! I don't want to hear you talk that way. What makes you so bitter? What do you talk that way for? Your mother, Jack, and that poor old man your father!"

"He's not my father," I said.

"Not your father!"

"No," I said, and sitting there in the motionless swing on the dark gallery, I told her what there was to tell about the pale-haired and famish-cheeked girl who had come down from Arkansas, and tried to tell her what my mother had finally given back to me. I tried to tell her how if you could not accept the past and its burden there was no future, for without one there cannot be the other, and how if you could accept the past you might hope for the future, for only out of the past can you make the future.

I tried to tell her that.

Then, after a long silence, she said, "I believe that, for if I had not come to believe it I could not have lived."

We did not talk any more. I smoked another half a pack of cigarettes, sitting there in the swing in the dark with the summer air heavy and damp and almost sick-sweet around us, and trying to catch the sound of her breath in the silence. Then after a long time I said good night, and went down the Row to my father's house.

This has been the story of Willie Stark, but it is my story, too. For I have a story. It is the story of a man who lived in the world and to him the world looked one way for a long time and then it looked another and very different way. The change did not happen all at once. Many things happened, and that man did not know when he had any responsibility for them and when he did not. There was, in fact, a time when he came to believe that nobody had any responsibility for anything and there was no god but the Great Twitch.

At first that thought was horrible to him when it was forced

435

on him by what seemed the accident of circumstance, for it seemed to rob him of a memory by which unconsciously, he had lived; but then a little later it gave him a sort of satisfaction, because it meant that he could not be called guilty of anything, not even of having squandered happiness or of having killed his father, or of having delivered his two friends into each other's hands and death.

But later, much later, he woke up one morning to discover that he did not believe in the Great Twitch any more. He did not believe in it because he had seen too many people live and die. He had seen Lucy Stark and Sugar-Boy and the Scholarly Attorney and Sadie Burke and Anne Stanton live and the ways of their living had nothing to do with the Great Twitch. He had seen his father die. He had seen his friend Adam Stanton die. He had seen his friend Willie Stark die, and had heard him say with his last breath, "It might have been all different, Jack. You got to believe that."

He had seen his two friends, Willie Stark and Adam Stanton, live and die. Each had killed the other. Each had been the doom of the other. As a student of history, Jack Burden could see that Adam Stanton, whom he came to call the man of idea, and Willie Stark, whom he came to call the man of fact, were doomed to destroy each other, just as each was doomed to try to use the other and to yearn toward and try to become the other, because each was incomplete with the terrible division of their age. But at the same time Jack Burden came to see that his friends had been doomed, he saw that though doomed they had nothing to do with any doom under the godhead of the Great Twitch. They were doomed, but they lived in the agony of will. As Hugh Miller (once Attorney General under Willie Stark and much later Jack Burden's friend) said to him when they were discussing the theory of the moral neutrality of history: "History is blind, but man is not." (It looks as though Hugh will get back into politics, and when he does I'll be along to hold his coat. I've had some valuable experience in that line.)

So now I, Jack Burden, live in my father's house. In one sense it is strange that I should be here, for the discovery of truth had one time robbed me of the past and had killed my father. But in the end the truth gave the past back to me. So I live in the house which my father left me. With me is my wife, Anne Stanton, and the old man who was once married to my mother. When a few months ago I found him sick in the room above the Mexican restaurant, what could I do but bring him here? (Does he think I am his son? I cannot be sure. Nor can I feel that it matters, for each of us is the son of a million fathers.)

He is very feeble. Now and then he has the strength to play

a game of chess, as he used to play with his friend Montague Irwin long ago in the long room in the white house by the sea. He used to be a very good chess player, but now his attention wanders. Or on good days now he sits in the sunshine. He can read his Bible a little. He is not strong enough to write any more, but occasionally he dictates something to me or Anne for a tract which he is writing.

Yesterday he dictated this to me:

The creation of man whom God in His foreknowledge knew doomed to sin was the awful index of God's omnipotence. For it would have been a thing of trifling and contemptible ease for Perfection to create mere perfection. To do so would, to speak truth, be not creation but extension. Separateness is identity and the only way for God to create, truly create, man was to make him separate from God Himself, and to be separate from God is to be sinful. The creation of evil is therefore the index of God's glory and His power. That had to be so that the creation of good might be the index of man's glory and power. But by God's help. By His help and in His wisdom.

He turned to me when he had spoken the last word, stared at me, and then said, "Did you put that down?"

"Yes," I replied.

Staring at me, he said with sudden violence, "It is true. I know it is true. Do you know it?"

I nodded my head and said yes. (I did so to keep his mind untroubled, but later I was not certain but that in my own way I did believe what he had said.)

He kept on looking at me, after I had spoken, then said quietly, "Since that thought came into my mind my soul has been still. I have had it in my mind for three days. I have held it there to be sure by the test of my soul before I spoke it."

He will never finish the tract. His strength fails visibly from day to day. The doctor says he will not last the winter.

By the time he is dead I shall be ready to leave the house. For one thing, the house is heavily mortgaged. Judge Irwin's affairs, at the time of his death, were tangled, and in the end it developed that he was not rich but poor. Once before, almost twenty-five years before, it had been heavily mortgaged. But then it had been saved by a crime. A good man had committed a crime to save it. I should not be too complacent because I am not prepared to commit a crime to save the house. Perhaps my unwillingness to commit a crime to save the house (assuming that I should have the opportunity—which is doubtful) is simply a way of saying that I do not love the house as much as Judge Irwin loved it and a man's virtue may be but the defect of his desire, as his crime may be but a function of his virtue.

437

Nor should I be complacent because I tried to make amends, in a way, for a crime which my father had committed. What little money did come to me from my father's estate should go, I thought, to Miss Littlepaugh in her foul, fox-smelling room in Memphis. So I went to Memphis. But I found that she was dead. So I was denied that inexpensive satisfaction in virtue. I should have to get whatever satisfaction I was to get in a more expensive way.

But I still had the money, and so I am spending it to live on while I write the book I began years ago, the life of Cass Mastern, whom once I could not understand but whom, perhaps, I now may come to understand. I suppose that there is some humor in the fact that while I write about Cass Mastern I live in the house of Judge Irwin and eat bread bought with his money. For Judge Irwin and Cass Mastern do not resemble each other very closely. (If Judge Irwin resembles any Mastern it is Gilbert, the granite-headed brother of Cass.) But I do not find the humor in this situation very funny. The situation is too much like the world in which we live from birth to death, and the humor of it grows stale from repetition. Besides, Judge Irwin was my father and he was good to me and, in a way, he was a man and I loved him.

When the old man is dead and the book is finished, I shall let the First and Third National Bank take the house and I don't care who lives here afterward, for from that day it will be nothing to me but a well-arranged pile of brick and lumber. Anne and I shall never live here again, not in the house or at the Landing. (She doesn't want to live here any more than I do. She has let her place go to the Children's Home she was interested in and I imagine it will become a kind of sanatorium. She's not very complacent about having done that. With Adam dead the place was not a joy but a torture to her, and the gift of the house was finally her gift to the ghost of Adam, a poor gift humbly offered, like the handful of wheat or a painted pot in the tomb, to comfort the ghost and send it on its way so that it would trouble the living no longer.)

So by the summer of this year, 1939, we shall have left Burden's Landing.

We shall come back, no doubt, to walk down the Row and watch young people on the tennis courts by the clump of mimosas and walk down the beach by the bay, where the diving floats lift gently in the sun, and on out to the pine grove, where the needles thick on the ground will deaden the footfall so that we shall move among trees as soundlessly as smoke. But that will be a long time from now, and soon now we shall go out of the house and go into the convulsion of the world, out of history into history and the awful responsibility of Time.

ABOUT THE AUTHOR

Born in 1905 in Kentucky, educated at Vanderbilt University, the University of California, and Yale University, a Rhodes scholar at Oxford, ROBERT PENN WARREN made his literary debut as a member of the "Fugitive" group of young Southern poets. Since then, he has taken his place as one of America's most multi-faceted leading men of letters. As editor of *The Southern Review*, he deeply influenced the development of Southern writing. As critic, teacher and anthologist, he has played an important role in American higher education. Above all, however, his name will endure as a poet and a novelist whose works have been accorded a rare combination of critical and popular recognition. He has been awarded both the Pulitzer Prize for Fiction and the Bollingen Prize for poetry, to name but two highlights of a career graced with honors.

Bring out the books that bring in the issues.

☐ "THEY'VE KILLED THE PRESIDENT" the search for the
   murderers of John F. Kennedy   Robert Sam Anson   2525   • $2.50

☐ GUILTY, GUILTY, GUILTY   G. B. Trudeau   2677   • $1.25

☐ WHO RUNS CONGRESS? Mark J. Green,
   James M. Fallows and David R. Zwick   8151   • $2.25

☐ THE MAKING OF THE PRESIDENT, 1972
   Theodore White   8344   • $2.25

☐ QUOTATIONS FROM CHAIRMAN MAO TSE-TUNG
   Stuart A. Schram, ed.   10059   • $1.95

☐ THE ECO-SPASM REPORT   Alvin Toffler   10181   • $1.75

☐ BURY MY HEART AT WOUNDED KNEE   Dee Brown   10277   • $2.50

☐ SOCIALISM   Michael Harrington   10907   • $2.95

☐ QUESTIONS AND ANSWERS ABOUT ARABS AND JEWS
   Ira Hirschmann   11199   • $1.95

Buy them at your local bookstore or use this handy coupon for ordering:

Bantam Books, Inc., Dept. EDM, 414 East Golf Road, Des Plaines, Ill. 60016

Please send me the books I have checked above. I am enclosing $_____
(please add 50¢ to cover postage and handling). Send check or money order
—no cash or C.O.D.'s please.

Mr/Mrs/Miss_____

Address_____

City_____State/Zip_____

EDM—12/77

Please allow four weeks for delivery. This offer expires 6/78.

REACH ACROSS THE GENERATIONS

With books that explore disenchantment and discovery, failure and conquest, and seek to bridge the gap between adolescence and adulthood.

☐	BONNIE JOE, GO HOME Jeanette Eyerly	2490	$1.25
☐	NOBODY WAVED GOODBYE Elizabeth Haggard	2670	$1.25
☐	THE UPSTAIRS ROOM Johanna Reiss	2858	$1.25
☐	THE FRIENDS Rosa Guy	8541	$1.25
☐	RUN SOFTLY, GO FAST Barbara Wersba	11239	$1.50
☐	SUMMER OF MY GERMAN SOLDIER Bette Greene	10192	$1.50
☐	HATTER FOX Marilyn Harris	10320	$1.75
☐	THE BELL JAR Sylvia Plath	10370	$1.95
☐	IT'S NOT THE END OF THE WORLD Judy Blume	10559	$1.25
☐	I NEVER LOVED YOUR MIND Paul Zindel	10561	$1.25
☐	PARDON ME, YOU'RE STEPPING ON MY EYEBALL Paul Zindel	10871	$1.75
☐	I KNOW WHY THE CAGED BIRD SINGS Maya Angelou	10842	$1.75
☐	RICHIE Thomas Thompson	11029	$1.75
☐	MY DARLING, MY HAMBURGER Paul Zindel	11605	$1.75
☐	WHERE THE RED FERN GROWS Wilson Rawls	11288	$1.50
☐	PHOEBE Patricia Dizenzo	11295	$1.25
☐	ELLEN: A SHORT LIFE, LONG REMEMBERED Rose Levit	11496	$1.50

Buy them at your local bookstore or use this handy coupon for ordering:

Bantam Books, Inc., Dept. EDN, 414 East Golf Road, Des Plaines, Ill. 60016

Please send me the books I have checked above. I am enclosing $_____
(please add 50¢ to cover postage and handling). Send check or money order
—no cash or C.O.D.'s please.

Mr/Mrs/Miss_____

Address_____

City_____State/Zip_____

EDN—12/77

Please allow four weeks for delivery. This offer expires 6/78.

Bantam Book Catalog

Here's your up-to-the-minute listing of every book currently available from Bantam.

This easy-to-use catalog is divided into categories and contains over 1400 titles by your favorite authors.

So don't delay—take advantage of this special opportunity to increase your reading pleasure.

Just send us your name and address and 25¢ (to help defray postage and handling costs).

BANTAM BOOKS, INC.
Dept. FC, 414 East Golf Road, Des Plaines, Ill. 60016

Mr./Mrs./Miss_____

(please print)

Address_____

City_____ State_____ Zip_____

Do you know someone who enjoys books? Just give us their names and addresses and we'll send them a catalog too!

Mr./Mrs./Miss_____

Address_____

City_____ State_____ Zip_____

Mr./Mrs./Miss_____

Address_____

City_____ State_____ Zip_____

FC—6/77